ΩMEGA CHRONICLES

VOL. 1

THE SUPER CYBORG

MACK WELLS

Omega Chronicles Vol. 1
Copyright © 2024 by Mack Wells

Library of Congress Control Number: 2024924936

ISBN
978-1-964488-38-7 (Paperback)
978-1-964488-39-4 (eBook)
978-1-964488-37-0 (Hardcover)

CHAPTER 1

Women are like precious gems; treat them right, and they will sparkle forever, but treat them poorly and that sparkle will fade.

A large explosion blows out of an office building glass an rubble rain down on the streets below inside the blow out building a woman stands in the center of the inferno a, strange glow surrounded her, from a device that she wore on her wrist.

She pulled herself free of the fire and the wreckage and turned off the force field. Then started to frantically look around for the man that had save her, it was incredible for he had taken out the six men that had come for her in seconds.

It was shocking at how strongly the man fought despite the fact that he had been shot, and he would've made it if one of the kidnappers hadn't of set off an explosion.

When she spotted him, she could see that he was hurt badly, both his arms and legs looked crushed and he was bleeding badly she frantically did everything she could to keep them alive.

He awoke taking in a large breath of air, and coughing up a little blood. He, looked around. He was only half conscious, and saw someone overlooking him, he thought he was looking at an angel, who had come to take him away.

It was clear, he wouldn't last long without medical attention. Suddenly, firefighters and paramedics were coming to help. The young woman was still fixated on the man until one of the paramedics put a hand on her shoulder, she turned to them as they said. "We need to get him out of here." But she told them. "No take him to the lower floors of the building I will take care of thing from there."

They all were about to argue but insisted that it was the only way to save him, as she said this she moved to the side and talked into the same device that saved her from the explosion "I've found the perfect candidate for the Super Cyborg protect."

CHAPTER 2

A few hours later, the young man brought to the lower leaves of the building being stabilized, by several doctors until the young woman from before steps in, ready to get to work on saving her hero's life.

That moment on herself and the Cyber Corp Doctor's went to work on the man as he now dreams of the advents that lead to this outcome.

Chris Striker had just landed in America though his entire life he had lived in Okinawa where he learned an ancient martial arts called Raion no Kiba an old marital art that very few knew, and the only reason he was chosen was because his Sensei was his Mother's, a man that might of been old, but he was the strongest marital artist around, though none knew this for he kept himself away form all only training those he dems worthy.

Now here he was in America after finishing his training though he couldn't figure out why his Sensei wanted him here but he never questioned his motives.

"Chris Striker?" Came a voice from afar, Chris looked over and saw the one that called out to him, a woman by the name Elise Pryer part of the company insisted that that he work for them as security despite the fact that he insisted that he not use guns.

Elise walked over to Chris holding a tablet, "It is good to finally meet you in person Mr. Striker."

"Thank you Miss Pryer have you got everything I ask for?"

"Yes sir, your room is ready, though your requests were very unusual." "I know, but you all came to me, and I refuse to use guns of any kind." "Yes I understand this, but you will be the bodyguard of Miss Minawa Ivy, and she is one of, if not the biggest VIP of Cyber Corporation, so forgive me if I am skeptical." "Well you would lead the way we can get started, and I can show you just what I can do."

With that said the two left the airport to Chris's new home and job working as a bodyguard for Minawa Ivy it was weird that she had contacted him and insisted that he be her personal bodyguard but sense she agreed that he wouldn't be using any type of gun and the money was good.

A limo drove up in front of a a building a woman got out talking on a phone, "I know General Bishop I promised another one, but you did say I could chose the next candidate, No I am not stalling I just have to be careful on this one for that metal is very hard to come by and the next one is going to be not only the strongest but the most powerful. I have to be careful who I choose or they could lose there minds."

General Bishop she was talking at that moment hung up on her she shook her head a she put away her phone that man is going to be the death of hers, she then moved into the building and noticed thatcher bodyguard had arrived.

She had chosen this man from a reference from an old friend someone you don't question no matter what, but he was easy on the eye.

"Hello Miss Minawa my name is Chris Striker, and it." "Yes, I already know, I'm the one that chose you for your skills so lets see just how good you are?"

With that Minawa went about her day with Chris always close behind, and in little over a mouth Chris had proofed that he was a man of his word he didn't needs guns or any firearm the man was a living weapon.

Though things were about to get bad for everyone real fast, as one day a General Bishop came to see Minawa he was not happy at all, he had been waiting to long for the woman to finish her final project and yet she still tells him that this trip was pointless that she still doesn't have it.

"You are telling me you just can't pick someone already." Bishop asked mad about the wait for the last, Minawa sighed as she was getting mad herself.

"Like I told you over the phone I have to be careful who I choose for if I don't the mental strain would tear their minds, apart."

The General glared at her for a moment then he looked to Chris who had been standing an attention, behind Minawa through there meeting. "What's with the statue, he hasn't moved sense we started?"

"His name is Chris Striker and he is my name security guard."

"Then shouldn't he be in the security room."

"Not him, I hand picked him for his marital skill, and power."

"Martial artist you say, but what weapons does he specialize in?"

"None he is strictly hand to hand, but anyway we need to return to our discussion." The General sneered at this to witch Chris noticed.

A few hours latter Minawa and the General exited the conference room to witch as usual nothing resolved but Chris through the whole found he didn't like this General at all, and little did he know the General was up to sometime that will change his life forever.

As the General was leaving, on the other side of the building six men were moving equipment around the loading dock, a dock worker approach them asking what they were delivering?

The group only looked from what they were doing for a moment as one of them pulled a gun from the box they were moving in, and with pinpoint accuracy fired one for each one of the dock workers.

"Get the rest of the equipment off the truck we have work to do."

Chris was working though some of the security files, when he noticed, what was going on the docks, he hit the button for them alarm but nothing happened he then checked the phones but there was nothing, and at that moment the power went out.

"This is not good."

Back with the men at the docks one of them was working on a computer shutting down all the power to the building and locking it down at the same time, the group moved on into the dark wearing night vision googles to navigate the darkened building.

Minawa was working in her lad when the lights went out she looked up from her work and before she ran out she put something on her wrist, and headed to the door to find out what was going on, but once she reached the door to the lab, it was blow out, thus knocking her to the ground.

Six men stormed in blending guns and wearing full tactical equipment, they surrounded her the night vision glowing in the dark.

"Professor Ivy, you are coming with us." One of the men stated as one of them grabbed her pulled her to the door but then something shot through the da, knocking the weapons from there hands, as they frantically trying to figure out what is going on, someone runs through, and grabs Minawa and runs around the corner.

Minawa at first couldn't tell what had happened it was still to dark to see, but then whoever it was spoke. "Are you alright Miss Ivy." It was Chris but how was he doing this in the dark.

"Yeah I'm fine but how are you able to fight in the dark?"

"As my Sensei, used to say, one does not need eyes to see."

Minawa was about to ask what he meant but Chris put a hand over her mouth to quite her as the men had manage to pull there weapons out of the walls where they had been embedded, without word spoken between them they went back trying to find there target.

Chris started to move both himself and Minawa in the dark and the woman was amazed he maneuver them through the dark so easily, he was even more amazing then she thought, but then a shots rang out and Chris pushed them both to the ground.

Minawa felt something drip down on her face she tried to see in the dark, but all she saw was a silhouette of the man, he moved in a flash and she found herself in what she assumed to a closet, and once the door shut she could see the flashes of gunfire but she heard the sound of the men yelling out, it went on for what seemed like forever until it all got quit.

The lights all came back on and she turned to door and was about to open it when it flew open and Chris lead against the door he was shot up badly but when she saw the men they were beaten and only one of the six was still conscious, but he wasn't about to be going anywhere as he was pinned to the wall by a knife.

"That was incredible Chris you took them all out in the dark with your barehands."

Chris just gave a half smile as he was still shot a few times in the fight but he was going to wait for he still had some questions for these men.

He turned back to the one that was still pinned the wall, "Okay buddy who do you work for and why have you come here?"

Chris said this as he and Minawa still in front of him but the masked man said nothing Chris then removed his mask and the man glared at Chris.

"You haven't stopped us we always have a back up and we always finish the job."

The man started to laugh confusing the two, until he tore open his shirt showing a digital count down Chris turned to Minawa who was about to grab him as she pressed a button on the device she took from her lab, but it was to late as the explosives each one of the men had on blow out the side of the building.

CHAPTER 3

It was a few days later when Chris awoke, yelling out from the nightmares of being in an explosion. As he became more conscious, he cried out, and he moved a hand to his face, but felt something was very wrong with his hand. He then sat up looking at his hands. He cried out again—his hands didn't, look like his hands anymore. They were mechanical skeletal version of his hands. And not just his hands, but his arms were mechanical too. He whipped the covers from his legs to see how much of himself was like this, and, to his shock, he found his legs where also mechanical.

Chris was truly in shock—half of his body was made up of shiny mechanical components. On top of that, not knowing how he got here! Just as he was starting to lose consciousness again, at the sight of his new limbs, as a nurse walked by his room, and noticed that, he was sitting up. She called out, for the professor, and when she walked into Chris's room. She greeted the new cyborg, as she took a seat, next to his bed, adjusted some of the monitors beside his bed. "How are you feeling?" she asked.

Chris lay back down, and looked up at the nurse. "I'm fine," he said. "But what's going on? What happen to, me? Where am I?"

"Well if you remember my name is Minawa Ivy, and you are in a military base a few miles, out of the city limits. As for what had happened to you. What is the last thing, you can remembered?

Chris thought for a minute then said, "I remember six armed men. I went after them, but then, at the last minute, they blew up the whole building and..." Chris trailed off as he looked at the young woman beside him, and recognized her. "You!" he said. "You were the one that they were after. And that must also mean that you, where that angel I saw."

Professor Ivy smiled warmly at him. She was flattered that he had thought, she was an angel, then she told him. "Yes, I am, and I am grateful that you saved me."

But Chris turned away, as he said, "I didn't save you; I failed."

She smiled at him again. "You did not fail. If you hadn't come, there is a good chance that I would be dead by now, or, worse yet, they could have gotten what they wanted."

Chris sat there still feeling as if he had failed. But he had other questions for this women. "Just how much of me is cybernetic?

"Yes," Professor Ivy started. "Your body was badly hurt. The only way to save you, was to replace a large amount of your body, with metal components. As you can see, both your legs and arms had to be replaced, as well as a large amount of your chest, and back, including some of your internal organs, as well as your left eye and left side of your head. You are now a cyborg—part human and part machine. The metal that your cybernetics are made of, is a very rare metal, that I got from an asteroid. The metal will also protect, what is left of your flesh. You are, in fact, very lucky, that I had enough metal left, on hand to complete the job."

"So what happens to me now?" Chris asked.

"Now comes rehabilitation. You have to learn, how to use your new body. Are you ready to get started on your rehabilitation?" Chris nodded, as Minawa called to the nurse.

CHAPTER 4

The nurse entered with an empty wheelchair. "May I, take you, to rehab?" she asked.

Chris looked at the chair and then back to her as he slowly slide off the bed. He reached out and, he grabbed the arm rest, and maneuvered his awkward body into the of the chair. As soon as he was settled, he looked at the armrest, and realized that he'd bent it, though he didn't notice, until he sat down, and saw the bent arm rest.

Chris looked up at Ivy Minawa. "Sorry," he said.

"Don't worry; it's to be expected," she said."

As the nurse wheeled Chris down the hall, Minawa said, "There are some clothes for you to wear in the rehab room; you won't need that hospital gown any longer."

A few minutes later, they arrived in a large room. The walls of it were padded for some reason, and Chris was soon to to found find out why.

Minawa turned to the nurse with a sly grin, and the nurse seemed to hold in a laugh as Minawa told Chris to get up. "I'll help you get dressed," she said. Chris was a little hesitant, at this, at first, but Minawa whispered, "You have nothing to be embarrassed about, sense— I am the one who worked on you."

The part of Chris's face that was still flesh turned redder then, his new cybernetic eye. But Minawa persisted, and soon he was almost dressed. "Try to get up," she said, "so I can pull these pants all the way up."

Chris hearing this, didn't like the thought of her seeing him naked, but this didn't bother Ivy as she told him again, "try and get up" so he reluctantly pulled himself out of the chair, but the second both his feet touched the ground, he was lunched from the ground high into the air. He, hit the ceiling, and then bounced back down, and hit the ground again. He started to get up again, but, the second he got his footing, he was launched into the air again. Minawa and the nurse started to laugh, seeing him bounce off the walls.

He finally hit the ground with one finally bounce, and didn't move, from the spot, knowing what would happen if he tried. He did manage, however, to get his pants on. Laughing, Minawa, finally, walked over to him, and leaned down, and put something on the back of his neck. Then she stood back up as she and said, "Try it again."

He sat up slowly, almost afraid that he would be flying again. Then, he turned to the young scientist as he asked, "What the hell, was that all about?"

Minawa smiled as she told him, "You are now, a lot stronger, then any human can imagine. The slightest move can send you flying off."

"What did you put on the back of my neck?" He he asked as he felt for the device.

"It's a limiter, designed to bring your strength, and power down, to a more manageable level, —at least until you can learn how to control your new abilities. Then we can remove it."

Ivy then, started to walk to the door of the room.

After word Chris carefully stood, "Where do we go from here?" he asked.

"We're going to the rehab room, so you can get started with his you're rehabilitation."

Chris wobbled to on his feet as he asked, "Isn't this the rehab room?"

Minawa turned to him, but kept walking to the door as she said, "This room is just for your first steps. Now that you are on your feet, the real thing starts."

Chris and Minawa then went into a room that was, full of heavy, weight equipment, and other types of things that Chris couldn't tell what they where.

Minawa turned around to face him as she smiled. "Let's get started!"

For the next few weeks, where spent adapting Chris to his new limbs.

Finally, after the third week, Minawa thought that it was time to remove the limiter. Chris was hesitant. "I really don't don't know about this, Professor Ivy," Chris said to her, as she removed the limiter from the back of his neck.

"You'll be just fine, and for the last time please just call me Minawa."

"Yes, Minawa," Chris apologized.

Minawa led Chris to a large punching machine. He had been working with this machine, and his progress had been monitored on a computer. Minawa walked over to the computer, and Chris stepped into position in front of the machine, and got into a fighting stance as Minawa said. "Hit the pad."

Chris quickly struck the pad, with a single punch, and the numbers went off the scale. "Excellent," Minawa said seeing numbers go up.

"Wow! I wasn't even trying!" and Chris told her.

"Okay—this time give it everything you have!"

Chris got into his stance again, and reared back, and struck the machine so hard that it shattered.

"Amazing! Far beyond my expectations," Minawa said with pure excitement in her voice. "Now it's time for the some speed tests." Chris and her, walked over to the large running track. Chris got into position and Minawa got ready to time him. "Go!" she yelled. Chris took off. He was like a bolt of lighting shooting, around the track.

CHAPTER 5

Several days later, Minawa and Chris were once again at the track. After Minawa timed the latest trial, she turned and noticed that a group of men had entered the room, and were watching her work. The largest in the group approached Minawa. He was a large black man, wearing a military uniform with lots of metals across his chest. He gestured to Chris, who was flying around the track. "It appears that your, new project is going well, Professor Ivy."

Minawa turned to him, and then turned back to cyborg running around the track. "He is more than a project. He's stronger, and faster, then than any of the other cyborgs I've created. He's the best, General, and he's also like no other guy I've ever met."

Minawa caught herself on the last part of her sentient as she spoke, thinking that she had just said a little too much. The general hearing what she had said. "It's not a good idea for you to get, emotionally attached to your projects, you know."

Minawa, glared at the large man standing next to her getting mad at the, General's comment, as she told him. "I know what I am doing. I have the authority to do, whatever I want with my projects."

The general stared down at her as he told her, "It's no longer, you're project now— it's ours. And, now that its, physical training is finished, my men will, work on his weapons training."

The second Chris he heard "weapons training," he skidded to a stop. "What are you, talking about?" he asked the general.

The general turned to him. "I said, it's time to begin your weapons training."

Chris's rage shot up hearing this. As he stared at the general, almost yelling at him, he said, "Never in a million years will I ever use a gun!" The general seemed to, take this as a insult, and said, "Since you are working under my military jurisdiction, you are going to learn to use the weaponry assigned to you."

"Minawa!" "Who does this guy think he is? He can't tell me, what I can and can't do!"

She answered quietly, "This man is General Jerald Bishop, a high-ranking General officer in the U.S. army, you met on your first day at Cyber Corp."

But before she could finish, the cyborg glared at the man as he said, "I don't don't care if he's the president himself, he can't make me use weapons I vowed never to use."

The general turned to one of his men, and ordered him to take control of the cyborg. But Chris said to the general, "I am not going anywhere with you, or your men, besides. My sensei used to say that when you rely on a weapon that doesn't understand the difference between, right and wrong, you too will stop understanding that difference.

General Bishop could not believe, the trash, this guy was spouting. "He's talking about honor, sir!" Minawa almost yelled. "It is that honor that guides him."

General Bishop looked at the cyborg with raised eyebrows. "What's your name, again? So I can have it carved into your headstone.

Chris looked over at Minawa and then back at the general, "You can call me Cy."

"Whatever?" General Bishop said as he shook his head. He looked at his man and jerked his head toward Chris—a silent order for them to overtake him.

Minawa, though stepped in so there wasn't going to be a fight. She stood in between the cyborg and the general addressed them both. "Wait."

She then pointed out; that right now the cyborg was still hers. The C.C logo that stood for Cyber Corp. witch was the name of her company was still on his shoulder.

"But, if you want him that badly, I'll make a deal with you."

"What deal?"

"You get seven of your best men, and arm them to the teeth. We'll set them up against Cy, who will be unarmed. If he wins, he and I can com and go as we see fit. If he loses, I will install the micro- neuron- barrier, into him just like I have with the others. That will insure that he will obey your orders explicitly."

The general thought about it. He knew his men were well trained, and believed they could easily take this guy out.

"Well, General, do we have a deal?" Minawa asked as she held out her hand to him, to seal the deal.

Bishop then shook her hand as he said, "All right, you have a deal. Tomorrow, mourning, 0800. You know where to go."

"Yes, sir," Minawa finished almost sarcastically, as the general turned to his men and signaled them to leave.

As soon as they were out of sight, Minawa smiled as she said. "Cy, I like that."

"What!" Chris turned to her. He was almost mad at what she had gotten him into.

"Cy. It's an interesting nick name for you. I like it."

"That doesn't matter right now. What does matter is what have you gotten me into?"

"What, would you rather I install that micro- neuron- barrier, and turn you over to the general?"

"No," the cyborg simply said.

"Then you are, just going to have to fight all seven of those men."

"Do you really think I can do it?" Chris asked and. Minawa kissed him on the cheek and said, " I have faith in you. And you have something those soldiers don't—honor."

CHAPTER 6

The next day at 0800, Cy and Minawa met the general, and his men at a large complex where this little contest of there's was going to be held., Cy was amazed to find a small town inside the complex. "What is this place?"

"It's a training ground where soldiers, learn to fight in residential areas," Minawa answered him.

General Bishop said as he turned to the cyborg. "I will give you a ten-minute head start, then my men will come after you. The rules are simple: if my men beat you, Minawa then installs the chip that will make you obey my commands, but, in the unlikely chance that you beat all seven of my men, I will allow you, and Professor Ivy to go wherever you want."

"The clock is ticking." General Bishop, finished.

Cy then turned to Minawa, and she just winked at him. "Go!" she said, and he shot off into the town area.

The second Cy was out of sight, General Bishop ordered his men to go. With a salute and a "yes, sir" they ran off.

"What happened to the ten-minute head start?" Minawa yelled at the general.

Without even looking at her he said, "There are no head starts in war."

"That's not fair," Minawa protested, .

"War is never fair."

Minawa looked into the town and prayed that Chris would be all right.

Cy had just jumped on top of one of the buildings, to get a better look around. He would wait there, until it was time, but he didn't have to wait long because right then his cybernetic eye detected, something coming his way. He turned around to see a missile coming his way, he had no time avoid it.

The explosion blew him into another building. He was furious with himself as he pulled himself, out of the rubble. He should of have expected that the general wouldn't give him the ten minutes.

Cy scanned around the area to find where that missile had came from. When he located the spot, where, the soldier who fired the missile was, he jumped from the hole he was standing in, and came crashing in, on the soldier.

The soldier jumped back when the cyborg came down, and tried to fire off another shot. But Cy grabbed the launcher with one hand and bent it in half.

The soldier dropped the launcher, and pulled out a handgun. He had time to get off only one shot, in a the blink of an eye, Cy caught the single bullet, and threw it back at the soldier.

The soldier fell to he ground as the bullet bounced off his forehead, for—Cy had managed manage to throw the bullet with such precision, that it hit a single pressure point. The impact had, only knocked the man out, for Cy had no intention of killing anybody.

Below him, the soldiers' commanding officer, was telling, four men behind him, as they moved on, to be careful, and watch out for anything. While the officer was still speaking, Cy jumped down silently, and grabbed each man, and rendered them unconscious as he moved his way to the front of the line.

The officer turned when he heard a slight sound, and he found that his men were down. And, before he could react, Cy came down knocking him out cold, "Six down, and one to go." he said, not even breathing hard.

General Bishop was not happy about this at all, his men were taken out with in only five minutes of the ten minutes that was supposed to be the Cyborg's head start.

He grabbed a walkie talkie, and shouted into it, "It's time!"

Minawa turned to him as he said this, wondering what he meant, but she was about to get her answer. While the cyborg was looking for the last soldier, he heard something coming up from behind him. When he turned, he was slammed into the ground, by a giant claw.

Minawa could not believe what she was seeing from the observation area. The general had sent in one of the specially designed mobile tanks. This one was designed to look like a giant scorpion, but instead of a poison tail it had a gun turret. Minawa glared at the general, as she yelled at him, "This is against the rules! It was just supposed to be seven armed men, and that needs at lest four people, to run it!"

The general responded, "This tank is special. It can be run by, one person. Not only that, but one of my best men is in that tank, and he has never let me down before. Now we'll see just how good your cyborg really is!"

Minawa was now worried about Cy, who was being held up by the claw that had hit him. The gun turret turned and locked on to its target—Cy. Just as, it was about to fire, Cy reached over and grabbed the claw. He started to force it open, and right as the tank fired, the cyborg broke the claw that was holding him he plummeted to the ground unharmed.

He landed on the ground as the cannon fired. He, rolled under the tank. The soldier manning the tank moved around trying to find Cy, the man inside the tank cursed to himself for not being fast enough, but as he was still trying to find the cyborg, he heard something that sounded like metal being torn.

Just as the tank turned, Cy climbed onto the side of the tank, and reached his cybernetic hand into the tank, and grabbed the soldier's head. He pulled the man out of the tank, and threw him down.

Cy jumped down from the tank, and landed next to him, looking down on the man that was once in the tank.

The soldier looked at the tank, he was throw from, and then yelled, "Look out!" Cy at first didn't respond thinking it was some trick, but then he heard the sounds of gunfire from the tall gun of the tank firing, from its tall gun.

Cy was hit hard by the missile that fired, and was slammed into a nearby building that then crashed down on him.

"*No!*" Minawa yelled in from the observation deck, as she watched Cy get buried alive. Then she turned to the General. "How did the tank move without an operator?" she asked.

General Bishop said nothing. It was more interesting to see her upset about this. He knew all about that tank, the second its pilot is ejected, the tank goes into automatic kill mode, destroying anything that moves.

But Bishop and Minawa both suddenly noticed that the rubble where the cyborg had crashed was moving. Then, bursting out of the rubble, was the cyborg. But something wasn't right as— his body seemed to be glowing, a black aura surrounding him.

Cy let out a roar, that almost sounded like some kind of wild animal had just been released from its cage. The general and Minawa watched in awe as a the fiery black aura surrounded him until it focused into his left fist surging around it. They watched the cyborg then shoot forward. In a the blink of an eye, his fist impacted the tank blowing it away in a fiery blast.

Minawa was running down to the battle area. Just as she arrived, Cy jumped out of the fire that was left from the explosion.

"Crap!" He yelled as he shook himself off, and kicked some of scraps of metal out of the way.

"What is it?" Minawa asked him.

She watched as he tore the burned shreds of his shirt off his body. "That was one of my favorite shirts," he said to her, with almost a comical sad expression.

Minawa just sighed and shook her head. "I'll buy you a new one," she promised.

She then turned as General Bishop who was walking up to them. "You've got three weeks, to do whatever you have to do, then the cyborg is mine," he said. Then he waved them off as he turned around, and walked away, mad as a hornet, angry that his men had been beaten.

CHAPTER 7

The next morning, Chris was packing his things when Minawa came in, his room carrying a large black trench coat. "What's the coat for?" Chris asked.

"It's a magnetic cloaking coat. It will shield you, and allow, you to walk though a metal detector for officious reasons.

Chris put the coat on, and Minawa then handed him some sun classes and a cap. Then she stepped back, to take a look. "Now that looks cool," she said.

"I don't know," he said, "do you think that the cap is a little too much?" But Minawa told him that it was perfect.

xxx

At the military base, General Bishop, had his men standing before him. The seven men were sporting a variety of injuries, but otherwise they were okay. But Bishop, was not happy with them, "You all are worthless," he yelled. "You were beaten by a guy, who had no military training!"

But, before he could finish his rant, one of the soldiers spoke up, "We could not fight against a, cyborg with enhanced strength. Not only that, he seemed to know some kind of martial art!"

General Bishop turned to the soldier, and asked him to give him his gun. "Why?" the soldier asked. and Bishop just yelled at him again and ordered him, to give him his gun. The soldier handed Bishop his handgun and Bishop then held the gun to the soldier's head, and fired.

The soldier fell to the ground, as Bishop then threw the gun too his body, and turned to the rest of the men. "Anyone else have any more excuses?

"No, sir," they all said in unison. With that, Bishop turned and started to walk off. "Good, and don't fail me again."

xxx

Chris and Minawa, walked into the employee garage that was in the building they were attached to the military complex. Chris was carrying four heavy looking suitcases, but he was carrying them with ease. When he saw Minawa's car he about dropped the bags, —it was a beautiful red dodge Dodge Viper. Sr she turned to him, and told him to put the bags in the trunk.

Minawa pushed a button on her keys, and popped the trunk. After he put the bags in the trunk, they climbed into the car, and drove off.

As they left the military base, Chris asked, "So where are we going?"

She smiled that knowing smile of hers as she said, "I have a place set up for us I don't think its a good idea for you to be to far away from me I mean you are still my top security guard."

Some time later they stopped in front of a large house, Chris was about ask if this was her place when someone opened the car door on his side, as a women welcomed him to the home of Minawa Ivy.

At first it was hard to believe that this was Minawa's home it was huge and there was a training area in the back as Minawa had prepared for his arrival and wanted to do more tests on his strength.

The inside was just as amazing as the outside for it had a voice controls for the whole house and everything was top of the line.

After he was shown to a room Chris finally had a chance to relax for it had been a troubling time being remade into a cyborg and the wonders of how this kind of technology actually works, but for now he would find that out for tonight he was relishing finally getting a chance to sleep in a bed but the moment his body hit the bed it broke under his weight.

The crash brought Minawa and some of her people to the room and upon seeing Chris in the broken bed they all couldn't help but laugh.

CHAPTER 8

The next day after the craziest of the night Chris and Minawa thought it would be nice to go out, for the day Chris headed toward Minawa's car, but she stopped him. "We're not taking the car" she said.

"Then what are we taking?" Chris asked.

She walked over to him. "Pick me up," she said, and Chris gave her a weird look. "Do it," she urged.

So he picked her up the way a groom picks up a bride, and asked, "What am I supposed to do now?" "Jump!" she said. "And put everything you have into it."

He then remembered his training with Minawa. He knew that he could jump long distances, so he thought that this might be a fun opportunity to see just what he could do. He took a couple of steps back, and then leaped into the air. He was right—this was fun, for he leaped over 300 feet in the air.

"This is incredible!" He he yelled out as they soared through the air.

"This is nothing," Minawa quietly said; "just wait till you gain the Hyper Mode."

"What?" Chris said.

"Oh nothing," she replied as they landed in front of the site of the events that had changed Chris's life. He had wanted to come back to the spot to see how bad it was.

As Chris put Minawa down, he walked over to the edge of the pile of rubble of what was left of the building. *How could anyone have survived such an explosion?* he thought. Then it hit him—how did Minawa survived?

He turned back to her. "How did you survive?" he asked. asking her this questions.

She answered by raising her hand to him and showing him the field generator on her wrist. "It generates a protective shield," she then told him. "It only has enough power to shield me from the explosion—and only for a brief period … But it was long enough for me to climb out of the rubble to help you."

Minawa then lowered her head in shame. "I'm so sorry for not being able to help more during that time, but —I was too scared to react fast enough."

Chris moved over to her, as he saw a tear trickle down her face. He put a his hand to her chin making her face him. He smiled at her. "There is nothing you could of have done to prevent my injuries. I'm glad to be alive. And, I'm the one that who choose to be your security guard, so don't blame yourself."

Minawa smiled at him. She felt a little better and was happy knowing that he cared. He kissed her forehead, and smiled back at her. "Besides," he said, "if you want to blame anyone, blame the maniac's who had suicide bombs!"

Later, the two of them went into a near by mall to look around and to get something to eat. While they were talking, Chris's cybernetic eye detected something, and his attention was diverted from Minawa. Minawa noticed this and asked, "What's wrong?"

"I think I'm detecting a silent alarm that's been set off, and it's close," he responded. Minawa and Chris looked around, then she saw two people with guns walk inside a jewelry store. They both where holding large bags as they pointed their weapons threateningly at the store clerks warning them not to do anything funny. Apparently the robbers didn't know about the silent alarm.

Minawa turned to Chris with a smile saying. "What do you say, we teach these guys a lesson they'll never forget?" Chris nodded and Minawa continued, "I'll be good cop, you, be bad cop."

"But I want to be good cop," Chris whined.

"Just come on," she finished, pulling him off his seat.

The two men headed for the doors with their loot in hand when Minawa stepped in front of the door blocking their exit. One of them yelled at her, "Get out of way or I'll shoot you!"

Minawa very politely said, "Return what you stole, and turn yourselves in or you will be sorry."

The two men looked at each other, and then back at Minawa, who just stood in front of the door, unarmed and seemingly with out a care in the world. The two of them could not help, but laugh at this, because she wasn't very intimidating.

"Don't you laugh or you'll make my boyfriend mad!" she said in a cute tone. This made the men laugh even harder. "You're only a girl!" one of them said. at this, then saying "bring it on, girl."

"If that's the way you feel…" Minawa said. Then she turned quickly to Chris, and shouted, "Take them!"

Chris jumped out of no where, and grabbed the two men. He slammed them both against the wall holding them both up by their shirts. The men, yelled, and kicked as they struggled, but could barely move. They did manage, however, to hold up their guns, —right at Chris's face, and chest.

"You guys shouldn't do that! It will only piss him off!" Minawa kindly told the two men. Despite the warning, they still fired at Chris, but the bullets bounced off his body. The only thing that they did succeeded in demolishing his sunglasses—he would need a new pair!

When they stopped firing, they looked in shock at the cybernetic eye that focused on them. The eye was glowing red. "He's some kind of freakin' robot!" one of the men yelled.

Chris did not like being called a robot, as he tightened his grip on two men. "I am *not* a robot!" he growled in his throat.

Chris's grip on the two men tightened, and the two men started to bleed from tightness of the impact of Chris's cybernetic hands. The blood started to run down his arms.

Minawa, seeing this, said, "You guys have one chance left to live. You could can turn yourselves in, and forget what you saw today, or I'll snap my fingers, and he'll snaps your necks, well boys what we'll be!

She then leaded up against Chris's shoulder preparing to snap her fingers. "Well, boys, what will it be?"

The two men gave in. "We give up!" Chris dropped them to the ground, and right then Chris and Minawa heard the police arrive on the scene. Chris shook his head thinking that it took had taken them long enough.

"We'd better get going," Minawa said as she saw cops coming through the nearby entrance to the mall.

Chris looked at the robbers. "Fools without honor," he said. "And they broke my sunglasses!" He grabbed Minawa's hand. "You're, right, we'd better get going."

Just as they turned to run, Minawa noticed a pair of sunglasses in the shirt pocket of one of the robbers.

She quickly reached down into his pocket and snatched them out. "You won't need these where you're going," she said.

"Come on, Minawa," Chris yelled. He was already at the mall entrance to the mall. She jumped up and, ran over to him. He took her in his arms and jumped up into the air.

While in the air, Minawa, noticed something coming they're way said, "Chris, look out!"

The moment that she said it something slammed into them, Chris managed to keep Minawa save as they crashed into a building and out the other side.

They rolled to a stop Chris looking around trying to find what had hit them his cybernetic eye then detected a large power source coming their way. He turned to Minawa, told her to run as a huge mobile tank crashed right on top in front of them.

CHAPTER 9

People in the street screamed and ran in panic, as they saw the large tank land. The tank moved right up in front of Chris. He didn't move an inch as he watched as a monitor came out of the front of the tank.

General Bishop's face appeared on the monitor. "You both must return to the base now!" He said to them as the tank took a step forward.

"What?" Minawa asked. "But you said we had a week!"

"You both have jeopardized, national sincerity with your antics. I saw what you two did in that mall. Now I have no choice, but to terminate everyone here. And, after that, I want you two back at the compound."

"You can't be serious!" Chris yelled out as the tank's gun moved to point to some of the people. "You can't kill all these people just because we helped stop a couple of criminals! That's ridiculous!"

"You have no one to blame, but yourself, Cyborg," Bishop said in an emotionless tone.

Acting on that Chris pushed Minawa out of the way, as he moved in front of the tank. He plunged his fist right down the gun barrel right as it fired. Immediately, Chris and the tank were engulfed in an massive explosion. Miraculously, no one was hurt—except for Chris, who was on the ground.

The people watching, at that point, thought that Chris had been destroyed, but Minawa told them all to look again. They all watched in awe as Chris came walking out of the fire. Other than the fact that most of his clothes were burned, he looked all right.

Minawa, though, still asked anxiously, "Are you all right?"

"I'm fine. But we'd better go get back to the corporation, and tell that crazy general that we quit, because there is no way that I'm working for a mad man like him."

Minawa agreed. "We need to go back, to my lab first."

"Why?" Chris asked as he turned to her.

"Because there is something that we need to get out, so the general can't use my cyborgs, anymore. I know he has been using my cyborgs as assassins. He calls them assassinords. That's the reason I made you, —so you could help me get them back."

But, before she could tell him anymore, a large clawed hand came out of the fire and grabbed Minawa, and lifted her into the air. Then a huge robot jumped out of the fire.

Minawa screamed. "Chris, this is one of the assassinords!" Chris was about to attack when the assassinord held up it's other clawed hand. Its claws lashed out like tentacles, and attacked Chris, slashing at him until one claw stabbed him right in his chest. Chris fell to the ground with sparks flying.

The people watching as the Assassinord grabbed Minawa, and then the robot turned to them and, in a monotone, said, "No witnesses." When Chris saw this, he rolled over on his stomach, and started dragging himself toward the robot, but the robot had hurt him badly, so he could barely move. Then Chris saw that the assassinord was about to attack.

Something snapped inside of Chris. He could not take anymore. He let out what sounded like a lion's roar as his cybernetics performed self-repair protocols. Hearing the roar, the assassinord turned to Chris.

Before the assassinord could react, Chris jumped in the air and, in one move, sliced off the assasinords hand that was holding Minawa. Before she hit the ground, he caught her.

She looked up at Chris as he put her down, and jumped at the assassinord. Chris's arms, and legs were glowing like fire as he spun around the large robot's arm, and then finally landed on it.

When the robot tried to get him, Chris jumped into the air. The assassinord raised his arm up, and Chris yelled out to it, "Go ahead, and use your cutters on me. See what happens after I made those cuts on your servos. Just try and kill me!"

Just as the assassinord tried to use his tentacle-like cutters, his arm exploded. At the same time, Chris destroyed the assassinord, cutting the large robot right down the middle using only his metal hands.

The assassinord split in half as it blew up in a fiery blaze. Chris then turned to Minawa and helped her to her feet asking. "Are you okay?"

"I'm okay" Minawa told him, "but I wonder if you're okay. What happened just now?"

"Honestly, I don't know. One minute, I was on the ground half dead, and then the next thing I knew, I was up and fighting harder than ever before." Chris finished his sentence as he turned to the fiery metal that was all that was left of the assassinord. Minawa, at that point, wondered to herself. *Just how strong is Chris going to get?*

Suddenly, all people that witnessed this started to come out of hiding and at this Chris and Minawa thought that it was time to go. As they flew through the air, Chris asked Manawa, "Is it okay that we left the way they we did?"

Minawa said, "We had no choice. If we didn't, the general will never truly, give up. He will now follow us to the ends of earth, if he has to."

Chris thought about this for a minute. "What did you mean when you said, that you made me to help you find other cyborgs, what did you mean by that?"

"Yes…" Minawa started. "You see, you're not the only cyborg I've made. In fact, I've made twelve—all with different powers, and abilities. They've all been placed all around the world. And the worst thing is that a lot of them are our age, and they're still being used as assassins."

Chris could not believe what he was hearing. How could someone use anyone—but especially someone young—as an assassin? Minawa then told him, "It makes sense in a way—who would suspect a young person to be an assassin? Before anyone can react, it's too late."

Chris thought about this for a while as they headed for the Cyber Corp building. He still could not help, but think how inhuman a person would have to be to turn young people into assassins. He knew he had to help Minawa get them back no matter what.

CHAPTER 10

When they landed in front of the Cyber Corp building, Chris looked up at the tall building in front of him.

"Okay," he said, turning to the women next to him, "how do we get to your lab from here? It's on the thirtieth floor? We certainly can't go in the front door now that the general properly probably wants us dead!"

"Do you trust me?" Minawa asked with a smile.

"I do," Chris answered.

Instantly, Minawa then moved behind him and jumped onto his back Rapping her arms, and legs around him, and just said "Then start climbing."

"How?" Chris asked looking at the building.

"Just dig those metal hands, and feet of yours into the building, and you can climb it without a problem."

The cyborg then moved over closer to the building. He looked up, and then he looked down at his hands. He then slammed his left hand into the wall of the building. His fingers digging into the concrete with ease. Then he slowly started to climb up the side of the building.

As he was climbing, he asked Manawa, "What are we going to do when we get in your lab?"

She looked up, as they climbed and said, "It looks as if you are going to have to fight off the guards long enough for me to get the design specs from the computers.

"So, I'm the distraction." He stated this more of as fact then than a question.

"Yup!"

Chris shook his head as he climbed. "You know, sometimes you can be a real pain in the butt."

"You got it! But you know you love me though," she finished as she hugged him. Chris let out a low growl, under his breath as he continued to climbed.

When they made it to the right floor, Chris punched at the window, but it didn't break. "It's reinforced," Minawa told him. But then she pushed at the glass and it just opened. "The windows and doors of the building have a DNA scanning system."

"They will open only if you're an employee of the corporation. They remain locked if anyone else tries to gain access." she stated with a smile as Chris growled at her again for making him look foolish.

They both jumped in, and Minawa told Chris, "Go, down this hallway and cause as much destruction and chaos as possible. I'll head straight for my lab. Meet me there in five minutes. It's down that way and to the left."

They both then said, "Be careful," in unison, and they ran their different ways.

Chris ran down the hallway and then stopped as he saw a camera. He jumped up and hung on the ceiling and yelled into the camera, "Come and get me!" Then he tore the camera off the ceiling. This action seemed to set off a chain reaction.

For it seemed that every alarm in the building went off at the same time. He waited for a few minutes unit he saw a bunch of men, ran running toward him. Then he smiled as he said, "Catch me if you can!" With that, he ran off with the men right behind him.

Meanwhile, Minawa had just made it to the door to her lab. She gained entry via the DNA scanner, but,— something exploded out on her.

Chris was still running when he stopped dead in his tracks. He, knew that Minawa was in danger. He shot off to in the direction of her lab, taking out the guards left and right as he shot past them.

Chris made it to the lab in seconds,—just in time to see General Bishop standing over Minawa's body. The cyborg seemed to vanish as he whirled into action. He grabbed the gun from the man's hand,

and crushed it as he threw the general against the far wall, with easy knocking him out. He then took Minawa, inside the lab, shutting and bolting the lab door behind them.

He held Minawa in his arms. She was still breathing. Her hand was pressed tightly over a bullet wound in her chest. "Are you all right?" When she moved her hand from the bullet wound, he knew he had to do something.

"Don't worry about this, I'll be all right" she told him. "Just go over to the far wall, and push against it."

He did as she told him and pressed against the wall. It slide open to reveal a young woman. She stood there without moving. Chris, then turned back to Minawa. "Who is she?"

"Do you remember, what I told you about the metal that you're made of?"

"Yeah. What about it?"

Minawa gasped. It was clear that she was struggling with her pain. "There was, in fact, quite a bit of that metal. I have made twelve other cyborgs besides you."

"What's this got to do with this girl?" Chris was confused.

"That girl is in fact an android. She will help you, track down the other cyborgs. Go, find them," Minawa then said. "She will awaken in twelve hours. At that time, she would will obey your commands."

After Chris heard this, he realized that Minawa was planning on staying behind. She had probably planned to from the start.

"There is no way I'm going to just leave you here," he said.

Minawa forced herself to her feet, as she said, "Chris! I want you to take that android, and go!" She yelled as loud as she could as she held herself up against wall.

"Minawa, please," Chris begged. "You need to stop talking like that. I need to get you some help."

But Minawa glared at him as she said, "Chris, you listen to me now. If you love me, as much as I love you, then you will do this for me. And you should know that there is a larger reasons that I made you as strong as you are. One of those reasons is to find those other cyborg's. They need you more I do."

She turned to him, and yelled *"Go!"*

But Chris still refused to leave her, so she then stood herself up and, despite the pain she was in, turned to him. "Chris, this is for your own good, and the good of those girls out there." She looked him straight in the eye and said, "Code 6225." The second she said those numbers, Chris stiffened up saying, in a static almost robotic tone, "Code confirmed. Awaiting commands."

"I want you to take this android and go two miles from the building and then reboot," Minawa told Chris.

The cyborg then stated, "Command confirmed." His voice retained that static tone. He picked up the android, and turned to the door that was still bolted shut. He grabbed the door, and tore it off its hinges with ease.

The cyborg then ran to the nearest window. He hadn't been able to break the glass before; however, now, with one kick, he shattered the glass, and jumped out the window.

As they plummeted to the ground at incredible speed, the cyborg didn't even try to grab the building to slow down their descent. He simply, slammed to the ground, with incredible force, cracking the concrete under his feet. He didn't even acknowledge the impact; he just ran off in a blur of speed.

Meanwhile, Minawa was working with the last of her strength, erasing all the data on herself, Chris, and the other cyborgs who were scattered around the globe. As she worked, she heard something behind her. Turning as quickly as she could, she saw General Bishop standing in the doorway.

"What do you think you're doing, Miss Ivy?" he said in low tone.

"I'm making sure that my work is never used for your plans," Minawa said as she sat back in her chair breathing hard.

"My plans are for the good of the world, Miss Ivy. I just want the best for our world. Why can't you see that?" Bishop said as he started walking towards her.

Minawa smiled. "Well, let's see what you think of this." Minawa pressed one last key on the computer and then her arms fell limp, and she slipped to the floor.

Bishop heard a computer voice say, "Self-destruct system has been activated. You have one minute to evacuate."

Bishop turned to the woman lying next to the computer. "The crazy bitch set the self-destruct!" he said in disbelief.

After traveling for about two miles, Chris came to a halt. He still held the android girl in his arms as his systems rebooted. He could see the Cyber Corp building in the distance. He was about to run back to the building, but, suddenly, the whole building blew up right in front of him.

Chris stopped dead in his tracks and fell to his knees in pure shock. He sat there still for a few moments holding the android in his arms. As he watched the building burn, he found himself unable to move. Quietly, he let the android slip from his hands and rolled to the ground.

That's when he let out a roar of animalistic rage. He started to slam his metal fist to the ground again and again in a blind rage. Then he got up and, leaving the android behind, ran at lighting speed back to the building and he stormed to the building and slammed straight into the burning inferno.

A couple of seconds passed before Chris let out another animalistic roar —this time from in the middle of the burning inferno. Just then, as an explosion erupted from the middle of the blaze. Chris roared out Minawa's name. The power that he let out in that one roar vaporized what was left of the building.

Chris was standing in the middle of a large crater that was once the building's foundation. There wasn't a scratch on him, although he was breathing hard, and had his hands on his knees to hold himself up. He had used up so much energy, he finally fell to the ground unconscious, as a silent tear fell from his eye.

Some time later, Chris came to. He found himself still in the crater, and he had no idea of how much time had passed since the explosion. He looked around realizing, that there was nothing left. He let out a long sigh and jumped out of the crater, landing right next to the android. Wondering how she had got there, he slowly picked her up, and turned to look at the crater one last time before jumping into the air.

CHAPTER 11

When Chris finally made it back to Minawa's house the sun was just starting to rise. He stepped into the house with the android still in his arms. One of Minawa's many servants came up to him and asked what happened to Minawa?

"Minawa's dead," he told them quietly and just as he finished, they heard a reporter's voice on the TV in the next room. The station was broadcasting a special report about Cyber Corp.

Chris, and the group ran into the living room, and the reporter on the television said, the Cyber Corp building, had been destroyed by one of their cyborgs that got out of there control. General Bishop, explained what had happened.

The cyborg had not only destroyed the Cyber Corp building, but had killed, Professor Minawa Ivy in the process. Now the general was posting a reward for of $1 million for the cyborg— dead or alive.

Chris could not believe what the general was saying. The general was framing him for the death of Minawa, and placing a reward for his capture. This was too much to for Chris to take. For the life of him, he was going to make that man pay for what he had done. He, reared back, and punched the TV, with more force than he had ever let out.

The punch didn't just destroy the TV, but the wall behind it, and half of an automobile outside. The cyborg stood there for a second breathing hard. Minawa's maids were in a state of pure shock for they had never seen power like that before.

"Now that you have that, out of your system, it's time for us to go." The cyborg heard a voice say from the kitchen. They all turned around as they saw the android walk into the living room.

"Hello, everyone," the android said. "My name is Ellis, and it is time for Chris and I to go."

Chris raised an eye brow asking. "Go where?"

"It's time for the two of us to go, and find those other cyborgs. It's also time for me to take you to your new home, —at least until you can get this whole mess straightened out."

Chris looked down at the floor, and then at the girl standing in the doorway. "All right. Let's just go," he said in a sad voice. He, walked over to her, and put a hand on her shoulder. She, smiled up at him.

Chris turned to the Maids. "The police may show up soon. You can tell them that I escaped from here, and ran off."

He then went back to his room and gathered some of his things. Before he left, he turned to them one more time. "Christopher William Striker is dead," he said. "From this day on, I will be known as Cy." Then, taking Ellis with him, walked out the door, and went to his car and drove off. He barely heard his aunt uncle and sister wishing him luck.

It was late at night, by the time they stopped, in front of a large building. Cy, and Ellis got out of the car, and headed up to the front door. Cy didn't think anything of it because he was still so very upset.

He was so upset that he didn't even see the sign in the front of the building that read, International School for Girls. Cy just followed Ellis with his head down as they walked into the building. There didn't seem to be anyone inside.

Ellis still led Cy to one of the upstairs rooms, and knocked on the door. A young woman answered, she was rubbing the sleep out of her eyes, but, when she saw who was at her door, she almost screamed. She grabbed both of them, and flung them inside her room, slamming the door behind her and locking it securely.

"I was expecting, the both of you after what I heard on the TV," she said. "I couldn't believe, about my sister being killed by a cyborg.

"You don't believe any of it, do you?" Ellis asked.

"Not a word for, I know my sister, would never make anything that would hurt anyone," the girl said. Then she saw the cyborg just standing there with a sad expression.

"What's wrong with him?" The the teen girl asked Ellis.

"He is still upset," said Ellis. "He has just lost Minawa and his life all in one night."

The girl walked up to Cy and smiled as she said. "You know, my sister often e-mails to me about you and how great a man you are. So you should realize that she probably died thinking about you."

Cy looked up to at her and, with a low voice, asked, "Who are you?

"I'm sorry," the girl said. "My name is Samantha Ivy. I'm Minawa's younger sister."

"No, I should be the one apologizing," said Cy, "because, I failed to protect the woman I loved, I don't even deserve an excuse. In fact, if it hadn't been for Minawa, I would already be…" Cy struggled to finish his sentence. Finally he said, "So I'm going to save you all the trouble of being near me and just leave."

He turned and moved to walk back to the door, but Ellis and Samantha both tried to stop him.

"You can't leave now," Samantha stated as she tried to push the cyborg back. "Not with a one million- dollar reward on your head. There are probably bounty hunters of all kinds just waiting to get their hands on you."

"I don't care!" Cy yelled at the two girls as he pushed them aside and shot out the door. He moved down the stairs and out of the building moving so fast that no body saw him run out.

Ellis and Samantha both knew they had to get him back, so, after Samantha got herself dressed, they both went out of the building to look for him.

Hours later, the sun had risen, and people were moving about in the streets. Cy had been out to check out the area and was now walking down a sidewalk on his way back toward the school. He held his head low so you couldn't see his face. All that was visible was his red glowing eye.

As he walked on, he heard a girl scream, but didn't react to it. No one did reacted, for that mater. As he continued down his path, the screams got louder. Finally, he heard the girl's cry for help. For a split a second he thought that it was Minawa calling to him.

He stopped in front of the school shed, and banged on the door. "Is everything all right?" he yelled. He heard a muffled cry for help, but then he heard a man's voice yell, "Piss off!"

That's when Cy reared back and punched the door in. Inside five guys were nearly on top of one girl. But what Cy really saw was someone hurting Minawa. Without even thinking, he rushed at the five guys and beat them within an inch of their lives. making them regret what they where doing.

Cy then dragged the five beaten bodies out of the shed. They were alive but badly hurt. He throw the lot of them into a trash bin.

The girl was so grateful for what Cy had done, that she didn't even notice the fact that he was a cyborg. His face remained sad, as he realized that the girl wasn't Minawa.

Suddenly, Ellis and Samantha came running over to him.

They had been looking everywhere for him. They both asked him if he was okay. But the way he looked at them made them wonder if he was ever going to be okay again.

Cy looked at them, then looked up at the sky. As as the two watched him, they saw him smile at the sky. Finally, he then turned back to them and said, "It's all right, girls. I'll be fine. I just needed some time to myself." They made sure the young woman was okay. She insisted she lived nearby and could make her own way home.

Sam asked, "Are you going to find those other cyborgs my sister made then?"

With a warm smile, Cy said, "Yes. It is what she wanted form me.

"Then you two should follow me," said Sam. "I have something special to show you."

They followed Sam back into the dorm, and right down to a hidden base that was hidden underneath the building.

Cy and Ellis where amazed at the sight of all the of technology. Sam told them that was why her sister sent them to her. Minawa, had designed, this huge complex underneath this school dorm, so that Cy and Elis would have a place to bring the cyborgs when they found them they would have a place to stay as well.

"That's great!" Cy stated, then turned back to Ellis, and asked her. "When can we leave and search for the first cyborg?"

Ellis then said, "The first cyborg should activate in about three hours."

"That's good," Cy said. "That gives me time to shower and get some rest. I haven't slept in two days." Cy then went back up to Sam's room where he had left his things. He grabbed some stuff from his bags, and then turned to Sam and asked, "Where are the showers?"

"There is a small problem. I wasn't expecting my sister to ever make a male cyborg."

"Where are you going with this?" Cy asked.

"Well, you see, all the cyborgs that my sister made were female, so this is an all all-girls dorm."

"So what am I suppose to do?" Cy asked.

Sam told him "If you waits a minute," Sam told him, "I'll deal with it." A little bit later, Sam was standing guard in front of the showers so no one would disturb Cy. After Cy got out of the shower, he went back to the underground complex to his new room that Sam had provided for him.

Later, Ellis ran into his room and told him that the first cyborg has had appeared on the tracking device. Cy looked up from his spot on his bed as he asked, "Where is it located?"

"California," Ellis said. "And her code name is Sniper."

"Sniper," Cy stated. "What kind of name is Sniper?"

"It's because her cybernetic powers reside in her eyes, for— she can see in any spectrum of light, and she can shoot beams from her eyes that can stun or even kill her opponent."

"Well, now the big question should be how are we going to get there?" Cy said. "I mean, my car can get us there, but it would take some time."

Sam smiled. "Wait a day," and she said. "I'll have something that will get you to California in a few hours." Cy agreed but was a little skeptical.

The next day, Cy, and Ellis, carrying their traveling gear, walked into the school's garage where Sam had told them to meet her. There was a van in the garage, but it didn't look any different from any other van, Sam greeted them. "Watch!" she told them. "This baby can fly!" The wheels rotated and disappeared inside the vehicle, and the van started to float in the air.

Cy looked awe stuck. "Is it difficult to drive?"

"It's as easy to drive in the air as it is on the ground," Sam told him.

As Cy looked at the modifications to the van, he told Sam that, "You must be as smart as your sister."

"I'm good," Sam said, "but nowhere near my sister's level of intelligence. I could never do what she did with you and the other cyborg's she built."

Cy then looked at his hands as he remembered Minawa. He sighed and then looked back up to Ellis, and told. "We had better get going. We have a long road ahead of us." Cy, and Ellis stowed their gear and got into the van. When Sam didn't join them, Cy asked her, "Don't you want to come?"

"Hey, I'm a lover, not a fighter." She winked at him, and he shrugged as he and Ellis took off into the sky. Sam had been right—the van was easy to "fly."

CHAPTER 12

It was only a few hours latter that they arrived in California at a spot that Ellis's tracking system indicated was near the origin of Sniper's signal. Cy carefully landed the van in an alley and then drove it into a parking garage.

Cy and Ellis took a walk around the city to get the lay of the land.

Cy was a little nervous as he walked down the streets. Even wearing a trench coat and sunglasses, he felt uneasy as the two of them moved on. He was grateful that Ellis looked like a normal person.

Suddenly, Cy thought of something. He turned to Ellis as he said, "The general currently controls these other cyborgs, right?" Ellis nodded. "Well, what's stopping him from telling them to go after me?"

Just as he said this, Ellis's tracking system detected the cyborg they were looking for was active. "Get, down!" she yelled, grabbing at Cy. As soon as they jumped to the ground, a huge beam blasted across the building behind them. Rubble from the building crashed on top of them.

Cy clambered out of the rubble holding Ellis in his arms. "Where'd that come from?"

"I don't know. Sniper can hit an object from over 500 miles away."

"That's just great!" Cy yelled out. "Then there's no telling where they are!" He put Ellis down.

xxx

Meanwhile, miles away from them, on top of a tall building, a man was yelling at a young woman.

He was very upset with her for missing her targets, but she told him in an emotionless voice that there her targets' reflexes were faster than she had anticipated. "Don't miss, again" the man said, and she nodded affirmatively as she got back into position.

When the girl looked again, her targets were gone. She scanned the area, but found no sign of them. She then noticed a hole left, from where they were meaning. *They must have they had gone underground,* she thought to herself.

Sniper told her handler this as she switched to infrared to track them underground. She saw the cyborg man running at incredible speed along the underground tunnels heading their way as he carried the girl in his arms.

"Target found," she stated as she fired a blast that tore apart the streets.,

xxx

Cy was running as fast as he could go as the beam tore through the tunnel. Ellis yelled out to Cy , "If we keep going like this we should come up under the building that Sniper is on."

"Yeah—if we don't get blasted first!" Cy finished,

xxx

Sniper was still blasting away, but then stopped. Her handler asked "What's wrong?"

"They're right under this building. I can't get a shot.

The handler wondered what to do next. "Where are they now?" he asked Sniper.

She used her scanner. "They're moving toward us at an alarming rate."

Her handler then said, "When they get to the roof, finish them."

Sniper watched carefully. Just as Cy and Ellis came into sight, she fired, blowing half the roof clean off with a monstrous blast.

Sniper's handler looked at the spot after the dust cleared. At first he and thought Sniper had gotten them, but then he hears Sniper say,

"The target is above you!" He looked up just in time to see the cyborg come down and slam his fist right on the remaining part of the roof.

The force of the impact destroyed the roof causing them all to fall through to the first floor below. And after the dust cleared, Cy walked over to the now unconscious Sniper. He picked her up and carried her to his van., Ellis trailing at his heels.

Just as they made to the van, the TV and news crews arrived at the scene. Cy jumped into the van and switched on, the van communications system. Sam came on, the screen. "I see you've got the first cyborg," she said. "If she's still unconscious, you'd better lay her on the bed in the back of the van."

"Well, anyway," Cy said, "now that we've got this girl, what do we do with her? Once she wakes up she'll probably try to kill us again."

He then looked at the girl again. She looked pretty normal—no metal parts. He still could not believe that people would turn a girl into a weapon. Sam's voice came over the communications system. "Look in the glove box," she said, " and take out the small device what looks like a button. It's a neuro-disabler."

He looked and found what she was talking about. "What do you want me to do with it?"

"Put it on the back of the girl's neck," she said. "You'll see a connection." Cy bent over to her, and pulled her hair back. He placed the device into the connection and watched as, a jolt of electricity shocked through her.

Cy turned back to Sam. "What is that thing?"

Ellis said, "The device must of have burned out the micro-neuron-barrier chip that was controlling her."

Sam said, "That's exactly what it did."

Just then, they noticed Sniper stir. She awake and looked, around. As soon as, she saw Cy, she smiled as she jumped at him giving him a crushing hug. "You're my hero!" she said.

Cy slowly managed to pull the girl off him, as he asked. "How do you know me? We've never met until today!"

"I don't know," she said, "I do know is this—I've seen you're face a thousand times in my dreams."

Cy wondered how that could it be. "Ah, that is my fault.

"So you're connected to the other cyborg's— that's how you're able to track them," Cy asked.

Ellis nodded. "That's exactly right."

Sniper interrupted them. "What happens to me now?"

Cy said, "For now we're going to take you back home to the school with us." As he sat started the van. But before he took off, he turned to her, and asked, "Do you have another name that we could call you other than Sniper?"

"All I can remember is Jennifer," the young girl answered. "Beyond that I can"t remember anything else."

"That's terrible," said Ellis. "How sad not to know your past."

Cy also felt bad, but also felt angry also at whoever for the one that had erased the girl's memories—he didn't think Minawa would have done that. This made him even more determined than ever to find each one of Minawa's cyborgs.

xxx

Sniper's handler crawled painfully out of the rubble of the building and watched the van lift into the air. He crawled out of the rubble and pulled out a communicator, and said. "They got Sniper."

CHAPTER 13

A few days later, Sniper—or Jennifer, as she preferred to be called— was getting used to her new home. It took her a while, but she was learning to use her powers again, and she had been using them to watch Cy when he was training.

One afternoon while Jennifer was watching Cy, through the wall (as a cyborg, she had X-ray vision), Ellis came up behind her, and asked, "What are you doing."

Jennifer jumped and, turned to the android, and said. "Nothing," she said as she blushed a little for being caught spying.

"Whatever," Ellis said. "I need to talk to Cy. You wouldn't know where he is would you?"

"There—in the training room," Jennifer said, pointing without thinking.

"Really," Ellis stated with a sly smile. "And how would you know that when the door to the training room is shut?"

"Well … I." —" Jennifer started.

Cy walked out of the training room and asked, "What's going on?"

Jennifer turned to him as she said, "Ellis wanted to talk to you,." while trying to hide the blush on her face.

"Yeah," Cy said. "What is it?"

"Another cyborg tracer has been activated."

"Where is this one?"

"New York," Ellis finished.

Later that day, they all were getting in the van when Cy asked Sniper said, "Hey, Sniper, do you really want to come with us?"

"I do," she responded. "You never know—I might be able to help."

Cy then noticed the look on her face. "Something wrong?" he asked.

"Could you call me Jennifer? Ever sense you found me you've been calling me Sniper, even though you knew I told you my real name."

"Sorry," Cy apologized as he turned back in his seat. Jennifer as she sat back down and Cy took off for New York.

She thought though this as they flew all the way to New York and after landing they started there search Cy was walking a few steps ahead of Ellis and Jennifer when Jennifer, who had remained quiet throughout the trip, asked Ellis, "Do you know if anything about Cy? Like what his real name is?"

But before Ellis could answer, Cy asked, "Ellis, what do you know about this cyborg we're tracking?"

Ellis stammered a bit as she said, "The cyborg's name is Mimic and— she can look like anyone or anything she wants. Not only that, she can create solid holograms of herself so her enemies aren't just fighting one cyborg but an entire army of them."

"Great," Cy stated. "How do we find someone, who can look like anyone?" He scanned around the area, hopelessly.

Jennifer said, "Maybe I can find Mimic with my cybernetic powers."

Ellis then said "That's not a bad idea," Ellis said. "If you can scan for the energy that Mimics gives off."

"Good," Cy said. "We'll have a better chance if we both look for her." They both began to scanned around the area until. Suddenly, Jennifer yelled out, "I found something. There is a large energy level over there!" And she pointed in the direction of the power. Cy looked in the direction she was pointing. He could also detected a high level of power, but nothing else.

"Good job, Sniper," Cy says said as he picked her up along with Ellis. "Hang on, ladies!"

They made it to the top of a building, and looked down. Jennifer pointed to a man walking down a street. "That can't be the cyborg," Cy said. "They were all suppose to be female, aren't they?" He looked at Jennifer and Ellis.

"They are," Ellis answered, "but, remember, Mimic can look like anyone."

"Okay," Cy then said, "I'll go get her!" He jumped from the roof, and landed right in front of the man that was supposed to be Mimic, but, when he did, the people in the area saw him land.

Some of the people ran, but three tough-looking guys realized who he was, and remembered the million- dollar reward on his head. The guys thought they could take him, because they ran over toward him and tackled him. But Cy didn't even move or seem to notice there their weight on him as they bounced off.

They caused only one problem—Mimic had ran, and Cy hadn't been able to see where she went.

Jennifer, and Ellis saw Mimic start to run away. They yelled down to Cy and pointed to where she was going to. Cy leaped out, and landed right in front of Mimic, and grabbed him or her. He, jumped up onto a building and then jumped from building to building, until he landed on the roof with the others. But, once he got there, Mimic got free of his grip, and jumped back.

Mimic changed into her true self and there was— a young African American girl. "Hey, do *not* interfere with my job!"

"What job is that?" Cy asked.

"It's classified!" she said, and then she split herself into five clones of herself, and attacked him.

Jennifer and Ellis watched as the five cyborgs attacked Cy. But he wasn't fighting back—just dodging her strikes. Jennifer then asked Ellis, "Why isn't he fighting?"

Cy heard her as he dodged Mimic. "I can't strike a woman no matter what!"

"Wow, he's a real gentleman," Jennifer said to Ellis. "I thought they were extinct." Jennifer said joking to the cyborg.

"What!" Cy yelled out just as he got punched by one of the clones. He fell off the building. Ellis and Jennifer watched in horror as Mimic's clones tumbled after him, still in pursuit. Ellis and Jennifer made there way to the street, and watched as he keep dodging Mimic's doubles.

Cy yelled out up to them, "Don't just watch—*help*!"

"All right!" Ellis then said, and she threw down the device that would free the cyborg. Cy barely caught it as he does a spin to avoid another strike. Then he yelled out, "What good will this do, if I can't tell which one of them is the real one?"

"Hold on," said Jennifer, "I'll tell you which one."

Jennifer scanned each one until yelled to him, "Behind you!" Cy propelled himself around the girl and, landed behind her, and placed the neuro-disabler on her neck. As soon as the connection was made, the device shocked her, and she fell to the ground as, and her clones disappeared.

Cy picked the girl up, and just as Jennifer and Ellis arrived. "Good job," said Ellis.

But something was bugging him Cy. "I wonder what job this girl was supposed to be doing?" he asked Ellis and Jennifer. "And where is her handler?" Just as he said this, the girl in his arms woke up. Cy looked down at her in his arms as he said, "Hello, little lady."

She looked at him and smiled as and said, "You're the hero in my dreams!"

Cy could not believe it it—she said the same thing that Jennifer had said, when she was awakened. He then turned to Ellis and, who she just shrugged her shoulders.

Cy put Mimic down and introduced her to Jennifer and Ellis. He then asked her, "Do you remember your real name?"

"I'm April," she told them Cy, Ellis, and Jennifer then noticed that the people around them were beginning to stare. A few of them were, talking about calling the police. Cy thought it would be a good idea for them to get going, and so he grabbed the three girls, and jumped into the air.

When they landed next to the van, April told them she could not believe how Cy could fly like that. But she figured that, since, she could change her form, it was to be expected that he had powers too. Still, this had to be the coolest thing she had ever seen.

Before they got into the van, Cy said, "Our job isn't done yet—we still have to found find out what Mimic's mission was."

They all agreed, and then they called Sam for help. Cy and asked her, "Can you hack into the general's files and find out what Mimic's target was?"

It took Sam a few minutes, but her face on the screen looked back at them with a worried look as she said, "She was supposed to kill an ambassador who is visiting New York, and I think they're going to try anyway even though we just got Mimic."

"Okay," Cy stated, "We've got to find this ambassador and protect him, from any of the other men. Sam, can you get us all the information we need to find him?"

Sam looked at her computers again, and said, "Sorry—there's no more information."

But April asked, "Why don't you just ask me?"

Ellis said "You shouldn't remember anything from when you were being controlled."

"I don't remember everything, but I do remember something about a statue surrounded by water if that helps."

After hearing this, Cy, Ellis, and Jennifer all looked at each other, and then said in unison, "The Statue of Liberty!"

They made it just in time to see the ambassador walk out of the statue with four guards on each side of him. They watched as a large truck drives up in front of the statue and then a large robot stepped out of it. The robot stood had large rotating guns instead of hands and stood at lest twelve feet.

Cy and the girls knew they had to stop that thing. "Get in front of the ambassador, and protect him," Cy said to the girls. "I take care of the robot!" As he jumped in the air and slammed down on the robot.

Cy punched the robot several times and managed to get it out of the way of the people. April—Mimic watched as Cy fought the robot. To her he seemed to threw it around like as if it was nothing but a child's toy. The ambassador seemed to realize the cyborg was, trying to keep that robot from killing him.

Cy jumped up onto the robot's head, and grabbed it, and tore it off, and threw it away from the body. Then he jumped to the ground as the robot fell right behind him. Cy then walked back over to the girls. "Is the ambassador okay?"

"The ambassador's fine," said Ellis.

"Are you okay, Cy?" asked Jennifer.

"I'm fine," he told them. "Watch out, though, here comes the ambassador. We'd better go *now!*"

He picked up Ellis and threw her onto his back, and then he grabbed both Jennifer, and April. He, jumped into the air, leaving the puzzled ambassador and his men on the ground. All they knew was that Cy was a hero.

CHAPTER 14

Cy, and the girls returned to the complex shortly after leaving the Statue of Liberty. Cy went straight to his room for he had wonted wanted to send an e-mail to his family letting them know he was doing okay. As he he typed the letter on a computer, April came into his room and said, "Samantha told me to bring this to you.," As she put a cup of tea on his desk.

"Thank you," he said to the girl. He took a sip and said, "It's superb." Then he noticed that April was looking like as if she wanted to ask him something.

"What's on your mind?" Cy asked, .

"Jennifer said that, when you captured me, you didn't try to fight back. You just dodged my blows."

"Yeah. So?" Cy said as he took another drink of his tea.

"Well why didn't you fight me? I mean, I could of have killed you, you know."

He sighed as he told her, "You were not yourself, and it would be dishonorable to fight a warrior who doesn't know what he or she is doing, —not to mention that it goes against his my code to strike a woman." Cy then sipped his tea again, and smiled at her.

A light blush appeared on the young woman's face, and, just then, they both heard Samantha's voice was over the intercoms of the complex calling them to the main computer lab.

When Cy, Jennifer, and April made it to the lab, Ellis and Sam were waiting for them. Sam said, "I have good news and bad news."

"The good news is that another cyborg tracer has been activated."

Ellis told them, "And this one is in Washington DC."

Sam then said, "The bad news is this cyborg has been assigned to assassinate the president of the United States. "

"The general himself has sent this cyborg. His plan is to have the cyborg kill the president, and make it look like you did it, Cy."

There was a dead silent in the room. Then Cy said, "We won't let that happen." As he turned and headed for his van. The three girls followed right behind him.

Upon arriving in Washington, they headed straight to the White House. Cy was walking a few steps ahead, and of his little Jennifer and April soon started to talk to Ellis.

"What is Cy's full story?" April asked. "I mean, why is he doing this? Why is he risking his life for people he doesn't even know? Not that I'm not grateful, but…" April's voice trailed off.

Ellis looked at both of them and told them, "He is doing this to keep a promise." And that's all I'm going to say. If you want to know anything else, you will have to ask Cy.

"Enough gossip, girls," Cy said as he turned to them. "We've got work to do!" He then pointed out over to the fence of that surrounded the White House. "Sniper, please scan the area for the cyborg we're after."

"Okay, Cy," she responded, and began the scan immediately. Right then she noticed something, but, just as quickly, it was gone. This confused her greatly.

Cy turned to Ellis, and asked, "What powers does this cyborg have?"

"Her name is Mirage," answered Ellis. "She has thermoptic camouflage, to— make herself invisible. She can also project and control force fields."

Cy turned back to Sniper Jennifer. "Try thermograph vision," he said.

"What's that?" asked April asked.

"It is a type a vision scan that might be able to see Mirage even if she is using her camouflage," he said. "With it, Jennifer might be able to see Mirage even in her invisible state."

It didn't take long. As soon as Jennifer switched her vision, she saw the cyborg heading right into the White House. "Cy, it looks like she's following right behind a tour group." They all knew they had to get to her before she was got to the president.

Cy and the girls managed to get to the tour group. Jennifer kept an eye on Mirage, who, apparently, did not realize she had been spotted. April then asked Cy, "How do you plain to do to get this cyborg?"

Cy looked at her and said, "I've got one idea. When we pass the Oval Office, I want you to take the form of the president. Get Mirage's attention, and lead her back outside. If things get rough, we don't want to start a firefight inside the White House."

"What do you plan to do when I lead her outside?" April asked.

"Once you're outside, I will find a chance to hit her with the de-control device. Then she'll be out of the general's control." Cy pulled out the device, tossed it up in the air, and caught it again.

"Besides, we have to keep the girl occupied," Cy stated, "because, once she turns on her shields, we'll never get another chance."

Once they reached the office, April managed to get out away from the group. When no one was watching her, and then right when the time was right she changed, using her hologram capabilities, and appeared as the president. Mirage moved closer to the image of the president. April began to lead the way out of the room, down the stairs, and out of the building. Using a communicator ear piece, she kept in contact with Jennifer, and the others to know where Mirage was to know that she was following her.

Just as Cy had planned, Mirage she followed her right back "the president" outside, . As soon as they were clear of the building, Cy, using his own thermograph vision, readied himself, and then shot forward so fast that Mirage didn't even notice his presence. He slapped, the neuro-disabler on her neck, shorting her out.

Cy caught the girl before she hit the ground. "We'd, better get out of here, before things get out of hand." They all agreed.

Later, after they had all met up at the van, they waited for Mirage to wake up. She slowly opened her eyes, and looked around. When she saw Cy, she said, "You are the hero of my dreams!"

Cy shook his head, . He looked at Ellis who just laughed. Then he turned back to Mirage, and asked her, "Do you remember your name?"

Shyly, she said, "My name is Megan."

Cy offered the girl his hand up, and said. "Welcome to the family." She took his hand, but, when he pulled her up, she bumped right into his chest. The the girl then jumped back. Her embarrassment over, his contact showed on her face.

Megan stepped back. At first Cy thought that she was scared of him. "Hey, we're all friends here," he said kindly.

Megan nodded her head, but, before they could say anything else, Ellis said, "Hold on! I've just detected an another cyborg in the Rocky Mountains!"

Cy smiled, and turned to Megan. "Well, it looks like you aren't the only one coming with us today!" He smiled. "Buckle up, girls!" And as he climbed into in the driver's seat, and revved up the engine.

CHAPTER 15

Some time later, Cy, Ellis, Jennifer, April, they and Megan were they found themselves traipsing through the the woods. "Man, this sucks!" April complained, . "I hate the forest. There is no sidewalk, no cell reception, and, to top it off, no bathrooms! I don't do forests!" Angrily, she pulled yanked some brush out of the way.

"What are you talking about Mimic, April?" Cy asked., "This is nothing compared to what I went through during the years I trained in the mountains." He then turned to Ellis. "What are we up against anyway?"

"This one is very interesting," Ellis started. "This one can take on the molecular structure of any material she comes in physical contact with."

"What?" Both Jennifer and April said confused. Then as they looked at Ellis in confusion, when Megan said, "It means that, when she touches something, she becomes like it."

"Oh," they both said.

"Quiet!" and Cy said, pointing to a cabin up ahead. Ellis nodded, indicating she was, that the cyborg was inside that cabin.

Cy, turned to April. "Can you disguise all of us using your holograms?

"Sure," she answered, "but you'll all have to stay within a thirty-foot range."

"Do it," Cy told her. She focused around her and each of them, changed to the point that they didn't recognize each other. But, with Cy, she charged him to the so much that his cybernetics were gone. He looked at his hands and then back at April. He looked as if he was about to cry at the thought of being human again, but he turned away from them and told them, "We'd better get going."

The girls looked at each other. They had seen the look in his eyes. They followed him up to the door of the cabin.

Cy knocked on the door. Sure enough, a young woman answered the door, and greeted them kindly. "What can I do for you?" she asked.

Ellis tugged on Cy's coat to get his attention. "This is the girl we're looking for," she whispered to him.

Cy nodded as he looked at the girl. "We were out hiking and we got lost. There's no cell reception out here. Do you have a phone or something we can use?"

The girl looked at them, and then turned to look inside, and looked at the a man who was setting sitting in a chair at a table inside the cabin. He looked at the "guests" and spoke to the girl: "Go ahead, and let them in for an a awhile."

"Come on in, and make yourselves at home," the girl said, and they all walked in. The girl disappeared into another room. Jennifer, April, and Megan sat on a small sofa. Cy sat down with the man at the table, and told there story how he with his three sisters had gone hiking and got lost.

The man seemed to buy there their story, but something about this guy was giving Cy a bad feeling in his gut. It was the same feeling he'd gotten when he'd seen General Bishop for the first time, —and he didn't like it one bit.

Just as Cy finished his story, the girl from before came back into the room with hot drinks for everyone. After Cy took a sip, he asked, "Has either of you heard of a person named Jerald Bishop?"

The man jumped out of his seat, and his eyes almost shot out of his head when he heard that name. Cy made a half smile when he saw his reaction. The guy spat out a question, "Who are you guys really?"

Cy stood up. "Well, I'm the one who's going to give back the lives that the general took."

Right when he said this he started to walk toward the man, and, as he did, the man yelled out, "Absorb, get them!"

Cy turned to watch the girl. She touched the iron stove, and her body changed to a metallic black. Suddenly, she ran at Cy, and tackled, pushing him straight through the cabin walls. They rolled ,on the ground and slammed into a tree.

The trunk of the tree shattered when they hit it. Escaping falling timber, Cy jumped into the air and landed on a branch in a nearby a tree. From there, he watched as the girl got up, charged at the tree he was sitting in, and, slammed her fist into it. Again, the tree trunk shattered, the causing it to fall to the ground..

Cy jumped out of the way before it hit the ground Absorb thought she had gotten him, and she turned to take care of the others. But, right then, Cy came flying down from the treetops, and grabbed her from behind, witch wasn't a good idea, because, once he grabbed her, she touched his metal body, she changed again to match his metal.

Absorb broke his grip in a flash and hit him so hard that he went flying high then slammed into a large rock, which shattered at the impact. "Dang!" Cy yelled as he got up, "that girl hits hard!" He rubbed his chin.

Absorb was heading right toward him as he got up. He readied himself for her strike, but her punch was stopped short by some unseen force.

He watched as Absorb punched again, and again, but the unseen force was too strong. That's when Mirage—Megan—appeared in front of him.

"Thanks," he said. "See? I knew you could help out!" Right then, a large blast hit Absorb and she was blasted forward. Cy, and Mirage jumped out of the way as the girl slammed into the rock that was behind them, but the impact had no affect effect on her because of the power she had absorbed from Cy.

Absorb looked coldly at the others. Just like the others before, there were no signs of emotion.

Confused as to the source of the blast, Cy looked to where it came had come from. He saw Sniper run down the mountain toward them. When she reached Cy, she said, "*You* might not hit a girl, but *I* certainly don't mind."

Cy laughed and said, "That may be true, but right now this girl is a lot stronger than all of us, and it would take something pretty large to stop her."

Then, from the tops of the trees, they heard April yell out, "How about this?"

They all watched Mimic, April jump from a tree. As she flew through the air, she changed into a large elephant, and then she slammed down onto Absorb. Quickly, she changed back to herself and fell back seemingly exhausted, .

Cy walked over to both the two girls.

Absorb seemed to be unconscious. He then picked up the girl and turned to the others. "That"ll work for now, but right now, we had better get this girl to the van, and get her deprogrammed before she wakes up!"

He told Sniper Jennifer to help Mimic April back too, for she seemed a little out of it. They all made their way and so Jennifer helped the girl back up to the mountain where Ellis was waiting for them. They were pleased to see, they all saw that she had knocked out Absorb's handler.

"All right! You got her!" Ellis said, with relief.

"Yeah," Cy said, "but I wouldn't of have been able to do it without everyone's help. Let's get back to the van."

Later, on their way back to the dorm, Absorb came to and asked, "What happened? And why does my body ache so?"

Ellis sat down next to her and said, "Well, let's just say it's something none of us will ever forget. Not to mention that you have been under the control of a evil man for a long time."

"Who are all of you?" Absorb asked. The girls all introduced themselves. When they got to Cy, the girl said, "You are the hero of my dreams!" Everyone laughed and groaned!

"I'm called Kim," said the cyborg.

"Well, Kim, welcome to the family," Cy said. "Why don't you as the girls get to know one another.

He didn't mind the girls getting close to one another, but he liked to keep his distance. He never even wanted to give them his real name.

When they would ask him, he would tell them that it didn't matter. They never liked that response, but they never could get anything else out of him.

CHAPTER 16

Several days later, Ellis ran into Cy's room and interrupted him as he was writing to his family again. "Another cyborg tracer has activated," she shouted.

"Where?" he asked, already shutting down his computer and grabbing his gear.

"In Mexico," she said as he stood heading toward the dorm to round up the others. "This one is one of the most dangerous of all of them because of its strength. It's called Force," she finished in a low tone.

When the two of them got to the others, Cy said, "We're off after another one, girls!" Then, as they headed toward the van, he said "It's going to be a tight fit on the way back with the six of them in the vehicle! We're going to have to come up with another mode of transport!"

It didn't take long to arrive in Mexico. Together, they walked through a small town where a large celebration was going—The Day of the Dead. People thronged around them dressed as skeletons and ghosts. Suddenly, Ellis pointed and yelled out, "There she is!"

Cy looked over the people trying to see what she was pointing at and had spotted. Then he saw a little girl that who looked no more than ten years old.

"That can't be her," Cy said, turning to Ellis. "A little girl couldn't be called Force!"

"Just watch," Ellis told him. The man and she moved closer to a small store. The man ordered the girl to destroy it.

The small girl punched forward and nearly shattered the building, with one strike. People ran out, at fear for their lives, .

Cy decided to act. As she had just nearly destroyed a building he jumped over across the street and grabbed the girl.

She squirmed around trying to get free of his grip. Cy had never felt such force come from a little girl before. He held onto her for as long as he could, until the girl pushed free and punched Cy so hard he was slammed into the building across the street. People around the area started to scream run from the area.

The tall man who was Force's handler saw this realizing who Cy was. He ordered Force to destroy the cyborg. "Affirmative," the girl said as she shot over to where Cy had fallen. Just as she was about to hit him again, when Force stop in midair.

Cy looked over to Mirage Megan and said, "Thanks. How long can you hold her?"

"Not long," Megan answered as she held the struggling girl with obvious difficulty in a force field bubble. Finally, Force punched one last time at Mirages Megan's force field. Megan winced as the little girl broke free and went flying at Cy again. But he jumped out of the way at the last second, and the girl slammed into the rubble behind him.

He turned just as she rocketed out of the rubble and punched him with incredible force. Digging his feet into the ground, Cy turned the force of her attack against her, and, using her momentum, threw her onto the top of a building.

"Are you all right girl?" Cy yelled to the girl. He was sorry for throwing her so hard. He got his answer when she walked out to the edge of the roof and said, "It will take more than that to stop Force!" She then jumped at him and punched him across the at his face. But the second strike missed, as did the next ones.

As the others watched, Jennifer got an idea. She turned to April. "Can you turn into the man that who was leading Force—her handler?"

"Why?" April asked.

"Because each cyborg is programmed to obey the handler. So, if you take the form of her handler …"

"She'll listen to me if I turn into him!" April said finishing Jennifer's sentence. Quickly, as she clapped her hands together to activate the transformation that would change her into the tall man who controlled Force.

"That's a good idea, Jennifer," Kim said. "And, while April keeps her busy, I grab her and absorb her power!"

They put there their plan into attack action. April, in the form of Force's handler, ran over to and positioned herself close to Force just as the little girl was about to hit Cy again. Then, April yelled, "Stop!"

Force stopped in med mid punch, her hand right in front of Cy's face. But, her real handler had revived and had figured out what was going on. "No!" he yelled. "It's a trick! I'm your real handler!"

But Mimic, still in the form of Force's handler, yelled back, "No! *I'm* your real handler!"

Force didn't know what to do or who to listen to. She just stood there confused until Kim came up behind her and grabbed her, absorbing all of her strength before she could react.

As Force fell unconscious in Kim's arms, as Cy took a breath from the fight and turned to the tall man that who had been with Force. In a flash, Cy was against the handler, holding him up in the air by his shirt. "I have a message for the general," Cy said to the frightened man. "Tell him I'm going to find all these of his cyborgs and free them! If he has a problem with that, tell him to stop me himself—if he has the balls for to try it!"

Cy then threw the man down. "Get out of here before I decide to use your head for a soccer ball!" Cy said. The man stood and ran off as fast as his legs could take him. April, still in the man's form, started to mock him, but Cy said, "That's enough." He turned to Ellis, glad to see that she had just installed one of the neuro-disablers on Force's neck. Now free from the general's control. He smiled feeling pretty good that they had got another in there their little family.

A few hours later, they landed in the dorm parking lot, right as Force was coming to. As the girls watched her, they realized that she was actually a young woman—older than she had appeared when she was under the general's control. Innocently, she looked around.

Jennifer was the first to say to greet her. "Hello," she said gently. "What's your name?"

"I'm Rebecca," said Force. "Where am I?"

The others then explained their story to the newest member of their group. Cy got out of the van and opened the side door. "Hurry up, girls! We can't stay in the van all night!"

When Cy spoke, Rebecca looked at him, she jumped from the van, and tackled him to the ground. Hugging him to the breaking point, she said, "You are the hero of my dreams!" "My hero."

The others couldn't help but laugh. They knew how strong Cy was was—and now he was being choked to death by girl—again! After he pulled the excitable girl off him, he told her, laughing, "It's nice to meet you too!" As he got up, he muss her hair with his hand. She smiled big at him as if he was greatest thing in the world. Cy smiled back as he turned around thinking how he could use a nap after all the happenings of the day.

Later that night, Cy was lying in bed in his room looking up at the ceiling thinking about all the things that had happened in his life, and thinking of the things that he was going to do if he found the general again. Finally, he fell into a deep sleep.

Cy awoke the next morning to the sounds of screaming. He jumped up and opened his door. Force — Rebecca—ran by him laughing. She was holding what looked like a whole jet engine.

He grabbed it from her with one hand and asked, "What do you think you doing?" Samantha then ran up to him and told him, "That girl took the engine right out of my shop! I'm trying to make a new vehicle for you to use."

Rebecca seemed up set that Cy had spoiled her fun. "I was just having a little fun," she complained. "This place is boring! Cy apologized somewhat sarcastically to her for not providing enough entertainment around here. "But we have to keep a low profile," he explained with even more sarcasm, " or bad people will come and take us all away."

"Sorry," Rebecca said, and the cyborg then told her to go help Samantha out and put the engine back. He handed the motor engine back to Rebecca. Samantha thanked him.

"Any time," he said.

CHAPTER 17

A few days later, with the help of Rebecca, Sam finished there new vehicle she invited everyone to meet in the garage. What they saw when they got there they could not believe believe—it was the biggest RV Cy or the girls had ever seen.

"What is this?" Cy the male cyborg asked.

"This is your new traveling vehicle," Sam said proudly.

Cy then pointed out, "That's awfully big! We're trying to keep a low profile!"

"I know," said Samantha, "and I've planned for that."

She then pressed a button on the vehicle's key, and the enormous vehicle vanished before their eyes.

The girls stood in awe, and Cy laughed. "What else can it do?"

Sam said, "Not only can it fly and hit speeds beyond the speed of light, it cannot be detected by any monitoring system."

"You're a genius," Cy told her.

"I still don't hold a candle to my sister Minawa," answered Sam. The girls then asked who her sister was, but, before Samantha could answer, Cy yelled out, "It''s none of your business, so don't get into it now. He then left the garage.

"What was all that about, Samantha?" Megan asked. "All we asked was who your sister is." "Come with me," said Sam. They followed her to a room in the building.

"Okay, listen my sisters name was Minawa Ivy and she was the one that built the lot of you as for anything else you're going to have to get it out of Cy." Sam started, again not getting any real answers..

xxx

A few days later at breakfast, Ellis came in to announce that she'd detected another activated cyborg tracker. As everyone jumped up and prepared to head for the new RV, Ellis stopped them. "We won't need to drive anywhere," she said.

"Why not?" Cy asked.

"Because this cyborg," Ellis told him, "is only down the road!"

Cy and the other girls had trouble believing that a cyborg was right down the road, but they had to make sure, so they all went outside. When they were in the small front yard of the dorm, Cy said, "Okay, girls, split up into two groups."

Force, Absorb, and Mirage (Rebecca, Kim, and Megan) headed one way, and Ellis, Sniper, and Mimic (Ellis, Jennifer, and April) headed the other. Before Cy went off in another direction, he said, "If you find anything, report it to the others."

Later the three girls , Ellis, Sniper, and Mimic were walking down the a street when they noticed a limo parked about fifty yards down the away. Ellis detected that the cyborg they were looking for was in the limo.

"Scan the limo, Jennifer," she said. "Tell us what's in there!"

Jennifer performed the scan. "There's a girl about eight years old. And two big guys who don't look human at all."

"The girl has to be the cyborg we're looking for," Ellis, said. The three girls then called the others and gave them the location.

When he got the call, Cy did a back-flip onto the roof of a nearby building. He got the call he looked around and saw the spot where Ellis and the others were, and he jumped in the air to get to them. On his way, he told the three girls to do what they can could to stop that the limo and get the girl out.

The girls got together and they advised a good plan, then they put it into action just as the limo pulled out of the parking space and began to move along the road. Ellis ran in front of the limo. The limo driver slammed on his brakes and stopped inches from her. Just then, Sniper ran by and shot out each tire from of the limo.

Mimic then changed into a large version of herself and tore the back door off the limo. As she did, two large assassinords came out of the limo. As they moved, their skin tore off their bodies, revealing what looked like two walking tanks. Then, they increased in size by ten.

When April saw this, she shrank back to her original size out of fear. The assassinords pointed there their arms at her, and their arms turned into canons.

When the assassinords fired, the girl was engulfed in a dust cloud. Sniper and Ellis thought that Mimic had been killed, but, when the dust cleared, they saw that she was all right, for she was was enveloped in a dome-shaped force field. The assassinords didn't know what to think, but the girls knew what had happened. it as Mirage as she appeared next to April and said, "It looks like we got here just in time!"

Force jumped from a building and slammed down onto the shoulders one of the assassinords. She tore it off as she jumped down from the large robot. She laughed as the assassinord started to chase her, and as she flung the his arm in the air mocking the robot.

Rebecca then ran behind Kim, who was just standing in one spot as she became made of the asphalts of the street. The assassinord slammed into her and shattered. As the pieces clunked to the ground, Kim just brushed herself off and turned to Rebecca, . "Are you all right?"

Rebecca turned to what was left of the assassinord and stuck out her tongue out. "I'm fine," she said, "but that was a stupid robot."

The other assassinord seemed angry that his partner was had been destroyed, but, just as he was about to attack, Cy jumped down and slammed down hard on the assassinord, destroying it.

"Did I miss anything?" Cy said as he looked at the six girls, .

"Nice timing as usual," Ellis told him as she walked over to the limo to check on the cyborg. The girl she seemed to be in a trance trance-like state.

Ellis looked back up to Cy. "This cyborg must have been programmed to obey orders and that's all," she said.

They burned out the chip that was controlling the girl. Cy pulled her out of the limo. "Time to go, girls. Before the people start to come out to find out what all the noise was."

Later, back at the dorm, Cy and the girls watched over the new cyborg. As she was waking up she turned to her actual age, as Rebecca had done. She appeared to be about the same age as Rebecca.

The girl awoke and looked around at the other girls. They greeted her and introduced themselves to her. "I'm called Destiny, and it's nice to meet you," she said.

She then saw Cy who just smiled at her. Destiny jumped on Cy and hugged him. "T hank you for saving me," she said.

And Cy just said, "You're welcome." He then put her down on the ground. "This is your new home, Destiny. You can feel safe here. You are among friends."

Later, Cy watched as Destiny and Rebecca played a friendly game on the computer. It was reassuring that the girls could still have fun even knowing that they were no longer fully human.

The next day, Cy walked into Sam"s lab. Destiny was there with her. "Well, what are you two up to?" he asked.

"See for yourself." said Sam.

Cy saw that Destiny had found a little hurt bird. The bird was resting on a soft cloth and was obviously seriously hurt. Destiny hovered over the bird, and, coming from her hands, were lights that seemed to be healing the little bird.

Cy could not believe this girl possessed the power to healing. But just then, the bird stood up and fluttered its wings. It then took off and flew around the room. Sam turned to Cy as Destiny followed the bird around the lab. "That's not all she can heal. She can repair electronics as well as heal flash and bone."

"That power's going to come in handy when we're in a large battle," Cy said as he watched Destiny play with the bird. But he also wished that all the cyborgs could be as free as the bird. He knew that the general would continue to hunt them down until they are slaves again. But Cy would never allow that to happen.

CHAPTER 18

As Cy watched Destiny play with the bird in the lab, Ellis ran through the doorway looking for Cy and Sam. "Oh, there you are," she said, breathing hard. "A new cyborg tracer has been activated. But this one was is different—it's at the bottom of the Pacific Ocean.

Sam knew what that meant. "Get the other girls, Cy, and meet me in the garage."

A while later, Cy, Sam and the seven girls were standing in font of the large RV that Samantha made and, Sam said, "This cyborg is not only at the bottom of the Pacific, but she's protecting the Ggeneral's underwater sea lab, but you guys don't have to worry about a thing for this RV cannot only fly, but it can go deeper than any known sub."

Cy took over: "So then, we have two jobs. One is to get this new cyborg, and two destroy the sea lab without hurting anyone in the sea lab."

Sam said "Right." Then she threw something at Cy and said, "Here!"

Cy caught a pair of flippers. "What are these for?" he asked.

"They're to help you swim. If you haven't noticed, your feet aren't exactly made for swimming!"

Cy looked at his feet. They were skeletal and had holes in them so they would not be good for swimming at all.

"You may be right about this," he told Sam. "I'll take them." He then turned to the girls. "Let's rock," he said, as they all got into the large RV.

Sam yelled out to Cy, "I have one more thing for you!" She threw something fist sized at him and he caught it.

"It's a bomb," she said. "You can use it to take down the sea lab."

Cy thanked her again. He climbed into the driver's seat, and the large RV shot off.

Soon, they were flying over the ocean. When their detection instruments indicated that they had reached the right spot, Cy flew the large RV right into the ocean. The vehicle went deep. Cy then landed the RV close to the sea lab, and he moved over to the air lock.

Cy took off his trench coat and started to put on the flippers that Sam had given him. Just before he went out, Kim asked him, "Why aren't you taking off your shirt?"

He turned to her. "I have my reasons. Anyway—the rest of you stay in the RV. I'm the only one that can survive at these depths. If I need your help, I'll call you. Until then, stay close." Cy then jumped into the water.

The girls watched him swim off. April—or Mimic—turned to Ellis and then asked, "What's he hiding?"

"I know that Cy's the good guy and that the General's the bad guy, but why is Cy so determined to help all of us?"

Meanwhile, Cy was now swimming under the sea lab. He installed the bomb in the structure that supported the lab and then swam over up to the side of the sea lab. Suddenly, he slammed his weight into the side of the structure to get the attention of the people inside.

The people inside, who could see Cy out of the window, began to yell. The leader yelled out that the Cyborg was outside shaking the whole lab they then ordered their cyborg to go out and destroy Cy. She swam out and headed toward Cy. Just as he slammed into the lab one more time, the cyborg known as Aqua slammed into him and crashed him into the side of an underwater mountain.

Aqua swam back toward the lab, but, when the sediment cleared, Cy was no where to be seen. Aqua looked around but did not know where he he'd gone, until Cy suddenly burst out from underneath her and grabbed her from behind.

As Aqua struggled to get free, she pointed her hand back behind her at Cy's head. A burst of water hit him with a powerful force, blowing him back. He shook it off quickly. "What was that?" he yelled into his communication system, but, before he could recover, Aqua shot another blast at him. At the last second, Cy swam out of the way.

"It's water under high pressure," Ellis told him through a the com link. "She can focus water into a deadly weapon."

"Great, thought Cy as he was hit again. The force of the water slammed him right through the side of the sea lab. He could hear the man in charge of the lab: "We're taking on water! Everyone Evacuate!"

Cy shot out of the break in the side of the lab and swam around and behind, Aqua. As soon as he knew that the sea lab was completely empty, he hit the detonator for the bomb and blew up the sea lab, . Aqua turned just in time to see the lab collapse.

As she turned around, Cy appeared right in front of her and put the neuro-disabler on her neck that burn out her chip. She fell back, and Cy caught her, and just the the RV drove up beside him.

"You did a good job, Cy," came a voice from one of the girls in the RV. Cy swam into the air lock of the RV and walked in still holding the unconscious Aqua. Once inside the RV, he put her on one of the beds. Then he walked over to a bag that had a change of clothes for him and headed to the bathroom in the RV to change so he could and get them all back to the dorm.

Before he entered the bathroom, Megan stopped him and asked him, "Would you tell us about how you became a cyborg?"

He looked at her and then said, "Maybe some other time." And, with that, he went into the bathroom. A minute later, he came out and drove them all back to the dorm.

Upon arriving back at the dorm, Aqua woke up and looked around. But then she did something that the other girls had never done—she attacked them and then ran past them out of the room. Just when she turned a corner in the hallway, Cy grabbed the girl by the back of her shirt and picked her up off the ground.

Aqua kicked and screamed, but when then she heard him Cy say, "I will not accept any of you fighting each other. We are now a family. You got that, girl?"

Aqua looked back up at him as he put her down. "I'm sorry for over reacting."

Cy then told her, "Don't apologize to me—apologize to the them." She turned to the other girls and told them that she was sorry for over reacting.

Cy put his hand on her shoulder and said, "That's a good girl." And then he turned, but, as he walked off, there was a light blush on Aqua's face. The other girls walked introduced themselves to her, and Aqua told them that her name was "Beth."

CHAPTER 19

Cy and the girls landed in an isolated area on a beach. Four of the girls—Megan, April, Kim, and Rebecca Rebecca—ran out wearing bathing suits. They threw their gear down onto the sand and yelled out, "The beach! The beach!"

Cy, Ellis, and the other three girls came out and walked over to them. They didn't seem too happy. "We came looking for our new cyborg sister—not to have fun," Jennifer stated.

"We don't have time for this," said the only male cyborg. "We have to get going."

Beth came up and took his hand. "So where is the cyborg anyway?" she asked.

"The girl is located at the base of the volcano," Ellis told them all as she pointed to the nearest mountain.

Cy nodded as he and the others started off. As they walked, Megan, April, Kim, and Rebecca were moaning quietly about not being able to have any fun, as they followed Cy and the other girls to the base of the volcano.

"We can have fun after we find this new cyborg," offered Jennifer.

"That's strange?" Ellis stated.

"What?" asked Cy.

"Well, I'm still detecting the cyborg, but the signal is coming from the sky rather than then from the volcano."

"What is this cyborg's power anyway?" asked April.

"This one is also one of the more powerful ones," said Ellis. "She"s code named Firebomb. She has the fire power to control fire, and can survive in temperatures as hot as the sun."

Cy thought of something and then asked Sniper Jennifer to help him out. "I have a theory," he told her. "Please use your infrared scanner and check out the sky."

Cy and Jennifer both looked skyward until Jennifer's scanner picked up something. It looked like a ball of fire, but, as it came closer, Jennifer and Cy saw that it was a flaming girl.

The flaming cyborg shot down a fiery blast that almost hit them. The entire group watched as she flew around for another shot, but, before she could attack again, Cy jumped into the air and grabbed the girl. The the heat from her was almost more them than he could take.

When his clothes started to burn he yelled out to Aqua. "Beth! Send up some water!" Beth looked frantically around. She saw a small pond, she ran over and put one hand into the water, and pointed her other hand at Cy and Firebomb. She let lose a large blast of water.

The water hit Cy and Firebomb, and they crashed into the side of the volcano. Cy rolled over and got up. He looked around, but the girl was nowhere to be found. He looked at his clothes—his trench coat and shirt was almost gone.

Just then, Firebomb shot out of the ground and fired a searing blast at the cyborg. He blocked with his arms as the fire burned off the last remnants of his coat and shirt.

Cy knew he had to stop this girl fast, so he shot himself through the fire and then jumped over her. As he sailed through the air just over her head, he put the neuro-disabler devise on her neck. The device that shorted her out, and her fire around her went out as she fell to the ground unconscious. Cy fell next to her.

The others arrived just as Firebomb succumbed to the device. As Cy struggled to his feet, Beth was the first to walk over to him. She looked at his body. This was the first time the girls had seen him without his shirt.

They could not believe the scares he had on his body—never mind how much of his body was cybernetic.

Beth was also the first to ask, "How did you get those scares?"

The question snapped him out of the daze he was in. He looked at her with a sad face, but he just got up, turned away, and started to walk back to the RV.

"Why don't you girls take Firebomb back to the RV," he stated not even turning to look at them, .

The ride back to the dorm was eerily quiet. The girls were still in shock. They could not believe the scares on the male cyborg's body and the extent of his cybernetic body. It was unreal even to them.

It was no wonder that he didn't want to talk about it.

Firebomb soon wake up. She looked at Ellis.

"What's going on?" the girl asked. "Why is everyone so quiet?" The girl asked.

Ellis turned to her, "Keep it down. I'll explain everything when they we arrive at the dorm."

Firebomb looked at the man driving the RV and said. "Hey, that's the guy who was in my dreams!"

Megan told her he'd been in all their dreams. "But he's not in the mood to talk to anyone right now," she said.

Firebomb didn't know what was going on, but she remained quiet. When they arrived at the dorm, Sam was the one to tell her what was going on, and Firebomb, who told them all that her real name was Ashley. Finally, Cy had left them, left them right after they arrived.

Later, Ashley found Cy in the last place the girls would ever think to find him him—in the music room of the dorm. He was strumming a guitar. Ashley walked over to him, she noticed his sad expression. "I'm sorry for what happened," she said to him. "The others explained to me about what happened to you."

Without turning or looking up, he said, "Don"t worry about it, ; it wasn't your fault. I just feel that ladies like you and the others shouldn't be exposed to things like the scares on my body—it's just not right."

"That's for us to decide, isn't it?" Then sat down at a piano. "Can you play that guitar?"

"A little."

"Do you wont want to play a little with me?""

Cy then started to play to show that he did. Ashley soon joined in, and the two started to sing together as well.

As they sang, some of the girls in the dorm heard them and followed the sound to see who it was. When they looked into the music room window, they all got a shock to see Cy playing the guitar and singing with one of the girl cyborg's. They were both very good.

A few more of the girls joined the little group outside the music room. "What are you doing?" Destiny asked.

"Shush," said Jennifer and pointed into the room they saw Cy singing and playing the guitar with while Ashley sang and played the piano.

They were all happy to see him smile again. Just when the song ended, the entire group went in clapping for both of them. The two performers seemed embarrassed because they didn't think anybody was listening, let alone half the dorm. Lucky for them that none of the teachers was around at the moment.

Destiny went over up to Cy. "I didn't now you could play so well!" She was very existed, .

Cy laughed. "I learned to play when I was young."

The girls were all were very impressed at on how good he was. Several of them asked if he and Ashley would play for them again.

Cy looked over at Ashley and checked with her, and they both sat back down for another song. Soon everyone completely lost tack of time until Ellis stood up, shocked. "Anther cyborg tracer has been activated," she shouted.

CHAPTER 20

There was a lot of moaning when the music had to stop, but they all got up and headed to the RV. On the way Ellis filled them in. "Our next desMegantion witch happen to be is in central Africa. This cyborg has the power of super speed. We have our work cut out for us."

When they arrived at their desMegantion, they went to a near by village where they heard rumors of a ghost that moved at sonic speeds. That's when they knew they had their girl. Following the directions of the residents, they headed off to the area where this ghost had been seen most.

It turned out there was a large military complex close to the area where the ghost has been seen, and, as they watched the complex, Cy and Jennifer could of sworn they saw something ran toward out at sonic speeds.

Just then they heard a voice behind them. "You can *never* win!" They all turned to see a girl standing there. She gave them all a cold stare. Before they could act, they found themselves all tied up in energy bindings.

Cy and the girls could not believe the speed of this girl. Then when Ellis spoke up: "We should have expected this from the fastest of all the cyborgs."

Cy turned to the girls then looked back to where Speed Demon had disappeared. "Rebecca," he said, addressing one of the girls closest to him. "Once I brake break free, I want you to free the others, while I take care of this new girl."

"How are you going to do that?" asked Rebecca.

Cy didn't answer. He simply broke free of his bindings and shot off after Speed Demon, who ended up following Cy. In a second, they were both gone. Rebecca broke her bindings and freed the others. They all looked around but could not see Cy or the girl anywhere.

As they tried to decide what to do, Ellis got a call on her com-link. It was Cy. "Where the heck are you?" she said.

"You won't believe this," he answered, "but I am now running across the ocean Atlantic Ocean with the Speed Demon right on his my tail."

Speed Demon kept calling out to him saying, "There is no escape!" Cy turned his head and told her that he wasn't about to give up so easily, as he shot off even faster after her.

Meanwhile, thirty minutes had passed and the girls were now wondering where Cy was. But, suddenly, he called to Jennifer over their com link. "Jennifer! Prepare a nero-disabler. I'm coming back around."

Sniper stood watch and right then she saw Cy and Speed Demon coming toward them at an unbelievable speed. Jennifer held out the neuro-disabler. Cy and Speed Demon ran by in a blur. Jennifer felt nothing, but the device disappeared from her hand.

Cy timed his movements just right and let Speed Demon get right up to him. Then he jumped backwards spinning in the air. As he went over the girl, he placed the neuro-disabler on her neck and it shorted her out. As she fell, she rolled hard. Because of the sonic speeds they were going, she rolled like a rag doll across the land escape. Finally, she slammed into a fence.

Breathing hard, Cy jogged up to her to see if she was okay. He picked her up and saw that she was breathing; the crash hadn't seemed to hurt her badly.

He carried Speed Demon back to the other girls and told them what had happened.

Beth spoke, "I didn't know you could move so fast!"

He laughed. As they all traipsed back to the RV, he told them about practice sessions with Minawa—about how excited she had been when he'd broken the speed of sound. But he caught himself before he went on about his past. "I still don't feel right telling anyone too much about my past," he finished.

As Speed Demon began to wake up, the girls were begged him to continue with his story. But he kept refusing. When Speed Demon saw the man carrying her, she blushed a deep red.

The girl didn't say a word, but she had heard the conversation. Cy set Speed Demon on one of the benches in the RV. "But why won't you tell us?" she asked Cy.

"Because, my past isn't important," he answered. But then he realized who he was talking to—the new girl!."

"Hi, the name's Kate," she said. "I'd sure would like to know more about you."

"No way," said Cy firmly. "You all don't need to know about my past or what I went through before this."

"Well, Cy," said Ashley, " it's like I said before—that's for us to decide." isn't it?"

"For the last time, *no.*" Cy moved over to the driver's seat and started the RV. Once they'd lifted off for their home at the dorm, they didn't say anything after the conversation stopped.

When they arrived at the dorm and the girls prepared for the evening, they explained there their situation to Kate. They also and explained a lot more of what they knew about Cy, even though they knew he would disapprove. They even told her about the scares on his body. But Kate had thought that his story and it the scars was cool— that it gave him character but he didn't feel that way.

CHAPTER 21

Late one night, Cy heard a knock at his door. When he answered he Ellis standing at his door he asks "What brings you out here?"

For a moment she couldn't answer as she saw him in his state of undress but she quickly shook it off as she said.

"Yeah, A new cyborg tracer has been activated. This one's in Japan. Her code name is Blackout, and she can fire electromagnetic pulses— E.M.P's for short— and control electrical forces.

Cy didn't hear her after she had said the cyborg was in Japan he had been lost in memories of his time there until he finally asked.

"Where in Japan is this cyborg?" he asked.

"Okinawa. Why?"

Cy was shocked when he heard this and realized that he might have to go back to his old training ground. "What's wrong?" Ellis asked.

He turned to her almost stiffly. "Nothing. I'm fine. Why don't you call the others? I've got to do something. I'll meet you all at the van." He then walked off.

Shortly after, they were all gathering into RV. As Cy took his place in the driver's seat, Rebecca and Destiny where the first too notice the look Cy had on his face. It was as if he was in a world of his own. "Cy, is something wrong?" asked Destiny.

"It's nothing," he told them as they started to lift into the air.

Ashley yelled out, "That's it! I've had enough of this! You're going to tell us what's wrong, or I'm going to castrate you with a fireball!"

That got his attain attention. "All right, I'll tell you. I grew up in the mountains of Okinawa. It's where I learned my martial arts." He went on to tell them about his sensei, who had become like a grandfather to him. He told them about his sensei's granddaughter and how very close they were. Through the whole thing he kept his real name to himself.

The girls were happy to hear him talk about his past, they could tell that he was still leaving key parts of the story out.

After they landed in the mountains, Ellis lead them around for some time until they came to through a wooded area to a set of old old-looking stairs that seemed to go on up the side of a mountain forever. Half way up, some of the girls started to complain. "Do we really have to climb all these stairs?" Aqua asked.

"Well, we might as well turn back if you girls are too tired to make it," said Cy.

"You're not helping!" said this Ellis, grabbing his arm. "And, unless you want me to tell them the real reason you want to go back, you'd better tell the others to get the lead out!"

"How could you know about my past? I never told you!" Cy whispered to the little android girl.

"I am not only connected to the other cyborgs, but I am also connect to you, so I know your whole past. I have just been respecting your privacy," said Ellis. Cy, stared wide-eyed at her. Then he turned back to the others and said, "Come on, ladies, you can make it! It's only a few more steps." He gave them a half-hearted smile.

An hour later, they all reached the top of the steps. They're where they saw a shrine protected by two large double doors. "Should we go in?" Rebecca said asked. She was about to punch the doors in, but Cy stopped.

"If we're going in, we're doing this right," he said.

"And how do we do that?" the small cyborg asked.

Cy reached up and rang a bell. "This is how," he said.

"What do we do now?" Kate asked.

"We wait," Cy said as he sat down on the steps.

After some time, Kate started to pace back and forth. She was not very patient. Finally she yelled out, "Are they going to let us in? It's been, …what … an hour?"

Cy looked at her. "This is a shrine. We need to be patient." Just then, the doors opened.

"Finally!" Kate said, about to run inside. Cy stopped her. "You should let me go first."

He walked in slowly and looked around, but something was wrong. There was no one around. The cyborg girls slowly followed him in. Cy turned back to Ellis and asked, "What exactly is this girl's power again?"

Before Ellis could answer, an electrical blast came down out of nowhere. Cy was just barely able to jump out of the way. And, thanks to Megan, who instinctively held her shield up, saved the other girls from the blast.

As the dust cleared, they saw the one who had fired the blast.

A young Japanese girl was floating in the air near them. Using electrical fields, she flew around the large temple. Finally, she landed near Cy and took up a fighting stance, that he recognized. She ran forward and started to attack him. Her moves were incredible; she was almost as good as he was.

The girls were all yelling at him to fight back because all he was doing was defending himself from her attacks. Finally, he started to fight back. The moves of both combatants were becoming more and more intense.

Electricity started shooting from both of them. At one point, it almost looked as if the two of them were enjoying themselves—until they all heard a man's voice yell out, "That's enough!" Both Cy and the cyborg girl stopped in med mid attack.

Blackout, turned to the man and bowed. Cy and the others looked over at the man as he walked over to them. He was wearing the traditional Japanese robes of a master martial artist. He had his arms behind his back as he approached Black out first. " Good job, Sakura-chan."

He then walked over to Cy. When the cyborg saw him, he just bowed and said with an awed voice, "Sensei."

Several of the girls approached them. "What the heck is going on?" asked Jennifer.

Cy said to his sensei, "I would like to know that too."

Cy's sensei turned around and started to walk back into the temple. Then he turned and as he said, "I will explain everything over a nice hot cup of tea." Then to Blackout he said, "Sakura-chan, fetch our guesses guests some tea for me. I will take them to the *dojo*."

Sakura bowed. "Yes, sensei."

Later they all found themselves in a large room. Many swords and other Japanese stile weapons, decorated the walls. They all had to remove their shoes before entering, and the girls were all having a problems sitting the same way that Cy was, for he seemed so natural sitting on his knees in front of his sensei.

A few minutes later, Sakura came back in carrying a tray with tea. She was wearing a summer kimono decorated with flowers. She handed her sensei a cup first, then handed one to Cy. By way of explanation to the girls, she said, "The first cups goes to the master, and—my senpai."

The girls all whispered to each other; they were unfamiliar with these Japanese customs.

Cy and his sensei both turned their cups before taking a drink. The sensei took a breath and then said, "Well, Chris-san, apparently a lot has changed since the last time you were here."

The girls' eyes lit up when they heard the aged man call the cyborg "Chris. Maybe this was his real name"

Sensei then told him "I am proud of you for what you have done for these girls, —freeing them from the control they were all under. But you must realize that sometimes, in order to free someone, you may have to fight him—or her.,"

Cy bowed. "I realize this now, and I will remember that. But right now I would like to ask— how did you meet Blackout?"

The cyborg's sensei smiled and took another sip of his tea. "I met her about a month ago. She was wreaking havoc around this area, I was able subdue her and free her mind. I brought her here where I began to train her as I trained you."

"All right!" yelled Ashley in the direction of the sensei, apparently angry that she'd been left out of the loop. "That's it! I've had it!,"

"You can't talk to the Sensei like that!" Cy yelled.

"I wasn't talking to the old man," she yelled back. "I was talking to *you*. I am sick of all the secrets you have been keeping from us. We want to know everything about you—*now*."

Cy didn't say anything. He just got up, turned, and walked out of the room. The sensei took another sip of his tea. "It looks like as if Chris-san has kept a lot of secrets from all of you. Perhaps maybe you should all stay at the temple until Chris-san realizes that it is dishonorable to keep secrets. This is a perfect place to stay until your next cybernetic warrior appears. You may all have full access to the temples grounds, including the hot springs."

"But Cy would never agree to staying here," Ashley told the man.

The sensei just sipped his tea again. "Just tell him it is a request from of his sensei."

Sure enough, once the girls told him, staying at the temple was his sensei's idea, he agreed. But he wasn't happy about it. He turned to Jennifer.

"Please go and get the RV and put it in the court yard. And take Ellis with you so she can call Samantha and tell her what's going on." He then turned and walked off.

Later, Cy was lying in the hot springs thinking of the events of the day. He thought about his reunion with his sensei and the way the old man had spoken to him. Had he been trying to tell him that it was being dishonorable to the girls to keep all those secrets from them?

The question really was, was he ready to tell them, his whole story or not?

He was so consumed with his own thoughts that he didn't hear someone enter the springs. Suddenly, he heard a soft voice.

"May I join you, *senpai*?"

Cy about jumped out of his skin. He turned to see Sakura with a towel wrapped around her slim figure. He turned back around with a blush on his face.

"Don't any of you girls have any sense of decency?" he asked her.

"*I* certainly don't have any use for it."

Cy looked up to see as Ashley enter the spa with the others close behind. And the towel Ashley had draped around her had barely been able to covered her as she made her way into the spring.

When the girls were all settled, they felt really relaxed. This was there first time most of them had been in a hot spring, and they all had to agreed that it felt like heaven. The water seemed to relax them more then than they had thought possible.

"So why have you been so indifferent to everyone?" Sakura asked, finally. "doesn't seem honorable. Sensei has told me about the time you spent here, but I do not see the man he told me about in the man I see before me now."

"You don't know what I've been through—or what I am going through. I can never be close to anyone now."

"Why can't you?"

Cy grabbed Sakura's hand and held it in his as the other girls watched.

"Because I can't feel anything anymore. I can't feel the warmth of your hand in mine. Every part of my body that is cybernetic is numb. That's part of the reason I've been so indifferent to you. The other reason is that," ..." he paused a moment. "I've lost the one love of in my life," he said quietly. " I cannot bear to lose another."

Sakura leaned over and kissed him on the part of his cheek that still was made of flesh. The girls seemed to get a little mad angry at this. "You felt that, didn't you?" Sakura questioned.

Cy touched the spot that Sakura had kissed. He had felt it. A tear fell from his eye and slid down his cheek. He put his hands in front of his face. He seemed lost, and then he looked up at the others. "I'm sorry," he said. "I didn't know you all cared so much for me."

"What's not to like? You saved us all!" Beth shyly said as she pried from behind one of the other girls. She was a little embarrassed about being naked with him.

"How about this?" this Jennifer started, suggested. "We all promise to always be by your side, and you promise to no longer keep any more secrets."

"All right," Cy said. As he laughed a bit, as they all leaned forward and put out their hands, and he shook them one by one. Cy and the girls then all laid back into comfortable positions in the water. But, before Cy could get comfortable, Ashley asked, "Well?"

"Well, what?" Cy asked.

"Well,… Aren't you going to tell us your story?"

"Here?" Cy asked.

"What better place to open up about yourself than in an open open-air bath," Sakura said encouragingly.

Cy sighed. "Alright."

He told them the story of how he had become what he is. About his romantic times he had with Minawa. When he was finished, he looked at the girls and noticed that most of them looked as if they were crying.

"Are you guys okay?" Cy asked, uncertain of their reaction.

Megan dried her eyes and said, "Now I understand why you were where being so distant. If I lost the love of my life like that, I would be indifferent to everyone too. And, it's so romantic that you want to fulfill the last promise you made to the one you love—to rescue all of her cyborgs."

"It's not only that," Cy said. "It's just the right thing to do. It is not right that the general has been using all of you to do his dirty work."

At that and moment, Ellis shot up out of the water. Everyone looked at her. Several of the girls asked her if she was all right.

"Another Cyborg tracer has been activated," she said. "Her name is Ice Storm, and she's located …" Ellis paused for a second and then turned with a cold look, "…Antarctica." Cy shivered a bit as he was reminded of the cold.

CHAPTER 22

As Cy, Ellis, and the girls were gathered in front of their RV in preparation for leaving for Antarctica, and as Cy's sensei joined them. He stood before Cy, the cyborg bowed and thanked him for everything. He, had a feeling that his sensei had planned this encounter to help Cy get closer to the others.

The aged man shook his head. "I have done nothing that deserves your thanks; however, I think the fates have brought you here to reestablish your honor.

They all then bowed again to Cy's sensei and said *"sayonara"* to him as before they piled into the RV.

A while after they took off, Cy seemed to be more at ease with himself—as if a large weight had been lifted off his shoulders.

After three days of traveling, they all arrived in Antarctica. Ashley was the first to speak. "Just how cold is it out their?" she asked.

"The average summer temperatures range from -5 to -31 Fahrenheit," Ellis said."

Ashley did not like the sound of that for —she hated the cold. "I think I will stay here in the RV where it's warm," the girl said.

Cy just a dug out the cold-weather gear that was stowed in the RV for such occasions. "This shouldn't take long," he told the girls. "And we'll be back in the warm summer heat in no time. Let's go!"

After some time in the snow, Ashley was really starting to hate this place. She was even falling back from the others. Some of the other girls were just getting jealous of the younger girls, Destiny and Rebecca, who were both huddled close to Cy as they walked through the snow.

Suddenly, Ellis then yelled, "Their she is!"

They all looked to where she was pointing. Cy could see the girl, who was skating across the ice with determination. He told Jennifer, "Please scan the area to find out where she is going."

Jennifer looked and said, "She seems to be heading to a small research station on the ice."

Cy wondered for a minute about what Ice-Storm plains to do, but Ellis said, "She's planning on destroying the research station."

"How do you know that?" Megan asked.

"I know because I'm connected to the global net. Ice-Storm has been sent here to destroy that research station so a company can use the area to drill."

"Then what are we waiting for?" Cy asked. "We've got to stop her before she gets to the research station." Cy told them and then turned to Kate. "Follow me," he said. "With your speed, we can catch up to her easily." Then he turned to Ashley. "You're coming with us. Your fire powers may be needed to stop this one."

"The rest of you, head back to the RV and prepare for the newcomer," Cy said. Then Cy, Kate, and Ashley took off at top speeds.

Meanwhile, Ice Storm was still skating across the frozen ground when she felt a disturbance on the ice. She turned in time to see Cy, Kate, and Ashley coming straight at her. She prepared herself as she fired an ice beam at the intruders.

Ashley saw it coming and fired a fire blast of fire to stop the ice beam. The odd thing about it was, however, that there blasts were of equal strength. Neither of them could not believe there the other's powers.

Cy and Kate ran around Ice Storm as she and Ashley exchanged blasts of fire and ice. Cy was trying to apply the neuro-disabler device to short her out, but Ice Storm kept turning before he could get close enough. Suddenly, when he got close again, she managed to freeze him in a block of ice. But Kate used that to her advantaged as she shot around Cy and put the devise device on Ice Storm's neck. It stopped her cold.

Ice Storm fell on the ice. Ashley landed and walked over to her. "That was a good bluff you and Cy pulled off," she said."

Kate then realized that Cy was still frozen. Immediately, they went over to him and Ashley started to melt the ice. When enough was melted, Cy fell to he ground shaking.

"I didn't think cyborg's could get frostbite," Cy said as he struggled to stand up. Ashley though picked up Ice Storm.

"Are you sure you're okay, Cy?" Kate asked as they headed back to the RV.

"I will be, when we get back to the RV, and get to a warmer climate," said Cy. "Right now, I wish I wasn't made of so much metal because every bit of it is ice cold!" Cy yelled out.

As Ashley carried Ice Storm, she though couldn't get it out of her mind that she had seen her the cyborg some place before.

Later, when they got back to the RV, the girls immediately saw that Cy was cold. They grabbed him and put him to bed and tried to warm him up.

"I'll make you a hot bath when we get back," Beth told him. "That should warm you up faster,"

Cy thanked her, and then he turned to Sakura., "You can drive us back to the dorm," he said. She agreed and went to the driver's seat.

As for Ashley and Ice Storm Ashley had put Ice Storm in one of the beds. She was looking at her she still couldn't remember where she had seen Ice Storm, but she was sure she had.

When they got back to the dorm, Ashley found Cy in the shower room. He was still suffering from the cold. "Ice Storm is awake," said Ashley. "She wants to know what was is going on."

Cy was about to explain what to do when Beth arrived and told him that he had no time to greet the new cyborg for she was going to run him a hot bath. "Ashley, can you explain everything to Ice Storm."

After Ashley finished talking to Ice storm. She found out that the new member of the family was named Melissa. Ashley explained everything that was going on, but there was one thing that Melissa knew that the others didn't. Ashley was her sister! This, of course, shocked the others for they could barely remember their own names let alone remember if they still had a family. Their lives were so different now. After all that had happened to them, they kind of all felt like family—and Cy was like the big brother to them all.

As for Cy, he was now lying back in a hot tub inside the dorm gym. Quietly, Beth came in and joined him in the hot tub. They were both enjoying the warm waters when Ashley ran in holding Melissa's hand. " Melissa is my *sister*!" The other girls crowded into the room.

Cy got up out of the warm waters and walked over to the new comer. Melissa didn't know what to think of him. She could barely believe the man standing in front of her.

A cyborg man wearing a swimsuit. He had scares on about every part of his body that was still flesh, and yet he was the guy she had seen in her dreams. When she greeted him, Beth yelled out, "Get back in the water! You're still not warmed up enough!"

"I'm fine," he told her, but Beth wasn't about to listen. Finally, Cy apologized to Melissa and returned back to the hot tub.

"What did I do to you?" Melissa asked him.

He smiled at her. "You froze me in a block of ice."

"Oh my god—, I must have, but I don't remember it." Melissa told him.

Cy laughed and said, "You don't need to apologize. You had no control of over what you were doing, so it's okay."

"But I still feel responsible for what I've done," she said.

Cy shook his head. "You've done nothing. You should of have seen what the others did to me, before I freed them!" He laughed at that thought as the others around him started to blush at the thought of hurting him worse than what Melissa had.

Later that day Ellis entered Cy's room as he was in the middle of meditation she took one step toward him when his one eye opened and his cybernetic one lite up.

"Let me guess anther tracer's been activated?"

"Yes," the android answered, .

"Where is this one—Rome or something?"

"You're not going to believe this," she replied.

"Where?"

"The moon."

"What!!!!!!"?"

CHAPTER 23

"The moon!" Cy yelled to Ellis. "How in the hell are we going to get to …" He stopped mid sentence.

"Samantha!" he yelled.

"The moon?" she said. "No problem— just, take the RV."

"It can fly all the way to the moon?" Cy asked.

Sam winked at him. "It could take you there and back while it's still in second gear."

"Well, in that case," Cy said, he turned to the girls, "let's get going!"

As they loaded into the RV, Cy sensed a nervousness among the girls. "Okay, what's up, girls?" he asked.

"I know we are going to the moon," Jennifer said, "but where would a cyborg be on the moon?"

"At the moon base, of course," Samantha told him them as she stowed some extra "moon gear."

Rebecca, who was, as usual, with Destiny, asked, "What's a moon base?"

He Cy looked at them. "It' sounds likes a military complex or a place for the military to do there work, but I've never heard of a military base on the moon."

"It's a heavily guarded secret of the government," Samantha said, slamming down the lid of the last gear compartment.

"I have more input," offered Ellis. "This cyborg is known as Gravity. Her strength is gravitational force."

"Figures," Cy said, then he clapped his metal hands together. "Well, we'd better get going."

On their way, Cy and the girls admired the views of space. None of them had ever seen anything like it— the millions of stares that blanketed the sky it was breath taking, and they couldn't believe the beautiful view of Earth. But, when they saw the moon close-up, they just stared in awe.

When they flew around to the dark side of the moon, they saw the base hidden in the shadows of the of the moon. They landed near the base, but out of sight.

"I don't like this, Cy. It's too quiet," Sakura said.

"I agree." Cy stated "In fact, I should go in by myself.

The girls all protested. "No way," said Kim.

"It's too dangerous," Melissa finished.

"I'll be okay," he told them. "I can get in and out before anybody knows I there."

Destiny and Rebecca then got in front of him and hugged him. "Don't go," cried Destiny.

"You'll get hurt," said Rebecca.

"I'll be in contact with you the entire time. I'll be okay," he assured them.

Cy went out through the air lock of the RV and walked—or moon jumped—to the entrance to the base. He had to force it open to get in, and he had to force it closed. There was no one around. Before he walked forward, a bit he contacted the girls and told them that he was in.

"The cyborg you're looking for is in the middle of the hole complex," Ellis told him, "so be careful. There may be traps."

"You girls need to relax," he said. "I can handle anything that comes my way."

The entire complex was completely deserted. It was eerily quiet. It looked as if whoever was had been in the base left in a big hurry— almost like as if they knew that he was coming. Cy, found the cafeteria. There was food still on the plates. The people must have just got up and left.

The cyborg then made his way to the center of the base. There he found the girl—Gravity—encased in a large, clear tube. Ellis had told him that her special powers were connected with gravitational forces. It looked as if she was the one that sustained the gravity for the whole base.

Right before he was about to break her out of the tube, a screen on the wall blinked to life. The general appeared on the screen. He greeted Cy.

"How have you been, Mr. Striker? Still mourning over Minawa I see, and fulfilling her last wish to get all of her cyborg's back and free them of my control."

"How is it you are still alive?" the cyborg asked. His shock was only greater that the general knew what was going on—and knew his real name.

"There were ways out of that building that Minawa didn't even know about. But, as for you and the cyborg's—you know that they are no longer any use to me. Because of you, they can no longer be put under *my* control."

"Then that's good for me!" Cy said as he jumped and shattered the tube that encased Gravity. He grabbed the cyborg away from the shattering glass, and they both landed on the floor.

"Oh, Mr. Striker." The general said with a smirk. " I have one more thing to tell you. The reason that this base is deserted is because, I have installed a bomb that is going to blow you all away in 10 seconds."

The general then started to count down as numbers flashed on the screen.

Cy started running as fast as he could, with Gravity in tow. He raced through the base toward the exit. In the background, they could hear as the general kept counting down.

Cy didn't think he would make it, out but then right as the general said "three," Cy crashed through the door and they ran straight for the RV. He opened the door and yelled out, "Megan—*now!*" There was a furious explosion. The entire base was leveled; taking everything with it—or so it appeared.

xxx

Meanwhile, on Earth, General Bishop seemed happy with himself. He had destroyed *all* of Minawa's cyborg's with one bomb. *"Now it's time for things to move in the direction they're supposed to"* the general thought to himself, and he turned to leave. But, suddenly, the computer detected a life sign on the moon.

"Impossible!" the general said out loud, turning to view his instruments. Sure enough, they were all still alive, safely encased in one of Mirage's force fields.

"Damn!" The general cursed to himself. He turned to a man in a lab coat. "What can we do now?" he asked his top scientist.

"Don't worry, General." The scientist said. "I will take care of them—or, in fact, Mr. Striker will take care of them, … when I take control of him!" With an evil grin on his face, he held up a microchip.

xxx

Cy stood up slowly inside Megan's bubble. "Is everyone okay?" he asked, looking around him.

He heard encouraging answers. Then Megan said, "We'll all be fine as long as I keep my arms up and maintain the force field."

"What are we going to do now, Cy?" Rebecca asked.

Cy looked around at the moon and the stars. "Honestly, I don't know. The RV looks totaled."

After the girls had applied a neuro-disabler device to Gravity, she had fallen asleep. Now Gravity started to wake up. She looked around. Even though she had been controlled, she could hear and see everything that had been going on. Also, so she knew how to get them back to earth.

"How about I get us back to Earth?" Gravity stated getting everyone's attention, Cy and the girls looked at her, and Jennifer asked her, "How are you going to get us back to Earth?"

The girl clapped her hands together and then raised her hands to the sky. Still in Megan's force field, they all started to be lift off the ground. Some of the girls started to panic, but Gravity said, "Don't worry! I know what I'm doing! Megan, keep the force field up."

As they all then shot up into the starry sky and headed back to Earth, Kate could not believe they were moving as fast as she could run, which was close to light speed. Cy called out directions to Gravity, who changed course as she told him to call her Victoria.

They landed right in front of the dorm, and Megan about fall fell over from exhaustion. But Cy caught her and picked her up. She thanked him, and Cy told her to forget it, he turned to others and asked again if they were okay. Everyone appeared to be fine, if a bit overwhelmed.

Cy turned back to Victoria. "Okay," he asked her, "how did you know how to use your powers so fast? The others almost had to spend time relearning how to use there their powers. What makes you different?"

"I have always known how to use my powers because I have been conscious through the whole thing, — even though I couldn't act. You see, my powers where used to keep the gravity stable on at the moon base."

Cy shrugged at this as he carried Megan inside. Some of the girls thought that she was milking the fact that she was tired just so he would carry her for a while, . He carried her to her room, and laid her down on her bed, and told her to rest for a while. He knew how it must of been pretty tiring it must have been keeping that field up for so long. She told him that she was okay, and thanked him for everything. But before he left, he told her that he would check on her in a while.

The next day Cy was setting sitting on a couch in the TV room of the dorm. Megan and Kim, sitting on ether side of him, they had fallen asleep with their heads on his shoulders. Sakura came in and handed him a cup of tea.

He took it very carefully so as to not wake Megan and Kim. And as he took a sip, Sakura asked quietly, "What are you going to do now that you have gathered all the cyborg's?"

Cy thought for while, "I don't know," he whispered. " Minawa never mentioned what to do after I got them all."

"I have an idea," Sakura said. And she explained it to him.

"Sounds good," said Cy. "Would you ask the girls to meet us in the gym after supper?"

So, the girls gathered in the gym, all wondering what Cy and Sakura had planned.

When Cy and Sakura walked in, Cy was holding a boom box. He set it in front of them the girls. Sakura spoke: "Good evening, girls. Cy and I have decided to start training everyone in the martial arts so you all will be prepared the next time you meet up with the general."

Cy took over: "We thought we would begin by demonstrating a few moves before we get started."

Ashley asked, "What's with the stereo?"

"I thought you would never ask," the male cyborg said, and he turned to Sakura and nodded. She pushed a button and music filled the gym. Cy and Sakura then demonstrated an amazing fighting routine to the beat of music. It was a combination of dance and combat moves.

The girls didn't get it at first, but then Jennifer stated, "Look at them, they're moving the same!" Cy and Sakura moved in perfect unison as if they had a psychic connection.

After the song was over, the girls ran over to them jumped up clapping and cheering. They could not believe how good Cy and Sakura both were! Cy addressed the girls, "This is a result of our careful training. We plan to train you the same way."

"The first step is teaching you all the proper moves and rhythm. Once you all are able to move in complete unison with us, that's when we will start the advance combat training." Cy told them.

"You guys want us to learn to dance?" Melissa asked.

"No, we want you to learn rhythm and teach you how to move in harmony," Sakura said. "By the time we are finished, you'll all be able to move as if we're all one." Sakura finished.

"The first stage of the training will last for several months," Cy explained. "At first, you'll all be like a bunch of people with two left feet—you'll be, falling over each other. But, by the end of the training, you will be moving with Sakura and me like we are all part of each other."

CHAPTER 24

After the training session for the day that evening, Cy headed out to a café that was close by. He was wearing his trench coat and sunglasses and was sitting at one of the tables having a tea. He really needed this just some time boy himself to get his mind back together.

xxx

Back at the dorm, Ashley walked up to Samantha. "Where's Cy?" she asked.

"He went out for a while he said something about going to a near by cafe."

"Really. Why didn't he ask us if we wanted to come with him?" the cyborg girl asked.

"He needed some time for himself, —that's what he told me," Sam said.

"But, still, he shouldn't be out there by himself," Ashley said.

"He's a big boy," Sam told her. "He can take care of himself."

xxx

At the café, Cy had just finished his tea when a large man came up to him and said, "Hay— you're that cyborg freak with the million-dollar bounty on his head, aren't you?"

Cy didn't even look at him; as he got up to leave. As he started to walk toward the door, the large man put his hand on his shoulder. "Where do you think you're going?" he said.

Cy turned to him and adjusted his sunglasses. "I'm going home. And, if you know what's good for you, you'll let me go."

The man laughed. "There's no way the rumors about you are true—that you can smash a building down with one hit."

Cy laughed and said, "Now that's funny. How people tend to blow things out of proportion. Besides, it was *two* buildings that I smashed in!" Cy then walked around the man and continued to on toward the door.

Once they were both outside, the man pulled out a gun and fired it at Cy. The bullet got nothing but thin air as Cy seemed to vanish in a flash. He had jumped in the air. He landed on top of a building, and rolled to a stopped, and got up fast. Then he jumped down off the building and into an alley. As he started to walk out of the ally, he again felt a man's hand on his shoulder, Cy turned fast, prepared for anything, but saw it was only one man—a different man. Cy lowered his guard as he asked, "Now what do *you* want?"

The man smiled sinisterly. "What *I* want is what General Bishop wants." And, before Cy could think, the man pulled out a strange stun gun and hit Cy with it. Cy yelled out an electrical scream before he fell to the ground and powered down.

The man then signaled two assassinords to take Cy away. Meanwhile, on top of a nearby building, a crow screamed out as it flew away. The man looked up and saw the crow, but thought nothing of it as the Aassassinords took Cy away.

Immediately, the crow flew to the dorm and landed., Kate, who was outside at the time, saw the bird change into April and falls to the ground. Kate ran over and helped her friend up, for she seemed a bit stressed over something.

"What's wrong, girl?" Kate asked. But all April could say through her sobs was something about Cy, and being captured as she started crying.

xxx

Elsewhere, Cy was laying on a table still unconscious. The man who had captured him stood over him. He was a scientist named Doctor Connor. He held in the palm of his hand a microchip that would mark the end of the all the cyborg's for good.

xxx

At the dorm, the girls heard the entire story from April. She had followed Cy because she was worried about him. She told them about the man who took him, and they all agreed to split up and start looking for him.

They all spent the rest of the day and the whole night looking for him, but had no luck. They were all very worried about him and had no idea what that man had done to Cy.

They all met back at the dorm at breakfast hoping that one of them had some news, but, sadly, they had none. Suddenly, Samantha burst into the cafeteria and told them to take a look at the TV. What they saw on the news was something rampaging in the downtown area of the city.

The girls saw Cy moving away from the dust that was left of a building he had just destroyed. They knew then that someone had to of have done something terrible to him for him to be acting like that. They knew that they had to stop him before he truly hurts someone.

"Sam," said Sakura, "keep in touch with us as we try to stop Cy."

They all ran out of the building and used Victoria's power to get them to where Cy was.

As they flew over the city, they saw an explosion erupt. They knew it had to be Cy. They landed, and started to converged on the male cyborg. But, when he turned around and said something they never thought he would say to them.

"Destroy Minawa's cyborg's" His tone sounded almost dead.

Instantly, they all knew that he was being controlled by someone. But, before they could do anything, the male cyborg clinched his fists as he began attacking them at mind-numbing speeds. They all managed to get out of the way.

As the fight started, Sakura and Rebecca where the first to realize that he wasn't using his full power against them.

Sakura know knew because she was so familiar with his moves, and Rebecca knew because she knew his strength. Together, they did something unexpected—they both stood together about fifty yards away from him.

"You are our protector," Sakura stated.

"Yeah, we care about you," Rebecca finished.

Cy moved toward them slowly at first, and then he began to run. "We won't fight you, Chris," Sakura said as she closed her eyes. All the other girls yelled for Sakura and Rebecca to move out of the way, but they remained in place waiting for Cy to collide into them. But the strike never came.

Sakura opened her eyes and saw his metal hand shaking right in front of her. She turned to look at his face.

He looked like he was fighting against himself. He stepped back holding his head as he started yelling, "Out! Get out of my head! I won't hurt them anymore!"

The others girls didn't know what he was talking about, but, elsewhere, Doctor Connor was yelling into a communication device telling Cy to kill all the cyborgs. But, no matter what he said, Cy would not listen. Dr. Connor turned up the power to his communication chip, making Cy yell out in pain. Then stopped and stood straight as he said in cold tone, "*Destroy!*"

Rebecca was standing near him. Forcefully, he picked her up.

"Destroy!" he said. "Destroy! Destroy!" He said over and over in a dark voice, he started to crush the girl in his arms.

The others were about to stop him when Rebecca spoke up, "No! Stop everyone—, I can get through to him, I know it."

The others did stop. They watched as Rebecca just tried to reason with the controlled cyborg.

"Your honor is your strength," Rebecca said, struggling to breathe in Cy's tight embrace. "And, because of that, you can do anything, —no one can beat you."

"Rebecca's right, Cy!" Jennifer yelled out, . "*We* may not have been able to break through the control of the general's chips, but we all know that *you* can."

Cy suddenly dropped Rebecca, and she landed hard on the ground. She looked up at him. "They are right, you know— you can do anything."

Cy grabbed his head again in pain. "You may have taken over my body and my mind," he yelled at his controllers, "but there is one thing that you can never take away from me—."

"My honor!!!!," he yelled out as the girls circled him.

Doctor Connor addressed Cy: "You can never brake my control chip." As he turned the power to its max.

Cy yelled out even louder as the pain hit him, but the girls kept motivating him to fight. Finally Cy stumbled to his knees. "I'm sorry. It's too much. I can't do it.

Beth was the next to yell. 'No, or, can't' isn't in your vocabulary! You can do anything.!"

"You are the greatest man to ever live! You can beat this," Melissa called out.

"Yes!" Cy said quietly. He stood tall as he roared out to the sky. "I can beat this—s" Cy yelled, "there is no way I'm going to let these animals control me. I won't let this stop me! I won't let him make me hurt my girls again!"

Suddenly, something unexpected happened. A beautiful sky blue aura surrounded him then slowly changed color from a sky blue to a dark black. And, with one last roar that sounded like a lion's roar, Cy bowed his head. The chip in his head blew out of his head and landed at his feet.

xxx

Meanwhile Doctor Connor, could not believe the power surge his instruments detected. Just as he was trying to figure it out, his computer blew up! He then frantically tried to figure out what had happened. "Could it be true?" Just before the computer blew, he could have sworn he'd seen a black lion's face on the screen.

Cy now stood up straight. The girls surrounded him asking if he was okay, but he didn't answer them. He just looked around the area until he seemed to move in three different directions. Then he disappeared. The girls looked around and could not figure out where he had gone.

"Can you find him, Jennifer?" Melissa asked.

"I'm trying," Jennifer said, "but he's moving too fast for me to get a proper reading, of where he went to."

Just then, she detected an area of increased energy. She pointed up, and all the girls watched as a man was thrown out of a second-story window. He rolled to a stop in front of them.

The man struggled to get up, but his legs seemed to be broken. "I was just following orders," the man yelled. "It was the general who made me do it!" Cy jumped down to the ground and landed near the man. He seemed furious as he walked towards the doctor.

"You made me hurt them!" Cy shouted as he picked the doctor up and threw him through a shop window.

The doctor was cut up, as Cy grabbed him and pulled him back out of the shop. Cy then threw the man at another shop window. The doctor begged him again and again to stop, but as Cy continued to beat him.

Finally, Victoria then yelled, "Cy, stop! Please—you're going to kill him."

Cy turned to her. "I have to kill him. He has destroyed my honor, —destroyed my pride. He has destroyed everything that I have lived for, I have to kill him to get that back."

"No. You don't, Cy," Sakura said. "It wasn't *you* who was hurting us—it was *him!*"

"But it was still my body that hurt you all," Cy explained. "He used me to hurt you all, so he must die!" Cy then hit the doctor into a wall.

The scientist was now covered in blood. He looked up at Cy and begged, "Please don't kill me. I know things about the general that could help you all."

Cy picked him up by the neck and shook him. "Just what kind of information could you know that would give me a reason to let you live?"

The girls now run over to surrounded Cy trying to stop him from further harming the doctor. They latched onto him with all there their worth, but trying to stop him in the state that he was in now, was like trying to stop a bull elephant, from charging.

In all the commotion, the doctor was able to choke out three words: "Minawa is alive!"

Cy and the girls' grips weakened.

"What was that?" Cy asked, in shock. He eased his grip on the doctor's neck.

"I said, Minawa's alive, —*and* you have a daughter." Cy dropped him, and he coughed as he slid down against the building and hit the ground.

Cy could not believe what he was hearing—and nether could the girls. Cy looked down and then up again, his red cybernetic eye growing brighter than ever. He pulled his fist back and let out a roar as he punched at the scientist. The girls all yelled out, "No!" but, when the dust cleared, they saw that Cy's punch had hit the wall right next to Doctor Connor's head.

Cy glared at the doctor. "It's just not worth it," he said. Then he turned to the girls. "Get this jerk out of my sight—please." He turned to April. "And please get all the information this jerk has on Minawa and my daughter."

April nodded. "I'll do my best."

Connor's looked up at the African American girl. "What are you going to do to me?"

"I'm going to make a copy of your memories," she said.

"What?" the injured man exclaimed, confused as to what she was talking about.

"My cyborg name is Mimic, witch means that I can copy anything— even the memories of people. But too bad for you, —it is a painful process, and it will probably put you in a coma for two weeks."

"You can't do that to me! I'm the chief scientist of the U.S. government!" Connor said, begging.

April laughed. "You should have thought of that before you tried to control Cy."

She grabbed the man's head with both her hands. Electricity shot around his head as she took in his memories. Once, she got what she wanted, she let go of his head. He fell to the ground unconscious.

April turned to Cy and said sadly, "You do have a child, and Minawa is alive, but you won't like what you see when you get to her."

"I don't care!" Cy yelled as he turned to the girls. "We are going to get her *now!*"

"Don't you think you've been through enough today?" Ashley asked worried for the man.

The male cyborg turned to the fire cyborg and yelled. "I don't want to hear any arguing! We are going."

"But," —" Ashley started.

Cy interrupted, yelling out, "*Now!*"

Cy then turned back to April. "Where is Minawa?," he asked quietly.

"She's in a large building about twenty miles from here."

"Then that's where we're going," he said as he picked her up. The glow appeared on his body again, and he took off into the sky.

"Victoria," Ellis yelled out, "we have to follow him." The gravity cyborg powered up and got the group of cyborg's into the air to follow Cy.

"Why does Cy seem so mad?" Destiny, asked Sakura. The Japanese girl turned to the healer. "It's because that scientist, in one brief moment, took away everything that he believes in, —his honor and his loyalties to us. And, to top it off, he just found out that the woman he loves, may still be alive. It would make anybody angry. We all seemed to forget that, under all the metal, there's still the heart of a man in pain."

CHAPTER 25

Cy, Ellis, and the cyborg girls all were soon hovering over a large building. Cy directed them to land on the roof of the on a building right next to the large building. Then Cy turned to Jennifer. "Please help me scan the building."

They both scanned the building from top to bottom.

They saw that the building was heavily guarded. There were several rooms in the building that were protected from their sight. They knew that Minawa and Cy's child must be hidden in one of them.

Cy turned to the girls. "I'm going in. April, Megan, Kate, you're all coming with me. April, you're going to turn into Doctor Connor's and lead me in, and Megan, you will follow us in using your invisibility. Lastly Kate, you're going to run in right behind us to look for my kid. As for the rest of you, you will wait for us here and be ready to serve as backup."

Some of them didn't like idea of Cy doing this, but his plan did seem to be the best idea to get in and get out as fast as possible.

"All right, let's go!" Cy said, as he Megan, April, and Kate made their way down to the front of the building.

April changed herself into Doctor Connor's in a flash of light., and Megan walked next to Cy and vanished. Kate hid waiting for her chance to run in.

April, in her disguise, walked into the building with Cy right next to her. To their surprise, General Bishop was standing in the lobby waiting for Connor's return. When he saw April in the form of Connor, he yelled out, "It's about time you got back here."

Cy and April walked over to the large man, who spoke to them. "So does this mean that the other cyborg's are destroyed?"

"Yes they are," April said in her Connor's disguise.

"Good," the general said plainly. But then he looked at Cy and noticed something. "Connor, is this cyborg really under your control?" he asked.

April looked at the general and said, "Isn"t it obvious."

"I guess," the general said slowly. "But now I want you to program him to obey *my* orders, not yours."

" Yes, sir," Connor's said. "But first I have to take him to my lab for the reprogramming."

"Just hurry!" the general told him as he turned around and left.

"Yes, sir," Connor said. And, still in Connor's form, April stuck her tongue out as he had his back turned away. "Jerk," she whispered.

"Watch it," Cy whispered back.

After April led the way to the lab and they were safely inside, she finally returned to her own form, as Megan reappeared.

Kate soon shot in through the window and said, "I've checked out the entire building. There are two rooms that I could not get into, and one, said Nursery on the door. The sign on the other door says Computer Room.

"You did a good job, Kate," Cy told her, and he turned to Megan and April who were now looking through the computers in the lab.

"Minawa's in the computer room," said April. "And the kid is in the nursery.

Cy nodded. "Can you get us in there?"

"I can," April told him.

"All right then," Cy began. "April and I are going to get Minawa. Megan, and Kate, you two are going after my kid." They all left the lab ready for their missions.

Minutes later, Cy and April were standing in front of the computer room when Mimic said, "The General is the only one allowed in this room, so it has to be the room where Minawa is" She then changed her hand to mimic the general's and placed her hand on the entry scanner. The door opened, thanks to her abilities.

When the two of them walked into the lab they both heard a woman's, voice say, "I've been waiting for you."

Cy looked around the room. He knew right away that it was Minawa's voice, but he couldn't see her.

"Where are you?" he asked in desperation. Just then, a bank of overhead lights came on. "Look up," Minawa said. Cy looked up, and what he saw almost made him fall over.

Minawa floated in a huge glass tube. She was nude and almost all of her body was gone. There were wires and tubes going to and from her body. She looked up at him and smiled. "It's been a long time, love."

Cy walked slowly up to the tube and touched it. "What have they done to you?" he cried in anguish.

She just looked at him sadly. "General Bishop did this because he wanted my intelligences."

Just then, they heard General Bishop's voice. It seemed to come out of thin air. "You should be happy that she's alive, because, when we found her, she was pregnant. The child, was very interesting considering that she was a mix between a human cyborg and an alien."

"What?" Cy asked looking around the room. April was standing right beside him. He knew it was really the general's voice he was hearing.

"She didn't tell you, she's not from Earth? That she's an alien?" The general said in a mocking tone.

Cy turned to Manawa. "Is this true?"

She nodded, "My, sister and I came to this planet to look for help, but, when we got here, our ship was damaged so we could not get home. We tried to get it repaired, but General Bishop found us out and had other plans for us. All he wanted was our technology. So he forced me to make powerful cyborg's out of young women. But, when I met you."—"

Cy finished her thought: "You found someone who was strong willed enough to free you and the other girls."

"No," said Minawa sadly. "I found, a man like no other, —an honorable man that can, not only free the cyborg's that I had made, but free my world as well."

The general's voice rang again saying, "Striker, you'd better get that thought of you taking her from me out of your head, because she can't live without being hooked up to those computers."

Cy could not take it. A, blue glow formed around him as he roared out, and pointed his fist right at the speaker where he was hearing General Bishop's voice. Out of what seemed like a reflex action, Cy shouted, *"Shotgun!"* and, simultaneously, a blast of energy shot from his hand. It sounded like a shotgun blast.

The beam of energy destroyed the intercom speaker. The blast scared April, but Minawa acted like she had been expecting this. Cy now stood with his fist still pointed straight out, his arm still smoking from the blast.

When he snapped out of the shock, he moved back to Minawa who seemed to be smiling at the fact that he had just fired what looked like lasers out of his fist.

"What was that?" Cy asked.

"It's what you called it, —shotgun," Minawa told him. "And that is only a small portion of what you can do."

As Cy shook this off, he said, "It doesn't matter what it's called because, right now, we just need to get her you out of here."

Minawa shook her head. "No, Bishop was right. If I'm removed from these computers, I will die."

Cy could not believe, what she was saying. "There has to be something we can do?," He pleaded.

"There is nothing that can be done now," Minawa said. "And, because of that, I must ask you to end my life. I don't want any more innocent people hurt because of my technology."

Cy couldn't move. He was too shocked. "Chris," Minawa said softly, "you told me once that you would do whatever I asked of you. And now, as you, would say it would be dishonorable to not do as I request. If you, still love me as much as I love you, you will do this last thing for me." Minawa finished her statement with almost a yell.

Cy lowered his head as he nodded knowing what she was saying was true. But April spoke up. "There is no way you can kill her. You have never killed anybody—you haven't even *thought* about hurting any innocent people. Wouldn't killing a women, go against everything that you believe in?"

Cy looked down sadly at this as Minawa said, "You promised me that you would do anything I asked, no matter what it was, Chris. This is my last wish, and I know it's hard, but this is what I want. I don't want to be used like a tool to hurt so many. Please do this one last thing for me."

Cy nodded again and as he reared back his fist.

April yelled, "You can't!"

But Cy shook his head. "No." Looking up at Minawa. "This is what Minawa wants, and I must do this for her. It must be this way. May god forgiven me for this."

As he finished speaking, the air itself seemed to come alive with energy. April had to stand back because the power he was give giving off was almost suffocating.

A lone tear slid down Cy's face as he pushed his fist forward in what seemed like slow-motion. When he hit the tube, he yelled out a battle cry, *"Screaming Bullet!"*

Minawa smiled to at him and mouthed, "Good-bye."

The energy from the punch, vaporized both Minawa and the tube. It also blew an enormous hole in the side of the building. In fact, the force of the blast shot straight outside. When the other girls saw it, they then knew something big was happening. But, as difficult as it was, they followed Cy's instructions to stay put and waited for his orders.

Meanwhile, inside the building, Cy stood breathing hard, standing in front of the hole where Minawa once was. April walked up and stood next to him., "Are you okay?" April asked.

"I will be once we get my daughter out of this place." He said.

April nodded in agreement. Cy moved over closer to her and wrapped an arm around her. Together they and looked up and jumped straight up through the ceiling and landed next to where Megan and Kate were.

They had been wondering what that the huge explosion was, but, when Cy burst through the floor, with April, they knew everything would be fine. He turned to them. "Is my daughter in that room?" he asked.

"Yes," said Megan.

"But we can't open the door," said Kate.

"Stand back!" Cy said, and he used his power to force the magnetically sealed doors open with ease. Both Megan and Kate stood wide-eyed at this.

As they walked into the room, Megan and Kate asked April how he Cy got so much stronger. "Girls, you wouldn't believe me if I told you," April said still in a little bit of shock herself.

The nursery it appeared set up for just one infant. At first Cy and the three girls couldn't see anything, but then looked around the room and saw a nurse hiding in the corner. When they walked over, the nurse held a bundle in her arms.

"Are you Chris Striker?" She the nurse asked as she looked up as him.

He nodded.

"Then this belongs to you," she said as she hands him the small bundle. "Her name is Maylu, and she is only three months old."

Cy took the bundle and held it in his arms. He and the girls peered at the baby. The baby smiled up at him. Cy was sure that for the moment the baby saw him she knew he was her father.

Cy turned back to the nurse, and thanked her for everything, and told her to leave for her own safety. He then turned to the others. "Hang on to me," he told them.

The three of them grabbed him, and then, holding the baby in one arm, Cy fired off another Screaming Bullet , which vaporized the wall. They all then jumped through the hole.

Cy landed next to the other girls on the roof of the building next door. He addressed them all: "We have a surprise for all of you," he said. "Take a look at the newest member of our group." The girls were very excited. Cy continued, "It is now our job to take care of this baby." Cy told them and they agreed.

Rebecca was the first to ask if she could hold the baby, —for their trip home?.

"Sure," Cy said. "But be careful." Cy handed the baby to Force-Rebecca, and the others started asking if they could hold her too.

"Rebecca asked first," Cy told them, . "You will all get your chance when we get back home. I want to get there as soon as possible. But, now that we got my kid we need to get home."

As they where about to take off, a large robot slammed into him, crashing him through the roof of the building all the way to the ground floor.

The girls looked down into the hole hoping that Cy was okay, but he was far from okay. As he looked up, he heard, General Bishop's voice come from the robot.

"What do you think of Minawa's latest power suit design?" He said to Cy. After Cy moved some rubble out of the way, he stood up and saw the general inside the large battle suit.

Before Cy could make a move, though, the general used the battle suit's whole hand to grab Cy by the head and throw him through the wall. He landed outside where he rolled to the street curb he looked up as the battle suit walked up to him. The general slowly going into a run and slammed him Cy into the wall.

The general walked back, and Cy could hear Bishop laughing inside the suit. Cy knew the general believed that the cyborg can't win. "I'm going to make you pay for destroying my computer!" Bishop said to the cyborg.

"That wasn't a computer!" Cy said. "That was Minawa! And nobody has the right to turn a human being into a computer."

"She wasn't human—heck, she wasn't even from Earth." The general punched at the cyborg. But Cy stopped the power suit with one hand as he yelled.

"You can't talk about the woman I loved like that!" He punched the battle suit, with monstrous force, but it didn't even move.

"Do you truly think you can beat a battle suit that was made by the same person that made you? Think again!" He pointed his arms out and fired hundreds of missiles at the cyborg. Cy jumped into the air to avoid them, but they turned up and hit him hard blowing him hard directly back to the ground.

Bishop pointed out his arms again, but this time let out a fiery blaze that engulfed the cyborg. The general then turned back to the building where the other cyborg's were.

"Who's next?" he yelled out.

Before they could answer, from the flames they heard a battle cry coming from the flames. Then they saw Cy walked out of the blaze.

His clothes were nearly burned away. He stepped out the flames and glared at the man in the battle suit as he said, "You leave them alone! The only cyborg you need to fight is me!"

Cy's fingers clicked like a shotgun being cocked as he formed them into a fist. April knew what was coming. "Take cover!" she yelled to the others.

"Why?" asked Ashley.

"Just get down!" Mimic yelled as they all scrambled for safety.

Jennifer started scanning the energy levels. She could not believe the power Cy, was admitting. When April yelled at her telling to get down she snapped out of fear induced daze and hid with the others.

Cy reared back his powered up fist. The battle suit started to run at him. Just as he got to him, Cy punched the center of the suit yelling out, "*Screaming Bullet!*"

The force of the blow, and the energy that was released were so great that it destroyed the battle suit was destroyed immediately. The force shot, General Bishop out of the flaming suit. He slammed into a wall on the other side of the street.

After the explosion the girls made their way down to the streets. Cy walked over to the badly burned man lying in the street. He picked up the man and reared his fist back again ready to strike him down. But, before he could, Sakura yelled, "Don't kill him!" she yelled.

"Why not? For what he's done, he deserves it. He has taken everything from me. He even made me kill Minawa— so tell me why can't I kill him!"

"Because, if you do, you'll be no better than he is," Sakura told him.

Cy looked at the man before him. "I knew you were weak," said the general. "You just don't have in you to kill me, and that's what makes you weak."

Cy growled at the man before he lowered him down. "I am not weak; I value life. You are the one who is weak, for you treat life like it is a disposable commodity. You use people as if they have no worth. People are only valuable unless they are used to destroy other life."

"Ha!" Bishop laughed, "What other point is there in life but to fight?" Cy shook his head, for he knew that this man would not listen to him. He started to carry him off.

"Where are you taking him?" asked an anxious Ellis asked.

"I'm taking him to a hospital."

"Why?"

"Because it is the right thing to do."

After depositing the general in a nearby emergency room, they started their way back home. As they traveled, Kate asked, "What are we going to do now?"

"We are now going to go to Minawa's home world, for we still have a job to do," Cy told them. Then he explained everything that they had learned from when he talked to Minawa. "Now we have to go into space to stop a tyrant there."

CHAPTER 26

When they got back to the dorm it was late at night, but Cy, followed by the girls, still went straight to Samantha's lab. He found her typing at her computer. She looked up as he entered. "Is everything okay?"

Cy gave her a half-hearted smile, and then as he explained everything that had happened. It was difficult to tell her and even how he had found out that he was a father and that she was an aunt. She seemed very surprised by the news. It was even more difficult to tell, her that Minawa was now dead—and he had been forced to kill her with his own hands.

Surprisingly, this did not upset Sam, for she knew that this is what her sister had wanted, After Cy finished his story, Sam smiled as she leaned back in her chair, as this is what she was wanting for.

"What are you smiling about?" Cy asked.

"I knew that my sister was thinking of a way to free our people, and now it looks as if she has done it."

Cy then asked the big question: "How long will it take to get a ship ready to travel to your home planet?"

Sam smiled up at him. "We could leave now if you guys hadn't destroyed the RV!"

"Hay, that wasn't our fault. We didn't know that the moon base was rigged to blow like that."

Sam sat back down. "I know, but it will take at least two to three weeks to get a ship ready. And then it will take two months to get there."

Cy thought for a minute, wondering what to do. He then looked at the sleeping baby, Maylu, still in Rebecca's arms. Then he turned back to Sam. "Do you think, while you get a ship ready, I could take the girls and my myself, and my new baby, home to my family for a while?"

Sam then stood and put a hand on his shoulder. "That will be fine, and it will give me the time, I need to get things ready. And, besides the girls would love a chance to meet your family." She then turned to the girls, "Wouldn't you?" she asked. They all looked at each other thinking of a chance to meet his family, and turned to Sam and agreed. "Then it's settled," said Sam. "In the mourning, I will arrange a flight to take you all there."

"How can you do that?" April asked.

"I can do anything with a computer," she Sam told her. "In the meantime, though, can I hold my niece?"

Cy smiled at the girls. "You all need to get, some sleep and get your things together for tomorrow."

After that, they all headed out of the lab to get ready, for tomorrow was going to be a busy day.

The next mourning at the airport, Cy was once again in his trench coat, hat, and sunglasses. Victoria was the one holding his baby. as they all went in the airport and sure enough there tickets were wanting for them.

The only thing that worried them was Cy walking through the metal detectors, but, thanks to Minawa's trench coat design, he walked through it with no problems, and, once they were on the plane, things went without a hitch.

When the airplane landed, there was a bus waiting for them. Sam had arranged it, for they looked like a school group visiting the area.

After a long ride, they all arrived at Cy's home. Cy told Victoria and the girls to hide when he knocked on the door of his house, for he wanted to surprise his family.

Cy knocked on the door, and his sister opened the it. "Hi,", he said as he removed his sunglasses.

Salina threw herself into his arms and yelled out to his their aunt, when she saw him. Angela ran over when she saw his face, she jumped and hugged her nephew. "Ouch!" she said. As then found.

She took a step back as Will joined the group and embraced Cy.

Cy took a step back from the porch and his family and said, "I have a surprise for you." Then he turned to the porch. "You can come out now, girls." And the twelve cyborg girls plus the android Ellis slowly came out of hiding. Cy introduced them all to his aunt, uncle, and his sister, witch it did surprise them thinking that things were going to a little tight in house tonight.

"The accommodations might be a little tight," said Angela, "but you are all welcome."

After the introductions, they all went into the kitchen. When they were settled, and Cy explained the whole story to his family. His aunt and uncle were shocked about how those girls had been used. They were also very surprised and the fact that he now had a baby from Minawa— and that the general had kept Minawa alive like as he he had. But, before they could continue, the baby, started to cry. Victoria started to rock her trying to quiet her, but soon she realized that she the baby was hungry. Not only the baby— but the others were hungry too. They realized that they hadn't eaten anything sense since they had left.

So Chris's Angela stated, "If you all can wait for a bit, I'll make you all some supper."

After they all ate supper, they retired to the large living room, and talked about their adventures around the world.

Finally, all the travelers—plus Salina— fell asleep in the living room. Angela, and Will looked at all of them sleeping soundly in a pile. They watched their nephew in the middle, sound asleep. "He"s quite a boy, isn't he?" Will said.

Angela agreed. They retired to their room for a good night's sleep.

The next mourning, Angela and Will woke to a quiet house. The living room was vacant—only a few blankets were left folded neatly on the sofa. Outside, however, they heard the sounds of fighting outside, and loud music playing.

They went outside to find Cy and the girls doing their exercises. Angela asked, "What are you all doing?"

The male cyborg said, "Don't worry, Aunt Angela. There just doing our mourning exercises! We can have some breakfast when we're finished?"

Soon, the whole kitchen was abuzz with activity as all the girls tried to make their own breakfast. The bathroom was also busy. Ellis went up to Angela and apologized for all the ruckus, but Angela told her not to worry because —she liked all the activity in the mourning.

A couple of days went by, and the girls found that they liked hanging around Cy's family. They even started to pitch in and help with the house and yard work. To Cy's aunt and uncle, it was like having an army around the house day and night.

The only thing that bothered the girls was the way Cy's sister didn't believe in his code or anything else that made him special in there their eyes. In fact, one day, while the girls were doing some of there exercises, Salina came up, and approached them. "How do you live with yourselves knowing that the whole world is after you just for because of who you all are? Why do you bother living at all when you don't know anything about your pasts?"

Sakura walked over to girl. "There is no honor in just giving up, Salina. You must keep fighting for what you believe in, no matter what, you have to keep fighting."

Destiny joined Sakura. "We may not know our pasts, but we can all have a future with Cy because we promised him that we would stay by his side forever."

"Whatever," Salina said. "You know, you all are crazy." She then turned and walked back to the house in a huff.

Cy watched her as she approached him. Apparently she hadn't seen him standing at the door, because she ran into his chest. When she looked up at him, he smiled. "You know," he said, " crazy is only how you look at something. What might seem crazy to one person might seem perfectly sane to another."

Salina scoffed at that and went on with her business for the day, which was to go out witch was going out with her boyfriend Zack.

xxx

When Zack saw Cy and the girls for the first time, he asked Salina, "Shouldn't we just turn your brother and those girls in, for the reward?"

"No! My aunt and uncle would never allow that—they would hate me for it."

"But think of the money!" Zack said. "We could leave and live anywhere we, want."

CHAPTER 27

After the group spent another two weeks of enjoyment with Cy's family, Samantha finally contacted them to say she was just about to arrive in a ship that was bigger than his aunt and uncle's house. "Good thing there's a big backyard!" she said. Sam hovered the craft over the house and then landed in the backyard. Fortunately, the ship landing behind the house, it was stealth rigged, so no one saw it come in. But they could hear it and whipped up a furious wind they had to hurry and get on it when it landed.

When Sam stepped out, she asked them what they thought of it. "This is the ship my sister and I traveled in when we journeyed to Earth. I've finished the repairs."

"This is great!" Cy said as he and the girls came out to greet her. They were ready to go.

When Melissa asked the big question, the one they all were thinking: must of them where thinking "what What are we going to do, for the two months that it's going to take us to get there?"

The male cyborg shrugged as he just said, "We can all get to know each other a little better." He was half joking, but the idea made them all blush witch that the male cyborg seemed to have missed.

Finally, Sam broke things up. "What are you all waiting for? It's time to get going!"

They were about to get on board the ship, when they all heard sirens. They turned and saw four police cars screech to a halt in driveway, lights flashing and sirens wailing. "We've been found out!" Cy yelled out.

Policemen stormed into the backyard, guns drawn. "Don't move!" yelled the officer in charge.

Cy looked at his sister. "Did you do this, Salina?" he asked. His sister shook her head no.

Then Cy turned and saw, Zack stepping out of one of the police cars. "There they are, officer," the young man said to the officer in charge, "just as I said."

Ashley was about to attack, but Cy said, "No. We're not going to fight the police."

"Well," what are we going to do then?" she snapped back.

Right before Cy could answer, the cops opened fire on them.

Cy acted in the blink of an eye. He caught every bullet fired at them, and when the firing stopped, the male cyborg stood in front of the others, with his fists, across front of his face. He glared at the men for firing at them without an order, then he opened his hands and let the bullets that had fired fall to the ground at his feet.

This act shocked the police officers for Cy had moved so fast to catch the bullets, they hadn't seen it happen., Cy turned his head to Megan. "Put up a shield between us and the police." Mirage razed her hands in the air, placing the invisible shield around them.

Cy turned to his family saying. "Sorry for the short good-bye, but we have to go!"

He reached through the shield and took his baby from Angela's arms. "Good luck," she whispered to him.

As soon as they were on the ship and in their places, Samantha took off. The second the ship lifted off, and the second it took off it vanished in the sky leaving the police officers to wonder what had happened.

Zack ran over to Salina. "Why did you let them go? We just lost a million dollars!" Saline turned to the young man and slapped him across his face. "We're through!" she said, and stalked off into the house.

xxx

Meanwhile in the ship Cy had just strapped his looked at Maylu, who was strapped in a sleeping tube that Sam had made just for her. The baby would remain asleep for the entire trip. Sam thought it would be easier and safer that way.

The male cyborg then sat down next to the girls, and laded back in the set. He reclined in his seat and then asked Sam, "Are we going to get sleeping tubes too?"

"I didn't have time to make one for everyone," she told him, "and, besides, they don't work very well on cyborg's for some odd reason." Sam told him, Cy sighed at the thought. "This is going to be the longest two months of my life!"

On the second day on the ship, Kim, watched as Cy and Sakura who were both sitting on the floor facing each other with there their eyes closed. "What are you two doing?" she asked them. But they didn't answer; they seemed to be in some kind of trance.

Kim asked again, but still they didn't respond. Sam turned to Kim from her seat. " They can't hear you."

"Why?"

"They're both doing a type of training called shadowing. I'm not completely sure how the whole thing works, but it has something to do with their martial arts training."

Inside their minds, Cy walked up to Blackout, Sakura and assumed a fighting stands stance. "Are you ready, Sakura-Chan?" he asked.

"Any time you're ready," she responded. Then they shot into a sparring match. Their moves were almost impossible to follow until Sakura fired an electrical blast that shot Cy out of the minds-cape.

Cy fell back scaring Kim who was watching them. When Cy looked back up at Sakura, he said, "That was impressive! I didn't expect that last blast."

"I don't believe you," she said. "I think you're holding back—I just can't tell how much." Nevertheless, she smiled at the complement. "Same time tomorrow?" she asked.

"Sure, thing." He nodded to her.

Kim finally got their attention. "Could you guys teach me that thing you were doing?"

"What thing?"

"That shadowing, thing you where doing—it looked neat."

"It's kind of, difficult to learn, but, if you're willing, I could teach you," responded Cy.

The girl smiled happily, but the smile disappeared when he said, "I can't teach you right now, but Sakura can."

Kim smiled again when Sakura said, "I might not be as good as Cy, but I'll do my best."

So, the next day, Sakura was doing her best to teach Kim the shadowing training technique, but it wasn't easy. At the same time,Cy was trying to get a little of his own training in by dancing in the main hall of the ship, which wasn't very big. He was having trouble with the bigger moves.

Just as Cy stopped himself from bumping into a wall, an alarm went off in the ship. Cy and the girls ran to the control room, asking Sam what was going on. "The' instruments are picking up something enormous in front of us," she said, "but 'I can't see anything.

Look! Jennifer then pointed out the window. "There! I see something!"

Cy looked and saw something coming right at them. Sam saw it to. "It can't be," she yelled. They all watched as the a ship came into few view. It looked exactly like 'theirs. "But that's impossible," said Sam.

The ship seemed to be coming strait straight at them. Cy yelled, "Move!" Sam changed direction, but the other ship, remaining in front of them. Just as everyone thought the two ships were going to collide, there ship seemed to disappear into nothingness.

Cy and the girls opened their eyes to see that they were inside what looked like a huge cargo bay of a very large ship. They couldn't see anyone outside. Cy turned to the girls. "I'm going to have a look around."

"I'm going too.," Sam stated.

Cy, agreed, but then turned to Rebecca. "Will you come too? Your strength could come in handy." The girl nodded. Cy turned the others. "Stay on the ship and watch your backs." They wished the small group good luck."

Cy, Sam, and Rebecca walked out of the ship and carefully surveyed their surroundings. " So, Sam, what do you think?" Cy asked.

"I don't know," Sam said. "Maybe the ship's deserted. It may have picked us up by accident."

Rebecca then pointed out to a door on other end of the cargo bay. Cy and Sam both saw it, and Cy spoke into his communicator. "We're were going to look farther into the ship. If we're not back in an hour, to send Jennifer and April to come looking for them for us."

The three of them headed for the door at the end of the bay. As they walked on, Rebecca noted that there were what looked like crayon drawings done by little kids all over the walls. Sam noticed a metal sign that read , "Watch Your Step."

"I wonder what that could mean?" she asked Cy.

Suddenly, when as they entered a narrow passage, Cy felt the floor under him move. "Jump!" he yelled out as he grabbed Sam and Rebecca and leaped over a huge trap door that was sliding open. When he landed on the other side, Rebecca looked down into the trap. There where huge metal spikes at the bottom pointed directly up at them. "Do you think they're trying to tell us something?" Rebecca stated.

"Well, we can't go back," Cy said. "It looks like we've got to keep going on."

As they continued, Rebecca noticed a second sign. It read Losers Ahead.

"Wonder what that could mean," Sam said.

Cy pushed the two girls down. "Duck!" he yelled. Pushing, them to the ground, a Two dozen razor-sharp blades shot out from the walls on both sides of them. The girls looked up at Cy, who was on top of the two them. "Loses a head," Cy said. "I don't know what's worse—the traps or the bad puns." We'd better keep moving."

Soon the passageway opened into a large, high-ceilinged room. Before them was a twelve-foot statue of a man with a sword strapped to its his back. The weird thing about the statue was the crayon drawings all over it. It looked as if like a bunch of kids had drawn on it, . As they approached it the statue, Sam noted the writing at the bottom. "There's a riddle printed here. It says we must solve the riddle to live.," she said.

At that moment, the statue came to life and swung its sword out. But Cy and Rebecca jumped back as Sam rolled under it the blade. The statue it swung its sword down at Cy. He caught the blade with both hands, and he yelled out desperately to Sam, "What's the riddle?"

Sam looks looked at the riddle. "What walks on four legs in the mourning, two in the evening, and three in the afternoon?"

Cy almost lost his footing as he tried to think and fight the statue at the same time. "What the hell does that mean?" he yelled as he went down onto one knee struggling with the large statue's sword.

That's when Rebecca shrugged. "A person," she said. Abruptly, and right when she said that the statue stopped fighting and kneeled before Cy.

Sam turned to Rebecca, . "How is that the answer?" Sam she asked.

"Well, a person crawls on all fours when a baby, walks on two in a adulthood, and uses a cane in old age."

Sam and Cy looked at each other before as they realized the truth in the answer. But Rebecca noticed the statue start to move again. "Look out!" she yelled as it swooped its sword at them. Cy caught the blade in mid swing. As he struggled to hold the blade, the lights, dimmed and doors opened all around them. What looked like small people holding guns came running out, and surrounded them. One of the taller ones approached them, and said, "You may have gotten through our traps and riddles, but you won't get through us!"

Cy looked around at the creatures. Then he frowned. "I don't fight kids!" he said.

Both Sam and Rebecca looked at him. "Kids?" said Sam.

"Yeah," he stated. "These are all kids."

Just then, the tallest one spoke up. "Yeah were kids. What's it to you?"

Suddenly the lights came back on, and Sam and Rebecca saw that they *were* all kids. Some of them didn't look any older than seven or eight.

"Where are your parents?" Cy asked. "And do they know that you're using those dangerous weapons?" Cy asked the kids as He pushed one of the guns out of his face.

"You have no right to talk about our parents because your group *killed* them all!" the boy said to the cyborg.

"I don't know what you're talking about, kid," said Cy. "This is my first time into space."

The kid pointed his gun up to the cyborg as he yelled out, "You lie! I'll never forget the day you, cybernetic monsters, destroyed my home and my family, —killed everybody on my planet."

Cy looked at the boy sadly. The boy was doing his best to hold back his tears, but some of the younger ones, hearing his words, could not help but cry. Cy was about to say something to the boy when an explosion erupted, shaking the whole ship.

"What was that?" Cy yelled out, Another kid ran into the room and spoke to the older boy. "We've hit a meteor shower! We wont last long, if they we don't do something fast, !"

The older oldest boy said, "Show me!"

Another kid said, "Hey, what are we going to do with the intruders?"

The oldest one said, "I don't have time for them right now!"

Cy, Sam, and Rebecca watched as all the children left, Cy turned to Sam. "Follow them—see what you can do to help."

"What do you won't me to do, Cy?" Rebecca asked.

"You return to the ship," he said, " and tell the others to come, and help. But tell Ellis to stay with the ship, —and watch over my baby,"

"Yes, sir," said Rebecca, as she ran off.

"You don't have to call me *sir*," Cy yelled back to Rebecca as she ran back the way they had come.

xxx

On, the bridge of the giant ship, the kid who was navigating was doing his best to avoid the meteors, but he was having a tough time. Sam burst in and told the boy to move. She pushed him out of the way and sat in the navigator's chair.

Sam looked at the controls for minute and then she started to navigate them the big ship through the storm with ease. Even so, two of the kids pointed guns at her face. Finally, she turned to them. "I'm trying to work here, kids," she yelled. "Leave me alone or we're all be dead!" She yelled at them. The kids jumped back and lowered their weapons.

xxx

Cy and the rest of the kids had remained where they were. They were doing their best to stay stable, but the ship was being knocked around. Suddenly, right then a large section of the wall started to fall on a group of the kids.

Cy jumped under the spot, and caught it. Cy looked at all the kids. "Move!" he shouted at them. They appeared to be too scared to move, but then they seemed to disappear. Cy turned to see Kate standing next to the group that was had almost been crushed by the wall. Kim came up next to Cy and absorbed the strength of the metal wall. Rebecca came to his other side, and, together, they helped him throw the metal slab to a save safe place.

Soon the other girls joined him. "What took you all so long?" he joked.

"I thought I told you to be careful," Beth told him, and they all had a laughed.

Sam had finally finished navigating the ship through the meteor shower and was walking out from the bridge when the kids surrounded all of them again. Some of the cyborg girls went into fighting positions, but Cy told them to stand down. "We won't fight kids.,"

The oldest boy, who seemed to be the leader, stepped forward. "I won't fall for this," he said to Cy. "You and your robotic friends were the ones responsible, for destroying our entire world and killing our parents."

Cy looked at the boy's eyes, and saw the pain the boy was in.

One of the other boys said, "They can't be the ones! These guys helped us! Not one of those monstrous cyborgs that destroyed our planet would think about helping people!"

But the lead boy would not listen. He, charged at the male cyborg and started to hit him again and again.

The young boy yelled at Cy as he hit him, "it was you. It was you!"

The boy yelled over and over again the cyborg girls were about to do something to stop the boy, but Cy motioned for them to stay back.

The cyborg then knelt to the boy, and hugged him as he the boy still kept throwing punches. Finally the boy gave in, and started to cry in Cy's arms. "Why did my parents have to die?" he sobbed. "Why did that monster kill them?"

Samantha realized what was going on. The monster who was responsible for taking over her world was also the one responsible for destroying these kids' home world. He must also be conquering other worlds now.

The boy was still crying in Cy's arms. Cy spoke quietly to him. "I promise that I will take care of this monster. I will make him pay for everything— all the people that he has hurt or killed. I will make him pay a thousand times over." Cy looked up to the ceiling of the ship, his cybernetic eye glowing bright red.

Sam and all the cyborgs gathered together in front of their ship. They were getting ready to leave., Sam was talking to one of the kids, who was explaining that the reason they could had not been able to see the ship at first was because that their whole ship's cloaking device not only shielded them, but also acted like a mirror to fool there enemies.

Some of the children were asking them to stay, but Cy and the girls still had a mission to complete. The boys wished them all luck on their journey. All the girls were on the ship. As Cy stepped in, he turned to the boy that was in fact there leader. "Be strong for the others," Cy said, "and become an honorable man."

The boy smiled, and thanked Cy for helping them. "Good luck!" he yelled as the ship lifted off the ground of the cargo bay and back into space.

As they were flying back through space, Cy sat on the floor meditating. He thought about the kids on that ship, and how scared they had been of him, and the others. Could it be, that the monster that had destroyed their planet those kids spoke of was a cyborg, like him?

Cy could not think of that, anymore. He had to find a way to get stronger to prepare for their arrival on Minawa's and Samantha's home world.

Cy knew that his body was now cybernetic and so limits were had been built in. But that didn't mean he couldn't train his mind with intense mediation. So, Cy spent most of the trip through space in meditation. As for the girls, Sakura was able to advance they're training by teaching most of them the shadowing technique to increase their training. After some time of traveling through space, they landed on a planet far from Earth.

CHAPTER 31

Sam landed their ship on planet Titan far from any sign of life. Cy asked Sam, "Why are we landing so far away, from any life?"

"It's because we don't won't to draw any attention to ourselves. There are a lot of bad people in this world."

"So how are we going to find anybody on this planet, if we're so far from any people?" Rebecca asked, .

Victoria answered her, "By flying you and the others in the air!"

Cy looked at them. "I can handle flying on my own."

Exiting the spaceship, they all took to the air. Megan held on to Cy's baby Maylu because of her force fields, Megan eagerly agreed because she liked holding little Maylu..

As they all flew over the area looking for any sign of life, Cy was started to think that the whole planet was abandoned, but then Sam yelled out for them to land. Her village was right below them. Cy landed first in the village, and then the others came down beside him. But, as they looked around, the village seemed to be like a ghost town. There was no one around. Cy turned to Sam and was about to asked where everybody was, when something hit him. Shocking him, he fell over like a rag doll.

The girls ran over to him. Ashley shook him a couple of times, but he was out like a light. Ashley turned to Sam. "What happened to him?" she asked.

Sam pulled a small dart off out of the back of Cy's neck. "It's a Nero neuro-disabler. He's going to be out for a while—but who—???" Right before Sam could finish, they heard someone yell out.

"We got him! That man is out.," yelled a female voice.

Sam and the girls turned to see who had yelled out. A woman appeared before them. Sam stepped in front of the girls and asked, "Why did you do that?"

The woman who had shot Cy said, "He's a man. All men are evil."

"You don't understand," said Sam. "He's here to free us from the cyborg who has become your enemy." "Sam? Is that you???" the woman said in surprise.

"Marie?"

"What are you doing with this man?" Marie asked. "And who are these other girls?"

Sam sighed as she told Marie that these girls were cyborg's, and that they have had all come to help them against the enemy cyborg. But, before Sam could tell her about Cy, another woman yelled out, "We have four flyer's coming our way! Everyone hide!"

Sam tried to tell Marie some more, but Marie said. "Hide! There are some heavy hitters coming our way."

They all started to head indoors, but Destiny yelled out, "What about Cy?"

One of the women grabbed her and said, "Who cares?" And she ran inside a building and locked the doors. A few minutes later, four very powerful-looking male cyborg's landed and started looking around.

"Are you sure that you detected high power levels in this area?" One of them said.

"Yeah, I detected at least a dozen levels right here." Just then, they both detected something. They looked over and saw Cy getting up rubbing the back of his head.

"Did anybody get the, license number of that truck?" Cy said quipped. He looked over at the men looking at him as he asked. "Who are you guys?"

"Hay, man; are you, one of the new recruits?" one of the cyber men asked.

"New recruit? What are you talking about?" Cy asked as he rubbed the back of his still-throbbing head.

Right then, the men realize something was wrong—that this guy couldn't be a new recruit. "So you are not here to help Lord Titan out?" one of the cyborgs asked.

"Lord Titan!" Cy yelled in response to hearing that name. "Is that the guy responsible for destroying the planets in this area of the galaxy?"

"Lord Titan, doesn't destroy, he conquers," one of the four men said to him, and. Cy realized right then that these guys were his enemies, and he jumped into a fighting position. "I don't care what this guy does, I came to this planet to take down this punk Lord Titan!"

The cyborgs didn't know what to think at this point. They had never had to fight a man on their own planet, but this cybernetic man was threatening their lord and master, so they attacked by flying around the intruder cyborg as he stood still.

The people hiding in the buildings, could not believe Cy. He was just standing in one spot as the four men flew around him. It didn't look as if Cy had a chance against the Titan's elite squad.

"Cy can take these guys easily," Jennifer stated. "There levels are nothing compared to his."

One of the other women said, "There is no way that he can take all of them.," But, before she could finish, Cy clotheslined, one of the cyborg men, and slammed him to the ground, and punched down crushed his head with powerful blows. The three men that were left looked on in awe. Cy had taken, down one of their men in two swift movements.

The three remaining cyborgs flew around Cy and then stopped, their feet barely touching the ground around him. Their hands split open revealing lasers. Just as they fired, Cy let a half smile across his face. The beams seemed to go right through him, which meant the cyborgs had to dodge their own beams. They all looked at each other as to discover what had happened. They hadn't even seen him move—but they knew he had.

They noticed the ground under him had been moved witch means he did move, but to fast for them to see, "That's impossible!" One of the cyborgs said, .

"No one is faster than me!" another said as he attacked, but his punches went right through Cy. The man then yelled right into his face, "Fight me already!"

Cy then put his fist right through his enemy's chest. Blood and oil poured out of him. The cyborg man looked at the other in front of him, and coughed some blood up. "*what the fuck are* you?" he gasped.

"I'm the one that's going to free this planet of evil!" Cy stated grabbing the cyborg's head. "And, one more thing," he continued, " you shouldn't swear when ladies are present." And, with that, he snapped off the cyborg's head and threw it to the ground next to the body.

Cy looked up to at the last two remaining cyborgs. One of them was really freaking out, as the other was getting ready to attack "The one freaking out turned to the other guy, "they don't pay me enough for this," he said, as he flew off.

But Cy looked at both of them and turned to the girls, who were still hiding. "Hey, girls," he called, "which one of these guys should I let live? One of them has to get a message to this Titan guy."

He heard them Sam yell back, "Let the one who's not freaking out live."

Cy smiled. "All right. I'll use the new long range attack I learned while we were still in space." He laid his hand across his upper arm and, made a fist, and yelled out, "*Shotgun!*" Thousands of small shots came from his fist. It was like a variation of his Screaming Bullet, only hundreds of blasts instead of one, and in smaller shots.

The shots hit the one cyborg that was flying away. He immediately fell to the ground and blew up when he hit the ground. The last remaining cyborg saw this, he shook his head. "I have not seen anything like this,—not since I saw the Titan himself fight."

Cy walked straight up to the other last cyborg, and looked him in the eyes.

Cy could tell just by looking at this guy that he had killed many people in his lifetime, and had not regretted any of it. The guy then punched Cy, but Cy caught it in his fist and held it before it made contact. Staring the guy down, Cy asked, "You don't care at all, what you have done to these people, do you?"

Cy seemed enraged at this guy whom he held at his mercy. He slammed the cyborg to the ground. "I want you to go, tell your boss that the cyborg that Minawa Ivy has made, has come to take him down!"

Cy slowly let the other cyborg up, but still had his arm in a tight grip. But before he let him go, he said, "One more thing." Then Cy tore off the cyborg's arm, in one move. The other cyborg screaming screamed in pain. "That's for thinking that, women are weak. They're, a lot strong, then you'll ever know."

"You'll pay for this," the Cyborg man threatened as he flew off, holding the stub where his arm had been.

Cy throw threw the arm down saying, "What a waste of a good arm!" He watched the cyborg fly out of sight, and turned to sees his cyborg girls, running his way. "Do you think I went a little overboard?" he asked them sheepishly.

"No," Victoria started said. "I think you did just fine."

Cy noticed one of the women walk over to him. She said, "If you think, just because you took down four of the elites, that we would all fall into your lap, think again."

"I'm not here just so you can fall into my lap with gratitude," Cy stated. "I'm here because it's the right thing to do. No one should feel that he or she is superior to anyone."

Marie joined the group and scowled at this man in front of her, as she said, "You may be strong, but you haven't faced anything like the Titan. He'll crush you."

"Who is this Titan?" Cy asked.

Sam then came up and told him, "He's the reason you where sent here."

The village elder then walked over to the male cyborg, though she seemed young to be the elder of this village"I am the Village Elder. And there is no way that we are going, to trust a man to do anything in this village."

Cy looked at her., "I have not come here to hurt anybody. I have just come here to help."

"Then prove it," said Marie. "Go to the eldest of our people,—our Supreme Elder—and tell her your story. If she believes you, then we will allow you to help us."

Cy took a deep breath. "All right, if that's the way you want it, I'll see this person." He turned to Sakura and Victoria. "You two will come with me to help me convince this person that I have come here to help."

But then elder Marie told him, "No, just me, I will be the only one going with you on this journey."

"Why, can't the others come?" Cy asked.

"They will remain here as hostages, to prevent you from running away."

"I won't run away," he Cy told her. He turned back to the cyborg girls, who were all giving him worried looks. He assured them that everything would be all right and, that he would hurry back as soon as he could. "Sakura, you are in charge until I got get back." Some of the girls yelled at him asking why Sakura should be in charge. "She has, a little bit more experience. ," he told them.

Cy turned back to the Village Elder and asked her, "How long will it take us to get to this Supreme Elder one of yours?"

The women looked coldly at him as she said, "About two days."

Cy about fell over when he heard this, but then asked, "How about if we fly?,"

The women gave him an odd look, as she said, "It would take a couple of hours, I guess, but we don't have any means of flying."

"Oh, yeah?" Cy stated as he scoped up the women in his arms and took off into the air. The Village Elder screamed the entire way. The cyborg girls sighed as they watched Cy fly off into the distance; seeing this some of them were thinking, how lucky the Elder was as they watched Cy fly off into the distances.

<h1 style="text-align:center">CHAPTER 32</h1>

The warrior whom Cy had let go turned messenger finally made it back to a large city called, Cyber City. This was the only city on the planet, and the only place on the planet where there was any technology. The warrior flew straight through the city to the center of it where the largest building was. He landed outside the building and ran.

The warrior burst through the double doors of the Titan's main office yelling, out. " We have intruders on our planet! Another man has come, —a cyborg! He's going to kill you, Lord Titan!"

The Titan looked up from his throne. Four women sat around him—all wearing next to nothing. The Titan sat back in on his throne. His face was in shadow, but you could see his eyes glowed in the darkness around him. And as he came into the light, he looked as normal as any human: his hair was as gold as the sun; his face seemed to glow with handsome beauty; and, to many that who looked upon him, he was perfect. But his eyes seemed to always give off a constant aura of pure evil.

Lord Titan looked at the warrior who had came into his throne room without an invitation, and who was dripping vital fluids all over his floor. "What are you talking about?" boomed Lord Titan. "No man would ever challenge me! I am the ruler of this galaxy!"

"That's just it, my lord, this guy isn't from our galaxy! He is alien to our world, and a powerful cyborg. He, tore through my men like they were nothing, —just look at what he did to me!" The warrior says as he holds pointed to the nub where his arm had once been.

Titan looked at his soldier. In, a smug voice, he said, "So what? One little invader is hardly worth my time, but I will send the Cyber Force. They will be enough to take care of him,—and anyone else foolish enough to challenge me on my world."

The warrior knew that the members of the Cyber Force went beyond the elites. He figured they could cope with this new enemy.

"Oh, one more thing," Lord Titan said. The soldier, looked up to his lord, he watched his eyes glowed red. "Don't *ever* come into my throne room again unannounced and dripping your fluids all over my floor!"

"Please forgive me, my lord," the warrior apologized.

But the Titan eyes fired a beam that hit the warrior and vaporized him in an instant.

The Titan then turned to his left and said, "Did you get that, Captain Cyber?"

A large, muscular man walked out of the shadows and said, "Yes, sir." He looked almost human except for his cybernetics, which made him look most demonic.

"Four of my men are ready. We will have this matter handled before the end of the day."

Titan smiled as he resumed his seat on his throne. "Good, I want the remains of these intruders at my feet." Captain Cyber bowed before heading off.

xxx

Several hours later after Cy left, the cyborg girls where still trying to convince the women in the village that, Cy was a good person. But, no matter what they said, the women could not accept that Cy was a man that they could trust. Just as they were about to give up, Jennifer detected something coming their way. She focused her attention outside and detected five powers heading toward them.

The other girls watched as the group flew toward them. Jennifer scanned each one, and was surprised to find that, out of the five, there were only three that had high energy levels. When they all landed, there leader stepped forward, and introduced himself as Captain Cyber of the Cyber force.

Sakura looked at this man. He looked demonic. He had two straight horns, one coming out of each side of his head, and reddish colored skin. Of all the warriors standing before her, he was mainly cybernetic.

The other Cyber Force members started to introduced themselves. The first, Time-Stopper, he was the shortest of the bunch. He stood at leased least three feet tall, and he had four eyes, two of them on each side of his head. The second cyborg called himself Steam Shovel. He stood a good eight feet, and had large, claw-like shovels claws for hands. Then there were Turk and Drive, the two tag team members of the force. Drive was long and thin, and looked built for speed. Turk was shorter, but still looked strong enough to take down anybody.

The cyborg girls all looked at each other not knowing what think. The Cyber Force members continued to introduced themselves and they posed, as if they trying to impress the girls.

The Cyber Force cyborgs seemed to be annoyed that the girls, didn't act impressed, by their display. Time- Stopper yelled out to the cyber girls. "Hey, do you not know who we are? We are the Cyber Force—the greatest group of cyborg's on this planet. Our leader is, Lord Titan, and we can't be beat by a bunch of weak little girls."

xxx

Meanwhile, Cy had flown the whole way with Marie kicking and screaming, for she was not happy being held by a man. But, then when she saw that they had arrived, she yelled out to the male cyborg that the Supreme Elder was at the top of the mountain peak up ahead. Cy landed in front of a large but old-looking building.

"Is this really where your elder lives?" Cy asked as he looked at the large building. But Marie didn't answer him. She just walked up a broad stone staircase that led to the entrance to the large building. Cy followed her. At the door, they heard a beautiful women's voice say, "Enter." The doors opened slowly, and they entered. The cyborg saw that the outside of the building may have looked old, but the inside looked like something out of NASA., Marie looked back at the cyborg, who stood awe struck. She asked him, "What are you waiting for?" He shook off the daze he was in and walked in behind the women.

xxx

Back at the village, Rebecca was the first to respond to the Cyber Force as she yelled out. "Weak! Who are you calling weak? Kim and I can take, all of you guys on at the same time!"

"Rebecca's right, girls," Kim taunted the warriors. She touched a nearby rock, taking on its stone granite- like characteristics. "Let us have a little fun!" Kim said, and stepped forward with Rebecca, .

Time-Stopper laughed at the thought of these two girls, beating him. He turned to the other Cyber Force warriors. "Stand back, boys, I'll, take care of these weak little girls.

Time-Stopper walked toward the two girls. It was obvious how easy it would be to defeat the girls. But Rebecca jumped twenty feet in the air, as Kim absorbed herself into the ground.

Time-Stopper was in shocked, when Rebecca shot down toward the ground, and Kim shot up from the ground, and both of them slammed to the ground where Time-Stopper had been, —but he was gone.

"Where'd he go?" Rebecca asked as she looked around. Kim pointed at Time-Stopper, he was standing leisurely a yard away from them, and was ready to fire a blast at them.

"How'd he get over there?" Force asked.

"I don't know!" Absorb, stated. "But he's not going to stop us!"

Time-Stopper then fired his blasts at them. But, when the dust cleared, *they* were gone.

Time-Stopper looked around, but saw nothing until he looked up,—and saw both girls about to strike down at him. Just as they were about to hit him, however, he smiled, and yelled out, "Time freeze!" and pressed a button on his wrist.

At the same time Kim and Rebecca were about to, punch they were stopped in there mid air. Time-Stopper couldn't believe their speed. He then started to run, and made it to a hiding place behind a large rock before the timer on his wrist hit zero.

When it did, Rebecca and Kim were instantly unfrozen. Continuing with their attack, they struck at— nothing.

Jennifer yelled out, "This guy can freeze time for everyone around him, with some kind of device on his wrest wrist. It's got a fifteen-second timer on it, —I managed to scan him right before he disappeared."

Kim and Rebecca looked at each, other and smiled. Knowing that they both had the same idea and, they shot out in different directions.

xxx

Cy walked into the cavernous building, and looked around. Every surface was covered with computers, and other electronic devices. There where scanners of all kinds all around him, and monitors that had displayed pictures of what appeared to be locations all across the planet.

Just then, the woman's voice he'd heard before, told him to stand still for a moment. He stood in the middle of a circle on the floor, and a light appeared from one of the devices on a nearby workbench. The light made its way, all the way up and down his body, and, when it went out, the woman's voice said, "Very interesting."

"What's interesting?" Cy asked.

"It seems that you were remade by Minawa Ivy.

"You knew Minawa?" The the male cyborg asked.

"Know her? I' am the one who taught her everything she knows about cybernetics."

A light then came from the far wall, and Cy turned and watched as a woman walked into view. She looked to be in her early twenties. She walked right up to him as he asked, "Who are you?"

She smiled as she said, "I' am the Supreme Elder of the planet."

"You have, got to be kidding me," Cy said. "You look to far too young." Cy almost wanted to laugh.

The, woman's smiled intensified as she stated, "Actually, I'm over two hundred years old."

The cyborg asked, "How is that ever possible?"

"I'll explain that later," the woman said. "But first, let me introduce myself. My name is Lorelei, Head Scientist and Elder to my people."

Cy smiled at this, still not sure what to think.

The women then asked, "How is Minawa doing?"

"She's dead," Cy sadly stated sadly. "Killed by a mad man on the planet Earth."

Lorelei looked down and was obviously grief stricken. "Oh," she said, "Oh that's to bad."

"Before Minawa died," Cy said, " She told me to come to this planet, and stop this guy who has taken over the planet."

"That would be the—Lord Titan," Lorelei, said to him., "He's considered by many to be a Super Cyborg— one who cannot be beaten by anyone."

"Yeah, I heard some of his elite warriors mention something about that."

Marie then approached Cy and Lorelei. "And anyone who has ever tried to oppose the Titan, is now dead." she said. "There is no way that …—"

Before she could finish, Lorelei spoke up. "That is enough." She put her arm between them. "I believe in this warrior to be telling the truth. If Minawa choose this man to become what he is, then maybe he might be able to free us, from the Titan and his rule over us."

"But he's a man!" Marie yelled. "Men can *not* be trusted." The woman pointed to the cyborg, who took a step back from her. Cy was about to say something to her, but Lorelei interrupted him and spoke to Marie. "Marie, you need to realized that we are in desperate times, and desperate times comes call for desperate measures."

xxx

Back at the village, Time-Stopper came out of his hiding place, and slowly looking around. He detected Kim and Rebecca coming his way, and, right when they appeared, he pressed his time freeze button. When he looked at them they were inches from him, about to strike him down.

Time-Stopper could not believe their speed, and power. He had never thought women could have such abilities. He started to power up his eyes, but his early warning device went off, so he started to run. Just as he moved, time started again.

Force and Absorb both, hit the ground in an explosion. When the dust cleared they saw that he was gone. Jennifer yelled out to them, and pointed saying "He's behind you."

They both shot after the short cyborg, Force jumping into the air, and Absorb, seeping into the ground. Time-Stopper saw them both coming right at him, and, right as they hit, he closed his eyes, and pushed the button again.

Once again, he slowly opened his eyes, and saw them frozen both just inches from his face. He ran off, and, when the time ran out, once again, Kim and Rebecca hit the ground.

Turk and Drive started to laugh at Time-Stopper because all he was doing, was running from two "weak" girls. Turk yelled out to him, laughing, "You don't' need any help with these little girls do you?"

Time-Stopper yelled back them, "I can handle this, and I'll proof prove it!"

As Rebecca and Kim started back after Time-Stopper, he raised his hands up, and yelled out as he powered up, and right then. Suddenly, a blue fog surround the two girls as they both stopped in mid air.

"What's going on here, I can't move!" Rebecca growled as she struggled to move, against some hidden force.

"I don't know!" Kim answered. "But I think it's some kind of paralyzing force, that the little shrimp's creating."

xxx

Meanwhile, Cy was giving this Lorelei women a funny look. "You're going to make me stronger than I could ever image? How?"

"Come with me and I'll show you." Lorelei lead him to a large room that held even more electronic equipment than the room they'd been in. There were also twelve table beds arranged in a circle, and an additional one in the middle. There were wires connecting the outside tables to the central one, almost as if all part of a system of some kind.

"What is all this?" Cy asked.

"I'll tell you," Lorelei said, "But, first, tell me one thing. Are there other cyborg's with you that were made by Minawa right?"

Cy gave her another funny look. "Yeah," he said, "twelve of them—and an android too. Why do you ask?" Lorelei then put her hands together, and just said, "Perfect." She left Cy to wonder what this weird women was thinking about.

xxx

Time-Stopper now had Kim and Rebecca right where he wanted them. He walked right up to them and smiled evilly.

"What are you girls going to do now? Not so cocky now, are you?" he said as he slapped Rebecca on the face.

She glared at him, and said, "You wouldn't be cocky either if Cy were here."

"Yeah, she's right," Kim yelled out to the little man.

Time-Stopper walked over to her, "Yeah, right," he said, and started touching the young woman. When he grabbed at her breast, he asked, "Where is this great guy now, and why doesn't he stop me?"

" Kim turned away so she wouldn't have to look at him, while he was doing this to her. As a tear slipped down her face, she heard something for a second, and she opened her eyes to see Time-Stopper take a step back.

He had a shocked look on his face, as Ashley landed behind him with one of her hands glowing with fire.

Right then Kim, and Rebecca could move again and they both watched as the short man turned to ash. He, reached out to her as his head slid off his shoulder, and rolled over to her feet.

Absorb and Force felt no regret at what they saw—the monstrous cyborg had got what he deserved. The other members of the Cyber Force were in shock, because they hadn't expected Time-Stopper to be beaten so fast, and by a young woman no less.

Steam Shovel stepped forward. "I'll go next" he said. As he flexed his muscles, as steam shot out of the sides of his arms as he flexed them.

"You'd better not fail," threatened Captain Cyber. "If you do, it will be the end of you!"

Steam Shovel laughed. "I'll be able to take these little girls out with no problems!" He walked over to Ashley, whose hands were still glowing with fire.

Ashley looked up at the eight-foot giant without fear and gave him a half smile. "You want a peace piece of this?" She waved her fiery hand at him.

Ashley was still hit hard, by Steam Shovel's shoveled claw-like hands. She slammed several times into the ground, before coming to a stop.

"Ashley!" Melissa yelled out. She turned to Steam Shovel, and saw his evil smile. He knew that he had hurt the girl. Melissa, Ice Storm reared back her hands, and fired an ice beam, at Steam Shovel in an attempt to freezing the giant in his place.

When Melissa looked at the block of ice, there was something wrong— for there was no one in it! Jennifer scanned the area, before she could find him, Steam Shovel appeared in the middle of the group of girls. He, slammed both his shovel-shaped fists at the ground causing it to erupt, knocking the girls back.

The cyborg girls tried to run in different directions, but Steam Shovel grabbed Kate and Beth, swung them around three times, then slammed them together before dropping them to the ground.

Then he went after the others. He grabbed Sakura, and Victoria as they were about to fly off. He grabbed them both by the leg slamming them to the ground and stomped on them, and used the momentum from that to run over to Megan and April. Megan, who still was holding Maylu, touched April's shoulder. Right before the behemoth could grab them, they both disappeared.

"Where'd they go?" The giant yelled out as he looked at the spot were they had stood. He looked around dumfounded.

CHAPTER 33

"Cy, let me explain something," said, Lorelei. "Those Cyborg's and the android, that Minawa made, are part of your main design.

"What?" Cy asked. He was confused as to how they could be part of him.

"With this circle of tables," she explained, "I will be able to connect, you to those Cyborg's."

"What does the android have to do with it?" The the cyborg asked.

"She will act as a power converter that will convert all of their power into you," Lorelei answered. "This will make you stronger than you ever thought you could ever be. It will also increase their powers in return."

"Why do I need this?" asked Cy. "I'm already stronger than any man can possible possibly be."

"Yes," said Lorelei, "you're strong, but you're no match for Lord Titan."

Marie joined the conversation. "You don't know what he is capable of. He is the reason that most of us don't trust men."

Cy turned to her. "Why don't you judge me for my actions, not for what you think I am?" Cy stated. As he stood in front of the women, he saw, something that she would probably never admit.

"Fear."

There was a deep resolve of fear in her eyes. Even though she was acting strong, this woman in front of him was scared of him, —and probably all men., Cy now knew the reason why he had come here. It was to show the women on this planet, that not all men are evil. Not all men are out to hurt women. Some even hold dear the same honor system that he holds.

"That's enough, Cy," Lorelei stated. "You now have to go get, those other Cyborg's, and your android and bring them here, so we can start on making you strong enough to beat the Titan." She then pointed to the door, letting him know that he had better hurry back.

Cy nodded, saying, "I'll return as fast as I can." And he shot out the door he entered the mysterious building.

xxx

Meanwhile, Steam Shovel was still looking around for those two girl cyborg's who had disappeared. Suddenly, Turk yelled out to him, "They're behind you!" Steam Shovel turned around just as April appeared, and, in a flash of light, hit him with a square across his face that knocked his head off.

"What do you think of that, you big metal freak?" Mimic, April yelled. She had taken his own form in order to battle him.

Stem Shovel's head rolled along the ground. But, unlike Time-Stopper's head, Steam Shovel's head, functioned. He knelt down, and picked up his head, and clicked it back onto his neck. Everyone was shocked. "That wasn't too bad, girl," he said, " but it lacks my mechanical strength." He hit her so hard that she lost her form, and slammed her into one of nearby home's.

The others where now in real trouble. Stem Shovel, in a flash, ran over to Beth, grabbed her head, and slammed her into the ground. He then turned to the youngest of the group, Destiny, who had no defensive or offensive abilities. But, just as he heaved a great punch, his hands where stopped by an unseen force.

"What the hell?" Steam Shovel yelled as he slammed, the girl again and again, but to no avail. What was stopping him? Megan then appeared, still holding Maylu who had fallen asleep totally unaware of what was going on.

"You're not going to hurt any more of us," Megan told him as, he was still tried to brake break her shield. On the surface, it looked like as if Megan could hold up forever, but, in reality, she would only be able to hold him for a few minutes. That's how strong Steam Shovel was.

Just as Megan's shield went out, though, Steam Shovel just stopped in his tracks. When Megan and Destiny saw why, they both yelled out his name, "Cy!"

"You came back!" Megan said. When the others heard that name, they look up from where they has been thrown.

Ashley started to laugh as she looked at the monster cyborgs. "You're all going to get it now!" she said.

Both Turk and Drive seemed in shock, but mainly Drive because he was the fastest of their group, and he didn't see where this cyborg had come from. The fact that Cy had stopped Steam Shovel's attack with just one hand was also a big shock.

Everyone watched as Steam Shovel fell to the ground completely incapacitated with one unseen strike. Cy stood up, and looked at the girls. They had all been beaten pretty badly. He looked up at the three who had been left unharmed. "Destiny," he stated, "you and Megan help the others while I take care of these guys."

Destiny, and Megan run over to the closest one witch happened to be Ashley, and as Destiny went to work helping their cyborg sisters; Cy, didn't take his eyes off of the three members of the cyber force who still seemed most interested in taking out Cy right now.

"Do you want to take this guy down fast and hard?" Drive asked his fellow warriors. "Or slow and painful, for what he's done to Steam Shovel?"

Turk growled in his throat before saying. "Fast *and*, painful!"

"Then let's *go do* it!" And with that they both shot forward and started to fly circles around the cyborg shooting past him at incredible speeds.

Captain Cyber watched his two best men fly around the invader, but. Cy didn't move as the two of them blew past him, his thick, black trench coat blowing in the wind they created. None of the Cyber Force warriors, could not believe this guy wasn't making a move.

Drive flew right at Cy, and, for one brief moment, he thought he saw Cy move. Turk flew at Cy as well, and then, so did Turk and both took to the air. "What's going on here, Drive? Did he move? I thought he moved?"

"I don't know," said Drive. "Let me get a reading on this guy. Maybe we can find out where we stand." Drive scanned the cyborg but only got a reading of 50,000, which was low by their standards. "Let's test him," Drive said.

Turk then pointed his hand at Cy. The Cyber Force warrior's whole arm opened up reveling a, cannon. He manipulated the mechanism and fired a huge laser—one that seemed like it would surely obliterate his enemy.

"Look out, Cy!" The the girls yelling out to him, and he knew that Destiny had worked her curative magic on them. Just, now completely recovered by Destiny, right as the laser beam was about to hit him, he just knocked it off course with a single strike from his hand.

Turk and Drive were in shock when they saw this. Turk had never seen anyone other than Captain Cyber and the Titan do that. It seemed impossible for this guy to do it too.

"Hey, Turk, let's hit him with our tag team strike!" Turk said.

"Great idea," answered Drive. "He won't be able to stop that!" They both stood back-to-back, ascended into the air, and yelled "Tag team strike!" Then, both turned into a huge swelling mass of light and spun down at Cy.

The cyborg looked up and smiled as he disappeared. Turk and Drive stopped in mid air and looked around for him. "Where'd he go, Turk?" asked Drive.

"Hey, morons, look behind you!" Jennifer yelled out from the sidelines.

Turk turned around to see Cy floating inches from him. "Just who the hell are you?" he asked Cy.

"You can call me Cy. and I'm the cyborg who came here from Earth. I was build by Minawa Ivy to take down the Titan, and free these people from his rule."

"Ivy!" cried Turk. "That crazy bitch of a scientist who thought she could build a cyborg stronger than Tit … —"

That was all Turk got out before Cy hit a hole right through him in a flash.

"Don't you *ever*, badmouth Minawa again!" Cy roared out. "You don't even have the right to say her name!" Then he spin kicked Turk in half. The body fell to the ground and blew up in a fireball. Cy looked at Drive, who was stunned at what he had seen. Cy had taken down Steam Shovel and Turk with only a few moves.

"I'm bad," Drive said. "But I'm not *that* bad!"

Drive was about to fly off when Captain Cyber yelled out, "Stop! I'll take care of this." He stepped into the battle, but stopped when he watched the cyborg land next to the strange cyborg girls.

"Are you all right?" Cy asked the girls. Sakura walked up to him and just hugged him. The, others soon joined in. "What"s wrong?" he asked as when he realized that some of them seemed to be crying.

"We were all so worried about you!" Jennifer said.

Cy smiled as he told them, "I would never leave you all."

He patted Sakura on the back. "Step back a bit, girls. I have a lot to tell you. But first I have to take care of *two little* problems." he said And he turned back to Captain Cyber and Drive.

Captain Cyber started to laugh. "It's been a long time sense anyone has opposed me," he said. "It's going to be fun bringing you to your knees!"

"Sir," Drive said as he landed behind him. "Somehow this guy can hide his true power from us."

"Of course, you fool," Captain Cyber yelled out. "You're looking at a rare fighter there. I bet when he gets going he'll have a power of 60,000."

"60,000!" Drive gasped. "That's crazy! He said, he was made by that crazy scientist Minawa." Drive said as he looked at Cy. Cy gave him a look of killer intent, as Drive remembered what Cy had done to Turk when he had badmouthed Minawa, and covered his mouth hoping that he didn't hear him say it.

Cy glared at Captain Cyber. The enemy cyborg stood at least eight feet tall, and the horns on his head, made him look intimidating. But

Cy ,knew he could take the cyborg out easily. He turned to the girls. "Get ready," he said. "We're leaving as soon as I take this guy down."

Cy got ready to attack, but, when Captain Cyber appeared right in front of him and punched him into the ground. Cy kicked him right as he was recoiling.

Suddenly, both warriors vanished in a flash. The only one who could see them now was Jennifer, she started to tell the other girls what was happening. It appeared that Cy looked like he had the upper hand, —until Captain Cyber hit him, sending him spiraling into the ground where he skidded into a nearby lake.

The girls watched Captain Cyber standing at the shore of the lake. He appeared to be waiting something. "You're doing great, captain!" Drive yelled out. "He didn't see that one coming!"

"Quiet, you fool!" said Captain Cyber. "I'm trying to concentrate.!"

Just then, Cy appeared, in front of Captain Cyber and punched right through, him. The horned warrior had disappeared. Cy realized that he had hit an after image. The captain then appeared and kicked Cy. He vanished, and then reappeared, and kicked him, again. They both disappeared in a fury of punches and kicks as they shot into the air and then returned to the ground.

They were all over the place., Drive seemed to think that the captain would be able to beat this guy. Suddenly, both fighters slammed into a double punch that sent the two fighters tumbling backwards. Cy rubbed the spot on his face where Captain Cyber had hit him. "That wasn't too bad," he said to his opponent. "You are a great fighter."

"Why don't you stop fooling around with me and show me everything you've got?" Captain Cyber said. "I know that you can hide your power, and I know what your doing you're trying to save your power for when you fight Lord Titan. But you won't get past me unless you show me everything you've got!"

Cy looked a little shocked as Captain Cyber said this. *"How does he know that I'm hiding my power? He thought."* *I haven't even told the girls that, I've never given my fights everything I have.*

"If you don't show me, all your power, I will have Drive destroy that village, —and those girls of yours— while we're fighting," shouted Captain Cyber.

"Go on, Cy, show him that you don't take threats like that!" Beth yelled out.

Cy looked over at the girls and then back to Captain Cyber. "All right, it will give me a good work out, and we won't waist anymore time."

The cyborg from Earth then flew up into the air. He hit his fists together, and powered up to what he has called his hyper mode. He roared out as he powered up. At first Captain Cyber didn't look intimidated.

"Watch out, Captain," shouted Drive. "His reading is over, 60,0000!" Cy saw panic in the captain's eyes.

Drive yelled again, "It's at 117, 0000!—only 3, 0000 away from *your* max."

Jennifer watched this unfold and could not believe it either. "Cy's, power level was is 150, 000!" she called out to the others others. They were just as shocked, they could barley believe it. "And it's still rising.!" she said in disbelief.

"No wonder he beat those other guys so easily," Rebecca said as she watch as Cy continued.

"It can't be!" Captain Cyber yelled, as he saw the reading was now at 160, 0000 and Cy told him.

"This is just the beginning.," Cy yelled back.

Captain Cyber could not have expected this, that there was a cyborg stronger than he. The horned warrior, roared out as he flew up into the air. Then he slammed himself into the ground.

Ashley yelled out to Drive, who was freaking out, "It looks like your friend is having a nervous brake breakdown."

"He's just taking a time out for a minute," answered Drive. "You just wait. He'll be ready to take down your friend, in no time." But the girls noticed that his voice was shaking.

Captain Cyber finally burst out of the ground holding a huge bolder over his head. He threw the rock with all his might at Cy, but he the Earth cyborg was giving off so must much energy that the bolder shattered as it hit him, and little pieces of it flew around him. Captain

Cyber pointed both hands at Cy. The hands turning into huge cannons. The captain firing two plasma cannon blasts at Cy, but where stopped by his power, witch now was glowing red.

When Cy finished powering up, he stared at Captain Cyber, he drafted back in shock. Jennifer on the ground was still taking readings on Cy's power level. She was shaking like crazy in disbelieve. "How high is it, Jennifer?", Kate asked in awe at what she was seeing.

"180,0000!!!" Jennifer yelled out.

"180,000," Beth said in awe. "That's crazy! How did he get that strong?," Beth asked as she watched Cy cross his arms as his power steadied.

Captain Cyber was too shocked to move. He had never came come across a warrior who was this strong. He didn't know what to do. Suddenly he had a revelation. "I know what you are," he stated slowly. "You're, your not an ordinary cyborg—your a *Super Cyborg!*!!"

"Call me what you want," answered Cy. "The out come of this fight will be the same. You are going to pay for all the pain and suffering you have caused these people."

Cy watched as the realization hit Captain Cyber. The giant was shaking all over., "Now that you realize that you can't beat me," Cy ordered, " I want you or Drive there" he said as he pointed to Drive who was wigging out at this, " to give your Lord Titan a message: That the cyborg that Minawa Ivy built, has come to fulfill her wish, and— to free her people from his reign of terror forever."

Captain Cyber looked at Drive, and then back at Cy, wondering what he was going to do next Cy was watching them like a hawk. Cy knew the captain was having trouble deciding what to do. He also knew they both could tell that he was completely on guard even in the his precarious possession he was in.

All of a sudden, both Captain Cyber and Drive took off like a bats out of hell, flying off as fast as they both could move.

Cy watch them both with a half smile. He turned to the village, and yelled out to the people, "How many men does it take to deliver a message?"

From out one of the homes, a young girl stepped into the street. "One," she yelled. The girl's mother snatched her back inside.

Cy yelled out, "You're right!" And he disappeared only to reappear in front of the flying Captain Cyber.

Cy screeched to a stop in front of the powerful cyborg, forcing him to also stop. Then he flew forward, getting Captain Cyber closer to the village. Cy wanted the people to see him destroy, one of there oppressors.

Drive was now completely out of sight, and Captain Cyber, now was looking into the face of his death, — he was looking into the face of a warrior like none, he had ever seen before, … one who refused to hurt others or allow innocents to be hurt, a warrior that who didn't care if the whole world was against him.

Time seemed to move in slow motion for Captain Cyber as he heard the Super Cyborg in front of him roar out, *"Screaming bullet!"* Cy punched the captain, and, in that instant, the one warrior who had caused so much pain was gone in a blinding flash of power. There was nothing left of Captain Cyber except an outline of his body on the side of a mountain a mile away.

Cy then landed and was immediately surrounded by the cyborg girls. "How did you get so strong?" asked Jennifer. The girls hadn't been able to understand how he could have gained so much strength during their three- month trip.

"I can't really explain it," Cy stated, "but, as I was meditating, something happened. Whatever it was, it made me, stronger than I ever thought was possible. I'll explain more on that later. Right now, we have to get ourselves to Lorelei's place."

"Who is Lorelei, and why do we need to go to her?" Destiny asked.

"So we can *all* get stronger," he answered.

The, the girls looked at him like as if he was crazy, and Kate asked, "Why? Don't you think, that you're strong enough as it is? I think you can take down anything."

Cy grinned at her. "No. According to the elder of this planet, I'm not strong enough to beat the Titan." "That's crazy," Melissa said. "If this Titan freak is stronger than you are right now, he must be some kind of monster."

CHAPTER 34

Back with Drive, he had just made it back to Cyber City. With much difficulty, he made his way to the Titan's palace he ran into into the main hall, guards helplessly on his tale as he ran into the Titan's room yelling out.

"Lord Titan!" Drive gasped, falling to his knees. "Lord Titan! Captain Cyber has been destroyed!" Drive huffed as he came in on the Titan, who was being bathed by four slave women.

Titan , looked up at Drive angrily and asked, "Why didn't you stay and fight with the captain?"

"I would have, my Lord but, …"

Drive's voice traveled off as the Titan stood. The women put a tied a robe around him. "Coward!" said the Titan.

Titans eyes started to glow red, and Drive panicked. "Forgive me, my lord," he begged.

But Titan was not in a forgiving mood. As he was about to fire his death beam, Drive said, "Wait, my lord. The Super Cyborg from Earth sent a message for you."

"Speak, fool, before I change my mind!" Titan roared at him as the glow in his eyes faded.

"He told me to tell you that the cyborg made by Minawa Ivy has come to free the women of this planet."

"Minawa Ivy!!" The Titan yelled out. "That scientist that who got away? She and her damn sister managed to get off my planet, —and now she dares to trifle with me? I swear I will destroy this cyborg, and prove to these disrespectful women that *no one* can beat the Titan!!"

xxx

Cy had just finished telling the girls the whole story of how, with Lorelei's help, how the girls can could make him stronger—and how they'd become stronger themselves in the process. He'd explained that Ellis was the key to the whole process. The girls agreed that making Cy stronger was the best plain of action. "Well," said Sam, "I don't know what you are all waiting for." Immediately, the girl cyborgs; and Ellis the android, who carried Maylu; Sam; and Cy sped off to see Lorelei, the Supreme Elder.

xxx

Titan was now ready to handle this problem by himself. He ordered what was left of his men to stay, and watch the city, —and to destroy anyone or anything that came their way. "I'll be back soon," he told them. "This shouldn't take long! I'm going to take down this cyborg … I will *not* let him threaten our way of life!"

As the Lord Titan flew off, one of his lieutenants told the other men, "You all heard him! Take up your positions!" The other men ran off in different directions to be ready for anything.

xxx

Cy and the others had just walked into the Supreme Elder's building and had been invited to her lab. When they followed Cy, to where she was, the girls, could not believe how young she looked.

Lorelei greeted them, and Cy asked again, "Just what do you plan on doing with all of us?" He still wasn't completely sure he had understood what she had explained to him.

"Follow me and I'll show you." She lead them all into the room with where all the beds were. "Girls, each of you lie on one of these tables in the circle. Cy, you lie on the table in the middle. And, Ellis, you put that helmet on and sit next to Cy. When you are all ready, we will begin."

152

When Ellis and the others lied down on the tables, Lorelei attached wires to two points on the cybernetic half of Cy's head. "Are the rest of you ready?" she asked.

Jennifer said, "We're as ready as we're ever going to be."

Lorelei walked over to a console and addressed Cy. "You may experience some momentary discomfort." Cy said, "Just do it. already,"

Lorelei pushed the a button that activated the system.

Cy roared out in pain, as power surged through him. The cyborg girls were about to get up to help him, but Lorelei said, "Stay put. If you move now, you could put Cy's life at more risk." So, the girls remained where they were. Just as quickly as it started, it stopped, and all was quite again. But Cy was unconscious.

"What did you do to him?" cried Sakura. "Why isn't he getting up? *We* can all move!"

Ashley grabbed Lorelei and said, "You had better not of have hurt him!"

"If you will all calm down," Lorelei said, "I will explain everything. You see, Cy needs some time to reboot his systems. He has to process a great deal of power, there is allot of power he has to go though, now that you all will be sharing an electrical link."

"But we don't feel any different," Beth said .

Lorelei stated, "You won't feel it, until Cy wakes up in about two or three hours."

"Two hours?" Rebecca said. "What are we going to do for two hours?" Rebecca asked.

Sam walked over to the small cyborg and said, "For starters, we should go back to the village, and make sure the people stay safe. Lord Titan probably, knows that his captain was destroyed, and he will be mad as a hornet, and itching to take revenge."

They all thought that was a good idea, but Sakura told Sam, "One of us should stay and watch over Cy until he wakes up."

"Agreed," Sam stated, . "Sakura, you can stay, and watch him."

The girls all protested— that they all wanted to stay with him—, but Sakura told them, "It was my idea, so I get to stay until he wakes up."

"Oh sure!" Ashley yelled said, pouting. "You seem to know what's good for all of us, and you always seem to be able to spend more time with Cy than the rest of us."

"That's only because I know more about him, —because I trained with his Sansei."

Samantha then said, "Lorelei and I will watch Maylu while the rest of you hold up at the village until Cy wakes up.

Lorelei agreed. "Be careful," she said as Victoria powered up and prepared to take them back to the village at top speeds.

Sakura watched them all leave. Once they were out of sight, she walked over to Cy's unconscious body. *I wonder what is going through his mind?* she thought.

She was about to hold his hand when Lorelei saw her reaching toward him. "Don't touch him," she warned.

"Why can't I hold his hand?" Sakura asked.

"In his current state, he is in he is generating a lot of power. You would be overloaded by the counter flow of the power surge."

Sakura looked back at Cy, who seemed to be sleeping soundly. Little did she know that, as peaceful as he seemed, he was really having nightmare after nightmare in this state.

Cy was dreaming of all the events that had happened, to him. It was as if he was reliving them again— how he had lost, and gained so much. Some of the dreams turned into nightmares, when he began to dream of the recent history of the planet Titan. Cy was able to see the events of what the Titan had done to these people, how he had raped, so many of the women, and killed off most of the men who had tried to stop him. Cy was able to see it like he watching the past, he didn't know he was doing it but he saw how the Titan had taken control of the planet and killed off almost all the male population. He saw the real reason that the women were afraid him, —Cy—and why they had no reason to trust him. Cy realized that for the way they were treated not a single man on this planet had an ounce of honor or loyalty to anyone. And Lord Titan was the worst one of them all. But the fact that shocked Cy the most was the fact that Lord Titan had been built to defend the planet, but, instead, he had taken control of the planet for his own selfish reasons.

CHAPTER 35

Lord Titan himself was blasting through village after village looking for the Super Cyborg who had taken out his Cyber Force. Now he wished he had let Drive live, so he could show him the way. But it really didn't matter to him, he could just destroy the whole planet if he wanted to. He would just move on to anther one, and take it, it would be no small feet for him.

xxx

The cyborg girls made it back to the village faster than it had taken them to get from the village to the Supreme Elder's sanctuary. "I can't explain it," said Victoria. "But, when we connected to Cy, I felt different— stronger in a way." The others all agreed, that they all felt a little stronger too.

Jennifer then turned to the skies as she detected something with enormous power coming there their way. Kate noticed Jennifer staring out into space. "What's wrong?" she asked,

Jennifer took a few steps back as she said, "I think I just detected the Titan."

"The Titan!" said Ashley. "Where is he? Is he close?" Ashley asked,

" No. He's still miles away, but I just got a glimpse of his power, and it is mind- blowing," Jennifer told her.

"Then that means that he left the city, and I have an idea," Melissa said. "Gather 'round, girls."

Melissa figured that the Titan was definitely the strongest being on the planet. "If he's away from the Cyber City, we can probably take control of it," she told them. "But we'd have to split up to make it work."

They all agreed. It was decided that Jennifer, Ashley, Melissa, Victoria, Rebecca, and Kim would head off to the city while Destiny, Beth, Kate, Ellis, April, and Megan would stay to protect the village. With Megan's force fields, there was no way anyone was getting by them.

xxx

Elsewhere The Titan had just destroyed an entire village in his search for the Super Cyborg who had destroyed his Cyber Force. But he was having no luck finding him. Suddenly, however, he detected several powers heading toward his city. Somehow he knew that they were the ones that he was looking for. Without another thought, he shot off with death in his eyes.

The six girls were making good time. with Victoria's power enabled them all to fly swiftly. It was easy going until Jennifer detected, something with enormous power heading their way. "Victoria, slow down a minute so I can get a proper reading, on something," she said. They all stopped in med mid air as Jennifer scanned the area.

At first, she had thought that the power she detected was Cy. She figured he had waken up early.

But she was wrong. The second that Jennifer realized who it was, she yelled out, "Victoria! Get us out of here, now! As fast as you can go! It's, the Titan!" Victoria took off like a shot as he came into view, but the Titan then immediately saw them, he disappeared from sight.

"Can you still see him?" Ashley asked, but, when Jennifer looked back, the Titan was gone. Suddenly, however, he appeared in front of them. He hovered with his arms crossed, and, even though they had never seen him before, they knew him from the power he seemed to emitted that he was the Titan.

Lord Titan was a very handsome, and a very strong-looking man. He had long blond hair, the face of a male supermodel, and the body of a Greek god. But, unlike Cy, he had no sign that he was a cyborg at all.

"Good afternoon, ladies. It would seem that you are all cyborg's. I understand you have different powers, and abilities. And that would mean that it was *all* of you who killed off my great Cyber Force." The Titan said spoke in a voice that would make some women melt.

"So what if we are!" Ashley yelled out to the Titan with no fear.

"Then it means you all must die!" Titan said in a calm yet threatening tone. But, before the Titan could act, Victoria focused a gravity ball at the Titan, and sent the Titan flying to the ground in an instant.

"Good shot!" said Jennifer as the girls cheered. Victoria brought the girls, to the ground—only to see the Titan as he dusted himself off and laughed at the futility of their attack.

"If that's the best you six can do, then you all are as good as dead," he exclaimed coldly.

Victoria could barely believe it he had taken the full force of the gravity wave—and it didn't even scratch him. They watched as the Titan smiled. Instantly, he vanished from the spot he was standing on and appeared in front of Ashley. He punched her, but Ashley caught the punch. Titan punched with his other hand, but she caught that one too, and they both erupted with a surge of power.

Fire surrounded the girl as their powers clashed. Then a dome of fire surrounded them as Ashley's power increased. When the Titan saw some of the hair on his arm start to burn, and he broke away. He didn't want his perfect skin tarnished.

"That is quite impressive, little girl," Titan spoke. "You can produce enough heat to actually singe the hair on my arm! You should be proud of yourself." He clapped a few times in retrospect.

As Titan was still gloating, Rebecca punched at the him, he ducked under her punch. As he ducked, Kim came up at him from the ground. But, once again, he dodged it the blow like it was nothing at all. This futile battle continued until Melissa froze one of his arms, causing him to get sustain blows by both Rebecca's and Kim's next strike.

Both girls looked carefully at the fallen Titan. He wasn't moving at first,, but then his eyes shot open and he jumped up, and struck down both Kim and Rebecca with his arm still frozen.

"That was an impressive strategy, but still futile ," Titan said to them, and then he pointed his frozen arm at Melissa. The ice shattered as his hand, and his arm seemed to opened and change into what looked like a cannon.

"Let's see what you think of this!" The cannon charged up, as he yelled *"Plasma Cannon Fire!"* She had no time to react, it happened like as if it was slow motion.

The blast shot right through Melissa. As the others watched in horror, as she fell to the ground hard. It was a sight that Ashley, or none of them would ever forget.

xxx

Back in Lorelei's sanctuary, Cy jumped up at the exact same time that Mellissa fell. Sakura, saw him jump. and asked "Lorelei? Why did he just jump?"

Lorelei walked over and carefully connected him Cy to a monitor. The readings indicated that the link connection between Cy and Melissa was breaking. Lorelei turned to Sakura, with alarm in her eyes. "It looks like Melissa is dyeing," she said.

"This is real very bad," Samantha said. She was still holding Maylu in her arms. As the baby awoke and started to cry, when Cy jumped again. It was almost as if she was feeling the experiences of others.

"What will happen if Melissa dies?" Sakura asked.

"If she dies before he comes back on line, it is possible that he and all of you will die, as well—from the shock of the brake break in the link."

"We have to get Destiny to Melissa as fast as we can," Sakura said. "I'm sure she can heal her even if she's close to death. But how can we get her to Melissa in time to save her?" Sakura asked, and then she said " Even if I flew at full speed, I might not make it in time."

Lorelei thought for a minute, and then looked at the unconscious cyborg. "I have an idea," she said. "Your powers are based on electricity, aren't they?"

"Yes, they are," Sakura answered, "but what does that half have to do with anything?"

"Well," Lorelei stated, "do you remember why I told you not to touch your cyborg friend in the condition he is in?"

"You said he was generating too much power … that it could kill me," Sakura answered.

"That's right," Lorelei said. "If you were to take his hand, it might be possible to ramp up your powers to a new level."

Sakura didn't like the look on Lorelei's face. "There must be a risk," she said as she was about to take Cy's hand in her own.

"It might empower you, or it might kill you," Lorelei finished.

Sakura then looked at Cy lying there and then said. "It is the only way I can buy Cy enough time to recuperate."

She grabbed his hand. As bolts of electricity shot into her, she had never felt so much power. The flashes of light were, so bright that it lit up the entire lab. Beams of light were shooting out of the windows of the building. As Sakura screamed out.

Just then Sakura, was thrown off him, from the power serge. She slammed into the wall of the lab. Lorelei and Sam ran over to her. Sakura's eyes shot open. She got up as electricity flowed around her. She seemed to be covered in blue light, —from the power she was letting out. She laughed and said, "It's incredible! It feels like every cell in my body has been empowered!" The power was so great that it started to shatter some of electrical equipment in the lab. Lorelei yelled out "Stop! You're going to wreck my lab!"

Sakura stopped and thought of what she had to do. "Tell Cy when he wakes up to come and help as fast as he can. I have no idea how long I can all hold off the Titan." She then disappeared in a flash.

xxx

"Sister!" Ashley called out. She ran over to Melissa and held her up trying to wake her, she Melissa fell limp. Ashley cried out in anguish, "Cy, help us!" Jennifer started to move away from Rebecca, and Victoria.

Kim asked, "What's wrong?" Rebecca was looking down and she seemed to be crying. She was giving off a power that they had never seen before.

"You monster!!!" Force screamed out as she raised her fists to the sky. Titan just laughed at this, but his laugher was cut short as Rebecca shot forward, hitting the Titan in the gut. The impact sent him flying skyward.

He had just stopped himself in the air when Rebecca appeared behind him, and elbowed him in the back sending him hurtling back to he ground. The impact of his landing was so strong that it left a crater! Titan looked up to see Rebecca slam her fist right into him. She threw a barrage of punches that caused the Titan to dance around like a rag doll.

She grabbed him by the leg and spun him around throwing him straight into a mountain side. He slammed so hard an impression of his body remained in the mountain. When he looked up, Rebecca punched him straight through the mountain, and out the other side where he rolled violently to a stop on his face.

Rebecca now stood breathing hard looking at what she had done. The others could not believe their eyes and wondered where her power had come from.

xxx

Back at the village, Destiny was helping Megan with some there of their scanning equipment that they brought to scan the area. In a blast of electricity, Sakura appeared and said. "Destiny you're needed badly!" Destiny didn't even have a chance to answer. Sakura just grabbed her hand and they disappeared. Megan didn't know what

xxx

"The fight isn't over!" Jennifer yelled out. "Titan is still very much alive. Rebecca was awesome, but she didn't even put a dent in his power." They all looked, and watched the Titan get up, and dust himself off. He look over to the girls, as he said, "Again, girls, that was indeed impressive. You girls are defiantly strong, and powerful, but you all still don't hold a candle to me."

The Titan's hands started to change again, he prepared his plasma cannon for battle. He aimed and was ready to fire, but right before he fired unexpectedly found his hand frozen again. He looked at his hand wondering what happened he turned to where the blast came from and saw Melissa standing as if nothing had happened to her, and next to her were Destiny, and Sakura, both looking ready to fight.

The Titan had no idea what was going nor was he to happy having his hand frozen again.

"How many of you cyborg girls are there anyway?" Titan almost yelled, . "How did that other one get healed?" Titan wondered to himself, but at the moment it didn't matter at all, for he was going to kill them all before they cause him anymore trouble, The girls knew they had not defeated him as he broke the ice around his arm and ready himself for battle again.

"It seems I got here just in time," Sakura said as she walked forward to the Titan.

Ashley watched her, and asked, "What do you plan on doing?"

"I plan on beating this guy to a pulp."

"You saw what he did to Melissa with just one stroke," Ashley stated. "It will take all of us, just to hold him back I don't even— you can't hold him back alone."

Sakura gave Ashley, a confident look as she started to power up. Electricity flowed around her, and, when Jennifer saw her and scanned her level, she almost had a heart attack! It was just as strong as Cy's had been when they arrived on the planet.

"How did you get so strong?" Ashley asked.

Sakura turned to her saying, "I just held Cy's hand." And then she walked over to the Titan.

Titan lowered his cannon arms as Sakura came to him. He gave her a half smile that sickened the other girls.

"Your not bad, girl," Titan said to Sakura, "Why don't we forget this fight? And become one of my slaves." His hand returned to normal and he offered her his other to her as if in peace.

Sakura slapped his hand away and said, "Do you think I'm going to fall for you just because you think that you're the god's gift to women?"

"Well, if the shoe fits …" Titan told her.

But Sakura wasn't amused. "Idiot! You might think that you are the god's gift to women, and all that other crap, but the real fact is that you are the ugliest being I have ever met! Beauty may be, only skin deep, but evil is to the core."

The Titan was outraged when he heard this. No one had ever refused him before, nor has anyone called him ugly. He was thought by many to be the most perfect being in the universe. "That's it!" he yelled. "No one talks to me like that!," He jumped forward and the two engaged in a furious fight in the sky, . The two warriors shooting around like two beams of light. Unlike with the others, Sakura was able to hold her own against the Titan.

Jennifer watched in amazement wondering how Sakura had become so strong. The fight was heating up as Sakura hit Titan with a magnetic pulse blast, that sent him careening to the ground. When he hit, he looked up just as Sakura charged up a huge electric ball. Just as she was about to throw it, she saw the look on Titan''s face. He looked as if he believed he was still in control of this fight, … as if all the damage that she had inflicted on him was having no effect at all.

When the electric ball hit Titan, it erupted into a huge explosion that left a large crater. The cyborg girls cheered, thinking that Sakura had beaten the Titan. But, once again, Jennifer knew otherwise, and so did Sakura. They both knew, that kind of power would not be enough to stop him, and they were right. As the dust cleared, they saw the Titan smiling like as if nothing had happened to him.

Sakura glared at the Titan. *What kind of monster are we dealing with?* she thought. *I hit him with my most powerful attack, and he took it like it as if it were nothing.* That's when she realized that maybe not even Cy, could beat this guy, and it was becoming clear that they all might not make it out of this alive.

The Titan, at that point, disappeared in an instant, and reappeared in front of her. Hitting her with an earth- shattering punch that sent her flying out of control to the ground. He was about to fire his cannon again, but a blast hit him hard, knocking him out of the sky. As he got up from the ground, another blast hit him.

As Sakura got up, she looked to see who had joined the battle. Jennifer was blasting the Titan with every thing, she had. As she pushed him back, she screamed out, "I have had enough! I'm going to blast you into oblivion!" But, just when it looked like as if the Titan would finally fall, he boosted his power and redirected the blastoff him. The blast, shot back, hitting Jennifer into the ground hard.

Titan then advanced to Rebecca, who had hurt him first. He, hit her so hard that she crashed into a mountain side just as she had before. Next, he went to Ashley, but she ducked under his punch and kicked him into the air. That turned out, however, to be a bad move, for he turned his arm into the a cannon and fired it down at her. In a blinding flash, she was down. He then flew over to Destiny, who was still standing next to Melissa. Titan was about to strike her down next, but, Kim, whom the Titan seemed to had forgotten about, came out of the ground and hit him with an upper cut that sent him back into the air. Kim turned to Melissa. "Get Destiny to the others and help her and get them back on there feet. I'll hold off the Titan for as long as I can."

Kim slammed her fists to the ground and absorbed the strength of the planet. Suddenly, the ground erupted, and two huge stone hands came out of the emerged and grabbed the Titan, crushing him.

Destiny made it to Ashley first, and in seconds she was back on her feet. "thanks" Ashley said. Destiny ran over and helped Rebecca next, but, unknown to them, the Titan saw what was going on though a crack in the stone hands. He realized that he had to destroy Destiny, the healer, or this fight could go on forever. Just as Destiny moved over to Sakura, the Titan exploded out of the stone hands.

Kim was thrown back from the blast and landed in the arms of Sakura, she helped her back to her feet. The girls gathered together, and Sakura said, "He may have been able to beat us one at a time, but let's see how he handles all of us at once."

"Ha!" Titan laughed from the sky. "You little bitches don't know what you're *really* dealing with! But I plan on showing you just what I can do! Up to now, for you see I have been fighting, all of you with only one percent of my maximum power!"

"You lie," Jennifer yelled as she walked over to the others. "I would be able to detect it, and I'm not getting any kind of readings like that."

Titan laughed again as he roared out a metallic roar. He stretched out his arms and legs, and Jennifer's eyes went wide as she saw the power readings go up. She then realized that, if she had felt this right away, her head would of have exploded. The Titan's, power erred out and threatened to blow out her scanners, and her eyes almost blew up.

Jennifer looked over to the others with a terrified look and said, "We don't stand a chance in hell."

Sakura said, "I knew that already, but we have to hang in there, for as long as possible."

"Are you crazy?" Jennifer yelled out. "I have never detected anything like this guy, and I thought I had seen it all before. What I read, was definitely just the tip of the iceberg. We can't win, and it would be suicide to try."

Sakura thought for minute and then looked up at the sky. She felt something, it was faint, but it was there. Cy was about to wake up.

Sakura turned to the others and said, "We have to fight."

But, before she could do anything, they heard the Titan simply say, "Bang." They hadn't even seen him approach. And they as he pointed his figure, the girls didn't even see the beam of energy. It was as if time had stop for them.

An explosion then hit them, as soon as they could see again, they saw realized that only one of them had been hit, and it was the one that could not be healed by Destiny, —Destiny herself, her body lay on the ground smoking.

Seeing one of their friends fall so hard, was almost too much to bear. Sakura yelled out in frustration and shot forward in a rage determined to avenge their friend. She punched at Titan with every thing she had, but he was now dodging with ease. It was as if she was standing still against him now that he had his power up.

xxx

Meanwhile Cy yelled out as he shot sat up quickly. Lorelei detected this, turned to her instruments and watched as his power raged out of control. Lorelei didn't realize it, but he had felt Destiny falling, and it was enraging him even in his state of unconsciousness.

"What is happening to him?" Sam asked shielding Maylu as Cy's power raged on and.

Lorelei said, "Something must of have happened to one of the others, but it should be okay because I think he is waking up."

"How is that okay?"

"You are just going to have to trust me."

xxx

The Titan finally acted. He, and hit Sakura hard, causing her to fly back into the air where there fight had lead them, again. The girl screamed at him, "I'm going to avenge my friend even if destroys me!" She powered up a huge electrical ball that was a hundred times bigger than the first one she created.

Jennifer yelled out to the others, "Take cover! This one's going to be big!"

When Sakura threw the electrical ball, Titan just gave her a half smile and said, " Stupid woman." He simply kicked the ball out into space with ease.

Sakura watched in shock. She could not believe this guy was so strong. That had been everything she had. That last blast left her weakened. So she had no idea if she could hold him off any longer.

Titan smiled again. "Well, are you finished humiliating yourself?"

Sakura could feel tears swelling up in her eyes as the Titan floated in front of her and smiled that evil smile that the girls detested. He grabbed Sakura by the neck, and threw her into the ground. When she hit the ground, dirt and rocks erupted from the impact.

The Titan floated down slowly and plunged his hand into the ground and pulled Sakura out. She appeared to be unconscious, but, when Titan punched her in the gut, her eyes shot open as she coughed up blood. Titan said in a seductive tone, "I was just checking your reflexes. They seem just fine." Sakura tried to pull herself free, but his grip was too strong.

Titan turned to the other girls. "Why don't you come over here and help her? Don't you see that she is in pain?" But the others could barely move from seeing one of their strongest get thrown around like a rag doll. Rebecca was about to jump forward to help, but Ashley grabbed her arm and shook her head no, because she knew that the Titan was way too strong.

Rebecca reluctantly stepped back, as they watched in horror as the Titan roughly grabbed Sakura's left breast.

Tears fell from all the girls' eyes as he did this. Then he pulled her right to his face, and said, "This is just the beginning, little girl." As Titan back handed her across her face and punched her.

Sakura winced from the impact. She screamed out, "Cy, help us … please …"

Titan laughed at this. "Go ahead and scream as much as you want. I like the screamers—that makes this all the more fun! And, when I'm done with you, I'm going to do the same to your friends over there too." He looked over to the scared girls.

The Titan started to punch Sakura around; he liked seeing bruises on his bitches. He kicked her to the ground, and kicked her again and again causing her to curl herself into a ball trying in an effort to protect herself. But the Titan picked her up again, licking his lips. "Prepare yourself for some real fun," he said as his hands started to move down over her body until she screamed out in agony.

xxx

Cy, at that moment, was still lying on that the table. Suddenly, his cybernetic eye started to glow. It became like a beacon as he woke up. He sat up abruptly. He seemed enraged as he got off the table and started to walk to the door of Lorelei's lab. Lorelei and Sam didn't dare approach him. They could both feel the power that radiated off him, but it didn't seem to bother his daughter, who rested in Sam's arms. In fact, she seemed to be at ease form her father's power.

"I can feel it!" Cy said, .

"Feel what?" Samantha asked, .

"I can feel all their pain. I felt Destiny die." His fists clenched so tight that sparks shot from them.

Lorelei quietly said to Cy, "If you can get Destiny back here, I might be able to heal her, but only if you get her back as soon as possible."

Cy nodded. Then looked up and called out telepathically, to Kate, letting her know that he had awakened. He could sense that the girl was happy to hear his voice, but wondered how he was sending his thoughts. He just told her that he didn't exactly know either, but, when he woke up, he could just "feel" the minds of all the girls like they where standing right next to him.

He told Kate to meet him where Victoria and the others were, and for her to move as fast as she could. She agreed and shot off in an intent.

"Take care of things while I'm gone," Cy stated to Sam and Lorelei., "I'm going to kill this Titan freak!" The second he said this he vanished.

xxx

Seconds later The Titan was about to finish off Sakura, when an explosion erupted, quite nearby. Titan and the girls looked over to where it came from, and the girls' hearts felt like they were about to explode when they saw Cy standing up slowly and walking away from the smoke and flames. He looked around and then approached the Titan, who immediately dropped Sakura, to the ground. The Titan smiled and walked over to Cy thinking that, sense he was a man, that he had come here to help him with the destruction of these rebellious women. But Cy's face was filled with rage—at Titan. As the Titan turned to face him, Cy said nothing. He just hit the Titan and sending him flying off into a mountain side.

The cyborg then walked over to Sakura where she lay on the ground. He, took off his trench to cover her. She looked up to at him as he did this, and, with tear- filled eyes, and said, "Thank god you came. I knew you would."

"Shhh … don't talk," Cy told her, . "I will take care of everything now." He turned to look at the Titan just as he burst out of the mountain side in a rage. He had never been struck like that before by any man or women, for unlike Forces strike his hurt.

"What are you doing?" he asked Cy. "Why would you hit me like that? Are you defending these stupid little bitches?" Titan yelled out to the cyborg as he flew back over to him, " Don't you know that men are the greater gender?"

"Ha!" said Cy. "You're one to talk. The passed hour these women have been giving you a run for your money!" Cy told him, the Titan did not like this comment. But then Cy heard his name spoken in a weak voice. He turned and saw blood pooling out around the center from under his trench coat as it lay across Sakura.

He knelt down to her, and put his hand over the injury in an attempt to stop the bleeding, but it was no use. Sakura whispered to him,, he heard Sakura tell him "It doesn't matter right now. You must, stop the Titan. He is a true monster. He has shown no honor to anyone."

Cy looked over at the Titan who seemed to be enjoying Sakura's pain -filled pleas. It was clear that it didn't matter to him that she was dying.

"Don't talk," Cy told Sakura. " Kate will be here any minute. She'll take you and Destiny to Lorelei, and she will get you both fixed up like new." But then another blast shot right through Sakura's body.

Cy was blown back from the blast, but saw the Titan shot her he yelled out and turned to face the Titan. "There was no need for that— she is no longer a threat to you."

Titan just shrugged and said, "What does it matter? She would of never have been mine anyway, and any bitch who refuses, me must die."

Cy could not believe this guy the Titan got his kicks by hurting others—especially women. It was a game to him.

"Form what I heard," Cy stated, "you're the one who killed off most of the mhen on this planet—after you where made, so you alone would be the only male on this planet. Expect for the thirty or so, men alive to follow your direct orders."

Titan laughed again. "Yeah, that's right! I killed off the men so I alone could rule over the women of this planet. In fact, if there is a male baby born, I'll strangle it with its own umbilical cord."

"You have no honor!" Cy roared out. But then Sakura coughed. Cy looked at her. Titan looked at her, too, realizing that she was still alive. Titan scoffed at this, and said, "Women can be so persistent. They just don't know when to give up."

Cy glared at the Titan, and then went back to Sakura. The others, had gathered around her as well. They were trying to think of something to do, but felt helpless. Sakura looked at Cy with a weak smile and said, "I want to tell you something that Sensei said to me one time."

"You shouldn't waste your strength," Cy told her. "Wait until you're better, then tell me."

But she grabbed his arm in a death grip saying. "No, I have to tell you this now. Sensei told me that when one forfeits his honor they forfeits there right to live. Titan has shown that he has no honor, So he has no right to live, so don't hold …"

Sakura didn't finish. She just fell limp on the ground, and her hand released its grip on Cy. But, before her hand touched the ground, Cy grabbed, it and said, "I'm sorry, Sakura." He moved her hands to his as he seemed to be shaking with rage and sorrow, he then placed both her hands together over her chest and pulled his coat over her head. Then he stood and faced the Titan with a killer intent radiating off from every surface of his body.

Titan noticed the emblem on Cy's shoulder, and he then knew who had made him. "Now I see," Titan stated. "So you and those girls there where made by Minawa Ivy—, to kill me. I see now that she was highly over ratted. She should never have believed, to think that a weak looking cyborg like you could possibly beat me."

Titan raised has hand, and it opened to reveal the plasma cannon.

"Look out!" Victoria yelled. But, when the blast was fired, Cy hit it out of the way, and it hit a rock, blowing it up. The others girls could not believe it. Titan couldn't believe it either.

He fired again , and again, but Cy diverted each shot like as if it was nothing., Titan was stood in disbelief. Not only was Cy knocking away his shots, he was deflecting his shots, away from the girls.

"Who is this Cyborg?" Titan thought, but then a monstrous thought crossed his mind: *What if this cyborg is a super Super Cyborg, like me?* He shook that thought off as he asked, "Why did you come here? To free the women of this planet? It has nothing to do with you, —so why?"

"Because it's the right thing to do. People shouldn't be enslaved. They should be free!" Cy paused for moment then said, "Also, because I promised Minawa I would. I owe her my life, so I will take back her planet, for her and for the honor of her people."

Once again, the Titan heard "this honor crap" from Cy. *What is honor but a crutch for the weak?* Titan thought. And then he said, "Well, if you're going to free the women of this planet, I guess you will use them as I have, for, at the core, all men want one thing, —and we both know what that is, don't we? And witch makes us the same in the end. So why not you join me instead."

"We are nothing alike!!!" Cy yelled out in a rage. The thought of him being anything like the Titan sickened him. "You destroy and kill anything that doesn't suit you. *Me* I will protect the innocent and destroy evil in whatever form it takes."

"Then prove me wrong," Titan said.

"With pleasure," Cy shot back. Then they both went into a fight that no one could see, —not even Jennifer. In an instant, Cy kicked the Titan right in the face causing him to jump back. The combatants now glaring at each other. Titan robbing the side of his face.

"It has been so long sense since I have felt pain," Titan said, as he was rubbing his face. He then lowered his hands, and clenched his fists. "For this pain that you have given me, I will pay you back a hundred fold."

Cy had no time to block as Titan shot forward, head butting him, sending him flying back to the ground. But he caught himself, and shot back up kicking, sending the Titan straight up in the air.

The Titan stopped himself and fired, his plasma cannon. Cy jumped back to avoid, the blast, but it changed directions and followed him, Cy then caught the fiery cannon ball. The blast pushed him right into a mountain side and the blast and Cy started to eat away at the mountain.

Cy pushed back as hard as he could, and pushed the blast straight up into the sky where it flew off, into space. He shook his hands , because he'd been burned a bit by the heat that the blast had created. The Titan smiling. "Is that the best you've got?" he asked.

"You truly think that you can beat me don't you?" said Titan with a smug look on his face. "Then let me tell you that you can never win this fight!"

"We'll see about that, Titan. Remember, I was made into a cyborg, to take you down—and that's exactly what I plan to do." Cy pushed himself forward yelling out, "*Screaming Bullet!*"

Cy's punch hit the Titan hard. He had never felt anything like it. Up till now, he had felt he was unbeatable. With that strike from Cy, and with that strike their fight continued. Like two bolts of lighting, they shot around the sky. In a way, it was beautiful. But, because the fate of a planet lay in the balance, it was not to be admired.

As the others, continued to watch the lights, given off from the fight between Cy and the Titan. The Titan then landed a blow, making him spiel downward.

He slammed into the ground, making a large crater. The Titan, shot down and landed, glaring at the cyborg, he looked unconscious. But, right as the Titan reared back to finish the job, Cy back flipped out of the crater, and the Titan punched the ground so hard that it erupted in an explosion.

Cy landed a few feet away, and watched the an eruption of the ground, but then the Titan shot up, and they both went back into there their fight, exchanging blow for blow in the sky and across the water and the land.

As there fight continued, Cy was starting to have trouble keeping up. At one point, Titan vanished and reappeared hitting him hard in the face. But the second punch, was caught and he spun Titan around, and threw him to the ground. Titan, though, wasn't out yet. He flew right back up and they continued, until the Titan suddenly jumped back. Cy had no idea what he was doing, when the Titan said, "This has been quite an interesting fight, but I can't have another cyborg almost as strong as me around. It could be quite irritating. But, before I kill you, you should know that, once you're gone, I plan to have my way with every one of those girls of yours. And then I'm going to kill them. I tell you this to show you that, no matter what you do, you can do nothing to stop me. " "So, let's stop playing around. We both know that neither of us is fighting at maxim strength. Why don't we stop with this game, and fight each other with everything we have?" The Titan stated smiled smugly.

"All right then," retorted Cy, " but let me tell you that you're making the same mistake as that so-called captain of yours made."

Cy retorted, but Titan didn't seem to be intimidated as he stated, "That's because I know that you are holding back about 2 percent, —maybe 4 percent of your max, —as I am only using only about one percent of my maxim power. And now I will show you just how hopeless of a fight this is!" The Titan started to focus his power into one of his hands, and then razed it. He then threw a blast straight down in front of the cyborg. Cy though barely managed to move out of the way as an enormous power split the ground behind him. The split continued for miles.

"What was that?" Jennifer said as her vision came back on from the blinding flash of light that had been given off from the blast.

"I don't know!" Victoria stated, for they had felt it all the way to the elders sanctuary as if it was had happened right next to them.

When Cy looked back at what the Titan had done, he started to think how insane this all was. *Just think*, he said to himself, *not long ago I was just a normal guy who just started my job as a security guard, and now here I am, half a galaxy away, fighting for my life and the lives of hundreds on a planet that I didn't even know existed!*

The Titan seemed ready for anything. As Cy reared back, a red glow appeared around him as he focus his power into his next attack. The Titan stood ready as he Cy shot forward and yelled out, "*Screaming Bullet!*"

Cy's momentum was incredible, but, when he got close, the Titan just raised his hand and caught the punch. But the bullet continued.

The power that they both were letting out was, blinding—until Cy pushed himself even higher as the bullet continued. The Titan started to get pushed back. He realized that the flesh on his hand was started to peel as the bullet approached. So the Titan pushed himself under Cy and pushed him off, and the momentum of the bullet though continued on and tore through everything in its path as it went up and continued into space.

The cyborg girls realized how much the last attack had taken out of Cy. Signs of exhaustion and pain were evident on his face.

Kate, carrying Sakura and Destiny, had just made it to the sanctuary of the Supreme elder. She slammed her fists against the large doors, and, without warning, they opened nearly causing her to fall off balance. She then heard a voice say, "Hurry. We don't have a lot of time to save Sakura and Destiny."

Lorelei told her to put the two girls on the tables she had readied for them. As soon as she laid the girls down, and Kate watched as the beds seemed to come alive and started to work on the two girls.

"Good," Lorelei said as she watched the machines work. She turned to Kate and said, "You had better get yourself back to the village." Kate agree and vanished in a flash.

xxx

Back at the village, April was keeping watch when she heard a crash where the village kept their food supplies. When she walked over to it she was met up with Megan who had also heard the crash to.

They, saw a huge hole in the side of the warehouse, and they could make out five unknown people in there, tearing the place apart.

"Who's in there?" April yelled out.

When she said this, five people jumped out in blurs. They, all landed at the edge of the village square. The two girls were shocked to see that it was the Cyber Force with their leader Captain Cyber—somehow they had come back.

"Say, 'welcome back' to the Cyber Force," Captain Cyber yelled out.

"How can this be?" said April. "We all saw you destroyed by Cy! he vaporized you and he took out the rest of you as well?"

"Those are good question!" Captain Cyber said. "And I have some a good answers for those questions," Captain Cyber said, "when your cyborg friend destroyed us, he failed to see that the most important part of my body —my head—detached, my head shot off before it was completely destroyed. "

My head then flew back to the city where the rest of me was repaired. Then I was able to get the others repaired and ready for action in time to see Lord Titan starting get into his fight with that pathetic cyborg, you call Cy."

"So what do you plan to do now, that you've got yourself and those losers back together?" Megan said cheekily.

"Well, sense you asked, we plan on killing you and the others in your group while Lord Titan gets your friend."

Captain Cyber then turned to his Cyber Force and said, "Attack!" But, right as Turk and Drive shot forward, Megan put a field around them and blocked their advance.

Beth came running out of the cooking area. She had been planning to make Cy his favorite foods for when he got back. She saw Megan and April in a shield bubble being attacked by what looked like a rebuilt Cyber Force.

She ran over to the village well and yelled, "Hay, jerk-face, why don't you all cool off?" And she pulled the water out of the well with one hand and focused it into a deadly water stream that blasted Turk and Drive out of the path of Megan and April.

When Megan and April landed, Beth ran over to them and asked, "How did those guys came come back?" April said to her, "It seems that these guys are built like New York cockroaches—you have to step on them real hard."

"So what are we going to do?" Megan said to April with a worried look. "There are only three of us here, and there are five of them! We're out numbered."

Kate appeared and said, "It's four against five now."

"Where have you been?" Beth asked.

"I had a few errands to do," Kate said. "Cy told me to tell you that we' should go back to the Supreme Elder's sanctuary where it's safe."

"A lot of good that does us now," said April. "We can't leave with these guys around!" She pointed to the Cyber Force, who didn't seem to like the fact that the girls where ignoring them like they had before.

"Do you girls mind?" Time-Stopper yelled out. "We're trying to have a fight here! Do you girls think you're getting away with what you all did to us before?" Time-Stopper yelled out.

"Give us a minute, punk," April said in her sassy tone. "And, besides, you have bigger things to worry about."

"Like what?" Mildew asked.

"Like me!" And April used her mimicking power to change into a T Rex. She roared right in Time- Stopper's face. He had never seen a beast like it, before, and he almost freaked taking a step back..

"Attack!" Captain Cyber yelled out. Turk and Drive flew around April in her T Rex form, and flew straight to Beth for some pay back for what she had done to them.

Kate ran right at Captain Cyber and circled him until a cyclone formed around him. Megan looked at the enormous man that was Steam Shovel. He flexed his muscles as steam came out of his head.

Megan laughed and said, "Is that the best you can do? Blow steam?"

Steam Shovel roared out and slammed both fists down on her, but they where stopped by her invisible force field. He continued to strike at the force field, but to no avail.

Beth watched as both Turk and Drive flew at her. As, she held up her hands, and steam surrounded her. Turk and Drive flew right into the stem to find her, but they could not see anything and were lost in all the steam.

xxx

Cy had just been hit hard and had crashed back down to the ground. He looked up as the Titan shot down and grabbed him by his head and slammed him into the ground. Ashley was about to jump in when she saw this, but Melissa stopped her. "You don't stand a chance," she said.

"If we don't do something, Cy is going to die," Ashley shot back. "He can't keep up with that freak anymore." Ashley shot back.

Right then, in their heads, the girls heard Cy's voice say, "I do need your help, and I have a plan."

The five girls lessoned to his plan. At first, the girls didn't think it would work, but Cy told them, "Trust me. It's a perfect plan."

xxx

Captain Cyber could barely move in the cyclone, that Kate had created. He had thought that these girls would be easy to beat, but, for some odd reason, they all seemed to be stronger than before.

The girls noticed their increased strength too. They seemed to be taking care of these guys, more easily than before. April then yelled out to the others, "It most of been when Cy got powered up! We must have been powered up too!"

"It's just like as Lorelei said!" Megan exclaimed as she threw a force field around Steam Shovel, and lifted him into the air, and slung him around in the bubble, and then slammed him into the ground.

Beth, still hidden in the steam, and attacked Turk and Drive with *Ninja* precision. And, right when Turk got hit, he punched forward— but he hit Drive in the face instead of connecting with Beth. Drive yelled at Turk.

"You moron, that was me!"

"Sorry, man, but I can't see a thing in this steam," Turk told him.

Drive looked around and said, "Then let's get rid of it!" He spun around to blow the steam away.

When the steam cleared and they saw Beth, they both flew at her. But, right before they got to her, she raised her hand and sent a as a jet stream of water at them. They both jumped out of the way, but not before Turk got hit.

The stream went right through his arm. Then Beth raised her hand up and pointed it at Turk. At first, he thought that it did nothing—until his arm fell off and dropped to the ground.

He yelled out in pain as black blood and other mechanical flowed out of his arm. When he looked back at the girl, she was smiling as if what she had done was nothing. "You're dead!" he yelled out to the girl.

Kate was still running around Captain Cyber. Finally, he was able to grab her in mid run. He hold her out by her throat and told her, "You can not beat me by running around!"

Kate smiled and said, "Okay, how about if a I vibrate your body until you fall apart?" She grabbed the arm that was holding her body and started to vibrate. Captain Cyber finally had to let the girl go—or risk falling apart.

April was still chasing Time-Stopper, who now had developed a mind numbing fear of giant lizards. He stopped and looked around thinking that he was being whipped by a young woman like her. He looked around. She had disappeared again.

He started to wonder where she had disappeared to, when someone taped him on the shoulder. When he turned around, he was looking at himself.

"Hey, big boy," the duplicate said in a girly version of Time-Stopper's voice. And then his duplicate blasted him with one his own attacks.

The real Time-Stopper went flying, and slammed into a near by tree, and fell to the ground. He looked up in time to see his double come flying at him. His double then rolled into a ball covered in metal spikes. Time-Stopper jumped out of the way as the ball slammed into the tree.

xxx

Cy was still fighting with the best of his abilities, but was at the end of his rope. He knew the girls had to act soon with his plan or he was finished.

Suddenly, Cy heard Victoria yell out to Cy form the sky. "Move out of the way!" When he did, she let out a gravity wave at the Titan that left a crater around him, and made him nearly hit the ground for the force was more than he had ever felt.

Titan, could barely move, but was able to watch as Cy yelled out to Ashley, "Do it now!"

She powered up her flames to the max as she took off and flew around the Titan creating a spiraling tornado of flame.

The heat was intense. Titan yelled out at the top of his lungs, "Stop this! It is foolishness! You can not stop me with heat! No one can stop the Titan, —I am invincible."

xxx

The cyborg girls that were where fighting the Cyber Force. Suddenly, felt intense heat coming from somewhere. The fighting stopped and so did the Cyber Force they all tried to see what was going on.

"It's Ashley!" April said. "It has to be!" They all saw a spiral of flame heading skyward. The Cyber Force could not believe what they were seeing. Drive yelled out to Captain Cyber, "What's going on?"

"How, should I know?" Captain Cyber yelled back as they watched in awe as the spiral of flames seemed to grow in intensity.

"Man," said Beth. "It's miles away and yet I can feel the heat as if I was next to it!" The girls also could till tell that Ashley was being empowered by Cy to increase the intensity of her flames, just like there powers had been increased.

Megan yelled out, "Everyone get over here! If the flames increase anymore, we will melt in the heat too."

The four of them ran over to Megan, and, with a single move, she placed a shield around them and the entire village. She was able to knock the Cyber Force out of the village—with the shield she had adapted her shield to exclude them.

The Cyber Force watched in horror as the flames seemed to wash over them, completely vaporizing them by in the flames. This time they wouldn't be coming back.

Cy had grabbed his trench coat when Kate took Sakura away. He held it up as Ashley cut loss her flames. He knew it would hold back the flames and protect him and the four girls behind him.

Victoria was still doing her best to hold the Titan at bay, but Ashley's flames were getting too intense for her to stay where she was. She was finally forced to fall back. The second that, happened, the Titan was free of the gravity force and he fired a blast at Ashley. The shot stunning her making her fall to the ground.

When the flames faded, the Titan stood up in a crater of molten rock, and his body looked like as if it was made of molten metal. "You are all going to pay for this!" he shouted.

"Hey, Titan!" Cy yelled out. "Chemistry 101, —what happens when you rapidly cool heated metal?"

"What?" the Titan said.

Cy yelled to Melissa, "Fire away!" And she fired an ice blast right at the Titan. He roared out as steam came pouring out from every part of his body.

When Melissa let up, there was a glacier where the Titan, had been standing. Cy and the girls let out a sigh of relief knowing that the battle was over. Cy fell back against a rock. "Are you okay?" Jennifer asked.

He looked up to her. "I'm fine—just a little tired. I'm just, glad that you're all okay."

Rebecca moved over to him. She sat next to him and sat between his legs, and lad her head against his chest. "What did you mean when you asked the Titan what happens when you cool heated metal?" the girl asked.

"Well, Rebecca," Cy answered, "when you cool heated metal it solidifies."

"What does solidifies mean?" Rebecca asked, but she couldn't pronounce the word right, and Victoria pitched in., "It means that the metal becomes hard, which also means that the Titan will never move again."

CHAPTER 37

Cy and the girls rested for a minute trying to catch their breath. The five girls sat near Cy and watched him breath with his one eye closed. He seemed to be about ready to pass out. Finally Kim asked, "What are we going to do, now that the Titan is dead?"

Jennifer shrugged as did Ashley, Melissa, and Victoria.

Rebecca and Kim looked up to Cy when he said, "We still have work to do, —we now have to help rebuild this world." He then stood up slowly. Rebecca and Kim moved so he could get up, but, right then, Jennifer detected something coming from the ice the that encased the Titan.

"It can't be?" !" She said, and then yelled, "Watch out!!" As she pushed Cy out of the way, as a beam came out of the glacier.

The beam missed Cy, but it went right through Jennifer, who stood where he had been. Cy yelled out to Jennifer when she fell to the ground. Melissa fell down before her friend, and she checked her to see if she was still breathing. She nodded to Cy, saying she was barely breathing.

The glacier started to crack, then it shattered in an explosion of ice crystals. The Titan stood before them again—but all of his flesh was gone. He looked like a robotic skeleton— almost as if he was a full version of Cy's bionics.

He looked at all of them with cold, robotic, glowing red eyes. Looking into his eyes was like looking into the eyes of death itself.

Cy was about to act when, the Titan acted first. He fired a blast right at Rebecca blasting her right, back into a rock. She managed to yell out to Cy right before she hit, but the blast turned her body into a black disfigured version of its self.

Victoria, and Kim watched in horror as their friends where being slaughtered in front of them. Then they heard Cy yell *"No more!,"* They looked over and saw him standing in front of the Titan, his body shaking with rage.

"No more … no more, … *No more!*" he repeated.

As Cy yelled out the finally word, as a red aura of electricity charged around him. The sky even seemed to react with his rage as it turned dark. Lighting struck around Cy. The metal on his body flashed gold once then twice, and then Cy let out what was to them an immense roar. The metal on his body seemed to be on fire as it changed to a shimmering gold, and the once red glow aura changed to a blue and then to gold.

Kim and Victoria took a step back from him, and Melissa, who had been in a catatonic state from what had happened to her friend, finally looked over and saw the transformed Cyborg.

The Titan had never seen anything like this before, —metal was not supposed to change color, and what was with the golden glow around him it was truly unnatural.

Cy looked over at the Titan with a look full of rage. Never taking his eyes off and while glared at the Titan, without turning he said "Victoria, take the others to the Supreme Elder's sanctuary. She may be able to save Jennifer and Rebecca."

Victoria, however, was still in shock. "Do it now!" Cy shouted, breaking her from her unmoving state.

Victoria shook herself out of her shock and said, "Yes, sir!" She flew over to Rebecca's body.

"Are you all right, Cy?" Kim, asked.

He just gave her a half smile and said. "Everything is all right now. You need to get to the elders sanctuary, that's all."

Kim nodded as she walked over to Ashley and Melissa and helped Jennifer up. When she slowly opened her eyes, she saw Cy still staring down the Titan. Quietly, she said, "Be careful." And Victoria lifted them all into the air and started to fly off.

When the Titan saw them go, he laughed. In an icy, metallic voice, he said, "If you all think you will get away form from me, you are all *dead* wrong!" He pointed his hand out as it changed to the plasma cannon and started changing up. Cy saw this and, in a flash, he was in front of the Titan.

"What?" Titan blurted out. Cy stood in front of him and grabbed his hand and crushed it back to its original form.

"You don't know when to quit, do you?" Cy yelled as he started to crushed Titan's hand. Cy continued to yell as the Titan tried to free himself from Cy's grip. "First, you killed Destiny. And then you took down Sakura and Jennifer. And now you have shot Rebecca! That is unforgivable!" Cy yelled out to Titan.

Cy let go of the Titan's hand as their power increased. The Titan rolled his hand and readjusted it. "How did you get this incredible power?" The Titan asked. "It's true, isn't it?"

"What's true, you sick freak?" yelled Cy. "That it is time for you to die?"

"No," said Titan, "is it of the black flame?"

"How should I know?" responded Cy. " I barely know how my cybernetics work?" Cy finished.

"If it is what I think," Titan informed Cy, " then you shouldn't be alive. No cyborg could be made of that metal. It would reject anyone made of it and— it would kill them with in minutes."

"Then I must be a special case, because it hasn't hurt me in the least." Cy told him. "But that doesn't matter right now. All that matters is that today you die for all the wrongs you are responsible for. You will die for all the people on this planet that you have hurt. You will now know the horrors they have all felt. I will make you feel all of their pain, and suffering that you have inflicted on them!"

Cy yelled out the last part of his message as he shot forward and hit the Titan into the air. While the Titan was still in the air, Cy grabbed him by his head and legs and slammed him across his knee.

The Titan yelled out in pain as Cy spun him around and throw him. The Titan tumbled around and then stopped in mid air glaring at the now transformed cyborg. The Titan, seemed furious, as he fired a plasma beam from his fingertips, but Cy moved so fast that his movements looked like blurs.

"How can it be?" The Titan yelled out in a rage. "How can you dodge at this range!!!" ?" Titan yelled out for he was only a few feet away from Cy. Titan fired blast after blast at Cy, but he Cy dodged them as if the Titan was standing still. *How can it be that I keep missing him?* Titan thought. Then he and yelled out, "why Why can"t I hit you?"

"Maybe it's your rusty body that makes you too slow?," Cy said with a half smile. The Titan was outraged and fired a blast at Cy's face. This one hit its mark, but it didn't have the effect that the Titan wanted.

As Cy moved back to face the Titan, he said, "You may be able to destroy whole planets, but you can't destroy what I am." With a half smile.

"What are you?" the Titan asked with fear now in his voice.

Cy stared straight at him as he said, "I am the, answer to all living things that cry for peace. I am the personification of honor, loyalty, and dignity to all who want it. I am ally to all that is good, and the a nightmare to all that is evil."

xxx

The girls, who were still at the village, and the other villagers there, all started to relax when the flames subsided and Megan put down her shields. They were all wondering if the flames had meant that the Titan was dead?.

They got their answers when Victoria, with Kim, Melissa, and Ashley arrived. The girls were immediately concerned with the fact that Rebecca and Jennifer were so critically injured.

Kate asked "What happened?" Ashley started to tell them what went on, at the battle field, and when she was finished telling them, what had happened. The girls could barely believe it. No one had ever heard of a man fighting for such a cause.

"What are we supposed to do now?" Beth asked.

Victoria told them, "We *all* have to get to the elder's sanctuary. , Cy said that she will be able to heal Sakura and Destiny—maybe she can help Rebecca and Jennifer too.

Jennifer, who was being held up by Kim, weakly said, "We need to hurry. and get her fixed up Cy may still need our help."

"Ha!" Ashley laughed. "Cy doesn't need our help anymore. He is now in a league of his own. There isn't anything that can beat him now."

xxx

Meanwhile, back on Earth, the cyborg's Sensei was sitting at a table near the temple when a young girl walked in. She wore glasses and was in was dressed in non traditional clothing. "I'm home, Grandfather," she yelled out. "I'll get your tea ready now." She walked into the kitchen, and made him a cup of tea, and, when she came back, she noticed the look on her grandfather's face. He didn't look right. So she asked him, "Grandfather, what is wrong?"

The old man looked at his granddaughter and said, "It's Chris."

"He's not dead is he?" the girl said with fear in her voice.

"No, that's not it. I fear, he has just gained a power that most men can't even fathom."

"Isn't that a good thing?"

"Not necessarily. The kind of power I'm talking about is uncharted territory for Chris. Right now, he's doing his best to hold on to himself, for there is something else that has been awakened within him— something very dark. And at the same time, this dark something is what gives him the power needed to fight at the level that he is now at. I only hope that he can remain himself after this fight."

xxx

Cy and the Titan were glaring at each other as lighting struck around them. Cy yelled out, "You know I have never fought anyone, just so I could hurt them. But you ... *you I must kill!*"!"

The Titan still had regained some of his composer composure as he thought of something. "You do still realize that I am still not fighting you at my max, don't you?"

Cy gave him a half smile. "So what? Neither am I."

"Then let's go to a place where we can fight with full strength and power."

"And where would that be?"

"In space. You *can* survive in space can't you?" the Titan asked.

Cy's glowing blue red eye grow grew brighter. "Yes I can. In fact, I recommend that we go to the asteroid belt around this solar system."

The Titan agreed, and they both shot off into the sky like two bolts of lighting.

xxx

As the girls flew to the elder's home sanctuary, Jennifer weakly looked to the sky as she felt something. She spoke quietly to Ashley, who was still helping her as well as Kim. "There are two large powers heading into the sky." Ashley stopped and looked and up. She saw what looked like two lighting bolts going into the sky, but they seemed to be going up instead of down.

"Hey, guys," Ashley yelled out. "Look! I think that one of those lighting bolts is Cy!" They all agreed that it was Cy, but why was he going into the sky?

xxx

The Titan and Cy landed on an asteroid. Staring each other down, they both got into there their fighting stances, ready to attack at any moment.

As they stood ready, a nearby asteroid smashed into another one. The collision produced a shower of rock debris. As the cloud of debris passed by Cy and Titan, the smaller rocks shattered when they impacted the two warriors. It was as if the power they were giving off was so strong that anything that touched them would vaporize. This was a signal for them to attack, and like two colossal warriors they fought like nothing the universe as had ever seen.

xxx

When the girls made it to the Supreme Elder's sanctuary, they found her watching a bank of monitors. She smiled at them and pointed out two beds where Sakura and Destiny lay, undergoing treatment. The girls were ecstatic to see their two friends looking so much better.

Then Lorelei addressed them: "Put Rebecca and Jennifer on these two beds. They'll soon be all right." Victoria did as she was told.

Right before they where about to asked what to do with Rebecca and Jennifer Sam and Ellis, who was carrying Cy's baby, walked over to them, and entered the lab. They were glad to see all the girls together, and glad that they were all receiving such good attention from Lorelei. "Look at this monitor," Sam said to the girls. "Lorelei, has a surprise for you."

When they all looked up at the large monitor, they could hardly believe their eyes. They could see Cy was fighting the Titan—and they were in orbit! Victoria asked, "Why do they look like blurs and flashes of light?"

"It's because they're moving faster than the human eye can see. He is, even moving too fast for all of you, to see properly," Lorelei told them as they watched on in awe.

xxx

"You can never beat me!!"! My cybernetics are superior to all!" the Titan yelled out as they fought on, but Cy didn't care what the Titan said to him. All he cared about right now was finishing off this freak for all he had done to his friends.

Cy and Titan shot through hundreds of asteroids as they fought. The light show they gave off could even be seen from other planets in their night skies, —it was like an aurora in space.

After what seemed like hours, the Titan became infuriated. He fired an enormous blast at Cy, making him crash down, into another planet. The explosion was monstrous as Cy burned through the planet's atmosphere., Titan yelled out in victory, thinking that he had defeated the Super Cyborg for sure.

"Ha!" he cried. "Super Cyborg, indeed! You must have been lying about the metal that you're made of!" Titan looked back at his planet. Now that, that cyborg was gone, he could start work on taking out those others before they got any ideas.

xxx

The girls cried out when they saw Cy crash into the planet. Right then, Sakura and Destiny awoke and they asked what all the commotion was. Sam told them what had happen to Cy, and they where almost in tears when elder Lorelei suddenly yelled out, "Look!"

When they looked at the planet where Cy had crashed, they saw another explosion erupted out of the planet's surface. It almost looked liked as if the planet was going to explode.

The Titan turned when he felt the explosion, and he saw a golden light shoot off of the planet and travel through the atmosphere. Cy was back, and he didn't seem too happy.

His clothes were torn up, but, other than that, he was fine. In fact, he seemed even stronger! Cy tore off the rest of his shirt. "That was one of my favorite shirts!" he said in an a growl.

"You!" Titan blurted out. "I thought you were *dead*, cyborg! You could have fled, and I would have never known!" He flew back to the cyborg.

"No way!" Cy told him. "I would never abandon my girls—my gems—and, besides, it is time for the reign of the Titan to come to an end.

Titan sneered at this remark. "How dare you talk to me like that? No one talks to the Titan like that."

He shot forward and there fight continued on. They were like two mighty gods of war, fighting in the heavens, shooting across space, neither of them giving in to the other until the, Titan yelled out, "Cyborg, you will never win!" and he hit him Cy into an asteroid.

"You see?" said Titan, laughing. "You're your nothing but a low-class cyborg, and a low-class animal."

Cy stood on the asteroid as if nothing had happened to him. "I would rather be an brainless beast than a heartless monster like you, Titan."

The Titan sneered again, wondering how this worthless cyborg could be so strong. It was bad enough that those girls had been able to strip him of his beautiful flesh, but this cyborg was actually giving him a run for his money.

xxx

Back at Lord Titan's Cyborg City, what was left of his men were trying to find there their lord. Their computers, were not much help. Suddenly, one of his men yelled out, "I found him! He's fighting in space!"

Another cybernetic man ran over, to the scanners and saw the readings they were off the scales.

"Incredible!" he said.

"I wonder who he's fighting." said another, .

"I don't know," said the first cyborg. "But his power is just as great as Lord Titan's. No —wait—it's actually a bit greater!."

"That can't be possible," The second cyborg said, and, right then, all of their equipment started to overload. Then everything in the whole city started to overload. The power that Cy was giving off was too much for anything in the city to take.

xxx

Cy and the Titan continued fighting it out. They fought as if nothing else mattered to them, because nothing else did. As they cut through hundreds of asteroids. Suddenly, something happen Cy vanished and reappeared behind Titan. He slammed his enemy into an oncoming asteroid with incredible force. When the Titan got into position to attack Cy again, his target was gone again.

"Lose something, Titan?" Cy stated from behind his opponent. Titan turned around, but Cy was gone. Titan felt someone behind him again. Titan turned and punched violently, but got nothing but air.

"You think this is funny? Toying with me like this?" the Titan roared out, his aggravation starting to show.

"There's nothing funny about this, Titan," Cy stated as he appeared around the side of an asteroid.

The Titan clenched his fist in rage. "For everything you have done to me, I will pay you back a hundred times, —no, a thousand times." ," he roared. His metal feet slammed into the an asteroid that he stood from the force of his power.

Cy glared at the Titan and got into his fighting stance. But then he stood back to a normal standing possession. "It's done," . He stated very casually.

Everyone back on the planet heard this and Lorelei thought Cy had lost his mind with all the new power, but The Titan was the one to asked, "What do you mean, it's done?"

"This fight is over, Titan," Cy stated. "You are losing power with every blow. Right now, you're no longer a challenge to me. You have fought a warrior who is superior to you, and you have lost."

The Titan would not except accept this. "It's not true!" he roared out.

He jumped from the asteroid and shot forward with in rage.

"Fool." Cy said as he watched the Titan fly in his direction. Just as the Titan was about to reach his target, Cy held up his hand and right when Titan was about to attack in a flash Cy yelled out *Screaming Bullet!!!*"

The bullet hit the Titan with incredible force, striking him right in the middle of his chest. As time seemed to move in slow motion, the Titan's entire body shattered. His head spun away from his body. It was all that was left of him. The bullet that Cy had fired at him filled the Titan's head with all the images of all the pain and suffering that he had caused throughout out his life. It was a fate worse than death. Cy gabbed his the head as it floated by. "You will now have to exist with the images of all the pain and suffering that you have caused for the rest of eternity, Titan." And he threw the Titan's head into the deaths of space, forever to live with the pain of his terrible deeds.

"I will have my revenge!" the Titan's head yelled out as it was shot through space.

Cy watched until the Titan was out of sight, and then turned back to the planet. As he neared the planet surface, he could already hear there cheers as he flew toward the the people.

CHAPTER 38

By the time Cy returned to the planet Titan, everyone knew he had defeated Lord Titan. Everyone ran outside to greet him as he returned to the planet, for the biggest welcome he could ever have imagined. The girls had trouble finding him because the cheering crowds were so thick. They looked around trying to see him as he came down, but they could not find him, they notice the crowds coming there way cheering for they had heard from Lorelei that Titan had been beaten and before Cy even started going back to the planet the people rejoiced that the tyrant who had put them into slavery for so long was now gone for good.

"Finally!" Jennifer yelled out, "Here he comes!"

The girls looked to the sky, and, sure enough, there he was floating down like an angel coming down from the heavens.

He landed softly a few feet away from the girls. As he started walking towards them, the gold color of his cybernetics gleamed in the light. But the metal still shinning gold, but the scares on his body where, still showed his human side.

The girls tackled him with hugs and kisses, as the rest of the people —mainly women— cheered for him. They all realized just how unbelieving they had been to in him, and begged for his forgiveness. But he told them that there was nothing to forgive … With a tyrant like the Titan around, he probably would hate men too, had he been in their position.

Cy looked at his girls and realized they were healed. He turned to Lorelei, the Supreme Elder, and bowed to her, and thank her.. "You have my deepest gratitude," he told her.

"We should be the ones to thank you—for freeing my people from Lord Titan," Lorelei told him. "We will be forever in your debt."

"You already have thanked me," Cy stated, "with your healing powers. My girls—my gems—are all well."

"So what are we going to do now?" Sakura asked.

"Now we start rebuilding this planet," Cy stated. "I will start by renaming the planet. It will no longer be called Titan. It will be called by a name that is more suited to its people, who will be dear to me forever. I would like to call the planet Gem, for you have all become more precious to me than any gem."

The cheers from everyone were deafening. The people where grateful to the male cyborg—not only for beating the Titan, but for giving their world a new name. But Cy knew that he and the girls still, had a lot of work to do, for rebuilding a the planet was not going to be easy.

The next few days, Cy and the cyborg girls went to the ruins of Cyber City to get parts and equipment for the villages so the people could build new homes and plant new fields of crops. But, as they worked, Lorelei was planning something big for Cy.

One day, during a break from their work, Cy was playing his guitar for some of the children in the village. Lorelei approached him. "What's up?" he asked her.

"Would you be interested in entering a tournament that's being held on a planet not far from here?"

"I don't do tournaments. Besides, the fight would be unfair, because of my cybernetics."

"It's an anything-goes fight to the finish," Lorelei told him. " The only rule in this, is that you must fight with everything you've got. Whoever comes out alive is the winner."

"So you' want me to risk my neck on in a tournament that has no prize at the end of it?" Cy asked. "No, there's a prize at the end."

"And what, pray tell, is this prize?"

"Let's just say it's enough money to help fix up our planet," Lorelei explained, "with enough left over so I could start work on getting our planet's population back to normal.

"When is this tournament?"

"In two days," she said, smiling sweetly. "Will you do it?"

"I'll think about it," he said. After I'm done here, I was going to the beach with the girls, and the best part is that we get the whole place to ourselves."

"Really!" Lorelei stated as if planning something. "The beach you say?" An evil glint shone in her eye.

Later that day after there work was done, Cy and all the fourteen girls, including his young daughter, were at a beach that was pretty close to the village where they were staying in.

The girls were dressed in bathing suits ranged from one's to two peaces of variety of styles and colors. Cy though just wore a normal pare of black trunks. He went without a shirt; he didn't feel uneasy anymore about the girls seeing the scares on his body. In fact, they all had been telling him that his scars make him look real cool and tough.

Cy had just laid out a few large blankets that was big so there would be enough space for all of them to lie down. The girls seemed to be excited. They finally got getting a chance to relax. It seemed to them that they hadn't had a chance to stop moving for a second sense they started their journey to Titan—or Gem, as it now was called.

Beth, and six of the girls were playing in the water while the three youngest of the group were playing in the sand with Cy's daughter. and himself and the rest were lying on the large beach blankets getting some sun. Cy looked like he had fallen asleep—until he heard a large group of women scream out his name.

Cy shot up thinking that something was wrong, but, when he looked around, he saw that his girls where fine. Then he looked over across to the other side of the beach. A group of inhabitants from the village were approaching. They didn't seem in any distress. "Is there anything I can do for you ladies?" he asked them politely.

One of them moved over to him and sat right in his lap and ran her fingers in circles around his metal chest. This didn't make the cyborg girls around him too happy. The woman then said, "There is one thing we would like you to do?"

"What?" Cy asked as he swallowed hard.

"Well," the women in his lap cooed, "sense you destroyed, Titan and his men, that means there are no more men on this whole planet, right?"

"Yeah," Cy stated, starting to get the point.

"So," said the young woman, "now we need your help in repopulating the planet."

Cy realized right then what they wanted from him. The thought was interesting, but … "Sorry, ladies, …"

The rest of the women, started to beg, as they circled him. He still refused them, but , since they had never met a man that who had actually refused to have sex, they became even more interested in him. They all found it alluring to the point they had to have him.

The cyborg girls where starting to get irritated by these aggressive women. They wanted to keep Cy to them selves. Sakura, Ashley, and Victoria were the first ones to start moving the women off away from Cy. Then the others joined in. Finally Cy yelled out, "I have had *enough!*" And he jumped up and ran off. But they were persistent and ran after him, each one determined to be the first ones to have him.

Cy ran as fast as he could. He knew who was responsible for all this craziness. Blasting off in a mini tornado of sand and flew off, he landed at the door to Lorelei's sanctuary. He, ran through the doors and headed to her lab where he knew he would found find her. When he opened the doors to the lab, he found her packing a bag as if for a trip.

She turned to him and asked, "Have you decided if you're going to fight in the tournament or not?"

Cy, however, though wasn't in the mood for this talking about tournaments. He yelled out, "You planned this, didn't you? You knew the women would run straight to me, didn't you?"

"I don't know what you're talking about. It is only natural for the people to want to be with their savior. What's so bad with about that?"

Cy thought minute and asked, "This device that you want to make that has to do with repopulating the planet … what does it do?"

"That's right, I didn't tell you what it does," said Lorelei. "Well, let's just say it will make our lives a lot easier."

"And, let me guess … you need the money from the tournament to build this machine, don't you?" Cy asked.

"You guessed it. You're, the only one with a ship that can take us to the tournament too," Lorelei finished.

Just then, they heard knocks on the door to her lab. Then they heard the voices of the women from the beach. They had found Cy.

"Miss Lorelei, is the Super Cyborg in there with you?" It was clear from the screams of the women what they were after., we all wait a peace of his meat" the women screamed.

Cy turned to the elder, who had a big smile on her face, when she said. "What will it be, Cy? Do you want to go with me to the tournament? Or do you won't to get it on with the whole planet?" She finished with a sly smile.

Most men would jump at a chance like this, but Cy wasn't like most men. He had his morals, and a code of honor, that he had sworn to keep up. So, he sighed and said, "I'll go to the tournament." He hung his head down in defeat thinking that, out of all the enemies that he had faced, the only ones that had beaten him were a bunch of women.

"Excellent!" Lorelei stated, . "The people of this planet well will owe you, for this, and, in fact, I will found find a way to repay you for this."

"Whatever," Cy said. "Just call off the army of sex- driven women already. If they get in here, they'll tare tear me apart."

The Supreme Elder then held up a device and her voice went out over a loud speaker, : "okay Okay, everyone, he agreed. You can back off."

Cy realized they then that he had been tricked into entering the tournament. He asked Lorelei, "You all was in on this little plan of yours?"

"Everyone," she said laughing. "Even the cyborg girls were in on it."

Cy took in a breath and let it out. "All right, when do we leave for this tournament?"

"Tomorrow morning," the Supreme Elder told him. "So be ready."

The next morning, Lorelei and Ellis were waiting for him at his ship. Some how, Ellis had talked the elder into bringing her, even though the other girls weren't allowed to go. Cy walked over to them and said, "Even though I have agreed to do this, it doesn't mean that I'm going to enjoy myself."

Right before they left, the cyborg girls came to him to wish him luck, and to give him a present. To help him remember what he's fighting for, and they presented him with a T-shirt and told him that they have had been working on it, for a while.

When Cy held it up, he saw an insignia on the shirt.

The words "Super Cyborg" were written across the back, and on the front it had the initials *S* and *C*.

Cy smiled and asked, "What this was this for?"

"A super hero needs an insignia!" Beth told him. "To let people know that he is a hero."

Cy thanked the girls as he removed his trench coat and T-shirt and put the new one on. It fit him perfectly, almost as if it was made for him—which it had!.

Cy, Ellis, and the Lorelei then got onto the ship. As they took off, the girls yelled out for Cy not to loss..

Hours later, when they arrived at the asteroid where the tournament was being held, Cy could not believe the types of fighters that were there from all over the universe. He asked Lorelei, "Why didn't you just ask one of them to fight the Titan?"

"Don't you think we tried that already?." The Elder told asked him. "Every fighter who went up against him was beaten."

Cy was kind of shocked hearing this. He could not believe that, with all these different types of fighters, that none of them could beat the Titan, . *Then that would make me one of the strongest fighters in the universe,* he thought.

After they registered Cy in the tournament, they had some time before the fights began. They decided to look around. The tournament was being held on a large asteroid that had lots of people on it and shops galore.

That's when Lorelei ran into someone she knew—, he was a scientist named Torok. He knew all about the most recent history of the planet formerly called Titan. He hadn't done anything about Lord Titan's horrible reign because he thought it was beneath him to help such a low-class planet. He believed that he was higher than most of the people in the universe.

"Well," Torok stated, , "I see that the Titan has finally realized that he didn't need such a low-class scientist on his planet and kicked you off it, right?" the man said to her, .

Lorelei laughed as she said calmly said, "The Titan is dead."

"The Titan can't be dead!" the scientist said. "No one can kill him! It is imposable! Only a warrior like the one I made can do that." And then a cybernetic warrior walked over to Torok. "Let me introduce Pike," Torok said. "He has won this tournament two years running."

"Ah, he looks like a overgrown toaster!" Lorelei huffed., "And I know for a fact that Cy can beat this guy with one hand tied behind his back. He did beat Lord Titan and threw his head into deep space where we will never see him again."

"Is that a fact?" quipped Torok. "Well then would you like to place a bet? If my cyborg wins the tournament, then you will come and work for me,— and if you win ...""

"*When* we win," Lorelei butted in, "you have to pay for all the parts I need for a project that I'm working on." She whispered the amount in his ear.

His eyebrows shot up, then he sighed. "That's fine by me, but don't get your hopes up, little girl. My cyborg design is perfect—unlike that piece of scrap iron behind with you."

They shook hands to seal the deal. Cy and Pike glared at each other. They, too, seemed to want to fight, to see who was truly the greater fighter. Cy, for the first time since arriving, was actually looking forward for to this fight.

When it was time for the first mach, Cy was found himself up against one of the strangest fighters he had ever seen. He wasn't even close to a human. He had an elongated head and no eyes for what Cy could see, and his body looked almost reptilian with a long spiked tail.

Cy greeted his opponent with a bow, and then got into his fighting position awaiting the referee's call. When the fight began, Cy shot forward ready to fight this alien, but right when he attacked with a huge punch, but, his fist went right through the alien's chest. Cy pulled out thinking that he had killed this the alien, but the alien laughed and asked, "Is that the best you've got?"

Cy watched as the opening he'd made in the alien's body healed up. Suddenly, the alien roared as it ran at him. Cy back flipped four times and just barely able to avoided its attacks. Then Cy jumped back, and shot forward. He caught the alien off guard, and punched him so hard that he shot out of the ring and crashed straight through the arena and out of the stadium where he crashed into the spaceport.

The alien stumbled to his feet and stuttered out, "That was nothing," …" before he fell to the ground unconscious.

Most of the people in the stadium stared in shock. As the ref declared Cy the winner, he told Cy, "We haven't, seen any fighter do that since a warrior who fought here years ago. His name was, "Shark Bait."

Cy left the ring and joined Lorelei. "Who's this Shark Bait?" he asked her.

"I'll tell you later," she said, "Now you should watch, it's Pike's turn. You should watch this match."

Cy looked at the fighter and his opponent and just said, "I don't have to watch. " I already know the out come of the fight," ." Then he walked off to get some info on about this Shark Bait warrior.

Pike was able to take out his opponent in less than three moves, and the tournament went on. Both Cy and Pike took out there their opponents with ease, each one showing more strength with each fight. In the next-to-last fight, Cy was up against a warrior that looked half fish and half human. He had a dower dour look on his face though, like he didn't care about anything. But Cy readied himself for whatever was to come. If he had learned anything from these fights, it was to expect the unexpected.

The moment the bell rang announcing the start of starting the match, match to begin Cy ran at the fish-man and kicked him right into the air. "Sorry," Cy said as the fish man was thrown in the air.

"I wouldn't have kicked him so hard," Cy said the ref, " if I had known he was so weak!" But the fish-man stopped in med mid air, and his whole out look changed. He seemed to become feral and vicious, and , with a single move, he filled the whole arena with water.

The people in the stadium was were saved though, the. The water stopped right before it got to the top. Cy was caught off guard as he fell into the water. Right then, the fish-man shot right at him hitting and hit him hard, . Cy spun in the water. H, he shook it off, but the fish-man came at him again, attacking him with unimaginable fury.

Cy knew at that moment that he had to get the fight out of the water, so he focused his cybernetic eye. Suddenly, the whole arena was engulfed in a red flash of light that blinded the fish-man momentarily.

Cy jumped out of the water, and into the air focusing his screaming bullet. When he fired it, it blew the water right out of the arena. The fish-man fell to the ground outside of the ring for a ring out.

Cy slowly landed on in the ring, as the ref declared him the winner of the match. The crowd cheered for Cy. As Cy was soaking the adulation up like a sponge, he really was having fun. But what he needed was a real challenge.

Before the last fight between Cy and Pike was going to start, the fighters had a thirty minute brake So Cy and Lorelei went to get something to eat.

"Cy, you're doing great!" Lorelei said as they were having their meal. "Just one more fight and we will win the tournament!" After they ate, they walked around the tournament grounds. They met up with Pike and his creator. No one spoke, as they passed each other, but both Cy and Pike seemed to stop for an instant and glare at each other.

Ellis noticed this as she caught up to the two, . "What's wrong, Cy?" she asked.

He seemed to snap back to reality and said, "It's nothing." And he turned back to look at Pike. *This next fight is going to be real interesting,* he said to himself.."

When it was time for the match, Cy and the others hadn't arrived at the arena yet. The ref called out, "If Cy isn't here in the next five minutes, he will be disqualified!"

Torok laughed at this as he said, "Why not go ahead and decide the winner for us now? It seems that they chickened out— like I knew they would! Nothing can stand up against my great creation."

But, just then, Cy jumped down from the top of the stadium and said, "Sorry we're late we. We had some communications to take care of, —we had to let our friends know about the match."

Torok laughed again saying, "It doesn't matter! My great creation will tare you apart either way."

"Is that so?" Lorelei said as she and Ellis walked over to him.

"Yes! And, after he wins, I will be known as the greatest scientist in the universe!

"We'll see about that," Lorelei told him.

As the match was about to begin.

Cy assumed his fighting stance, watching as Pike just stood in one spot with his arms crossed like as if the fight didn't matter at all. Cy was almost insulted by this. As soon as the ref rang the ball bell, to go Cy decided he, might as well start it big. He ran at his opponent and punched once … then twice … Pike didn't even try to block.

Cy backed off with an angry look saying. "I know you're fast enough to block those punches." Pike smiled at this. "It's because those punches of mine aren't strong enough to hurt you, isn't it?" Cy asked.

"Well," …" Pike said as he shrugged his shoulders.

"Well, you'd better block when I start using my real strength," Cy told him.

Then as Pike yelled out, "This isn't a game!" And he punched the Cy back onto the corner of the ring.

Cy looked up in time to see Pike's wrist flip back to reveal a cannon. Pike fired a blast that almost hit Cy, but he jumped out of the way as the blast flew by the him. Cy, then used his shotgun blast, but Pike jumped out of the way. Nether one of them realized that their projectiles had turned and followed them until both looked back and saw their blasts aimed right back at them. They both shot skyward, and with the beams followed.

Both Cy and Pike flew around the arena until they flew right at each other. They shot straight up as both of their blasts hit each other beneath them blowing up in , which caused a massive explosion.

Ellis and Lorelei both wondered if Cy was all right, but, when they started to see explosions erupt in the sky, they knew that he was still fighting Pike with everything he had. But, when Cy came crashing down from the sky, they panicked, and Torok laughed thinking that his greatest work had won the battle. When he saw Pike flying down after him he knew he had this fight in the bag.

Cy crashed hard into the middle of the ring. He jumped out of the way just in time to avoid Pike slamming down into the ground. Cy shook off the impact, and couldn't help but laugh. It had taken this entire tournament, he found a real match—in his the last fight. Pike did a half smile as he was thinking the same thing.

The Super Cyborg started to focus the power that resided in his body. The metal of his cybernetics flashed gold twice before it he gained his Super Cyborg mode.

Pike had never seen such a transformation, and Torok had never seen metal change color on a whim like that. He leaned over to ask asked Lorelei, "What's going on?"

She laughed and said, "He has now transformed into a true Super Cyborg."

"What's that mean?" the confused man asked.

"It's nothing really … only that his speed, power, and abilities have become ten times more sensational than before."

"It can't be!" Torok said as he looked back to the at Cy, who now was surrounded by a golden glow around him that made him look almost unstoppable.

Torok turned back to Lorelei. His smile increased, but he shook his head and said, "It doesn't matter. Pike still has not used his full power yet either."

"We shall see," Lorelei finished with a, returning his smile.

Cy was ready to go, but Pike started to laugh, .

"What was so funny?" Cy asked.

"It finally happened! A warrior has come to match my power!" Pike told him, and then his body transformed too. But his transformation was more mechanical than Cy's. When it was done, he looked a lot like some kind of robotic animal—but none that Cy had ever seen.

It stood up right and had long metal claws and teeth. As the cyber beast stepped forward, Cy took a step back. When the beast opened its mouth, it fired a beam that hit Cy dead on and nearly blew him out of the ring. The back wash of the blast ran through, the stadium and blew away most of the people in the stands.

As things settled down, Pike had thought that he had beaten the Cy. But then Cy yelled out, *"Screaming Bullet!"* Cy jumped up after him.

They both slammed into a mid air battle that was more intense than their previous fight. The whole stadium was being lit up by the power they were both generating. The people, as they staggered back to their seats in the stadium roared their excitement. They had not seen a fight this exciting since "Shark Bait" had fought in the Universal tournament all those years ago.

Lorelei and Ellis seemed just as excited as the rest of the people in the stadium seats, but Torok was starting to get a little nervous. He had never seen a fighter like this Super Cyborg. His creation had never had a fight last this long before.

Cy and Pike were fighting hard, but this fight was different from Cy's other fights. This time, he wasn't fighting for his life. This was a fight between real warriors who fight for the sere sheer enjoyment of it. As the fight continued, Cy was hit hard and was sent spiraling down to the arena.

He crashed right in the middle of the ring again. As he slowly got up and tried to steady himself, he realized that the fight had taken its toll on him, and the crash had roughed him up pretty badly.

Pike landed and said, "Now it's time to finish this fight!" Cy watched as the monster's mouth opened *his mouth opened and started to charge his attack, "Come on, Chris,"* Cy thought to himself, *"you have to find a weakness in this attack! ,*As Cy watched as Pike get ready to fire the attack, he saw his opening. He stood tough, ready to strike. Just as Pike fired his attack, something unusual happened. The beam went right through Cy, and he vanished in a blur. Pike looked around, stunned.

"I'm right here!" Cy yelled out form the left side of Pike. Cy fired his screaming bullet, and Pike was blown out of the ring. He crashed into the wall surrounded the stadium.

The ref yelled out, "Ring out!" He climbed out of a hole he had been hiding in since the fight had gone airborne. T, decreed the Super Cyborg the winner of the tournament.

Cy raised his arms in the air in victory, but, as he stepped off out of the ring, he walked over to Pike and helped him up and said, "That was a great fight. We should do it again sometime."

"Yeah, we should," Pike said as he got up. "But I have one question—how did you know I was blind on that side?"

"You see once I see a particular technique I can usually see a weak point like that, I can usually find a way to use it to my advantage. Like my Sansei used to say, 'A warrior is not bound by a single technique.'"

Pike thought of about this as he said, "Truly, you are a great fighter." Then he turned and to walk away. "I'll keep training and get you the next time," he finished.

Torcok about had a heart attack when he saw his greatest cyborg get blown away. He never thought in a million years that his cyborg could be beaten like that.

Lorelei yelled out. "He won! He won!" As Torok walked by, she turned to him and said. "Well, it looks like I won our bet."

"I'll forward the funds I owe you through the space network," Torcok said, and turned to walk away.

Lorelei yelled out, "You had better not back out! Because, if you do, I'll get my Cy after you!" The man cringed when he heard this, but kept going.

When they left the tournament, they stopped at a neighboring planet so Lorelei could purchase the parts and elements she needed for her project. Then they headed back to their planet Gem for a well well-deserved rest.

CHAPTER 39

It had been three years now since the Super Cyborg had left his family. And a lot had changed during that time. For starters, his sister Salina had found a boyfriend. When she told her boyfriend about Chris, she made him promised that, when he returned, that he would not, give him away.

One day, while Angela was working in her garden, she heard something out in the neighboring field. When she ran out there, she could feel something large flying down to the earth she could feel some hot air currents, but she couldn't see anything. But, when she saw the ground cave in as if something large had landed on it, she knew that her nephew had returned.

She watched as a door seemed to open in thin air and the cyborg walked out of the invisible ship along with a dozen girls, including his daughter Maylu, who had just turned four years old and was happily walking right next to her father.

Angela realized something, none of them didn't seemed any older than when they left. It was as if time had stopped for them when they left, but at that moment she didn't care.

"Hi, aunty! We're back!" Cy said as he stood in front of her. When she didn't seem to notice him, he asked, "Are you all right?"

She just happily yelled out, "I'm just glad your back!" And she hugged him as hard as she could.

After they had settled in and told the story of all that had happened on their trip, Cy told his aunt and uncle that, sense they were still wanted, by the government for crimes they didn't commit, that he couldn't stay with them for long. "But, Sam has a nice place all set up for us somewhere. I just can't tell you where it was is. I don't want to risk putting all of you in danger."

The family all understood, but asked him to at least keep in touch as he had done when he was gathering the girls from around the world. Cy agreed, but there was one thing that was bugging his family—why hadn't he aged any.? So they asked him to explain.

"I was wondering that myself," he stated. "But the Supreme Elder of on the planet Gem told me that it is the metal that I'm made of and the fact that so much of my body is now cybernetic. In other words, the girls and I will never get any older than what we are now."

Will and Angela, we're shocked at first, but thought of this as a good thing. But Salina, didn't like the idea that he was never going to get any older, because it meant that he was going to live a lot longer than she was.

When it was time for all of them to leave, Will and Angela were sad at having to see him leave again, it was like saying good-bye to their nephew all over again. They did know that he was going to be all right because, he had so many people to watch over him.

They watched as the ship lifted off again, to parts unknown.

After a not-so-long journey, Sam yelled out, "We're here!" Cy and the girls looked out there windows. What they saw they could barely believe. There was a huge flying island with one large building on it. Sam said, "Minawa was always one to plan ahead. This place was made with the latest in antigravity technologies."

"This is amazing!" Rebecca said.

Destiny said, "It's our own private place! We'll be save safe from anybody who might try to attack us."

They all liked the idea of being safe, but the first thing the girls wanted to do before they settled on the floating island though was hit the nearest mall! They had, after all, been being gone for three years! They needed to check out the latest fashions before they got settled into there their new home. Cy finally gave in to them and told Sam to find a place to set down near a city and let them have a little fun. In fact, he decided to join them.

After Sam carefully landed them on the outskirts of a city, they hit one of the biggest malls they could had ever seen. Kim, Sam, Jennifer, Destiny, Rebecca, April, and Megan were standing in line to see a movie, but Melissa, Victoria, Kate, and Beth, along with Cy and Maylu, went shopping for clothes. Cy, though, was not enjoying himself as he watched the girls look at clothes. It was a good thing that Sam gave had given them all plenty of money, but Cy never asked where she got so much had come from. Right now, though, he was wishing that he had stayed with Ashley and Sakura, who had stayed behind with Ellis to watch the ship. He was left carrying all the bags, and, with so many of the girls in the shopping frenzy, it was quit a lot! The girls had helped Maylu pick out some clothes too, and, when she spied a doll in a toyshop window, she could not resist getting it because she had never had even seen one before.

After the shopping, they met up with the other girls after their movie in the food court, where they were enjoying a good meal and talked about everything they'd seen. But, little did they all know that someone was looking for them.

A few miles from the mall, three cybernetic looking men were walking straight down the street. One was large—at least eight feet tall,—and looked more robotic than the others. One wore, a helmet that covered his whole face. To the point, you could not see his face, the third one looked almost human expect except his arms and legs where looked like coils tightly bound together to form his limbs..

The three walked on, through anything that stood in their way. They walked right through buildings as if they were nothing. And, as they walked through the streets, several cars crashed in front of them. A, police car, screeched around a corner, and headed toward the three men, but the one wearing the helmet pointed his hand at the car and fired a light beam that cut the vehicle right down the middle. The halves of the car crashed into opposite sides of the street.

As they these men approached the mall, the big guy asked the one wearing the helmet, "Are the ones we're looking for in there?"

"Wait a minute. I'll check," said helmet. Lights started to flashed around his helmet as he scanned the building. And then he saw the cyborg they were after in the middle of the mall. "Bingo!" he said.

Cy had just finished his third whole pizza, and was spinning the pie plate, around and asking the nearest waitress if they had free refills. Sam nudged Maylu, who then turned to her father and said in her four-year- old way, "We shouldn't yell in a place like this, Daddy."

Just then, the three men made it to the level right under where Cy and the others were. The one with the coil bound limbs said, "It's time for us to have our revenge on that worthless piece of trash! Let's take him down, Spectral!" he yelled out to the cyborg with the helmet.

"With pleasure." Then he turned to the other cyborg and said, "Coils, let's do this!" And as a beam started to power up form from Spectral's helmet.

Cy and the others suddenly felt the whole place start to shake. "Either I've had too much coffee or the room is shaking," April blurted out.

Cy then yelled out, "Megan, shields!"

More than half the building blew up in a fiery explosion. Cy and, the cyborg's all flew out of the explosion in a shield bubble. They managed to save some of the other people in their shield as well. Victoria using her powers flew them all away from the site of the explosion.

Cy flew back to the building to see if he could find out what had caused the explosion, but he couldn't see anything that might of caused it. But, suddenly, from the bubble, Jennifer then yelled, "Look out!" Cy turned to her and then back to the building as he saw a glow coming from something—or someone. He, powering up, realizing someone was there.

A beam fired at him, he moved out of the way before it hit him. He turned to Victoria, who was still holding the bubble full of the people as well as the other girls. "Get everyone to safety! I'll handle this!" Victoria tried to say something, but Cy yelled, "Go!!!"

She just turned and flew off. Maylu yelled out to her father, "Be careful!"

Cy turned to back to the building, as three men broke out of the building rubble and flew after him. As they then stopped high in the sky, he looked them over he couldn't help but notice something familiar about these guys, but he couldn't place it. He just knew, these guys from somewhere.

"Who are you guys anyway?" Cy asked?"

"You don't recognize us, do you?" the big guy said. "The name's Megaton. And these guys are Spectral and Coils." Megaton then he pointed behind Cy. "The two behind you are Shriek and Gatling." Cy turned to see two other cyborg's standing on a building near by. One looked as if he was wearing strange armor with unusual devices on his hands. The other had two large gating Gatling guns on his arms and missile launchers on his shoulders and back. But, even after Cy learned their names, Cy could not place where he had seen these guys before.

"Well, if you can't remember us, then we will tell you!" said Spectral. "You killed us in that building four years ago!"

Then it hit Cy—these guys were five of the six men that attacked Minawa and blown him up those four years ago. The thought of this brought back memories that enraged him. *Who, would go to the trouble of rebuilding scum like them?*

"I beat you all once," Cy yelled at them, "and I can do it again! But weren't there six of you guys?" Cy asked.

"There *are* six," Megaton told him. "He'll be along shortly."

"But first we get to have our fun with you," Gatling said as he fired dozens of missiles at Cy from his shoulder launchers at him.

Cy managed to dodge each one, but he was hit in the back by one of Spectra's light beams. Then Megaton slammed him straight through three buildings. Cy ended up embedded in the wall of the third building. He looked up just in time to see Shriek about to let loose with a sound blast, but, to Cy's surprise, his enemy was suddenly hard by a gravity wave, that sent him flying off the building and crashing into a car below.

Shriek glared up at the girl who had hit him. He scanned her to see which one of the 12 twelve cyborg's she was. He found her to be the one that was code named Gravity. He grinned as he fired a sound blast from his hands that sent him flying back to the top of the building.

"You know, girl, we don't have to fight," Shriek told her. "We just wont want *him*!" And he pointed to the Cy, who was pulling himself free of the building.

"In that case," said Victoria, you've got to get through me, if you wont want him."

"And you've got to get through me," another voice said.

"And me too," said another.

"And don't dare forget me!" said yet another, as all the cyborg girls all said one by one as the rest of them landed on different building tops, around the five enemy cyborgs men..

The Super Cyborg looked up around at the girls, and asked, "Are the people okay?"

Jennifer said, "They're fine, but who are these guys?"

"They're five of the six men who tried to kidnapped Minawa but blew themselves and me up!" Cy told her. When the others heard this, they turned back to the men ready to fight. But then they heard a new voice say: "If you think that your girls can take my boys, then you're crazier than you look, boy."

Cy and the girls looked to the sky and a saw a man fly down. He didn't look as mechanical as the others. In fact, he looked almost like as if he belonged on a farm, wearing those overalls.

"Even if your so-called boys are strong," Cy stated, "we still outnumber you thirteen to six. And, if you think that thirteen is an unlucky number, then you hadn't faced us yet, you robotic redneck."

"We'll see, boy, … we'll see," the leader of the other five stated. "You're going to find out that six is your unlucky number! You will not beat us again! I am Mondo, the leader of, the Insidious Six! Mondo go get 'them, boys!" Mondo yelled out in his country tone.

"Split up, girls!" Cy yelled out, . "Let them come to you!" The girls scattered into the city in all directions in the city , leaving the Super Cyborg to face Mondo.

The girls split into groups of two, all except Rebecca who was off by herself., Kim and Kate were running down an alley, wondering if it was a good idea to split up. But they trusted Cy's judgment. Suddenly, Coils, jumped down from the a roof top and landed in front of them. The girls jumped back in surprise.

"How are you ladies today?" Coils asked smiling. "Fine, I hope." Coils stated with a smile.

As the girls got ready to fight, Coils just raised his arms up. The two didn't know what to think until he threw his arms down again, and both of his arms split into dozens of tentacles. The cyborg looked like a mechanical squid.

"This might be a little bit harder than we thought," Kate stated with a shaky voice, not wanting to even think what the guy could do to with all those tentacles.

"Don't worry," said Kim. "We can take this over grown squid!"

Jennifer and Victoria had just run into Spectral. And as Jennifer scanned him, she noticed that he didn't have a face at all under that helmet. Victoria asked, "What do you see?"

"This guy doesn't have a real face," she said in a surprised voice. "The helmet is his face!"

"That's right, girls," Spectral said. "You can thank that son of a bitch cyborg friend of yours for that."

"That's funny," Victoria said, "because Cy told us that the guy was a coward who tried to run after he saw his buddies get their butts kicked."

Hearing this made Spectral furious. He charged the light beam cannons in his arms and fired them. Jennifer, though, fired her eye beams at the same time. The beams hit in a stalemate; their there beams were even.

Beth and Melissa were just suddenly hit hard. The force of the blow nearly falling plunged them into, the river that ran through the city. The two girls looked at their opponent just and right as they did he fired off another sonic blast. But, this time, Melissa made an ice shield. Unfortunately, it didn't hold up , against Shriek's sonic blast. The ice shattered, knocking the two girls into the river.

April and Megan were having a hard time against Gatling. Even with Megan's shields at their max, she could barely hold off the endless barrage of missiles and bullets he was firing at them. The guy would not let up, and the mechanical beast was laughing at their desperation.

"What do we do, April?" Megan yelled, still holding back the barrage. "I can't hold him back forever!"

"If I knew what to do," answered April, " do you think I would be in this shield with you? I mean, look at this guy! He's a walking tank! He's probably got more missiles than we have ideas."

With Gatling firing down on them, they didn't think they would ever … get out of this until April thought of something. "Megan, do you think you could hold the shield while I'll take us both into the air?" she asked.

"That shouldn't be too much of a problem." Megan said. April then changed herself into a large bird and grabbed Megan and flew into the air. Gatling kept firing at them as they took to the air, but now it was harder for him to get a lock on them because they where moving to so fast now.

Rebecca walked alone through the street thinking that she should of have stayed with some of the others instead of going off by herself.

Right as she was thinking about this, something hit her hard sending her flying into the side of a building and out the other side. As she dug herself out, she heard someone with a very deep voice say, "Oh, how I hate fighting women!, '"

Rebecca, jumped out of the rubble. "You think just because I'm a woman you think you can beat me that easily? Well, let me tell you, a little dynamite goes a long way!"

She yelled out to the eight -foot giant that now towered over her.

Megaton laughed at the girl thinking. "There's no way you could take me on by yourself!" To prove that he meant business, he slammed both of his fists down on her. The ground under Rebecca's feet smashed in. To Megaton's apparent surprise, she was holding his fists back.

"You still think this is going to be easy, big guy?" Rebecca roared out as she started to pull up both his fists with apparent ease.

"Actually, I did!" he roared, as he pulled back his fists and swept under her. He grabbed her leg and swung the girl upside down.

Megaton laughed at her attempt to get free asking, "what do you think of this."

Rebecca looked crossly at the giant, "Oh yeah? Well hows this!" She swung back and then kicked, his elbow, making him drop her. The instant she hit the ground, she jumped at him, punching him in the groin, causing him to drop to his knees in pain.

"Ha! You want small? That was probably the smallest target I ever hit! I was lucky I hit it at all! 'You're, not so, big guy!" Rebecca laughed.

Megaton stood back up furious at her comment as she shot forward sending a spin kick at Megaton. She got him twice in the face before he fell to the ground.

The two beam attacks from Jennifer and Spectral had fired were still evenly matched, until, suddenly, Spectral used his helmet again firing another beam. This beam came from his whole face, forcing Jennifer jump out of the way. "You can fire beams from your face too?" she shrieked.

"What do you think of that, ladies?" he said as he fired at both the girls. As the blasts came at them, Victoria grabbed Jennifer and took them both into the air. But right when she did Spectral took to the air as well firing blast after blast at them. Finally, when he fired an extra large beam, it looked as if the two girls had had it. But they were all amazed when a large fireball knocked the beam out of the way.

Spectral looked around to find out who had introduced the fireball. Suddenly, a firry beam of light shot up from the ground in between Spectral and the two girls.

They all watched Ashley as she landed with her arms crossed. Spectral seemed to like the idea of another player in this game, —until Ashley turned to Victoria and Jennifer and said, with a wink. "Your fighting up till now has been pitiful. Cy would be very disappointed in the two of you."

"Hey, give us a break! This guy is tough!" Jennifer told Firebomb Ashley. "But thanks for the save, Ashley. We could use some help, were not much of fighter like you are."

Ashley turned back to their opponent, gave him a half smile, and as she got into her fighting stance. "That is true," she said.

Spectral thought that this girl most must be, crazy to think that she could beat him alone. To prove it, he shot over to her in a flash and began fighting throwing punches at the girl at incredible speeds. But the cyborg girl blocked each punch as if he was standing still.

At the same time, April was still in the form of a giant bird, holding Megan who still had her shield around them as Gatling fired everything he had at them. The girls knew they had to think of something or this guy was just going to wear them down. That"s when Megan tried something. While still holding the shield with one hand, she used the other to make a shield disk in the other. "April, can you fly us in a quick pass by Gatling?"

"Sure!" She nodded her head as she shot forward. And as they flew by Gatling, Megan throw the disk at him. The disk cut into his thigh. He fell to one knee as he roared in pain and fired a barrage of missiles every which way in a mad rage.

"You two can't avoid my power forever!" Gatling roared out to the female cyborg's as he stood back up watching them fly skyward.

"April," Megan asked, "do you have enough, left for a power dive?"

"I do, why?"

"Drop me then!" Megan yelled, .

April then nodded as she figured out what Megan was thinking. She let go of Megan.

Megan dove straight at Gatling, as he fired at her shields. When she was about to hit him, April shot under Megan, grabbed her, and the two shot past the cyborg's guns, cutting them off his arms.

"You little bitches!" Gatling cursed. "Look what you've done!" He kicked at the broken guns. "You're going to pay for this!" And he opened all of his missiles ports. Hundreds of missiles shot out of him and came screaming toward the girls. April flew as fast as she could with Megan holding the shields up around them, but, with so many missiles being fired, it was only a matter of time before they were struck down.

Beth and Melissa tried to get out of the river, but every time they tried, Shriek fired another blast of sound across the water, making them jump back into the water. Beth was able to handle underwater travel, but Melissa wasn't made for underwater combat and was having difficulty. As Melissa began once again was running out of air, Beth had an idea. She then motioned for her to make a barrier of ice to hold air. So, Melissa in made a large dome of ice and both girls came out of the water. Gasping, Melissa was catching her breath she asked, "What are we going to do?" She knew that ice barrier wasn't going to hold for long.

Beth said, "If we can get him in the water, my powers might be enough to stop him." Aqua stated, "His sonic waves will be muffled in the water— he might not be able to make a direct hit."

"Not a bad plan," said Melissa, " but how do we get that boom box with an attitude into the water?" Melissa exclaimed, Beth was about to explain her plain when the wall of the ice dome came down upon them.

Beth and Melissa both jumped into the water to escape the blast, but they still knew they had to get Shriek into the water with them., Beth had figured out how to do it. She motioned to Melissa to shoot an ice beam at her beam of water. When they fired the stream of water and ice at Shriek, it nearly took him out, but he was forced to the edge of the river, which gave Beth the perfect opportunity to strike. She spun the water around her making a tornado. As the power of the tornado expanded, it finally forced Shriek into the water. Now that he was underwater, Beth knew she had him.

Kim and Kate had just watched a cyborg turn, from man to squid-man. Long tentacles came out of Coil's arms and legs, that lashed at the girls like mad. Kim jumped out of the way as they came down at her, and Kate shot around as fast as she could to avoiding the metallic tentacles, they which turned out to be faster than even ,Kate herself. One of the tentacles grabbed her by the leg, and she fell to the ground. Coils dragged her to him rapping his coils around her crushing her.

To save her friend, Kim tried to absorb the strength of the bricks of the walls making her body look like the bricks of the nearby buildings.

She slammed into Coils as hard as she could, but all she hit was the other side of the wall as Coils moved up in the air. He used his tentacles to grip to the wall as he climbed. The second Kim was up again, Coils grabbed her too and started to crush her. Things did look too good for Kim and Kate.

The other girls were also all in a fix. The five cyborgs had the girls where they wanted them. Shriek had proven that, even in the water, he was still stronger than the two girls. To top it off, he could breath under the water! Gatling had managed to get April and Megan back to the ground as his missiles fired on and on.

Spectral had, with ease, managed to strike down Ashley, Victoria, and Jennifer to the ground with his power over the light. He simply blinded them leaving them helpless. And Rebecca was up against a wall, —literally. Megaton, after Rebecca had struck him, had shot forward and, with one hand, grabbed her and slamming her against a wall, crushing her. It appeared that the five cyborgs (of the Insidious Six) were going to finally beat the cyborg girls.

Cy had been fighting Mondo—leader of the Insidious Six—the entire time. He started to feel that his Gems where in trouble, and he knew he had to do something or they would be finished.

"What's the matter, boy?" Mondo laughed. "You know those little girls of yours, are in a tight spot?"

"Yeah, they are," Cy stated. "So it's time for me to stop fooling around with you and your men!" As Cy roared out at his enemy, his metal turned gold as his power rose And at the same time, the girls felt his power too. As Cy transformed, all the girls' started to glow. The pupils of their eyes changed in to resemble those of a cats, and all of their powers seemed to increase in proportion as Cy's powers increased. Simultaneously, the girls yelled out as they felt their new power. They all broke loose from each one of their opponents, and began to fight harder than ever before.

Mondo wasn't impressed by Cy's transformation. He just fought on and then blasted Cy into under ground. Then he shot down after him. The ground shook as the two fought under ground until Cy was hit out of the ground back to the surface, with Mondo right behind him.

Cy was able to stop himself right as Mondo got to him. Cy hit with the force of an 8.0 earthquake.

Kate's powers increased so much that it enabled her to vibrate her body until it metal parts got so hot that Coils had to let go of her to keep his tentacles from melting. But he still had Kim—or so he thought. Kim absorbed the properties of his metal coils. She was able to squeeze Coil's tentacles so hard he had to let go, and she landed safely on the ground.

As soon as Kite Kate hit the ground, she saw Kim go escape from his coils, and she knew what to do. Coils was about to make his move on her when she vanished in a flash. He looked around until, she ran around him, tying him up in a flash with his own coils. He yelled out, "I'll get you for this! This won't hold me forever!"

"I know, you over grown squid!" Kate blurted out. "But it will hold you long enough for Kim to do her thing!" She then pointed to the wall of the building next to them, which looked as if it was alive.

As the walls at ether side of him started to move, Coils yelled out, "Stop!" But the walls continued to move until it had completely enfolded Coils crushing him flat in an explosion of fire.

Kim came out of the ground to see her handy work. She turned to Kate and said, "Not bad, partner."

"Not bad, yourself.," Kate stated.

Beth swam around Shriek, trapping him in the her whirlpool. Melissa took a deep breath, and dived down swimming over, and fired an ice beam that froze him in a large block of ice that crashed into the water. When the ice block floated to the surface, and Beth swam at it full speed, shattering the ice—along with Shriek—into a thousand pieces.

Still underwater and exhausted, Melissa could not hold her breath any more. She tried to make it to the surface, of the river but the current was too strong. She was to deep she started to fall under, but Beth grabbed her swimming the rest of the way, when they hit the surface. Beth yelled out, "Woo! That was some party, a Melissa!"

Melissa gave her friend a dirty look, and just said, "Shut up," as she coughed up some water.

Spectral had taken Jennifer and Victoria down in one shot. As Ashley prepared to put an end to the situation, she watched how cocky this guy was, as he dusted himself off form taken down two of her friends.

Ashley focused her flame into her right hand until it started to glow red hot. Then she threw it straight at Spectral. It was obvious that he didn't seem to think that she could stop him. He shot forward to meet her attack.

When they struck, it looked like as if Ashley got hit the hardest as she crashed on into the top of a building. She looked back up at Spectral as she tried to get up. He was laughing at her pain as she tried to get up. But, just right then, his head fell off! He caught it as he stated.

"Ooooch *shit!*" His body then blew up., Victoria and, Jennifer saw this and Ashley cheered as they watched the bits of Spectral fall to the ground. "Jerk-off," said Victoria.

April was still in the form of a giant bird. As she flew up with Megan around Gatling, Megan kept firing disks at him. Gatling fired everything he had back at them, but the shields blocked every shot. It was as if the shields had minds of there their own. The two girls flew around Gatling like lighting! But the girls' shots seemed to be missing their mark.

"Ha! you You misted me!." Gatling yelled out."

"You just wait!" April called out. And, right then, all of Gatling's guns fell off in hundreds of pieces. He then mat the girls as his vision started to blur. As he started to fall apart. The last thing he said was. "Stupid little girls." And then he blew up.

April landed and shed her bird disguise. Megan looked at what was left of Gatling. The girls shared an exuberant high five as each uttered an enthusiastic "Yes!"

Megaton was still crushing Rebecca up against a wall. She by screamed out as loud as she could, but she could feel her body giving way.

"Give it up, little girl," taunted Megaton. "You don't stand a chance against me! My strength is greater! And, besides, there is no way that I'm going to be beaten by an underdeveloped woman."

That was too much for Rebecca to handle. She grabbed Megaton's large hand that was holding her throat and pulled back his fingers until they snapped off. Megaton reared back holding the now stubs that remained. He watched mechanical fluid and oil squirt from the holes where his fingers had been.

Megaton stepped back from the girl and watched her throw his fingers away into the dark. The girl looked at him crossly with her eyes glowing like fire.

"Does it make you feel big for making fun of me?" Rebecca yelled out to him. "It's, not my fault that I stopped growing! I'm a cyborg, but there is one thing that you don't understand."

"And what is that, little girl?" Megaton asked as he stood ready to take her down.

"That I am, the strongest of all the cyborg's. And you should know that I am a force not to be reckoned with!"

Rebecca finished as she ran at Megaton. He just said, "We'll see, little one." And he ran at her as well.

They both ran at top speed. It looked as if Megaton would run right over Rebecca, but, right as she was about to be hit, she jumped forward right at Megaton's chest. She burst right through him leaving a gaping hole in his chest.

She skidded to a stop spun around to a stop and stood up as Megaton turned to her. He looked down at the hole in his chest, then he looked back up at her and growled. He ran at her again. She didn't move as he roared out, "You'll pay for this!" And right as he came within an inch of her, he blew up. Parts of his body, flew around her, but she didn't move. She grinned, as his head rolled over to her. He opened his eyes.

"I'm going to get you for this, you little bitch! No one makes a fool of Megaton!!" he yelled.

out to her "Whatever." Force Rebecca shrugged as she jumped in the air, and came down fist first, and crushed his head.

Mondo was still fighting with Cy. Suddenly, someone came up and grabbed Mondo's legs. Cy looked down and saw Sakura. "What's up?" she said as she spun Mondo around and threw him off to the side.

Mondo finally stopped himself and flew back up saying. "This fight doesn't concern you! If you want to live, you had better, high tail it out of here."

"Same old unhealthy obsession, right, Cy?" Sakura stated. The Super Cyborg flew next to her, and then the others started to show up. Mondo could see them on the roof tops and in the sky.

Ashley flew to Cy's side and then turned to Mondo saying, "Your buddies where created with inferior craftsmanship, —they didn't have any balls!"

"My Insidious Six have been destroyed?" Mondo nearly roared. Then, as he started to laugh in an insane way. Parts of his fallen comrades started appeared out of nowhere and flew to him and attached themselves to him, making him bigger and giving him the powers of his fallen cyborg subordinates. Before everyone's eyes, Mondo was turning into, a super version of himself. "Now you will face Super Mondo, the perfect form of the Insidious Six," he yelled.

Cy and the girls all flew back a bit in shock, but Ashley regained her composure and flew right at Mondo. As she did, Cy yelled out, "Wait!"

But she told him, "I've got this guy!" She punched, Mondo, but he didn't even move.

"What the— …?" Ashley started punching him again and again. But all her effort was in vain. Finally, she looked up at him, fear and shock on her face.

Mondo grabbed the girl and threw her straight to ground at top speed. When Melissa saw this, she jumped down to help her sister, but right when she got near Super Mondo fired a light beam that sent her flying into a building.

Mondo then slammed down on Ashley slamming her into the ground. Sakura then shot down kicked Super Mondo in the head, but it didn't even faze him. She kicked and punched him again and again, but he was too strong. Super Mondo then grabbed her with the coils that where now attached to his back and threw her out of the way. He raised his arms up and fired hundreds of missiles, witch took out the other girls easily.

Cy flew down in a rage. He had transformed to his Super Cyborg form, but still even in that form, his punches had little or no effect on Super Mondo.

He kicked at Super Mondo, but Mondo grabbed Cy's leg in mid kick, punched him in the groin. Cy roared, out but then the behemoth slammed him to the ground. Cy back flipped to get away, but, in a millisecond, Super Mondo was on him. He grabbed his head and threw him into the air. As Cy flew, Super Mondo punched and kicked him before he even hit the ground.

Mondo then blasted Cy hard. Together, they crashed right into a scrap heap. "This is the perfect place for your demise," Mondo stated. Cy just lay there knowing he was about to die.

Through his pain, Cy heard a voice in his head. "Call to them, Chris." Cy heard a voice in his head say. "Minawa?" Cy said recognizing the voice.

"Tell them to give you their strength!"

Cy didn't know where her voice was coming from, but he knew better than to argue with her. Slowly, he stood up. He tore off what was left of his shirt, for it had been torn to sheds form the last blast, and he called out to the cyborg girls, "This is our last chance, girls!"

Without knowing how, they heard his call. They all pointed their hands to the sky as their power found its way to Cy.

As they did this, Super Mondo was preparing to attack Cy again. Just before he fired, Rebecca came up behind him and, grabbed him, pulled him back, then kicked him into the mid air. He landed against a wall. That didn't stop him, though, for, as soon as he was back on his feet, he shot over and hit Rebecca to the ground and stomped down on her. As he stood up, Super Mondo heard what he thought was a lion's roar. He turned to see Cy's power raging out of control. His metal seemed to be burning with a black flame, but it wasn't hurting him. And that was not even what made Super Mondo take a step back, —it was his eyes! They had turned to cat's eyes. And Cy's teeth had grown out so they were like those of a wild animal.

Cy let out a roared again as the black flame around him became so hot that it melted the metal in the scrap yard heap into a red liquid.

"What do you think you're doing?" Super Mondo yelled out.

But Cy didn't answer. He just issued another deafening roar. The other cyborg's looked up at him. They all thought that he looked monstrous, but they weren't afraid. Super Mondo, however, thought it was like looking into the eyes of the devil himself.

He wasn't going to be stopped by this Super Cyborg, though. Without wasting a second, Super Mondo, shot forward and punched at Cy. But Super Mondo's, fist started to disintegrate from the power

Cy was emanating. This infuriated Super Mondo, as he punched again with his other hand, only to have the same thing happen.

Cy roared out again as he punched, his screaming bullet. This time, the bullet was surrounded by the black flame that seemed to had remained burning around the Super Cyborg. As it hit Super Mondo, he yelled out, "This *can't* be happening!"

Super Mondo's body disintegrated in a flash of black flame. Cy, roared out again as the black flame burned around him. Suddenly, the flame then took on the form of a monstrous black lion. And, on that day, something was awakened—something with monstrous power and killer instinct. Something that none of them could of have believed to be real.

After the power raging in him calmed down, Cy went to gathered up his Gems. They were all unconscious form the power loss, they had suffered. He placed them all gently on a roof top to wait for Samantha to come pick them up.

CHAPTER 40

When Samantha arrived in a small ship, Maylu came running out to her father and gave him a hug. He happily hugged her back as she asked, "Are the others okay?"

He turned to where the others lay, then turned back as he smiled and said, "They well will be fine."

xxx

Meanwhile, in a hidden lab, a scientist and a very large man, whose face stayed in the shadows, could not believe what they had just seen, for they had been monitoring the whole fight.

"Sir, did you see that?" The scientist said to the man in the shadows. "When he called to the other girls, it seemed to make him stronger. But what was that black flame?" the scientist said to the man in the shadows.

"Yes, I saw," said the man. "But, remember, we never intended for those six to win—only to us in assessing the of power of those cyborgs and nothing more. And that they worked well, for now I know that I have nothing to worry about. This time when I fight that cyborg, I will humiliate him in front of, all of those reject cyborg girls. I will make him pay!"

"You are so right, General Bishop."

xxx

Cy had resumed his training at their new home, on a flying island. One afternoon, during a training session, with the girls, Sam came running out of the main building. "We have a big problem.," she called out to everyone.

Megan and Beth looked at each other. "What now?" Megan asked."

"You all have to see this for yourselves," Sam said. "Meet me in the control room." Sam then looked at the girls and asked, "Where's Cy? He has to see this too." But the girls had no idea where he had gone.

"Well, I guess he can see this later," and she ran to the control room. When they all gathered, Sam then sat in front of a a monitor. "I had recorded this a few minutes ago," she said as she pressed a button.

No one could believe who appeared on the screen. It was the general—but he had changed. He was now a cyborg, although he looked more like a robot. He was wearing a long black cape that moved in the wind as he spoke.

"You people knew me as General Jerald Bishop, but, thanks to that cyborg Chris Striker, I have become the thing you see before you, —I am now a soldier, willing to stop his acts of terrorism. Right now, I'm standing in the middle of an arena that I built, here in this open field for one reason. I want to fight the cyborg Chris Striker, in a tournament. I will show the world what will happen if anyone else interferes with me. Here is a little demonstration of my powers."

The cyborg General shot into the sky. The camera changed panned to show a small city. As the cyborg General flew over it, he fired a strange beam into the center of the city. Buildings exploded in a mass of red light. When the light faded, the city was gone.

General Bishop then appeared in front of the camera again. "This is just a sample of my powers. This tournament will begin in five days. Don't start thinking that my actions today are evil. This demonstration was is merely the only way I could think of to lure Chris Striker, the cyborg, and his followers into the open. But, if the cyborg Striker fails to show up, I will not be responsible for my actions. See you in five days, Chris Striker!" The screen then went black.

Samantha looked back to the girls and saw the fear in their eyes. They had just seen what the General did it was just unbelievable, he destroyed a city with one shot. Suddenly, Cy then made himself known to the others as he spoke up from behind them. "Don't worry, it won't come to that," he said, for he had seen the whole thing.

"What do we do, Cy?" Victoria asked.

"We fight!" he responded. "We have five days, and I plan on using those five days to find a way to stop him. This time when I fight him, it will be to the finish."

Hearing this,, made them think that surely Cy could beat the general, but little did they know that Cy knew for a fact that the general was, by far the stronger combatant. But he had a plan; he just hoped that it would work.

xxx

At the arena The general stood like a statue in the middle of it his arena wanting for his match with Striker. He looked to the skies and decided he'd give the people a little going away present because he planned to take control of the planet Earth after he was done with Striker. He felt that the world needed a leader like him. He shot up into the sky and into space to the asteroid belt. Then he blew up several large asteroids and sent them down to Earth where they rained down like fire. Amazingly, they didn't cause no harm to the people. The general watched his handy work. He would be thinking this time he would be the victor.

xxx

Cy in question was sitting in a lotus position remembering that his limits were built into, his body. He knew that, but he had to find a way to get stronger. Suddenly, he detected something. He got up and walked to the edge of the island. Using his enhanced vision, he scanned the surface of Earth and scanned the area, where the general was. He detected a large mass of people heading in that direction.

Jennifer and Ellis, along with some of the others, came up to him. "What are you doing?" asked Ellis.

"There's an army heading right toward the general's location," he told them.

"Are you sure?" Jennifer asked.

Without turning around, he said, "See for yourself." She walked next to him and scanned the surface of Earth. Her sense of vision was even more powerful than his. She could see the army as if they where right next to her. The others wanted to see too, so Ellis told them to hold on. She went over took Jennifer's hand, and, immediately, the others could see what Jennifer was seeing.

General Bishop had just landed back from his trip into space. The army advanced on his position, determined to take him out in revenge for his destruction of all those people in the city he destroyed as an example to Cy. When the general saw the army, coming, he flew out of the arena for he didn't want it damaged.

As he flew, the army commander thought he was running away. But then the general stopped and turned around. The commander gave the signal and they all immediately opened fired, it was a rain of bullets, tank fire, and missiles from jet fighters as they flew overhead.

"To think that I used to work for these fools!" said the general as he flew over, the raging battle. "But now I have the power of an army myself, and I can crush these hopeless fools!" The general easily absorbed all the fire aimed at him.

Cy and the girls watched from their floating island. The whole area was covered in dust and debris. Finally, the commander gave the order to cease fire. He had to yell three more times before the message was acknowledged.

As soon as the soldiers stopped firing and started to calm down, some of the men began to laugh. They thought that there was no way that the general could of survived. But the situation soon became clear to the commander as he looked through some binoculars and saw that the general was very much still alive.

"It can't be!" one of the men said as he, too, saw the general still standing like as if nothing had happened.

The general laughed as he asked, "Is that all you've got?"

The men started to panic. As they and started to run, the general raised his arm up and then pointed it around in an arc around his body, shooting off a beam that eradicated everything in its path. Nothing was left moving or alive.

xxx

Cy let out a lion's roared as he saw this. He slammed both his fists to the ground, making the girls step back from him in fear. Ellis was about to say something to him when he got up and stormed off. When he was out of sight, the girls agreed that it was scary to see he him so angry.

xxx

Sam was in still in her lab when Cy came storming in. He grabbed her arm and said, "We need to talk!" Sam had no idea what was going on.

"What's this all about Cy?" Sam yelled, obviously frightened.

Cy grabbed Sam roughly by both shoulders but then backed down as he slammed both hands on ether side her as he bluntly told her, "Remove my limiters!" he shouted, his face just inches from hers.

Still scared, Sam tried to laugh a bit not to show her feelings on her face. "What limiter?" she asked. "You don't have any limiters."

Cy slammed his fist into the wall next to her. Then he sheepishly pulled his hand out of the hole. "You know what limiters," he said a little more quietly. "The limiters that control the amount of power I can let out at one time."

Sam didn't want to make him any angrier, but she told him, "Those limiters are there for a purpose. They regulate the amount of power that goes through your body. Without them, your internal temperature will keep going up until.." —"

"I know that!" Cy interrupted. "But I have to fight with everything I have at this tournament! I owe it to Minawa to stop the general once and for all!"

Sam lowered her head as she said. "All right. "I'll do it," she said. "But I need Ellis's help—and the process will take at least two days to compete."

"That's fine," Cy said with some relief. "That gives me three days to relax with my Gems till the tournament," ."

At that moment, Sam called Ellis to the lab. Sam told her about Cy's plan. Ellis screamed, "Are you craz— y," " Cy covered her mouth before she could finish.

When Cy let Ellis loose, she said quietly, "Are you crazy? Without your limiters, your power will be mind blowing! But the strain on your body might kill you!"

"Don't you think I know that," he yelled. *"Just do it! Now!"*

Ellis and Sam looked at each other quietly. They both thought that this was a bad idea, but they started work. The process required that Cy be anesthetized. Just before they put Cy under, he made them both promise not to tell the others about what they were doing. They didn't want to agree at first, but, in the end, they gave in and promised that they wouldn't say anything.

As the next two days passed, the others were only told that Cy was going through a process that would make him stronger, . When he finally came out of Sam's lab and greeted the girls, he looked a little different to the girls, but they just thought that meant that he was stronger, so they didn't think much into of it. "Let's go have some fun, girls," he said. "We have three whole days before this tournament of the Ggeneral's begins, so let's live it up."

This change in his attitude freaked some of the girls out, but the others thought it was a great idea. They hadn't had any fun for a while, having been being stuck on this boring island for so long.

Cy smiled and said, "The sky's the limit! I will take you a anywhere you all want to go I will take you." Beth was the first to yell out out—as usual— "The beach!"

Ashley agreed and said . "The beach sounded sounds like a great idea! The last time we went we were interrupted by all those women!"

The others heard Ashley they agreed that on their first day of fun should be at the beach—and this time they would not be bothered by any interlopers! As soon as they had gathered a few things, they where off on their three-day adventure.

Thanks to Samantha, once again they were all going to have a private beach in Florida all to there selves. This so Cy would not have to hide even though he was still wanted by the government for the murder of Minawa witch he was innocent of.

Upon arriving at a beach, Beth ran straight to the water and splashed under the waves. When she came up, she yelled out that the water was great. Some of the other girls ran down to the water and splashed in too. Cy and the rest of the girls just walked down to spread their blankets at the edge of the water. Cy thought about the chaos they had encountered and set up the beach blanket like he did last time they'd been at the beach. *But,* he thought to himself, *the last time they we were on a different planet. It should be quieter here.*

Maylu then asked her dad if she could join Beth and the others in the water. Cy said, "Yes, but be sure to stay with others. Be careful now.."

Sakura smiled at Cy seeing how caring he was to his daughter. And after Maylu ran off, Cy lay back on the beach blanket with the girls who hadn't gone into the water. Ellis was one of them. As she looked at Cy, she understood why he was doing this why he was giving them this time to enjoy themselves. It was because she knew deep down that he was going to die in this fight with the general, and was letting them all have this one last time with him before his end.

Right then Victoria broke Ellis out of her thought as she asked her if she was going in the water she then nodded that she would like to join them.

There first day at the beach was uneventful, just filled with fun and relaxation. The next day they decided to go to an amusement park.

xxx

As the general at this time was still standing eagerly awaiting for the day of his tournament, city officials were holding a large a press conference nearby. They were trying to come up with a way to stop the general. Suddenly, a large man burst his way into the room. As the cameras turned to film him, he said, "I will fight the general at his tournament—and I will beat him.

This large stranger had a body that looked like as if it was craved out of marble. To prove himself to be strong enough to accomplish his stated task, he and punched a hole in the brick wall. One of the government officials said, "You may be strong, but the general was able to destroy an entire city by himself!"

The large man laughed and said, "If this general is, in fact, a general, he probably set bombs ahead of time to be ready for the army. All the power that this general has is nothing but show of his military might and nothing more."

"If that is the case," said another official, "then we hope and pray that you can beat him.,"

The first official then said, "I think you might be able to beat the general! What's your name?"

The fighter assumed a strongman posse. "I am the world master of martial arts, Ryan Omit, but you can all call me The Crusher because, I will crush this general like the fool that he is."

xxx

One day before the tournament and, Cy and the girls where out relaxing on a beautiful mountain top having a picnic. Cy and Maylu were having a sparring session as the others watched. Even though Maylu was only four years old, and was not cybernetic, her abilities went beyond her youth.

Jennifer scanned both of them as they sparred and could not believe the levels. It didn't seem right that a little girl who wasn't a cyborg should have so much power. But, coinciding her breeding, she decided she wasn't all that surprised.

Maylu suddenly shocked the girls again when she did a double spin kicked against her father and knocked him to the ground. He looked up a little shocked. He hadn't expected that her level of ability would be so high after only a few lessons.

After she did this Maylu looked at her father. "Did I do something wrong, Dad?" she asked.

"No," said Cy. "You didn't do anything wrong. In fact, your doing great!"

She ran over to her father and gave him a big hug. She was always happy to have such a strong father. And she loved that he was teaching her his fighting style so that she could continue his legacy—and her mother's.

At the end of her lesson, Maylu happily ran to the girls and said, "Did you see me? Did you see me?"

Victoria said, "Yes, I did. You're, going to get to be as strong as your father before you know it!" The four four-year-old, happily hugged Victoria and then went to the others telling them how good she was getting. She shocked her father, however, because she began calling all the girls "mother."

He was about to say something to her, but decided against it. In a way, he realized, all those girls was like mothers to his daughter. They were all helping raise her. He was counting on the fact that they would continue to raise her even if he didn't survive this fight. As he promised himself that he would make sure that he if losses he would take the general with him.

xxx

The general was still standing in the same spot in his arena where he had been for the last five days. He hadn't moved at all since his little adventure into space.

Meanwhile, behind some rocks, a news crew hid. A, reporter spoke at a whisper as his cameraman filmed. "It's almost time for the general's tournament," said the reporter, "and it seems that nobody is going to show up— they're all afraid for their lives." But suddenly, a limousine pulled up next to the reporter. The cameraman focused on the door as the so-called martial arts master exited the vehicle. Crusher yelled out "General your going down" but the General didn't even move.

The Crusher motioned to the news crew to follow him to the ring. The reporter was a little hesitant at first. He was afraid of the general. But he and his camera man slowly moved over to the ring and started to interview the "champion." "It's going to be a piece of cake to beat the general," bragged The Crusher.

XXX

Meanwhile Cy had just put his Super Cyborg shirt on, and then put his black trench coat on over it. It made quite a striking outfit. When he walked out of his room, he was greeted by the girls and, his daughter, "What do you all plan to do?" he asked them.

"We're coming to cheer you on, of course," said Jennifer.

"No," said Cy. "I don't think that's a good idea."

"It's no use arguing," Sam said. And, in the end, Cy had no choice but to let them all go with him.

He then pointed to Victoria in question. "Ready to get us off the ground.?" he asked.

Victoria then saluted like a soldier. Then she focused her powers and everyone who couldn't fly started to left off the ground. Cy watched as his daughter enjoyed being lifted up in the air.

Cy turned to the rest of the company and said, "It's time to go!" And they shot off to the general's tournament.

The Crusher was was in the process of taunting the general. He was accusing the general of being a faker and saying that all his strength was nothing but foolish ticks. But, no matter what The Crusher said, the general did nothing but stand as still as a statue.

Then the reporter and his cameraman, who had been filming this standoff, suddenly caught sight of something coming from the sky. The reporter told his cameraman to get a shot of it, and, as the camera focused on what was coming their way, the cameraman turned to the reporter and said, "You are not going to believe this!"

Everyone in the area started looking up. They saw over a dozen, people flying in the air. Most of them appeared to be young women. As they prepared to land, the reporter asked The Crusher what he thought of what they'd just seen. "It must be some kind of trick or something," The Crusher said, " because it is physically impossible for people to fly."

As the reporter looked at the group, he noticed the cyborg that was wanted by the government for the murder of a scientist. He turned back to The Crusher and told him about Cy and the reward. The Crusher seemed happy to hear that the $1 million bounty was still in effect.

The Crusher pointed as Cy touched down. "Hey, you, cyborg!" yelled The Crusher. "Once I'm done with the general, your going to be next!"

Cy looked at the man. Then he and turned to the others girl cyborgs and his family and asked, "Who is this guy?"

They all just shrugged. But Sam knew. "He's The Crusher— the greatest martial artist of in the world!" he blurted out.

"Ha, this lug is the greatest?" Cy laughed. "His level doesn't even register on my scans!"

The Crusher was about to attack Cy for saying such things about him, but the general yelled out over a loudspeaker from the ring in the arena, "It is time!" The Crusher turned to Cy and said, "That punk general just saved your hide 'cause, right now I have to go put the smack down on him!" He pointed to the general.

As they watched The Crusher and Cy enter the ring, the girls were thinking how much of an idiot this guy was. They figured that the general would knock The Crusher out in less than two seconds.

"So which one of you is going first?" the general called out. Cy was about to step up when The Crusher yelled out, "I will be going first!" And to prove to them that he meant business, he jumped from the ring and, pulled a large rock out of the ground, and crushed it with his bare hands. He was trying show them that they were weak compared to him, but the only response he got from them was confusion.

The reporter tried to tell everyone that the The Crusher was the world's best chance to beat the general, but Cy and the others didn't think that everyone there was working with both oars in the water.

Cy tried to tell The Crusher that, if he challenged the general he was going to get killed, but The Crusher and the reporter just shrugged and didn't pay attention." thinking that he was just crazy.

The general was getting impatient. "The match must begin now!" he yelled. "Which one of of you is going to fight him me first? The Crusher stepped back up onto into the ring and said, "I am going first!"

Everyone watching around the world—for, this battle was televised—the people watching at home were thinking that it was going to be an easy win for The Crusher. They had seen him punch a hole through a brick wall before, and beat many strong opponents.

The Crusher got into his fighting stance. Then the general said. "Let us begin," growled the general. The Crusher ran forward and struck the general right in the head with a single kick, but the general didn't move an inch. The reporter and the camera man and the people watching were just thinking that The Crusher had just moved too fast for the general to block.

The Crusher attacked again with a barrage of punches and kicks, but still it didn't seem to have no effect on the general at all. The Crusher yelled out as he went in for his finishing move. "This is where it ends!" But the general back handed him right out of the ring. The Crusher slammed to the ground.

The spectators stood in shock. If anyone had blinked, he would have missed the strike.

The general turned to the Super Cyborg and said, "Are you ready now, fool? Or do you think that I have to fight another inferior opponent?"

"Why not?" Cy asked. "You seem to be good at bullying the weak, General." Cy said as he stepped into the ring and got ready.

The reporter was freaking out. He had never seen a man get hit that far away before. The Crusher came walking back sore as hell. The reporter saw him he stuck his microphone under the defeated champion's chin. "What happened, champ?" he asked. "That guy threw you like a rag doll."

"That was nothing," said The Crusher. " I just tripped is all,."

The reporter turned back to face the camera, and said, "Folks, The Crusher will get another chance after this next fight is over." Then he turned and the reporter asked The Crusher. "What do you think of this cyborg? Do you think he stands any chance at all?"

The Crusher laughed and said, "This fool is going to be put down in less than a second!" They both turned back to Cy and the general.

As they watched, the general had just shouted, "Go!" And he and Cy flew at each other at incredible speed and slammed into a tussle of punches and kicks that left The Crusher and the reporter—and everyone else watching — in shock.

Cy did a couple of back flips and disappeared. The reporter and The Crusher looked around but, they couldn't find him. When the general disappeared as well they didn't know what to think.

Jennifer was watching the fight. She could see more than the reporter. She noticed that both fighters seemed almost evenly matched, but, right then, the general hit Cy back to the ring. That's when the reporter and spectator could see them again, too. But right when the general looked like he was about to finish Cy off, Cy disappeared and reappeared behind the general. He punched forward but got nothing but air, as the general, too, disappeared momentarily. The battle went on this way for quite some time. They were fighting so fast that it was almost impossible to see them—unless, of course, you were a cyborg. Luckily, for the others they were able to see the fight because they were linked and thanks to the link they shared they could see through Jennifer's eyes.

Cy spun like a tornado right at the general and kicked him hard sending him flying. But stopped himself and shot over in an instant and head butt the general and grabbed him and smashed him back to the arena. The reporter and his camera man saw General Bishop slowly get back up with a half smile on his face as he watched the cyborg landed in the arena. Cy seemed to be enjoying himself just as much as the general was.

"This has been a good fight, cyborg," the general said, " but I think it's time to stop kidding around." The general crossed his arms. Using holograms he split into four images of himself. Each one shot to the four corner of the ring.

As the reporter and The Crusher watched the general do this, and the reporter turned to The Crusher and asked, "How'd he do that?"

"It's a trick using mirrors and stuff," The Crusher stated, trying to act smart.

Megan was listening to the broadcast. "How thick can this guy be?" Megan she said, "It's not a trick, it's science! It's the use of holograms and laser technology to make the holograms solid. But the real question is, can Cy beat four generals at once?"

Cy was smiling as he watched the four generals surround him. He didn't seem to as worried as the girls where. "No way!" he said. "This trick won't work on me!"

"We'll see about that!" One of the generals copies said. And they all attacked at once. It was a furious fight with four against one, but Cy seemed to be holding his own against them. He fought as if they were standing still. He managed to hit each one down. When he throw the last one into a four-way pile up, and then he told Bishop, "Pull yourself together!" Slowly, the general's copies disappeared, leaving only one lying there not moving.

April cheered thinking that Cy had won. Ashley yelled at the girl, "The general's only playing dead. He still has a lot of power left!"

Sakura, who was standing next to Ashley, agreed. "Watch, April," she said, and they all watched as the general stood back up like as if nothing had happened to him.

"I think that was a good enough warm-up, don't you, think Cyborg?" the general stated as he got up, Cy agreed.

The reporter, The Crusher, and the camera man all seemed in shocked that the general considered the fight so far as only a warm-up..

Cy crossed his arms as he started to power up. He roared as his metal turned to golden. He remembered what Sam had told him after he had awakened—about how to unlock his limiters. There was a verbal trigger he had to say to do it. Cy took a deep breath.

"*Heaven's, Gate!*" Cy yelled. His power ramp up more than it ever had before. He was letting out so much energy that he was causing the entire arena to shake. Cy roar as his power shot up. He raised his arms to the sky as the power increased.

Cy's Gems all could not believe what they were seeing. When he was finished powering up, Cy didn't even seem like himself. They knew that his power was mind blowing, and they thought for sure that Cy was going to win easily. But then the general started to power up too, and he seemed even more powerful than the Super Cyborg! In fact, his energy was so great that Megan had to put a shield around all of them so they wouldn't be blown away by the force of the power that the general was releasing.

The reporter and The Crusher looked at both fighters in awe. Both warriors seemed to be glowing with power. One was gold and the other was black.

Cy walked over to the general and stood right in front of him glaring at him.

"So," the general started, "are you ready to continue the game, Cyborg?"

"Bring it on," the Super Cyborg stated, and they both disappeared in a flash. They fought each other with such intensity that the sheer force of their blows shook the whole arena.

As their fight continued, something started to happen—General Bishop seemed to be getting the upper hand. It seemed he was moving faster than Cy. " What's wrong, Cyborg, having trouble keeping up?" the general taunted.

Cy turned around, not expecting this. And, as soon as the fight started up again, Cy started showing the general what he could do as both of them moved faster and faster. Even Jennifer was seeing blurs.

"Don't adjust your TV's," the reporter stated into his microphone as the crew struggled to shoot the two fighters. "These fighters are really moving faster than the human eye can see!" Flashes of light shot around the ring.

General Bishop now maintained the upper hand as he punched Cy at lighting speed. He held Cy to the edge of the ring with one hand, but, right when Bishop raised his hand to strike a finishing blow, Cy vanished in a flash. General Bishop stood ready and waiting for Cy to reappear, but, when Cy did reappear, he caught the general off guard and hit him back. Both warriors vanished, as they were now fighting in the air again at levels that most men can't even fathom.

The reporter and his crew had no idea where the combatants had gone. The arena had gone quiet. Suddenly, The Crusher yelled out, "There they are! There in the broken part of the ring!" As he pointed to the spot, he then said, "It's another one of their tricks! When it's my turn again, I won't fall for such childish tricks!"

The reporter just played along thinking that The Crusher may be right. But when they felt an explosion that shook the ground. The camera man said, "There they are, ... in the air!" The two of them looked up to see flashes of light striking each other then braking off. The reporter yelled out, "Shoot them!" But the cameraman told him that it was still hard to focus on them.

Cy spun as he kicked the general in the head. Then grabbed his leg, as he fell back, and threw him down. But General Bishop shot back up without even hitting the ground. He head butted the cyborg then fired a blast from his fingers that made Cy fall back. But he blow off the blast and stood ready. Even though he was starting to breath a little hard, he stared down the general still ready to fight at any time.

General Bishop watched and asked, "Is the game too hard for you?"

Cy just glared at him. General Bishop then said, "Let me make it easier on you." He shot up into the air, and Cy followed. The general's his hand shot open into a cannon ready to fire. But he wasn't aiming at Cy, he was aiming at the arena. Cy turned to the others yelling out, "Get away from the ring!" the general fired an enormous blast at the ground destroying the ring.

The cyborg girls made it away from the ring just in time. They all could not believe what the general had done.

Kate had just dropped The Crusher and the reporter and his Camera crew, who had all just missed being crushed by the general's attack. "It's time for you to leave," Kate said, "Things are about to get heavy."

The reporter adjusted his tie as he said, "No way! We have a responsibility to the television audience."

Kate shrugged. "It's your funeral." And she turned to leave.

"If you think it's so dangerous," The Crusher yelled out, "then maybe you should consider leaving! Just let me deal with the general! I should be the one to stop him because— there is no one stronger or better looking than me."

Kate started to laugh at the man's ignorance. "There is only *one* man in the world who can stop the general's rampage—and that's the man who is fighting him now!" Kate shouted at the The Crusher. Then, right before she flew back to the others, she smiled and told him, "Besides, Cy is *way* better looking than you!" by a long shot" as she then took off.

"Do you believe that girl?" The Crusher stated. "She thinks that cyborg freak is better looking than me!"

Cy and General Bishop slowly landed. Breathing hard, and sized each other up. For their second round, general Bishop asked the cyborg, "What do you think of the whole world being our arena?"

"So it's the last one standing who wins?" Cy stated asked, stretching his arms.

Impatiently, the general responded, "It is time to continue the game." He shot forward and fired laser shots from his fingertips. "Last one standing," he affirmed.

Cy flew back. As the beams came at him, the whole demolished area was being lit up by the general's blasts. The reporter yelled at his camera crew, "Get close! Get close! I want a better shot!" But his camera man was being hesitant because of the explosions.

Cy finally reared back and fired a full-power shotgun blast that stopped the general's blasts in their tracks. Both warriors then, collided in a mass of power and strength. Each fighter dared the other to push back.

The sere force of them grappling together shook the ground under their feet. Eventually, the ground under them started to give way. The force of it was so great it could be felt for miles around.

"It's incredible!" Sakura yelled out. "Not only are they equal in power, but in strength as well!" She was trying to get a grip on herself as the ground shook under her feet, and the others were really starting to freak out as well. Cy's and General Bishop's fight intensified pummeling each other with strikes that would surely shatter most mountains.

xxx

Far across the galaxy, Lorelei watched form her monitors, she had been monitoring what was going on, on Earth for some time. She herself could not believe the power readings that she was getting. Even more startling, both warriors' weren't getting weaker they seemed to be getting stronger.

XXX

Cy struck the general hard as they were fighting back up in the air. The general sending him flying toward the ground at incredible speeds, but he recovered before he hit the ground and shot back up. But, then he saw Cy starting to power up his screaming bullet.

He laughed at the thought of Cy firing his screaming bullet at that angle, for, if he did, he could very well destroy a big part of the planet.

The others watched, also aware of the grave danger. "Cy wouldn't do that, would he?" Rebecca asked. "I mean, he might be crazy … but he's not that crazy … right?."

As Cy reared back his fist. Just as everyone thought he was about to fire, he vanished. General Bishop looked around not knowing what had happened, but then Cy appeared right in front of him.

"*Noooo!!!*" he yelled. But the bullet hit him in a mass of power that shattered the top half of his body. The back wash of the bullet's force even flew outside the planet's atmosphere.

When the blast subsided, Cy's metal body was steaming badly and his cloths started smoking from the heat that he was giving off.

When what was left of the general hit the ground, most of the girls cheered thinking that Cy had won. But some of the girls weren't cheering. They knew something wasn't right. As they watched Cy stare at what remained of the general, they realized that Cy wasn't looking too good after that last screaming bullet..

The reporter then signaled to one of his cameramen, who trained his camera on Cy. The reporter, too, thought that the cyborg had beaten General Bishop. He went in font of the camera and said, "Well, folks, it looks like General Bishop has been defeated by this cyborg who has been wanted by the government for some time. It also looks like The Crusher won't get his chance to fight the general after all." As he closed out his report, he finished as he turned to look and see if he could get a interview with the cyborg.

Jennifer was scanning what was left of the general when she yelled out to Cy, "Watch out! He's about to regenerate!"

"Regenerate?" Cy thought. And just then, what was left of the general's body underwent a transformation. To everyone's amazement, the general hoped back to his feet. The reporter and his crew all stopped in their tracks.

Wires began to shoot out of the general's neck until a new torso appeared. More wires shot out to form the lower half of the General's body as they started to form into new arms. When he was whole again, General Bishop smiled at Cy. His expression said it all: "Is that the best you could can do?"

As General Bishop started stretching out his new limbs, Cy asked, "How did you do that?"

"My body is a living computer that is monitored constantly. Any injury that I sustain is instantly detected and repaired. So, in other words, you can't win!"

"Then I'm just going to have to try harder!" Cy roared. But General Bishop started laughing as he said, "That won't happen, Cyborg. I know what you did—you pushed almost all of your power into that last attack. That means your fight is over!"

"That's *not true!!!*" Cy yelled out in frustration. His power began to rise.

General Bishop smiled saying "That's the way, —fight till your body gives out." And they both shot forward letting loose in a fight that could have only one winner.

"This isn't good," Samantha stated to herself. *"Cy was hoping that last attack was going to finish it, but now he's fighting on fumes, and not only that his body's starting to overheat, —and that's not the worst of it."*

The girls turned from watching Cy and looked at Sam. They could see the fear on her face. and Kim asked, "Sam, What''s wrong?"

Sam lowered her head as she told them. "If Cy continues, his body will overheat. There's no way to stop it. When his body hits 600 degrees, he will blow up."

When they heard this, the girls were in shock. "We have to stop the fight," said Melissa. Some of the girls nodded in agreement.

But both Ashley and Sakura disagreed. "No," Sakura told the rest of the girls, "This is Cy's decision to make."

"Are you both crazy?" Melissa almost yelled, . "If Cy continues to fight," —" she paused as she thought of what will could happen.

Ashley finished her sentences, "He will die," she said sadly. "But I think that was his plan from the start— that, if he couldn't stop the general, at least he would take him with him." Ashley looked out at Cy where he was fighting as hard as he could. She could see his body literately starting to burn up. And as she watched, she said softly, "But, still, it is his decision to make, and not ours."

"How can you be so cold?" Melissa yelled out at her sister, .

But Victoria then laid a hand on Melissa's shoulder and told her, "Your sister is just as upset about this as you are. This is hard on all of us, but Cy is fighting for what he believes in, and that is just the way he is."

Melissa began to cry. "But he just can't die on us! He saved all of us. He gave us our lives back—and now he is just going to die?" She fell to her knees in grief.

"He is just that kind of man," Victoria finished. "He would sacrifice everything to protect the ones that he loves the most," Victoria finished.

"Maylu! Where's Maylu?" Samantha suddenly yelled out.

Speechless, as April then pointed to the battle field where Cy and the general were fighting. Finally, she said, "There she goes— she's heading to her father!"

"Oh no!" wailed Victoria. "She must of have heard us saying that her father was going to die!" She watched helplessly as they all watched Maylu fly to her father.

Cy was now blasting his shotgun blast at the general. With each shot as he yelled out, *Double Barrel!*" and each blast was ear spiting— like a thousand shotguns going off at once. As the general was being pushed back, he yelled out and made a electrostatic shield around himself. As the shield got bigger, it pushed back Cy's blasts away as if they were nothing.

The general's shield moved right up to the girls, who where watching from quite a good distance away. Cy's temperature was now at five hundred and ninety five degrees —he was just ten degrees short of blowing. He drifted forward preparing to pounce on the general at any second. But, suddenly, Maylu came flying out of nowhere and kicked the general right in the head. The four-year-old girl's strength was immense; for the general was kicked straight out of sight. almost like he was hit by a train in that spit second.

After she kicked the general, Maylu turned to her father, who, at that moment, had used up the remainder of his strength. She tried to hug her father, but, the second she touched him, she burned her small hands on his hot metal body.

The small girl pulled back as her father told her to "Stay back,—I am too hot to touch!"

But Maylu still tried to get close to her father. "I don't want to lose my Daddy! I want you to stay with me and not die."

General Bishop had just finished digging himself out of the mountain side where Maylu's attack had sent him. He was wondering what had hit him. He looked over at the cyborg he was down on one knee with his daughter his body to hot to move, and was surprised to see him trying to fend off the embraces of a little child. *Could a child have such strength?* At least he knew that now he had his chance. He knew the cyborg could no longer defend himself. All of his major functions had seemed to have shut down, leaving him helpless—so helpless, in fact, that he couldn't seem to keep the child from burning herself on his body.

General Bishop flew up and positioned himself over the cyborg. Before Cy could react, the general grabbed Maylu by the back of her shirt. He tucked the screaming child under his arm.

"Put her down!" The cyborg yelled, but, when tried to move, he found it impossible.

"Cyborg," Bishop stated, "now is the time for you to feel the humiliation that you have given me. You are going to watch helplessly as this child and those girls over there die with you. You will be unable to stop me."

"*Noooo!*" He could deal with his own death, but the thought of harm coming to the girls the thought of that terrified him more than anything.

General Bishop then turned to the skies. "It is time!" he cried.

Out of the skies came the Insidious Six. They landed next to the general. Cy looked up in horror. "It's not possible!" Cy he said.

General Bishop, looked at him and said, "I had them rebuilt. Not only that, I made them stronger. And, there is another surprise," ..." he gestured to the skies just then doubles of the six cyborgs came down and landed, each next to the original version. The Insidious Six Plus Six now surrounded the girls. They were ready to strike at their general's command.

Ellis who watched as the doubles came down thought that now was the best time for her to act. She slipped away and stepped around to the general. As, he taunted the Cy, she then jumped and grabbed him the general from behind, rapping her arms and legs around him, forcing him to release Maylu. The second the child was free, Maylu ran back over to her father's side. Cy watched wondering what sort of a plan Ellis had in mind.

"You General Bishop, you have made a mess of things," Ellis said. "But you will now be destroyed with the explosives I have placed in my body as a last resort. You will die for all the misdeeds you have done." Ellis yelled. Still hanging on to the general, she powered up her body. It began to glow as the general tried to shake her off. But it was no good. She had a death grip on his body.

Just as Cy yelled out, "Don't do it!" the general, with Ellis on his back, swooped up into the air. Immediately, they were engulfed in a massive explosion.

Cy tried to move again to see if Ellis was really gone, but he had not recovered from his power loss. He still could not move his body. He was helpless. As he watched the dust finally cleared, Cy was shocked to see General Bishop was still —alive and unscathed— as he return to Earth. The general just dusted himself off as he looked down at the head of Ellis lying on the ground. He picked it up saying, "Annoyances!" And he throw the head away.

Cy tried with all of his might to move, but still nothing he had no power. His rage was gaining new heights. He could not take much more of this.

But the general was going to make sure that Cy and the girls would experience the worst. He turned back to the Insidious Six and their doubles and said, "Kill them all, but do it slowly." Then he smiled.

"*Noooo!!!*" Cy yelled. But it was no good, . The doubled Insidious Six Plus Six attacked with brutal cruelty. Megan was barely able to put a shield around herself Destiny, and Sam. Because they had no defensive powers, but it was almost no good because both versions of Gatling came right at her and started firing everything they had, but she was willing to hold them off for as long as she could.

Sakura and Ashley flew off as the two version of Mondo came after them. To make it worse, they where both now the super versions of him, so fighting them was almost impossible.

"These guys are defiantly stronger than the last batch," Rebecca yelped between gulps of air as she tried to hold back Megaton.

"Really, Beck?" Kim butted in, sassy as ever. "What was your first clue?" As she absorbed into the rocks ready to fight the other Megaton.

After about thirty minutes of non-stop fighting, the girls slowly started to show signs that they where getting tired. The doubles of the six where just toying with the them to begin with, and Cy knew that soon they where all going to die, and there was nothing he could do. His body just refused to respond. His daughter had even been grabbed again by the general. "I'm taking her alive," the general said to Cy. "I will use her for myself!"

The reporter, meanwhile, could not believe what he was seeing. The fight was horrible. For him and his crew, seeing those girls being pummeled was almost too much to watch.

Sam was still inside of Megan's shield. When outside of the shield she heard a small voice say, "Help me!" Sam turned and saw what is it was that is was Ellis's head

"Take me to Cy … please," begged Ellis, "Please … Cy needs all of your help to win this fight."

Sam nodded as she left the safety of Megan's shields. As she skidded to the ground, she grabbed Ellis's head. Then jumped back to her feet and ran through the battle field where everyone was fighting.

Jennifer fired an enormous blast at one of the Spectral copies as Sam ran around the beams trying to get close enough to Cy to throw Ellis's head to him. Sam yelled out as she ran. "This is crazy! I'm a scientist not a fighter."

Ellis kept saying, "You're doing fine!" When Sam got to a good spot, that she felt it was safe, she reared back and threw Ellis's head right to the Cy.

Cy was in a daze. He didn't know what to do anymore. Minawa had told him to protect the girls, and now he watched them as they were all about to die. Sakura, Rebecca, and Ashley, out of the twelve, were still able to defend themselves to some extent. And little Maylu was crying her eyes as she fought, wanting her father to help her. But still Cy's body would not responding. He cringed as he heard the general say, "Play time is over, boys. Kill them all!"

Cy yelled out again as he fell over trying to move, when, out of nowhere, Ellis's head came rolling over to next to him. "Ellis," Cy croaked, "But how?" He saw her look up to at him.

"Cy, let it go," Ellis said to him.

"Let what go?" Cy asked, confused.

"You can't reason with this man! He believes that the more weapons you have, the stronger you will be. But you are different. You have honor, pride, and dignity. But, most importantly, you must remember it is not a sin to fight for the right cause. "

"You said it yourself on planet Gem when you fought the Titan, —never in your life have you fought anyone just so you could hurt them. This is a time like that one! So, remember that you are not just normal cyborg or some robot, —you are a man who will fight for what he believes in. Tell him who you are! Show him what you are,…"you are— "

Before Ellis could finish, General Bishop stomped down on her head and crushed it. Cy hadn't even seen him approach. The general laughed, "This has been a very interesting day."

Seeing the General do this made him think, he knew Ellis was just an android, but she had learned the meaning of protecting life. And, then he thought of what had just happened that despite his strength, she still died for him.

Cy felt his rage starting to burn up inside of him. He could feel a strength that he had never felt before. Suddenly, his body started to move again, and, as he stood, he shocked the general. Cy stood with new found strength. He stared down the general and said, "Ellis is right. I will never hold back again. I'm done holding back for I am not some machine! I am a man— and a martial artist! *I AM CHRIS STRIKER!!!*"

CHAPTER 41

As soon as Chris yelled out his real name, Chris's body started to change, as his power exploded out the ground slammed around him. As his arms and legs started became empowered, the metal seemed to come alive. Metal pistons seemed to change into metallic muscle. Spikes grew out of his forearms and his legs. The metal changed colors as well turning and ended up a dark red.

Three spikes came out of the side of his face, and as his cybernetic eye changed to a glowing lens that went on and off as he blinked.

General Bishop could not believe this transformation. Chris looked more animalistic as claws now protruded from his hands and feet.

Chris slowly stood up and walked to the general. He stood in front of his opponent and he let out a animalistic growl. General Bishop, though, didn't seem too worried. In the a blink of an eye, Chris's daughter was back in her father's arms. The general could not believe how it had happened.

Maylu was so happy to see her father as she hugged him, and a strange glow emitted from him his body instantly heal the burns on Maylu's hands.

"I'm done playing with you, general," Chris growled as he held his daughter tight with one arm.

General Bishop was furious. He punched right down at Chris with all his might, but connected with nothing but air as Chris vanished.

The Cyborg girls who were still conscious could not believe Chris's strength. He had made it to a whole new level, —he was in his Supreme Super Cyborg mode.

Chris appeared close to the two Megatons who had Kim and Rebecca right where they wanted them. The one who was attacking Rebecca picked her up with one hand and held her out saying. "Don't come any closer or I'll crush this brat!"

Chris didn't even flinch as he held out a fist. Power started to surged through it. Megaton took a step back in shock.

"What's the matter, didn't you hear me?" Megaton yelled as he held out the girl's body. But Chris didn't answer. Instead, he just flexed out his fingers in a flash. And at that moment, Megaton's head blew up in a monstrous display of power. As the behemoth went down, Chris shot forward and caught Rebecca before she hit the ground.

Chris then vanished, appeared next to Destiny. He left Rebecca there with her, then shot back over to the other Megaton. He kicked him so hard in the head that it that his head twisted right off.

"After all the time we spent trying to kill these guys, he does it in one blow!" Ashley said in shock. They all watched the carnage unfold, Chris took out two more of the doubles of the Insidious Six using only one arm.

When what was left of the Insidious Six threatened him, Chris looked each one over, and he then looked at Maylu. "Are you ready, sweetie?"

She nodded. "I am, Daddy." He then throw her in the air. As the group came at him, he dispensed each one as if they were standing still, taking out four more of them.

When they were all down, Chris opened his arms and Maylu fell right into them as gently as could be. "That was fun!" she said, laughing.

Chris looked at what was left of the once large group of enemies. There were only six left. "Not being paid enough for this are you, boys?" Chris was not about to let any of them leave this battlefield alive. As they retreated in different directions, he shot off like a rocket after them. He flew up to one of them and said, "I will never forgive any of you for what you have done to my family!" The Six's strategy of separating was useless. Cy took out each one easily, one by one—even while holding Maylu! He then slammed the last one to the ground with a single punch.

General Bishop was furious. Chris Striker had taken out his warriors far too easily, making a fool of him again. Chris glared at the at the black cyborg. Then he yelled out to Kate, who had just been healed and put back on her feet by Destiny. "Kate, come take Maylu." Kate shot over and took the four year-old from him, then she shot back over to the others—but not before glaring at the general.

Chris now turned all of his attention to the general, who seemed all too ready to fight again. Chris faced the general showing no sign of even breaking a sweat, even after beating all twelve of the Insidious Six Plus Six.

"Ha! You think you've seen what all that I can do?" General Bishop laughed as he sent a barrage of punches at Chris, at incredible speeds. But every one of his punches missing its mark.

The, reporter and his camera crew were still trying to broadcast the events of the day. To them, it looked as if Chris wasn't even moving—and they couldn't even see the general anymore.

As there fight intensified, Chris started to take control of the fight. The punches of each combatant seemed to be in sync with the punches of the other. At one point, the general reared back and punched straight at Chris, but he stuck a mountain side as Chris vanished in a flash.

General Bishop was starting to lose his patience. as he power up and blasted the mountain away with a single blast he yelled out, "I'm going to kill you!" Chris was making a mockery of him again.

The general then thought this through. As he calmed himself down, he walked back over to Chris. Smiling he said, "You have had better not get too confident! I have yet to show you what I am truly capable of!"

The cyborg girls started to get a little worried as the general said this. Melissa stood in shock saying, "He's bluffing. He can't have that kind of power!" But, just then, the general started to increase his power to its max. It blew all of their theories out the window. The force of the power that the general was letting out was like a hurricane. The of energy vaporized everything in its path like a nuclear blast

When the general was finished, he asked Chris, "What do you think of me now?"

"Is that all you've got?" Chris coldly stated, unfazed by his opponent's power.

General Bishop shot forward and punched Chris at such speeds that the others couldn't even see him move. But they could feel the impact of the punch under their feet.

With that strike, General Bishop smiled thinking that he had caused a serious blow to Chris Striker, but when he opened his eyes and smiled that's when he soon know something was wrong. Chris dealt a blow right in the general's solar plexus. The general lurched causing him to winch forward, but then Chris struck him with an upper cut that caused him to fall back to the ground in pain. Each time the general tried to get back up, he fell back down. He started to cough up blood and mechanical fluids.

"How is this possible? thought the general in awe. *He only made contact with two punches!"* He tried to get up again, but fall fell back. *"Why am I so damaged?*

When the general finally got himself back together, he appeared to be almost afraid. He took a step back. That's when Chris asked, "What wrong? Wasn't this what you wanted? A real fight with the Super Cyborg?"

Bishop shook his head in disbelief. "You're not the same man that I remember from when Minawa was still alive. You're different now. Is this the power, that Minawa was talking about before she died?," He stopped in the middle of his thoughts and shot up into the sky. He threw his hands up into the sky, and they changed into two large cannons. As he started to recharge he laughed hysterically. "This is the end of everything! I'm going to blow up the Earth, —and you and all those defective Cyborg's!"

As the girls saw this, they didn't know what to think. If Chris didn't act soon, the Earth and everything on it was going to be destroyed. They looked at Chris, but Chris wasn't moving! He just watched as the general laughed. Suddenly, the general fired a blast that was impossibly large. "Say good-bye to the Earth!" he yelled.

Everything seemed to be moving in slow motion as the blast came down toward Earth. Everyone watched on in horror. As the blast came right up to Chris, but right then he yelled out, *"Screaming Bullet!"* And Chris sent out a blast of his own. The blast hit and the force of Chris's bullet exploded into the general's blast and sent it right back at him. But, also the back wash of the force of Chris's bullet blew a blast of wind back and threatened to engulf everyone back in a hurricane of wind. When Megan saw it coming, she put up a shield just in time, and the blast wave shot around the shield.

"No way!" the general yelled out as he saw his blast coming back to him. There was no time to avoid it. He yelled out in pain as he was engulfed in his own blast.

The rest of the blast flew out into space. Seconds later, everyone dug out of the dust and debris that surrounded Megan's shields. When they got out, Rebecca yelled out, "Wow, that was incredible! There is no way, that the general lived through that!"

"Don't get to cocky, Rebecca," Jennifer told her as she pointed to the sky. "The general's not dead yet—but he is badly hurt."

As Jennifer spoke, Ashley was looking at Chris, who didn't seem at all worn out. She wondered what his secret was. And she thought his new look made him look even more magnificent than he ever had been.

General Bishop was not having a good day. His body was all most completely destroyed. He yelled out to Chris furiously, "I'm not finished yet!"

Just as the general was about to regenerate himself, Sam yelled out to Chris to finish him off quickly.

But Chris turned to her and gave her a half smile. "No," he told her, " no I'm going to make him suffer for a little while longer."

The girls all yelled out to him to, "Finish him off!" "Destroy him!" But still Chris refused to act. He just watched as the general finished his regeneration. The general's fury was very apparent now. As he yelled out, his metal body started to grow in strength and power, and he crashed down right in front of Chris and yelled out. "You will not humiliate me like this!" the general shouted. And he punched at him

Chris, but missed each time he now had power, but his body was too big … his fighting was awkward!

Finally, Chris sent a well-aimed punch right into the general's stomach.

The general reared over to the ground in shock. He was now badly damaged—even worse than the first time Chris hit him. He looked at Chris with fear in his eyes. Chris just smiled at him as if he was nothing but an annoyance to him now.

"You're not a man—you're a monster!" Bishop yelled in fear. Then he fell over again and coughed up more blood and mach fluid. He tried to get himself repaired before Chris could strike him again.

"Monster!" said Chris. "I'm not the one that who turned young, innocent women into killing machines! I'm not the one who killed a woman whose only crime was just wanting to help her people. And not only that, but you blamed me for her death to cover your own monstrous plans. Now you tell me, general, who is the monster is?"

Chris punched the general so hard that he spun up into space out of control. As he looked back down at Chris, a blast from Chris's shot gun came right at him and blasted right through him.

But the general was far from dead as he made his way back to Earth. When he had nearly arrived, Chris grabbed him by the neck and then slammed him down to the ground. Chris reared his fist back ready to finish the job. But before he threw the punch, the general said "Wait!"

"Why?"and Chris asked.

"Because there is a very large explosive device inside my body. It's for a last resort—just as your android Ellis's was—but mine is capable of destroying all life on this planet. If you destroy me now, it will set it off killing everybody and everything on the planet."

Chris stopped and thought for a moment. "Well, then," he said, "I guess I'm just going to have to destroy you someplace where that bomb won't cause any damage!"

"And where would that be?" The general asked with a smug expression on his face. It was clear he was thinking that there wasn't such a place.

"Outer space," said Chris.

"*Noooo!*" The general yelled.

As Chris turned to his Gems, and his daughter. "Good-bye," he said quietly. "I love you all." Then he turned quickly and shot up into the sky.

Because Chris knew this war would still end in his death. He had known all along, from the second that the general had gained his new power, that the general had was armed with a huge, destructive bomb in him from the second he gained this new power.

The girls screamed out to him not to go, but he was out of sight before they could do anything. When Chris flew far enough away from Earth, he looked at the general said, "This is for Minawa." And he slammed his fist through the general's body. Instantly, they were engulfed in a massive explosion. It was so large, that it could be seen half way around the planet.

The cyborg girls could not contain their emotions. They all wept uncontrollably. Sam fell to her knees. "I should of never removed his limiters. If I hadn't, then maybe he would still be alive."

Sakura turned to her and hugged her. "Don't say that," she said. Then she picked up Chris's daughter and held the crying child in her arms. "Chris had no regrets in his decisions, He did everything he could to protect all of us. In the end, it was the ultimate sign that he loved all of us."

Ashley walked over and yelled out angrily to Sakura, "Well, what are we going to do now that Chris is gone? Where do we go from here?"

The Crusher, the reporter, and his the camera crew, at that moment, decided to show themselves as they come out of hiding. They approached the cyborg girls. "What happened?" asked the reporter.

The girls and the others looked over at them. With moist eyes Sam said, "This doesn't concern any of you. We just lost a great man and a great hero."

"Ah, ladies, I'm okay," The Crusher said as he walked over to the girls. "I'll take care of everyone." That's when Rebecca ran over to him jumped at The Crusher, and punched him hard, and sending him flying.

He looked up shocked, just in time to see her run at him again. She punch at him again. Finally, Sakura yelled, "Stop!"

But her warning was too late. The super strong cyborg punched at Crusher, but when the dust cleared, fortunately, he was able to dodge the blow. When The Crusher looked up at the girl, she had tears in her eyes. She broke down completely and fell to her knees and started to cry. "I want my Chris back," she cried.

Melissa went over to the girl and kneed down and cradled Rebecca in her arms. "Everything will be all right," she said,

But, through her sobs, she said "It's *not* okay without Chris with us."

Meanwhile, out in space, a body floated unmoving … until it suddenly shot up, spun around, and shot back to earth.

The girls hadn't seen anything, but they did hear something crash behind them. They all turned, but all they saw was a giant dust cloud. At first, they hoped it was Chris. But then in an instant Jennifer yelled, "It's not Chris!" They had no time to move before a beam shot through the clearing dust at them. At first, it appeared that the beam had missed them all, but then they heard Rebecca yelled out, "Melissa's been hit!" They turned to see, the fallen Ice Storm next to Rebecca holding the fallen cyborg.

Destiny ran over to her fallen friend and looked her over. There was a large hole in her chest. "She's hurt really bad," Destiny said as she started her work.

"Ah, it seems my aim is as good as ever.," Someone said. As the dust finally cleared, no one could believe what stood there. They were all sure that the general had died with Chris—but then there he was. "I can not die, even if my body is destroyed. I will always come back even stronger than before."

Ashley watched as the large man laughed at them. She then turned to her sister who was still laying on the ground as Destiny did her best to save her. Melissa began to cough up blood, and Destiny yelled told her, "Hold on, girl!"

Ashley could not believe what was happening. First Chris died at the hands of this freak—

But, before Ashley could finished her thoughts, something else crashed down in front of the girls.

"How dare you attack them?" roared a familiar voice. "They have nothing to do with our fight!"

"*Chris!*" the girls yelled when they saw him. But he turned to them with a look of fury. "Stay back," he told them. "This fight is far from over."

They obeyed and backed off, knowing that things were going to be all right now that their Chris was back.

"What do you see in those clones anyway.?" the general asked with a smug look. The girls didn't know what to think, when he said this.

"What do you mean, clones?" Chris asked not understanding what the general was talking about.

"Don't you think it's strange that a woman who believes in protecting people as much as Minawa did would, turn innocent young women into cyborg's?"

"The thought has, crossed my mind," Chris told him, .

"Well," the general began explained with a great deal of smugness, "Those girls where never real to begin with! Each one of them is a clone, —a piece of Minawa. She changed them all to look different. And *that's* why they all like you so much!"

To know that they were all nothing but clones this was almost too much for the girls to stand to know that they were all nothing but clones.

"They are more than just clones," Chris then yelled, "they are my family, and I love them *all* more than anything in this world!"

Bishop laughed. "How amusing, … to think you love them. But now this has to end!" And it was obvious that he was about to attack.

But Ashley was furious. Ashley yelled out, "I have had enough of this!" she yelled. "First we almost lose Chris, and then my sister falls before this freak!" She glared at the general. "You're dead, you monster," she roared. Suddenly the flame surrounded her. It started out red and then changed to a flaming blue as it became hotter than it had ever been becoming even hotter then before.

"It can't be?" !" Sam said in a shaky voice. Ashley had gained a hyper mode of her own. Sam watched as Ashley then yelled, "Bishop!!! " "You'll pay for what you did to my sister!" Then she shot out a huge fire ball. The general was engulfed in flame. But Ashley wasn't finished with him. She flew around him creating a fierily tornado just as she had against the Titan, but this time the flames were ten times hotter. As the fierily tornado raised into the sky, it looked like the skies where a blaze as if hell was pouring from the heavens.

Ashley's screams of rage could be heard from inside the fierily tornado. Chris and the others now had to retreat inside Megan's shields, for now it was too hot to be anywhere near the flames. Even the reporter and The Crusher and the camera man had to be in escape inside the shields.

Chris yelled, "Stop, Ashley! You're going to set the world a blaze!"

"I'm not going to stop until I'm sure that the' General is dead!" Then she flew out of the twisting inferno and worked up another enormous ball of flame. This caused the twister to explode.

"I did it!" Ashley yelled as the flames started to subside. But, to everyone's amazement, the general jumped out of the flames and said, "Only *I* decide who leaves here alive!" And he back handed the girl. She went flying and crashed hard into the ground seemly unconscious.

General Bishop landed close to her. "Nothing can kill me—I am invincible!" His hand opened to the cannon and started changing up. Just as he fired, Chris jumped in front of the weapon, taking the hit. The force of the blast blew his right arm off and spun him around crashing him to the ground. His arm landed fist first in the ground next to him.

Chris had landed on top of Ashley, and they both seemed unconscious. Chris slowly got up, some of his blood poured out of his blown arm socket. Some of it dripped down on Ashley. Chris turned to the general still ready to fight—even with one arm.

"Ha, Ha, Ha, Ha, There is no way, Striker, that you can fight anymore. You are finished!"."

They all knew it was over there was no way that Chris could fight anymore. And, deep down, he knew it too. The general had won.

Chris watched as the general pulled back his fist in the same way he does for his screaming bullet. He was surprised to hear the general say, "I'm going to finish you with your own attack."

Chris fell to one knee and slammed his fist against the ground in desperation, "What' *is* this?"

General Bishop asked, "You're not going to fight back?"

"What's the point?" Chris told him. "You have won!"

The general laughed again. "How boring! I was hoping the end would be more dramatic. But, if this is it, then so be it."

As Chris watched, as the general powered up his screaming bullet. Chris thought to himself, *Sorry, everyone, I wished so much that I could do it.*"

"Don't tell me you're giving up like that?" a voice said from out of the blue.

"Who's there?" Chris said as he looked around.

"What, you forgot about me already? I'm hurt."

"Minawa?" he said.

"That's right."

"But how?" He asked still looked around, wondering where she was.

"Do you remember when I put the limiter device on your neck?"

He nodded.

"Well, that device was actually a device that connected my mind to your computer half of your brain. When my real earthly body was destroyed, my mind and my very soul were transferred into your mind. They lay dormant —until you activated this new form."

Chris could not believe this—that Minawa was still alive, ... sort of. Granted, she was in his head ... but her spirit was alive.

The general interrupted this exchange between Chris and Minawa. "What wrong?" The he yelled. "Has your fear caused you to go crazy?"

Minawa's voice was strong and clear inside is head: "Chris, don't lesson to him. You can still win!"

"But, Minawa, I only have only one arm left."

"So, that's all you need, to take him out," she said. "There is no way he can beat you for— you are truly the greatest fighter that will ever exist."

Hearing those words made him feel strong again. As he took a deep breath, right then a jet flipped out on his back to, which increased the power of his bullet. Chris readied himself as he reared back his left arm. "This fight is far from over!" he roared.

When the general saw this, he actually felt excited, for he was going to achieve a win that no one would ever forget.

Everyone watched when the two warriors shot forward, both roaring out simultaneously, "*Screaming Bullet!*" When the two fists clashed, fist to fist the shock wave was like a sonic boom.

The energy that seemed to soar around them was so powerful it began to tear the ground away under their feel. They all felt that those two warriors were going to reshape the whole planet if they kept this up. As the blast wave hit them, causing them to hit the ground hard.

The reporter yelled out to his camera crew "Keep shooting! This is truly the fight of the century!" The wind blew around like a hurricane.

Chris was doing his best to force back the general's fist, but the general's screaming bullet was just as strong as Chris's. Cracks started appearing on Chris's his body, meaning that his cybernetic body was literally braking apart.

"What's wrong with you!" Minawa yelled out. "You shouldn't be falling back! You should be able to push the general back easily!"

"It's too much for me. Can't you see that I'm at my limit?"

"I don't know where you got that idea," she shot back. "You are far superior to that freak in every way. You can not be stopped by, him. Right now there are over a dozen people over on that rock ledge that believe in you, so — do not let them down!"

Chris let out a lion's roar as he pushed everything he had into his screaming bullet. He succeeded in pushing the general back, but, unexpectedly, the general powered up his bullet to match his.

Minawa thought of everything she could to get Chris to push it harder, but it wasn't working. The general was still pushing him back, and Chris's body was starting to brake apart.

The cyborg girls watched Chris struggling to hold on with all his might. Finally, Rebecca yelled out, "I'm not just going to lie down and die! I'm going to fight back!"

She turned to the others. "So what if we're clones? It doesn't make our lives less important!"

Something unexpected then happened to Rebecca. Her body, started to gain a glow, just as Chris's had attained his higher form. She shot over up at blinding speeds and landed behind the general. And she began firing off what looked like screaming bullets, but they were but not as strong as Chris's. Even though the bullets didn't stop him, they did make him fall back. The others watched in amazement. Up until now, Rebecca couldn't been able to fly. "It must of have been the hyper mode?" ," Sam thought said as she turned to the others. And she saw them, too, started to gain the golden glow. They were all willing to stop at nothing to help Chris. As they gained their power, they took off toward the battle. Sakura though was the last one to take off. But before she left, she turned to Sam and Chris's family. "If we don't make it out of this alive, take good care of Maylu for us. She may become even stronger than any of us some day."

Sakura turned and flew over into the battle. She started firing down at the general to try and take him down, but, even with everyone firing at him, there blasts where like nothing to him, and he was able to blow them off without even losing his concentration on his fight with Chris.

"Leave them alone, General," yelled Chris as he saw the general turn his attention momentarily to the girls. "This is our fight!!!" Striker yelled. "

"Anyone who gets in my way will die!!" Bishop yelled back

Chris then tried to tell the girls to back off, but they told him that they wouldn't let him fight this alone— they reminded him that they were his family. If he was going to die, they would go with him.

"These sentiments are making me sick.," General Bishop stated. "I bet that pushing yourself so hard, Striker, is really started to get to you! I bet all of those wounds, are really burning!"

The general pushed forward again, blowing off the girls one last time. It now looked as if the end was near. It looked as if Chris had given it his all. But Minawa yelled at him again, "Don't let up!"

"I've given it everything I have!" he told her, as his body started breaking apart. But right then a large fire ball hit the general pushing him off balance. Chris looked up and saw that Ashley had fired the fire it.

"Do it *now!*", Minawa then yelled.

Chris roared out and fired off everything he had into his screaming bullet. The general saw it coming. "It can't be the end!" he said shocked. Everyone watched in awe as his body started to vaporize and fall apart … all the way down to the last microchip!

The last bit of Chris's bullet shot off into space. As the blast subsided, there was nothing left of the general —just the canon left from screaming bullets the two warriors released. Chris slowly floated in the air after the attack was over. He smiled as he fell to the ground and reverted back to his normal cybernetic from. Then he was laughing at the fact that he had won.

CHAPTER 42

Ashley landed right next to Chris as he was getting up she hugged him tightly, saying how happy she was that he was okay. It was way out of character for her to be showing so much affection, but it wasn't long until all the girls turned and piled onto on the poor man. They were all so glad that he was okay.

When they all finally calmed down, they backed away from Chris. They knew how tired he must be. In fact, Ashley was the one that got to help him up she then put his only arm over her shoulder to stabilize him. Kate ran over to retrieve Chris's other arm, witch was still slammed into the ground some ways at the battle site.

Sam came up to them reassured them all that she and Destiny will could fix Chris up like new. Just then, The Crusher and the reporter and his cameraman ran over and the reporter asked Chris and joined the group. "What happened?" shouted the reporter, digging out his microphone. "Where did the general go?"

"He was destroyed by my daddy." Maylu proudly said as she pointed to her exhausted father.

The Crusher yelled said, "That is impossible! A murderer can't be a hero! I'll prove it, by beating this cyborg and getting the reward from the government."

When they heard this, the cyborg girls surround Chris protectively ready to fight off anyone who would try to hurt him. Megan spoke to The Crusher: "You would fight a opponent that can not fight back?"

"Lesson girl, he's not worth protecting.," The Crusher told them her.

But anger rose in the hearts of all the girls. "We wouldn't trade Chris for anything," said Jennifer speaking for all of them. "Chris is a guy that we wouldn't trade for anything."

The reporter held his microphone out to all the girls and asked, "Just what is your relationship with this cyborg?"

Chris, at this point, had fallen unconscious from exhaustion. Ashley released her hold on Chris and let him lean on Sakura. Then she took the microphone from the reporter. "We're all his wife's."

When the reporter heard this girl say that all twelve of them where this cyborg's wife's he asked "Is this true?"

"It's true," said Jennifer. And all the girls agreed. "If you have a problem with that," she continued, "it's just too bad." Then she turned to Victoria. "Can you get us out of here?"

"Sure thing," said Victoria, as she focused her powers and took all the girls, Chris, off into the air leaving the television crew and The Crusher in shock.

xxx

After Chris won the battle that shocked the world, Chris was cleared of the charges against him, and the bounty on his head was removed. Investigation even proved that General Bishop was the person responsible for Minawa's death.

It was only a week after they had returned to their island haven that they received an unusual guest. A, plane landed on their island. Three men disembarked; two of them were wearing the Cyber Corp. logos. The third , just by looking at him, you could tell that he was a lawyer. When Kim and Kate two of the cyber girls went out to greet the guests, the lawyer asked, "Is there a Mr. Chris Striker living here?"

"Well Yes,"unless there is anther flying Island around here, he's here," Kate told the man hesitantly.

"Good," he said. " and he said "My law firm represents Cyber Corp. These gentlemen are the CEO and the CFO of Cyber Corp. We have some important business with Mr. Striker."

"Well," Kite Kate started. "he is in the dojo training with some of the others," the lawyer then asked "could you show us where that is?" "We'll take you there."

When they entered the dojo, they found Chris was doing a little tai chi, as the some of the girls sparred. The guests watched as the warriors all seemed to be moving to the beat of the music.

The lawyer walked up to Chris and introduced himself and the officers of Cyber Corp. "Could I have a word with you for a moment?" the lawyer asked.

Chris though seemed to be entranced by the music all the way until the song ended.

Sam turned to the lawyer and asked "what do you want? All of the charges against Chris have been dropped."

"That's not why I'm here." the lawyer said, then he turned to Chris. "You remember that Cyber Corp belonged to Minawa Ivy, don't you, Mr. Striker?"

"Of course," said Chris. "That's Minawa's company—where she built my new body." Chris stated as he walked over to the lawyer after finishing his warm up.

"Well, Mr. Striker," said the lawyer, "you've been a challenge to track down. We're here to tell you that it seems Miss Ivy left you the company and all rights to it."

When the lawyer said this, Chris could hardly believe him. But about fell over as the lawyer showed him the will that contained this information. Her will was dated back to the time when she had first created him.

Chris looked up at the man, "Is this really true?"

The lawyer assured him that this was no joke and Chris was now the owner of one of the biggest corporations in the world. "But there is a catch," he said. "If, by any chance, that the share holders are able to proof beyond a shadow of a doubt that you are not a man but a robot, or being dishonorable in any way, they can take back the control of the company.

Chris laughed at this. Minawa sure was something else. She new that those corporate fools would try anything to get her company.

Using his honor code as a basses she would able to make sure that no one would be able to take her company away from him.

The CEO then spoke up. "This is why we are here with this Lawyer —we are here to prove that you can't be honorable because you are nothing but a machine—a robot that looks human."

Chris was shocked. "What's your name?" he asked.

"I'm Kentia Matzo, CEO and a major shareholder. We're not going to take this lying down! We *will* find a hole in this contract!"

Chris faced the Japanese man. His cybernetic eye scanned the man as it focused on him. "I will be running this company for now," Chris said. "And my first order of business will be to fire any dishonorable people who don't believe that I am, in fact, more of man than anyone can see."

"You can't do that!" Kentia stated as he turned to the lawyer for help.

"It looks like he just did." said the lawyer.

With that, Chris turned on his metals heel. "Good day to you all, I will be going down to that Cyber Corp. tomorrow."

As he walked back to the plane, Kentia yelled out, "You haven't seen the last of me!"

Chris just waved his hand behind him as he walked. "We'll see," he said quietly.

The next day, Chris, Samantha, and the other cyber girls flew to the main corporate headquarters, witch happened to be in Japan to Chris's surprise. A large limo big enough to hold all of them comfortably.

When they arrived, at the Cyber corp. building they where greeted, very well by the staff. Many of them knew who Chris was because of Minawa. She had talked about him a lot when she was still alive, and that was a good thing because that put so many of them were on his side.

When they entered the, board room, the board members where all talking about their new boss—Chris. They had heard that he was the man who saved the world from a crazy general, but they still didn't want him to head up their company. The conversation—which was being carried on in Japanese—stopped as Chris, Sam, and the girls entered the room. Chris noticed them bad mouthing him in Japanese. They must have assumed he didn't speak the language.

Chris turned to them saying and addressed the group in Japanese: "Don't try and think that, just because I am half American, that it meant that I don't know what's going on. I know, that you have been planning on taking the company away from me, by trying to go over my head."

This shocked them all, for it seemed that Striker knew more about running a company than they thought. What they didn't know was the fact that Chris plans on building up the company by doing something he had always wanted, and which was giving the people an affordable security agency that they could count on. He would still make money on new technologies. He planned on calling this agency the "C.C.S.A"—"The Cyber Corp. Security Agency."

The board members could not believe what they heard. They tried to convince him otherwise, but Chris had already made up his mind, and the fact that his girls were behind him 100 percent. The board members gave in and agreed to this knowing that they had no choice—Chris owned over 70 percent of the company, and it didn't appear that they could prove him dishonorable or other than a human, so it was out of their hands.

Over the next few days, Chris worked to set up his new plans. He would run the company in name only, and Sam would deal with getting clients for his new security agency.

CHAPTER 43

Late one afternoon, three of the girls April, Megan, and Kate decided to take some time day off. They enjoy the sights that Japan had to offer. After April saw a club that just opened, she could not resist going in. When the three of them walked in, April felt at home, for the whole place was jumping with music and dancing.

After an hour in the club, Megan was went to the bar to get them something to drink when she noticed something strange. There was a large black man standing at the counter, and, when he turned around, what she saw she could not believe.

There was the General Bishop! But there was something wrong, for he looked human again. Megan at this panicked and ran straight back to the others who were talking to some of the people who had recognized them from the tournament. Megan ran up to them and frantically tried to tell them what she had seen, but April and Kate had to tell her to calm down so they could understand her. Megan took a deep breath. "The *general*," she said, "is sitting at the bar!"

Kate and April looked at each other and then back to Megan. Then laughed. "That is impossible," Kate said.

"Yeah," said April. "We all saw Chris killed the general weeks ago."

"If you don't believe me, then go look for yourselves," Megan told them. Kate and April walked casually over to the bar; they too were shocked. He was sitting at on a bar stool. Suddenly, he looked over at them and gave them an evil smile and wink at them.

Kate and April about jumped out of their skin when they saw him. Then April said, "We have to contact Chris, *now!*" And they ran off.

xxx

Chris was walking down a hall on his way to talk to Sam about a few things he wanted to work through when he heard three of the girls call out to him through their communications link.

What he heard he could not believe. He tried to tell them that it was impossible—that he had watched as the general was vaporized. But, when they gave him a link to their vision, he saw him, for himself. Chris was confused, however, to see the general in human form.

Before he could find out any more, there connection went dead. Chris yelled out to the girls a couple of times and tried to get them back, but it was useless … the connection was lost. So he tried to call to some of the others but he couldn't get a signal. It was as if someone was jamming the signals. But that was supposed to be impossible. To Chris, there seemed to be a lot of impossible things happening right now, and he wanted answers, he took off.

xxx

When the signal was lost, Kate, April, and Megan the three of them looked back to where the general had been sitting, but he was gone. The girls, thought their best plan would be to get out of there and head for home.

xxx

Sakura and Victoria were out doing some shopping. They had just bought something that they had thought Chris would love, when out of nowhere someone seemed to jump in front of them knocking them over. When they looked up, they could not believe what they saw. The general, —in human form—was looking down on them with cold eyes.

"How have you girls been?" Bishop asked them as they stared in shock. He smiled, "Bye," he said, and as he ran off.

Victoria shook off the shock and said, "After him!"

They both jumped up and ran after this general look-alike. They ran as fast as they could, but, just as mysteriously as he appeared, he disappeared, leaving the two of them lost and confused.

The general taunted the rest of the girls, too. They all had an encounters with someone who looked and acted like the general —even though they all knew that he was dead and gone.

xxx

Chris and Sam made to her lab. "Have you heard what's going on?" he asked.

She turned to him from the computer that she was working. "Yes! Each one of the girls has had an encounter with this general look-alike. What's worrying me is that the encounters have occurred simultaneously!"

"That is impossible!" Chris said in shock, not believing what he was hearing. How could the general's look-alike be in so many places at once? Just as he asked himself this question, he heard a woman's voice say, "I may be able to answer that question."

Chris turned to see the Supreme Elder Lorelei of the planet of his Gem. She was, standing right behind him.

Chris immediately asked, "How did you get here?"

Smiling, she said, "I used the door." She pointed to the door behind her, which Chris had only known as a door to a closet. Unbelieving, he ran over to the door and opened it. He was shocked to find himself looking into Lorelei's lab on Gem.

Chris turned back to her. "How did you do this?"

"I put an inter-dimensional gate on a door at my lab so I could travel to Earth with ease."

"I'll have to take your word for that one, Lorelei." ," Chris stated, unsure of how that sort of system might work. He shut the door back and then asked, "Do you really know, what's going on here?"

"Yes, I have a answer, but it's kind of elaborate." Lorelei told him as she moved over to a computer. She put in a disk, to the machine, and pictures of the city of Tokyo appeared on the screen. The city was filled with multicolored dots. "The blue dots are normal people, the red are cyborg's," said Lorelei.

"And the black dots?" Chris asked.

"The black dots represent something new that has appeared. I believe these beings have taken on the form of this general of yours. But the most interesting part has to be that these general look-a-likes are made up of nanites." Lorelei finished with a not-to too-happy look.

Chris looked at her. "What the heck are nanites?"

Lorelei shook her head and right before she lowered her head.

"Nanotechnology," Sam said. "Nanites are microscopic machines. Together, they can do almost anything, —including from together to make this general look-alike."

"This must be the general's last resort." Chris said realizing how bad this was getting.

Lorelei then gave them even worse news: "At the rate that these nanites are multiplying, they could cover the globe in less than two weeks."

"They can do that?" Chris asked perplexed at this development.

"In fact, they can do that and more. " Lorelei exclaimed, "If my research is correct, it's possible that they could even alter things at a molecular level, which means that they could alter the whole planet and change it to match there requirements."

Before they could say anything else, Chris shot out of the lab to find the girls and tell them of this predicament. He flew through most of the city trying to find them. Having no luck, he finally stopped and sat down on a bench to think. After a moment, he looked up. There was the general look-alike walking up to him.

"General Bishop?" Chris blurted out.

"Oh, I'm not the General," the look-alike said as he approached. "You may call me Black. I assume that your scientist friends have all ready told you what we are?"

"Yeah," Chris said and then realized what he said. "We?" he said.

"Yes, we," Came another voice. Chris looked to his side. Another Black walked up to him. "We are the destroyers," said the second Black. Then another Black appeared. "We're also the creators." More and more

Blacks started appearing, and Chris began to get very anxious as so many of them came out of no where.

"What do you want?" Chris asked.

"Our first job, before we remake the world, is to, destroy Chris W. Striker."

After saying his name they all attacked at once with incredible power. Each seemed to have the same powers as the original general, but they also had some powers that he hadn't had. For example, like every time Chris hit one down, two more took the fallen Black's place. To Chris they would multiply each time he punched one it looked as if each punch shattered his target into thousands of ants put together that seemed to shatter and simply reassembled themselves. And, it was almost impossible to read their movements. Just as Chris hit one of the Black clones to the ground, hundreds of them started coming out of everywhere fighting him like crazy.

The fight was like ants attacking a single peace of food until they all came at him at once over powering him holding him down. They all started to say in unison, "It is inevitable—no one can go against our procession, … our perfection."

"Screw this!!!" Chris yelled out. He transformed to his Supreme Super Cyborg mode, exploding out with power. The Black doubles were all thrown off him. He stared them all down as they seemed to study this new form. They still, all surrounded him, however. It was one against a million. And, even in his new form, he would have a hard time beating them all.

"You can not win!" All the Black clones said in unison. They came closer to him ready to pounce at any moment. Chris knew that his new supreme mode was strong, but he wouldn't last long against all of these opponents. Just then, he heard Minawa's worried voice, "Maybe we should leave and think of some way to beat them without getting our circuits rearranged."

For ever sense the fight with the general, he could talk to her freely.

"Maybe you're right," Chris said as the Black clones came at him. Chris suddenly shot skyward. But something happened that he hadn't expected—they all took off after him like a swarm of black bees.

One of them flew right at Chris and plunged his hand right into Chris's chest. Black started to consume Chris's body. At first, Chris didn't know what to do as he started to feel himself slowly lose consciousness. But when Minawa yelled out, "Don't give up!"

Chris bolted awake and punched the Black out of his body, and then he punched the Black to the ground, others came at him, attacking him at from all sides. Chris was still holding his own even against so many opponents, but Minawa told him, "You can't keep this pace up forever. You have to get back to the island and find out if these things have any kind of weak point."

Chris knew that, if he left the fight now, they would just follow him no matter where he went. He contacted Sam on the island. To see if she and Lorelei had any additional information he could use. She did, indeed have a plan, but the thing was she was amazed that Chris could talk to her while he was fighting all of those things.

"I managed to get in contact with Jennifer and Beth," she said. "I sent the two of them to the general's old base to see if they could find out anything on this, Black nanites thing. Just hang in there while they work on this." Sam finished.

"Yeah! Give me the hard job." Chris stated, as he punched another clone down. *This is going to be a long day"* he thought to himself. As hundreds of them general look-alike came at him, he readied himself and fought them all like mad.

Jennifer and Beth walked through an empty base. It was apparent that no one had used it for quite a while. And as they looked around the complex, suddenly a large robot came at them from behind. It had tank treads for feet and large claws for hands, and right next to its head was a cannon. The thing roared out', "Terminate!" as it came at them. They both ran the second they saw it, but it was faster than they were. "It looks like the general left this big guy here to keep trespassers out!'"" Beth stated to Jennifer.

"You think?" Jennifer almost screamed as she ran. But, suddenly, she jumped, spun around, and fired an eye beam at the behemoth. It barely fazed him. Beth saw a fork in the hall in front of them . "Jennifer," she said, "let's split up!" .

The robot stopped at the fork point where the girls had separated. It yelled out in frustration. As Jennifer was running down the hall, she passed a room marked Computer Lab. She stopped and opened the door. This sure enough was the place that they were looking for. She went to the biggest computer and hoped that it still worked. As she began to boot it up, she heard Beth yelled out, "I could use some help! This crazy robot is still chasing me!"

She fired a few water steams at it at high pressure, but all it did was push the robot's shoulder back a bit. She cried out again, "I could really use some help here!"

"Just give me a minute!" Jennifer, Sniper yelled back, as she looked through the computer as fast as she could. Just then, she found what she was looking for. She pressed a few keys and pressed Enter. The robot then immediately stopped in its tracks. Beth turned to it and slapped her attacker and said, "Stupid robot!" The robot fell over. Scaring her, she took off to the lab. Jennifer was looking through the programs in the computer. Finally, she found a file called Black. When she hit opened it, the general's face appeared on the screen. Next to him was that mad scientist who had almost taken control of Chris.

The general spoke: "If we both failed to stop Chris Striker, this new program, Black, will stop him for sure. Its power is limitless."

Hearing this made them both girls cringe. But then Jennifer found another file that contained information about the design of the nanites. When the two girls looked thought the design, they found what they were looking for, —a weak point to the Black program.

They both called back to Sam, told her the good news, and sent her the information.

"Good work, you two," said Sam. "I'm sending the others to help Chris against the Black clones."

"We'll meet them there." Jennifer finished as they took off.

xxx

Sam turned to the others, "Let's get going, everyone."

"We shouldn't take Destiny," Ashley stated. "She is still the only one of us without a hyper mode." Ashley stated.

"No," said Sam. "We may need her to heal Chris if he's going to use the information we got."

Destiny looked up at them a little worried. Ashley did have a point— that she was the only one out of the group that had not attained the hyper mode yet. It might be dangerous for her to be at this fight.

Sakura looked at the girl and said, "You'll be okay, as long as you stay close to Megan." Megan walked next to her. "You're going to be just fine—you're in good hands.."

Destiny nodded her head and agreed. "I would do anything to help Chris."

xxx

Chris, though, was not looking good. His body was badly beaten. His supreme mode had been completely maxed out. He was breathing hard, and the Black clones could tell that he would not last much longer. He was determined, though, to win, no matter what. Just when he thought things couldn't get any worse, the Black clones all pointed there hands at him. He didn't like the way this looked … and then as there hands started to give off an electrical charges.

Chris readied himself for what ever they had planned. But, when they all fired a plasma blasts at him, he thought that he was finished. The blasts hit him hard, and, for a moment, he managed to hold it them back, but, when more of them fired, it was too much for him to handle. Chris was blown down toward Earth. He crashed right into a building, making half a of it come slamming down on him.

The Black clones started towards the rubble ready to finish off what ever was left of the cyborg. But, suddenly, what seemed like lighting struck down more than half of the Black clones. More of them were hit by ice and fire as well. And, finally, as laser blasts and other things took the rest of them out—or so they thought.

The cyborg girls all landed around Chris and started digging him out of the rubble. But, as they worked, Jennifer noticed the remains of the black clones starting to reassemble themselves. "Let's make this fast, ladies!" she cried.

Finally, they got Chris out of the rubble. He was barely conscious. Right then, the Black clones, had formed themselves back together, and started firing on all of them. Megan though got a shield up just in time to stop the attack, but she would not be able to hold them for long, for there where just too many of them to hold off.

"Okay, Jennifer,"said Sakura, "where's the weak spot on these things?"

Jennifer peered through the shield and searched among the clones. "See that one with a red crystal on his forehead?" She pointed to one of them. "He's the Black Control. If we take him out, the others will fall."

There were so many of them around that getting to one individual looked to be impossible. And Chris was now out like a light from fighting the Black clones for so long. The girls, had to do something before Megan's shields gave out and all of those Black clones would overpower them.

"Well, everyone," Ashley stated, "if we're going down, well going down fighting, —right along side our man."

Melissa turned to her sister and actually agreed with her. The the two of them, cleared the shield and ran into the mob of Black clones, and started fighting them off like mad. Sakura tried to tell them to stop, but it was too late. She just shook her head and shrugged and said, "Well, it looks like we're not going to do this the smart way, so let's just kick some but, while we still can."

She and the rest of the girls took off into the fight, but Megan and Destiny stayed behind to watch over the still-unconscious Chris. Destiny looked him over. His body was seriously thrashed. He was even more damaged than he'd been after he'd fought the general. But at least he was still in one piece. When she touched his arm to try and get him on his feet, it broke off in her hands.

"Crap?" !" she said quietly. She was trying to start fixing him but she knew it would take at least an hour to get him back to full power, and it didn't look as if the others where going to last that long. It was going to take a miracle to get them out of this one, but a miracle wasn't about to happen, for, even though they were all fighting off the Black clones, they where being overpowered by sheer numbers. And that wasn't counting for there strength for each one was as strong as the original general.

After what was seemed like an eternity to the girls, they where all beaten down. Megan was barely able to maintain the shield. She was starting to think that this was the end as she watched, as the Black clones started to come toward her and Destiny. And Chris was still out cold.

Megan turned to Destiny. "Do you have any ideas?" she asked. "Because I'm about out of power, and it's only going to take a matter of minutes before those Black clones get to us."

Destiny slowly shook her head. Megan's shields. Finally, the shield fell and pushed Megan back into the wall, knocking her unconscious. Destiny was now the only one still able to do anything. She had limited power, and she didn't know what to do. Hundreds of, the Black clones surrounded her, aiming cannon hands at the her and at the body of Chris. As they discharged there weapons, Destiny threw her body over Chris, determined to protect him from the blasts. But, at that same moment, she screamed out Chris's name. As she did, she, finally transformed to her hyper mode. Now empowered her ability to heal at an incredible rate. An explosion of healing power hit Chris and the girls, healing them instantly. As they started to get up they saw Destiny had gained the hyper mode.

Both Destiny and Chris were engulfed in a blinding glow that pushed the Black clones back. Chris stood up as Destiny continued healing him and regenerating his metal. The glow then seemed to cover him entirely and, almost making him look like a robot as the metal of his body seemed to come alive and cover him. When the process was finished, Chris now opened two mechanical glowing eyes. As he looked in one direction and then another, he looked almost like a metal beast. He flexed his new metal muscles as if testing them. He had attained his perfect supreme mode. When he saw what the Black clones had done to the others, he finely roared out, "Look at what you've done to my Gems! You will *all* pay for this with your very lives."

The Black Control was not impressed. "I still have the upper hand in this fight. I still out number you a million to one."

"Oh yeah?" Chris stated calmly as he reared back his fist, saying. "We'll, then let's even up those odds a little bit." And he fired a screaming bullet that eradicated almost all of the Black clones at once.

This shocked the Control. Then he realized that half of his clones remained—he could just make more.

"Foolish man," Black started. "Our abilities far surpass yours. I could destroy you with a single move!" Chris started to laughed hearing this. "Really? Well, if you're so tough why didn't you notice the hole I just shot through you?"!"

"What?" Black yelled out. He looked at his stomach and saw a hole going right through him. He looked back up at Chris, who knew Black hadn't even seen Chris make the shot. He knew the Black Control was now confused.

The Black Control raised his hands to the sky, as all the Black clones ran at him. Fusing together into one huge body that towered over Chris. Together, they were as big as a, skyscrapers.

The cyborg girls positioned themselves behind Chris, though he seemed to be enjoying himself. They knew he wanted to beat down this general wannabe. Chris flew right up the giant's body until he was in front of the face. But the giant grabbed him and absorbed him into its self faster then Chris could make another move.

When the girls saw this, they reacted fast. Sakura flew up in a rage, firing off an enormous E.M.P, (electromagnetic pulse) that made the giant fall back. Ashley flew over him shooting off a stream of heat so hot that it would of destroy anything ease else. The giant fell back, but the giant stood back up like it didn't feel the heat at all.

The rest of the others soon joined in the fight. Suddenly, to everyone's amazement, the giant toppled over. It held its head as if in pain ... as if something was attacking him from the inside.

"It's Chris!" Victoria yelled out. "He's still fighting that big freak from the inside!" And, sure enough, Chris burst out of the giant's head holding a crystal in his hand. Black tried to reach for it, but right then Chris snatched it out of his reach. "Not today, big guy!" he said as he crushed the crystal in his hand. When he did, Black seemed to roared out in pain, and as his enormous body started to melt. The giant disappeared in in a wave of black as he fell apart.

Nothing was left of Black but a pool of dying nanites. Chris watched them. "It seems that, without its main power crystal, it can't keep itself together so to speak," he said as he dusted the remainder of the crystal off his hands.

"Chris, that was amazing," Beth said as she and the others joined him. They all looking at the new form. "You don't think this is permanent, do you?" Beth asked.

Chris looked at all of them and laughed saying. "No, I can go back to normal at any time—but not right now."I'm not ready yet."

"Why not?" Megan asked.

Chris smiled, and, with no indication of whom he was talking to, said, "I'm not wearing any clothes!" the transformation had burned away my clothes."

He turned and started his way back to the Cyber Corp. building as if nothing had happened.

The cyborg girls where in shock because for his new form covered him in so much metal to the point he looked decent even without clothes. Chris looked back at the girls. "Are you all coming or what?" They shook off the shock and took off after him.

CHAPTER 44

A few days after the defeat of the Black, a young Japanese woman walked slowly up to the Cyber Corp. building. She carried in her pocket a picture of a five-year-old little girl and a ten-year-old boy playing together. The wind blew by her she looked up at the building. She sighed. "Chris-chan."

Beth and Ashley were making their security rounds around the building when they got a call about a girl who was starting a ruckus in the lobby. When they went down to the lobby, they saw the girl. She looked like the typical college student. Her shirt seemed to be a little big on her—, the sleeves seemed to be too long as they almost covered her hands. Her hair was cut short and seemed to stick up as if she had just gotten out of bed. The girl appeared to be looking for something or someone. Ashley was the first to approach the girl. The girl was babbling in Japanese, it seemed that she didn't speak any English, but there was one word that caught Ashley's attention: when she said. "Chris-chan. ," Ashley knew then this girl was looking for Chris.

Ashley tried to tell the girl that Chris wasn't in the building. But of course they where the only ones unable to speak Japanese so Ashley did her best to tell the girl to wait at the lobby that they would get back to her latter but the girl seemed insistent to speak with Chris now, she started to run past Ashley and tried to get toward the elevator. Beth, however, caught the girl. "No one is allowed to go inside this building without permission from Chris."

The girl was obviously becoming quite angry. And then she did something that caught both Ashley and Beth off guard— she performed a take down move on Beth that looked exactly like one of Chris's moves. She then ran past the fallen and surprised girl and into the elevator.

"Did you see what that girl did?" Beth yelled out in shock as she started to got back up. "She used one of Chris's moves on me!"

"Yeah, and I thought that Chris was the only one that knew that one. He told us he learned it from his sensei —from his martial arts training," Ashley said as she and Beth took off after the girl.

xxx

Chris was just landing on the roof of the building in Japan. He was thinking to himself how crazy things have had gotten since the Supreme Elder of Gem had found a way to jump from planet to planet with her multi- dimensional gate. And, was, impressed with his new and improved form that she had to insisted on studying it in great detail.

Sakura landed beside him saying. She knew what was on his mind. "It's okay," she said in an effort to calm him. "You know the way scientists are—when they find something new to study, nothing can stop them from figuring out how it works."

Chris sighed deeply. "Yeah, but does she have to treat me like a science project? I mean, I thought Lorelei and her team would never finish with me!" They both walked into the building not knowing what was going on inside.

xxx

Megan was heading to where all the commotion was. She had heard that someone had gotten to the upper levels of the building. She ran until she found the girl, and then she cut the girl off and caught her inside a shield bubble. When Ashley and Beth caught up, they thanked her for the help and told her to bring her the girl back to the lobby so they could figure out what to do with her.

The girl kept yelling Chris's name over and over and was punching the bubble with all her might. But Megan's shield couldn't be broken by a normal human..

After they'd gotten the girl to calm down, and have a sit in the lobby. They did their best to asked her what she wanted with Chris, but sense the girl didn't speak English, she seemed unable to answer them. But, suddenly, Chris walked into the lobby. "What's going on here? Why are you all away from your posts?"

That's when he saw the girl. "Oh … Neneko-chan!" he said quietly.

When the girl heard him say her name, she turned to him and stood up, the others heard Chris say her name it made sense as to why the girl was here in the first place they knew each other but form where?

Neneko slowly started to walk over to Chris. "Chris-chan," she said again. She raised her hands and cupped his face. At first, the girls all thought the girl was going to kiss him, but right then she slapped him across the face as hard as she could. "*Baka!*" she said, along with a swift stream of Japanese that the girls couldn't follow. *Baka*, they knew, meant stupid!

The girls sprang forward to protect Chris, but he raised his hand to stop them. "I think I deserved that," he said. Then he turned to the girls. "Can you leave us alone for a while?"

Later after things cooled down Chris and Neneko, were sitting on the couches in the lobby talking, the girls had left the room prier to Chris's order but they stayed in the doorway of the lobby and watched as the two talked, as they talked Ashley turned to Sakura, who had joined them, "What are they talking about?"

Sakura told them, "it seems that Neneko is Chris's childhood friend." "She's the granddaughter of Chris's sensei. They grew up together in the temple where I stayed for a while."

The girls' Japanese was improving, and they could understand bits and pieces of Chris and Neneko's conversation. Soon, they were all saddened to hear that Chris's sensei was dying. Neneko had been sent to bring Chris to hear her grandfather's last wishes."

Chris didn't move as he absorbed this. Neneko, was quietly weeping. Chris stood and said, "I will go to respect Sensei's last wishes."

Neneko hearing this stood and bowed saying. "*Arigato*, Chris-chan," she said.

When she said this Chris's four year old daughter Maylu ran into the lobby. She ran past the girls and headed straight to her father holding a picture she had drawn. It was a portrait of Chris and the girls. "Daddy!" shouted Maylu.

Neneko didn't know what to think about this girl, but when she said "daddy" to Chris she turned to Chris with a look of death. She, seemed ready to pounce. "Whose girl is this, and why is she calling you Daddy?" she asked in rapid Japanese.

Chris gave her a nervous look. "This is my daughter," he said.

Neneko turned to him. "When did you have a kid?"

Chris told her, "It happened some time after I became a cyborg. Her mother was the one who saved my life."

Neneko asked, "Where is this woman now?"

Chris just looked at the happy girl in front of him and then back at Neneko. "She's dead … …" "She died three months after Maylu was born."

"*Sumimasen*," she apologized. She couldn't help, but see the sadness in his face realizing how hurt he seemed when he said this.

"Don't be." Chris said as he picked up Maylu and sat her in his lap. "I still have the others, and they help take care of her, so things have petty fun around here. We have made a good family."

Chris turned to the others, whom he knew was had been watching them, and told them, "I must go with Neneko to the temple to hear my sensei's last wishes. I will take my daughter with me."

"No way—I'm going with you," Sakura stated as she entered the room.

"This is a personal matter, Sakura. I need to take care of this myself." ," Chris told her.

"Sensei helped me out too," Sakura told him. "He took care of me before you knew about me."

Chris sighed and said, "All right, but just you." He turned to the others. "I'm sorry—I can't have all of you coming along. This, is very personal."

The others all nodded in agreement for they knew that his sensei was like a second father to him and that he needed this time alone. But they all still planned on following him to make sure that he was safe, especially with that Neneko girl around. For some reason, they did not trust her.

xxx

Later, Chris, Maylu, Neneko, and Sakura where walking up the steps of the dojo at the temple. Neneko asked, "Why does this girl have to come too, Chris?" She gestured to Sakura.

Chris was about to explain when Sakura answered for him, "Sensei is just as important to me, as he is to Chris."

Neneko had forgotten that she could speak Japanese too as they continued, Sakura then asked Neneko, "Just how long have you known Chris for?"

Neneko turned to Chris and then back to the cyborg girl. "I've known him sense I was born though. He is five years older than I."

"So that means that you are still in college, doesn't it?" Sakura asked her with a smug look.

"I am, but that is none of your business anyway."

"Hey," Chris said to the two arguing girls. "Why don't you two keep it down. This is a sacred temple after all."

"Yes, Chris," they both said in unison.

Upon making it to the top of the temple, the four of them were shocked to see the other girls waiting for them. They were talking to someone else who was already at the temple.

"What the hell are you girls doing here?" Chris asked. "I told you all to stay at Cyber Corp. and wait for us!"

But when he saw who they were talking to, he got really quiet. The two of them stared each other down.

Shivers ran down all their spines as Chris and this man stared at each other. Their auras became visible as they mentally fought. Finally, Neneko said, "This is no time for the two of you to fight."

Chris and the man scoffed at each other and turned to head for the room where Chris's Sensei was. Neneko sighed and shook her head.

"What was that about?" Jennifer asked Neneko, as she looked at the others. "Who was that big guy anyway?"

"The big guy's name is Akurei," said Neneko. "He's my cousin, and he's been Chris Kun's rival ever sense he came to this temple." Neneko told them.

The girls did a double take for Neneko had just spoken English for the first time. "You speak English?" Melissa yelled out.

"Of course. If you haven't realized, Chris is half American. I had to learn English, as part of my training," Neneko stated to the girls.

"But why didn't you speak to us at the Cyber Corp. building," Victoria asked?

"Because I didn't know any of you," she stated in a calm voice.

Chris walked straight to where his sensei was in the main dojo living quarters. When he saw his master lying on the photon on the floor, he could not believe how his sensei looked. The master had always seemed so strong— to him and now he seemed as weak as a child. Chris moved close to him and called to him.

His Sensei turned to him, and smiled and said, "I'm glad I got to see you before I died, my boy." Suddenly, Akurei entered the room and moved to the other side of Sensei and greeted him. Sensei looked at the two of them and said, "The reason that I called both of you here is because that I know that my time in the light draws to an end, but I wanted to see my two most promising students to hear my finale wishes."

"First, I want the two of you to end your rivalry."

Akurei looked up at Chris and then back down at his Sensei and said insincerely, "I will do my best, Sensei," he said in a insincere way.."

There Sensei then turned back to Chris and said, "I have something important for you to do. As you know, Neneko's parents died when she was young, so I am all she had left. So I ask you when I die, I wish you to look after her."

Chris knew where this was going and said "I will make sure to take care of her," Chris told Sensei.

"Good," his Sensei said, and then he turned to Akurei, who was still giving Chris a death glare. "And you, Akurei," he said, his voice weakening, "must promise me that you will make sure to help Chris take care of Neneko." Then he turned back to Chris. "And you must take care of this temple, for I am giving this temple and everything in it to the both of you."

Chris was shocked at this statement, for the temple was worth just about as much as his Cyber Corp. building. He bowed in agreement to Sensei, as did Akurei. they both agreed to take good care of the temple and everything in it.

There Sensei smiled and said, "I am glade I can leave this world knowing that everything will be fine." He laid his head back felling asleep for the last time, with a calm smile on his face.

Chris and Akurei both bowed their heads out of respect. Then both stood. They knew that there sensei had lived a good life. Akurei then smiled to Chris and said, "Sensei's dead. So let's cut our losses and sell this place for all it's worth."

Chris about fell back hearing this. "Are you feeling all right?" he asked in astonishment.

"I'm feeling fine," Akurei stated. "but I just don't have the time to take care of this place. And I doubt you have to time either. So, it's just better if we just sell it, and be done with it." Akurei told him.

"How can you say such things? And in front of the master's body?" Chris said asked, still in shock.

"Listen, you have no say in the matter, for Grandfather, said this run-down place is ours, and I say we cut our losses and sell it!," Akurei stated then walked over to Chris and put a friendly arm around his shoulder. "After we sell it, what do you think of letting me take care of Neneko? You seem to have enough women as it is—, and it's not like you can really please her in any way."

Chris pushed Akurei away from him and said, "Forget it! I just promised Sensei that I would watch over her. And, unlike you, I back up what I say."

"Hey, you think, just because, Neneko hung around with you when you were kids that, you think she waits wants to stay with you, now?

Get serious! You're a cyborg freak! I doubt she would give you the time of day!" Akurei gave Chris a smile that made Chris's skin crawl.

Neneko finally stepped between them and said, "I will have none of this. The two of you will not fight in this room or anywhere around this temple. Those are the rules here, and besides *I'll* decide who I will go with. I will go with Chris and respect Grandfather's last wishes. Now you two have a lot of work to do, so get going!"

Neneko yelled out the last part of her speech, making Akurei and Chris to jump to attention and run out the door to prepare for her grandfather's funeral.

"Wow, Neneko, where do did you learn to control Chris and that big guy so well?" Beth asked, amazed at the girl's confidence.

"When you grow up around guys as strong as them," said Neneko, " you have to be strong yourself or you just get left behind. Besides, I couldn't have them fight around my grandfather, —even if he has just past passed on." Neneko spoke with sorrow in her voice. "I am very alone now," she finished.

xxx

Later, after Chris and Akurei had put their Sensei to rest, they had some unfinished business to take care of. Akurei did not like the idea of Neneko going with Chris, and Chris didn't like the idea of Akurei selling the place against Sensei's wishes.

"You know, Striker," Akurei started, "if you agree to my terms, I won't have to mess you up."

Chris was now wondering what Akurei could be thinking— that there was no way that Akurei could beat him in fair combat, but, then again, Akurei had never been one to play fair.

"Listen, Akurei, there is no reason that the two of us should fight over something so trivial."

"No, Striker," Akurei said taking a step toward him. "You know, I thought maybe time had made you open your eyes and realize that honor has no place in the real world anymore. But no, you're still the self-righteous fool you've always been! It's truly pathetic."

"You're the one who's pathetic, Akurei," retorted Chris. "You think honor' is a weakness—but it's a strength. Honor defines who I am and makes me strong. Hell, without it, I wouldn't be the man I an am today!"

"Ha!" Akurei laughed. "You mean a cyborg freak of nature like you are! You who will never live a normal life again!"

Chris didn't want to take this any further. "We will continue this conversation tomorrow," he said.

He started to walk off.

But Akurei yelled, "You're also a coward as well as a fool! That's all you'll ever be!"

Chris didn't stop. He just flew off into the sky.

xxx

Sam and the cyber girls had seen the whole argument and were angry at Akurei for trying to make Chris fight him. Akurei should know that a human would not stand a chance against a Super Cyborg.

As they all walked past Akurei, Rebecca turned to Victoria said, "That guy's got some screws lose or something."

Victoria told her, "Keep it down, he might hear you."

"I may not be as strong as a cyborg," said Akurei, " but at least I'm *real* and not some clone!" Akurei stated as he heard Rebecca's comment.

When Rebecca heard this, she turned around with tears in her eyes remembering what the general had said about them. She wanted to attack Akurei right then and there. But, before Rebecca attacked him, surprisingly, it was Ashley who stayed calm saying. "Ignore him, Rebecca. A man ,like that doesn't deserve a women's time of day."

Akurei laughed at them saying. "Whatever, makes you fakes feel better," he said. And he turned walked off in the other direction.

After everyone had settled in for the night, Chris had decided it might be a good idea to visit the hot springs. As he was walking quietly out the door, when his four year daughter came out of one of the rooms and asked, "Where are you going, Daddy?"

"I'm heading to the Hot hot springs. Do you wont want to join me?"

"What's a hot spring?" The the little girl asked.

"Let's go get you a change of clothes and I'll show you."

Then they headed quietly out of the building.

Maylu smiled at the wide expanse of the springs she smiled at the steaming water—it looked like a large swimming pool to her.

Chris helped his young daughter get washed up, before she got into the water. When he was sure she was okay, he then told her to go on ahead, he then undressed himself and, wrapped a towel around his waist, and went got into the hot spring water with her. When he saw his daughter playing in the water, it reminded him of old times when he was young.

The cyborg lay back in the water. It was amazing how good it felt. He had he always loved the springs they always did make him fell better, and now the water was actually good for his metal parts too, for it cleaned him better than anything else.

Neneko, meanwhile, was still awake talking to some of the older girls telling some them about some of the good times she had spent with Chris back when he was young. Neneko, of course, had known Chris before he was cyborg, and, for the girls, hearing about his past was like getting to know him all over again. Jennifer then made a suggestion. "I hear there are some killer hot springs here," she said. "Let's go there!"

Chris had been in deep thought about how it was nice to see Neneko again after all these years. Then he laughed to himself. *It hasn't really been all that long*, he thought. *But it seems like an eternity. That always happens when I leave this place.*

As the girls got ready to get go to the springs, Ashley turned to Neneko, who had just removed her glasses so she could remove her shirt, and asked, "Just how close are you two anyway? I mean, you grow up together, right?"

"What do you mean by that?" Neneko asked as she started to blush at the thought?.

"I mean, you two grew up together, even though, Chris is older than you. So I'm guessing that he and you bathed together as kids sometimes, right?" The the fire girl stated in a suggestive way.

The question and the boldness of Ashley's words made the young girl nearly drop her things, but she held onto her shirt that she had just taken off close to her. She remembered the past and thought about all the times that Chris had been there. But then Ashley started talking again, snapping the girl back to reality. "That is none of your business," Neneko said to Ashley. "And, for the record, I don't know you well enough to divulge such personal Neneko then thought of something that she had wonted to asked Chris but was too afraid because she thought it was to much of a private matter to Chris. Suddenly, she asked, "Just how much of Chris is cybernetic?"

The five cyborg girls looked at each other. Smiling, and Sakura told her, "We would love to *tell* you, but how about, instead, we *show* you!" They all then pushed Neneko out of the building and through the gate that led to the spring. It was a good thing that Neneko had just wrapped a towel around herself because what she saw made her blush from top to bottom. There was Chris sitting in the water at the edge of the spring. He was sleeping. He was in the springs holding himself out of the water with both arms, and little Maylu was playing in the water, without a care in the world.

Neneko could not believe it. She knew Chris was a hard sleeper, and she didn't won't to wake him in the condition that he was in. But then the other girls came up behind her. "What do you think?" Ashley asked.

Neneko turned to them and whispered loudly, "You all knew that he was in here, didn't you?" They looked at each other and then back to Neneko. Ashley said. "We did, for we have a communications connection with him, and sense our trip into space we knew Chris was heading to the springs."

"So that's why you all lead me here," said Neneko. "We have got to get out of here, before he wakes up, and finds us in here with him!"

But then Maylu saw them and yelled out, "My momma's are here! Have you all come to play in the warm water too?"

Sakura snickered a little as she waded in the water. "We have," she told the child.

Maylu innocently smiled, then said, "It's too bad Daddy fell asleep." She pointed to the sleeping form of her father.

"Sakura!" Neneko yelled called out again. But then she covered her mouth, afraid that she was going to awaken Chris. She watched the others go into the water not even caring that Chris was still sleeping very close to them. Jennifer then told her, "Don't worry. Once Chris is asleep, nothing less than a sonic boom could awaken him."

"That isn't the point," Neneko yelled said quietly, trying to get them to stop getting to close to Chris. "I can't believe you're all are so bold! What if Chris wakes up and finds you all in the buff!"

This situation was starting to get to Neneko. She seemed intimidated by the appearance of the cyborg girls. They were all very beautiful, and had perfect bodies. Neneko turned away from the others and was about to leave, Chris then decided to wake up. He sensed that there was a lot of noise for it just being him and Maylu.

Chris opened his eyes to a big surprise. There, in front of him, were Jennifer, Melissa, Sakura, Victoria, and Ashley. They were were where staring straight at him.

He about jumped out of his skin—or his towel—as he jumped out of the water. As he landed unsteadily on the stone patio, outside the spring and backed right into Neneko. As he turned to her, he turned to see the shock in her eyes. There she was standing there wearing nothing but a thin towel—in front of the guy she had known she liked even before she liked boys.

The blush on her face told Chris to look away. He turned back around, but there where the others—and his daughter staring at him. Maylu, being naive and young, was clearly wondering what was wrong.

Chris then did the only decent thing a guy could do in this situation. He just walked around Neneko and started to walk back to the dojo. But Ashley flew ran after him and stood in front of him. "Where do you think your going?" she demanded.

Chris looked at Neneko, who still seemed to be in shock at the situation. Then turned back to Ashley. and said "I should go," he said. "This is situation is difficult for Neneko. The last thing I want right now is any misunderstanding."

"Oh, come on, Chris," Ashley said with a cheeky grin. "This isn't the first time you've seen us in the buff— and, besides, you told us before that we're like family. And Neneko is one of us now, isn't she?" Ashley said with a cheeky grin.

Chris once again started to move past Ashley, but then he heard a small voice say, "Stay."

He stopped in his tracks and asked, "What was that?"

Neneko summoned all her courage and turned to Chris. "Stay, I don't mind."

Chris looked straight at her as his cybernetic eye focused on her and asked, "Are you sure?"

She turned to him and said "I am," she said. "We are family too. We were raised together, so it is okay. Besides," she said as she looked at the cybernetic parts on his body, "I want to know exactly what happened to you. And I want to know about the mother of your daughter. I don't think I would will get another opportunity to asked."

Neneko breathed out hard as she realized what she had just said. Her nervousness was apparent she was so nervous that it was showing all over her. Chris smiled and said, "It seems that the others here have started to rub off on you. You are becoming just as bold as they are—when it comes to me that is."

Chris returned to the water, and Neneko watched the steam rise from each part of his body just from the heat of the the metal.

Neneko slowly got in too. She kept her distance from Chris, but she watched him carefully, for it was the first time she had a good look at how much of him was cybernetic. It was an amazing sight. She watched as each part moved in perfect onion, with the parts of him that were still flesh.

Neneko then jumped as Chris started to talk. He started to tell her his whole story. He told her at what had happen to him, how he stopped six armed men and when he was about to get out, they blow up the building. He told her how Minawa saved him and how he had saved her her from living in a glass tube. As he spoke of Minawa, a tear ran down his face.

Then he told her about Ellis and how she was the one who had really pushed him into supreme mode. He told her about the general and how much the General did to them and how he controlled the cyborg girls.

Neneko now had a lot to think about. She now understood that Chris had been through a lot. And she understood now why he hadn't contacted her for so long. And after Chris finished his story, she once again summoned up her courage to asked Chris, "Can I take a good look at your metal?"

Because ever sense she saw him again this thought had ran though her mind just what was that metal like but To her surprise, Chris told her to go ahead and take a good look. "It doesn't matter," he said. "I can't feel any of the metal parts anyway. "Watch what you touch, though, not all of me is made of metal." He half joked.

Her nervousness was going crazy considering the possession that they were in, but she thought that she would never get anther chance to check out his cybernetic body.

She slowly inched her way toward him, and, with the five cyborg girls watching her every move, she finally got a good look at the cybernetics that made up Chris's body. The cyborg girls began to giggle and laughed a bit.

Neneko looked up at him and asked, "How much of you is cybernetic?"

"About 70 percent," He told her as she reached out to touch him.

Her expression reflected her shock. When she herd this, and thought of him being this way for good was a lot to take in, when she finally touched one of his arms, he didn't even react. She expected him to react but he didn't even move she slowly ran her hand down the metal arm feeling how each part went together. When she reached the tip of his hand, she intertwined her fingers in his. She thought that he would feel her hand in his, but he didn't react.

Neneko moved her attention to his face. She noticed that his face was part flesh and part metal. At least half of his entire head was metal. She looked at his chest. There were spots on the cybernetic part of his body where she could see all the way through him.

She saw the scares on the flesh of his body, and she couldn't resist moving one of her hands along the length of one of the long scares. But, when Chris jumped at the contact, she moved away quickly.

"Sorry.," Neneko said as she moved away from him.

"Don't be sorry," he said. "Though I'm cybernetic, I can still feel a little—but there are times that this body feels so numb that I just wish that I could curl up next to a warm body, … just to know that I'm not alone …, that I am not a robot."

CHAPTER 45

Later that night, after they, finished up at the springs, Chris was sleeping soundly next to his daughter. Maylu, who had come into his room earlier because she had had a bad dream about losing her father to a monster. Little did the child know how close to the truth that dream had been.

Suddenly, Chris opened his eyes, sensing danger. He quickly moved Maylu out of the way as a large beast crashed through the wall into his room. It stood stood at lest ten feet tall. It was thick and muscular, but its body was as black as night. Even with his night vision on, it was difficult for Chris to see the intruder. All he could make out was an outline of the beast and the glowing red eyes.

"Who are you?" Chris yelled as he looked at the beast before him.

"I am your destroyer." The beast said in a familiar voice.

"Akurei!" Chris said as he recognized the voice, but the beast didn't answer. It just attacked. It slammed its fist down at the ground, but Chris grabbed his daughter, jumped up, and spun in the air, and throw the window, landing on the ground outside.

Chris put his daughter down. "You go hide, little one," and she ran off. Chris stood ready as the beast he was now sure was Akurei stepped out, through the window, destroying the wall in the process.

"What are you doing, Akurei?" Chris asked. "And how did you end up like this?"

"Wouldn't you like to know!" Akurei told him as he stood in front of Chris ready to strike.

"There is no way you can win a fight with me," Chris warned Akurei. "Your flesh and blood is no match for my cybernetic strength."

"That doesn't matter anymore," Akurei stated, in a near growl. "And, as for an answer to your earlier question, what I want is you dead!"

"Why, Akurei?" Chris asked. "There haven't been any problems before. Why start now?"

"There were always problems with you, Chris, ever sense you came here. You took everything from me— my grandfather's love, and respect, … even Neneko. Everything seemed to always fall into place for you, and, every time I fought you in those days, you always beat me like it was nothing to you! And now, when you come back, Grandfather decides that it be, you to take care of Neneko and — not me, a member of her own family."

"Sensei just knew that I would take good care of her and this place," Chris said, trying to reason with Akurei, who was stepping closer as he talked. "Sensei probably knew that you had planned on selling the temple to make money, and that was never Sensei's plan." "He wanted this place to stand the test of time and remain here forever."

Akurei was in front of Chris now, glaring down at him like the way a predator looks at its pray. "None of that matters anymore, for, when I kill you, everything that was given to you, will be mine."

With that, Akurei punched Chris so fast that Chris didn't even have time to think. The blow blasted him right out of sight of the temple.

Akurei, obviously thinking that there was no way that Chris could get back in time to stop him, walked to the edge of the temple and raised his hand in the air. He pointed his fingertips at the center of the temple. His finger nails opened, and power started to charge in his fingers. But, before he fired, Chris flew back at top speed and slammed his fist right into Akurei's head making him fly off into the air and crash back into one of the temple buildings.

The girls, who were inside sleeping, where awakened by the crash. Jennifer scanned around the area and looked through the walls. She could and saw the fighting going on outside. She turned to the others and said, "There's a fight outside, —Chris is fighting some kind of monster!"

Chris was now flying over the spot where he thought Akurei had landed. He looked around and yelled out Akurei's name, but there was no answer, —until a hand burst out of the ground and grabbed him, by the leg, picked him up upside down, and swung him around and then slammed him to the ground. Right as Akurei was about to finish the job, an electrical blast hit him from behind.

"You, leave him alone!" Sakura yelled as the others ran up behind her. "No one hits our Chris and gets away with it!" Sakura yelled as the others ran up behind her.

Akurei laughed at the thought of Chris having to rely on these little girls to save him. This made Ashley mad enough to fly forward at Akurei. Just as she punched him, there was a loud crack from her fist, and she reared back in pain.

"What the hell are you made of?" Ashley yelled as she rubbed her hand.

Akurei laughed again at the absurdity of their efforts, for he knew that he was indestructible and that no little cyborg was going to stop him now.

Akurei then turned back to Chris, but he was gone. It appeared that Chris, had left the girls alone. But then he heard someone yelled Akurei's name. He looked up to where the voice was coming from and saw Chris coming straight down on him at full force. Chris slammed down on his opponent's face, crushing his head in. Akurei fell to the ground. Chris turned to others asking, "Are you all okay?"

"Yeah, we're fine, Chris. What was that thing?" Victoria asked.

"It was Akurei," Chris told them. "It looks like he did something to himself in order to fight me hand to hand."

Jennifer walked over and scanned the thing that was once Akurei. "It looks like some kind of mutation, and whoever did this to him, was defiantly a genius in DNA research."

"So what do we do with him now?" Melissa asked.

"Now we take him back to the island and let Sam study him and see if she can find out who or what made him." Chris stated. He then turned and yelled out to Maylu, "It's safe to came come out!" Maylu came running straight to her father. He picked her up and held her close as he turned to Victoria. "Go ahead and take what's left of Akurei to Sam."

Victoria walked up to the body and saw that his whole head had been smashed in by Chris's strike. She saw how the skull was so totally smashed to the point it didn't even look as if he had a head any more.

Chris saw Victoria spacing out and said, "Today, girl." As she snapped back to reality and focused her gravity powers. She lifted the body into the air and took off like a beam of light.

"Now what do we do, Chris?" Rebecca asked curiously.

"Now we go back to bed, and, in the morning, we deal with cleaning up this mess." The girls looked around at the mess that Chris and Akurei had made in there little tussle. It seemed that half the living quarters was destroyed. That meaning they were going to have a long day tomorrow.

xxx

The next morning, Neneko was told what had happened. Somehow she was able to sleep through the whole fight. Chris joked with her about how she had always been like that, even when they were young. She could always sleep through almost anything anything—just like him.

Neneko slapped him on the shoulder saying, "Chris, I can't believe that Akurei has been turned into some kind of mutant."

Changing the subject, Chris nodded and said, "Sam should be able to find out just how he did it." He then clapped his metal hands together and said, "Enough talk, now it's time to fix this place and return it back to its former glory."

He and the others all went to work on fixing the damage done to the temple the night before. Neneko watched as the cyborg girls used their various powers as they worked. It was an amazing sight to behold, especially seeing little Rebecca left three hundred times her weight!

"It's amazing, isn't." Chris said to Neneko, "Heck, you should see what Maylu can do!"

"What do you mean by that? She's only four years old! There's no way that she— ..." but before Neneko finished, Chris pointed to where Maylu was helping Kate out with the rubble from the collapsed buildings. Once again, Neneko was amazed. The four-year-old lifted up a rock that was at least three times her size, and, with speed to match her strength, the child moved the large rock and threw it off away from the edge of the temple with what looked like ease.

"Like I said, it's amazing," Chris finished, and then went back to work himself.

By the early afternoon, they had finished fixing the temple. What would have taken normal people at least two days, to fix up Chris and others did in less then half a morning. He told the girls they had done a great job. "Now that the temple is back to snuff," he said, "you should head back to the island and take the rest of the day off."

"And what about you, Chris, aren't you coming back?" Beth asked with a sad look.

"I've still got work to do here, and Neneko has to go back to school tomorrow. I want to find out if she has been doing well."

"That's right," Kate stated to the only human girl in there their group, "you still have to finish school! Don't you miss Neneko?."

"Yes, I do. I wasn't as lucky as you girls, —I have to get an education because I'll have to work for a living."

Chris laughed a bit as they argued, thinking how they all ready sounded like one big happy family. Finally he had to interrupt in the middle and said. "Okay, ladies, that's enough. We have more important things to do."

Chris turned to the cyborg girls and told them, "When you all get to the island, you need to ask Sam if she has found out anything about the mutant Akurei."

Sakura said, "We'll contact you as soon as we know anything."

Ashley asked, "When are you going to meet up with us?"

"I'll be there latter on today, so don't worry. I know how you all worry about me," he said.

"Oh, one more thing, girls, take Maylu with you. I think, it looks like she could use a nap." When Maylu heard the word *nap*, she shot up and said, "No nap, no nap no nap!"

Chris then knelt down to her level and said, "You need a nap if you plane on having more fun with everyone latter."

Maylu smiled at her father and hugged him. Then ran to Sakura, who picked her up saying and said, "Ready to go?"

Chris watched as they all flew heading toward their floating island home. Just before, Destiny took off she gave Chris a sad look. He turned to her and asked, "What's wrong?"

She jumped a little because she didn't expected that question, but then shook her head real fast and said, "It's nothing." Then she turned to the others and took off after them.

xxx

In her lab on the island, Sam was studying the remains of Akurei, trying to figure out just who had made such an abomination. Victoria soon joined her and asked, her "Have you find found anything, yet?"

Sam shook her head saying. "No, the mutant genome is hard to figure out, but there is some good news. Since this mutant's head was intact, it means that I can scan its memories for anything that can help us find out where it came from."

"Wait, did you say that its head was intact?" Victoria asked shocked.

"Yes, I did. So?"

"Well So … Chris crushed its head in. That's how he killed it!"

They both went into the adjoining isolation room and looked at the body lying on a the table in the isolation room. Its head had regenerated! Just then, all of Sam's monitoring equipment went crazy, and they both ran back to the lab. When they looked back through glass wall of the isolation room, Akurei was standing right in front of the glass of the isolation room there, breathing hard onto the glass.

When the others landed on the floating island, they could tell something was very wrong. Sparks where shooting out form Samantha's lab. Jennifer went to infrared and saw that there was a large man standing over two people in the lab.

Sakura turned to the others and gave orders: "Jennifer, Ashley, Melissa, Rebecca, Kim, come with me. The rest of you stay here, and scout around,." they agreed as they ran in, Megan, Beth, Kate, April, and Destiny watched as the others ran off. Worry was clearly marked on their faces.

Inside the lab, it was dark as night. Jennifer had to be their eyes. Suddenly, they heard someone scream. They ran toward the sound, and, in the flashes of light that came from an overhead light that was swaying back and forth and blinking on and off, they saw him in the flashes of light.

The red glowing eyes told them that it was Akurei—healed and ready to kill. When he took a step forward, something caught their eyes. It was what he was holding in his hand. When the light swung to illuminate the beast, the girls saw he was holding Victoria's lifeless body.

The sight of their friend's lifeless body and in the arms of the monster that stood before them made them all shake with fear and shock. Ashley, though, was not about let this go unpunished. She powered up and turned to the others saying, "Are we going to just stand by and watch as this monster kills us?"

They all looked at her and then, nodded in agreement that they where not going to give up without a fight and, they readied themselves to fight to the end. No one gets away with killing one of their teammates.

Outside Megan, Beth, Kate, April, and Destiny the others watched as blasts of all kinds started to shoot out of the lab.

"What the heck is going in there?" Beth asked.

"I have no idea, but I intent to find out," April yelled out. The group was about to go in when they heard someone yell out."Wait!"

They turned to see Sam. She was covered in what looked like blood, and was she in deep shock. Kate asked, "What happened?"

Sam took a deep breath before she screamed out, "It was Akurei! He woke up and attacked us!"

Her voice softened. "He killed Victoria. It was so fast that I didn't even see it." She then fell to her knees and cried.

"I barely managed to get away. He's a monster—a demon that no one can stop!" Sam then started to mumbled how nothing can stop this demon and then said words that didn't make any sense.

An explosion then erupted again form the lab, blowing a large part of the building away. Everyone could see the demon Akurei holding up Rebecca with one hand. Kim was on Akurei's back trying to absorb some of his energy, but he wasn't stopping—if anything, he was getting stronger.

Akurei then threw Rebecca as hard as he could at Sakura, who seemed to be badly beaten. Both girls slammed into a wall from the force. Jennifer then jumped right at Akurei and fired a point blank beam right at his head, but it didn't even faze him. Akurei just back handed her and she slammed into a wall. Then he moved over to her and crushed her against the wall.

Ashley fired up every thing she had at the beast as this went on it didn't do any good. He just walked through the flames at her. Ashley screamed out as Akurei grabbed her by the head, and, with one swift move, snapped her neck. The girl fell to the ground like a rag doll.

Kim was still holding on to Akurei. She kept him from being at fell power, but that didn't last long. Akurei reached back and grabbed her and slammed her against the back wall, witch exploded from the impact.

Akurei then turned to the others. The look in his eyes said he was out for blood. He vanished for a moment and then appeared in front of the five girls. He raised his hands up and punched down at them all at once, but his blow was stopped by Megan's shields,. The force of one blow, however, was enough to take up all of her power, and she fell to the ground powerless to hold back his attack.

Akurei yelled out, "Prepare to die!" He raised his hand again, and a strange aura appeared around his body.

When Destiny saw this, she grabbed the only two she could get to in time— Maylu and Sam. The three of them vanished, just as the whole island blew up in a fiery blaze.

xxx

Chris was just walking away from the campus after dropping off Neneko when he fell to his knees and roared out in pain. He held his head as he fell to the ground shaking. Neneko heard him and and ran back to him. "What's wrong?" she asked, falling to her knees next to him. But he didn't answer. He just stood up and looked to the sky in an emotionless state. Then shot into the sky, at an incredible speed. Neneko watched him fly wondering what was wrong with him.

Chris flew as fast as he could. He knew that something was monstrously wrong. He made it to the island just as it blew. The sight of this would be etched into the back of his mind for the rest of his life. He stopped, unable to move as he watched the island fall. There was no way anything could survive, that blast—not even a cyborg.

Right then, he saw, Akurei fly away from the falling island. The sight enraged him far more than anything he had ever experienced. He shot over to him before Akurei could get away and appeared right in front of him. The explosion still lit up the skies. Akurei stopped to see the fire that was in Chris's eyes—he could see that Chris was burning mad.

Chris could never forgive such an act. Akurei had, destroyed them all—Jennifer, Sakura, April, Megan, Victoria, Beth, Rebecca, Kite, Kim, Ashley, Melissa, and Destiny, and not to forget Samantha and little Maylu.

Chris let out a lion's roar that seemed to shake the very boundaries of creation itself. Akurei laughed. He had been waiting for years to see him Chris angry.

Akurei roared out, too, to mock Chris. But, when Chris's rage hit its peck, he changed to his Perfect Supreme mode, shedding his clothing during the process. "I'm going to make you pay for this! *You're dead!*"

"Bring it on, Striker-san!" Akurei stated, egging the cyborg on. As the two shot forward, both reared back as Chris yelled out, "*Screaming Bullet!*" He let out everything he could at Akurei, and, when their fist's hit collided, there was a monstrous shock wave that broke the sound barrier.

The energies that they released were incredible as they both pushed forward. Just as Chris thought he was making some headway, something unexpected happened. Chris's hand and half his arm shattered.

He never thought that flesh could match his metal. Chris flew past Akurei and paused. Then looked at what was left of his hand and arm except for a metal spike.

Chris looked back at Akurei, as he pointed his hand at Chris. Akurei's finger nails opened up and he sent blast after blast at Chris. Chris tried to block the blasts, but to no avail. The blasts were slowly eating away at his metal body.

As his metal was being, eaten away he realized that whoever made Akurei like this had to have known about about him inside and out.

All of a sudden, Akurei disappeared and then reappeared in front of Chris. He cupped his fists together and slammed them down on Chris, hitting him straight to the ground with such force that the impact made a crater around him.

Akurei slowly landed right next to Chris, his whose body was now nearly destroyed after only a couple of moves done by Akurei. The mutant grabbed Chris and picked him up by the neck. He laughed as he told him, "My plan has worked perfectly! By letting you beat me, I was able to get to your island and destroy it, as well as those cyborg bitches of yours."

When Chris heard Akurei say this, Chris's eyes shot open as he lunged forward and wrapped his arms around the mutant and shot into the sky.

"What the hell are you doing, you freak? Let me go!" Akurei yelled out as Chris went faster straight into the sky.

"I plan on, execute you in space!" cried Chris. "I know for a fact that no human can survive in space without a spacesuit or cybernetic lungs." Chris thought he had won once he hit the upper atmosphere. But something was wrong. Akurei was just smiling. It, was impossible, but Akurei was fine even in space.

Akurei burst free of the cyborg's grip saying, "If you think, being in space can stop me, you're dead wrong, —and in fact, your just *dead!*" Akurei stated hitting Chris with a beam of energy that came, right out of his mouth. The beam blasted Chris with a monstrous force that sent him flying straight to the moon, where he crashed with such force that it almost change the moon's course.

Chris was lying in a crater made from the impact. He reverted back to his normal form. Since he had torn out of his clothes, he lay there nude.

Akurei also landed on the moon and started walking toward Chris. He was laughing as he said, "This is a perfect way for you to die, — alone and naked … far away from anyone who can help you."

"At least I will rejoin the girls now, and, I can see my Minawa again," Chris said with a cough. The mutant then started to charge up a power beam in his hand. He aimed it right at the cyborg.

Chris watched. He knew the beam was about to fire, and he felt he was ready to die. But right then Destiny appeared right next to him. "You're not going to die yet! We still need you!" She touched him, and they both disappeared in a flash. The beam found its target, but succeeded only in destroying a large area of the moon's surface where Chris had laid.

"Striker, you have a coward's luck!!!" Akurei roared out as he saw them disappear.

xxx

Akurei turned back to Earth and thought, he would have some fun sense Chris was gone, he knew that nothing could stop him, and he flew back to where Neneko was. She still had no idea where Chris had gone. Suddenly, Akurei landed in front of her smiling he grabbed her "Chris is no longer a problem, so now you must come with me."

"Chris-san can't be stopped by you your lying!," Neneko yelled as she fought against the mutant's grip. But her punches didn't even faze him. He grabbed both her hands with one of his and picked her off the ground. "It's useless for you to fight. Nothing can stop me. My body is indestructible and ever growing."

Tears rolled down Neneko's face thinking about Chris. How could he have been beaten? She felt so helpless now. How much she wished she had some of the cybernetic powers like those cyborg girls.

xxx

Meanwhile, at the wrecked sight of the floating island, eleven beams of lights shot out of the remains heading toward their target.

xxx

Suddenly, something hit Neneko, who was still being held fast by Akurei. The girl found herself surrounded in a strange light. Akurei was angered to find that he could not get past the light.

xxx

Destiny had just landed on the planet Gem with Chris. She fell to the ground exhausted right outside the sanctuary of the Supreme Elder Lorelei, who ran straight to them. She could see how damaged Chris was. He, was a work of cybernetic art; nothing should be able to do this to him. She then turned to Destiny who had propped herself up against the outside wall of the sanctuary. "Who did this to him?" she asked the exhausted girl.

She took a couple of deep breaths before saying, "A mutant monster did this, but he was more like a demon than anything else."

Lorelei then called out for help, and a young girl walked out of the sanctuary. She was Lorelei's new apprentice, Nodoka. She was a shy-looking girl who was a little clumsy and apologized a lot. When she ran out of the lab, she tripped over Chris's nude body and fell on top of him. When she realized that he was a man, witch wasn't difficult considering that he was naked, she jumped off him.

"Why is there a naked man here?" Nodoka asked. She seemed to be scared out of her mind.

"This man is Chris Striker, the Super Cyborg, the saver of this planet. And right now he needs our help. He is badly hurt and needs repairs, so help me get him into the lab and onto a table so we can start working on him."

The elder spoke with an intensity that it removed all of Nodoka's fears. She bent down and helped her teacher pick up, the unconscious cyborg. Together, they carried him inside and set him on a lab table. The elder started working on him immediately. While she worked, she yelled out for Sam to help out, Nodoka was still a little shocked at what had happened. With new powers from Lorelei, Destiny had managed to get Sam and Maylu off the island to the safety of Gem.

While Lorelei and Sam worked in Lorelei's lab on the planet Gem.

Neneko awoke to find herself surrounded in light. She looked up and saw eleven of the twelve cyborg girls standing around her.

"What's going on?" She weakly asked.

They all spoke in unison as they said: "Our bodies have been destroyed, but a part of us has survived, —the part of us that contains our powers, in witch we now give to you."

" We only ask that you use these powers to fight alongside Chris as we have. We ask you to love and protect him."

Neneko nodded as she watched them all speak as if they were one. Then Ashley stepped up and said, "You had better take good care of him, or else you will answer to me!" As they turned back to beams of light and shot into her.

Akurei punched at the ball of light that shielded Neneko, but he couldn't penetrate the powerful aura. Suddenly, something shot out of the ball and flew into the sky. It was Neneko. She looked the same, but she felt incredible, for she now had all the powers of the eleven of the cyborg's girls. She could feel the powers coursing through her. She had never felt so alive—almost as if she had been reborn. But she could still feel the others deep inside her telling her everything that she needed to know about how to use their powers.

Neneko turned to Akurei. "Time for you to pay for what you did to Chris-Kun and those girls, Their powers are now mine, and I intend to use them to take you down!"

Akurei laughed at the thought of her even trying to beat him with the weak powers of the cyborg girls. He had been able to beat each one easily, so it shouldn't matter if all their powers were in one body. That would be easier for him and saves him some time.

Neneko, though, was not in intimidated. "There is more to me, than there was with them, —allow me to show you!" And she then forced her hands forward, letting out a gravity force that was stronger than anything Akurei had felt before.

The force of the gravity that slammed down on Akurei was so strong that it slammed him to the ground, creating a crater around him. It was then that he realized that the forces in this girl were greater than forces that had been in the the originals.

"Do you see now, Akurei?" Neneko started. "Not only do I have their powers, but the powers are magnified ten fold in me!"

"It still won't save you!" Akurei yelled out as he jumped up. Then digging himself into the ground. Neneko landed and looked around at the spot where he had stood, and there was nothing but a hole. She then felt something moving underground. She jumped in the air as Akurei tried to grab her, but he missed as he joined her in the air.

Neneko now had the perfect chance to stop him. She started to engage all the powers at once. When she got going, Akurei was hit with fire, ice beams, water, and electricity.

The blasts blew Akurei through four buildings and then slammed him into a fifth with incredible force. His impression remained in the side of in the building. Akurei shook it the attack off, but, before he could get himself free away, Neneko appeared in front of him and hit him with a right hook that blasted him through the rest of the building. She then appeared behind the building and slammed Akurei to the ground with a double- fisted punch.

xxx

Lorelei and Sam watched as Chris's eyes slowly opened. All of a sudden, they shot open wide and he jumped up and began to transform to his Perfect Supreme mode. "Why didn't you let me die? I failed them all! I should of have died with them!, I deserve to die! There is no way that I should go on, —I don't deserve to live!" He yelled as he picked up a large computer and prepared to throw it in anger. "Why did you save me? Why?"

Everyone started to panic. They were afraid that Chris was going to kill them. But, just then, he just put down the computer and fell to his knees unable to stop the tears from steaming down his face. He changed back to normal.

The Supreme Elder walked over to him and put a hand on his shoulder. "It will be all right. I will make the pain go way, so don't worry."

"I failed them all," Chris said as he looked at her with a tears going down his face. "My honor has been destroyed with them. I have nothing worth fighting for anymore. They are all gone."

"You will fight again. I will make sure of that," the elder said. She pushed a spot on the back of his neck and he shut down. She then patted his shoulder as his eyes seemed to stare into space. "I am truly sorry, Chris."

Lorelei then turned to Sam and Nodoka. "Help me get him back on the table," she said.

They did so, and Sam asked, "What did you do to him?"

"I reset his systems, for I plane on removing his memories of the cyborgs that where lost today from his memory" she told them.

Both Nodoka and Sam looked at each other. "Is that a good idea?" Sam asked. "What if he finds out?"

"You all saw the way he reacted," Lorelei said. "There is no way that he would be willing to fight again if he thinks that he failed them. I feel right now that this is the lesser of two evils. I just hope that someday that he will forgive me." With that, she placed a wire to his head that led to a another computer and started to work. When she was finished, Chris would think that, Neneko had had the eleven powers to start with, for Lorelei had been monitoring Earth and had seen the powers go into the girl. When she reactivated him, Chris would "remember" that it was only him his daughter Sam and Destiny who had fought alongside him through all the fights they had been in.

CHAPTER 46

Chris sat up and rubbing his head. "What happened?" Until it all came back to him. Akurei had nearly killed him, and then Destiny had saved him. "How did I get here?" Chris asked, looking around realizing he was on, the planet Gem.

"It was Destiny," said Lorelei. "When I fixed her a while, back, I gave her a new power to, —teleport. So, right before the island blew up, she grabbed your daughter and Sam and transported them here. Then once she did that she transported, to where you were and brought you here right before that mutant got you."

"That's great!" Chris started. "But how come she looks so tired?" Destiny was lying against the wall sleeping.

"It's because she transported three people across the universe! That takes a lot of power, so she needs some time to rejuvenate."

Chris then remembered Neneko. "And, Neneko—is she okay?"

Lorelei told him "She's fine right now, but she's fighting Akurei, and I'm afraid that she won't last long."

"Than I've got to get down there and help her!" Then Chris paused for a moment before asking, "Do you have a pair of pants I can borrow?"

xxx

Neneko had thought that she had beaten Akurei with that last attack, but, when he shot out of the crater that he'd made, she realized that this fight was far from over. She saw the attack coming and readied herself.

She was fast enough to block his attack using a force field, but the impact that Akurei hit her with still felt like a tank smashing into her.

Neneko flew back holding her stomach, and Akurei shot forward again and punched her so hard that she crashed onto the top of a building.

She started to get up, when Akurei came down and stepped down on her. He moved down close to her face. His hands were her crushing down on her chest. "Well, isn't this cozy? You actually didn't think that you could beat me, did you? I told you before—my body is indestructible."

"You are a true demon, Akurei," Neneko grunted out, as she tried to get Akurei off her. But it was like having a full-grown bull on top of her.

"You should just join me and stop thinking about that fool Striker," Akurei said. "Besides, you should have seen the way he begged for his life! He crying like a baby."

A tear went down Neneko's face as she yelled, "Chris would never beg! I know him, —he would of have died spitting in your face!"

Right as she said this, she absorbed herself into the roof of the building and disappeared. Enraged, Akurei jumped up and slammed into the building and landed on the ground inside. He looked around trying to find her. His roar echoed throughout the building as he started to power up, his energy raging out of control.

Neneko had managed to go straight through the building. She ran out of the front door of the building just in time, for, the moment she ran out, the whole building blew up. Akurei shot out of the inferno roaring, out "Neneko! Come out, and fight!"

People around the building started screaming and running for their lives as Akurei fired beam after beam out of his hands destroying everything around him.

xxx

After Chris asked if he could get a pair of pants, Lorelei the Elder said, "Wait a minute. I'm not finished with you yet."

"Just what did you have in mind woman?" Chris said as a chill went down his spine.

"Don't worry. It's only something that will make it easier for you if you to remain the way you, are."

Lorelei said as she walked over to a large metal door that led into an adjoining large room. A monitoring window separated the two rooms.

She asked him "Please step inside this room,"

He rapped the sheet around himself as he started to walk over to the door, but the elder cleared her throat indicating that he could not take the sheet with him. She then held out her hands for him to give her the sheet. He just shook his head and said, "You girls just like seeing me naked, don't you?"

"It's okay, because— I'm a doctor," said Lorelei.

But when Chris throw the sheet off himself it misted Lorelei and fell around Nodoka's shoulders. The young woman freaked out and yelled, "Man germs!" She ran over to the edge other side of the room.

"What's with her?" Chris asked as he, walked past Lorelei into the next room.

The elder told him, "She's still like a lot of the people on this planet, —they are afraid of men."

Chris nodded thinking that he'd have to work on that.

He then walked into the center of the room and asked, "Is this okay?"

Lorelei said, "That's fine."

"What do you plan on doing to me, anyway?"

She started to do some calculation on a key board before she stated, "I plain on upgrading your body. With this upgrade, you well will become stronger than ever before."

Right before he could ask how, Chris was engulfed in a ball of electricity. He roared out as the power shot through him. It felt like his whole body was on fire. One thing was for sure—he was in more pain right now than he had been at any other time in his life.

xxx

Neneko ran to the end of an alleyway. She'd had no idea that Akurei was strong enough to destroy a whole building. She watched as the people running around the area fearing for their safety. Then she started thinking about Chris and how he wouldn't be hiding if he were in her place. He would think of a way to stop Akurei—or at least to slow him down. She looked out of the alleyway just in time to see Akurei, standing in the street. Just then a bus drove toward him and stopped in front of him. Akurei picked up the bus easily., Neneko could see there were people inside, so she knew that she had to do something. Just as, Akurei threw the bus, Neneko jumped out and caught it in mid air. Then she yelled out to Akurei, "If you want a fight, then you're going to get one!" Gently, she put the bus of screaming people down, and then charged up as much power as she could. She turned and fired it at Akurei, but he too fired an enormous beam from his hands. Akurei's blast was bigger than Neneko's. It took everything she had to hold him back. How she wished so badly that Chris-san was there with her right now. She knew she couldn't last long.

Chris was yelling out as he was still in the throes of his upgrade. He was engulfed in energy. As he yelled out in pain, the energy finally erupted in an explosion inside room. A blinding light filled the room, and, when it finally subsided, Chris was down on one knee. Smoke was rising off him as he slowly rose.

Nodoka and Sam had both expected him to look different, but, when he turned to them, there was no change in his body. "He looks the same to me," Sam said.

Lorelei laughed and told them. "Look closer," she said.

Nodoka and Sam saw the difference, but Chris still didn't. "I don't feel anything different … what's so funny?" he said in frustration.

The elder said, "Look again."

"Look behind you!." Sam said.

When he turned around to look, something caught his eye. It was swaying back and forth. He grabbed it wondering what it was was—and then it clicked: he had a metal tail that looked like a lion's tail.

"I have a tail!" He yelled out. He look up at the elder. "Why do I have a tail?"

"Come on out and put some clothes on and I'll tell you," Lorelei told him. When he came out of the room, Sam handed him some a new clothes, then she left the room. They looked like his normal clothes and fit perfectly. The pants even had an opening for his new tail. This meaning that the elder had planned for this new addition. When he was fully dressed, Lorelei said, "The new outfit is special. From, now on, when you transform to your higher levels, the fabric of your clothes will fuse into his the metal of your cybernetics. You will no longer be naked!."

Chris asked again, "Why do I now have a tail?"

"It's a secret," she told him. "You will find out, when you get back to Earth to help Neneko."

"That's right!" he almost yelled. "Neneko still needs help,— but how do I get back to Earth?" Chris asked.

"You get back there the same way you got here," Destiny said as she sat up from the spot where she was resting, .

"Are you sure you're ready for the trip back?" he asked her.

She told him "It's no problem," she said.

Just then, Sam went to fetch Maylu, who had been playing with some of the children in another room. When the child joined them all in the lab when she, ran over to her father and jumped up into his arms and gave him a big hug.

"I wish you luck," Lorelei said. "I have been watching Neneko and Akurei on my monitors. You need to get there fast." Destiny then said "guys hold on tight."

xxx

Destiny landed them safely near the site of the battle between Neneko and Akurei. Chris turned to an exhausted Neneko and asked. "Are you all right?"

When she saw him, she could not hold herself back. She jumped and engulfed him in a crushing hug.

"I knew you where okay," she cried, as she squeezed him, .

But Chris said, "There's no time for that." And he pulled her off him. "I have to handle Akurei right now."

Akurei stopped himself short of leaving the Earth's atmosphere. He roared out now knowing that Striker was back. He shot back down to Earth and hovered over the cyborg.

"Chris Striker, I thought you ran away like the coward you truly are!" Akurei said with a laugh.

"I didn't run—I just needed a little up grade before I faced you again."

"I don't see anything different about you?" ." Akurei said. "What did you get an up grade, on your luck? Because you're going to need it to face up against me again!"

"Oh, yeah," said Chris. "Check out my new tail!" The cyborg stated as he let his tail out form under his coat. He swayed it elegantly back and forth.

When Akurei saw the tail swaying back forth, he laughed so hard he almost about lost control and fell over with laughter.

Chris, however, though did not think it was funny. For, if Lorelei thought it was going to help, it would. He roared out saying, "I'll show you what I can do now!" And he started his transformation into his prefect Supreme Super Cyborg mode. Then, he shot forward with his "screaming bullet." But Akurei moved to the side at the last minute. He grabbed Chris by his new tail and spun him around, and then threw him right into the side of a building so hard that it left a gaping hole in the wall of the tenth floor in the side of the building.

Chris moved some rubble out of the way as he got up. *I wonder how Akurei managed to do that?* he wondered. *Lorelei the elder said that I would be a lot stronger, but I don't seem to be any different.* He yelled out "What's wrong?"

xxx

Lorelei, though, did hear him, —through the satellite link. Nodoka turned to her and asked, "What's wrong? Why isn't Chris getting any stronger?"

"Just wait," said Lorelei. "It'll start soon."

xxx

Chris saw Akurei fly up to the level of the tenth floor. "Well, I'm not impressed with your performance," Akurei said. "Your, new tail your, just makes it easier for me to catch you, as any other animal!"

Chris took a step back knowing that his opponent was right. But somehow he knew that he had to win no matter the cost.

As Chris flew at Akurei again, hitting him with a barrage of punches that put them both in a ball of lighting. But an explosion erupted, and Chris was shot out of the ball at high speed. He crashed through and on the roof of a lower building, where he reverted back to his original state and lay there unable to move.

He felt like such a fool. When rolled over on his back and looked up at the night sky, he hadn't even realized that night had fallen. When he looked up at the night sky, he noticed the full moon, as he thought of his friends and loved ones. He knew Neneko, Sam, Destiny, and Maylu were watching him. But then something happened. As as he looked at the moon, he started to hear his heart beating in his chest like a drum. Suddenly, his body felt as if it was on fire. He felt his body start to expand.

He tried to stand back up, but fell back to the ground. As he started to transform, his metal parts seemed to shift and grow. His hair changed from its normal black to a fiery red as it grew into a mane, around his face, starting to change, gaining cat-like features. Chris looked at his hands as they changed into large metal paws. He kept growing and changing, until, finally, a seven-foot, cyber lion stood where the human cyborg once had.

The cyber lion roared in its mastery, as the moon shown shone in the distance. When Neneko Sam Destiny and Maylu saw this, they could not believe it. The beast had all of Chris's cyborg looks, but now what looked like two jets were mounted on ether side of his shoulders. Chris looked like a enormous, well-armed, metallic lion cyborg!

Chris's roared echoed around the city. Then the beast noticed Akurei standing in amazement. Letting out a low growl, that seemed to make his chest vibrate, the cyber lion jumped off the building and headed right for Akurei. The beast gave no warning as it pounced on Akurei it roared once and then ran off into the city emitting more roars as he ran.

As Akurei stood back, he realized that Chris had become nothing but an animal. He also realized that the beast had control of Chris, so Akurei felt that he still had a good chance of beating his rival. Akurei turned around, as he took off after the cyber lion, which now seemed to be terrorizing the city.

"This is not good!" Sam told the others., "Chris has lost his mind in the transformation!" The four girls knowing they had to think of a way to snap Chris back into reality before he hurt someone—or himself. "We have to find him, before Akurei does," she said, turning to the others. But then she asked, "Where is Maylu?"

"Oh, no!" Sam said as she looked around, for she had only put her down for a moment after Chris transformed.

Neneko said, "She probably went after Chris. So, if we find Chris, we find her. And the best way for us to find them is to split up, and search the city."

They all agreed and took off in different directions to look for them both.

The cyber lion, which was once had been Chris Striker, ran through the city at such incredible speeds it created a sonic boom as it ran, shattering every window it passed. Suddenly, however, it stopped dead in its tracks and sniffed the air. Then it jumped to the side as little Maylu walked out of an alley.

"Daddy?" she spoke, calling to her father. But her cries fell on deaf ears as the enormous lion roared out to the sky firing some kind of beam from its mouth, scaring the child, who covered her ears and fell to the ground shaking. But, when the blast subsided, the lion looked down at the shaking child and felt sympathy for her. The lion kneed down and gently licked the child's face.

Maylu laughed as she felt the big cat's rough tongue. She looked back up to the lion as it stepped closer to her. The cyber lion seemed to be purring—almost as if it knew that the child in front of it was his child. Maylu was about to say something, when out of the sky Neneko suddenly came down. When she had seen the lion and Maylu, thinking that Chris was not in control, she was afraid he might attack Maylu. When she landed, the lion seemed to cover, Maylu with his body in a protective way.

When Maylu saw Neneko, she looked up at the lion and said, "It's okay." As she petted the lion's mane, the seven-foot animal stepped away from Maylu, who ran to Neneko. The lion then slowly walked up to both of them and looked at them both oddly.

Neneko picked up Maylu and held her close, afraid that Chris might attack. But Maylu told her, "Daddy remembers me and won't hurt me."

Neneko turned back to the lion, who was now standing an inch away form from her. He was sniffing her. Neneko closed her eyes and held Maylu tighter, but then she felt something rough and wet. She opened one eye and saw that the cyber lion wasn't going to hurt her—he was just licking her arm. Maylu reached out and petted the large beast as if it was a kitten.

"See?" she said childishly to Neneko. " Daddy remembers you too!" Maylu stated cutely as Neneko used her free hand to pet the cyber lion's mane.

"Chris, are you really in there?" Neneko asked the large beast thinking it might answer. But, no, answer came. All it knew was the fact that the people in front of it, was important to it somehow—and must be protected.

Neneko called to the others saying. "I have Maylu— and Chris is with us." When they asked how she'd gotten to Chris, "I didn't get him! Maylu did! You'll have to see it to believe it."

Meanwhile, Akurei had been searching the city for the cyber lion. When he saw a beam shoot up in the sky in the middle of the city, he knew that it had to be Chris, so he shot off in the that direction. When he arrived, he could not believe what he saw. The beast seemed to be timid around the girls. This infuriated, Akurei even more. Even when Chris was an animal, women seemed to flock to him like scared children for protection. *Well, I'll put a stop to that!* Akurei thought as he jumped and fired a beam at them.

At that very moment, the cyber lion sensed danger. He jumped in front of the girls just as a beam hit him hard in the chest. The girls gasped, but the beam barely moved the beast.

Akurei then jumped to the street.

"Look what we have here," Akurei taunted with an evil smile. "A new rug for my fire place."

The cyber lion roared out as it stood its ground protecting the women behind him. Even though, Chris being was in this state, for an odd reason, he could still remember everything that Akurei did, done—like destroying the others on the island. Everything that the monster had done was in Chris's subconscious. Because of this, the lion wanted blood more than anything.

Akurei was not about to be taken out by a stupid animal. As he roared out, his body grew and changed. He became more demonic and more powerful.

The lion was not about to wait. It charged head-on at the large mutant, but Akurei had a plan, for he believed that the beast was nothing but an animal running on pure instinct.

He started to tease the lion. He pretended like he was going to attack but he jumped over the lion and grabbed its tail. He swing the beast around like he had done before, throwing it right into another building.

"Daddy!" Maylu yelled out as she saw her father thrown. But Akurei wasn't finished! He fired an enormous blast right into the building, causing it to crumble down on the cyber lion.

Thinking that he had finished his enemy, Akurei turned back to Neneko and Maylu, ready to finish them as well. Just then, though they all heard a roar that shook the ground. They stood on as the cyber lion burst out of the rubble firing a large beam cannon from its mouth. It seemed that Akurei had enraged the beast beyond anything, for now it was blasting about like mad going more and more ballistic firing its mouth cannon again and again.

Thinking that he was no longer a threat Akurei dodged the lion's attack and continued on with what he had planned. Akurei reached out for Neneko, who was still holding Maylu. When the four-year-old screamed out for her daddy, witch made something deep within the heart of the raging cyber lion's heart melt.

The cyber lion stopped in its tracks as it seemed to focus on Maylu. It charged right at Akurei, its mouth cannon firing right at Akurei the blast was so precise it missed Neneko and Maylu but blew Akurei across the sky.

The cyber lion then roared out, " Maylu!" Another transformation began. The body of the cyber lion started to glow as it reared up onto its back legs. The animal kept roaring out as it changed from looking like an animal to being a more human form.

The explosion of power from this transformation seemed to go straight into the sky. As it parted the clouds, Neneko, Maylu, Sam, and Destiny felt as if they were seeing a god being born in front of them. When the transformation was finished, the cyber lion was no more— now stood before them a cyber lion –man. This was his Alpha Omega Cyber Lion mode.

This lion-man stood calm and still as the girls looked at his new form. Its body neither like a robot or, a lion, or a man. It didn't even look like a cyborg. It was a new being altogether … almost as if the metal and flesh had become one.

"Chris, are you okay?" Neneko asked as she looked him up and down as if determining if he was still the same person.

Chris moved suddenly making the girls jump back. Truthfully, they were a little afraid of what he might do. He then turned back to look at his hands. He, started to laugh. He raised his arms to the sky and yelled out, "I'm whole again!"

Neneko asked, "What are you talking about?"

Chris turned to them with a cat grin and said, "I can feel again! In this form, I am whole … complete." He turned to where Akurei was. He was ready to show the mutant what he could do.

"Wait here. I'll be back." He waved to them as he shot off into the sky nearly blowing them off their feet with his force.

Akurei was heading back to the little group. Raging mad, he yelled out, "I'll kill them all! Especially that overgrown cat! No one does this to me and lives!" But just as he was flying back, Chris appeared right in front of him with his arms crossed. Akurei stopped in his tracks.

"Ha!" Akurei laughed. "Was the cyber lion too much for you to handle?"

"Yeah … this is just another costume change for the weakling cyborg," Chris stated. As his power increased, and his hair blew as if in the wind as electricity flowed through it.

Akurei did not like Chris's new attitude —or his new body. The mutant, flew right at the lion-man. "Now the *real* fight begins," said Chris.

They both flew at each other for a finally strike. Their powers charged in their fists as Chris roared out *"Screaming Fist of the Beast King!,"* Akurei tried to match Chris's power with his fist, but Chris's was faster than he expected. As it hit Akurei's chest, Chris let out a lion's roar. Chris's fist tore into Akurei like a knife. As Akurei's body was shot back, it started to disintegrate.

"Shit!" the young Akurei said as he was thrown to the ground by a young Chris Striker. "Why can't I beat you? I'm stronger than you! I've been training harder too?"!"

Right then, their sensei appeared. "He beat you because you don't understand why he fights so hard. Chris- san understands something that you do not. Until you understand what that is, Chris will always beat you no matter how much stronger you think you are. Chris will always be stronger because he has that one thing you do not."

Akurei he fell back he realized what that one thing was—Chris had the will to protect those whom he loved. First there is his daughter, then Neneko, and then those girls. It was his will to protect them that made him so strong, —stronger than he could ever get, even with his new body. Akurei knew that no matter how much he tried, Chris would be the stronger no matter what.

Akurei roared out, "Striker!" As his body finally blew apart and crashed to the ground in a massive explosion.

Neneko, Sam, Destiny, and Maylu made it to the spot where the explosion occurred. They saw Chris—still in his new form—hovering a few inches from what used to be Akurei's body.

It was completely misshapen, and in fact Neneko covered Maylu's eyes from the sight.

"Chris. Are you okay?" Destiny asked as she took in the sight of Akurei's body.

Chris turned to the girls and smiled a cat smile and said, "I'm just fine. In fact, I've never felt better!"

Sam went over and examined the remains. She still wondered who had made Akurei into a mutant. "I'll take the body," she said to Chris. " I want to examined it back at the lab."

CHAPTER 47

Later Chris walked into Sam's new lab near the Cyber Corp building in Japan. "Have you found anything about Akurei's body?" he asked.

Sam just shook her head. "Whoever made him did not want anyone to figure out who he was, but I have to admit that I have to appreciate his work on an academic level. "

"The person who made him had to of have been either a genius or a certifiable nut, and to think that Akurei only needed one component to make him completely unstoppable."

"One component?" Chris asked.

"Yes," she answered as she, turned to her computer. "See this?" she said, pointing to the image on the screen. "The entire time you were fighting Akurei, he was constantly mutating and changing. He was unstable, because of the one missing component." She started showed him the sequences of Akurei's DNA, and how one component kept changing, Akurei with out the, one component and then with it to constantly rejuvenate at speeds that went off the charts.

"God all mighty," said Chris, " I could of never have beaten him if he had that type of power," Chris stated in shock. "Wait, you said it was missing a component?"

"So it was," said Sam. "But then I found it. Do you remember when you were under the control of a Doctor Connors? In the general's lab?"

Chris growled in his throat as he remembered.

"I'll take that as a yes," said Sam. "Well, when I looked through his lab files, I found some DNA samples there. The thing is, Doctor Connor's didn't create it, but he was studying it witch—means."—"

"Which means there might be a clue in Connor's lab as to the source of the sample, in his old lab," Chris finished her sentence.

"Exactly!" said Sam. "That's why I'm taking the next flight back to take a another look around Connor's old lab."

"You're not going by yourself, are you?" Chris asked, with concern in his voice.

"I'm a big girl, Chris. I'm pretty sure that I handle looking around Doctor Connor's old lab by myself," she told him. "Thanks for caring, though."She told him, feeling good knowing he cared so much.

"Still, I would feel better if you at least took Neneko with you."

"Fine.," Sam sighed.

Later, Sam and Neneko were on the next flight to Florida. Sometime after they landed, they went down into the area where Connor's lab had been. It still looked pretty messed up from Chris's attack. As they looked around, Sam told Neneko about Doctor Connor's and what he had done to Chris and the others.

"You mean to tell me that this Connor's guy took control of Chris?" Neneko said while she turned her flash light in Sam's direction.

"Yeah, it was pretty rough," Sam said. "But, from what I have heard, Chris was able to beat the doctor's control through his own force of will."

"Well, Chris-chan was always pretty tough, even when he was young."

As they continued to look around, something caught Sam's eyes. It was a scanner that looked like as if it had been used quite a bit. She examined it closely, with a PDA, she had, she was able to hack into the device. Suddenly, the whole wall next to them opened up reveling a newer-looking lab. When the lights came on, Sam just stood staring at something.

When Neneko walked behind Sam and saw what she was looking at, all she could say was, *"Nou."* "What?" said Sam.

"Sorry," said Neneko, "that's Japanese for *brain*." The two women stood staring for there in the light was a large brain in a strange-looking container attached to the wall.

"It's been a while, hasn't it, Miss Samantha Ivy?" a voice stated.

Sam walked up closer to the brain. She seemed to recognized the voice. "Doctor Connor's?" she said.

"Yes, —or what's left of me," said the brain, " after that Chris Striker friend of yours did to me."

"But, I didn't think that he harmed you that badly," Sam stated flatly as she looked at brain of Doctor Connor's.

"Well, he did. But this is only temporary—once I get my hands on that cyborg's body."

"That's disgusting," Neneko interrupted, "what are you, gay?"

"NO!!!" Connor's yelled out, "I mean I'll put my brain into his body, I will become unstoppable."

"Well, little man, you're going to have a hard time doing that without hands!" Neneko said with a laugh.

Witch she stopped laughing when she heard the laugh that emanated form brain. "That's where these guys come in," said Connor. Suddenly, the walls on either side of the brain opened, revealing four large and dangerous- looking biotech warriors. Before Neneko knew what was happening, Neneko lit up as she was electrocuted.

"Neneko!" Sam yelled cried. Then she turned back to the brain. "You'll never get away with this! When Chris comes to get us, he'll tear out your cerebellum!"

"We'll see about that," Connor's stated. As the four biotech warriors came at Sam.

xxx

Chris was in the middle of a deep meditation when he felt something troubling. As his eyes shot open he said, "Neneko, ... Sam," ..."

Right then, Maylu and Destiny ran into his meditation chambers Destiny said, "We felt it too."

Chris looked at both of them and stood up., "I have to go get to them—and fast."

"But what if by the time you get to them its to late, you can't get to them in time?" Destiny asked.

"I will get to them," Chris stated almost coldly. "Stay with Maylu. I have a feeling this might be very dangerous." Destiny and Maylu watched as he ran to the roof of the building as he took off into the sky.

Chris flew faster than he ever had before. He landed near a man whole cover that he new would lead him straight to where Connor's lab used to be. He moved the manhole cover aside and was about to enter the dark interior when he detected a strange life reading coming from the ground. Just then, a large bio beast crashed out of the opening.

It was the ugliest beast Chris had ever encountered. It stood a good twelve feet tall. It had four large, elephant legs that supported a body that looked like an enormous fish. To make matters worse,—it had a tail of a scorpions as well as its pincers.

The beast made of miss matched beast parts roared as it lumbered its way toward Chris. When the beast slung its tail down at Chris, the cyborg back flipped as the beasts tail slammed into the ground.

It roared out several times as it tried to get its tail free. As it did this, Chris thought it was a good idea to get moving, so as ran as fast as his metal legs could take him.

Chris then entered a large room that was in the underground sewer system. But there was something strange —there were metal orbs, each about a foot wide, hovered in the air all around the room.

At first, he didn't think nothing much about them. But then they all opened, and each orb became armed with a dozen metal spikes. All the orb started to spin toward Chris at incredible speeds.

Chris dodged past each one, avoiding them by inches. Then, he roared out, "That's enough! "Shotgun *Double Barrel!*" With this, he fired hundreds of beams out of both each fist. All the orbs were, destroyed instantly.

He stood in the mist of the dust, breathing hard when the beast from before jumped out at him and slammed him to the ground with so much force that it left a crater.

The beast flung its tail back and forth then slammed down at the cyborg, but it missed his head by inches. Chris then moved his legs under the fish- beast's belly and pushed it away from him with incredible force.

It roared out and charged at Chris. He readied himself and powered up. As he roared out, his golden hyper mode took over and he fired off a "screaming bullet" he shot into the fish-beast's mouth. The shot went right through the beast's body; blood and mechanical parts flew everywhere.

xxx

Doctor Connors and his other biotech warriors were in shock as they watched this through a monitor. They never thought that Chris had, this much power. Connor's then told two of his other warriors to take him.

xxx

Chris was wiping at the, fish yuck that covered his body. "This is beyond nasty," he stated. "I may never eat sushi again."

Chris then walked over to a large door that was at the other end of the room. He found it to be locked, so he just busted it down with one punch. On the other side of the door, there was another large biotech warrior. This room seemed to be standing in the middle of a large filtration system for the water in the sewer system. There where large waterfalls around them, witch made it hard to believe that they were underground.

The large biotech warrior looked more human then than the last one, but had a body as black as night. Its flesh looked as if it was starting to decompose. The only things holding it together were the metal spikes that were plunged into the warrior's body.

Right as Chris walked up to the warrior he elbow punched him, sending him skidding back, where he slide to a stop on the ground.

The strike hadn't hurt the biotech warrior, but Chris could tell the beast was aggravated as it got up without a problem and started to laugh as if what Chris had done was like nothing at all. Not knowing what to expect, Chris readied himself again. But, right as the beast was about to attack, something caught Chris's eyes. He punched at something that appeared for a moment and then disappeared. Whatever it was came up behind him again, but he detected it and punched at it again. This opponent was able to move fast, —so fast that Chris could barely detect it, let alone hit it. And it was giving off a large amount of electrical power.

Right next to the black biotech warrior, the fast one appeared. The other one looked like a walking corpse too, but this one had electrical transformers on either side of its shoulders and was wearing some kind of a mask covering his face.

"Who, or what are these you guys? And when was the last time you guys bathed?" Chris asked. He felt as if he was going to, pass out from the stench.

"I'm Spike," said the one with the metal spikes sticking in his body.

"I'm Electrocute," the other said in a wiry voice. He was laughing and jumping about madly. As Electrocute disappeared, and Spike put both his hands to the ground. As the metal of Spike's body touched the ground, the metal on the ground started to liquefy and move. It shaped itself into large spikes that shot out at Chris. Chris managed to jump out of the way, but then four spikes shot up around him and, before he could move, the spikes then melted around him in a cocoon of liquid metal.

Spike laughed and Electrocute danced around, madly charging up with, electricity. Suddenly, a voice came over a hidden intercom. "I need the cyborg alive, so— just capture him, don't kill him!"

Spike didn't like the idea, but shrugged. Chris's body appeared trapped in liquid metal, but it began to harden into an indestructible mass. Spike then said, "I'll take this guy in his metal coffin ba … : —"

Right before he touch the metal though something hit Spike hard, knocking him back against the wall.

Chris looked down. There in front of him was Maylu.

"Hi, Daddy," the girl said as she looked up at her father.

"Maylu!" Chris yelled, shocked. "I told you to stay home with Destiny!"

"Well, who, do you think brought me here?" she retorted as Destiny jumped down to the ground next to her and assumed a fighting stance.

"Sorry Chris," Destiny stated. "I tried to convince her to stay, but she wouldn't, so I came with her."

"Be careful, you two. These guys are tough stuff," Chris told them.

Spike was mad! He slammed his hands into the ground, and the ground erupted as a blast of metal spikes flew toward Chris, Destiny, and Maylu. But Destiny yelled out, "Not so fast!" She put her hands to the ground and then the eruption of metal just stopped.

Spike lifted his hands up and just looked at them. "What happened?" he asked. "How'd you do that?"

Destiny smiled as she rose up. "I used my nanites," she said. "I can produce them to stop your attack cold."

As Destiny smiled at the monstrous looking man, proud about her new abilities, Maylu yelled out, "Destiny! Look out!" And the little girl pushed her out of the way as Electrocute appeared and almost hit her.

The two girls landed out of harm's way as they saw Electrocute. He started to charge up yelling madly as wires shot out of his skin, and around his arms. The wires then formed into blades of light. The two girls froze in there tracks as the biotech warrior flung the wire blades at them.

They managed to avoid the first strike, but the wires seemed to have minds of their own. They followed the girls into the air and grabbed them and shocked them to the ground. Electrocute charged up as much power as he could; he seemed intent on barbecue the girls alive.

Chris could see what was happening, and hear their screams of pain it was driving him crazy. He struggled to break free of his metal straightjacket.

Electrocute then flung the girls into the air as Spike changed the metal on the ground into hot liquid.

Chris had had enough! He roared out into his prefect supreme mode as he exploded out of his metal prison in a mass of power that no one could believe.

In a blink of an eye, the girls where free of Electrocute. Chris punched him in the head so hard that his head shot off into the air. Then Spike was elbowed back into a drainpipe and impaled him.

Chris landed near the two shocked girls. When the head of Electrocute came down, Chris caught it. He and then held it up and turned to look up yelled out, "Connor, listen up! You'd better give back my friends or you'll end up like your biotech warriors here, —totally dead!" He then spiked the head to the ground.

xxx

Connor was in total shock. He had never seen a transformation like that. It was as if Chris's metal had come to life. The cyborg's power was unreal.

"That was nothing!" Sam stated to the brain. She was chained to the wall, she had been there since they had taken Neneko away.

A fourth biotech warrior came up to Sam. He, looked like just an old man. He smiled an almost toothless grin, and said, "Really."

"You just wait!" Sam said. "When he gets serious, you're all going down!"

"We'll see about that," said Connor's brain. "If he is now stronger, then I well be stronger when I take his body for my own,." said the brain.

xxx

Chris and the two girls where running through the sewers and underground tunnels. Destiny asked, "Are you sure that we're going the right way?"

Chris said, "Yeah—I'm sure that Neneko and Sam are down this tunnel." But, right, then, they ran into a dead end.

"What do we do now, Daddy?" Maylu asked as she looked up at him and grabbed his coat.

He looked around, not understanding what was going on. He was sure that he could sense that Sam and Neneko where close.

Right as he was trying to to find a way through the wall, the floor started to rise. Soon, they found themselves in a new room. The room was totally dark. Suddenly, a spotlight came on above them.

"Welcome, Striker," a voice stated from all around them.

Chris stepped forward and said, "Connor's?"

"Yes, Striker, … or what's left of me," said the brain as the lights came on revealing Sam chained to the wall, and a brain in a container attached to the wall, and an old man standing on the other side of it.

"Sam," Chris yelled out as he ran to her, but, right when he was about to grab her, a force field shocked him back. Sam screamed as she saw this, and Destiny and Maylu helped him back to his feet.

"Hurry and get him ready!" Connor's told the old man. Instantly, wires came out of the ground and tied Chris down and then shocked him.

Maylu yelled out to Doctor Connor's the brain, "Stop it, your! You're hurting my daddy!"

As Chris struggled to get free, Maylu started to ran to the old man ready to fight. Then, out of no where, Neneko appeared. She stopping the girl in her tracks. And as this happened, Chris managed to break free of the wires. He step forward. Neneko was giving him a death glare. He saw a strange device on her head and sensed that something was wrong.

"Miss Neneko" Maylu said But Neneko back handed the little girl to the ground. Maylu looked up, with tears in her eyes not knowing what was, going on. Neneko then shot forward, flying at Chris, and punched at him. He ducked under her strike then slide under her in a flash.

"Neneko! Don't do this!" Chris yelled. He knew she wasn't herself, but she continued to attack him with complete ruthlessness. Maylu yelled out for them both to stop fighting, but it was no use. Neneko seemed determined to end Chris's life.

Destiny had managed to get over to Sam. "Get me out of these chains," Sam said to Destiny.

"I don't know how to," said Destiny as she touched the field that surrounded Sam, which gave her a substantial shock.

Sam said, "You'll have to cut off the power."

Maylu turned to the bio monsters she knew were responsible for turning Neneko against her Daddy and screamed out, "It's all your fault!" All her powers rose to the surface and exploded with so much force that it shook everything as if they were in an earth quake.

But the old man asked the little girl, "What do you think you're trying to do?"

But Maylu was in a whirl wind of rage, and she continued to scream out, "It's all your fault!"

The old man raised his cane. It opened and shot out a red blast at the girl, but her power was too great. She was able to push the blast back, making everything that wasn't bolted to the ground rise in the air, shocking both Doctor Connor's and the old man.

Chris was still fighting with Neneko when Maylu let out her own, lion's roar. Surprisingly, it sent a shock wave that nearly destroyed Connor's chamber. It knocked the old man to he ground, and the device that was controlling Neneko started to deteriorate.

The old man reached for his cane, but Destiny kicked it out of the way. "Let Sam out," she screamed. But the old man smiled at her as he raised his hand to her face. Suddenly, his hand shot open and changed into a machine gun, right in front of her eyes.

"Crap!?!" Destiny yelled out, and she ran as fast as she could go, as the old man fired at her. She literally ran on the side of the wall to get away from the barrage of bullets.

The device that controlled Neneko loosened from the force of Maylu's power, and she was able to shake it off finally.

"Chris-san, what's going on?" she said, confused.

Maylu came up to her "Are you okay?' asked the child.

"I'm fine.," said Neneko.

Destiny ran by Sam, as the old man fired at the shield control, destroying it. Then destroyed the shield around her, but then the old man aimed at both Destiny and Sam. But Neneko fired her eye beams at the old man's machine gun hand. His whole arm burst into flame. Most of the old man's arm burned off, revealing that he was a robot.

"That's for thinking that you could control me!" Neneko yelled out to what was left of the old man.

But right then Doctor Connors started to laugh at all of them.

"This has been real entertaining," he said at last. "But I think it is time that I ended this."

"What are you going to end?" Sam said as Destiny freed her from her chains. "You're a brain in a jar!"

As they all watched, the brain, moved into the wall, and the whole room started to shake. Connor's continued to laugh and as the walls exploded in a mass of rubble. An enormous robot stepped out. It stood a good fourteen feet tall and looked like as if it had stepped out of a sci-fi movie. It had six robotic spider spider-like legs and four arms, each with its own weapon. Where the head should be was there was only a hologram projection of Connor's head.

"I think, you may have spoken to soon, Sam," Chris said as they all stepped back from the giant.

"Aw, man!" Sam screamed as she saw the giant and ran behind Destiny.

Chris, Neneko, Maylu, and Destiny readied themselves for combat as Sam stood behind them knowing that she couldn't fight him.

The robot then reared back its arm. "Die!" he shouted. It fired a cannon at them.

They scattered to avoid being hurt by the blast. Chris shot back as he said, "I have to fight as long as my body holds out."

"Yahh!!!" Maylu yelled out as she jumped in the air at the Connor's robot and fired her version of her father's screaming bullet. But hers wasn't as strong as his, the Connor's robot just back handed her away.

Neneko caught the girl, and they landed safely next to Chris. He shot forward at the robot and ran under its legs. He grabbed one, flung the fourteen-foot robot around, and threw it into a wall. When it was down, Neneko had come back into the air moved to Chris's side, leaving Maylu next to Sam.

She let out all of her fire power into the robotic beast. It momentarily disappeared into a cloud of dust, but it blasted through the dust and slammed Neneko into the wall.

"Neneko!!" Chris yelled out. He powered up into his prefect supreme mode and blasted himself at the robot. He struck the robot in the back, then shot around and hit it in one of its arms. The arm blasted off, but still leaving the robot with five more.

Chris landed and started to power up his screaming bullet. He was ready to end this fight fast. But so was Connor. The big robot leaned forward. The hologram of Connor's head disappeared as a cannon took its place on the shoulders of the robot.

Chris launched himself at the robot at the same time the cannon fired. He tried to punch through the blast, but it pushed him back. Chris yelled out, *"Power up!!!"*

'His screaming bullet shot though Connor's blast. Then Chris struck the giant robot right in the middle. The robot retaliated, and the force was blinding as they hit each other, but Chris was able to overpower the robot. He blasted the mechanical giant through the ceiling of the lab and through the street. The robot burst into the air and blasted straight into obit.

"You did it!" Destiny said to Chris.

"No, he's still alive."

"Even after all that?"

"Striker ..." Connor's yelled as he the robot turned around in space, "it seems you're stronger than I remember, but that doesn't matter. I will just focus all my power and destroy you with the Earth."

As Chris and the others stood at in the ruins of what was left of Connor's lab, all kinds of equipment started to boot up and glow. Chris knew that something wasn't right. "Run, girls!" he said. "I'm going to take down Connor's with a screaming fist of the beast king!"

The girls ran out of the ruined lab as fast as they could, as Chris started to power up. But, as he was transforming, Connor's, fired a beam attack from space. The blast vaporized everything in it path.

Maylu saw this and jumped up from Sam's arms. She and yelled out as she prepared shoot into the sky. As she stood there, Neneko came up beside her.

"Momma Neneko," Maylu said as she saw her, .

"Uses all your power to stop him!" And, together, they flew up into the sky.

The robot saw them flying to him. "You are all history!" But he was cut off as Neneko and Maylu slammed right into his giant body.

Maylu shot back toward Earth, but Neneko looked up at the robot's face and fired her eye beams right into its face. Then she pushed off of him. That was when Destiny appeared out of the clouds and jumped onto the robot and kicked the robot in the side, knocking him back.

The robots steadied himself after the blast. "I'm going to turn all of you into space dust!" he roared. Meanwhile, Chris had manage to finished his transformation before the blast hit him. And as the dust cleared, he stood ready in his new form. He roared out, and shot into the sky.

At the same time this happened, Connor's fired an enormous blast to the Earth. The three girls watched in horror thinking this was end, but then they saw that the blast was being pushed back.

"What *is* this?" Connor's yelled out, as he watched his blast start to erupt, and then blast apart as the cyber lion, shot through it. Chris roared out as he blasted right through the robot's beam.

Chris struck Connor's right in the center of his robot body roaring out, " *Screaming Fist of the Beast King!*" Then Chris's whole body shot through the robot and came out the other side.

"Damn you, Striker!" Connor's yelled out as the robot blew up, in a massive explosion that lit up the skies and blowing everyone back to Earth as the explosion lit up space.

Chris came too sometime later. He looking up. "Wow … to see four beautiful angels," he said, as he looked around at the girls for he was still in a daze.

When he said this, Sam was the first to blush, —she had never been called beautiful before. Neither had Neneko, who had to turn around before he snapped back to his senses.

"Daddy, are you okay?" Maylu asked her father.

He shook off the shock of the blast and stood up. When he got back on his feet, he saw Neneko and Sam hiding their faces looking away from him. He turned to Destiny and asked, "What's with them?"

"Oh, them—they're still in shock of from the blast.," Destiny said with a sly smile.

CHAPTER 48

They all returned to Japan after the defeat of Doctor Connor. When Sam returned to her lab, she told everyone that she had a lot of work to do. She had retrieved a lot of from Connor's lab. The data was in bad shape, and it would take her some time before she would could get any useful information from it. It might even take her a few years. She felt exhausted just thinking about it.

Neneko had went straight to bed because she had school in the morning and she was really behind in her school work, with all the craziness that' has been going on.

Chris wished her good night as she walked into her room when she walked in her room she looked around and saw her sawing project that she had been working on for awhile, she thought that she had better remember to finish it when she gets back from school.

The next day, Neneko started her routine. As she dressed, she then looked at herself in the mirror. She had not changed much, even after gaining the powers of those cyborg girls. She had hoped to become as beautiful as they where, but there was no luck about that. And, even with cybernetic eyes she still had to wear her glasses, which she didn't like. Still, she did have have one thing that she had wanted for such a long time—, she had Chris-chan, as she had called him when they were children. So that made things eraser for her, so she smiled at herself in the mirror, and then went to wake up Chris-chan for the day.

Chris's room was right next to hers. She just let herself in and found him sleeping on his futon in the middle of the floor. As always, all he wore was a pair pear of boxer shorts. He must have, been tossing and turning in his sleep because his covers had been kicked off. He was soundly asleep. She couldn't help but smile, for, even though so much has had changed, some things seemed to stay the same.

"Hey, Chris-chan, time to get up," Neneko said, kneeling down and shaking him. But he was determined to stay asleep. He just rolled over, swung his arm around, caching Neneko in his grip.

There she was, lying on his futon with him. One of his cybernetic legs going over both her legs, and one of his arms lay over her chest.

She turned to look at him with a blush on her face. Then she got up, determined to wake Chris.

Chris was suddenly sat up in his bed rubbing his face where a hand-shaped mark lingered. Neneko was standing over him with her arms crossed over her chest.

"What was that for?"

"You would not get up, and you know how mad Sam gets when you're late! And don't forget that you have to get little Maylu to preschool too. And you have to walk me to school as well!"

"Yeah I know," he said. "How can I forget when you keep reminding me? Every day when you wake me up at the crack of dawn!"

"Well I wouldn't have to get you up so early if you wouldn't take forever to get ready, what with your morning exercises and all."

"Well, a guy's got to stay in shape you know."

"What shape," she teased him back. "Most of your body is made of metal?"!"

"Neneko-chan', that's a low blow." ." Chris pouted.

The cyborg then finally got up and walked to his dresser and pulled out his clothes for the day. He then turned to Neneko, who was still in the room looking at him trying to hurry him up. "Maybe you should go out and let him me get ready."

The second he said this, she realized what he was talking about. She stood back up and walked out the door. After she closed the door, she leaned against his, door holding her hand to her heart. She could still feel it racing. It had begun racing when he had rolled over on her on the futon. She was still having trouble thinking, and she was glade that he had never noticed the blush thaw as on her face.

After dropping off Maylu at her preschool, Neneko and Chris walked together to her college campus. Despite the fact Chris was older than he looked, when they arrived, one of the teachers gave him a bad time about his clothes, thinking he was a new student. But, when he removed his sunglasses and revealed his cybernetic eyes, the teacher took a step back. Chris then wished Neneko a good day, and told her that he would pick her up later, when he got off of work with Sam.

Later that day, Neneko was in her school class with her friends Miu and Chika. They were sitting by the faulting vault horse.

"So, Neneko, what are your plains for this the weekend?" Miu asked.

"Nothing really. I was going do some training exercises with Chris-chan this weekend, but if you guys have any better ideas." …"

"You know I envy you," Chika told Neneko.

"Why?"

"Because you get to live in the same place as the guy who saved the world from that general freak. I mean, he's a known celebrity and— a hero! You have to admit that' is pretty awesome!"

"I don't think that it' is that awesome," said Neneko. " I mean I grew up with him, so it doesn't even seem that new to me—well, all except for the cybernetics parts and all."

xxx

While Neneko was in school, Chris visited Sam in her lab at Cyber Corp. He walked in to see Sam and Destiny still working hard on the information that they had retrieved from Connor's lab. "Did you get anything useful?" he asked.

"We got enough information," Sam said, looking up from her computer. "But the thing is, it's all encrypted. Even with my computers working on it, it could take weeks, months, or even years before it can decrypt it."

"That's just great." Chris said sarcastically, thinking that it was a waste of time.

"There is one thing I did find," Sam offered. "There was is a name that was being repeated a lot in the files."

"What name?"

"A last of name to be exact," Sam pause and turned away, and then looked back at him and said, "Bishop."

"Are these files old?" asked Chris.

"No," said Sam. "They're pretty current."

Chris seemed to have trouble believing this, for Bishop, was dead. What could all of this mean? First Connor's showed up, back from the dead. And now they were hearing Bishop's name again. Chris sat down. "So maybe we haven't heard the end of General Bishop," he said, obviously disappointed. "Maybe you'll get lucky deciphering those file, Sam," he said. "Or maybe the general will make the first move."

Destiny took a look at the clock on the wall and noticed how late it was. "Chris you're going to have to leave to pick up Maylu and Neneko unless you'll be late."

Chris saw this too and said, "Your right. Thanks. I guess I'll see you both tonight." And he headed for the door.

xxx

Maylu was sitting on the steps of her school waiting for her father to come when a teacher came out and asked the girl, "Is everything okay?"

Maylu smiled at the teacher said, "It's no problem. Daddy had a lot to do at work, so maybe he got held up." But right then Chris jumped down to the ground with a crashing thud right in front of them.

The teacher was in shocked when she saw Maylu's father come out of no where, but, when Maylu saw her father, she yelled out, "Daddy!" And she ran over to him. He picked her up, saying, " Sorry for being late."

The little girl laughed saying . "It's okay! You're here now and that's all that mattered."

"How did I get such a forgiving daughter?"

"I don't know,." the The four four-year-old shrugged. "Just lucky I guess!" She said with a laughed as her father tickled her for being so cute.

Chris then turned and jumped into the air leaving Maylu's teacher in disbelief. All the teachers secretly thought that Maylu had one of the greatest fathers around.

Chris landed, holding Maylu, at Neneko's campus right on time, for Neneko was just walking out with two of her girlfriends Miu and Chika. Chris know them both casually, form when they were young.

Miu and Chika had never met Maylu. When the three saw , Chris standing there holding little Maylu, Miu immediately asked, "Whose kid is that?"

"She's Chris's daughter," Neneko told her two friends. "Her mother died a while ago when Maylu was a baby. She was the scientist whom made Chris-chan's body.

The two girls where amazed but also felt bad for the little girl she didn't get to know her mother, .

"Hi, Momma Neneko!" called out Maylu.

Neneko looked at her friends and saw the shock on their faces.

She laughed uneasily as she said, "Maylu, has always called me that, —ever sense we met."

"What's up, girls?" Chris asked as he came up, to them.

"Nothing," Neneko stated uneasily. She was still uncertain about being called "momma" "We should be getting back to the temple now," she said, eager to get away.

xxx

He just shrugged and started to walked with her leaving her two friends, as she left she told them that she would see them tomorrow as she turned and waved goodbye.

Destiny and Sam were on their way home to the temple as well. They had taken a break from their tedious computer work to go out and pick up some groceries. Just when they where leaving the store, Destiny had decided to play a spin-the-wheel raffle game sponsored by a new hot springs that had just opened nearby.

Sam shook her head in disbelief as the indicator stopped on the grand prize! Destiny had won a free pass for a large group people to the new hot springs. On top of that, Destiny had been shamelessly flirting with the raffle vendor. Her cybernetics kept her looking young, and she constantly used that to her advantage

As they walked home with there groceries, Destiny eyed the grand prize ticket she got.

"Can you believe it, Sam? A free ticket for any number of people to get to the new indoor hot springs that opened down town?"

"Yeah, I know," said Sam, "But will we be able to get Chris to agree? He's the one who will decide if we go or not."

"He'll agree—you'll see.," Destiny said as she holds up the ticket.

xxx

"Absolutely not!" Chris yelled out when Destiny told him about the ticket.

"But why not? It would be fun?" !" Destiny said with a pout.

"Because we all ready have a beautiful hot spring right here in a temple where we live." In reality, Chris didn't like being out too much in public. He liked to keep his cybernetic life to himself. And he liked to keep his "family" private too.

"But, Chris, this place doesn't *just* have hot springs. It has sand baths, mud baths, steam baths, and even an indoor pool. We can all have fun."

Neneko heard this discussion and put in her own thoughts. "It would be fun to go out, to a place like this," she said.

Even Sam butted in. "Sounds good to me!" she chirped.

Chris was now being out numbered. If they could go so in the end, he sighed. He had no choice. "All right, we'll all go as a family."

As they all cheered, Neneko thought of something. She turned to Destiny and asked, "If Chris is coming with us, does that mean, it's mixed bathing?"

"*No!!!!* It's not!" Chris yelled out. Then he turned and walked away in a huff. But, before he stepped out of the room, he looked over his shoulder to look at the girls and said, "We'll all go tomorrow." And, with that, he walked out of the room. The girls were happy that he had agreed. But Neneko, deep down, almost wished that it was here would be mix bathing.

xxx

That night, Neneko was sitting in her small, private bathtub. It was in the bathroom that she shared with the other girls at the temple. As she sat there in deep thought, she noticed that she had forgotten to take off of her glasses. As she removed them, she suddenly heard Chris's voice outside her door. Quickly, she put her glasses back on. "Chris, is that you?" she asked. as she side his name at hearing his voice.

"Neneko, the faucet in my bathroom is broken. Can I use your tub?" And Chris just walked into the room.

Chris stepped into her bath and sat down in the water behind her. She could feel his bare body move against hers as he settled in. "Eep!" she said.

"This is a tight fit isn't it?" Chris said.

"What do you mean, Chris-chan?"

"What's wrong you? You and I used to bathe together all the time when we were kids?."

"That was when we were kids, … now we're—e …"

Chris then leaned over and whispered into her ear. She could feel his hot breath against her ear. as he spoke.

"Neneko, I want you. I wont want all of you. Do you wont me?" Chris he asked her in a seductive voice. Neneko that made her shook shake all over.

"I, —I, —I," —" Neneko stuttered out.

Suddenly, there was a great splash, and Neneko had gotten out of the tub. Neneko was out of the water into the shower, cold water running down her body as she said. "The bathtub is no place to fall asleep," she said haughtily.

xxx

CHAPTER 49

The next morning, both Neneko and Chris looked tired and out of it, from lack of sleep. Destiny and Sam where standing together with Maylu waiting for them to hurry up. Today was the big day—they were ready for their trip to the hot springs.

"What is with you two, today?" Sam asked as they finally made it to the limo that was going to take to the hot springs baths.

"I didn't get much sleep last night," Chris said.

"Me, either, I guess," said Neneko.

"Had too much fun last night, you two?" Destiny said with a sly smile.

They both shot awake saying in unison. "We didn't do anything like that.,"

"Come on you guys," Sam stated. "We're going to be late. The limo is waiting."

Upon arriving at the hot springs, Chris and the others were impressed. It was a huge building with a large glass dome over the top. They could barely believe that this place had nothing but baths and springs in it.

"*Sugoi!*" said Neneko.

"I agree—it's amazing!" said Sam.

Later Chris went immediately to the men's side of the baths, where he started to get undressed. As he was removing his shirt, he felt a number of eyes staring at him. He turned to see that everyone who were in the locker room was staring right at him.

"What are all of you all staring at?" he asked. "You act like you' have near seen a cyborg before!" When he said this, they all turned back to what they where doing, making sure that they minded their own business.

He walked over to one of the mirrors to see himself. What he saw was a clear remainder that he was not human anymore. He usually took this for granted even though others saw it as unusual. The cybernetics on his body were the only reason he was still alive.

"Well it can't be helped," he thought. *"it's the price you pay for the power that now I now have."* But the thought didn't make the feeling go away that he would always be different in the eyes of others.

Sam was enjoying herself. She felt a little guilty because she did still had a lot of work to do back in her lab, but, at the moment, she allowed herself some well-deserved relaxation as she lay back in the large pool-like spa and sighed.

Neneko turned to Maylu, who seemed to be staring into space. "What's wrong, Maylu?" she asked.

She sadly told Neneko, "I miss Daddy. I know he's here, somewhere, I wish he was here with us."

"Don't worry too much about Chris-chan," said Neneko. "He's probably enjoying himself just as much as we are." Neneko told the girl.

"But, Momma Neneko, wouldn't you like to bathe together with Daddy?" Maylu innocently asked.

Neneko was taken aback from by the girl blunt question. She blushed, and twiddled her fingers together nervously and said, "No, not really."

Chris was in a pool at the top part of the bathing area, close to the glass dome. From outside, it looked as if the whole place was covered in mirrors, but, from the inside, it felt like an open-air bath as bathers looked out into the treetops. For Chris, this was the first time in a lone long time that he had felt at ease, but that was about to change. For, climbing on the outside of the building, was something that resembled an impossibly large spider.

The top half of a full-sized woman. The back part was all spider. The mutant arachnid climbed right to the top of the dome.

While Chris was half asleep in the water, the Spider-Lady smashed through the top of the dome and splashed down right into the water.

Chris shot up when this happened. He could not believe what he was looking at, —it had to be some kind of mutant. Suddenly, it turned to him it said, "Chris Striker, I have come to kill you!"

"What do you want with me?" Chris asked, still not believing what he was seeing.

"I want you dead!" the Spider-Lady hissed.

"This is bad," Chris said to himself as the spider lady charged him. As men ran screaming from the pool, Chris jumped over the mutant arachnid and headed to the door. But the spider ran after him. Even though Chris had cybernetic legs, the spider—on eight legs— beat him to the door. Spider-Lady jumping in front of him hissing.

"Crap!" yelled Chris as he turned and jumped through the gaping hole in the roof. He landed on the side of the roof. He slid down over the glass dome and then jumped through one of the windows and crashed right into another area of the baths.

Neneko and the others where in the steam baths at this time. Sam was having the hardest time, for she wasn't used to the heat. But she had heard the steam baths where the best way to hold on to one's beauty.

"You know you shouldn't push yourself so much," Neneko told her, noticing Sam's discomfort.

Without warning, they heard a huge crash in the locker rooms, which were adjacent to where they were. A dozen or so women came running out of the locker room, holding their towels around them. One of the women screamed, "A giant spider!"

Another woman said, "Some guy's fighting it!"

"Giant spider?" Destiny asked as she looked at the others.

Neneko shoved Maylu at Sam and grabbed Destiny. When they ran in there, Chris was fighting a giant spider lady. Chris was wearing nothing but a towel around his waist.

"Chris-chan, what the hell, are you doing???" Neneko yelled out to him.

"Well, Neneko, what does it look like I'm doing? I'm fighting for my life! This mutant wants to kill me!" Chris yelled back to her as he jumped around out of Spider-Lady's grasp.

Spider-Lady saw him turn as he spoke to the girls and took the opportunity to shot her sticky webbing at him. She slung him around and slammed him into a wall.

"Chris!" The the girls yelled. Then Spider-Lady started to run toward the girls. She was then, ready to take them out too. But then they all heard a lion's roar.

"Beast form!" Chris roared out as the Cyber Lion jumped out of the rubble and roared again. "You will not hurt my family!"

The spider laughed as she said, "I thought your code of honor prevented you from fighting women."

"It does," Chris said in an almost growl in his cyber beast from. "But, even though you're a women, you're more spider than human, so my code of honor stays intact."

"Oh shi—i ..."

"You said it!" Chris roared. And, then he let out the blast roar at her that sent her through the wall and out of the baths thus vaporizing her.

After he was sure the mutant was dead, Chris turned to the others who were standing around him in awe. Still in the beast form, he said, "Well, this has been fun and all, but I think that I will stick to the springs at the temple from now on."

"Oh, you're no fun, Chris. This has been a great day," Destiny told him as she came up to him. "But I think we do have one big problem though."

"What's that?" Chris asked.

"You demolished the lockers, all of our clothes are torn up underneath all that rubble." She pointed to the broken wall and metal lockers.

"Oops." Chris growled, sheepishly as he took a few stepped steps back like a scared cat.

"What are we going to do now for clothes?" Sam asked, obviously them not liking the idea of riding all the way home in only towels.

Neneko then, with a timid voice said, "Well, Chris can fly in that cyber lion form. And he is big enough to carry us all. We could ride him back to the temple and I could use my powers to make us all invisible, —that way no one will see us, and no one would find out that we did this."

Chris didn't seem to like the idea of him being used like a horse by three naked girls and his daughter. "

"What's the problem, Chris?" Destiny said asked as she looked him up and down, . "You' *are* big enough."

"That's not the problem.," Chris said in an unsure tone. Right then, they heard people coming back into the locker room area.

"Come on! We need to hurry."," said Neneko.

"All right," he said as he kneed knelt down.

Hanging onto their towels as best they could, Neneko and Sam both slide onto Chris's body sort of sidesaddle for there their own reasons. But Maylu and Destiny just climbed right onto him. Chris seemed a little uneasy with this situation, but powered up his shoulder engines and shot out of the building and into the sky. Neneko used her powers to make them invisible.

The girls at first where a little scared and griped tightly to his mane, but, as he flew higher, they started to enjoy themselves.

After a short time, they landed at the temple. Chris really seemed out of it, as he let them off, and they wasted no time in running to their rooms to get dressed. They were half frozen from the trip.

Chris just walked back toward his room slowly. Still in his cyber lion form, he was still thinking about that spider mutant that had attacked him. Who sent it? And how had it tracked him?, Tracking him wouldn't have been that hard; after all, he was a bit of a celebrity now a days, but still he had told no one where he was going. Most importantly, who was making these mutants?

Chris had just tried to enter his room still in his cyber lion form and, hit his head on the door frame He shook himself out of his daze, laughing at the fact, he didn't change back to his humanoid form. When he did change back, he realized that he had forgotten his clothes back at the baths. *Ah, no matter*, he thought. *Nothing of too, great importance.* And he went into his room to put some clothes on.

The next day, as Chris was walking with Neneko to her campus, he still seemed a bit out of it. Neneko asked him if it was okay if she invited some of her friends to the temple, but he didn't answer. She waved her hand in front of him.

"What is it, Neneko?" He he asked.

"I just asked you if you don't mind if I have some of my school friends over for a while this afternoon. I need their help with my clothes designing protect I'm working on?"."

"Of course I don't mind," he said. "But you don't need have to ask me. The temple is as much yours as it is mine."

She agreed to that but knew that something was bothering the cyborg. "What is with you Chris-chan?" You've been out of it sense that spider mutant attacked you."

"I've just been thinking a lot," he told her. "It seems that there is someone out there who is going to great lengths to kill me, —and going to great lengths in keeping his or her identity a secret."

"Try not to think about it too much," Neneko suggested. "It's not like, it was another Akurei or anything. Besides, you can handle anything that, whoever -it-is throws at you."

"I hope you're right, Neneko," Chris said."

Chris went through the rest of his day still thinking about the mutants that had attacked him?

Neneko later returned home, and her friends where in Chris's room with Destiny and Maylu. They where in there because Neneko liked the lighting for working with her designs and fabrics.

Sam had made it back home from her errands before Chris, for he had to run some errand on the way back to the temple. She had heard the commotion in Chris's room and wanted to know what was going on, so she opened the door to find four girls all wearing ferrous clothes and variety of costumes. Two of the girls were Maylu and Destiny, and the other two where Neneko's friends Chika and Miu. "What's going on here?" Sam asked in a friendly way.

"This is a school project," Neneko told her. "I've designed and made the outfits that we're modeling— they're from famous anime films!" I've been doing this as a hobby for years," she continued. "I have also a few outfits for Chris-chan to try on when he gets back, but I don't think he will—he hasn't done this since we were kids."

Sam turned to Neneko as she reentered the room Neneko picked up a a sketch pad. She walked over to a corner of the room and sat on the floor and started to sketch each girl as they posed. She was quit skilled.

Chris was slowly walking up the stairs of the temple. He had a run-in, with another mutant on the way home. This one had been a plant mutant, Chris was able to kill it easily just by cutting its root, —but it had been quite a little fight. *How do they keep finding me?* he wondered again. *And who is making them?*

The moment he opened the door to his room, he found the group of women wearing outfits from famous anime films.

"What the hell is going on here?" He said in shock not knowing what was going on.

"Well," Neneko answered, "at the moment I'm sketching."

"Well that's great and all, Neneko, but why are all of you in my room?"

"The light is better in your room—and it's the biggest one," she said. "Turn to each other and hold each others hands ... and face me." She told Destiny and Maylu.

After there costume session was over, Chris joined the girls in his room. He was watching the TV while the girls were talking to Neneko about how good she was. "Yeah,", Chris said, "she was always, good at sewing. Even when she was little, she would make shirts and stuff for her family."

"That's right," Neneko stated with pride. "I know sewing like I know the back of my hand."

Destiny then held up an outfit and asked, "Are *you* going to try any of them on?"

Neneko shook her head no. "I'm fine just watching."

"That's no good, Momma Neneko," Maylu exclaimed, .

Even Neneko's friends agreed with her that she should try some on too.. Chika held up an outfit and said, "Try this one!"

"Really guys," Neneko stated, "I don't think they would look any good if I wore them."

Chris spoke up without thinking and without turning away from the TV: "No, don't do it, Neneko. All those frilly lassie stuff really doesn't suit you." When girls like you, try to look glamorous," he continued, " it just turns out looking bad. Beside Neneko, you never had much in sex appeal."

Neneko jumped up. She was furious, but tried to remain calm. "Don't you worry," she said. "It would will be a million years before you see any of *my* sex appeal, —even by mistake! And I wouldn't talk if I were you, besides I doubt any beautiful girls would give you the time of day."

"What was that?" Chris yelled finally dragging himself away from the TV.

He got up and stood in front of her. They glared at each other for a few seconds until Neneko said, "It doesn't matter." Then she turned to her friends. "Thanks, you guys. I'll be able to finish my project now." And she gathered her things and left the room.

"What's with her?," Chris thought to himself, but then he noticed Maylu and Destiny giving him, big sad eyes look. That made him take a few steps back, "What's wrong?" he asked them.

"That was mean, Daddy," Maylu said sadly to her father.

"Yeah, Chris didn't you feel how that hurt her?" Destiny added.

"What are you talking about?"

"Well, even without the heightened sensitivity to other people's emotions that Lorelei gave me when she added my teleport power, but I can sense the feelings and overwhelming emotions of those around me, and how badly Neneko was hurt, by those things you said to her. You may have been kidding, but it might of been only a moment. but it went really deep."

Chris was taken aback by what they said. Even Neneko's friends didn't seem to like what he had said to her.

Neneko returned to her room. She stripped off her clothes and stood in front of the mirror in her underwear. She pulled out one of her dresses that she had made, and held it up to her. But then she lowered it as she touch her chest wishing that she could look good in the outfit.

The rest of the night was quiet, but the next day things didn't seem to go be back to normal. As Chris, Maylu, and Neneko were walking to their schools, Neneko didn't speak a word to Chris.

All through, Chris was thinking about what he had said. He finally realized that he had gone a little to far. He determined that maybe he should apologize.

In the afternoon, Chris picked up Maylu and then headed for Neneko's campus. As they headed back, Chris started to talk about the day before, but Neneko ran off, saying that she had to pick up a few things. She was gone before Chris could say anything.

"Daddy," Maylu said, "are you trying to apologize for hurting Momma Neneko?"

"Well, honey, it seems that Neneko is still mad at me," said Chris. "So I should let her calm down a bit more before I try again."

That's when Maylu had a plan. When she got back to the temple, she got Destiny to help. Maylu and Destiny as they went into Neneko's room. When Neneko came into her room and found them, she asked, "What are you two doing, with one of my outfits?"

The two didn't say a word, they just crept closer to Neneko. By the time she realized what they had planned, it was to late. Against her protests, they forced her to put on the outfits.

Neneko was now sat on the floor breathing hard. Maylu and Destiny were laughing, and Neneko couldn't help but join in. Neneko was now in wearing one of own design dresses. It was a beautiful and elegant design, but, since Neneko wasn't as well endowed, as the girl she had designed the dress for, it didn't fit her well in the top.

"Now then let's go!" Maylu said.

"Wait a minute," said Neneko. "Where exactly am I going to go dressed like this?" Neneko asked.

"To Daddy's room, of course," Maylu said happily. "So Daddy will say you look pretty."

"Pretty," Neneko said, as a memory from the past came to her.

"Daddy is sad," Maylu said quietly. "When Daddy is upset, it upsets me."

"Maylu, dear," Neneko said, "your daddy won't be in his room this early. He has to work out, before he even shows his face around here in the afternoon." She looked at Destiny. "But thanks to both of you. Besides, I'm not even mad at Chris-chan any more."

"Then you'll forgive him?" Maylu and Destiny both asked.

"Of course I will," she said. "You both are such good girls." She hugged them both thinking that she should be thanking them, for reminding her of that day.

Chris was coming back from his training, when he saw Neneko sitting at the top of the grassy hill that overlooked the hot springs. She had changed back to her regular clothes.

"Hey, Neneko-chan," Chris said as he walked up at behind her. "Do you know how many times I have found you here over the years?"

"Really!" ?" she stated not turning to him.

"Yeah, I've found you here reading sometimes … or crying."

"What? When did I cry?"

"Yeah, well you cried that one time," Chris said, sitting down next to her. "Do you remember the first time you wore a dress to school? It was back in second grade—before we had to wear uniforms. You came to school wearing some frilly home made dress. The school bullies picked on you, the skirt wasn't long enough and most of the parts weren't sewn on right! But, no matter what they said, you remained quiet."

"That's right," said Neneko. "And you defended me, don't you remember?"

"I did?"

"Yeah, you did. You wailed, on one kid till he got a bloody nose. And then, later, when you found me here, you really tried to— …"

"Wait—did I do something?"

"Yeah—after I told you about the dress. My mother had started the dress. It was supposed to be a present for when I started school. But she died before she finished it. When I found it, I tried to fix it and I wore it anyway, to school even though I knew it didn't look good on me. After you defended me, you said."

"That it did look good on me. You and even said that I looked like a princess, —your princess." Neneko's eyes filled with tears.

"Yeah well, Neneko," Chris said. "what I said to you before well I didn't mean a word of what I said yesterday. I shouldn't have teased you. In fact, you are one of the most beautiful girls that I have ever met."

"Well, thanks Chris-chan," Neneko said as she had already gotten up, without Chris realizing it.

"Wait where are you????"—"

"I have to get dinner ready. It's my turn tonight." And, with that, she was off. Chris didn't see it, but, as she ran, she had a very happy expression on her face. It made her happy knowing now that Chris cared about her so much. Maybe there was hope that her fantasies about him might come true.

Chris's metal hands and feet made a crunching sound as he climbed the side of the hundred-story building. As he climbed, he dug his metal hands and feet into the side of the building. It had taken six years for Samantha's computers to decipher the files she had retrieved from Connor's computers. During that time, they had all been, attacked many times by mutant assailants who tried to take Chris's life. Also, during that time, Neneko had graduated from college and she and Chris had had a son together. Leo who was now four-years old.

"Tell me again while, I'm the one doing this, Sam?" Chris asked into to his built-in inter com, connecting to Sam's lab, where she and the others where watching everything through his eyes. "I mean, after six years, you finally tell me to climb this building to check and see if this was where Akurei was made?"

"Well," Sam said, "it took me a while to find any information in Connor's destroyed lab, —no thanks to you."

"I said I was sorry," Chris responded. "How was I, supposed to know that my Screaming fist would destroy half the lab?"

"Half the lab nothing," she argued back playfully. "You blew up half a city block! It was a good thing everyone thought it was just a gas explosion, or else we would of have had bigger problems than what we have! But, right now, that doesn't matter at all, does it? You just remember that, this building is the one where I think is making illegal mutant monsters like Akurei are being made. If the information that

I got from Connor's lab is right, we should find what we're looking for inside."

Chris continued to climb, "But why does it have to be me?"

"Because you're the only one who, that can do this!" Sam told him, .

"Then why can't I just fly?" Chris whined.

Sam shook her head at the monitor as she watched his progress. "That wouldn't work! We have to do this as quietly as possible, without guns blazing. So think like a ninja," she finished.

At that point, Chris made it to the ninetieth floor. This was where Sam had told him to enter the building. He looked at the window of the building, but there was something wrong— the window was fake. It was just tacked onto the outside of the building.

"You girls seeing this?" Chris asked knowing that the others we're watching too.

"Well, that's not suspicious," Neneko said in a sarcastic tone, as she watched him tapping on the fake window.

"Chris can you still find a way in?" Samantha asked as she leaned forward to the monitor.

"It shouldn't be problem," Chris told her.

He then grabbed the side of the building and tore into aside the fake window.

After he checked to make sure no one had heard him, he then jumped into the building. He replaced the fake window back as best he could. And then he listened to the girls scold him for making too much noise.

As he walked down the hall ways, he noticed something unusual— he had been walking for some time and yet he had not seen or heard anybody. The whole place seemed deserted.

Sam then said, "Maybe the hall way, is fake to too—like the outside window?"

Chris walked over to the, walls of the hallway and tapped on the walls. They sounded hollow, so he then punched right into a spot next to him. He, tore a large piece off the wall off, revealing that the whole inside of the building was a large factory of some kind. Human-sized tubes lined the walls. A railing separated the tubes from the computers in the center of the room. As he scanned the area, Sam noticed something. "Stop!" she yelled.

"Go back, Chris," she said. "There was a life reading in one of the tubes."

Chris turned back. Sam was right—there was a life reading coming from one of the tubes. It seemed weird for the other tubes didn't give off any type of reading and yet there where hundreds of them.

Chris leaped over the railing. He fell as he landed and skidded quite a distance before he ground to a halt before one of the tubes. He climbed up to the tube that was giving off the life readings. There was someone inside, but the tube was fogged up. Sam and the others saw it too. There, inside that tube, was a small female child. *She couldn't be no older than my son*, Chris thought..

Chris, tore the whole tube off the wall and jumped back to the railing. The others watched with awe and wonder as the Super Cyborg tore the door off of the tube. When he did, steam poured out and they all watched as a the little girl sat up.

She was nude, and had a network of wires attached to her small body. She did, in fact, look about four or five years old. The cyborg and the others in Sam's lab watched as she rubbed her eyes. When she opened them and looked at Chris, he saw that her eyes were as pale gray and somehow reminded him of the moon. He also noticed that a strange power seemed to emanate from her eyes.

The child didn't seem to be afraid of him at first. "Who are you?" she asked. In a voice no higher than a whisper.

The cyborg said, "I'm here to help. I'm going to take you some place safe.."

He took off his coat and wrapped it around her. As he did, he made sure to cut the wires attached to her without her knowing. And that's when every alarm in the whole place went off. Sirens sounded and the whole place seemed lit in a red light.

"Chris-chan, you have to get out of there *now!*" Neneko yelled out to into the inter com.

"You think!!?"

Chris grabbed the girl and ran headlong for the fake window. But, got close a wall going down covering his escape. When it slammed shut, he punched the wall in frustration.

"Blast it!" He yelled.

He then heard people coming his way. He turned to see what looked like military soldiers running toward him. He could not believe it, he never thought that the military would be in a privately owned building. But he had no time to think, so he reared back and slammed his metal fingers into the metal wall that was blocking his way. With one hand, he tore the wall out and threw it at the soldiers. They barely managed to get out of the way before it hit them.

The Super Cyborg then looked out to the open air. He looked at the girl in his arms and told her, "Hang on tight."

The girl griped him tightly as he jumped out of the opening in the wall of the ninetieth floor. The soldiers ran to the window and fired a few shots, but to no avail. One of them then took out an communicator and reported, "The cyborg got Program Number Eight."

Chris and the others heard the report, but they never heard the response: "You are all incompetent fools! That girl is important to my research. Don't worry about it, I will get her back, my way."

Chris was free falling at an incredible rate. Back in the lab, the girls who where watching though his eyes started to feel a little sick as they watched through his eyes.

Just as it looked as if he wasn't going to make it, he made contact with the other building across from the one from which they were escaping. He skidded half way down the building before he came to a stop.

He turned back to look at the other building and he couldn't even see the spot he'd jumped from. He then looked at the girl and saw that she had passed out.

"I don't blame you, kid," he whispered to her. " I probably of would have passed out too, if I was you."

xxx

Later when Chris returned to the lab, he gave the girl to Sam who did a few tests. She, in turn, gave the girl to Neneko, who then took the girl to find her some food, clothing, and a place to rest.

Later, Chris then appeared Sam's lab. "Did you find out anything about her?" he asked.

"Well, for one thing I found that her name is Hinata. It was on a necklace she was wearing. There was also a the number eight tattooed on her arm. I found where some unusual things about her blood, that bothers me, but, other than that, she seems really normal expect—for her eyes."

"Yeah, I know," said Chris. "There was something about them when I first saw them, … I almost felt like I was staring at the moon."

"That's just it, Chris, her eyes, they *are* like the moon, —they give off lunar waves."

"What in the heck are lunar waves?"

"They're the waves of energy, that are given off from the moon. They're, also what turned you into a Cyber Lion that first time, —when you got that the tail."

The thought made Chris think of something. "Wait a minute," he said. "Where's Leo?"

"Your son, he's with Maylu in the play area. That's where Neneko, put Hinata to play to   She didn't want her to be alone. Oh no!!!!!"

"Yeah, we better get in there before it's too late."

Chris and Sam, ran out of her lab as fast as they could going straight to the play area as fast as they could, hoping they had some time left. Chris then saw Neneko standing at the entrance to the play area.

"Neneko, where is our son?" Chris asked.

"He's playing with Maylu and that girl that you brought Hinata. "Why?"

They all heard the metallic lions roar coming from the play area, and the room shook violently.

"What was that?" Neneko said as she looked into the play area.

Chris ran in and saw his son already changing into the Cyber Lion. Hinata stood right in front of him, so scared she couldn't move. Chris jumped in front of his son to try and stop, the transformation, but it was too late. His five-year-old son, had already changed into a cyber lion. Unlike Chris, Leo had no control over this form. At any time, he could turn making into nothing more than a raging animal.

The good thing was that his son wasn't as strong as Chris. And the young cyber lion was only about as big as a real lion. So Chris had the advantage, but still it was going to be hard.

The cyber lion ran around in a rampage, but Chris jumped in front of him again and grabbed him. As he held his son down, Chris yelled out, "Neneko, stun him."

Neneko though was always a little hesitant to stun her own son, but she used a low beam through her eyes, and shot fast to get it over with. Instantly, the large cyber lion fell asleep then, slowly reverted back to a small boy.

Chris then looked around and saw the girl. She was shaking in the corner of the room. Chris picked up his son. "I'll take him to the infirmary," he said to Neneko and Sam. "Take care of the girls, and make sure that they're okay."

Maylu was surprised when Sam asked if she was all right. But she shook it off quickly as Sam asked her, "What happened?"

"I didn't see much. Just that, only, when that girl looked at Leo, he started to change."

Neneko walked over to the poor girl cowering in the corner.

"Its okay, sweet-heart. It wasn't your fault. It's, just that my son is a little allergic to the moon light that your eyes give off. Everything is fine now," Neneko said doing her best to calm the poor girl.

Hinata slowly moved over, and jumped up, and hugged Neneko. Even though she must have been frightened by all the things that happened to her, this must have been the scariest.

Chris was watching his son sleep in the infirmary when he noticed that, his entire left hand looked almost metallic. When Sam came in, to check up on him, she saw the metallic hand, too. "What's happening to my son?" Chris asked.

Sam lowered her head as she told him, "It's was, because of you, Chris."

"Me??"

"Yes, it's the metal that you're made of. You didn't notice, it but, when he was born, some of the metal was in his system. The good thing is that everything works all right with him. But he will eventually look like your supreme form. Each time he transforms to the cyber lion, the transformation will be magnified. The worst thing about it is the full transformation to his final form will be slow and painful."

"That's terrible!" said Chris. "Isn't there anything we can do for him?"

"No, ," said Sam sadly. "I'm sorry, but it's the metal that's going to cause him the pain. It's going to one day cover his body. The most amazing thing is that it will probably going to make him stronger than even you."

"Well then, I hope he can handle the pain, he will have to endure until his transformation is complete."

Just as Chris said this, his son started to scream out in pain. Not knowing what to, Chris tried to hold his son down, so Sam could give him some pain killer. Just as Sam was reaching for the medication, Neneko with , Hinata and, Maylu burst into the infirmary.

"Stop!" Neneko yelled out.

"But, Neneko-chan, our boy is in pain." said Chris.

"Then let Hinata help him," she told him. She looked at the girl. "Go on," she said.

Hinata timidly walked up to the bed, and stood next to Leo, who still cried softly because of the pain. Both Chris and Sam saw the girl's eyes start to glow. Hinata reached out her hand and then she touched him first on the chest, and then on the boy's metallic hand. They all watched as he seemed to relax, and with that his pain was gone.

Leo looked up at the timid girl, and smiled. It was the first time in his young life that he didn't feel any pain. Chris, Neneko, and Sam were amazed at this discovery.

"How did you know, Neneko??" asked Chris.

"Maylu told me that, when the girl first came into the play room, Maylu, had just fallen and hurt herself and twisted her ankle. Hinata did, that same tick to help her."

Sam looked at the girl closely, but the child was scared easily and ran behind Neneko's leg. "Do you know what this means?" Sam asked Chris. "This girl definitely is a mutant, but she isn't crazy like the others have been. I think that maybe this girl is the perfect mutant form—meaning that she might have powers close to yours, Neneko's, or Destiny's. She might even be the next step in the evolutionary scale. Do you realize what type of kids she would have if she was were to bare bear with your son? It might be the perfect new race."

"Time out, Sam," said Chris. "My son's only five years old! You're thinking way too far into the future for my tastes."

"Or mine," Neneko added.

"I'm sorry guys," said Sam. "But you have to understand that I have to see this at an academic level. I mean the genetic research that went into this must have been amazing."

xxx

On the rooftop of the building across from the Cyber Corp building, a large man stood watching the Cyber Corp building. Four others soon joined him.

"Sir," one of them the newcomers said, "Are we going to destroy the whole building?"

"Yes we are," said the first man. "But remember—our objective is to get Number Eight out alive, and kill everyone else in the building. Make sure it looks like an accident."

"Then let's stop talking and take it down, what are we waiting for,?" another said becoming impatient.

"Nothing at all, soldier. But first let's have some fun. Remember, we have to kill everybody in the building."

The five men jumped off the building. As they fell, they each turned into monstrous mutants, each one with there own special powers.

There leader became a beetle-like creature, with huge horns and a strange crystal, in his forehead. One was like a rhino, built like a tank. Another had a long neck. Tentacles grew out of his head, and, instead of hands, he had long blades. One was a living missile launcher. He had large organic missile launchers on each side of his shoulder. The last looked like some kind of mutant bear. But all of his hair was white as snow, and he had the head of a snakes.

The second they landed, they entered the building and began to tear things apart. The people working in the building ran the second they saw them, but running wasn't an option. As they tore through the building, they slaughtered everyone in there sight. The leader yelled out to them, "Hurry up! We don't have all day!" He just watched his soldiers tear the people into shreds.

As this was going on below, Chris was still watching his son in disbelief that he wasn't in pain anymore— all thanks to this mutant girl, who didn't look like a mutant. Suddenly, every alarm in the place started to go off. "What's going on, Sam?" Chris shouted.

"Chris, you will not believe this, but five mutants are in the building, and there they're killing everybody in sight."

Chris turned to look at the monitor, and when he did he saw them destroying, everything in sight as they moved though the building.

Chris turned to the girl and said, "They're after Hinata. There is no other reason for them, to be here. I'll go hold them off. You three take the kids and get out of here as fast as you can."

"Are you sure you can handle them alone?" Sam asked with concern.

"Don't worry about me," Chris said. "I can take care of myself. Just take the kids and get out of here!"

Chris then shot off out of the room and down the hall as fast as he could. He shot around each corner of the building like a crazed beam of light, and he skidded to a stop right in front of the bear mutant. The beast shot a dose of venom at him, but Chris ducked out of the way and it hit the wall melting it.

"Wow, that was one major spit wad.," said Chris.

"That ant't the half of it, Striker," the mutant told him with a hiss.

"You know who I am?"

"Yes, and, if you return Number Eight, we might consider letting you live."

"Fat chance of that! My son has grown quite fond of that girl now that he knows that she can lessen his pain. Even if it wasn't for that, I still wouldn't give her back."

"Then you will die, with the rest of the people in this building, when we blow it up."

"But the only way to do that is to— …" Chris stopped mid sentence realizing what these guys have planned to do. Immediately, he then jumped to the wall, and jumped around the behemoth, and ran off with the mutant right on his tail.

Chris knew what they planned to do. They were going to blow the reactor core that was housed in the basement at the bottom of there building. There was enough power there to blow the whole building up. Chris just needed to buy his family and the employees some more time. Little did he know, that their time was about to run out. For the mutants' leader had made his way straight to the top of the building where Chris's family was.

Neneko was the first to stop in her tracks as she felt the mutant coming their way at top speed. She then said to Sam, "Keep going with the children!"

But Leo cried to his mother, "Don't do it!"

Even he knew that this mutant was different and that she didn't stand a chance against it. But she yelled out, *"Go!!"*

Sam grabbed the boy and ran with the others as Neneko stood her ground. The mutant beetle came charging at her, but she readied herself. Right when it looked as if the mutant was going to hit her, the rhino looking mutant came, crashing through the wall and slammed her against the wall. The beetle kept going after the others.

Chris made it to the reactor room just in time to see the long-necked mutant discharging electricity through his tentacles.

He ran at the mutant, and jumped up, and kicked him right into the wall where he know it was electrified. The mutant absorbed a jolt of electricity from the equipment he slammed into, but he came right back at Chris.

"Don't!!!" Chris yelled to the mutant freak. He then spin- kicked the large beast and then grabbed it by the tentacles and spun it around and

threw it hard right into the other mutant that had just arrived. They both slammed into the opposite wall.

Both got back up. They positioned themselves for a charge, and Chris readied for the attack, but it never came. Chris wondered what was up, then he heard the screaming sound of something flying at him. He turned to see small missiles coming his way.

He had no time to get out of the way. They blew up in a massive explosion.

Neneko was barely able to move as the behemoth crashed her against the wall. She quickly moved her head to face him and fired a straight beam at the mutants right eye. He reared back in pain as blood shot out of the socket.

Neneko fell to the floor trying to catch her breath when the mutant stared her down with his now one good eye.

"You will pay for that, woman," The the rhino mutant roared out as he watched Neneko struggle to her feet and stand ready.

"Yeah, well I'm not as easy to beat as you seem to think, freak.," she retorted.

As the explosion in the reactor room faded, Chris could tell that the three mutants had thought they had killed him. But the Super Cyborg turned to face them down, his clothes badly torn.

He had, his arms crossed across his chest. Chris looked back up at the mutants mad as a hornet. He turned to the one who had fired the missiles at him, and, in an instant, he shot past him. The mutant didn't see him do anything, but Chris just turned to him and snapped his metal figures fingers. The mutant looked at his missile pods and he saw that they had been destroyed—as blood and other liquids came pooling out.

"No!!!" The mutant yelled. "This can't be happening!" As he tried to stop the flow of liquids, he added, "Do you realize what you have done?"

"Apparently, something bad for you."

"No," said the monster. "You don't get it— my body emits a chemical agent that is like nitro glycerin."

"Well then," said Chris, "I guess that means that I'm going to have to give the cleaning lady a raise after this one." And Chris aimed his arm at the mutant and fired a single shot of his shotgun.

The moment the beams hit the mutant, he blew up in a massive explosion of guts and gore.

Neneko tried to think of something quick when she saw the fire hose behind the behemoth. *Water!* she thought. She then just aimed her hand at it and it sent the water blast at her attacker. The blast shot him forward and Neneko ducked under him as the water blast him threw him right through the wall, and through the outside wall. He fell a good thirty stories before slamming face first into the concrete.

Neneko walked to the hole in the outside wall and looked down at the beast. She blew him a good-bye kiss, then she silently thanked Beth who had given her the power of water in the first place.

Chris was now ready for the other two, who now just wanted revenge for their fallen comrades. They where driven by rage as they charged him. He powered up to his supreme mode and made himself ready to fight. As the golden glow covered him, he shot back as the two punched him at the same time missing him by inches.

He then spun back and kicked the two on their backs. They both were pushed back by the hit, but shook it off fast. The bladed mutant went at Chris like mad as the other circled around, Chris looking as if he wasn't even trying any more.

Right then, the snaked-head mutant struck out his head and attacked the cyborg, but Chris disappeared and the only thing the mutant hit was his fellow mutant.

The tentacle mutant yelled to the snake headed mutant, "You should of have done a better job getting him!" "Let's see you do better!" screamed his comrade.

As they argued, Chris rose up to float right over their heads.

"If you two are done fighting each other, I think we should finish this. I have places to go and mutants to stop," Chris told them both form his spot in the air.

The two mutants were really starting to hate this cyborg. The bladed mutant took to the air using his own method of flight. He engaged Chris in a mid air fight that was so fast it looked like two beams of light fighting each other.

The snake-headed mutant then took his chance as he watched them fight. He stretched out his head again and attacked, this time hitting his mark.

The snake mutant wrapped his head and neck around Chris. The bladed mutant sliced at Chris, but something unexpected happened, —the blade broke right when it hit Chris's metal shoulder.

The mutant reared back as blood pored out of his blade hand.

"What the hell are you?" The now one blade -handed mutant said as he put his bleeding hand under his other arm.

"I'm the Super Cyborg, punk," Chris stated. Then as he yelled out, powering up, and snapped the snake mutant's head off breaking free of his grip.

The snake-headed mutant's head fell to the ground and wiggled around as his bear-like body fell to the ground, twitched twice, and fell lifeless..

The other tentacle mutant was not feeling very confident now that two of his team mates had been killed by one cyborg man, who wasn't even at full power yet. The odds are that he was dead, but he wasn't going down with out a fight. He still had one technique that might work of for him.

The mutant shot his tentacles at the cyborg, rapping him in tight electrified bindings.

"What's the matter with you?" Chris said. "You should be able to figure out that, tying me up won't work!" But, right then, the mutant electrified the binds.

Chris was being shocked, with enough power to light a city,.

"I bet you're getting a charge out of this!" the mutant told him.

But, even as he was being electrocuted, the cyborg smiled at the mutant as he told him, "I am getting a charge out of this, but I think you will get a bigger one out of this!," And, right then, Chris pulled his arm out and grabbed the sides of the mutant's head. This caused a reversal of energy. Chris barbecued the mutant with his own power.

Finally, Chris just dropped what was left of the over-cooked mutant to the ground where it shattered and smoldered. Then Chris pressed a button on the side of his head and asked, "I need an up date, everyone. What's going on?"

"Well Chris-chan," Neneko began reported, "I just blew a large mutant through the wall."

"How about you, Sam? What's your status?"

"The kids and I have, made it to the roof, Chris," she reported, " but we have a little problem and we could use your help."

"What is it, Sam, are you okay?" Chris asked in a panic, but then there was nothing but static and he knew he had to get the roof fast. Since he was at the bottom of the building, there was only one thing for him to do. He powered up and shot straight up throw the side of the building and landed on the roof.

Sam and the kids were trapped in the center of the roof. Sam was standing in front of the kids trying to protect them from the large beetle mutant. The mutant had just smashed her communications link. As the mutant moved in closer, Leo stepped in front of Sam and he readied himself to fight.

The mutant laughed at the thought of a little boy stopping him. He swung his arm and knocked the boy back against the ledge of the buildings roof. Hinata moved away form Sam. Sam screamed, "Come back!" but it was too late.

The mutant went after the girl as he said, "You're all making this too easy." But Hinata managed to run right to Leo's side, and tried to get him back up.

The mutant, however, then grabbed the girl. As she screamed, Leo shot up, and, despite his small size, he used a variation of the screaming bullet. "*Shock Bullet!*" he yelled at the mutant, shattering his whole left arm like it was nothing. But, as the mutant fell, he managed to slashed at Hinata's arm as he fell to the ground.

Seeing what the mutant had done, the boy went into a blind rage. The boy ran at the mutant, and grabbed him by the leg, and spun him twice before releasing the beetle mutant into the air and beyond the edge of the roof. The boy let out a roared for his victory just as, Chris burst out onto the roof. Neneko made it there at that moment too, ready to help. But the fight was already over by the time they got there thanks to their five year- old son.

The beetle flew and crashed hard into a building a mile away. He was hurt, but not dead. As green goo came out of his wound, he stood as he looked at his hand. It was covered in the blood of Number Eight. Maybe the fight hadn't been a total loss.

A woman was sitting in a dark lab when the door flew open. As light poured into the room, it illuminated a African American woman in her mid twenties. She looked at the damage of the beetle mutant.

"Well," the woman said with a scowl, "Did you get the girl?"

"No, I didn't," the beetle mutant told her angrily. "And I lost *all* of my men in the attempt! " "Why didn't you tell me that cyborg freak was so strong? And don't *even* get me started about his kids! The Cyborg's, son is one who did this to me, —and the boy was is only five years old! Now tell me that's, not messed up!!"

"You fool," she told him, "he and his kids have been enhanced by the metal that he is made of. How do you think he survives the speeds he runs at? He can even survive in space!"

Just then, the woman saw the beetle mutant's hand covered in blood. "Wait a minute," she said, getting up and approaching her creation for a better look, " what is that on your hand?"

"This?" the mutant started said. "This is just the blood that came from your precious little mutant girl, Number Eight. I managed to cut her up, pretty good before the cyborg's son threw me off the roof."

The woman seemed a little happier as she grabbed the mutant's hand and put it on a slab, on her lab table. She then grabbed a large blade and, right before the beetle mutant could protest, she cut off his hand with one quick slice.

"Why did you do that? I only had one hand left! What am I going to do now you bitch??"

"Well, now you can bare witness to my greatest work of genetic engineering yet—the creation that is going to kill that cyborg once, and for all and avenge my father's death!" she told him. "You see, I created that girl to contain the finally genetic code I needed to complete my greatest work of art."

The mutant watched her, as she scrapped the blood off his severed hand. Slowly and carefully, she processed the blood through a multitude of equipment that the beetle mutant didn't understand. Finally, the blood entered, and went though a tube system that went into a breeding tube that was growing the woman's greatest work. As the beetle mutant walked behind the woman he watched, something move in the tube.

Suddenly, a gray fist punched through the tube. As a low roar came from the broken tube, as the gray beast broke out in an explosion of energy that would put a power plant to shame.

There stood an enormous gray man. He was at least twelve feet tall, but proportioned to his size he had fists the size of watermelons. His eyes where as red as fire, but his face was, like that of a walking manikin.

"What do you think?" said the woman to the mutant. "Isn't he amazing? He is my newest super soldier. *He* well go and kill the Super Cyborg." He is mutant X." Then she turned to address her new monster. "Mutant X," she said, "your first order is to kill the mutant in front of you."

The beetle mutant didn't even have time to move. X grabbed him with one hand. The beetle mutant tried to get free of the beast's grip, but it was no good he had no leverage without his hands. X picked him up the mutant, kicking and screaming then, in one sickening motion, he crushed the beetle mutant's head. As the broken body hit the ground, its gooey green blood poured onto the floor.

"Excellent, X," the women stated. "Now go kill the Super Cyborg," And get Number Eight!"

X looked down at his master and said in an empty voice devoid of emotion, "Kill Super Cyborg."

xxx

Chris was still a little shocked that his boy was so strong. He began to formulate an interesting plan for his son. It was time for his son to start

366

martial arts training. And, from what Chris had seen of Hinata, he decided that she should be trained along side Leo.

Sam was calling clean up crews to clean up the mess that was in the building, and repair crews to fix structural damage. Chris, though, knew that the battle wasn't over. He knew that there was a storm coming, and that they have had to be ready for anything.

Chris was outside assessing the damage to the building, Hinata had joined him. She had started to treat, Chris almost like a father. As they were walking alongside the building, Chris ran right into someone very big.

Chris looked up to apologize, but when he looked up at the man he realized that something was not right with him. Has face was gray and his eyes were red as fire. He wore a large black trench coat, and had overly large, gloved hands. But the worst thing was the power that Chris felt coming from the man. The man himself was as empty as a corpse.

"Kill Cyborg, " the large man said as he reached out, and grabbed Chris. In one swift motion, X picked up the cyborg and threw the cyborg effortlessly into the wall, smashing him in a pile of rubble. Hinata was terrorized at this sight. She was shaking all over as the mutant stepped forward, as it said, "Get number Number Eight."

X' reached out his hands toward the small girl, but Chris burst out of the rubble. He used his screaming bullet on the large mutant, but the bullet, didn't even faze X. The mutant simply grabbed Chris again, and said, "Good-bye, cyborg," and threw him across the street.

Chris yelled out to Hinata, "Run!" And he flew over a building and crashed into the street so hard he cracked the concrete.

Hinata screamed out as the mutant grabbed her. He covered her whole face with his hand. She was only able to let out a muffed scream before she passed, out from the lack of air.

People gathered around Chris's cybernetic body as he lay unconscious. Finally, someone walked up and was about to see if he was okay when he shot up on all fours and then leaped into the air. He bounced off two buildings as he jumped to the roof of another building. Then he ran off as fast as he could. He leaped into the air yelling out Hinata's name as he went. But, when he landed at the Cyber Corp building, the girl and the large gray man was gone. But Chris noticed something on the ground, where the mutant had been standing. It was a business card, for the company where Chris had found Hinata. He crushed the card in his hand as he said, "It's on!"

xxx

Hinata woke up and found herself lying on a lab table looking up at a woman. The child was shaking all over. The woman smiled at her, but it still made Hinata shake violently in fear for her life.

"Don't be afraid, my dear," said the woman. "I'm the one that who made you. My name is Tiara Bishop. You should think of me like as your mother."

"Th.. —Then let me go," the girl said still shaking with fear.

"I can't do that," said Tiara. "You see, you will bring that cyborg here where my mutant can dispose of him properly."

"Why do you want to hurt him? He has done n.n.n.—n—nothing to you."

"Oh, Hinata dear, he has. That beast of a cyborg killed my father in cold blood," Tiara told the child. "My father was a great general, but that cyborg Striker made him look like a fool, so when my father went after him. He actually killed my father! So this is going to my revenge, and it will only be complete when my greatest work of genetic engineering—my Mutant X—finally kills that Super Cyborg!"

Mutant X then walked into the light behind Tiara, and Hinata screamed out in terror at the sight of it.

xxx

Chris was furious when he told the others, what had happened. He felt terrible as he was in his dojo he slammed his fist into the wall shacking the whole building. In pure rage he then roared out and slammed his fist to the ground floor shacking everything again.

"Chris-chan it will be all right," Neneko told him. "Sam is working on a plain to get her back, so calm down." , As he turned to her, she had never seen such rage in him before. It scared her, for it seemed that something dark had been awakened inside the cyborg to bring him to such rage.

"I'll calm down when I get that girl back and kill that freak of a mutant that took her!!!"

"Chris -chan, do you realize that this has to be some kind of trap?"

Chris turned to her as he headed out of the room. He stopped at the doorway as he said, "I don't care!"

Later, Sam found Chris getting ready to leave to get Hinata. She ran up to him and grabbed his arm. "You're not going alone, —you're going to need some kind of back up."

"I'll be fine, Sam. I can take care of myself!" he almost roared.

Sam, then without warning, slapped him across the face in her own rage.

"I'm sick of this macho bullshit that you're always spitting out! What happened to your that honor that you've always been so proud of?"

Chris glared at her. The slap didn't faze him, but it did make him mad. Then he turned away from her. As he lowered himself down, as his rage subsided, he realizing that his anger wasn't getting him anywhere.

"You're right, Sam, I was blinded by rage. If I plan on coming back from this one, I had better keep my cool. Thanks for slapping some sense into me."

"Good, because I'm going to be, your backup."

"What???"

"You need my expertise on this one."

"Why?"

"Because I can hack into any security system that's out there."

Chris shook his head but agreed, as the two headed out.

Sometime later, Chris was flying with Sam over the building that he had infiltrated—where he had found Hinata. He didn't know that, there unknown enemy was, waiting for them.

"Chris!" Sam yelled out to him. The speed at which they were traveling made it hard to talk unless you yelled.

"What?"

"You are going to have to do this fast, or they'll be all over us in a second."

"So what do you expect me to do, crash into the building?"

"That's exactly what I expect you to do."

"Well then, hang on tight," Chris told her as he flew up then dive bombed straight down at the top of the roof. At the point of impact, he ducked his head cradling Sam in his arms protecting her from the crash.

They both rolled to a stop inside the building as rubble and parts of the wall they crashed through came with them.

Tiara watched their landing through the monitors that were in her lab. "Release all the mutants we have in the building," she told one of her female lab assistant. "We'll see if the Super Cyborg can live up to his name." Even if he made it through the hundreds of lower -level mutants, there was no way the cyborg would manage to beat her Mutant X.

Chris and Sam now where running as fast as they could through the levels of the building. Sam had been able to locate where Hinata was by hacking—with her mini computer—into the network of computers.

"Chris, we need to take the elevator up ahead," Sam yelled to Chris as they ran. "It should take us straight to the level that Hinata is on."

Chris hit the button for the elevator but nothing happened.

"Blast," he said, " they must know where we are in the building by now. They've locked off all our ways down."

Sam then said, "There's still the direct approach!" The cyborg smiled as he knew what she meant. He slammed his hands into the elevator doors, prying them open, and then looked down the elevator shaft.

Chris then turned to Sam. "Hang onto my back!" As she put her arms around the back of his neck hanging on.

Sam could not keep herself from screaming a little, as they fell down the shaft, but then, about half way down, Chris slammed his hands against the walls of the shaft to slow them down. The elevator car was just beneath them.

Chris opened the elevator hatch that was at on the top of the elevator car, but when he did he saw at least five mutants standing in the elevator! They looked up and saw the two of them and roared out as they scrambled to get at them.

"Oh ... *No!* " Chris yelled out as the four mutants started to swarm out of the elevator at them. But Chris jumped up in the shaft to the door at the next level up. Sam was still holding onto his back. As she turned to see the mutants climbing the shaft, each one looked more monstrous to her than the next.

Chris managed to pry the elevator door open and jump onto the floor just as one of the mutants reached out for Sam's leg.

The two of them then rolled, and Chris jumped back to his feet. He fired a shot gun blast at their assailants, blowing off one of the mutant's heads with a single shot. Two others were knocked down the shaft. Chris, grabbed the doors to the elevator and crashed them together, jamming the mechanism of the door to keep anything else from getting in. He and Sam, could still hear the roars of the beasts trying to claw there way in.

"That was crazy!" Sam managed to get out as Chris turned to give her a hand up after she had fallen from the shock.

"Yeah, but I have a feeling that we haven't seen the last of those freaky things," Chris said. "Let's go!"

As they continued on, Chris detected something. He grabbed Sam's hand and they disappeared just as gun fire ripped through the room like made. Suddenly, a large mutant with electromagnetic rail guns for arms burst through the bullet hole –covered wall. When it saw that the two targets where gone, it looked around for them, but Chris and Sam had not left the room. Chris had grabbed Sam and jumped. They were now hanging overhead his hands and feet slammed into the ceiling. Sam was lying on top of him, clinging onto him her head facing down as she looked at the mutant freak. Just then, a drop of sweat from her face hit the beast. The mutant looked up, just in time to see Chris let go of the ceiling and swing down. He snapped the freak's head right off with his feet, and then dropped to the ground still with Sam gripping tightly around him.

"Sam, you can let, go of me now," Chris told her.

"Right," she stated. As she let go of him, she looked down at the mutant. "Man, those things stink!" she said. She pulled out her mini computer and told Chris, "We have only a few levels to go—and the stairs are close by." But then she noticed something on her computer, —there where at least half a dozen "things" moving around in the next level, meaning that there where a lot of them waiting for them on that level.

"Well, then I don't plan on waiting for anymore of them to get us," Chris said. "Let's just bring the fight to them. You just stay close and watch my back," he told her.

Sam nodded and said, "I'm going to stay so close to you you're going to think I'm your shadow."

They moved on down the stairs. When they came to a door a few flights down, Sam told Chris, "We have to get through that door, we need to go beyond this point, but there are a half a dozen mutants on the other side."

Right when Chris opened the door. What they saw it was like something out of a horror movie. Dozens of different mutants stood ready to attack, and all of them looking as if they could tare you apart with a single strike. When the mutants saw Chris and Sam, they roared out and headed right for them. Chris readied himself. Just as he was being surrounded, he let loose a screaming bullet.

The shock wave tore through a dozen mutants like a knife through butter, and blew more than half the building apart.

When it was over, Sam looked at the devastation. Mutant body parts and gore littered the area, and a huge hole had been blown through the building wall. The blast had cleared the way for them.

"Wasn't that a bit of over kill?" Sam asked, as they continued on. But then Chris stopped right in the middle of the destruction. Sam slammed into his back. "What's up?" she asked.

"Wait here," Chris said, as he turned to a door and opened it. When he did, he started to step back.

All Sam could hear where large heavy foot steps, as if something big was walking their way. When it appeared in the doorway, Sam about lost it. She had never seen anything like this monster.

"It's the mutant that took Hinata," Chris yelled out as it came at him.

"Kill Super Cyborg," said the mutant in its emotionless tone.

"Run!!" Chris yelled at Sam. When she'd first seen, the seven -foot giant, she couldn't move. Now finally got her legs to move. As she took off, Chris punched the beast, but it had little or no effect of the monster.

Mutant X back handed the cyborg. The large hand hit Chris like a wrecking ball. The force of the blow knocked Chris over, but he caught himself with a single hand and spun into a double spin kick. Each kick only seemed to enrage the monster rather than cause him harm.

Chris was running out of ideas so he decided to stop playing these games. *If, this freak can take my normal punches with no problems*, thought Chris, *then let's see it take a lions fist!* The cyborg yelled out as he changed from a normal cyborg to that of a Cyber Lion in a blink of an eye. He grow to the beasts size, but then past it by five feet he would have been too big for the room if he hadn't of blown two floors away earlier.

"Lets see how well you take an Alpha, Omega, Cyber, Lion, you mutant freak!" Chris yelled out as he punched the mutant so hard that this time it flew through the building, crashing through each room until it stopped itself just before it would have exited the building. Mutant X clinging to the building by one hand. As it started to climb back up onto its feet, the Cyber Lion roared out. Chris walked over to the mutant, kneed down, and grabbed X by the hand it was holding on with, and picked him up. X's coat was torn from the battle.

"Well, I happened to know," Chris said as he looked down, " that, if I can survive this fall, that you probably can. So I'll make sure that you don't survive this, by blowing you apart first!" He then brought his other fist to the beast's chest and said, *"Shotgun Double Barrel!"*

The blast that the Cyber Lion let out lit up the sky as it blasted out of the building through Mutant X's body. The blasts echoed all around like hundreds of shotguns being fired at once.

X's body was thrown about repeatedly until like a rag doll until the shots stopped. The Cyber Lion held out what was left of X making sure that it was dead, and then dropped it off the side of the building and watched it slam to the ground with a sickening thud.

Chris then turned back to Sam. She still seemed out of it from the shock of the mutant that almost killed her. Chris waved his hand trying to snap her out of it. Finally, she screamed out in pure terror as she grabbed unto onto Chris. But his size made it hard for her— she only hugged him around his waist shaking in fear.

"It's okay, Sam," said Chris, hugging her back. " I got the mutant. "You don't have to freak out about it, any more." Then he chuckled. "And, as interesting as this is seeing you act like a scared little girl instead of a scientist, we have to get going."

Sam then let him go and slapped him on the hand. "It's not funny! I was really scared of that freak, —and I'm not used to being *in* these battles!" Sam then looked around. "How are we going to get to the lab now?"

She then watched a cat like grin appear on Chris's lion face. He picked her up with ease ease. "What do you plan on doing?" she asked him

"I plan on taking the fast way down," he told her. He reared his fist up and then slammed down at the floor with his screaming bullet.

The blast blew them both down, and Sam, for the second time that day, wished that she had just stayed with her computer work, back at the Cyber Corp building. *This, is why I am* not *a field agent.*

They landed hard at the bottom of the building in an underground lab. Hinata was strapped to a table in the middle of the room. When Chris and Sam ran to her side, she weakly looked up at Chris and Sam.

"Chris, I knew you would come for me," the girl said. Chris looking down at her as Sam worked on freeing the girl from her bonds. When the girl finally sat up, she started to tell her rescuers that they had been caught in a trap, but it was to late. Silently, a very large glass tube came down around them, trapping them all inside.

Chris punched the glass, but it wasn't like anything he had seen before. His punches didn't even make the glass shake.

xxx

Meanwhile, outside the building, where Mutant X's body lay in the rubble. Suddenly, his body started to grow and change. Blades shot out of his fingers; replaced by five large blades. His body grew at an alarming rate. The mutant roared out as the spot where his heart was transformed into a large, pulsating orb on his chest. When he stood back up, he was as big as Chris in his Alpha Omega Cyber Lion mode. Mutant X stomped back into the building saying over and over, "Kill Super Cyborg."

XXX

Chris, Sam, and Hinata where trapped inside a the glass cylinder when gas started to flow onto it from vents in the floor. For Chris, this was no problem because his lungs where cybernetic. He knew, however, that he had to get Sam and Hinata out of there or they would suffocate.

Chris then heard a women's voice say, "I will let you out on one condition." Chris looked over through the glass at a woman standing on a nearby platform. He couldn't put his finger on why, but there was something familiar about her.

"Who are you?" He he asked.

"Me I'm doctor Tiara Bishop."

"Bishop!!" Chris said loudly. "As in General Jerald Bishop??"

"He was my father—and you killed him!!" The women screamed.

Chris could not believe this that the one that's been after him was the daughter of one of his most dangerous enemies.

"Now you have two choices, cyborg," the woman offered. "You either fight my Mutant X to the death, or you can watch your friends die in the tube next to you."

"All right, I'll fight him. Just let them out of here!" Chris said. Then, watching the two young women start to gag, he yelled, "They won't last much longer!"

The tube lifted off, and Sam and Hinata began breathing hard trying to take in oxygen. As they started to relax, Chris stepped forward. "Where is this Mutant X?"?" he asked.

She told him that "You have already seen him."

"You mean that mutant that I blew apart and dropped off this building?" Chris asked. "He's dead!"

"Oh really." I don't think so," Tiara said as a large creature walked up behind her. Chris recognized it was the mutant that he had thought he had killed, but he was different, —he was bigger and looked a lot stronger.

"What the Hell hell happened to him?" Chris said in exasperation.

Tiara laughed as she told him, "X is always evolving. Whenever, you kill him, he will come back stronger than before. There fore, it is impossible to stop him. No matter how many times you destroy him, he will always come back. He is the ultimate weapon." Tiara then turned to X. "Attack!" she yelled. And he jumped at Chris. But Chris managed to block the strike. The strike was so forceful, however, that the concrete beneath Chris's feet cracked.

X swung his bladed hands back and delivered an upper cut strike that sliced across at Chris's face leaving a bloody scar across his face and through his right eye. Chris had, to close that eye to keep the blood out of it.

Chris stumbled back holding his face as the blood poured from his cut. X then charged, but Chris sucker punched the mutant so hard that it went flying, and crashed through the wall. He exited the building and crashed outside the building where he crashed into another building. X started to get up, but Chris appeared in front of him with claws drawn. X hit him with a hay maker. X's bladed hands sliced right up his Chris's chest.

Chris started to feel light-headed. He knew X had done something to him, with that last strike. As Chris fell back, X jumped at him, but Chris managed to dodged his attack. That's when he noticed that X could not fly—he was just leaping! It wasn't a big weakness, but Chris had to work with whatever he had.

When X jumped back, from a rebound off another building, Chris grabbed X's bladed hand, and spun him around, and slamming him back into the building. Chris could see its frustration not being able to get to him.

xxx

Meanwhile, Tiara was watching the fight through her monitoring equipment. She was enjoying watching Chris get tossed around. She was surprised to feel someone tap her shoulder. Just as she turned around to see who it was, Sam punched her right in the face.

The woman fell to the ground with a bloody face. She looked up and realized that she had forgotten all about Sam and the girl.

"How dare you hit me!" screamed Tiara. "Do you know who I am? I am the greatest geneticists on the planet!"

"I not don't care who you are! Your going to tell that freak fighting Chris to stop, —or you're going to regret it!" Sam yelled to at the woman with rage in her eyes.

"Why should I save him? He killed my father."

"Your father was evil. He tried to destroy the planet and he would of have done it with you on it! The man was insane."

"My father was the greatest man on this planet. You have no idea what you're talking about," said Tiara. "And why should you care about that cyborg? From what I heard, he's somewhat responsible for the death of your sister! You should want his head just as much as I do, unless— …"

Tiara then stood as she finished her sentience: "…, " unless you fell in love with that him too?"

"That's none of your business!" shrieked Sam. "You tell that thing to stop fighting!"

"Don't you get it?" said Tiara. "Once I give it a order, it won't stop until that order has been carried out. So there is no way to stop it. And, once it kills the cyborg, it will then kill anyone else associated with him."

"No." " … Chris," Sam said as she watched the action on the monitor.

xxx

Chris was had just been hit hard again. He had been slammed onto the ground, X was pummeling him hard. The mutant slammed into the side of a building as he was being pummeled hard by X, he was still saying, "Kill Super Cyborg," over and over. It was starting to get on Chris's last nerves.

Chris stopped the last strike by catching both of X's arms, head butting the freak. As X fell back, Chris grabbed it and fell back to earth he shot down and punched it back into the air. X slammed onto the roof of a nearby building. As it stood up, Chris flew up and fired his shotgun, but something happened he didn't expect.

The blades on X's hands started to glow. When he swung them forward, making blades of pure energy fly though his shotgun blasts toward Chris and hit him. The blades felt like a thousand knifes knives going through him.

Chris fell to the ground hard. As he tried to get up, a monstrous pain went through his arm. He looked up to see that X had stabbed him with one of his bladed hands. X rose him up and Chris expected him the killer to say, "Kill Super Cyborg," again. But, instead X said, "This is the end." As Chris watched, a green liquid began to seep from the ends of X's blades. Then Chris realized that X's blades where poisoned.

Just as Chris understood that X was using poison, X plunged four of the five blades into Chris's chest. Chris could feel the poison ripping through his body. It was slowly killing his organic half. He looked up at X and saw, for the first time, emotion in those cold, red eyes. He saw the joy of killing him.

X felt a sense of satisfaction in killing the cyborg as he fell limp in his claws. The life was finally leaving the cyborg. X then flung Chris off his blades and watched him fall to the ground with an earth shaking thud.

"First objective compete," reported Mutant X. "Starting second objective: kill all associated with Super Cyborg." X leaped into the air.

xxx

From the monitors in Tiara's lab, Sam and Hinata had watched the monstrous thing kill Chris. For Sam and Hinata, it had been almost to painful to watch. Knowing that Chris was dead was like a kick in the gut to Sam. She fell to the ground holding her stomach feeling sick.

"Do you see that I have proved that organic manipulation is greater than cybernetics?" Tiara asked almost jumping for joy at the sight of the cyborg's destruction.

xxx

X landed right in front of the Cyber Corp building and crashed through the front door. "Kill Cyber Corp members," he said over and over.

Neneko had already seen the mutant coming their way. She was standing right in front of the freak, as it came into the building. She fired her optic beams at him, but the mutant was too strong. X stood his ground as he started to move forward through her beams as if they were nothing.

xxx

Chris, in the Alpha Omega cyber lion still lay positively dead. Or was he? One hand twitched! As the poison still flowed through his system, it was doing something else as it went,—it was opening up memories of the past. Eleven names popped into his head. As he remembered each one.

": Jennifer, April, Megan, Kim, Rebecca, Beth, Ashley, Kate, Melissa, Victoria, Sakura! "My cyborg girls!!!" He yelled out. His eyes shot open. Their names rang in his ears like a forgotten dream, —or nightmare.

Chris roared out as his wounds receded. An intense, black flame covered his body as he stood up. Rage filled his eyes. His lion's mane changed into black flame that surrounded him. With a fierce, low growl in his throat, Chris looked to the sky shooting off into the sky faster than he had ever gone before.

xxx

Neneko was hitting the mutant with everything she had— using fire, electricity, and ice. But everything, was no good the mutant's strength seemed limitless. Just as X raised his clawed hand to finish her, a flash of light shot through and hit X right out of the way and slammed him out of the building.

Neneko looked up to see Chris, but she noticed something seemed wrong with him, even beyond his enhanced appearance. When he looked down at her with cold eyes he growled at her, she stepped back with fear. But then he shot off just as fast as he had came in.

Neneko fell to her knees wondering what was happening to him, for she had never feared Chris -chan before. She felt paralyzed by the amount of killer intent given off by the black flame that now surrounded him.

The Cyber Lion flew at X as the mutant stated, "You're still alive?" But Chris had no time to think of this. He just hit X with so much force that it made the whole city seem to shake with fear, and sent the mutant flying.

X tried to regain control, but it was no good. X flew through four skyscrapers. The Cyber Lion clapped his hands together and slammed X to the ground. A crater formed around him form the impact. As X tried to get up, Chris flew straight down at him and yelled out *"Screaming Bullet Rapid Fire!!!"*

Each hit literally shook the city. The sound of each hit echoed everywhere. It was as if the Cyber Lion was everywhere at once. The mutant's body was being torn apart with each hit. With the last hit, Chris realized that he was no longer hitting anything. Only the blood covered street. Chris had pounded the mutant so hard that its body had been totally vaporized.

The Cyber Lion then let out a roar that shattered the windows in the whole area. The people around the area could barely stand the earth-shattering sound as the glass fell around the large cyber lion–man.

"What just happened?" cried Tiara. " I lost my mutant X's signal! But that's impossible!" Tiara yelled out as she watched her monitoring equipment go dead.

Sam looked up from the floor where she had been huddled with Hinata. As she realized what was happening, Sam dried her tears and began to laugh.

"Don't you dare laugh at me!" Tiara yelled at Sam.

"It would seem that X mutant is now extinct!" said Sam.

"That's impossible—there is no way that your cyborg could destroy my greatest work!" Tiara wailed. Just then, they all heard something walking into the room. The newcomer was radiating killer intent. "Nothing is impossible," said the newcomer.

"Chris!?" Sam yelled out. But he didn't acknowledge her. He just walked right past her and headed for Tiara Bishop. Sam had never seen him look as angry as he did now. He was furious about something.

"You!" he screamed at Tiara. "You made a child to use, in your own monstrous experiments! You created freaks of nature to fight for your revenge, against a man you know nothing about!"

As he got closer to Tiara, she started to actually feel a little afraid. She had never felt fear like this before and she didn't like it. She ordered what was left of her mutant minions to her and they fell from everywhere, ready to attack, Chris just kept walking forward. When the mutants tackled him, he just threw them off as if they were nothing. Tiara then saw the look in his eyes.

Chris's eyes were as white as could be. Rage seemed to radiate off him. Suddenly, he jumped up and landed inches away from Tiara's face. He stared into her eyes, and with a low growl emanated from his throat. Tiara cringed. Then she started to cringe as she knelt down to the ground. "Please don't hurt me," she begged.

The Cyber Lion slammed his fist into the wall right next to Tiara's head. The sound reverberated around the room. As she looked up, he removed his hand form from the wall. The the killer intent drained away from his body, and his color returned to normal. He turned around and started to walk off. Tiara stood back up. "Why?" she asked timidly.

"Because no matter what you have done to me, —or to anyone else," Chris said, " my honor forbids me form ever killing a woman, no matter how angry I am." Chris said as He turned to Sam, growled, and said, "Get Hinata. We're leaving. There is nothing more to do here. That woman won't be bothering us again."

"Are you sure, Chris?" asked Sam. "I mean, she did say, that she wanted you dead." Sam asked as she was trying to figure out, why Chris had seemed so angry.

"Believe me, if she tries anything else, she won't just get off with a warning," Chris said. "Now come on, I have something that I need to tell you, and the others when we get back to the Cyber Corp building" Chris growled.

Sam didn't argue. She took Hinata's hand and followed him. He was certainly angry at something. *It has to be something big for him to have done all of this*, she thought as they left the building.

xxx

As for Tiara, she still could not believe that that Cyborg had beat her greatest mutant. He must truly be a Super Cyborg to do that. *Maybe*, she thought, *my father is the one I should be mad at. The Super Cyborg could have killed me for all that I have done to him, but he didn't. He just left and let me live.*

xxx

Chris, Sam, and Hinata made it back to the Cyber Corp building as Neneko was starting to supervise the repairs to the building. As he entered the building, Chris grabbed Neneko by the hand. He cut off her greeting: "We all need to talk! Go get Destiny and call Lorelei. I want to talk to her too!" he then let her go and walked off.

"What happened to him?" Neneko asked Sam.

"I don't know?" Sam stated, "but whatever it is, we had better do as he says. Something happened to him in that last battle."

A short time later, when Neneko had assembled everyone in the meeting room. Lorelei was on a live video screen feed and Destiny, Sam, and Neneko, where sitting at a the conference table. When Chris walked in, he had turned back to normal, but there was a scar that was now across his face from where Mutant X had hit him. Chris turned to the assembled women.

"Okay," he said, his anger still apparent to all of them. "It's time for you all to confess!!!"

"Confess what, Chris?" Lorelei asked form the monitor.

"Confess what you have done to me."

"We haven't done anything to you, Chris-chan," Neneko said. Truly, she didn't know as she was still wondering what he was talking about.

"When I was fighting that mutant, he stabbed me. And, when he did, he poisoned me. It almost killed me, but, as I was losing consciousness, several names and memories of a number of female cyborg's, popped into my head. I want to know who they are and why they had powers like Neneko's."

The four women didn't know, what to say. They didn't think that Chris would ever remembered the other cyborg's that Minawa had made.

Lorelei sighed and told him about the other cyborg's that Minawa had made. She explained how they had combined their spirits and their powers into Neneko.

"Why can't I remember them?" Chris demanded of her.

"It's because, I altered your memories of them. I made you believe that Neneko had had the powers all along. Because when Akurei destroyed their bodies— ..."

"Akurei!!" ?" Chris, interrupting her. "He killed them?"

"Yes," said Lorelei sadly. "When he destroyed the floating island, he destroyed them. But, when he did, something spectacular happened. Their power management chips flew off, and found Neneko. All of their powers were transferred into Neneko, —that's why she has them now."

"So you tampered with my memories to make it look as if Neneko, had the powers all along. Why?"

"You were upset when you came too, after you fought Akurei," explained Lorelei. "For the first time in your life, you wanted to die. But I could not allow that. You are too important to all of us—we cannot lose you."

"So to keep me alive, you changed the memories I had of those girls," said Chris, his anger still apparent. "You didn't even give me the chance to mourn their loss!" Chris started to yell by this point.

"I'm sorry, Chris," Lorelei continued. "At the time, we thought we were doing the right thing. We never thought that— ..."

"That's right!" said Chris angrily. "You didn't think!" He turned to look at the women in the room with him. "You all thought that things would just go on as if nothing had happened—as if those girls didn't matter! Well, guess what!" "They do! And you have disgraced them all. Not only did you make me forget them, but you made yourselves forget them as well. It is as if they didn't exist in the first place."

When Chris said this, Lorelei realized that she had acted like the Titan by taking his memories away. And the Titan was the one she had hated for so long. She had manipulated Chris like the way the Titan had manipulated and controlled the people on her planet. "Chris, I am so sorry," she said. "I know now that we were wrong. Please forgive me … forgive us."

Chris turned to look at all of them. They all were quiet and were crying softly. He knew they were sorry too. But then Neneko looked up to Chris and spoke: "When I got all of their powers, I did gained something else, Chris-chan. I gained their experiences. I could see everything that they had seen and felt, and there was one thing they all shared in commend, —they all loved you. They all died loving you, and, because of that, they all agreed to give me all of their powers, knowing that I would take care of you for them."

Chris thought about this, but still felt hurt for what they all did to him. He wiped his eyes, and came to a decision.

"I'm going to leave for a while. I need some time to think this through. It is, true that part of them will always live on within Neneko, but you all kept this a secret from me, for over five years. You deceived me, and because of that I'm still not sure, I can forgive you. Just for now, I need you to leave me alone and let me think this through."

"How long will you be gone?" Destiny asked, worry in her voice.

"I don't know. At lest until my heart and my honor are repaired." He turned to look at each one of them. "Good-bye for now." he then walked out of the room leaving them looking after him in astonishment.

Once he left the room, they all could not hold back anymore. Sam, Neneko, and Destiny all broke down in tears. They all realized, how much they had hurt the man they cared for the most.

Lorelei was almost in tears herself, for she was the one who had made the decision to do this to him. She began to think of a way to make amends.

Chris walked out of the building. He carried all his worldly possessions in a pack that he had strapped to his back. Without looking back, he took off into the air as fast as he could go, heading off to a place that only he knew of.

It had been almost a month since Chris had left the Cyber Corp building, and the family he had there. He had settled into a large house on the island of Okinawa regain of, Japan. It was a quiet place that overlooked a small lake. He had managed to get a good-paying job, as a martial arts instructor. He, seemed to be doing well for himself. Because he was basically a celebrity for saving the world, more than once, he had immediately acquired almost more students than he could handle. Also, since he still looked very young, he was real very popular with the young women in the community.

After work one day, Chris was enjoying the night air on the roof of his large home, when a delivery man came to the door. When he knocked on the door, Chris jumped down from the roof. Since his home was three stories tall, he scared the poor delivery man half to death! There were luggage bags piled at the door he asked the delivery man, "What is this all about?"

"I'm just to delivery these bags to this address." The delivery man handed him a paper to sign, before Chris could say anything else he noticed the time. "Look I don't have time for this just leave them here and I will figure this out later." So he signed the papers and took off.

xxx

When Chris ran into the dojo, he noticed that his students all seemed a little off. As they where doing their drills, Chris returned to his own spot to at the front of the group. The boys noticed someone, walk into the dojo, but Chris had his back to the door and didn't see anyone. The woman walked up to Chris.

"Neneko?" Chris said in complete confusion and surprise. "What are you doing here?"

"I'm here to help you get through your problems," she said. "And I am your wife and I do have the powers of the girls you lost I thought maybe I could help you get over it."

"I don't need help," he told her. "Especially from someone who betrayed me." Chris told her as he turned his back to her and then faced his students to continue his teachings.

Right then, Neneko stepped in front of him and yelled right into his face, "It wasn't your fault for what happened! You at least remember them now, so there shouldn't be a reason for you, to be this upset."

"I left you all, because you all lied to me!" he said angrily. "You kept secrets from me, and you altered my memories as if I was some robot."

Both of them noticed Chris's students looking at the two of them, as if they were the latest drama on TV. Chris addressed the tallest boy, "Take over for me, son. I'll be right back." He led Neneko into his office to where they could talk privately.

The moment the door of his office was closed, Neneko started there talk again.

"We have been friends for as long as I can remember, and we even have a child together, who, I should remind you, is wondering what his father doing so far away from him! And you're going to tell me you can't trust me?"

Chris sat in his chair in his office and thought for a moment. "I'm listening."

Neneko then told him exactly what had happened on that day, when she got the powers of the cyborg girls.

She told him that, when they where destroyed, their power management chips, had come to life and saved her. When that happened, she had seen the girls, and they had told her that they where going to give their power to her—but on one condition. She had to promise to protect Chris. That's how much they loved him, Neneko finished.

Chris jumped when he heard these words. He and Neneko had known each other for a long time. He took a deep breath and sighed thinking that she was right that— maybe she had a point that she and him have known each other a long time, and that he had heard before, that those girls had given their lives for him.

Chris looked back up at Neneko and smiled. "Thank you for reminding me about, what is important. I still feel pretty hurt for what happened." Chris then stood and looked Neneko in the eyes. He took her hands into his and asked, "Would you mind staying with me until I my head back in order? And she was right he did have son and daughter that miss him too."

"Sure thing, Chris-chan," she replied with a smile. "I was hoping you would say that, —that's why I had mine and the kids things delivered to your house oh and I brought that Hinata girl as well!"

Chris just laughed. Neneko had always been that way, she was— always ready for anything.

After they agreed that Neneko and his two kids would stay, Chris walked back out into the dojo feeling a little better, than he had been in long time. Because of that, he went a little overboard with his students. Finally, Neneko had to step in and tell him to take it easy, but, by then, his students where too tired to move. They had all collapse form exhaustion.

"Good job today, everyone," he told the boys. "In fact, you did such a great job that I'm going to close the dojo tomorrow and let you all have the day off." He wanted the day for himself so he could get Neneko-chan and the kids settled into his place."

The only responses he got from the boys was groans as they where still trying to catch their breath. Chris then turned to Neneko. "Shall we go?" She nodded as she took his hand.

On their way home, Chris started telling Neneko about his time here. But Neneko had a few things to say to too for the kids had really missed their dad and the young girl that he had saved had become very attached to their boy Leo.

When they approached the three-story house, Chris showed the four to different rooms that they could use while they stayed. Chris was a little shocked when Hinata turned to him and thanked him for having them.

Chris couldn't help but smile as the girl seemed to become part of the family, Neneko saw this as the two went into their room, for the night.

As he slept, some time that night, the three children managed to sneak into his and Neneko room and into their bed. The next morning when Neneko woke, she found Maylu curled up like a cat at the end of the bed and Leo and Hinata both laid across the cyborg She knew that Chris, being the dead sleeper that he was, would never realize they were there. Like most warriors, he slept soundly and deeply. Neneko looked at the clock. Realizing that it was still early, she couldn't help smile for they really were a family.

Chris awoke first that morning to find his family asleep around him. Neneko, however, though had his head in against her chest, and her legs were wrapped around his body. He tried to move, but then felt Leo and Hinata behind his back. When he tried to slip down, he found Maylu at his feet. He was trapped at on all sides by his wife and the kids.

Neneko started to stir in her sleep. He watched her eyes flutter open. When she saw that Chris was awake, she immediately let him go, and apologized for grabbing him like that. He sat up in bed and asked, "What are they doing in my bed anyway?"

"I came in and found those three in the bed with you," she said, pointing at the still sleeping children.

He sighed again, and got out of the bed, before anything else could happen to him. Then he turned to Neneko and told her, "This had better not be a recurring thing, with those three or I'll kick you all out onto the street!" He half joked for Neneko knew that he was only joking. He would never really do that.

"Don't worry Chris-chan," she told him. "I'll tell the kids to stop sleeping in our bed. But I was hoping that we could all go out as a family, I mean you chose this area because we grew up around here."

"Yeah I did."

"Well, we can show the kids some of the places we went to when we were young."

The rest of the day went well, for the family, but, as they were heading home, something unexpected happened. As they walked, something jumped down from a roof top and crashed down on Chris. He was slammed hard onto the ground. Something hard grabbed his head and slammed it into the ground as hard as possible. Then, his attacker held him up by the neck and said, "This is a warning! Someone still waits to see you dead!"

It was a large man. He then started to crush Chris by the neck, but the cyborg kicked forward and broke free. He finally got a good look at his attacker, and was shocked to find that he looked like a normal African American man and was reality human—only super strong and was oversized.

"Who are you? And what do want?" Chris asked. He tried to figure this guy out, but then he realized that he looked very much like his old nemesis the general. "You must be the son of the general," Chris said, "Are you here to try and kill me like your sister did or is this a social call?"

"I'm here to give you a warning, Striker," said the man. " I do plan on killing you, but first I was planning on killing your little family over there." The monstrous man said as he pointed to Neneko, and the kids.

"You must think you're tough stuff to tell me this when we could fight it out now and save us, a lot of time and effort," said Chris.

"And where would the fun be in that?" said the attacker. "I want you to suffer until I decide to kill you—at my own leisure."

"Like father like son," said Chris. "Your family has given me more grief then I need. First your mad father tries tried to kill me in front of the world with his tournament, then his crazy daughter tried with mutants. So what's your thing going to be?"

"Me?" said the man. "Well I work with both mutants and cybernetics, to make something stronger than either of the two. My weapons are, kind of like Doc Connor's bio tech warriors, but with more zip. I call them cyber mutants." The man said with a snapped of his fingers.

"Great, another tech nut," Chris thought to himself. "So what's your name, anyway?" Chris asked the nutcase.

"John Bishop at your service. And, now that the introductions are over, I will leave you to wonder where I'm going to strike next." And, with that, he flew into the air. With a salute, he disappeared in a flash.

"Why is it that the craziest people keep showing up in my life?" Chris said to himself as he slapped his hand in his face in aggravation.

When Chris, Neneko, and the kids finally made it home, Chris appeared to be sick. As he sat on the floor next to his low table, Neneko asked, "Are you all right? You don't look too good."

Chris looked up to at her with a sad look. "Why does this keep happening to me?" he asked, "I mean, I have never done anything to anybody. All I ever wanted, was to protect the innocent, but, every time I do, some maniac appears and threatens the people around me. I mean, what does it take to be left alone?"

"You've been given great power, Chris-chan," Neneko stated. "And, because of that, you will always have to fight to live a normal life. There will always be those who threaten those around you, for there must be evil to match your good and pure heart." She put her arms around him. "It is the concept of *in yo*, which is like the Chinese *yin yang*, just as grandfather told you. Chris, if you don't take up the challenges that life puts before you, then who will? For only you are strong enough to stop them and protect those around you."

Chris stood back up and said, "I'm going to my room. I have some thinking to do." As he went upstairs, he knew that Neneko was right. If he didn't take up these challenges, that his life has put before him, who would? For he was, the only one strong enough to fight these mutants and monsters that have come for him.

The next day, before Chris left for his dojo, he told Neneko to help the kids prepare for their first lessons in the martial arts. He wasn't going to let those three go around without being able to defend themselves. He would take them to his morsel arts classes today.

When they arrived, they were shocked to find that someone had destroyed the dojo and everything in it. The building looked as if it was going to fall over at anytime. Chris noticed one of his students lying outside the building. He was looking pretty beat up. Chris ran to him.

"What happened here?" Chris asked his student.

"There were three of them," the boy said, struggling to breathe. "They came and destroyed the dojo. They fought most of your best students. We're all pretty beat up. The others are at the hospital. I was told to tell you, that they plan to destroy the things that you hold dear to your heart."

"What did they look like? Was one of them a large black man?" Chris asked. Before the boy could answer, him his student fall unconscious in his Chris's arms. Chris turned to his family. "Return to the house, Neneko, help this boy. I'll go looking for the ones who did this." He then turned to the sky and shot into the air at incredible speed.

CHAPTER 53

Neneko turned to the children. "Well, it looks like your training is going to have to wait until we get this thing handled. But first let's help this boy to a the hospital." She picked Chris's student up, as if he weighed nothing at all and she took him to the hospital. Then she used her cell phone to contact the police to tell them what had happened. She contacted some more people to clean up the destroyed dojo as she and Maylu, Leo, and Hinata headed for home. When she got there, she called Cyber Corp to report in.

Chris was having no luck finding any trace of the three that destroyed his dojo. It was as if they had dropped off the face of the earth. And he knew every inch of the area, where he lived, so he shouldn't be having this much trouble finding them. Just as he was about to give up, he saw it a large man walking down the street carrying the biggest sword, he had ever seen. Chris jumped up and landed down right in front of the beastly man.

When Chris landed, the large man stopped. "Are you one of the guys who destroyed my dojo and hurt my students?" Chris asked him.

The large man laughed a maniacal laugh that would send chills down a normal man's back. But Chris was too angry to care care. "Yes," said the man, "I was one of the men, ."

"Who are you?"

"You can call me, Rock," the large man said. As his body started to change into stone and became bigger even than he was before.

Rock swung his large sword around in an arc above his head like a spinning 'copter blade, and then swung the blade down at Chris with enough force to slit him in two.

But Chris managed to back flip out of the way. When he looked back up, Rock was running right at him with his large sword dragging the ground. Sparks flew from the sword as he ran. And, when he swung the sword up at Chris, it connected, the force of the blow was so great it blew him straight into the guardrail that ran alone side of the street, bending it down from the impact.

Chris had no time to recover as Rock ran over to him, and grabbed him by the head. Rock's hands were so big that they covered his Chris's whole face.

Rock picked him up, and punched him, three times in the chest. On the third strike, Chris coughed up blood. Some of his blood landed on Rock's face. With a sadistic grin, Rock slammed Striker into the ground head first cracking the street from the impact.

The cyborg yelled out in pain as Rock stood looking down at the fallen warrior and started to stomp down on him with incredible force,. Chris started to sink into the broken street. His cries of pain echoed around the area even though there was no one that could hear him.

xxx

Neneko, had returned home, to contact the cyber crop, she got an hear full form Lorelei about not contacted her sooner but she assured her that things were going to be all right. After that she had spent the rest of her time trying to reassure the children that everything was going to be alright, and Chris could take on anyone. Later she was sitting in the tube with her knees to her chest and her arms wrapped around them thinking though she told the kids that things would be alright but as it got later she started to worry about her Chris-chan.

She knew that Chris wouldn't take what happened to his Dojo lying down. She knew he would do anything he could to get whoever it was who had caused the pain and damage.

After she was got out of the bath, she put on one of Chris's T-shirts, which was what she usually wore to bed. On her, it looked like a night shirt for it went down almost to her knees. Neneko sat in front of her mirror. She sighed when she realized that she had not aged a day since she had gained the powers of the cyborg' girls. That meant, that she was a cyborg too. She had always hoped that she would gain some of their looks along with their powers, but she still looked the some same as she always had. And, now that she had cybernetic eyes, she needed to wear her glasses to disguise them, even if she didn't need them to see.

Neneko was fixing her hair for bed when she heard something from across the hall in Chris's study. She realized that she had not heard Maylu, Hinata or Leo in a while, and she got up and ran to the room where she had left them before her bath.

She found them both laying on the floor. When she checked them, she found they were unconscious— thankfully not dead. Someone had knocked them out. She looked around to try to find who had done this, then she heard a muffled laugh that sounded as if it was coming through a mask.

She turned toward the sound. He was a medium-sized man—about as tall as her. He wore a plain white mask that covered his face. He had long, blond hair, that went down his back, and he carried two curved blades, one in each hand.

"Who are you?" she yelled out to the man. " And what did you do to my children?" Neneko yelled out to the man.

"You may call me, Z, I am here at the bidding of John bishop, son of the late General Bishop," said the man. "And those two girls were not as beautiful as I, so I put them down. The boy tried to protect them but you see the results. I did them a favor. Anyone who is not as beautiful as I, should be put out of their misery."

"So, if you're so beautiful, why do you wear a mask?"

"Because, there is no one, worthy enough to see my beauty."

"And I say you hide your face because it is too horrible to look at," said Neneko boldly.

Z could not believe what he was hearing. How dare this impertinent woman call him ugly? "You will pay for that!" he threatened. "You aren't exactly easy on the eyes yourself, little girl." Z told her as he readied himself for combat.

xxx

Chris was lying in a deep hole, made by his own body's from a result of Rock's strikes. Rock stood over his handy work, thinking his victim was dead. But, suddenly, Chris shot up, aimed his arm at him Rock, and yelled out "*Shotgun Double Barrel!*"

The blasts hit their mark as they tore through Rock's body, but didn't make him fall.

Chris jumped out of the hole, and slammed both arms down on each side of Rock's shoulders. The impact was so great that the force dug his feet into the ground.

Chris Striker landed down and stared at the mutant thinking that this guy was solid. But, before he could act, Rock reached out for him. Chris back flipped. *I have to stop this guy now!* he thought. Time for my Supreme mode.

Striker yelled out as his body changed into the cat-like look of the Supreme mode. When he was at his full strength, he cocked his arm like a shotgun, ready to fire.

xxx

Neneko and Z were fighting it out, inside Chris's house, tarring the place apart. Z had not anticipated that this girl would be so good. He had been ready to fight Striker too, and this girl seemed to be just as good as he was, but not good enough.

Z managed to slash at Neneko, With a second slash, he cut through her shirt and slashed her body. When she recovered from the strike, she saw the bloody slash into her shirt and felt the pain of the cut. She recovered form the strike, now not only was she bleeding but her shirt was torn her white lace bra, was now revealed, but because of the fight that she was in, she had no time to think of her modesty.

Z laughed at her again with his muffled laugh, as he saw the state she was in, —blood was running down her hand as she stood breathing hard in her fighting stance.

"You have no chance to beat me, so I will honor you by letting you see the perfection in my face before you die," he said as he slowly removed his mask reveling that he was, in fact, very handsome.

"Ha!" Neneko laughed. "You think you're good looking? You have nothing on my Chris-chan."

"What did you say!" Z yelled out. "You think that monstrous cyborg is better looking than me?"

"Yes!" Neneko quipped. "And, I bet he's even better in bed than you are, freak." She was starting to breathe harder from exhaustion and pain.

"That's it, little girl," Z said in anger. "You're going down! No one talks to me like I'm second rate!" He charged her in blind rage, witch was what Neneko was hoping for.

Right when Z came close enough, she grabbed him by the shoulders, flipped him over onto his back, and against the wall behind her. But, in his rage, he wasn't as hurt as she was hoping for. He turned, slashing at her with monstrous speed and strength. But, when she was up against the opposite wall, she pushed herself off and over Z. She grabbed the ceiling with one hand and kicked him to the ground, and then swung down at him. But he held up his blades, at her ready to impale her. Neneko managed to stop in mid air inches away from his blades.

She smiled as she swung herself up. Then she, put her foot down right on Z's face. With all her strength she spun her foot against his face, and, to her shock, she watched half his face tear away.

Neneko jumped back to see, what she had done. She watched Z get up. Half his face was torn off. The sight of exposed bone and muscle on his face, almost made her sick.

"Look at what you have done to my beautiful face!" screamed Z, holding his hands against his face. "It's ruined!" Z said to her to. "You bitch! I'll make you suffer for this!" He lunged at her, slashing at her with pure cruelty.

xxx

Chris's opponent Rock was not going to back down. As he charged full force, and as, Rock swung his sword at him, but Chris caught it with one hand. The mutant tried to move, but it was as if his hand was an iron vise.

Chris smiled as he broke the sword with a twist of his hand and then threw the pieces of the blade, away. He ran at the mutant. They collided fist to fist, then hand to hand as they each pegged each others strength against each the other's.

The force of the battle shook the ground as they tried to push each other back, but then Chris yelled out, "You're not going to beat me!" as he crunched down on Rock's hands shattering, his hands into fine gravel.

The rock mutant roared out, as he stumbled back. He looked up at Striker who's look of rage made him think that he was finished.

Chris started to walk toward Rock, ready to finish him. Rock stepped back until he was up against a stone wall. Striker slammed his hand at into Rock's face and roared out as he pushed him to the ground. Chris crushed Rock's head with incredible force.

Breathing hard, Chris stood up and looked down at the freak's crushed head. Suddenly, Chris stood back up after crushing the freaks head, he heard a powerful explosion coming from his home.

"Neneko!" Chris cried, as he took off in the air leaving the crushed body of the mutant on the ground.

xxx

Neneko was not going well. Z had slammed her into the couch, and she was having trouble moving. "I'm going to skin you alive for what you did to me!" shrieked Z.

Neneko was not going to have let this happen. She had to get her Chris-chan to come back to Cyber Corp with her. And the only way, she was going to do that, is if she lived! She gathered everything she had left to prepare for a single attack that would finish this freak off for good.

First, she jumped off the couch and picked it up. This show of strength shocked Z. But he was more shocked as she threw it at him. He jumped to the side to avoid it then looked back to where Neneko had been, but she was gone.

Z looked around, but she was no where to be seen. Then something hit him hard against the wall. Neneko then appeared in front of him. Electricity charged around her as her eyes started to glow red.

This was far beyond what he had been told about her. She should be out of power by now, but her power was growing every second.

Neneko screamed out as she attacked him with unstoppable speed and powerful, fast punches and kicks, that were moving like beams of light over every inch of Z"s body. Neneko was tarring him apart with every strike. As her power, increased, fire, electricity, and other powers started to manifest themselves in pure brutality. She screamed out as she jumped back and then powered up, every power, that she had and fired it with everything that she had, blasting Z with everything, blowing an enormous hole in the side of the house.

Chris Striker landed a few minutes after the explosion, that came from his house. He ran into the house yelling out everyones names.

He found Maylu Leo and Hinata lying on the floor of his room. Then he find found Neneko lying next to the a large hole in the wall. Her body looking pretty beat up. He gathered her in his arms. "Neneko, are you all right,?" When she opened her eyes, she smiled a weak smile at the sight of him.

"Chris-chan, I knew you could not be stopped by anyone."

"Who did this to you?"

"It was a mutant sent by Bishop's son called Z."

Neneko still smiled at Striker as she fell back to the darkness of unconscious. Chris panicked as he tried to wake her again. At that moment he knew he had to get them all back to the Cyber Corp—fast.

xxx

Later, Sam was checking vital signs of the four as Destiny did her magic on Neneko. Chris waited outside of the infirmary waiting for any news of his family.

When Sam came out she removed her gloves, as he asked her, "How are they?"

"Well, Chris, I won't lie to you. The kids will recover with some rest, but Neneko's going to need some time to recover. She was pretty beat up, when you brought her in. She was lucky you got her here so fast … any second longer and not even Destiny could of have put her back together."

Chris turned away from Sam, angry with himself. Once again, he was responsible for getting people he cared about hurt. But this time there was still time, he still had a chance to make things right. He wasn't going to wait for Bishop's son's next move—he was going to make the next move himself, and take the enemy out, no matter the cost.

xxx

John Bishop was resting inside a strange cryogenic tube. His body had been almost altered almost beyond anything that looked human. Only his head and his left arm retained human characteristics.

His right arm was monstrously changed—he had five large claws where his fingers had been. And, on the shoulder of that arm, was an enormous eye that was looking around without any knowledge form the man as if it had a mind of its own (which it did!)

Chris landed near a building where Sam had told him to go, even though she hadn't wanted him to. He looked at the top of the building with a look that didn't match his usual calm. Then he forced his way, into the building, where he was met with some extremely nasty mutants.

They attacked him fast, in large numbers, but he was in no mood. He plowed through them with blood red eyes, fighting them and tearing them apart with cruelty that was unlike him. As he fought his way up to the labs, black flame seemed to surrounded him again, as he started transforming into his Alpha Omega Cyber Lion mode.

xxx

John Bishop's eyes shot open, while the eye on his shoulder was still looking around. John broke his way out of the tube, and started walking past his three top scientists, who stepped back, when they saw him. One even stated, " What have we unleashed upon the world?" John turned to them and said, " A god!" As he watched each one of them fall dead for reasons only he knew. He moved on.

xxx

Chris had just wiped out, what he thought was the last mutant in the building, but now, as he opened the door to the main lab, he encountered one more, and this one, looked stronger than anything that he had faced yet. The mutant John Bishop had just killed the scientist by just walking past them.

Striker had no idea, why but the second Chris walked near the mutant, he could feel himself getting weaker. He fell to his knees.

"What's happening?" Chris stated to himself.

"You have just bared witness, to my powers. I have the ability to absorb the embryonic energy of the Earth. Simply put, I can absorb the energy of everything and anything around me, —even from people. That is how I increase my strength." thus making me stronger."

"I guess that means you are following in your father's foot steps. He was also quite the control freak."

"My father was no control freak!" shouted Bishop. "He was a strategical and tactical genius! He could figure out an enemy's weak point just by watching his movements on the battle field. And what I have learned from my sister's mistakes, —I have learned your weakness, it is that you care. You care about the people that are around you, — your family, friends and… all those little irritants that seem to appear around you, all the time! But, with this new body I have, I plan to absorb not only the energy of the Earth, but the energy of the entire universe. And, when I absorb that energy, I will become a god. But don't worry, Striker, I plan on letting you bear witness to my godhood on this planet. You will see just how hopeless you are without your powers."

"*No!*" Chris yelled out. He tried to get up, but he fell back to the floor. His body felt so heavy like it was made of lead. His body also was usually able to absorb the energy that was around him for power, but just now he seemed unable to get the energy he needed, and, it seems that without the normal amount of energy, he was useless.

Suddenly, John jumped throw through the ceiling and landed outside in the street. From there he jumped to the roof of his building. He raised his misshapen arm into the air as he started to absorb the Earth's energy.

His absorption powers where so great that the people started to feel it, almost immediately. One by one, as they started to fall to the ground, not knowing why.

xxx

Even back at the Cyber Corp lab, Sam and the others, they could feel the power draining from their bodies. As Destiny's powers started to go out, she fell over. Sam crawled over to her and held her up, realizing that she had no pulse. She turned to a window and saw the stream of energy in the air. Before she fell under herself, she said weakly, "Chris, help us, please."

Chris managed to crawl to the roof of John Bishop's building, where he saw General Bishop's son absorbing the Earth's energy.

Striker saw the changes that John Bishop was going through. His body was growing and changing at a phenomenal rate. First his body morphed into a four-legged beast, and then his mouth became nothing but a holed mouth with rows of ragged teeth.

John's body now looked like a massive mix of bone and muscle. It was monstrously sickening to look at, and, when the mass fell off the building, Chris thought it had killed itself. But John suddenly become as big as the building, it spoke in a thundering voice:

"Bear witness to the greatest thing in creation! A man has now become a god! I will rain destruction across the universe and remake it in my magnificent form."

Chris was now at a loss. He could not move. *I have failed everyone,* he thought. *First Minawa and then the eleven cyborg girls that she had made. I have failed Neneko and my children, and now I have failed the world.* He was just not strong enough. He cursed himself for being so weak.

Just as he was about to lose consciousness from the lack of power, he heard a voice, yelling out to him.

"Chris, stop beating yourself up! It was never your fault in the first place. You are by far the most honorable man that I have ever met. And you're the must most foul hearty one too."

"Minawa?" Chris stated as he looked up and in front of him he could see a shimmering image of Minawa. The eleven cyborg girls stood behind her. They didn't seem happy with him for beating himself up so much.

"Do you still think that it was your fault that we all died?" Ashley stated from behind Minawa.

He nodded his head. Minawa, though, shook her head at this. "Well, know this, Chris: It was never your fault. If it was anybody's fault, it was Akurei's —and that General Bishop's. It was never your fault. How many times do we have to tell you?"

As Minawa said, this, the other girls behind her nodded in agreement. "Besides," continued Minawa, "We live on inside you, and, our powers live on in Neneko. So stop beating yourself up over it!" They all finished.

Chris looked up at them again realizing that he had been blaming himself for everything that had happened to them. They were right— if it was anybody's fault, it was not his. He knew they would always be right there fighting alongside him forever, as long as he fought for the right reasons they will always be right there fighting along side him forever.

Chris now stood up with new found strength, —a strength he didn't even know that he had. He looked up at John, the mass that had once been a human being. He saw shock on John's face. Obviously he had thought Chris was dead … that he had absorbed all of his energy.

Actually, the mutant mass, had seen a dozen women standing behind his enemy. It appeared that they, were the ones giving him their energy. Yes, the mutant mass could feel it, —Chris was taking back the energy that he had absorbed. But there was no way the cyborg could hold all that energy in that small body of his.

Chris roared out as his body changed to his Alpha Omega Cyber Lion mode. He continued to absorb the mutant's energy away from him, as he roared out.

"You know what?" Chris yelled out to the mutant mass. "For a long time now, I have been blaming myself for things that where never my fault. But I realize now, that what happened to those girls wasn't my fault. I also realize that what Lorelei did to me, she did it out of love … to protect me from myself. Because all this time that I have been blaming myself for what happened, and because of that, I have allowed a monster like you, —and others — to get stronger." He paused for a moment and stood tall in his Cyber Lion form. "Well no more!" he roared. "For I am back, and, this time, I will fight for the reason I became a martial artist, —for my honor and to protect those who need protecting. I will *never* falter again! And, you, you miserable mass of DNA, *you're dead!*!!"

As Chris yelled out the last part of his sentences, as he shot himself up at incredible speed, and punched his way into the mass in a bloody explosion, but it didn't seem to have any effect on the beast. John started to laughed at the ineffectiveness of Chris's actions, but then started to cry out in pain, because deep inside the mutant mass, Chris was tearing the mutant apart from the inside out. Chris, moved to the center of the beast as he yelled out, *"Screaming Fist Of The Beast King!"*

The roar the beast let out, before it fell was that of a thousand nails on a chalkboard. The beast exploded like an atomic bomb in a mass of blood and gore in a red mushroom cloud that could be seem seen for miles.

All was quiet after the explosion. The people still seemed to be dead lying on the ground, but, when Chris emerged from the gore, he looked to the skies as he yelled out *"Screaming Bullet Of Life!"* As he shot the bullet to the skies, letting out a ray of life energy that he had absorbed from the mutant mass.

The people slowly stood up, wondering what had happened. They would never know that, on that day, they had been saved by one man who finally realized that, even with all his powers, he found that the greatest one of them all was love, —the love that he had for the ones he had lost. He would always keep them close to his heart, and he would never forget them ever again.

Sam and Destiny awoke knowing that it was Chris who had saved them. Soon Neneko awoke along with Maylu, Leo and Hinata. The three of them, had never felt stronger. It seems that, when Chris used his bullet of life, the energy had healed every one that had been hurt during this ordeal.

The everyone ran out to find Chris. They flew out looking for him, they made it to the spot where he was, almost as if Chris had lead them there. They found him covered in a golden glow that made him look almost like some great god or true beast king.

Neneko finally spoke. " Chris-chan, are you all right?"

He turned to her and smiled as he said, "I'm just fine."

The women could not hold themselves back anymore. They ran at him and tackled him, in their excitement. They knew that they had their Chris back, and now there was nothing and nobody that was going to stand in his way.

CHAPTER 54

Chris was in dojo training his two children in tai chi. As Lorelei walked into the dojo, she called his name, disrupting his routine. He looked over at her wondering why she was on Earth in the first place. "Kids," he said, "you keep practicing while I talk to Lorelei for a minute."

"What exactly are you doing on Earth, girl," he said to the Supreme Elder of the planet Gem. "You should be on your planet taking care of your people!"

Lorelei looked sadly at the cybernetic man in front of her. She could no longer hold back. She jumped into his chest and wept. Maylu and Leo and Hinata stopped their exercises and ran over to see what was wrong. They both come to love Lorelei. "what's wrong?" Their father shook his head, not knowing what was wrong. "Go outside and play."

Chris held Lorelei then spoke as she cried into Striker's chest as she struggled to speak. "It's terrible …" she sobbed. "Our whole planet has been destroyed."

Chris could not believe what he was hearing. He held her at arm's length and looked in thew her face. "What do you mean, the planet has been destroyed?"

Lorelei tried to dry her eyes, as she tried to regain her composure. She looked up at him and said. "My home world was has been destroyed by … the Titan."

"Titan!" Chris said in shock. Then he said, "You had better tell all of us the whole story. Let's go to the house." As he led Lorelei to the house, Chris turned to his kids and told the children to fetch the others.

After they had all gathered to the house and Lorelei had been given some tea, as she managed to calm herself down as she told them the whole story.

Everything was going along fine. I was in my lab doing some calculations I've been working on. All of sudden, Nodoka my apprentice, ran into the lab and told me we were under attack! Using one of my monitors, Lorelei scanned the area. Right above their orbit, she discovered an enormous ship—bigger than anything that she had seen before. A swum of giant incest's flying out of it, and when they hit the ground they changed into human beasts running at them they reached there village, tarring everything in sight apart and killing everyone they got their hands on.

Lorelei had to think quickly; for she didn't have much time to plain. She called, for an evacuation of the area. She directed everyone who could, to head for her newly constructed ship. Since there were no men on her planet, the main, objective was to get as many of there children out of harm's way as possible.

As soon as the ship was full and Lorelei and the crew had made it to their stations, Lorelei ordered for them to take off. But one of the crew called out, "My Lady, we only have a hundred and fifty of the people on the ship."

Lorelei yelled back, "We don't have enough time to wait! Those animal things are coming this way. We have no choice. "

"Take off now!"

As the ship launched, the animalistic beasts grabbed onto the ship. Strangely, they where unaffected by the heat of the ship's exhaust. Hundreds of them clawed their way up the ship. They were like ants attacking a carcass. But, as the ship passed the planet's atmosphere and into space, the attackers fell off.

As Lorelei's ship passed by the space ship that had let out the swarming beasts, Lorelei saw on the main monitor someone floating outside the ship looking down at the planet. The person pointed both hands at the planet.

Lorelei couldn't see details, but even with what she got form the man's look she knew who it was when he raised his hands—the Titan!

The ship's crew watched the monitor in horror as, the Titan charged up cannons on his hands and fired twin beams at the planet, even knowing, though some of his troops were still on the planet.

The Titan's blast traveled to the planet as if in slow motion. Upon contact, the planet slowly started to crack. The whole planet then exploded into a thousands of pieces. The sight was almost too much to watch, —all of their worst nightmares had come true. All of the women and children that where still left on the planet were now dead.

They watched the Titan's sadistic laugh they could almost, hear him as he watched the explosion in a super nova. Lorelei's crew turned to her wondering what to do next, but they found her sitting in the captain's chair with her face in her hands. She was too shocked to cry.

"What are we going to do now, Elder?" Nodoka asked as she approached her captain.

Lorelei forced herself up as she flung her hair back and took a deep breath. "Plot set a course for Earth. Only the Super Cyborg, can help us now."

Lorelei finished her story, as the others listened in shock. Chris stood clenched his fists so tightly that they started to spark with power. He was remembering, back to the day he fought the Titan. He had actually thrown the Titan's head into deep space! There was no way he could of have come back. But, apparently, he had found a way. Upon further thought, Chris realized that this whole thing was definitely a trap to get to him.

Neneko saw the pain in Chris's eyes. "Chris-chan, what do you plain to do?"

Chris turned back to her and said. "What do think I'm going to do?" he asked not unkindly. "The Titan did this to get a rematch against with me. And, if that's what he wants, then that's what's he's going to get!!"

"Dad," Leo asked calmly and quietly, "do you think I can go? I would love to go into space with you?" Chris looked at his son and said, "No!"

Maylu then said, "It's because you're too young, Leo."

"That's right, and you're not going either," said Chris, surprising his bold daughter. "You're going to stay with my aunt and uncle."

"What?" cried Maylu in frustration. "But why can't I go? I went with you before …, what's the differences this time?"

"It's because this time around I don't think I will be coming back. I want the two of you to grow up as normal as possible. Coming, with me will not work. You two are staying on Earth, got it?"

"Yes, father," the two kids said in unison. They were sad at the thought of their father leaving, but they knew that he had to go and save the refugees from the planet Gem and save the rest of the universe from the Titan. He had to stop the Titan no matter the cost.

Chris then looked over to Hinata and said, "Now what do we do with you, little one?"

Sam then spoke up saying. "I will take her. I'm not going back into space with you this time. Someone's got to run Cyber Corp."

Chris agreed and then turned to Destiny and Neneko. "So, are you two going to coming with me or staying here?"

They both looked at him and then to at each other. Smiling, and said in unison, "We're going."

"Good," Chris stated. He turned back to Lorelei. "Well, it looks like you've got yourself an addition to your crew.

"Thank you, Chris," Lorelei said with an honorable bow. Then as she turned to Destiny. "Can you please transport us to the my ship? It's now in Earth's orbit."

Destiny shook her head. "I can't yet. I don't know the lay out of the ship. I might transport us right into a wall or a piece of furniture!"

"I think we should listen to her," said Neneko. " I for one don't want to end up inside a wall!" She moved behind Chris afraid that Destiny might transport them anyway.

"Well then," said Lorelei as she pulled out her communicator, " it looks like we've got to do this the hard way." She spoke into her communicator: "I need a pick up for me and five passengers."

As they waited for their transport, Chris called his aunt and uncle and told them what was going on. He explained his son and daughter would be staying with them for a while, and that there might be was a big possibility that he wasn't coming back. They understood, of course. Even though they were worried about their nephew, of curse and they were happy to take care of his kids.

"Good," Chris stated, then said, "Sam will drop them off as soon as she finishes things up here."his aunt and uncle told him to be careful and that they would miss him a lot.

Just as he was done talking to them Chris hung up the phone, a transport vehicle from Lorelei's ship had landed on the roof of Cyber Corp. They all went up to the roof. The pilot of the transport vehicle turned out to be Nodoka, Lorelei's apprentice witch now she had become the ships tech officer.

When Nodoka saw Chris walking to the transport vehicle she kind of cringed. He greeted her with an honorable bow, however, as he entered the vehicle. Destiny and Neneko sat down next to Chris, and Lorelei sat in the cockpit with Nodoka.

Hinata, Maylu, and Leo watched as the transport flew out of sight. As Leo watched, he made a vow to become a greater warrior then than even his father, what ever it took.

The transport vehicle shook like crazy as it flew thought the outer atmosphere and into space. When they landed, they exited onto the main ship.

Lorelei's people where waiting for her return. A small group of her female crew greeted her as she exited the transport, but, when Chris exited, they panicked thinking that he was one of the Titan's men. They jumped in front of Lorelei to protect her, holding out there fists the same way Chris did when he fired his shotgun blast.

Chris didn't know what to think, and was about to ask Lorelei what was going. But Lorelei told her crew, "Stand down."

As they lowered their hands, one of one of the younger women said, "He's a man! Men *can not* be trusted, —not one bit."

"It's okay," Lorelei said, "I invited him, and the others here to help. We need all the help we can get. Besides, you should remember this guy, —he's the one who took out the Titan the first time!"

"Well, you should of told him to have done a better job, because he's back, and now he's stronger than ever!" The woman said as she raised her hand to Chris's face.

Chris didn't like the way this woman was behaving. She was basically calling him a weakling.

"Hey," Chris yelled out, "how was I supposed to know that he would come back? I didn't think it was possible in the state I left of him in."

"Well," responded the angry woman, "you're supposed to be the great Super Cyborg! You should of have planned for this. Right now you seem to me to be the biggest joke I've ever seen!" The women yelled back to his face.

Chris was becoming angry. This woman couldn't be much older than his own daughter. He hadn't, come all this way just to be yelled at by a man-hating alien.

Lorelei moved between the two, breaking them up. "Save it for the Titan, and his group, you two."

The girl looked at Lorelei, then turned and walked off with in a huff. Chris could not believe that woman, and he asked, "Who was that?"

"That was Jura ," Lorelei answered. "She is the main security officer, for the ship and our top pilot. She is also the one you'll be taken taking orders from," Lorelei said thinking that things were about to get interesting if Chris stayed.

"I don't think so, Lorelei," Chris told her. "Right now, the only thing that I plan on doing is finding the Titan, and taking him down for good. This time, I'm not going to leave enough of him to fill a matchbox!"

Lorelei turned to Chris saying. "Before we face the Titan, there is one thing I would like you to do for me," she said sincerely.

"What is it?"

"I want you to come with me to the infirmary for a moment."

"Why?"

"Because I want to talk to Minawa for a moment."

Chris froze in his tracks. "You know?" he asked. But she didn't answer. She just lead him to he infirmary.

As they walked to the infirmary. "What are you two talking about?" Neneko asked nervously. "I thought that Minawa died years ago?!"

Chris shook his head. "She is still alive inside the cybernetic half of my brain. She downloaded herself in it without me knowing, and stayed hidden. During our fight with the general, she was awakened. Even though she is inside me, she prefers to stay quiet. Isn't that right, Minawa?" as he touched the cybernetic side of his head.

"That's right, Chris," Minawa said with her own voice through Chris's mouth. "And, Miss Neneko, it's so nice to finally get too talk to you," she said.

Neneko didn't quite know what to think about, this. Then a thought hit her: if Minawa had been inside Chris-chan's mind this whole time, does that mean that she had been watching when … She stopped herself in mid thought as she boldly asked Minawa, "Are you around when me and Chris-chan and I sleep together?"

Minawa laughed and said, "I am always around, and I'm happy to know that I'm not the only screamer when it came comes to Chris."

"Minawa!" Chris yelled to her. Neneko had stopped in her tracks. Her face was so red it would make a tomato jealous.

When they arrived at the infirmary, Chris and the other visitors were meet with a shock to find out that the only doctor on the whole ship, was so young. She didn't seem up to the task of being a medical officer.

"This is a joke, right?" Chris asked Lorelei, referring to the young woman.

"Let me assure you, Chris," responded the Supreme Elder, "this girl has an IQ of over two hundred. She understands more about taking care of things here than you'll ever know. Even though she's never cared for a man before, she is prepared to and lately I've given her male anatomy books so she would be ready to work on you if necessary, because all she's worked on has been women." Lorelei stated."

"Is that right?" Chris said, as he watched the doctor get herself ready to help with whatever Lorelei had planed for him.

The doctor walked to him and said, "That's right. I am the regarded doctor on this ship, and I'm going to help out Lorelei, when she works on you, and the other cyborg's that's with you."

Lorelei then turned back to Chris. "Take off your trench coat and lie down on the table." He did as he was told, but felt a little uneasy. "I don't want you to mess with my memories again," he said to Lorelei. Then, told Neneko and Destiny, "Watch her as she works."

Lorelei felt a little hurt hearing him say that, but still went right to work. She used an electric driver, to open the cybernetic side of his Chris's head. Neneko and Destiny where a little curious, as she did this and wanted to see what she was doing and moved closer. The young doctor stood next to Lorelei holding a tray full of tools. She also held a tray to hold the parts that Lorelei would remove from Chris. After Lorelei removed his shock damper from Chris's head, she reached into his head again with a pair of pliers and quickly removed a chip. Chris stopped moving and seemed to go into shock as he stopped moving.

Lorelei put the chip on the tray the doctor had and then said "Pie-way," addressing the young doctor, " take that to my work station and prepare my equipment."

The doctor did as she was told, and then Lorelei notice Neneko and Destiny looking at Chris. She could tell they were worried.

His face had a shocked looked on it, as if something had scared him. Neneko moved in front of him and snapped her fingers a couple of times. There was no reaction. Destiny then moved his hand up. The sound of the motors inside his hand was the only sound that they heard.

"He's not going to move, no matter what you do to him," Lorelei told them.

"What did you do to him?" Neneko asked.

"I removed his main possessor chip," she told them. "Without it, he is nothing but a cybernetic manikin. He can't move, and he has no idea what is happening around him. It's what I call status lock."

"You mean he doesn't know anything that's happened to him?" Destiny asked as she looked at him closely.

"Nope, it's kind of like being asleep without being able to wake up," Lorelei told her as she joined Pie-way at her workstation. Lorelei placed Chris's chip under her microscope and started to work on it.

"There it is," Lorelei said. With great care, she used a pair of tweezers to remove something from Chris's main possessor. She carefully put it on another tray that Pie-way had ready for her. "Be really careful with, that chip," she told the doctor. "It contains everything that makes up Minawa's heart, mind, and soul."

"That little thing, that you removed is Minawa?" Neneko asked in disbelief.

"Yup," Lorelei said happily. "And when I put it in our main computer, Minawa will become this ship's main computer."

Pie-way walked out of the infirmary leaving Chris still off-line.

Neneko asked Lorelei, "Are you going to put Chris back together?"

"I will after I finished putting Minawa into the main computer," Lorelei said. And, with that, she followed Pie-way out of the infirmary.

Lorelei entered the main computer room. Pie-way pressed a button on one area of the console and a slot opened on another area of the console. Lorelei took the chip from Pie-way and slid it into the slot. Just as she did, the whole place lit up as the computer rebooted.

xxx

Chris awoke some time later, feeling a little groggy. As he looked around, his internal clock started to reset itself. When his internal system let him know, just how long he was out, and when he saw that he had been out, for almost an hour, he stood up and asked Lorelei, "Was there a problem?"

"No there wasn't," he heard Minawa's voice say. He turned to the sound of her voice and saw her standing in front of him.

"*Minawa!!*" He yelled out, he ran over to her. "You're, alive!" But he ran right through her and slammed into the wall behind her.

Everyone started to laughed, Minawa included. She turned to him and said, "I'm a hologram. I'm using the ship's hologram projectors to project my form. It will be a while before I can figure out a way to make it solid, but for now at least I have a body to call my own again, —and it's this entire ship!" She raised her arms up feeling alive again.

"It doesn't matter, you're back," the cyborg happily said as he stood back up. "At least I can see you again. With you back, I can start living again."

Chris then looked over at Lorelei. "What are we waiting for? Let's go, take down the Titan once and for all!"

All of a sudden, however, the door burst open and some of the crew members, being led by Jura, walked into the infirmary. Jura pointed to Chris and said to the others, "See? I told you there is a man, on the ship. And not only that, he's a cyborg at that!"

The other crew members started to yell at Lorelei. One said, "How could you allow a man on this ship?" Lorelei tried to calm everyone, and Neneko and Destiny stood in front of Chris protecting him from the sea of rage that seemed to appear with the crew.

Chris had had enough of this. Lorelei had commissioned him on this ship to stop the Titan. His voice boomed over the female voices: "All you have to do is point me in the right direction and I'll take down the Titan."

Minawa then said, "We have been heading to where the planet Gem used to be. It seems that the Titan hasn't moved since he destroyed the planet. It's almost like he waits us to come to him."

"Good," Chris stated, "we can go deal with this, and then I can leave you all in peace, and— you'll never see me again!" With that, he turned and headed for the transport hangar to wait for when they arrived.

The crew members were still arguing with Lorelei when he left. They all still believed that they didn't need him at all.

Finally, Destiny had had enough. "Shut up," she yelled. They turned to the little cyborg to see what she wanted to say.

"You all have so much hate for men, but yet you all know that Chris would never hurt, any of you. He would rather die first. I known, he has never once hurt a women. Not only that, he's upset right now. I mean, come on, … he took down that Titan guy, once already. And he's beating himself up about the fact that he's back! Do you think he wants to be pushed around by a bunch of selfish, women who will never understand what he has sacrificed to get the power that he has? He can never feel the warmth of a women's hand in his again, —he well never know, what it feels like to be embraced by someone ever again! But you all don't care! You'll use him, and, when his job is done, you'll throw him aside, just like like a useless tool, —just like the Titan used all of you!"

When Destiny finished, she was exhausted. The crew members, looked at each other. Some of them remembered the day when Chris came to their world. He had fought with everything he had, to stop the Titan. Slowly, realizing the girl was right. Jura spoke for all of them. "Okay," she said. "We will give him a chance."

xxx

Chris stood ready in the hangar watching the stars. When he saw the Titan's ship come into view, he readied himself for battle. *This battle is going to be one for the history books!* he thought.

When Chris felt that he was close enough to the Titan's ship, he took off for the Titan's ship.

Chris Striker flew as fast as he could, slamming into the ship. "Welcome back!" he heard the Titan say.

"You're going to pay for destroying the planet Gem."

All he heard from the Titan was, "Follow the lights if you want to find me."

Chris ran through the ship, following the lights to the middle chambers. Finally, when he walked into the what looked like the main room. The walls of the large room were decorated with carvings that depicted every battle the Titan had been through during the time he had been in space.

Chris then saw the most recent one. It depicted the end of the planet Gem. He moved over to the picture and studied it. It showed the Titan firing a beam from his hand, but something didn't look right with the Titan, … He seemed much bigger.

"That one is one of my favorites," came a voice that seemed to come from everywhere around the room.

"Where are you?" Striker Chris yelled out.

"Ah, that is a difficult question to answer. In one sense, I'm everywhere around you. But I suppose what you are looking for is right here," the voice said as the ceiling opened up. What came down shook Chris down to his very core. He stood there staring for down came the head of the Titan. It was attach to wires and still looked exactly the way it had when Chris had thrown him into space.

"Ha!" said Chris. "You still don't have a body!"

Titan then laughed and said, "You don't get it, do you? This whole ship is now my body. And, with this body, I will destroy you."

"What, body?" Chris asked. Then, suddenly, he, realized what the Titan was talking about, —the entire ship was his body, witch meant that, if Chris cut the wires that attached Titans head to the ship, the Titan couldn't control the ship anymore, and he would be easier to kill.

Chris wasted no time. He shot forward and slashed at the head, cutting the head from the wires. Titan's head fell to the floor.

Titans head rolled to a stop, but, when Chris picked it up, Titan started laughing. "You'll have to do better than that!" The Titan's head flew out of Chris's hand and into the air. Chris Striker watched as bits and pieces of room, disengaged from their places, fly off and collected together and formed a large body for the Titan.

Titan's new body stood a good ten feet and was decorated all over with fire markings all. On his fore arms where what looked like dragon heads. There was another one, on his chest. Suddenly, a mask shot over his face covering the top half of his head. As the Titan took a step forward, Chris could feel the ship shake from the sheer weight of the Titan's new body.

Chris was not impressed. "You may have a few tricks, Titan, but I have some as well."

He charged up and roared out as he slammed his foot to the ground changing into his Alpha Omega Cyber Lion mode, roaring out as he changed.

They stood staring at each other, ready to attack at a moment's notice. But then the Titan roared out himself, —a heavy, metallic heavy roar that shook the ship again.

Chris roared out too as they charged each other, slamming together and fighting at lightning speed. But something was wrong. The Titan seemed to be faster than he had been before. Chris found himself slammed into the back wall. The Titan held him against the wall, by the neck and said, "It is futile! My power, has gone beyond what it was before. This time I shall be the victor!"

Chris Striker roared out as he tried to break the Titan's grip, but it was like a vice on his body holding him against the wall.

The Titan then pulled back his other fist and the dragon head on his fore arm moved over his hand and a strange energy charged up inside of it's mouth. The energy fired right in Striker's face.

The blast burned off a large amount of the Cyber Lion's flesh. Chris reared back in pain as the Titan let him go. Chris held his face as he tried to get his bearings, but he had been blinded by the blast.

"Now that I have your attention," the Titan said, "it's time to face the three-headed dragon." The other dragon head moved over the Titan's other hand, and the dragon head on his chest moved up and over the Titan's head. Finally, large leathery wings and a long tail folded out from the Titan's his back.

Chris's vision came back just in time for him to witness this transformation. As the dragon stepped over to him, one of the heads grabbed Chris by the neck and picked him up to face the middle head, which he moved on a long neck.

"You can never beat me ever again," said the Titan. "No matter what you do, no matter how much power you have, I will always be stronger. I am a god, remember. I can never be beaten." He glared at Chris. "Know this, Striker," he said. "I won't kill you. I will make you live forever, on that ship, with all those women. And they will hate you forever, because, thanks to me, they are ruined to all men. They will treat you like dirt, until you can't take it anymore, and then you will abandon your code of honor to protect those precious to you and destroy them all yourself. After you destroy them, you will join me, and we will rule this universe together forever."

"I will never do that!" Chris said, gagging for air. The dragon maintained a tight grip on his neck.

The Titan laughed again as he said sarcastically, "We'll see about that, Super Cyborg."

As the dragon's grip on Chris tightened, the beast also grabbed Chris's leg and started to tear him apart. Chris roared out as his leg and arm were ripped off as if his metal was made of ten tin foil.

xxx

Lorelei and some of her crew-members were watching there main monitor on the bridge of the ship, hoping that they would see the destruction of the Titan's ship, but instead the crew saw something get shot out of the side of the ship. When the image was magnified, the image they saw was Chris. He was back to his normal self and looked really beat up. Lorelei ordered her crew to pick him up, and get him back onto the ship. She planned for them to get out of this the area as soon as Chris was on-board, Neneko had already flown out and grabbed Chris. The second that she got Chris back on-board the ship, they turned and shot off at maxim speed.

xxx

The Titan watched them fly off, with a smirk on his face. *This is only the beginning of Striker's torment,* he thought. *When those Gem women see that he failed to stop me, they will torment him even more!* With that, the Titan turned to address twelve warriors who were assembled on the main deck of his ship. "It is now up to all of you to turn Striker to my side. I want to see that Super Cyborg destroy what's left of those women for me."

When they heard their orders, the warriors took off in their own ships. They traveled to areas around the universe to do their jobs.

xxx

Chris awoke sometime latter, to hear the sound of the women talking. He stayed still looking like he was still out. He heard Jura's voice yelling

418

at Lorelei, saying,. "Can you now see how useless this cyborg is? We don't need him at all!"

Lorelei responded, "We all underestimated how strong the Titan has become. There is no way that we could have predicted that Chris wasn't strong enough to beat him. But don't worry, I have a plan. I can make him stronger than he ever before."

When Chris heard this he bolted off the bed. "Lorelei, how can you do that?"

She turned to him, surprised that he was awake. Then she smiled and said, "Well, does that mean you're going to stay with us until you beat the Titan?"

"Don't worry, I'm not going anywhere, —until I teach that punk who's boss."

"That's good," Lorelei said. "Now come with me, to the hangar. Neneko, Destiny, are waiting for you there."

Lorelei and Chris then walked on past Jura as she said, loud enough for Chris to hear, "I still feel that we don't need the cyborg. We can handle things ourselves."

When the two arrived at the hangar, Neneko ask, why Lorelei wanted all of them here.

"It's because I won't to ask you a personal question about Chris here," Lorelei said pointing behind her at Chris.

"What?" Neneko asked.

"Now answer me truthfully," Lorelei said. They looked at each other, and then back to her nodding in agreement. "Have all of you kissed Chris at least once?"

The girls' face went red.

But Chris asked, "What does kissing me have to do with anything?"

"Because of the properties of your metal not only does it protect what is left of your skin, but turns your flesh into a conductor for transferring energy," explained Lorelei.

They all looked at each other, not knowing what she was talking about. So Lorelei turned to Chris as she said to him, "Look outside the hangar doors." She pulled something out of her pocket and the hangar doors started to open.

They panicked for a moment as the doors opened into space, but Lorelei said, "Don't worry. There's a shield around the opening. It lets things out, but not in." Everyone watched as a large asteroid floated by. "Chris," said Lorelei, "shoot that asteroid with his your shotgun and destroy it."

Chris watched the asteroid float by. It was at least as big as the ship. "There's no way I can could destroy something that big!"

"Just shoot it!" she said. Chris shrugged as he aimed and fired his strongest shotgun blast, he could muster, but, when the dust cleared away from the large asteroid, they saw that Chris's blast had only scratched the surface of the asteroid.

"Not bad," Lorelei said. Then she turned to Neneko and the others. "Now, ladies, focus your energies though Chris. You should already know how to do it."

The two of them started to charge their individual powers. As they did, Chris felt their power as if it was his own.

The feeling of focusing their power through his body was new to them. At first, it felt a little exhilarating. Their breathing became a little fast and shallow, —almost as if they where feeling a sense of sexual arousal from the experience.

Lorelei watched their reactions and was pleased to see it was working as she had predicted. "Chris," she said, "fire your shotgun again, and this time give it everything you have."

When he fired again this time, the energy blast was far beyond anything that they had seen him do, before. A, thousand beams shot out and hit the asteroid with such force, that it was completely vaporized. And the backlash was so strong that it pushed the whole ship back. When the asteroid dust finally cleared, everyone stood in shock at what he had just done.

It was incredible, the girls thought. They hadn't expected that, with their powers, he would be powerful without transforming to his higher forms.

"What was that!" Chris yelled out as he looked at his hands. He turned to Lorelei, who had a big grin on her face seemly pleased at what she had seen.

"You liked that, didn't you?" Lorelei said as she saw his reaction.

"Hell yeah, but what was that? Did I use their powers to maximize mine or what?"

"Well, as you know, the metal that you're made of has the ability to absorb energy," began Lorelei. "That's why you don't need an internal power source. Lately I have discovered that the metal has changed your flesh, making it, strong enough to hold up against the forces, that you go though. Not only that, but your flesh has become a conduit for transferring energy from flesh to flesh. In other words, each girl who has kissed you or," Lorelei's grin became bigger, "made hot, passionate love to you will become stronger. And that will make you, stronger. When they power up, to their fullest, you get stronger and more powerful too."

Chris and the girls where dumb struck. Basically, whenever Striker Chris gets to first base with, a woman, her power would make him stronger.

Neneko didn't like where this was going. "So," she said a little testily, "so the best way for Chris-chan to get strong enough to fight the Titan again, he's going to have to get a kiss from the entire crew of this ship?"

"That's right," Lorelei said in a singsong voice as she walked up to Chris. Smiling big, right in his face, and, with out a warning, she stole a kiss. Her kiss started playfully, but then turned into a passionate, heated kiss. As Lorelei deepened it, her kiss, she had difficulty controlling herself. Neneko stepped in and slipped between the two. Chris shook it off as Lorelei seemed to be holding herself back from the excitement she was feeling.

"I'm sorry about that," she said to them all. "It's just that it's been a while since I got to experience a kiss like that. I was about to lose myself there for a minute."

"Lose yourself?" Neneko yelled out to her. "You were ready to take him down, and do him right here!"

"Neneko, please calm down," Chris told Neneko before she blow up.

"Chris-chan," Neneko said in mock calm. She and then pointed to Lorelei.

"I know, Neneko-chan, but you have to realize that these are desperate times. And desperate times call for desperate measures."

"Yeah I know," she said, " but doesn't mean, I have to like it! I mean, you're supposed to be with *me,"me!"* Neneko said with almost a pout.

"Hey, what about me?" Destiny said, stepping up to Chris. If Chris didn't step in soon, they where going to start fighting over him.

"That's enough, both of you!" Chris yelled out. "You all need to know that I care for you both, equally, and I would do anything for you, so don't get it into your heads that, I belong to just one of you, do you get me?"

"Yeah," they said in unison.

He then turned back to Lorelei who was still enjoying the feeling of her kiss with Chris. "Are you finished with your experiments?" he asked her. " I would like to know where I'm going to be staying on this ship."

Lorelei straightened herself up and said, "Yes, about your living quarters. There is a little problem about that, Chris."

"What?"

"Well, you see, the rest of the crew, is definitely not going to like you staying anywhere near them, so," she paused a moment debating what to tell him, .

"Let me guess, they want me to stay as far away from them as possible, right?"

"That's right, so, if you wouldn't mind staying here in the hangar, …" Lorelei asked him, kept her hands behind her back and her head down, and dragged her foot back and forth in front of her.

Chris just slapped his face with his hand. *I think that I should of have expected this when I got on this ship with a bunch of man-haters*, he thought to himself. But, he said, "It will be all right. Besides, I didn't come on this ship for a pleasure cruise, I came to deal with the Titan. So living in the hangar won't be too bad. But how about my girls? Will they be getting rooms?"

"Don't worry, Chris," said Lorelei, "They will be getting, there own rooms real close to the hangar so you can see them every day."

"That's just fine," he finished.

But Neneko protested. "But Chris-chan, you can't stay, in this hangar like some sort of power tool, to be used when needed!" Neneko told him.

"Don't worry, Neneko-chan. It will just be until we can convince the crew of this ship, that I'm not here to hurt them."

"All right, Chris-chan,." Neneko said feeling down, "if you're sure about this."

CHAPTER 55

Chris spent a good amount of his time in the hangar, but he finally did get a tour of the ship. It was much bigger than he had originally thought. It was architecturally designed to hold a planets population witch meant that there was quit a lot of extra space because only a hundred and fifty, of the whole planet's population had made it on-board before the destruction of their planet Gem. From a combat standpoint, the whole crew was combat ready and fifty where children. But that was also a good thing, because it gave Chris a chance to convince the next generation that he wasn't a threat to them. It might be easier for him to ingratiate himself with the crew through them. But that turned out to be he easier said than done.

One day as Chris walked through the areas of the ship with Minawa's hologram walking next to him, he ran into Pie-way who was carrying a large pile of books. Obviously she'd had a lot of studying to do. Just as she came pass Chris, she tripped. Her load of books went flying, and she and the loud of books she was carrying fell, but Chris reacted so fast that he caught every one of them in mid air and then caught her before she even had a chance to hit the ground. She looked up at who had caught her and, with a dark blush on her face, she moved out of his grip and thanked him for saving her. "I'm all right now," she said. As she was taking her books back from Chris, he, noticed the title of one of the books.

It was a book about understanding the male anatomy, which made Pie-way's blush even deeper. She grabbed the books before he could look at any more of the titles. "Lorelei gave me these to study. I am the ship's doctor after all, and I have to understand how to help everyone on the ship." She then turned and walked at a fast pace to her room and the door slammed shut.

Chris could not help but laugh a bit, as he continued on his way. *It's not going to be too much of a problem to convince, that one that I'm the good guy*, he thought. But, as he went on, he ran into a group of girls who were talking about him. Even though they were whispering, he could hear every word they where saying. Then it hit him, … he knew who they where. They were some of the girls, that he had played his guitar to when he lived on their planet for those three years. They were talking about that very day. When they saw him coming, one of the girls, approached him and asked, "Are you going to be playing your guitar for the crew?"

When they said this, an idea hit Minawa, and she turned to him and said, "That is a great idea."

"What?" He asked unsure at what she meant.

"You see Chris, my people don't have music, so I bet if you started to play for them, they might start to think that you're a good guy."

Chris thought about this, and then turned to the girls who had asked him to play. "I'd love to play for you, but I didn't bring my guitar!"

"That's all right," Minawa said. "You left yours behind when you visited us before, and we saved it for you. It's here on the ship! I'll have someone bring it to the hangar for you."

Chris was surprised. "Well, then," he said, "would you all like it if I played during your dinner time?"

They all told him that they would love it. "All right," he told them, " don't tell the rest of the crew so—it will be a surprise."

The girls agreed to the idea, and took off. *I need to talk to Neneko about this*, Chris thought. *She can help.*

When dinnertime came, Chris walked into the cafeteria carrying his guitar. The crew-members who where there, didn't know what he was doing for they had never seen a guitar before. But the ones who did know, seemed to be quite excited. They were surprised to see Neneko was standing next to him. She seemed a little nervous.

Neneko swallowed hard and turned to Chris.

"Chris-chan, I don't know about this," she said as he sat down and started to tune his guitar.

"It will be fine, Neneko. Don't worry, Minawa's got you covered. She'll be playing the back ground music along with me."

When Chris started to play, Neneko took a deep breath and started to sing. Chris joined in, singing a duet with her. When they both started to get in to it, Chris stood as he played, and the two of them really started to, rock the ship.

Soon the crew-members started to get into it too. More crew-members walked, into the cafeteria wondering what was going on.

Chris and Neneko played four different songs, they— play rock and some slower songs, when—some of women wanted to hear more. They had feared Chris before; now they were warming to him, because he had given them music—witch means that they found a good reason for Striker to stay.

As Chris and Neneko where leaving the cafeteria, some of the crew-members asked them to come back tomorrow and play again. As they left, they ran into Lorelei. She was standing at the door of the cafeteria smiling. "Good job," she told them. " I think they really liked the two of you! But do you think that, next time, I could try and sing too?"

"No problem, Lorelei," Neneko told her. "In fact, that would be great! It makes me nervous to sing in front of people. I thought I was going to die when Chris-chan asked me to help him out with this."

"Well, I think you did a great job, and more," Lorelei said to them. But then her face went serious as she turned to Chris.

"Chris, I really need your help with something?" she said.

"What?"

"I need you to come with me, and some of the other crew-members. We're planning to land on a nearby planet to gather food and other supplies that we need."

"No problem," said Chris. "But what do you need me for, if it's just a supply run?"

"Well it's a trader planet, but the problem lies with the fact that my people are still seen as slaves on a lot of planets around here, so— ..."

"Oh I get it," Neneko said, stepped into their conversation, "you need Chris-chan with you, for protection. Am I guessing correctly that this planet that your going to, basically, trades everything—even people right?"

"That's right, Neneko," Lorelei said. Then she turned to Chris. "So, Chris, will you go down with me and the crew that's going— and pretend to be our master?"

"You know how I feel about that master thing, but, if it is to keep you guys safe, I'll do it."

"Do you mind it I go too?" Neneko asked, for she thought that her powers might come in handy.

Lorelei thought that was a good idea, and Chris then asked, "How many will be going on this little supply run?"

"There will be six of us counting you and Neneko."

He then asked, "Who are the others?"

"Nodoka, Jura, and Pie-way."

When Chris learned that Jura was to go, he began having second thoughts about this expedition. He knew, that Jura still didn't like him. But they really needed him for this, if the planet that they where down to, was like she said they really needed him with them.

"When do we leave?" Neneko finally asked. And Lorelei told her, "Tomorrow mourning."

CHAPTER 56

The next mourning, Chris was waited for the others at the hangar doors. It was easy, as he basically lived there, having nowhere else to go. Eventually, when the others came down to join him. He was shocked at their outfits! They where far from descent. The most shocking thing was that Neneko was also wearing a very revealing outfit. He never thought in a million years that she would wear something like that!.

"What are you guys wearing?" Chris yelled out at them.

"This is what the slaves have to wear," Lorelei told him. "Remember we're going down to the planet as your slaves. The people on this planet will trade anything—even people, —so it is understandable that, we have to look the part, … blend in. That's why we have to wear these, somewhat revealing outfits."

That might be true, Chris thought. *But their outfits barely cover their bodies! There is little left for the imagination.*

Lorelei then took a look at Chris and realized that he was going to need something to cover his face. The rest of his body was covered by his clothes, but any one of the Titan's men would recognize his face. Chris knew what she was thinking. "Don't worry," he told her, and as he slipped on his sunglasses and put on a hat. He turned to Lorelei and the others and and then asked, "What do you think?"

Jura told him, "You look like a cyborg wearing sunglasses and a bad hat."

"Jura, that's not very nice to say to him," Pie-way said. She turned to Chris. "I think you look fine," she said.

They all boarded the transport vehicle and descended to the surface of the nearby planet. The trip was smooth and they landed easily at a space port. When they disembarked, and walked out, Chris was shocked to see how lively the whole place was. He turned to Lorelei and asked, "How long are we going to stay here?"

"As long as it takes to get the things we need, master."

"Master!" Striker Chris almost yelled, as he looked at her.

"That's right, master," Lorelei said quietly, "and you'd better get used to it, because not only me, but everyone here well have to refer to you as master, as long as we're here, is that clear?" Lorelei said turned to make sure they had all heard her and that they would remember to call him by the title, master.

Neneko felt a little weird thinking that she has to call her Chris-chan "master," but it should only be for as long as they are were on this planet, so it shouldn't be too bad. Besides, it might be fun to think of it as a little game.

As for Jura, she was not enjoying herself. She could not believe that she had to call anther man "master." But she had to remember that, if she reveled herself on this planet, she could be captured or—worse—turned into a love slave for some disgusting man again, and the thought of that gave her chills.

Nodoka wasn't enjoying herself either, for she considered herself just a technician and nothing more. The thought of this cyborg man, helping them was making her feel even more afraid of men than usual.

Pie-way seemed to be the only one of the group who didn't mind the charade. Because she was the doctor of the ship, she knew she had to stay professional under these circumstances.

As they walked, through the city, Chris saw some men who seemed to be making business transactions. When he saw that they where selling slave women, he about lost it, but Lorelei told him to keep his cool. "Let's deal with the big problem first—meaning the Titan, —and then we will deal with this," she told him.

"Yeah, I know," Chris said with a growl in his voice. "But it doesn't mean I have to like it." Suddenly, Pie-way, informed them quietly that she had found a place that sold the things that they needed.

When they walked into the store, Chris Striker was shocked to see some men doing things to the women that sickened him. He felt like tearing the men apart. They were treating the women, as if they were animals. Lorelei, however, gave him a look that said he had to remain calm, and act as if it didn't bother him. He turned to Nodoka. "Do you have the list of the things that we need?"

Nodoka jumped back and stood with her arms hugging herself. She was a little unsettled at being in a shop like this too. But she managed to stutter out that she had the list. Chris pointed to the counter. "Go take care of our purchases," he told her. She walked up to the counter and handed the salesclerk the list of things they needed. The clerk turned to Chris, as the master of this slave, and said, "Well, you've got yourself quite the harem. I bet that you're a slave merchant. That's why you have such a big list of supplies here, right?"

"You have no idea," Chris told the man.

"Well," said the clerk, "I can get everything on your list here, but it will take a while."

"How long?" Chris asked.

"At least three days," The the man told him.

Chris looked over surreptitiously at Lorelei, who nodded her head. Chris turned back to the clerk and said, "It's not a problem. We will come back and get our supplies in three days."

As they started to walk out, someone stopped Chris at the doorway. It, was one of the men who had been trying out one of the slaves in the back. He looked pretty clean-cut, but Chris just gave him a cold stare, through his sunglasses. He really, did not like the feeling that he was getting from this guy.

"Listen, man," the guy said to Chris, "I couldn't help but over hear, your conversation with the store clerk, and I can see that you really are a man who enjoys his work, so.."—"

"So, what do you want?" Chris asked the man impatiently.

"Yeah, well I would like to buy one of the slaves you have with you," the man said as he pulled out a card that was used for the currency on the planet. Chris could tell the girls were all holding their breath.

Chris shocked the girls by asking him, "Which one do you want?"

When the man pointed at Jura, Chris Striker turned to her and stepped next to her and said to the man in a calm voice, "Well, she is quite the catch, isn't she?"

"Yeah, how does two hundred sound?"

Chris nodded as if in agreement, which scared Jura. She wasn't surprised, this would happen for all men were the same to her. But then Chris surprised her by saying, "Not even if you paid me a million! I would never sell any of my women. They are worth more than anything to me."

"Now let's be serious here," said the man, "they're nothing but women! And we all know women should be used for what they're good for, —making kids, cooking, cleaning, and … most of all … pleasure!"

That was the last straw. Chris had had it, with this, guy. He no longer cared if he compromised their cover. He hauled off and hit the guy right in the face so hard he flew, and hit a building on the other side of the street and landed on the sidewalk knocking the man unconscious. As the people looked over to see what was going on, Chris yelled out, "If I ever sees your face again, I will tear you in half!" He then turned to the girls and said, "It's time to go!" The five women followed him out the door and down the street.

As they searched for a place to stay, for the time being while their provisions order was being filled, Lorelei told Chris, "What you did was reckless and stupid! You could have gotten us all caught!"

"I'm sorry but that guy was ticking me off."

"Let me finish." Lorelei told him. "It was stupid—but it was really sweet. Thanks. But next time don't hit the guy, so hard that it draws so much attention."

They all had a laugh at the Lorelei's comment.

xxx

The man that Chris had hit got back up as if he hadn't been hurt at all. He cracked his neck back into shape and said to himself, *"Just as I thought—that guy was the Super Cyborg. Lord Titan will be pleased when I bring him his head and the women who are with him. But first I think I'll have a little fun with that sexy thing that he called Jura. She looked very sweet."* The man laughed thinking at what he was going to do to her as he took off to get some help with his plan.

xxx

Chris and his entourage finally found a hotel. When they entered, Chris walked up to the to desk to check them into a room. As he was about to ask for six rooms, Lorelei and Neneko both kicked him into silence. "We'd like one room for all of us," Lorelei told the clerk.

The desk clerk winked at Chris and looked at the five, "slave girls." "I'm sure you'll have a good night, sir," he said slyly.

Lorelei said dryly, out of earshot of the clerk, "You have, no idea as." And the clerk gave Chris the room key.

As they headed to the room, Chris asked, "Why did you and Neneko do that?"

"Did you forget that this planet is dangerous? You are our only protection! There is no way that I'm sleeping on this planet without you sleeping nearby. Besides it's going to be very interesting to see this room!"

As they entered their suite they where, surprised to see how clean it was. It looked like a love sweet suite. It was, indeed, big enough for all of them to be comfortable, but then the bed was something to look at,—for there was only one. But it was bigger then than any bed that Chris or the others had ever seen before.

It was round and looked as if it could sleep at least eight people comfortably. "Well," Chris started, "It looks like this is going to be home for the next three days." He went over and fell back onto the bed just now realizing how tired he was.

Neneko then hopped down next to him just as tired. But then Jura said, "I'm not going to sleep next to him!" Pointing at Chris, he sat up realizing that maybe, he should sleep on one of the couches, they'd seen in the outer room. As he got up, Lorelei stopped him. She turned to Jura and said. "Do you really want to risk sleeping here without some type of protection?"

"I don't need any protection," responded the angry woman. "I can take care of myself. I've got more skills, than you can ever imaged." Jura yelled out, as she turned away from Chris, and walked past Nodoka and Pie-way and out of the suite.

"What's with her?" Pie-way asked as she looked at the others.

"You know Jura," Lorelei said. "Once she puts her mind on something, she won't let up. She thinks that she's going to be okay, but she doesn't know, just how dangerous this planet is for a women. Why do you think I had Chris come with us? He's the only thing keeping the men here from, turning us back into slave,—or worse."

"Then we had better go after her," Nodoka said, as she looked over to Chris, who was already getting up to go after her.

"I should be the one to go after her," he said to the others. " I can find her a lot faster if I go alone." Striker told them.

Lorelei agreed. "We'll stay here in the room in case she came comes back," she said. Chris turned to the window and flew out into the night sky.

xxx

Jura was walking down the street, still mad at Lorelei, wondering what they really need that man for. *All he's going to do is slow us down, in our fight against the Titan*, she thought. *And, besides, it's all his fault in the first place! He should've finished off the Titan, the first time he fought him.*

Jura suddenly ran into someone big. She looked up and apologized to the stranger. "Sorry, I guess I wasn't watching where I was going." As she started to move on, he stepped in front of her.

Jura turned again, but the large man moved with her. "Excuse me," she said as she tried to move passed past him. But the large man grabbed both her shoulders and just said, "You're *not* excused."

Jura forced herself free of the man's grip, but, as she stepped back, she ran into the man who had tried to buy her at the market.

She stepped away from him as she said, "Don't you try anything, —I'll bust you up!"

The second man laughed. "I like them feisty," he said. Then he called to his large friend. "Turk take her."

The large man grabbed Jura and picked her up as if she weighed nothing. She kicked into the air, but could not escape. "Let go of me! "You'll be sorry for this!"

"Drake," Turk said referring to his smaller companion.

"What?"

"Are we going to take her to the Titan?"

When Jura heard the word *Titan*, she knew that she was in trouble, for that meant that these guys weren't human.

"Yes, we are," said Drake licking his lips, " but first what do you, say we break her in, and have a little fun with her?"

"*Nooo!*" Jura screamed out as Turk moved her into an alley. Drake followed. " Then, let me have the first go!" He took Jura in a tight grip and threw her down the alley. She slammed into the back wall. She got herself up quickly, but he grabbed her, and pulled her to the ground. Moving his way on top of her, and he started to tear away at her clothes. He laughed wickedly at the thought of what he was going to do to her.

When she was just about to be stripped nude, he readied himself as he saw tears steaming down her face. She knew there was no hope. But, just then, something grabbed Drake's head and picked him up and away from her.

When Jura felt that she was free, she opened her eyes to see, what had happened. When she saw Chris standing there holding the rapist by his head, she felt a relief that she had near felt before wash over her.

"Are you all right?" Chris Striker said to her.

All she could was just nod her head, as she tried to cover herself with her hands.

Chris moved the punk right to his face. "I don't think the lady enjoys your company," he said. Then he slammed Drake against the side wall, which broke and crumbled over the man.

Jura then yelled, "Look out!" As Chris turned in time to see Turk, who was about to slam his fist down on him. But Chris retaliated quickly, hitting the large man three times, so fast that he didn't react until Chris moved away, at which point, he fell to the ground and blew up in mass of mechanical parts.

Chris moved back over to Jura. He took off his trench coat, and wrapped it, around her. Then he stood up, and noticed that the first guy, he'd attacked was still alive, and was trying to get away. The cyborg jumped and landed in front of him.

"Where do you think you're going, little man?" he asked Drake.

"Ahh!" Drake yelled out, as Striker picked him up by the neck.

"So you like to rape women do you? Well let's see you rape a women in hell!"

Chris tore Drake's head off, with one swift motion.

Jura felt no repulsion, when she saw this, for she was glad, that man was dead. But when Chris walked up to her, and asked her again if she was okay, something inside her just broke. She threw herself into his arms and wept. "I'm so sorry for saying those terrible things to you and about you," she said as she gripped his shirt, tears flowing and she cried on him.

"Its all right, Jura," Chris said as he held her. "Those men won't hurt you any more."

Jura looked up at him with tears in her eyes. "Please don't to tell the others that this happened or that I was crying."

Chris nodded his head and told her, "No problem."

Jura continued to cry for some time before she managed to calm herself. It was the first time she had ever cried, and, for some reason, she felt better than she had in a long time even though the one person that saw her cry was a man.

Chris then slowly helped her to her feet and said, "We should get back to the others. They're still waiting for us."

Jura nodded as she stood up. But right before she could protest, the cyborg picked her up in his arms, and jumped into the air, and flew back to the hotel.

xxx

Lorelei was pacing the room wondering what was taking Chris so long. Just as she began to think she should go looking for him herself, they all heard something tap the window. Nodoka was the first to the window, which she opened. Chris jumped into the room holding Jura in his arms. She didn't look too happy. Quickly, the others noticed that she was wearing Chris's coat. Chris set Jura down. "What happened?" asked Lorelei.

"Don't worry, everyone," Jura said. "I was careless. I got lost and I fell down in a the river. If it wasn't for Chris here, who knows what might of have happened?"

"Is that true Chris-chan?" Neneko asked., Chris just nodded in agreement.

Lorelei sighed in relieve relief as she said, "At least you're safe, and nothing bad happened to you. But I hope this showed you that this place is dangerous without Chris—, he's our only lifeline on this planet."

Jura nodded and felt ashamed for what she had done. But, she didn't show it. Lorelei then suggested that they all get some sleep. "We have a big day tomorrow," she told them. "We still have two days until our supplies are ready, but that doesn't mean that we can just stay in this hotel, the entire time —we still have other things to do."

The next morning, the others were a little shocked to see Jura practically hanging on Chris. Even after they got up and left the hotel, and not only that, but every time they passed a man, she would grip him tighter. Neneko asked her, "What's with the change on of heart?"

Jura just said, "Lorelei said Chris is our lifeline on this planet, and I for one do not want to get separated from him again, while we're here."

As they walked through a shopping area, Pie-way was the first to stop at a toy store. When Chris saw this, he turned to her and asked if she wanted something there.

She jumped, not realizing that he was watching her. "No, of course not!" she said, scoffing at the very idea of waiting a toy or stuffed animal.

"Ha!" Chris laughed. "I thought that all little girls like stuffed animals."

"Not me," she responded. " I have more important things to think about than toys." She told him with her head up high, but Chris knew that she wanted one.

He turned to Lorelei, "Can you part with a small portion of our funds?" he asked her.

Lorelei, knowing what he had planned, handed him some cash. "You guys go into this restaurant here," he said, pointing to a place next to the toy store. "Find us a table. I'll be right in."

As he left them, Jura felt a pain come back, and a fear that she had never felt before. But Neneko told her, "Don't worry, that he won't be gone long."

"What makes you think I'm worried?" Jura scoffed. "I don't have to be afraid of anything on this planet!" Jura told her, trying to sound as if she wasn't afraid, but Neneko knew that she was. Jura's voice was even shaking.

They entered the restaurant where they were going to have their breakfast. Lorelei saw something interesting at a table across from there's, and could not reset checking it out. There was a man playing chess with a companion. His slave was standing behind him. She was average, but beautiful girl, about Neneko's height, but with a body that would make some men scream, and her hair was as red as fire. There was something unusual about her, but Lorelei couldn't figure out what. The other man's slave was also standing behind her master.

The two men were apparently playing for their slaves. Finally, one of the men said, "I forfeit the match. I'm trapped."

The other man just said, "Well, like I told you, there was no way to win against me."

"But that's not true! You can still win, sir," came Lorelei's vice behind one of the men.

When the so-called winner of the match turned to look at Lorelei he said, "So a slave thinks that she could do better than me? I don't think so."

"But I was just wanting to help," Lorelei told him as she pointed to the chessboard. "Your opponent still could win."

"So you think you, could do better? There's no way! And, a slave should know her place!" But someone stopped his hand mid way. When he looked to see what stopped him, he saw Chris.

"I would not recommend that if I were you." Chris said calmly to the man, as he let go of the man's arm. "What's the problem?"

The man looked at Chris carefully sizing him up. He noticed a few things. For starters, he was holding a large stuffed lion in his arms. It was at least as big as the young girl who was sitting at the table with the others that was —with the women who had disrespected him.

"If there is a problem," said Chris, " you take it up with me, —not with them." He put the large lion down, and turned back to the man.

"This woman thinks that she could beat me, at the at this point in the game, my opponent is at," the man told him.

"Lorelei, is this true?" Chris asked.

"Yes, Master." Lorelei meekly said trying to sound as a slave should.

"Well, then, I think there's only one thing to do." Chris said as he turned back to the man.

"And what's that?" the man asked.

"That's to let Lorelei here, play the game from this point, and beat you to prove that she is right."

"But, master," —" Lorelei started.

But the man said, "All right. And, if, she losses, I get her as my prize. That's my deal with my friend here!"

Chris turned to Lorelei, who seemed a little nervous. Then he turned back to the man and said, "All alright, you've got yourself a bet."

When the others heard this, they could not believe that Chris would bet Lorelei like that, and. Neneko and Nodoka ran up behind him. "What are you thinking?" Neneko whispered. "If she losses, we will have to give her to him."

Chris didn't even turn around to them. "Everything will be all right. Lorelei won't lose."

Lorelei sat down and picked up the game, where the other man had left off. And at first, the other man didn't seem happy about this, but then everyone could tell he was confident that knew that there was no way that a girl, couldn't win. But, as the game got on, both men were shocked to see the moves that they didn't know possible, in fewer than four moves, Lorelei won. .

As the man saw this, his shock was apparent, being beaten by a woman—never mind a slave! He stood and turned to Striker. "You have quite the slave! She's beautiful—and she's a smart one to boot."

Chris laughed as he told him. "You have no idea, just how smart."

"Well, like the bet, I lost, so here." the man said. He grabbed his slave lightly and pushed her toward Chris.

But Chris said, "This girl isn't *my* slave. It was Lorelei who won her, not me." And he gave Lorelei a sly grin.

The people in the restaurant could not believe that a slave could win another slave. They were surprised when the slave had taken a slave, but the man laughed as he said, "You're right!" And he pushed his slave toward Lorelei, "Respect your new master." Lorelei was still sitting in her chair obviously unconformable with this situation. But the slave girl walked over to Lorelei and got down on her hands and knees. The man said "You are quite the interesting person, allowing your slaves to have such freedoms," he said. At that moment the man know, that he was doing the right thing to keep his slave save form harm.

As Chris watched the man walk off, he realized that he hadn't given Pie-way her gift yet. He picked up the stuffed lion, and walked over to her. She, was sitting at the table with Jura and the others. He sat the lion next to her and told her, "This is a gift. I want you to take good care of it."

When Pie-way saw the lion, she was a little surprised, that he would get her anything, after what she had told him earlier, but he said, "It's all right act your age, now and again, you know!"

Pie-way slowly hugged the large stuffed lion and then looked up, at him and said, "Thank you. I will treasure it always."

Lorelei was still having a hard time believing, that Chris had just arranged for her to win her own slave. The girl before her was now her slave, the thought of it was just weird. And as she looked at the girl, she still believed that there was something unusual about her ... something special. But she still couldn't figure out what it was.

CHAPTER 57

While the others were still in the restaurant, the man who had given up the chess match was standing next to his partner, who had been waiting to meet up with him outside the restaurant.

"What do you mean you lost the match!" the man said. "The boss is not going to like this. You were supposed to win her! You guaranteed that you could win the bio-android."

"I'm sorry," said the loser. "If it hadn't been for that cyborg guy, and his pretty little slave, I would have won."

"Wait a minute, did you say cyborg?"

"Yeah— he was wearing sunglasses and gloves, but I could defiantly tell that he was a cyborg."

"Did he have a bunch of women with him?"

"Yeah." I think he did now that you menage it one of them was the one that won my slave?"

"You fool! That was, the Super Cyborg, —the one that Lord Titan, has been after. If we get him—and the bio-android—, just think of the rewards, that the Titan would bestow on us! We'd better tell the boss and see what he wants us to do next." With that, the two of them ran off.

Chris and company, plus their new friend, were back at there hotel room. Chris couldn't help but laugh at Lorelei's little dilemma. Her new slave still would not leave her side, even when Lorelei insisted that she didn't need a slave. It seemed that this girl had been made for one purpose and one alone, and that was to serve her master.

Lorelei turned to Chris and gave him a pleading look. Chris knew that Lorelei would never feel comfortable ordering around a slave. The girl was sitting quietly next to her new master. Chris just decided d to talk to there new comer.

"So girl," Chris started, "what's your name?"

"I don't have one yet," she answered, bowing to Lorelei. "Not until my master gives me one."

"Well, is that a fact?" He then turned to Lorelei and said, "Well, it appears to be up to you."

"I don't know what to call her," pleaded Lorelei. " I'm a scientist not a book of names."

"Well then, I'll give her one," Chris told her as he looked at the girl over. "How about *Ichigo*?"

"What?" Everyone said at the same time. But Neneko though knew what he was talking about.

Chris then said "It means *strawberries* in Japanese," he explained. "And with her red hair, it's the first thing that came to mind. Either that or I'm hungry."

"I like it." ," Destiny said as she took the young woman's hand and asked what she thought. But the girl seemed as if she was waiting for a reply from Lorelei, , who remained silent. Chris then asked her what she thought, and the girl meekly said, "I like it, but it is up to my master to tell me if, that is going to be my name or not."

Chris said, "Don't worry, if Lorelei's is your master and Lorelei is my slave, then that means that I hold a higher level of authority than she does, so which means that you are my slave too. It also, means that I can choose a name for you, and I pick Ichigo." he said with a smile.

The girl seemed overjoyed as she hugged Chris. Lorelei felt a little better that Chris had decided that he would take care of the girl. But there was still one thing that bothered her—why did this girl seem so different from the other slaves? What made her so unique?

Later on that day, Chris, Ichigo, and Destiny went out to do some more errands. This was one thing he was not looking forward too.

As they exited the store, someone slammed into Striker pinning him into the wall. It was the man who had lost the chess game in which Lorelei had won Ichigo form.

"What the hell is going on here?" said Chris. "What do you want?"

"I won't you, —and the girl," the man said to him.

"Well I'm flattered, but you're not getting me or the girl," Striker said as he tried to get free. But found that the guy holding him wasn't human, —he was some kind of alien, and was just as strong as he was if not stronger.

When he saw the another alien, go for Ichigo, Chris ducked under the arms of guy who was holding him and shot under his legs. Then he went back to back with him and swung his arm up, grabbed the guy from behind, and threw him at the second, guy making them both fall over each other.

Chris then ran out and stood between them, aliens and the girls, ready to attack at any time. But, when the two stood, they looked at each other. The first alien held out his hand. "If you think you've got power, check this out."

His hand seemed to burst open, but it wasn't cybernetic, but it was organic. Chris, took a step back in shock as he saw a strange energy charge in the organic arm cannon.

It fired, —like a Gatling gun, firing— a shower of organic bullets. To the alien's shock, however, Chris, Ichigo, and Destiny were still standing without a scratch on them. Slowly, Chris raised his arm and opened his hand. The bullets that had been fired fell to the ground.

"What the hell is going on here?" Gun-Hand said as he saw this. "I didn't even see him move!" He then turned to his partner and said, "Maverick, I think we've got some problems."

"I think you're right, Gun-Hand—, so let's go get the boss before this guy gets us."

They both agreed and ran off, Chris turned to the girls and asked, "Are you all alright?"

Ichigo was the first to say, "That was amazing. I have never seen anyone move that fast before."

Chris rubbed the back of his neck in embarrassment and said, "That really wasn't nothing special. I can move a lot fast then than that."

xxx

Meanwhile, Gun-hand Hand and Maverick ran into an alley, where they thought they were safe. Maverick then pulled out a communicator and called their boss. After the boss listened to the story of what had happened, he was angry at the two and on the screen a person in shadows answered, you could only make out an outline of the person, so you couldn't tell who it was, but they knew.

"But, boss," Gun-Hand whined, "that guy's crazy strong and fast! He caught my bullets like they were standing still!"

There boss wasn't going to have it. "If you can't beat him with brute force," he told the two underlings, "you will have to find another way!" With that, he disconnected.

xxx

When Chris and the others got back to the hotel, they told them what happened and related their experiences. Everyone was shocked that someone would be after them. They wondered what these people wanted and what would they want with Ichigo.

Lorelei knew there was more to this than meets met the eye.

Lorelei decided to find out, what they wanted with Ichigo, she started to run a few tests on the girl. When she conducted a full-body scan of the girl, she discovered the girl was a new type of bio-android that she had not seen before. Ichigo could actually reproduce. A, model like this one would be worth billions, on the black market. No wonder they wanted her so badly!

After, Lorelei explained the situation to Chris, they decided then that maybe they should go out and do some research to see if they could find out who had made the girl. As, they where all leaving the hotel, however, something made Chris stop. He scanned the area, as he felt something was off, and it hit him as he scanned, he saw the two men

443

who had attacked him and the girls. They were several miles off, and one was holding what looked like a missile launcher, but bigger.

"*Move!*" he yelled out, as he pushed them all out of the way. But he had reacted too late. The missile hit Chris, with an incredible force, shooting him back into the hotel, which then blew up in a massive explosion

xxx

"Got them!" The two men yelled out, as they headed over to pick up the pieces.

xxx

Neneko had put up a shield just in time, to protect the others, but she was worried about Chris. As she retracted, the shield, she yelled out, "Chris-chan!"

But there was no answer. Worry started to set in for Neneko as well as the others as they, looked for any sign of him, in the rubble. As bad as that was, they still had no clue as to what had hit them, until they heard someone yelled out to them, "Don't move or you'll join your friend in hell."

When they turned, they faced the guns of Gun-Hand and Maverick. The two, determined to take Ichigo this time. But, as they came close, they heard a muffled roar, and then the ground started to shake.

The girls knew what was next as the Cyber Lion, burst out of the ground roaring his metallic roar shaking the dust off its fur. When the Cyber Lion spotted the two men, he let out a low metallic growl.

Maverick and Gun-Hand took a few steps back when they saw the enormous lion. The lion, stepped forward, and the five women stood next to him as if they where about to order the beast to attack.

The two of them, knew they couldn't beat the lion. They just looked at each other and then jumped into the air. They landing on a roof top and ran off.

Chris shook a little as he growled, changing back to normal. But, when he did, they saw that the explosion did mess his clothes up, they where totally destroyed, which now hung on him like rags. Chris stood back up and throw what was left of his trench coat to the ground. "Those guys are going to pay for this," he said. "This was my favorite coat!"

"Don't worry, Chris-chan," Neneko stated. "We'll get you a new one, at the store here. We're just happy that you're okay."

"Yeah, I'm fine." He turned to Lorelei. "So, what's our next move?"

"Well," Lorelei stated, "the next thing we should do is go find Ichigo's old master, but, before we do that, we have to do a little shopping. We lost everything when the hotel blew up!"

Chris turned to Neneko and told her to take everyone. She nodded and lifted the others into the air. Ichigo was amazed when she was lifted up, and Lorelei said, "Don't worry, Ichigo. Neneko has the power over gravitational forces so she can fly, —or make others fly.

When they flew off, Chris took one last look at the wreckage of the hotel and then shook his head. *How can Titan's men, be so cruel?* And then he took to the air following Neneko and the others.

xxx

Gun-Hand and Maverick, had stopped running, Maverick had taken out his communicator and relayed their story to their boss.

Their, boss again, was not happy with them.

"What do you mean you failed? You morons had a simple job, —get that bio-android and the cyborg. How hard can that be?"

"We're sorry, boss," Maverick said trying to explain their failure, " but you should of have seen him! He was enormous!"

"Aw, stop your sniveling," said their boss. "I will take care of him myself!" The communicator screen went black again, and the two swallowed hard thinking that they were in for it.

xxx

Chris landed a few minutes after the others, and walked into the store. The girls where happy to find that the store owned was a woman, who seemed nice to them.

While Chris looked through the men's clothing, the girls where looked for something good to wear for themselves. As Chris continued to look around, the owner walked up to him, and introduced herself to him. She told him that her name was Rachel, and then said, "I have something in the back that you might like. It just came in."

Chris was little uneasy at first. He didn't feel right leaving the girls, but Rachel assured him that they would all be fine, that no one would bother them in her store.

So Chris followed the women, into the back where she then slammed the door behind him. He turned and yelled out, "What's the meaning of this?" but she just waved good-bye to him. Right then, a spike went right throw through Chris's chest. Silver fluid ran out of the wound. Chris turned to see what had hit him, came face to face with a twelve-foot-tall robot that stood on the other side of the room. The robot's arms were decorated in large metal spikes, which Chris knew it could fire upon its enemies.

Chris Striker tried to remove the metal spike from his chest, but, before he could act, the robot cleared the distance between them, and grabbed him, and slammed him against the wall, then slammed him to the ground.

The girls in the next room, had no idea what was going on, but, as they where still looking around all at once, alarms sounded. They didn't know what was going on until dozens of the Titan's police security officers came running into the store. The officers apprehended the girls. Jura, however, was on the other side of the store. She saw the officers take the others, and she knew that something wasn't right. She had to find Chris, but first she had to think. She ran out a side door to hide for a while.

Chris tried to get free of the robot's grip, but had no time to think. The robot picked him up and threw him through the wall. Chris rolled outside onto the street. People ran, when they saw the robot come outside. Chris Striker started to get up, when something hit him hard and he fell forward. The metal spike that was still through him forced him to fall to his side, and as more silver fluid came out of his wound.

He tried to stand again, to see who hit him; he didn't think it had been the robot this time.

He turned to find Maverick and Gun-Hand, standing behind him. Maverick seemed to be the one who had hit him with some kind of cannon, he didn't know what it was but it packed a punch.

Striker started to see in his cybernetic eye a examine of his vital signs. He learned that he had sustained, a critical energy loss. Minawa then came on the display trying to find out, what was wrong, but she was losing his transmission because, his power was draining. The damage done to him, wasn't helping much either. And it wasn't over—, as the robot came running out, with Rachael not far behind. And the officers came out holding the girls captive.

"What are you two doing here?" Rachael said to the two who finally had Chris right where they wanted him. "I told you, that I would take care of him." Rachael said.

"We didn't want you to have all the fun," Maverick said as he walked up and twisted the spike that was in Chris's chest, making him scream out.

The girls could barely watch this. As the officers held them, they cried screaming for the men to stop hurting Chris, but it was no use as they were forced to watch as Chris was being torn apart.

The robot then grabbed Chris again, by the arm and picked him up. Then grabbed his other arm and started to rip his arms form his body. The thought that he was going to die raced through Chris's mind, but he was not going down without a fight. He looked up to the robot, and kicked the robot's head so hard it flew off, rolled across the ground, and came rolling to a stop in front of Rachael.

Chris Striker fell to the ground, he slowly stood back up to see Gun-Hand and Maverick both smiling at him. They ran at him, and attacked him with everything they had, witch finished him off. They hit him into an alley and beat him down. They shot at him until they watched the glow in his eye go off and on, showing them—proof that he was dying.

The two stood over their handy work. One of his arms had been broken off and lay off to one side. Blood and other fluids poured from his body. Finally they used the spike that was still through him, and imbedded, him against the wall. As his eye finally went dark, he hung there the two of them turned and walked off after finishing there job.

xxx

When the five girls got to the police security office for the planets police, Ichigo was separated from the others and taken to Rachael, where she was planning on having her taken to her Lord Titan as planned. The others where going to be sold off as slaves.

xxx

Meanwhile, Jura was still looking around for any sign of Chris. After all the craziness, that had gone on, she got all turned around. That's when she saw a trail of strange silver liquid on the ground. She followed it until she saw the shattered remains of Chris in an alley. His body was impaled to the wall by a metal pike that had been shot right through him. The sight was mind numbing. She ran over to him and saw that he wasn't moving, and his eye wasn't glowing. The sight was almost too much for her to bear.

Jura might not of have liked men before him, but no one deserved this. She had to do something, but he was most certainly dead. Still, she felt she should at least try to remove the spike from his chest. With a heavy heart, she moved over to him, and grabbed the spike. But, when she did, Chris jumped and reached out to her, startling her.

She jumped back and then slowly looked him in the face as she asked, "Chris, are you alive?"

He slowly moved his head up, and looked at her. She saw a weakness in him that she had never seen before. He had always seemed so strong, and unstoppable, and here he was, with barely enough power to move. "Get Lorelei or Destiny," he managed to croak.

"I can't —they've been captured, by the Titan's troops."

He looked down at the ground and then back to her, and said with a cough, "Then you will have to fix me."

"How?" She she asked. "And with what?"

Chris looked up as he pointed with his one arm to the space port where their ship was. "You have to get me to our transport vehicle."

As Jura nodded. She tried to remove the metal spike that was holding him to the wall. It wouldn't budge. Chris grabbed it and slowly started to pull it out of him. The sound it made as he slowly pulled it out was sickening. When he finally got the spike out. It was covered in a silver liquid, that she did not recognize. Just as Chris was about to fell to the ground, she caught him and helped him to his feet. As they headed for the transport, she hoped that it wasn't too late.

xxx

The four captured women had been left in the a holding cell. They where losing hope fast. They believed that Chris was dead, and it was just too much, to bear. Their sprites were broken, and they knew it was only a matter of time before they would be sold off to the highest bidder. Suddenly, Neneko heard someone coming their way. Neneko know she had to do something, but they had incapacitated her powers by putting a neutralizer collar on her. But, she wasn't about to give up even if her Chris-chan was dead.

When the doors to their cell opened, she attacked, she ran at the man who stood there. But, stopped when he yelled out, "Wait a minute!"

She looked up and saw, that it was the man who had originally owned Ichigo form the start.

"What are you doing here?" Neneko asked as she steadied herself back.

The man looked around and then turned to her and said, "I work here as a security officer so I can serve the Titan as a spy. I am one of his top scientists. When, I heard you where all captured, I had to help." He then held out his hand and introduced himself to them. "The name's Doctor Turner. I have been working on a bio-android for the Titan, for years. My goal was to make the ideal woman that the Titan could use, for him to make a new world for himself. But, when I finished it, I couldn't bring myself to make her into a mindless slave like the way the

Titan wanted, so I gave her a will of her own. I wanted her to be able to make up her own mind about things."

"So let me guess," Lorelei asked. "The Titan didn't like that idea, did he?"

"No, and so I've been on the run, for a while. But, when you guys appeared during my chess match, I thought I could find a way for her to go with you, so I bet her in a match knowing you would beat me. The thing I 'hadn't planned on, was one of the Titan's generals being there."

Neneko was already making plans. "We have to get out of here, and go back to where we left Chris-chan and hope he is still alive.," Neneko told the doctor. "But this collar is preventing me from using my powers to get us out of here."

"Yes, that's right," the doctor said as he unlocked the collar. Neneko moved to the wall knowing they couldn't get out the front door. She punched the wall, busting it down, and then turned to the others saying. "Let's go!"

xxx

Rachael was sitting on a couch in her hotel room with Maverick and Gun-hand Hand waiting to hear for a communication from the Titan. Ichigo was tied to a chair with a gag in her mouth.

Ichigo was trying to say something to Rachael. Rachel got up and removed the gag she asked. "Do you have something to say, honey?" she asked sarcastically.

"You are a evil person!" Ichigo said. "Master Lorelei and Master Chris will come and save me." Ichigo said as she glared at the woman.

Rachael shook her head thinking how naïve this girl was. "Chris, Striker the so- called super Super Cyborg, is dead. And Lorelei is in lockup, soon to be sold to the highest bidder. So there is no way out."

xxx

Jura managed to get Chris into there transport without being caught. But they couldn't take off because, if they did they, would surely be shot down. Jura had to do something quickly because the trip to the transport

450

had damaged the cyborg greatly. Jura then got Chris as comfortable as possible, then she contacted there main ship. As she did, she started thinking that, if she had been nicer to Chris form the start, this might not of happened. Chris had only wanted, to protect them. All she had done was was treat him like dirt. Right then, she promised herself that, if he lived through this, she would treat him a lot better. By that time, Minawa appeared on the console screen. Jura had made contact with the main ship.

Minawa appeared and already knew what had happened to Chris. In fact, the whole ship was in an up roar. But nothing could have prepared Minawa for what she saw when she connected her video feed to the transporter.

Chris's body was badly beaten. He barely had the power to stay alive. He was missing one arm, and he was bleeding badly. At the most, she calculated, he had fifteen minutes of alternate power remaining.

"Minawa, thank god you're here," Jura said happy to hear her. "You have to fix him now!"

Minawa didn't seem too happy. "I'm still a hologram; I can't touch him. You're going to have to be my hands."

Jura looked at him and then back to Minawa as she said, "I can't. I'm not good at this stuff. I'm a warrior, not a, mechanic or a scientist."

"F-Ff-Fifteen fifteen minutes …" stuttered Chris as he looked up at her. "You have to g-get good."

"What?"

"Pl-plenty of time, time like a short of runic, sort of, rhyme …" Chris said, slowly losing himself

"Okay, okay don't lose it," Jura said to him as she waved her hand in front of him to snap him out of his daze. "Stay with me!" Then she sat in front of him as she turned to Minawa and asked, "What do I needed to do first?"

"First thing we need to do, is we need to find out the extent of the damage," Minawa said. "Rip off his shirt."

Jura blushed at this, but shook it off as she grabbed his already torn shirt and ripped it the rest of the way off revealing the bleeding silver liquid, that was still oozing out of the hole that was made by the metal spike.

"What is this?" Jura asked.

"It's called mechanical fluid," Minawa answered. "Mech fluid for short. Its fluid that helps his energy flow, and keeps his organics intact. With out it he will," …" she paused then said, "… die!"

When Jura heard this, she thought that she had no choice. She removed her own shirt, much to Chris's protests he told her that it was improper, but she told him to forget it, as she tore her shirt to strips, and wrapped them around his body bandaging him up.

"Well I stopped some of the bleeding," the now shirtless women said as she grabbed Chris's trench coat. She had helped take off him, when she tore his shirt off, she put it on. It might have been torn a little, but it was better than nothing.

"Yes, you did stop the bleeding," Minawa answered her, "but he is still losing power, so you have to reconnect the broken wiring to his heart. It is the only way to save him. And you have to do it before his back up power is gone."

"All right, all right," Jura said. "What do I do next?"

Minawa said, "Open the tool box in the locker and get out the soldering iron."

After Jura found the necessary tools, she looked at the damaged circuits inside Chris, and said, "This is impossible!"

"Don't worry," said but Minawa. "I will help you every step of the way." And the two of them got started.

xxx

As Neneko and the others, in the company of Doctor Turner, where flying through the sky looking for any sign of Chris, Doctor Turner told them to land at his lab. "It's nearby," he said, "and we can use my equipment to find Ichigo."

They ran in the moment they landed, Neneko realized the place was swarming with police, so she said, "Stand back—let me deal with this."

"What, are you crazy, girl?" shouted Turner. "There are too many of them! I can count twenty of them from here." But he watched her walk up to the officers unafraid.

"Don't worry Dr. Turner," Pie-way assured him. " Neneko can take care of herself." They watched Neneko approach the officers. When they, saw her, they yelled out to her to halt, but she didn't stop. And they pointed their guns at her, ready to drop her.

When she wouldn't stop, the leader of the group said, "Fire,!" The bullets bounced off an invisible force field. Neneko's, eyes started to glow, as she fired stun beams at each one of the officers, dropping them before they could think of what to do.

Neneko then turned back to the others and said, "It's safe to come out."

"That was incredible!" said Destiny. But Neneko didn't even have time to be embarrassed.

Turner was in shock. He figured that girl could probably take down an army by herself, it was no wonder her powers had been contained.

Turner opened the door to his lab and went right to work to find Ichigo. The girls stood around his computers watching. The good news was when he found her she was still on the planet, but he could tell that she was moving fast and was in the air. That meant that she was in a hover car, and whoever had her, was heading to the spaceport. They didn't have a lot of time left. Lorelei looked at the monitor thinking that, if only Chris was were with them, he could get to her faster than any of them.

xxx

Meanwhile, Jura was working as fast as she could trying to fix Striker's circuits. Weakly, Chris reported to her that his back up power was about gone, Jura said, "I've got almost all the connections made. This last one should be it."

"I hope so," he said, trying to sound confident for her sake.

Suddenly, Chris could feel his power returning. He remained still for a moment until he felt strong enough, as he stood up. He managed to hug Jura. "I knew you could do it!" he told her. "Thank you!"

"Now you can do the rest of the work yourself, right?" Jura asked.

"That's the plan, Aruj." He said to her.

"It's Jura," she corrected.

But he turned to her and said, "That's what I said, —Aruj." And he went back to working on himself.

A few minutes latter, he had his arm reconnected and was doing some more repairs. As he stood with his back to Jura, he said, "I'm seventy percent repaired, but I s-still having a p-problem talking straight."

"I can't believe that a woman did this to you," said and Jura.

"Everyone has the capacity for evil," said Chris. "Even women. Even m-me."

"No way," Jura yelled out. "You don't have an evil bone—or piece of metal—in your body."

Chris still did not turn to face her. "No," he said, "no that's not true even I have the capacity for evil. No one is immune to it. Even now, all I c-can think about is r-revenge."

He turned around to her with a look in his eyes, that she had never seen before. It startled her a bit, but she still stopped him from moving as she stepped in front of him and asked, "What do you plan on doing?"

"I plan on k-killing them all!" Chris stated coldly.

"These are serious guys, and you're in no condition to be picking a fight with them!" Jura said. "You're not up to full power."

"I'm ok-kayay kay," he said, " just a few bugs to work out … in … out … in." Chris shuttered out.

"Yeah, sure, listen to yourself! You can't even talk straight!" Jura was starting to get mad, as she yelled out the last part.

Chris then grabbed her by her shoulders and kissed her, full on the mouth. Then he stood back and said, "A man's got to do, what a man's got to do," He moved her a side, as walked around her, and headed for the door. But he missed the door and slammed right through the wall.

Jura stood for a few seconds in shock, touching her lips. She could still feel his lips on hers. It was something she had to admit she had never done before. She was one of the few who had never been with a man. She had only fought them. After a minute, she shook herself out of her daze, as she took off after Chris. "Wait up, you stupid man!" she yelled.

Chris ran straight back to the spot where he had been beaten up. Jura caught up with him. "You won't find them, here," she told him. "They're long gone."

"Find I will," he stated as a few sparks shot from his neck. He scanned the area with a the spectral scanner in his eye, and then he found the vehicle that they had used to get away.

"There they are," he told her.

"You found them?" Jura asked. "Can you see where they're going?"

"No problem," he said. "Hop on my back. I may not be able to transform right now, or fly, from the damage, but I can still jump."

Jura climbed on his back, as he leaped into the air, ricocheted off a building, and soared skyward.

xxx

The girls where flying, as fast as Neneko could take them. First, they where trying to find Chris, but, when they got there, they found that he was gone. Lorelei saw something near the area where Chris was taken, Lorelei ran up to the spot.

There was the silver fluid on the ground and Lorelei knew that it was from Chris. She knew he was bleeding to death. "We have to find him now," she told the others. "And we have to find Ichigo. If we don't find them soon, it may be too late." They took off into the air again.

xxx

Rachel, Maverick, and Gun-hand Hand where in their hover car on their way to the spaceport when Maverick looked out the rear window. He saw Chris jumping and following them on the heavily traveled route. The cyborg was jumping from car to car heading their way, "I don't believe it!" He said.

Rachel looked behind her, as she saw this, Ichigo turned as well. When she saw him Chris, tears of joy steamed down her face.

"We have to lose that thing!" Gun-Hand yelled out. Maverick floored the accelerated to the max, leaving, Chris and Jura in it's wake.

"We'll never catch them now," Jura said as Chris leaped onto another hover car.

But then Chris smiled as he noticed a paved drainage ditch along a nearby roadway. "There is still the short cut," he said.

Jura shook her head saying. "No way!"

"Trust me" he said.

Chris jumped a good thirty feet to the pipe flew along it until it went underground. Soon they were flying along in the pitch dark.

xxx

As Neneko and the others were flying, Minawa contacted them. "I have a good connection with Chris!" she told them. "He's okay, but he's not at full power. I can guide you to him. He's was going after Ichigo."

"Thanks," said Lorelei. "We're ready to follow your direction."

xxx

Rachel and her men finally made it to the spaceport and landed safely. They believed that they had lost the cyborg, but unknown to them he was closer than they thought. From their position in the drainage pipe, Chris reached up and lifted a manhole cover up under the hover car. As Chris started to looked around, as Jura asked, "Can you see them?"

"Shh!." " Quiet!" said Chris.

"Quiet? Do you know what just floated past me down here?" Jura said to him with a disgusted tone to her voice.

Striker moved the manhole cover aside and grabbed the threesome's hover car. Jura said, "What are you doing now?"

"Pumping iron!" He told her as he picked up the car. Inside the car, Rachel asked, "Why are you flying up? We're here already!"

"I'm not doing anything!" he said. "The car is moving on its own!" As they realized what was happening, it was too late. Striker threw the car as hard as he could. As it, crashed into the spaceport building, with the passengers screaming at the top of there lungs.

Chris helped, Jura out of the hole. He walked to the crashed hover car. Just as he was about to touch it, it shook and Maverick and Gun-Hand jumped out ready to fight.

"Okay, jerk-off," Maverick yelled out, laughing crazily. "You're about to get recycled!

Chris Striker laughed as he said, "Give it your best shot, laughing boy." The two shot into an enormous fight. While that was going on, Rachel managed to climb out of the hover car, and dragged Ichigo out with her. She was about to run away with Ichigo when Jura stepped in front of her.

"Where do you think you're going?" Jura asked as she stood in front of her. Rachel threw a punch, but Jura caught her arm and threw her aside with ease. "Watch it," she said. "You're out of your league!," Jura held Rachel down against the wall as she watched Chris tangle with Maverick and Gun-hand.

"Help me, you idiot!" Maverick yelled to Gun-Hand as he fought Chris.

But Gun-Hand told him, "I can't get a clear shot!" Right then, Chris hit Maverick right across the face sending him flying into the hover car, that they crashed blowing it up. Chris Striker turned around in time to see Gun-Hand, ready to fire at him again. Chris was still able to catch each shot fired at him with ease. When Gun-Hand stopped firing, he believed that Chris would soon kill him, but then Maverick ran up behind, Chris and pummeled him with a piece of pipe that he had grabbed from the wrecked vehicle. But Chris caught, the pipe in it mid swing, without even turning around.

"You rang?" Chris said as he threw Maverick over his shoulder. Chris held his opponent up by his neck. "You stabbed me in the back, you son of a bitch!"

Maverick said,thought "oh shi— ..." but he was cut off as as he was thrown into the air. He came down hard, and was impaled on a radio antenna that was at least a few stories high.

Chris Striker then turned his attention to Gun-Hand. As Chris walked up to him, Gun-Hand put his hands behind his head and said, "I give up! " "I don't want to fight you!"

But Chris continued forward. When he stood inches from him Gun-Hand, just jerked forward, making Gun- Hand to turn to run. But Gun-Hand didn't realize that there was a wall right behind him, and he slammed right into it knocking himself out cold.

"Baka!" Chris said as he grabbed Gun-Hand and tied him to a fence. Jura, who was laughing at the sight of Gun-Hand knocking himself out. But then Rachel took advantage of Jura's distraction and punched her right in the stomach. Jura fell over, against the wall, barely holding herself up. Rachel then took the opportunity to grabbed Ichigo and ran.

Jura was coughing and doing her best to let Chris know that Rachel was running away. Finally, she managed to take a deep breath. "Chris!" she yelled out. When he turned, he saw Jura pointing behind indicating that Rachel, was getting away with Ichigo.

Rachel ran right into the spaceport. Once inside, she yelled to her men, "Release the robot drones!" When they asked how many, she told "All of them! Don't let that Cyborg get me!" .

With that, Rachel ran on with Ichigo, to her space ship. She believed that she would make it.

Chris saw the robot troops come out of everywhere, in uncountable numbers, but he wasn't about to be stopped. He, shot into the army of drones, fighting each one like mad. He was still hurt, and his body was coming close to its limit. At one point, he fought several drones at once, tarring one in half and used the two have's like bats, swinging at the others in a rage.

Neneko landed, at the spaceport with the others. When Lorelei ran up to Jura, who limped from the side of the building, Lorelei asked, "Where is Chris? I think he's bleeding badly and losing power fast. If we don't stop him, he is going to die."

Jura then pointed in the direction of the army of drones. Lorelei and the girls couldn't see what was going on, but, when they heard

Chris roar out, they recognized him. They could not, however, get close enough to help him.

Chris was still fighting off the drones, when he saw Rachel's ship lift off, into the air. He roared out, "You are *not* getting away from me! I am truly *pissed off!!!!*"

He powered up as high as he could as he fired off a shotgun blast, that wiped out the remaining drones. Then, using every bit of power that he could muster, he shot into the sky. The force that he let out when he took off created a creator where he had stood.

Rachel was piloting her ship and feeling as if she had gotten away scot-free, but then an alarm went off, in her ship indicating that something was coming her way, and it was moving faster than anything that she had seen before. *It can't be, the cyborg*, she thought. *He's too damaged to fly!* But that thought was thrown out the window, when he burst through the wall of her ship.

The cyborg was glowing black as night, and his face didn't seem like the same face of a man who would never hurt anyone. He looked like a man who was, willing to do whatever it took, to get a job done—even if it involved killing.

Chris grabbed both Rachel and Ichigo, and jumped back through the ship's hall felling straight to the ground, with Rachel yelled out, "You're crazy! You're going to kill us all!"

"Sometimes crazy works!" Chris yelled, back. Then he turned around and held the two, close as he slammed into the ground with monstrous force.

Rachel, slowly sat up as the dust started to clear. She, and Ichigo where fine. Chris absorbed the full extent of the fall. "What the hell are you?" Rachel said to the dying warrior.

As this went on, Lorelei and the others seeing the crash ran to the site with fear in there hearts. Lorelei was the first to get to Chris. As she looked him over, the others grabbed Rachel, and held her so she couldn't get away.

"Chris, what is wrong with you?" Lorelei asked Chris, in a panic. "Where is your ancillary power?" Chris lay on the ground with his head in Lorelei's lap.

Jura asked, "What are you talking about?"

"His ancillary power!"

"Do you mean his backup battery?"

"Yes!!"

"Its dead," said Jura. "He used it up already." She turned to Rachel, who seemed as if she was still the winner, of this ordeal. But then Jura walked up to her and said, "This is all your fault!" Then she punched Rachel as hard as she could right in her face, knocking the woman unconscious.

Right then Destiny arrived from the main ship, ready to get started on Chris's recovery. She had been waiting on the ship for a call, and, when Minawa told her to go, she had left as fast as she could. But, when she saw how damaged he was, she turned to Lorelei. "I don't know where to start."

"I don't care where you start, just as long as it keeps him alive!" Lorelei shot back.

Chris slowly and painfully turned his head to them. With a weak voice as he said, "Good-bye. everyone. I love— ... ..." but he didn't finish. His head dropped limp in Lorelei's lap.

Lorelei grabbed him and shook him, saying, "You can't leave us like this!" She looked around for some way to save him. When she looked up, she saw Neneko starting to cry. She yelled at Neneko, "Stop crying! Get over here, and help me!" Neneko did as she was told, but didn't know what Lorelei had planned.

"Listen, Neneko," said Lorelei, "I want you, to use as much of your own power as you can, and shock him with everything you've got!!"

"What?"

"Just *do it!*!"

"All right," Neneko said. She took a deep breath and rubbed her hands together, to ready the charge. Then she put her hands on Chris's chest and ... ...

A shock exploded around her. But Chris's condition remained the same. "Do it again!" Lorelei yelled. "But with more power!" Neneko followed the Supreme Elder's orders, but Chris remained unchanged.

"Again!" Lorelei said. Neneko charged up more power, and fired it right at Chris's chest. This time, he jumped up from the shock as electricity changed through him, but his condition didn't improve.

Jura then pushed her way through the rest of the girls. She grabbed Chris and shook him. "I won't let you go like this!" she yelled yelling at him.

She Jura started to beat on his chest. "Live!" she screaming screamed at him. "I'm sorry for all the terrible things I said." But there was still nothing.

The others could not believe what they were seeing and hearing. Despite Jura's words, Chris didn't move. Giving up, Jura fell onto his chest, weeping. Suddenly, Jura felt his body jerk.

She sat up and watched. His one organic eye started to open. Then his cybernetic eye, started to glow slowly.

"Please say something," Lorelei whispered.

Chris opened his eyes. He saw the girls all standing around him, all with tears in their eyes. "What's with the tears?" he asked, not realizing that he had almost died.

When he spoke, they were so happy that he was alive, that they could not hold themselves back. They all jumped on him, hugging him tight. "Careful,I'm still petty beat up!"

"Sorry Chris-chan." Neneko said as she pulled away from him. She, wiped some tears from her eyes and said, "We where just so worried about you, … we had thought that you had …—" she didn't finish her sentences for she was still too upset.

"It's good to see all of you too," Chris said, as he tried to smile. "But, right now, I have a one monster of a headache."

As he lay back in Lorelei's lap, she told him, "Don't worry. We'll Chris have you back on your feet in no time at all.

CHAPTER 58

To everyone's astonishment, Chris was back on his feet in only one day, and things started moving in a positive direction. They managed to go, and pick up their supplies without incident. Rachel was now being kept in a holding cell back on the main ship awaiting there return.

Before they returned to the main ship, Doctor Turner invited them to go back to his lab. He wanted to talk to them before they left the planet for good.

"So, Turner," said Lorelei as they entered the lab, " what do you want to talk to us about?"

"Well you see," said Doctor Turner, "its like this: Ichigo, as you call her, is in fact a bio-android. I made her to help the Titan remake a world in his monstrous image, but I could not allowed him to do it. I have asked you to come back here, so I could ask you to take her with you, —to make sure that she doesn't fall into evil hands."

Lorelei looked at Chris and then turned to Ichigo, who had just walked in carrying a tray with cups of tea for everyone. Lorelei turned back to Turner and said, "It's not our decision to make. It's up to her to make that dissension, right Chris?"

"Right," Chris answered thinking the same thing.

Everyone looked up at Ichigo and she looked back, very nervous, for she was not used to making up her own mind, even though Doctor Turner had given her the ability to do so. "Take your time," said Turner.

Ichigo took a deep breath and said, "I would like to go, for you to show me the meaning of freedom, and making decisions for myself., I know that master Chris will stop the Titan once, and for all, and I want to see that day."

"Very well," Turner said. And then he turned to the others. "Please be careful up there. The Titan is dangerous. And there are other things in space that are just as dangerous as the Titan, himself.."

As they were leaving, Chris turned to Turner and told him, "Don't worry about a thing. I'll take care of the Titan very soon, and this area of space will be, free of him forever."

"I don't have any doubt in my mind about that," Turner told him as he shook Chris's hand.

When they finally walked over to Destiny and she transported them back home to there ship.

When they returned to the ship, they where greeted by all the woman, and they were frantic. They had heard bits and pieces of the story of Chris and how he had been hurt. They heard that it was Jura who had saved him. They wanted to know the whole story. Some of the girls volunteered to tell the story. But first Chris wanted to talk to Rachel about a few things, Neneko, and Jura followed him to the cell.

Chris walked in as Rachel was leaning up against one of the walls of her cell. When she saw Chris come in, she stood straight and said, "Well, look who decided to come down and see a condemned woman."

"I didn't come down here for pleasantries," he told her. " I came to ask you a few questions. If you answer them correctly, we might consider letting you go, back to your Lord Titan."

"Really?" Rachel asked letting it the word out slowly.

"Yes, but if you don't cooperate …, well, I can't be held responsible for your well-being."

Rachel laughed knowing full well that Striker can't hurt a women,—that it went against his code. But then he moved to his right. Rachel's face became pale as he said, "That's right. I can't hurt women, but the two lovely ladies behind me can. And, let me tell you, they are in a bad mood, for what you have done to me."

Rachel looked behind Chris at Neneko and Jura. They seemed almost eager to tear her apart at a moment's notice. She gulped as she turned back to Chris and asked, "What do you want to know?"

He found out that Rachel was the first in the line of the Titan's seven generals. He also found out that he had the smartest of the group.

One was a powerhouse of strength, known as Matrix, a robotic warrior that was the strongest of the seven. Then there was Speed Trap a true racing nut.

There was another called, Blade, but Rachel had no information on that one. Viral who was a living computer virus, and the last two led Titan's armada of ships.

"This is not going to be an easy trip," Chris said as Rachel finished telling them about the Titan's seven generals, but then he turned away leaving her.

"Hey, wait!" Rachel yelled out to him. "You said you would let me go, if I answered your questions!?"

"That's right," Chris started, "I did say I would let you go. And I am. I'm letting you go—to those two," Chris said pointing to Neneko and Jura, who were both standing there as they pounding their fists together.

"You see," continued Chris, "they're really upset, over what you have done. And they're not as forgiving as I am." Chris finished as he walked out, and shut the door. He heard Rachel yell out for him to wait, but it was to late Chris just walked off. As he left, he could hear Neneko and Jura beating the crap out of the women.

Chris arrived on the bridge, just in time to see a pod shoot out of the ship. He knowing fool well that Rachel was on it, and probably really beat up too..

Chris saw Lorelei sitting in the captain's chair. Chris, walked up beside her. "Why are all the women giving me strange looks?" he asked.

"Well, Chris, for starters, Jura told them about what you did on the planet. And, second they found out that you haven't bathed since you came here!" she explained. "Some of them are disgusted at the thought. They think that men don't know how to bathe themselves." she said as she got up from her chair.

"Well, you see, I can explain ..."—" Chris started.

"Don't bother,—I know all about it," said Lorelei. "Minawa told me all about it."

"Minawa!!" Chris yelled said angrily. He looked up to the top of the ship knowing that she was listening, but then he said, "It's not just that. I just didn't want to walk in on any of the other crew-members or passengers. I mean, there is only a single bathing area for the whole ship."

Lorelei then grabbed his hand and almost dragged him straight to the shower room. When they stopped in front of the door, as Lorelei pointed to the sign, witch about shocked him out of his mind. There, in bold letters, the sign read: Bath now co-ed, but only for Chris Striker.

Chris turned to Lorelei and said, "You have got to be kidding?"."

"No way!" Lorelei stated. "The crew has to get to know, you very intimately. And the best way for people to get to know you each other, is to bathe together, right?"

"I don't know where you get your logic from," said Chris, " but that is totally insane. I think you mean the way to know them better is to fight them? Chris said to her.

Then Lorelei slapped him on the back side. He jumped at her boldness. "Don't worry about it so much," she said. "Just get in there and start bathing, for all our sakes."

Chris put his hand on the door of the shower room, then stepped forward and then turned and asked, "Is there anyone in there now?"

Lorelei shook her head no. "But Neneko and some of the others will join you shortly," she said with a wink.

Chris wasn't feeling too confident anymore. As he had reasoned before, like he thought before most men would kill for this sort of situation, but him on the other hand, thought that it was impolite to bathe with women. *But,* he figured, *if they want it this way, there is nothing more I can do except get use to the idea of being around them all the time.*

Chris walked into the shower room, and slowly removed his shirt. He was thinking, in fact, a nice long bath did sound appealing.

He had not expected that the place would to be so big,— it seemed more like a spa than a bath house, for the whole ship, but if you think about it made sense.

There were large hot tubes, and rows of showers. The thought of just taking a fast shower did cross his mind, but the thought of a nice hot tub sounded all the more sweeter, so he just showered off and climbed into one of the bigger hot tubs.

As he lay back, he had to admit, he did feel a lot better being clean. And the heat made his cybernetics feel lighter.

As he lay there, he thought about how he had lost track of time, for it, had been a good two weeks since his arrival on the ship. Things had been pretty crazy, and he finally realized just how tired he was.

"Do you like it Chris-chan?" Came a voice from behind him.

He was so relaxed that he didn't realize who it was. "Yeah, it's great," he said without thinking.

He looked up behind him and there was was Neneko along with, Lorelei, and Pie-way and Jura were there. All the girls had towels rapped tightly around them.

"Sorry, I didn't think you guys would come in here. I'll leave." Chris stated.

But, as he was about to get out, Neneko said, "Stop, Chris-chan. It's okay. We just wanted to join you." He settled back down feeling as if he was breaking one of his rules of honor.

"Chris-chan, don't worry so much," Neneko said. "You, know, there is a such as thing as being too honorable." He had always been conscious of his honor. Even when they where kids growing up, that he would always insist on training harder and longer. Even her grandfather, his sensei, would have had to tell him to stop, for the day. But Chris would continue working on his stance or his guard.

"I only train hard so I can protect the ones I care for.," Chris told her. And then he said, "Besides, my honor is the driving force in my life. It is what makes me who I am. And no one else can take that away form from me." He settled back into the water.

CHAPTER 59

Chris was starting to feel really uneasy, as he lay in the hot tub. It seemed to him that all the women were inching closer to him. Suddenly, one of the girls beat them the others to the punch when—Pie-way swam right up to him and cuddled up next to him in the tub. "Thank you again for the stuffed lion you bought for me back on the planet."

Chris laughed uneasily as he said, "It was nothing—a girl like you has got to have fun and play every now and then."

Neneko and the others felt beaten, by the young doctor, but, before they could do anything about it, Chris jumped as he felt an incredible force coming their way. He stood out of the water, freaking out the girls, but had no time to react as an enormous robot burst thought the wall and slammed right into the midst of the hot tubs in the shower room.

The robot stood at least 10 ten feet tall. "I have come to challenge the one called Striker," he announced.

The robot looked as if he had been assembled from a mismatched group of parts. One hand looked normal for his size, but the other hand was skinny with only three fingers. His legs where the same way. But it was his face that stuck out for it looked like a large skull with red eyes that seemed to stare straight into everyone's soul.

Chris slammed his feet to the ground as he transformed to his Alpha Omega Cyber Lion mode.

He was about to attack, when one of the girls all screamed out.,

"Pervert!"And they all began throwing things at the mechanized freak. But the robot wasn't affected. He just fired something out of his hands that captured the girls inside large energy bubble.

"Let them go!" Chris yelled out, as he charged head long at the robot. But the robot caught Chris's arm, and threw him around in the air, then slammed him to the ground. The robot slammed his foot down on his Chris's chest.

"Listen up, Striker," the robot said. "I am Matrix, one of the Titan's greatest generals. I have come to challenge you to a fight. You will comply, —unless you want to see your pretty little bitches crushed like ants."

Striker looked over at the girls, who were still struggling inside the energy bubbles. He knew he had no, choice. "I'll do it," he said.

Matrix lifted his foot from Chris's chest. "In this fight," he said, " there will be no transformations or use of energy techniques. It'll be just fist to fist, … cyborg verses robot, got it!?"

"I got it, Matrix," Chris said as he stood in front of the robot. They stood eye to eye. Chris was still in his Alpha Omega Cyber Lion mode.

"You had better get it, because one little shot of that shotgun of yours and I will have the bubble those girls are in collapse in on itself, killing them," Matrix said as he pointed to the women in the bubble.

Suddenly, Chris looked up when he saw movement near the opening through which the robot had entered the bath house.

He could not believe it, —it was Rachel. Matrix must of have picked her up, on his way here to the spaceship. She smiled at Chris. "This is going to be a fight for the history books," as she said, used a device to control the bubbles the girls where in. She moved the bubble near the entrance.

Matrix then turned to the opening and looked out. He headed out and pointed to a near by planet. "We will meet there in one hour. I hope you're as strong as they say you are. I want a good fight!" Matrix finished as he and his captives disappeared in a flash.

Later, Chris Striker was heading to the hangar in his battle gear. A large number of the crew followed him pleading with him not to fight the robot. They believed that it was a trap.

He turned to face them saying, "I know it's a trap, but I intend to bring them back alive, or I'm not coming come back at all."

Then he flew off into space heading toward the planet and the spot where Matrix waited to meet him.

The girls were not enjoying their time in the energy bubble. Each one had, only a towel to cover herself. They did not like the way Matrix was looking at them—even if he was a robot.

"You know," Matrix began, "Lord Titan would love it if, after I beat the crap out of that cyborg, I bring him all of you as a present—dressed just the way you are."

Hearing this made Neneko feel lost. She had been trying unsuccessfully to break the energy bubbles with her powers, but, no matter what she did, nothing got through. And, having this freak look at her in this condition made her feel so violated. She tried to cover herself with her arms, and she kept her knees close to her.

As for the others, they all just wanted Chris to hurry up and get them out. Lorelei looked down at Rachel who had been left to watch them.

"I hope you're happy," Lorelei said to Rachel. "Not only did you kidnapped us, but you've taken away our dignity as well."

"I am happy," Rachel stated. "And, after Matrix kills your protector, you'll be brought to Lord Titan where he'll do unspeakable things to you."

As they where talking, Matrix had moved outside to his stadium, where he had planned on fighting the cyborg. Just as he was thinking about what he was going to do to him, out of the sky came the over grown Boy Scout.

Chris landed in his normal form. He looked at the energy bubbles containing his friends. Rachel came out of the ground standing next to them, seeming happy with herself.

Striker yelled to the girls, "Hold on! I'll get you out that real soon."

But Matrix laughed and said, "You'll have to beat me first!"

"Then that simplifies things!" Chris yelled as he charged. The two warriors attacked each other with thundering punches and kicks, but Matrix seemed to be the stronger of the two. To demonstrate, he grabbed Striker's next punch and threw him over his shoulder and into the seats of the stadium.

As Chris started to get up, Matrix ran up over the chairs at incredible speed. He slammed Chris against the wall hard, then he grabbed his arm and threw him straight back to the stadium floor where he landed with an earth- shacking thud.

Chris looked up in time to see Matrix jump at him, but they slammed fist to fist, each trying to push the other back.

Matrix laughed and said, "Is that all you've got? It would appear that, without your transformations, you're nothing!"

When the others heard the metal freak mock Chris, they yelled out for him to push the robot back. But, despite their cheering, Chris Striker was the one slowly being pushed back against the wall. Then Matrix punched him hard against the wall and threw him to the middle of the stadium floor again.

Chris looked up to see Matrix coming back down out of the sky. He rolled out of the way just in time, as the robot slammed into the ground making a creator in his wake.

Matrix jumped out of the hole and slammed into Chris as they grappled hand to hand again. As Matrix pushed Chris back again he laughed and said, "Is this all there it to the great Super Cyborg? If that is the case, you don't deserve to fight the Titan." And Matrix pulled back and then punched Chris to the ground with another earth -shattering strike that shook the area.

When the dust cleared, Chris Striker was lying on the ground, with sparks shooting out of his damaged body. But he managed to pull himself up to his hands and knees as Matrix roared "I have *won!*"

"All right, fine—you win," Chris stated. "Now let my friends go."

"*No!*" Matrix said as he turned around and started to walk to his captives. Rachel stepped aside as the robot turned to face Chris again. "These women will make fine trophies to give to Lord Titan," he said. " I plane on giving them to him dressed just as they are."

Chris, hearing this, felt all hope was lost, for there was no way, he could win. His honor was now gone. As he slowly stood and started to walk out of the stadium, the others yelled out for him to keep fighting. He heard Neneko say, "You can, still win!"

But, as he walked, he said, "No I can't." And he left the stadium.

"Ha, ha!" Matrix laughed. "It seems that I was right. Without those transformations, he's nothing, but a weakling. I am all robot, and he is only human."

Chris walked through the ruins of the planet, where Matrix resided. He felt that he had flailed them all — Neneko, Pie-way, Lorelei, and Jura. He flailed to protect them as he had promised he would.

"You know that you're a lot stronger than you're letting on. You know you can still win," came a voice from behind him. Chris knew who it was.

"Minawa, there is no way that I'm going to go all out," Chris told to her. He wasn't surprised to hear her voice, for he knew that she had kept a link between him, so they could talk to each other. "I swore that I would never use my full strength ever again. You know that it is too dangerous to do so."

"It may be dangerous, but right now it is the only way to save them!" said Minawa. "For, as I've told you, you can't live in the past, or you'll be doomed to repeat it."

Matrix was talking to Lord Titan. The Titan's image appeared on a large screen. He was expressing how happy he was, about what Matrix had told him about how he beat the Super Cyborg. He was also happy about the capture of his enemies. As Matrix showed off his captives to the Titan, Matrix had just told Titan how weak the human cyborg was. But, suddenly, the door behind him blew open and Chris walked in pounding his fists together with every step.

"Humans, aren't as weak as you think, Matrix," Chris said to him as he stepped up in front of the behemoth.

"You must have a death wish?!" Matrix said. Then charged at Chris. They slammed together as they blew outside into the stadium where Rachel raised the captives to the top of the stadium again so they could watch the fight.

The two had at it, tearing the stadium apart, but nothing seemed different about the fight. Chris was still being beaten down.

After a punch that sent Chris sliding into the wall, Matrix walked toward him. "Why did you come back? You should have known that you don't stand a chance in hell against me!"

"It's because those women, that you captured are important to me," Chris said as he pushed a large stone out his way. It had fell when he slammed into the wall as he walked out of the rubble.

"Important!" shouted Matrix. "What's so important about them? "There weak,—there only humans, and, after all, human's are weak!"

"They're not weak! There strong fighter's who will fight you and the Titan's men to their dying breath. But me—I have another problem," he continued. Chris hit Matrix so hard that he slammed to the other side of the stadium. As he shook off the shock of being hit, so hard, he saw Striker moving to him again.

"What the?" Matrix said not believing the power that Striker had put into in that last punch.

"You know, ever since I became a cyborg, I've felt like, I live in a world made of cardboard," said Chris calmly. "I'm always holding back, always afraid I might hurt someone or even kill someone. I can't even hold a woman in my arms without the fear of crushing her. But, in the end, it seems there is but one job for me, and that is to fight. And that provides us all a rare opportunity for you and the Titan to witness, just how much of a *Super Cyborg* I am!!"

Striker finished as he shot forward. As Matrix reared back preparing a punch, as Neneko detected that the energy levels were rising faster than anything up to the that point. She started to shake with fear, and that's when she screamed out to the others, "Cover your ears, ladies! Prepare yourselves! This is going to be big!""

Time seemed to move in slow motion as Striker punched forward at Matrix. When his punch made contact, the impact let out a shockwave, that not only knocked Matrix though, the stadium wall, but out of the stadium it blew the others girls free of the energy bubbles.

After punching Matrix, Striker disappeared. Rachel, who was almost deaf from the shockwave, said, "Striker had to of have transformed in order to do that to Matrix."

Lorelei walked up to her. Holding her towel around her with all the dignity she could muster, she said, "Chris did not transform. What you saw was only pure cybernetic strength."

Matrix was still flying through the ruins of the cities. He had just plowed through four buildings when Chris appeared above him, and clapped his hands together, and slammed the robot straight through a fifth building. Chris Striker then crashed down at Matrix, and punch at him again and again. "This is for treating my Gems the way you did!" He yelled out to Matrix angry about the impure way, he kept those girls it was no way to treat ladies like them, he then slammed down at Matrix's head again until his head mashed to the point all Striker was hitting, was concrete and broken metal parts.

The others, by now, had captured Rachel and tied her up. They had even managed to find clothing to cover themselves with. As they waited for Chris to return, but they did hear the sounds and felt the force of his strikes on Matrix. When they could hear nothing more, and they knew that Chris had won.

Right as they where wondering where he was, they heard him yell out. They turned to see him holding the remains of Matrix above his head. Then he threw the body of the once-strong, Matrix to the stadium floor, where it landed in a crumbled heap. Chris then jumped to the ground and walked over to the others, where he saw Rachel shaking like crazy in fear.

"Is everyone okay?" Chris then asked.

But Lorelei asked a question of her own: "Where did that strength came come from? I have scanned you dozens of times, and I have never detected anything that, indicated that you had that kind of power! It, makes no sense,—you should not have that kind of strength. It goes beyond anything that should be possible with cybernetics?!"

Chris didn't seem as if he cared what Lorelei was talking about. He asked Minawa to send Destiny to pick them up because they were all tired. In a flash, Destiny appeared, and transported them back to the ship. Once there, Lorelei stepped in front of Chris, and started to demanded to know where his strength had came come from.

"Back off Lorelei." He told her.

"I want to know, where that strength of yours came form?"

"You want to know where that strength came from?" Chris yelled, said. "Then ask Minawa." And he turned and headed off in the direction of the hanger.

CHAPTER 60

After that Lorelei, and the others had showered and had gotten dressed, they met on the bridge of the ship, where they knew they could talk to Minawa. Lorelei then called to her to come out. "I have a bone to pick with you," she said. When Minawa appeared, she didn't seem too happy about, telling everyone the secret that Chris had been keeping for so long.

"Minawa, you will tell me now," Lorelei shouted. "How can Chris be so strong? I did a dozen scans on him and never detected anything like this before."

Minawa took a deep breath as she started to tell them the whole story. " Back when Chris first became a cyborg," she began, "long before any of you met him, I had him train in a dessert area. I thought that we were far enough away from anyone or anything that might get in our way.

During the test, I found that he was going beyond, even my expectations in speed and strength. During one test of strength against some automated tanks, one punch to one of the tanks let out a shockwave that shattered a dozen of the tanks and sending sent parts and derby debris everywhere. Chris let himself get carried away. He threw two more of the tanks into the air. We didn't even know where they landed, latter we found that they fell on a town over hundred miles away. Hundreds of people were seriously hurt or killed, but the whole thing was covered up as an accident ... people were told that a cargo plane, had dropped its supplies while on a run. But for Chris he knew what he had done. He swore that, form that day, he would never use his full strength ever again—until today that is."

After hearing the story, they all understood why he had kept that strength a secret. With that kind of strength, he must be even afraid of himself sometimes.

xxx

Chris was in the hanger, he was doing a hand stand on one -finger doing push ups, when he felt Neneko's presence in the room. He jumped out the possession and asked, "Has Minawa told you the story yet?" She just nodded. "Well, now you know," he said, "that's why I never used my full strength."

"You should of have told us the story," she said, "and not kept it a secret from us, and— especially from me! I care about you more then than anything, you know that,." Chris turned away from Neneko..

"You don't know what it's like," Chris startedsaid, "to always hold back … to know that, if I let go, for even one moment, I could crush you. And, besides that, not being able to feel … it's like …"

Neneko thought of something she grabbed his shoulders and spun him around. When he was facing her, she forced a deep kiss on him she kissed him deeply and pushed him against the wall. When he tried to grab her, she took his arms and pushed him down as she pushed the kiss deeper.

When they broke apart, he was about to ask what had gotten into her, but she put a finger to his lips to quiet him. "If you're worried about hurting me," she said softly, " then let me do all the work. I'll feel for the both of us."

As she kissed him again, tarring his shirt. Whatever had gotten into her, one thing was for sure sure—he was in her control and there was nothing he could do to stop her.

As this was going on Minawa, who had the whole ship monitored, the two making love in the hanger. And that's when she got a seductive idea. She snapped her fingers and piped a feed of Chris and Neneko making love into every adult's room hoping to get a very interesting result out of it in the mourning.

Chris awoke the next mourning feeling exhausted and spent, for Neneko had not once let up on him as they lay in the make shift bed that he made out of mats. As someone tap him on the metal side of his head. When his cybernetic eye focused, he saw Lorelei standing over him with an unusual smile on her face.

"Lorelei, what are you doing in my room?" Chris said still half asleep.

She smiled again as she laughed and said, "You're not in your room."

The memories of the night before flooded in, to Chris's consciousness, and he was about to stand up, but there was something on top of him him—Neneko had fallen asleep on top of him. And it was a good thing they where had used his trench coat as a blanket for they were both nude.

He tried to shake her awake, but she waved her hand at him and said, "Chris-chan, let me sleep."

"You had better get up," he said. "We have company."

Neneko opened one eye, and saw Lorelei. She shot up grabbing the coat to cover herself. "How long have you been there?" she asked Lorelei.

Lorelei laughed. "Long enough," she said. "But that's not why I'm laughing. The point is how you two have really got the crew into an uproar."

"Uproar, what are you talking about?" Neneko asked, grabbing more of the trench coat. Chris to jumped for his pants, which surprisingly had survived in one piece.

Lorelei could barely contain herself, as she told Neneko what Minawa had done. A blush deeper than anything appeared on Neneko's face. She could not believe that the whole crew had seen her and Chris.

Chris, on the other hand, was shocked and angry at Minawa for, what she had done. He yelled out to her, but all he heard was her laughter, witch told him, that she had planned the whole thing. There was always a plan to Minawa's actions.

"What is going on?" asked Neneko, confused.

Before Chris could answer, Lorelei said, "Minawa planned on Chris breeding with the crew-members.

"What!" Was was all Neneko could say. She was in shock.

Lorelei was opened her mouth to explain, but Chris asked her, "What happened to that money, I won? I thought you were supposed to be coming up with something for you to build that would solve that problem."

Lorelei turned to him. "That device already did its job, for all it was supposed to do, was enable the women to bear male children again. That possibility had been removed at one time."

"Why?" Neneko asked as she started to look for her clothes.

"Because my people didn't want to risk a chance that another Titan would be born," She still had an interesting look on her face,—a look that made Chris move back away. He was almost afraid of her gaze.

"So you're telling me that you only want my Chris-chan to be, the one man on this whole ship? There is no way, he will live long enough to do the whole job."

Lorelei seemed amused by this. "Remember?" she said to Nenko. "Chris is not going to grow old! He is, as you humans put it, immortal. Haven't you noticed that, in all the years, you've been with him, that he hasn't aged a day sense you met, again?"

"I just thought that it was me," Neneko said. "He just always looked good to me."

"Well, don't get to worked up over it," continued Lorelei. "You'll never age any either! So I think that you two where made for each other,—or I should say 'of each other, sense you're both made up of the same metal."

xxx

After there talk with Lorelei, Neneko went to talk to Minawa. She was angry. When she got to the computer room, she yelled out, " Minawa show Show yourself!"

Minawa appeared. "What's wrong?" she asked simply.

"What's wrong?!" Neneko almost yelled. "You invaded our privacy."—Chris's and mine!"

"Listen, Miss Neneko," Minawa began, "I did that to show my people that men, can be controlled just as easily as women, I mean, come on, you had him right where you wanted him, and there was nothing he could do despite his strength."

Neneko thought that she was right, Chris-chan hadn't even dared to move. She had him where she wanted him even though he was actually strong enough to get out of it, any time he wanted.

As Neneko thought about this, Minawa turned away as if she was looking at something else. Suddenly, Neneko noticed that Minawa had focused her attention on one of the monitors. "What's wrong?" Neneko asked the holographic image of the woman.

"There is a large ship, coming our way," responded Minawa.

She paused for a minute, and then said with excitement, "It's one of our ships!"

Suddenly, alarms where going off all over the ship. Lorelei burst her way onto the bridge to find out what was going on. When she saw the ship right in front of them, she turned to a crew-member. "Can you hail the ship? I want to make sure it really is one of ours, and not some deception.

Neneko had run off to summon Chris, they soon arrived on the bridge, and stood next to Lorelei. Chris asked, "what's up, is that ship really one of yours?"

Lorelei turned to him and then looked back at the ship in front of them. "That's not just one of our ships," she told everyone. "That's one of the first ships to ever escape our planet and get away from the Titan before he conquered the planet.

As Striker looked at the ship, and right then one of the screens on the console in front of him came on. A woman appeared. She looked near death.

"Sister!" Lorelei yelled, as she recognized the woman.

The woman spoke slowly and quietly: "Please help us. Our life-support systems have been corrupted.

Lorelei turned to Chris to tell him to go, but he was already out the door, heading for the hangar. He, ran and jumped straight out the hangar doors and flew straight to the distressed ship.

Striker hit the ship and tore a hole into it, in order for him to get inside. After he was inside, he sealed the hole and ran as fast as he could to the bridge of the ship. There he found the woman that Lorelei had called sister. She looked at Chris with a worried expression. Obviously assumed that he was there to kill them all in their weakened state. Other crew-members were lying on the bridge, either unconscious or dead—he could not tell. He went to one of the consoles and called the others back on the ship.

As he was talking to Minawa and Lorelei, the women lying next to him asked, "Who are you?"

"I'm a friend," he said. The women seemed shocked at this statement.

"Minawa, what should I do to get the ship back online?" Chris asked.

Minawa said, "Plug your hand into the auxiliary communications port on the console. I'll use your link to the ship.

Chris reached out to do as he was told. *"No!"* yelled the woman. But it was too late. Chris plugged his hand into one of the the ports. Immediately, he was electrocuted, which shouldn't have happened because he was completely insulated. Minawa on the other ship felt the electrocution as well.

Minawa cried, "It's a virus! I have to sever our link before the virus infects me and the ship."

Minawa immediately broke the link. Minawa breathed hard a couple of times, after she severed the link she looked back at the other ship wondering what was happening to Chris.

Striker was still being electrocuted. Suddenly, however, a blast wave seemed to hit him and he was propelled back against a wall. When he hit the wall, the power seemed to come back on in the ship. He could hear the life-support, systems kick in. He watched, the crew-members as they stood back up with new life in them. Lorelei's sister walked up to Chris, but he just looked around quickly, and then ran off to a corner of the room, and slammed right through the wall into space. With the power back on, a force field would seal the hole and protect those inside.

Chris flew fast back to his own ship and crashed right into his ship and ran to the bridge, where he knew Lorelei and the others were.

Speaking in a robotic, metallic voice, he shouted, "Terminate all women on the ship!"

Jura, who had joined the others ran to the bridge, and saw Chris looming over the others. She yelled out to him, and, when he turned around, she thought he didn't seem like himself..

"Chris!" Jura yelled out again. He took a step toward her, when he ran at her, and grabbed her by the neck, and held her against the wall with such incredible force, that she coughed up blood from the impact.

Jura could not move as Chris's grip, became tighter. And a feeling of death came over her as she was about to pass out from lack of air, but then Neneko appeared next to Chris and threw him away from her. As he flipped over and landed back on his feet, Neneko asked Jura if she was okay. All Jura could do was nod as she held her neck and coughed again.

Neneko looked down at Chris, as he started toward her with a look of vengeance. But she stood her ground, not even in a fighting stance. Just as he was about to strike her, she raised her hand and slapped him across his face. It shocked everyone on the bridge, and it shocked Chris as well.

"Christopher William Striker, you snap out of it right *now!!*" Neneko yelled.

Chris shook his head a little bit and looked up at her as he asked, "Why did you hit me?"

Before she could answer, Chris suddenly yelled out in pain as another voice said, "No you don't! This body is *mine* now."

Neneko yelled at Chris again, "Fight it, Chris! You're being infected by a computer virus!"

Striker held his head as he cried out in pain, and stumble around. He slammed into a wall and yelled out louder. The uncontrollable pain would not go away.

"Get out of my head!" He yelled out as he started to pound his head against the wall in the madness that seemed to have infected him.

"Fight it, Chris-chan," Neneko pleaded. Chris yelled out as he started to punch the wall again and again. He yelled out his voice echoed throughout the ship. Soon, however, his body slowed down until it stopped moving. His cybernetic eye went black, and he went still.

"What just happened?" Neneko asked Lorelei, as she fell down next to the prostrate body of the man that she cared for most.

"He couldn't beat it." Lorelei said, "so he shut himself down, —he's off- line."

"You mean he's dead?" Jura said as she walked back toward Chris still holding her neck from the grip that he'd had her in.

"No, far from it," explained Lorelei. "It's as if he's put himself to asleep to keep himself from hurting anyone." Lorelei told her and then turned to Neneko. "How did you know that hitting him would snap him out of the control of the virus?" she asked.

"Oh that." Neneko said. "Well, when we where kids, I used to hit him when he got out of line, or when he wouldn't listen to me."

"So what are we going to do with him?" Jura asked Lorelei as she to looked Chris.

"We first get him to the infirmary, so I can see what I can do to help him stop this virus." Neneko then moved over to him to try and move him, but he weighed a lot more than she expected. The metal that he was made of was very dense. It took all three of them to drag him.

When they finally got to the infirmary, they laid him on a medical table. Lorelei then moved over to him and pulled a cord out of his head and plugged it into a computer. Then she started a diagnostic program. As she had suspected, Chris had cut off all of his motor functions to keep the virus from penetrating any further. But she also found that his will was weakening and soon the virus would have full control of his body. When that happened, there would be nothing that could stand in its way.

"What are we going to do, Lorelei?" A crew-member asked from the doorway. Most of the crew where starting to worry. They understood that Chris was strong enough to kill them all, if he wanted to, and they had heard that he had contracted a virus.

Lorelei shook her head; she wasn't sure what to do.

"This isn't like you, Sister." Came a voice from the group as Lorelei's sister walked through the door. She walked up to Lorelei and put a hand on her shoulder.

"Myra." Lorelei said as she saw her, "when did you get in here?"

"After that cyborg took the virus out of our computers, we hooked our ship with yours and I came aboard to find out what was going on," she told them.

""Do you know what else can we do to help Chris?" Lorelei asked her sister.

"He seems to has been put into a dream state, by the virus," Myra said. "I think the virus is keeping him in this state trying to take control of his body again."

When Lorelei heard what her sister just told her, she turned back to the computer and started to work on something. "If he's in a dream state," she muttered, "we may be able to see what he's dreaming about, and that might give us a clue as to how we can try and help him fight the virus."

xxx

Chris woke up with a start. As he looked around, he realized he was in the temple back home on Earth. *But, how can that be?* he wondered. *I'm, millions of miles away from Earth in space. And what's with that this virus?* But his thoughts were interrupted by someone moving next to him. He jumped up and saw what couldn't be there but was it was—.

Minawa, she was alive and well lying next to him in his futon. *But that's impossible,* he thought. *She was now the computer of the our ship!* But then he looked down at him self. In shock, he fell over as he saw that he wasn't cybernetic anymore—he was totally flesh and blood.

He could feel again, —his hands … everything! He started to think that maybe everything up till now had been just a dream, but what was Minawa doing here? He reached out and touched her. The feel of her skin was more than anything he could of have imagined … so soft and warm. This couldn't be a dream.

When she opened her eyes and looked over at him with a light smile on her face, he jumped back not knowing what was going on. But she stretched and said, "Good morning, Chris," in a sweet voice that made him feel like melting.

When Minawa saw the shocked look on his face, she asked him, "What's wrong?"

He just shook his head a bit and said, "Nothing." But then, as he rolled over, he bumped into something in the bed. When he looked, he found that it was Neneko. She was lying on the other side of him. As he fell on her she mumbled in her sleep saying, "I would love to do it again, but right now I just want to sleep."

The shock of this made him jump onto his feet. He again looked around to find that Minawa and Neneko weren't the only girls that was in the room. There, lying around him, was all the cyborg girls, —all alive and well. As they started to get up, they seemed so surreal to him. But still something wasn't right. As he moved by them, he heard one whisper to another, "What's wrong with *him*?"

Chris stumbled outside, and, sure as he had thought it, he was on Earth, and at his temple. *This makes no sense!* he told himself. *I'm in space, I'm a cyborg! Why have I woken up in such a state?*

"Chris, what's wrong? Don't you want to come back to bed?" He turned to see Minawa as she walked out wearing what seemed to be one of his shirts. It was two sizes too big for her delicate frame, and one of her shoulders was exposed.

"Minawa?" Chris said, "You're supposed to be dead, and so are the others. This can't be real. I was on a ship in space light-years away fighting some aliens …"

His voice trailed off as the girls came up to him.

"That must have been some nightmare?!" Ashley stated as she walked out.

"That's right, Chris," Sakura said. "You're not in space and you're not a cyborg. You're right here where you belong—with us forever." Soon all the girls came out with looks of sexual lust that he had never seen in them before.

Then something hit him.

"Wait a minute!" he told them. "I never told you I was a cyborg in the dream. What's going here?"

It's everything you have ever wanted in life, isn't it?" came a voice from above him. Chris looked up to see a man sitting on top of the temple.

"Hey, who are you? And what have you done to me and to them?" Chris asked, more confused than ever.

The man jumped down to the ground and walked to Chris. "I'm Viral," he said, "but that's not important right now. Here's what's important: this is everything that you have ever wanted. You have your flesh back. All the cyborg girls are here—and Neneko and the whole crew of the ship. They are all here to please you in any way a man could ever want or hope for."

Chris looked at one of the girls then turned back to Viral and said, "These are not my gems. They're not even real—they're just illusions … fakes!"

"They may be fakes, but, let me assure you, they can be as real to you as you want them to be," Viral said as he went to Minawa. She had stopped moving when he showed up. He moved her head to face him and he kissed her, and, when he did, she let out a moan of pure ecstasy that made Chris's blood boil.

"Stop it!" Chris yelled out. "You don't have the right to touch her, whether she's real or otherwise."

Viral turned back to Chris and smiled. "See? Anything you wan't can be yours in *this* world. Anything is possible for you here."

"Then I want' out of here, and back in the real world," shouted Chris. "I don't go for this virtual reality crap!"

"I'm afraid that I can't give you the real world. Lord Titan demands that I finish you and take control of your body," Viral told him. Then he continued, "I wanted to do this the easy way and let you live out your life in this world, but, if you want to do this the hard way, I can do that too."

Viral then changed his own body to look like Chris's cybernetic form. The thought of destroying the Super Cyborg by using his own powers seemed to be so poetic to him.

xxx

Lorelei finally got monitors tuned into Chris's dream. They watched as Chris was about to stand up against a warrior who had assumed all of Chris's own powers while Chris had none. Deep down, they all knew that Chris was going to have his hands full. And, as if they didn't have enough problems, the alarms started to go off all over the ship again.

One of the crew-members ran into the infirmary. "We have a problem!" she yelled.

Lorelei said, "Get in line! We have enough problems as it is! What else can go wrong?"

The crew-member turned to another monitor. They all watched as an armada of ships came their way. "They've found us Myra said in a shaky voice.

"Neneko!" Lorelei yelled out, "take as many of our fighters into the air and hold off these things for as long as possible."

Neneko looked at the image of Chris and then turned to Lorelei and said, "I want to stay and look after Chris-chan."

Lorelei said, "Don't worry. I have everything under control here. All you need to worry about is defending the ship. Besides, you're the only other cyborg that could possibly hold them off."

Neneko hesitated until Lorelei yelled, "Do it, *now!*" Neneko jumped as she ran out the door and headed to the hangar. Lorelei watched on another monitor how she wished that she was more like her sister. She did not feel as confident as she sounded.

Myra put a hand on her shoulder. "Everything will be fine. From what I have heard about this Chris Striker guy, he is plenty strong enough to take care of himself."

xxx

Neneko ran out to the hangar and started to yell out to crew. "Okay, ladies! We have a job to do! We have to defend this ship for as long as we can!" Neneko's voice echoed around as she told them what to do.

The crew readied the mini battle pods faster than they had ever done before and launched them into space ready to fight. As Lord

Titan's armada got closer, Neneko floated out into space; she was able to survive in space using her powers.

"Okay everyone," she said, speaking to all the crew-members through their communication systems. "We are out here to protect this ship. Chris is unable to fight at the moment, so it is up to us to hold them off for as long as it takes. We will not let him down!"

xxx

Chris was not going down without a fight. He assumed his fighting stance and readied himself to attack.

Viral mirrored Chris's stance. Chris attacked. Viral countered the attack so evenly, it was as if he was fighting his own mirror image. They exchanged blow for blow. But, because Viral had Chris's cybernetic body, Chris's, hands started to hurt after the first few strikes. He had no idea how he was going to beat this viral monster.

"How do you like fighting yourself?" Viral asked as he caught Chris's hand mid punch and then twisted his arm, making him fall to one knee in pain.

Viral then moved around Chris and, in one bone-breaking move, snapped his arm right out of its socket. When he let go, Chris stumbled back. Viral was surprised to find that Chris hadn't yelled when he dislocated his shoulder. He was shocked even more when Chris set the bone into place in one move—and one sickening sound.

xxx

When the women on the bridge of the main ship saw this on the monitors, some of them started to feel sick. They believed he must have a will of solid steel to be able to do such a thing to himself without even yelling out in pain.

xxx

The battle outside the ship was heating up too. Although Neneko could not use her fire in space, she was still not' helpless. She could still throw

487

lightning and use her laser eyes. She also had the power to duplicate herself so she could be in six or seven places at once. The women warriors, in their mini battle pods, were able to destroy many of the Titan's armada, but, still, as many ships they took down, it seemed as if there were more coming their way. The armada seemed endless, and the women never realized how much they needed Chris until that very moment. Some of them prayed that he would help them—and soon.

xxx

Chris readied himself again after relocating his shoulder. He had never been more determined to beat an enemy.

"I don't care what you do to me," Chris yelled. "I will never give up! Even if you break every bone in my body, I'll find a way to beat you."

Viral shook his head as he said, "Your determination is refreshing, but it is futile. You can think that you can beat me, but, in my world, I make the rules."

"This world might be yours," countered Chris, "but we're still inside my body, and you can't beat my will or my sprite, no matter where I am!"

Viral still shook his head at Chris's words, then he attacked in a flash of red. Chris felt an impact stronger than any he had ever felt in his life.

The punch almost made him pass out. He landed on his back and skidded on the ground. He landed curled up in a ball of pain.

"Well, Striker," chided Viral, "do you now give up your body to me?"

"I would rather die!" Chris said as he started to rise. But he coughed up blood and fell back down. "I know what you plan to do, after killing me," he said to Viral. "You plan to use my body to kill everyone on the ship. But I won't let you, no matter what you do to me, because I still plan to win this."

Chris managed to stand, but he felt as if he was going to fall over at any moment. That last strike had managed to hurt him seriously. As he stood, Viral attacked with pure cruelty hitting him hard again. Chris slid back to the ground.

xxx

Lorelei and the others could barely watch anymore. It was like watching Chris get tortured. They couldn't do anything but watch in horror. Suddenly, Myra 'asked, "Is it true, sis, that you still have the prototype mimicked beasts here?"

Lorelei turned to her and said, "We do! They're right here! She pointed to the console and Myra pulled out two chips they changed into a bird and the cat. "I need to talk with you." Two animals nodded.

"Good," said Myra. "I must tell you that 'it is up to you to save our friend. You are the only ones who can save him now. Because you are made of pure energy, you can enter Chris's body and help him to find his strength so he can beat this virus once and for all.

"Whoa, wait a minute," interjected Lorelei. "If they do that, they can't become themselves ever again. They'll be permanently fused with him forever!" She moved up.

The cat and bird knew this already for it was what they were made for, to help and strengthen those in need.

The bird and cat turned to Chris's body. They looked at the monitor that was showing them what was happening to him. They saw him get hit again and again. Viral was tearing him apart from the inside out. They knew that they were about to do the right thing. And they vanished inside cyborg's body.

xxx

Chris had managed to hit Viral with a few good shots, but he was on his last legs. He had no strength left. As he was hit again, he fell to one knee. His body was battered and bruised, and he was bleeding badly out of several wounds. He knew that he would not survive another barrage of blows. As Chris watched without hope, Viral raised his cybernetic hand and said', "*Shotgun!*"

Chris saw the beams coming at him. "Sorry for failing," he whispered as the beams hit him and shot right through him in a bloody spray. He slammed to the ground with blood pooling around him.

Viral moved over to him and checked his pulse to make sure that he was dead. When he felt nothing, he walked off with a feeling of satisfaction that showed on his face. But then he turned around because he sensed something happening. Chris's body started to glow. Two beams of light shot out of Chris's chest. Viral blinked. When he opened his eyes, he saw two women, bathed in light. They were standing on either side of Chris and were holding his hands.

"Who the devil are you two?" Viral screeched.

"I'm Mina," said one of them.

"And I'm Dita," said the other. "And we're here to tell you that it's not over. There is nothing that can kill Chris Striker—as long as there are people who love him more than anything."

Mina said, "We'll show you why this fight isn't over."

Mina and Dita's bodies both started to glow again. Then Chris's body also started to glow. When he stood, his wounds were healed. 'He looked at Viral, who was starting to take few steps back. Viral saw that Chris's eyes looked like cat's eyes.

"But this can't be!" shouted Viral. "All your powers are gone! This is *my* world! It runs on *my* rules!" Viral stared at Chris in disbelief. Then it hit him—it was those two. They were breaking the rules of his reality. Viral was pleased, however, to note that Striker still didn't look right. His face seemed lost, as if his mind was gone.

Mina and Dita each touched one of Chris's shoulders. Mina said, "It is time for you to understand just how powerful you are."

Suddenly, he started to glow. Then he roared out a lion's roar as he changed from human to his Alpha Omega Cyber Lion mode. Mina and Dita both turned to Viral who was freaking out. He had no idea how they had been able to altar his reality.

xxx

In the real world, in the spaceship, Chris's body started to change to his Cyber Lion form too, but, because this transformation was different, his cloths tore off as he changed. Myra 'was just thinking how interesting this was getting.

xxx

Chris still didn't feel as if he was conscious. He stood staring blankly at the cyber beast who was Viral clothed in Chris's image. Mina and Dita still stood next to him. Dita smiled and pointed to Viral. "You just wait," she said to the virus. "Once we fuse with Chris, he will be unstoppable." As she said this, their bodies turned to two balls of energy that shot around Chris's body several times before they shot into his hands. When they did this, two jewels appeared on the backs of his hands, a blue one on his left hand and a red one on his right.

Chris seemed to wake up right at that moment. He shook his head as he realized that he was still alive—but he was in his Alpha Omega Cyber Lion form! Then he noticed the jewels on his hands and wondered what they were. He got his answer when they started to glow and say, "We are now part of you, and we will help you from now on."

Viral was starting to get scared. He seemed to realize that, with those two helping him, Chris would be able to override Viral's ability to control the world he had created.

Chris moved toward Viral with a stern look on his face, ready to fight. But Viral would not have this—he attacked first.

When Viral punched, the shockwave that hit Chris was impossibly powerful, but it had no affect on the Super Cyborg. Chris smiled as he backhanded Viral to the ground. Viral seemed to be scared out of his mind by the power he felt from the cyber beast before him. He seemed more powerful than he had ever been before. It was as if he had been reborn during the fusion with those mimetic beasts.

The cyber beast's eyes glowed red as he approached Viral. His body was glowing black. "You know, Viral," said Chris, "we all have our inner demons, even if we don't show them. They are there, waiting to be released into the world."

"What are you talking about?" cried Viral. "What do you mean, inner demons?" Fear started to build up in him for the first time in his life.

"Let me show you," Striker said as he cracked his knuckles.

xxx

Neneko and the other fighters had been pushed back to their ship. Many of their pods had been destroyed; there were only four left that could fight. They were still trying to hold the line and keep the Titan's forces away from the ship, but now it looked as if they were at their limit. Neneko's body was bruised and battered, but she was determined to hold the line. For as long as she had breath, she would fight. She looked at the armada of ships that still stood in their way. She wished with all she was worth that her Chris-chan was there to help. She was sure that the battle would be over by now if he had been there.

In the infirmary, inside the main ship, the others saw Chris's image disappear from the monitor. They had no idea if he was all right or not, but they got their answer suddenly, as his physical body started to glow and then started to change again. As he stood, his fiery red hair shot straight up and took on the appearance of silvery fire as his whole body seemed to change from the red to silver—he was now in Silver Cyber Lion mode.

'No one said a word as he stood already knowing what had to be done. He bolted from the infirmary. In a split second, he was floating next to Neneko. When she saw him, her heart seemed to skip a beat.

"Chris-chan," she yelled out. He smiled at her and then turned to the armada of ships that stood before him. He clapped his fists together and roared, *"Power Shotgun!"*

This was not his normal shotgun blast. Not only was it bigger than anything he had ever fired, but each beam seemed to have a life of its own. Each beam sought out a separate enemy, but left the women's pods untouched as if it could distinguish friend from foe.

The destruction was becoming overwhelming for the Titan's armada. In the end, they retreated with only a couple of ships intact.

When Chris was finished, he turned back to Neneko. She collapsed in his arms with a smile on her face. "Arigato, Chris-chan." And she fell unconscious.

CHAPTER 61

"So, Chris, tell us what happened while you were in that dream state?" Lorelei asked after things had settled down and they could take a breath.

"I don't' know all the details," Chris said sadly, "but I do know that now Mina and Dita are a part of me. I can still feel that they are very much alive, but there's no way I can separate from them. The fusion is permanent."

As Chris finished speaking, Myra stepped up to him and circled him as if she was checking him out or something.

"Is there something I can do for you, miss?" Chris said jokingly as the woman looked up at his face and then looked him up and down as if she had never seen a man before.

"You are amazing," Myra said, and she hugged him tightly. Chris was in shock. He didn't even know this woman, and here she was hugging him as if he was a long-lost child!

"Myra, please, control yourself!" Lorelei said. "You haven't even introduced yourself!"

"Oh, yes, how rude of me," Myra said as she let go of the cyborg and straightened herself out. She bowed to Chris and said, "I am Lorelei's older sister, Myra." Myra winked, which made Chris take a step back. He was feeling a little nervous around this woman.

"Nice to met you," he said as he moved around the woman, who seemed to still be looking at him as if he were a piece of meat. Chris stood behind Lorelei and whispered to her, "That woman scares me."

"Don't worry," said Lorelei, "she scares me too."

"Sister," Myra said as she turned to Lorelei, "since we are safe for the time being, would you be willing to let me borrow this man for a while?"

But Lorelei shook her head. "No, I can't do that. He isn't a slave! He is our protector. If you want anything from him, you will have to ask him directly."

Myra then smiled at Chris, who seemed to be trying to disappear behind Lorelei. "Would you help me with something?" she asked. "One of the Titan's generals is on a nearby planet where my people have stationed themselves. He is terrorizing them." She batted here eyelashes at Chris and continued, "But this general enjoys a race! He has promised that, if one of us can beat him in a fair race, he will leave and never come back. So far, we have not been able to find anyone who can beat him.

"But, if I race him using this new form of mine," Chris finished for her, "I might be able to beat him, right?"

"Yes, that's right," said Myra. "But there's more. This general races on a giant cheetah that is indigenous to that planet. And he insists that our challenger also rides one of these large animals. No matter what we do he still beats us."

"So you were hoping that, since I can turn into a giant Cyber Lion, you could ride me and win this race to get rid of this tyrant?"

"That's right," squealed Myra. "Will you do it for me and my people?"

Chris moved out from behind Lorelei and faced Myra. "All right," he said, "but no funny stuff, you got me?"

"No problem," Myra finished with a smile. "Come on, we have to hurry. My ship is in the hangar. But, as they were leaving, Lorelei remembered something. "Whatever happened to Viral?" she asked.

"Oh him," Chris said, smiling. "We won't be seeing him again."

"Why? What did you do to him?"

"Let's just say he's fighting with some of my inner demons."

xxx

Meanwhile, deep inside Chris's mind, Viral was running for his life. His body was torn and battered, but he still was running. The look on his face was one of pure terror. An enormous beast ran right on his tail. It had glowing red eyes and a black fiery mane, and, when it roared, it shook every fiber in Viral's being. Viral yelled out for help, but no one would ever hear him. He would be running for his life for all eternity.

xxx

As Chris and Myra approached Myra's ship in the hangar, Neneko ran up to Chris. She had refused medical attention and had run after Chris despite Pie-way's protests that she was not healed yet. "Chris-chan, where to you think you're going?" Neneko said as she stumbled to him doing her best to stand on her wobbly feet, for she still felt dizzy from the fight.

Chris shook his head when he saw how stubborn she was being. "I'm going with Myra to help out on her planet with one of the Titan's generals who is terrorizing them. I'll be back soon. Please take care of yourself."

"Baka!" shouted Neneko. "Stupid! You've just recovered from that virus, and now you're going out to fight again?"

"Nen-chan, don't worry so much," Chris said, using her nickname. "Remember I'm a lot stronger now, and I'm not going alone. Jura and Lorelei are coming too. You just get yourself fixed up, and I'll be back before you know it." Neneko gave way and fell forward, still too weak to be up and about.

Pie-way guided Neneko back to a bed. "Thank you, Chris," she said. And then he ran back to the others who were still waiting for him to get back.

"Let's get going, Chris, we don't have all day," Jura said. They boarded Myra"s ship and headed off to the planet.

Everyone decided that Chris should change into his Cyber Lion mode before they landed, so as to not arouse suspicions with their opponents on the planet. After he changed, however, they came up to him with evil looks in their eyes, and he started to have second thought about their plans.

"Um, ladies, is there something I can do for you before we land?" he asked with a shaky voice not knowing what, exactly was going on.

But Lorelei smiled and held up a spray can of paint. "Stand still for a minute," she said.

"What?" he asked anxiously.

"Well you see," said Jura, "you look like a cybernetic lion, and I'm pretty sure that we can't have anybody on this planet recognize you. So we're going to make you look more like a *real* lion with this!" Lorelei held up the spray can. As she painted him to look more like a real giant lion, he couldn't help but feel as if he was just being made up to look cuter in their eyes. But, when they were finished, he looked exactly like a real,' giant lion.

When they landed, Myra seemed happy as she "led" Chris out of the spacecraft in his Cyber Lion form. He was one big cat, and it made her feel safe just having him walking next to her. One problem, though, was that his footsteps still sounded like metal hitting metal because of his claws, but, other than that, he did seem like just a normal lion.

The race would not be held until the next day; however, they had to go directly to the preliminary check-in. The judges couldn't even tell, as they inspected Chris, that he wasn't a real lion. He had to stay quiet even though he wanted to yell out! When they were finished, the judges directed them to the stable where he would be staying overnight. Chris wasn't looking forward to this!"

As they were heading to the stall, they saw the competition—the one who called himself Speed Trap. He looked more like a cheetah man. Indeed, he was leading a large cheetah. And there was a large *T*attoo on his shoulder, which meant that he worked for the Titan.

When Speed Trap saw Myra and her group, he could not help but walk over to them just to harass them. Harassment was one of his favorite pastimes. In this case, he knew that, no matter what they did, they could never beat him in this race, for he made the rules.

"Well," Speed Trap stated, "it seems you all finally decided to race. Too bad you've got such a poor excuse for a cat!" He scoffed at the large lion.

Chris started to growl at the fool for making fun of him. Speed Trap still just scoffed at him. But then Chris 'snapped at Speed Trap and roared at him. This shocked Speed Trap. He had never seen any cat on this planet snap at him. He could control any of them. That, in fact, was how he won all that time. But he was the only person who knew that.

Speed Trap backed off as the lion started to step forward in a protective move.

The lion growled louder as it kept approaching Speed Trap, who finally said to Myra, "It seems you have found a lion with a lot of spunk. This should be interesting." And, with that, he walked off a little unnerved by the situation.

"Did you see that?" Myra said. "He practically pissed himself when Chris came at him!" Chris seemed happy with himself as Myra continued, "This is going to be big. I've never seen Speed Trap back off to anyone before." She then looked up at the cyber lion. "You are incredible."

Chris gave her a cat like smile, as he said, "I was only doing my job. I can't have anybody poke fun of me or the people that I'm here to protect."

"No, I guess not," she said half laughing at the outcome. She rubbed him behind the ear, which made him purr and everyone else laugh.

That night, Chris was sleeping soundly in his stall, which the girls had made very comfortable for him, when he was awakened by someone moving around near him. He looked around thinking that it might be someone trying to sabotage them before the race. Chris looked up to see Speed Trap standing in front of him—and the man didn't seem happy.

"It's you, isn't it?" Speed Trap asked as he stood in front of the large Cyber Lion. "You're Striker, the one who's been giving my master so much trouble lately."

Chris didn't answer, all he did was nod his head. "Good," Speed Trap stated. "I was hoping that we would get a chance to race. This is going to be a good race, but I want something if I win!"

"What do you want?" Chris asked as he moved closer to the cat man's face.

"I want you, and the women on your ship, and the women on this planet to obey me," he said as he turned his back to Chris.

"I can't do that!" Chris told him with a straight tone.

"And why not? You seem to have some sort of power over women that neither I nor the Titan has ever had."

"It's because they don't belong to me," said Chris. "They are my friends, and my allies. We all respect each other. I have no say in what they do. But, I'll tell you what I'll do. I will give up my own freedom if you beat me." Chris sat back down in his corner waiting for Speed Trap's answer.

"That's not good enough," he snapped. "I want the women to surrender to me—not just you!"

But' another voice said, "We'll agree to your terms." Both turned to see who had spoken, and saw Lorelei and Myra standing by Chris's stall. They had brought food for Chris.

"You will?" Speed Trap asked happily.

"You guys don't have to do this," Chris said to them as he stood up on all fours.

"It's our lives," Lorelei said. "If Speed Trap agrees to leave this planet without any more lives lost, then we are all for it. Even if we risk our freedom."

"Then it's settled!" roared Speed Trap. "If you lose tomorrow, you're all mine to do with as I please."

"But remember," Chris said, "if we win, you have to leave the planet forever. And, if you lie to us, you'll have to deal with me in full force." Chris stared at Speed Trap crossly.

"Fine. I'll leave if I lose, but that's a big *if*," Speed Trap said, and he laughed his way out of the stall.

Chris then turned to the two women now standing next to him. He could see that they were unafraid that they would lose tomorrow.

"Are you guys crazy making a deal like that? You know he'll cheat knowing what's at stake!" Chris yelled at them.

But they both smiled. Myra said, "There is no way we will lose because we have something the Titan's men don't have."

"And what's that, may I ask?"

"Honor and you!"

The day of the race, everyone was tense to say the least. All kinds of racers were ready to put it all on the line. Chris looked at Speed Trap, ready in his starting position. Speed Trap turned to them and smiled. *This is going to be an easy win*, he thought.

They had decided that Myra would ride on Chris. She seemed very much ready, but Chris was not having fun. He felt like a pack mule, with the saddle and harness that he had to wear. But he steadied himself in his starting position.

Chris could feel the tension building in the air as they waited for the sound of the starting gun. When it went off, it was as if a stampede had been let loose, as hundreds of animals jumped out of the starting gate. For this race was unlike any that Chris had ever seen. It was an eight-hour race across unpredictable terrain through forests and mountains. It ended with a two-mile straightaway. It was predicted that not all the racers would make it to the finish line alive.

As they ran, Chris yelled out to Myra, "This race is going to be crazy!" He shot past a couple of the other racers, but Speed Trap was way out in front. It was going to take a lot to catch up to him, but they weren't about to give up.

Chris and Myra reached the forest area before Speed Trap expected they would. They were right on his tail, and it appeared that he was going to have to kick it up, or they might have a chance at beating him.

With Cyber Lion running right next to him, Speed Trap yelled out, "Watch your footing!" He then pulled out a staff and stuck it between Chris's front legs. Before Chris could react, he toppled head over paws and crashed right into a nearby lake.

When he popped to the surface, with Myra still on his back, he yelled out, "That punk tried to kill us!" Myra stated, "What did you expect? A fair race? With the Titan's men, expect the unexpected."

Chris roared out as he jumped out of the water, and ran fast to catch back up with the other racers. He was not about to let that go without a fight.

Speed Trap felt pretty sure of himself now, so he was taking it easy. Suddenly, however, out of nowhere, a flash shot past him. He was enraged when he realized it was Striker. Speed Trap roared out and kicked the sides of his cheetah making it run faster.

Chris and Myra and Speed Trap and his cheetah shot out of the forest side by side running at unbelievable speeds. But, as they ran, Speed Trap turned to them and asked, "Is that as fast as you can go?"

Chris turned up to Myra, and then turned back to Speed Trap. "What's it to you?" he asked.

Speed Trap said, "Nothing." And he pulled on the reins of his cheetah, and vanished in a flash leaving a shockwave behind him that blew Chris off his feet. He crashed into the ground and Myra went flying.

Myra got up. *Wow!* she thought. *If Speed Trap is that fast, then what hope do we have?* The final straightaway was coming up, and it seemed they had no hope of catching up.

But, with a raging roar, Chris yelled out, "It's not over yet!" As he roared, his body changed from gold and red to a shining silver—Silver Cyber Lion!

He walked to where Myra stood and said, "You coming or not?"

His form was almost overwhelming to her, but she quickly shook off any feelings of anxiety and climbed back on. Chris roared out again as he reared back—and they vanished in a slivery flash.

Speed Trap was so far ahead of them that he thought for sure that he was going to win. In his opinion, there was no way that they could catch up to him now. But that thought vanished fast when he heard something moving up from behind.

He looked back and could not believe what he saw. There was a silver Cyber Lion moving faster than anything he had ever seen before. Two jet engines propelled the lion and his rider forward like a silver lighting bolt.

"Oh crap!" Speed Trap yelled out as he buckled down and tried to move faster. He looked ahead to see the finish line. He looked back and realized that the distance between them was too great. "I'm going to win!" he yelled out in triumph. "The people on this planet are going to be mine forever!"

Chris roared once more as he forced his jets to move faster. As he came up on Speed Trap's side, the two looked more like angry lighting. They both crashed across the finish line. No one watching could determine who had crossed first.

Chris and Myra and Speed Trap and his cheetah slid roaring stopped a few feet beyond the finish line. Speed Trap yelled out, "I won!" But then an official announced, "After consulting our photographic evidence, we have determined that the official winners are Myra and her lion Striker!"

Myra could barely contain herself, as she cheered. We are *free!*"

But Speed Trap would not accept this. "There is no way that anyone or anything is faster than me and my cheetah!" he stated as he stormed over to Chris and Myra. He pulled out a large gun that had been strapped to his back. *If I can't win, then no one will win*, he thought. 'He aimed, but Chris moved between him and Myra. Chris growled and said, "If you're not going to keep your word, then you're not going to like what I'm going to do to you, little man!"

Chris growled again as he stared Speed Trap down.

Speed Trap scoffed and said, "This planet isn't worth my time anymore! I'm leaving!" He climbed back onto his cheetah and said, "This isn't over, though. Not by a long shot."

Then Speed Trap's large cat changed into a ship, and they took off into space.

Chris thought, *I knew something was off with that guy and his big cat.* He turned to Myra and smiled. She ran up and hugged the big lug, saying, "You're definitely one of a kind."

Later, Myra was addressing her people. "We will never have to worry about Speed Trap again! We have beaten him at his own game, and he is now gone for good."

When her people heard this, their cheers could be heard from space. There followed a huge celebration that lasted for several days.

Just as Chris and Myra approached their ship, where Lorelei was waiting for them, Myra said, "Can I ask you for one last thing before we leave?"

"What is that?" he asked. Myra put her arms around him. Before he could act, she kissed him with incredible passion.

Lorelei, seeing this, was incredibly jealous. She pulled them apart and said, "All right, enough of that!"

Chris was a little dazed as Lorelei pulled her sister off him. He had not expected either sister's reaction to him. Myra smiled as she licked the taste of the man off her lips, savoring every bit of it. *Now that is a man*, she thought to herself.

CHAPTER 62

After Chris, Myra, and Lorelei got back to the ship, Chris was lying in his bedding in the hangar, for he still didn't have a room of his own. He wasn't the type to complain; besides that, he sort of liked the peace and quiet that he got during his downtime. He was almost asleep when he felt something unusual. And, suddenly, all' the alarms on the ship went nuts. Chris stood in an instant and looked around just in time to see a man fly right into the hangar.

The man skidded to a stop right in front of him. As he turned to face him, Chris noticed that he wore samurai armor. He also wore two swords of different lengths, one on each side of his belt. The thing that caught Chris off guard was his headband, which had the Japanese *kanji*, or symbol, for honor on it.

Chris lowered his guard as he wondered what this guy was doing here. As Chris approached the newcomer, the samurai pulled out a sword, and held it at Chris, who took a step back not knowing what side this guy was on. But the samurai spoke in a noble tone.

"Are you the one they call Chris Striker?"

"I am."

"I am sorry," said the samurai, "but I'm here to kill you for the Titan."

"The Titan!" Chris stated. It didn't seem right that a samurai who wore the symbol for honor would be doing the Titan's bidding. '"

"So what," Chris asked, assuming a fighting stance. "Do you plan to kill me right here and now?"

"No there is not enough room for the two of us to fight here," said the samurai. "So I recommend that we meet on that planet." And he pointed his sword to the nearby planet. Then he stated, "We will meet at high noon tomorrow. There is a large temple on the planet. If you fail to be there at that time, I will be forced to kill the women on this ship."

Hearing this made Chris angry. "How can you wear the sign of honor and threaten innocent people?"

"I have my reasons," the samurai stated as he sheathed his sword.

The samurai turned toward the exit, but, before he left, Chris asked, "One last thing—what's your name, samurai?"

"Blade," he stated. And, without turning around, he shot back into space.

Right as Blade shot out of the ship, some of the others made it to the hangar in their search for what had made the alarms go off. As they came up to Chris, they asked, "What was all that about?"

Chris told them what was going on. "I have been challenged to a duel tomorrow on that planet. And, if I don't show up, the challenger will kill everyone on this ship."

After they heard this, Lorelei said, "Surely, this is a trap. The Titan just wants to get Chris to leave the ship! Then he can attack Chris—and us!—with an army!"

But Chris shook his head. "I don't think so. This guy seems different somehow from all the rest of the Titan's minions. Somehow, this guy has a deeper reason for fighting."

"Chris-chan," Neneko said, worried about him, "this is too dangerous. You can't go alone. You must take some of us with you."

Chris looked back at her. "This is an honorable challenge. I don't think this guy will go against his word as long as I don't."

"Yeah, I get that too, Chris," Lorelei said to him, "but we would all feel better if you took some of us with you.

Chris sighed and stated, "It should be okay if some of you come—two or three at the most will do."

"Fine," Lorelei stated, "then Neneko, Jura, and Nodoka will go with you to the planet tomorrow."

Once that was settled, Chris walked off to think about this duel. What was bothering him the most was the kanji that was written on Blade's headband. It meant "honor."

Chris had all sorts of questions: Why was this samurai working for a monster like Titan? Was there a deeper reason for it, or was this all just a trap set by the Titan? But the only way he was going to find out was to fight this warrior tomorrow.

The next day at high noon, Chris was standing before the samurai ready to strike. They both ran at each other. In a flash of light, they shot past each other. The samurai had his sword drawn, and Chris was in his Cyborg Lion mode, claws outstretched. As the samurai turned, his sword dripped with blood. Chris reared back and then his eyes became blank as he fell to the ground dead. As he lay there, the women of the ship stood around him in shock. They wept because they had lost him. And they wept because he had failed. All they could think of was all of them being ravaged and raped by the Titan. Slowly, the Titan's men appeared before them.

"Ahhhhhhhhhh!"

Chris awoke from the nightmare screaming. He looked around his sleeping area in the hangar and he looked down at himself. *I can't let that happen!* he thought. *This is a fight of honor. The Titan must be stopped, no matter the cost.*

In the transport vehicle, as they headed toward the planet, Chris was thinking that he should be doing this alone. *Maybe bringing these three with me 'was a mistake. What if my nightmare comes true? What if this samurai calling himself Blade is a better martial artist than I? Or, what if this is all a trap set by the Titan?* There was a lot to consider.

As he was sitting there, Neneko noticed his uncertainty. She leaned over and put a reassuring hand on his shoulder. He looked down and saw her smile at him. Her attitude was that this fight didn't mean a thing—that it would be another walk in the park for him. She had full confidence in him. Knowing that made him feel a little better.

When they landed, the four of them noticed that the planet the samurai had sent them to was in ruins. But, as he looked at some of the buildings, Chris couldn't help but notice that the planet seemed to remind him of his home in Japan.

Nodoka then said, "I can see the temple." As they headed right for the temple, they saw the samurai sitting in a meditative state holding his two swords out in his arms.

"Are you ready?" Chris asked.

Blade looked up at him and said, "This fight is to be between you and me. Why are they here?" He pointed to the women.

"They're just spectators—nothing more," said Chris. "They won't interfere, you have my word as a martial artist, and a man of honor."

Blade stood, accepting Chris's word, and put his swords back in their scabbards. Bowing, he told Chris to follow him. They walked to a clear area near the temple. They turned to each other, stepped back and bowed, and readied themselves. Still, Chris could not understand the samurai. Why was this warrior fighting on the side of the Titan? And why had the samurai brought Chris to this planet?

As if Blade had heard Chris's questions he said, "This planet was my home until the Titan came and destroyed everything and killed all my people."

Striker 'hadn't been expecting this. "Why work for him then, if he destroyed your people?" he asked.

"Because, when he first came to my planet, he beat me in combat. His victory put me under a contract that honor bound me to him. After he defeated me, he laid waste to my world and my people. Now the only way for me to be free of the Titan is to kill him—or to die by the hands of an honorable warrior who could beat the Titan. No matter how hard I've tried, I can't beat the Titan. But then I heard about you, a great warrior protecting a ship full of innocence's, determined to beat the Titan, at any cost. When the Titan ordered me to fight you, I knew I had a chance to find out if you would be the one who could beat the Titan. I am here to get my honor back in combat with a greater warrior than even the Titan."

After hearing Blade's story, Chris understood why this samurai wanted to fight him … to beat him. It was a matter of honor. It was the only way for his people to forgive him for what he had done. To both Chris and the samurai, this was going to be more than a fight to the finish. It was going to be a fight to see who was capable of finishing off the Titan.

Chris had his head down. He held his fists clenched so tightly they were shaking. When Blade saw this, he asked again "Will you fight me or not?"

Chris's head shot up as he yelled out, "Get ready for the fight of your life, Blade!"

Blade smiled as he pulled out both swords. He knew that this fight was going to be special. Chris knew he had to give him everything, but didn't think that he would need anything higher than his hyper mode. But, Blade sliced his sword through the air letting out a cut stream that shot out and seemed to cut the air around them. Chris was almost cut in half.

"I should have told you that you are going to have to go all out to fight me," Blade yelled out. Suddenly, his armor changed. He became sleeker and somehow looked more like a robot or cyborg. His entire body was now covered in blades, a reflection of his name. He was a living, breathing sword.

Chris had to change to his Alpha Omega Cyber Lion mode just to jump out of the way! But then Blade shot up into the air. Flying seemed to be no problem for him. Chris followed him. Blade slammed into Chris with incredible force sending him spiraling back to the ground.

Chris pushed himself up as he heard Blade yell out to him. "Stop playing like you're hurt, I'm not even trying yet!"

Chris stood fast, yelling out, "If you wan't to see everything that I can do, you got it!"

When he got back into his fighting stance, Blade was excited. He knew about the cyborg's transformations, but never thought that the cyborg would look this intimidating. He also knew that the cyborg was still holding back his ultimate form too. And he knew there was one way he was going to get it out, and that was by showing the cyborg that he was no pushover.

The two warriors vanished in a flash. Explosions blew up as flashes of light shot around the area. The three who watched were entranced at the power of the warriors as they shot across the sky. The two monstrous fighters both believed in honor. Chris's honor was to protect the ones around him; Blade's was to fight to avenge his people.

They both clashed like thunder and lighting, one not giving way to the other, and both determined to win one way or another. They fought blade to claw as they clashed circling each other, until Blade slashed hard at Chris faster than he could dodge, pushing him back as he blocked with both arms crossed in front of him.

"I told you before we started this that you would have to give it everything you've got to beat me!" Blade yelled out as he slashed again and again, pushing Chris back farther and farther.

Chris now knew that Blade was right. "Mina of the blade and Dita of the wing," he called out. Right then, his red lion's mane changed to silver fire as it stood on end. His body changed too, turning from red orange to silver. Bladed gauntlets appeared on each hand, and sliver blade wings appeared on his back.

"Silver Cyber Lion!" Chris yelled out. "Is this what you want?" Blade smiled as he let out two more strikes that did almost nothing. The girls watching were shocked, for this was the first time that they had seen Chris's silver form at its peak.

"Yes, now we can both fight at our best," Blade stated as he too went through another transformation. His armor seemed to shatter and reform around him changing from silver to gold. His swords molded to his hands.

Both warriors were now fighting at 100 percent. They stared each other down in classic fighting stance. Nodoka had seen Chris fight the Titan when she was a child, but this fight was like nothing she had ever seen before. As she watched, she got an idea for something that would help Chris and her countrywomen in their final fight with the Titan.

Striker and Blade still stared each other down waiting for a sign. Just as a piece of rubble fell, they both shot into the air at each other colliding in a flurry of punches and kicks that seemed to shake the planet under the feet of the women who were watching.

Neneko could barely believe that the man fighting in the air was the same man who had trained with her all those years ago. She remembered the day she met him. She had been only five years old; he was ten. Even as a child, he had trained like a man possessed by a demon. One day her grandfather, his sensei, had told him that the only way that he would finish his training was if he could shatter a large boulder that was at the temple where they grew up.

Her Chris-chan trained harder and longer than any other student. After four years, one afternoon Neneko had found him staring at the boulder. She was about to go to him when her grandfather stopped her. "Just watch," he said.

Neneko had watched as Chris stared at that boulder for a long while. Suddenly, he had yelled out and punched it right in the center with incredible force. Even though she had been a small child when it happened, Neneko still remembered the incredible blow Chris had dealt the boulder. The boulder had shattered.

Her Grandfather had told her on many occasions that he sensed that that boy would succeed in great things one day, that his skill in martial arts would go beyond any in the world. "He will one day become unstoppable," he had told her.

If he had told her then that she would be watching him fighting in space as a cyborg, she would have laughed. Seeing what he could do now made it seem that she wasn't looking at a man, but a god.

Chris and Blade still fought on as the planet seemed to be trembling at the force of their battle. Eventually, the two of them crashed down to the ground with incredible force like two falling stars.

A flash of light shot over the women. They had to cover their eyes from the blinding flash. When it subsided, they saw the two warriors still standing. They were both battle torn and beaten, and they were breathing hard, but they both knew that this was a fight to the finish, and neither was finished yet. Once again, they ran at each other with incredible force punching at each other as sparks flew from their cybernetic bodies.

Nodoka covered her eyes for she could not take any more of their fighting. "Why do men fight like this?" she cried. "It doesn't make any sense!"

Neneko moved over to the girl and said, "Because sometimes fighting is the only way for a man to find himself. Fighting is what drives some men, and defines them and makes them feel alive. But for Chris-chan, it's different. What drives him to fight isn't the thrill of the fight, but what he is fighting for—he is not just fighting for himself, he is fighting for all of us. That is what drives him, not' fame or glory … just for the honor of protecting those around him. So don't look away, for he is doing this for you. Winning this will mean nothing if he isn't fighting for the honor of protecting someone in need."

Neneko's words made sense to Nodoka. She looked back up at the two fighting cyborg's. After one particularly harsh exchange, both of them at the same time were sent flying back. As they both slammed into a large rock formation, Chris lost his Cyber Lion form and Blade lost his Blade form. But they weren't finished yet. They pulled themselves out of the rock piles and ran at each other like madmen.

Chris yelled out "*Screaming Bullet!*" as he struck. Blade ran with his sword in hand yelling out, "*Crimson Blade!*" The shockwave they generated when they hit was incredible. It pushed the women back in a cloud of dust.

As the three women pulled themselves out of the dirt, they looked around for the Super Cyborg. "Look!" Neneko yelled. The women turned to where she was pointing. Both warriors were lying on the ground. Both looked beaten or dead. But then they watched Chris slowly raise his hand in the air as he folded his fingers into a fist.

He got up and slowly walked over to Blade who was still on the ground, for he was close to death. That last strike had been his last. Chris held one of his arms, for it was badly damaged.

Blade coughed up blood as Chris stood over him. Blade smiled weakly at him, as he said, "Well done, you are a true warrior—one who fights for what he believes in and nothing else. That makes me wish I had known you before the Titan came to my planet. My people may have survived. But at least now I die knowing that there is a warrior in our universe who is willing to do whatever it takes to protect the people around him."

Chris looked at the warrior he had just beaten. *This was just what I needed before my final fight with the Titan—a fight with an honorable warrior*, he thought. *Now I believe that honor still exists in the universe.*

"Thank you for fighting with me," Chris said as he looked at the fallen warrior. "But why did you wan't me to fight you to the finish like this, when the two of us could have teamed up to take down the Titan together?"

Once again Blade smiled. "It is because this is your fight, and no one else's. The Titan is your mortal enemy, not mine, so it is only fitting that it be you alone who will defeat him. But, before you go, please do me one last favor, for I am not strong enough to make it on my own."

"Just name it," Chris said to him.

Blade raised his hand and pointed back to the temple. "Please take me back to the temple. That is where I want to die."

Chris nodded. As he bent to pick Blade up, the others ran to him. "What are you doing?" asked Neneko, worried about his condition.

Chris turned to the three of them and said, "This man is an honorable man. He wishes to die in a place of honor, and this battle-torn land is no place for an honorable warrior to die. I will carry him to the temple."

"Chris-chan," said Neneko, "if you haven't realized, you're pretty beat up yourself. If you try and carry this samurai back to the temple, it might kill you."

"No it won't," Chris sternly said. As he picked up the samurai and began to walk toward the temple, sparks flew from his body. It was difficult for the girls as they watched him force himself to move all the way to the temple. It was even harder to watch him walk up the steps to the temple, but, once he laid Blade on a stone slab inside the temple, they all felt relieved that he had made it.

Chris bowed his head in honor for this man's strength, for he had given him an honorable fight. Chris knew that, if they had met under different circumstances, they would have become good friends. But the Titan corrupted everything he touched, and thus the two had ended up fighting each other.

Blade turned to Chris one last time. "I have something to give you," he said weakly. He held his hand out and dropped something into Chris's hand. Chris looked at the paper. "That is where the Titan is hiding," said Blade. "I want you to go there and finish the fight—free the universe of his evil forever,"

Chris bowed again and said, "I will."

After those last words, Blade turned over and passed away peacefully in the temple of his people.

Chris stayed and prayed for the man for some time. Finally, he stood up as best as he could and turned to the girls. He made his way to them with more of a stumble then a walk, and said, "We have work to do." But then he could not stand anymore. He fell to the ground unconscious.

CHAPTER 63

Some time later, Chris awoke back on the ship. Pie-way was looking down at him as she worked on one of his arms. "How long have I been out?" he asked.

She looked up at him from her work and said, "You have been out for a few hours, but don't worry, we're already on our way to where the Titan's been hiding all this time. And, this time, we all have big plans for helping you out in your battle with him—or I should say Nodoka has a plan … in the hangar."

After his repairs were finished, he headed to the hangar. On his way, he met up with Neneko, who seemed happy about the big surprise that Nodoka had cooked up. When he entered the hangar, it seemed that half the crew of the ship were there.

"What's going on?" Chris asked as he moved into the group. Lorelei was standing next to Nodoka who was standing next to something large that was covered with a cloth.

"This is great!" Neneko said excitedly as she took her place next to Chris, who still didn't know what was going on.

Lorelei started to talk,

"As you all know, we are going to fight the Titan again. We now know where he is, thanks to Chris's last fight. Now, we all know 'that Chris and Neneko are the only ones of us who can survive in space, so Nodoka and I put our heads together and— "

Nodoka interrupted her,

"Well, more like *I* did," she said. "I came up with the idea when I was watching Chris fight." As she stood next to the large covered object, she turned to the crew and said, "This new invention will enable all of you to fight alongside our cyborg allies." With a dramatic flourish, she pulled the cloth off the large object to reveal a large cyber lion–looking mechanical suit.

The crew stood in awe as they checked out the suit, which looked like a large human cyber lion. This one looked quite different from Chris's Cyber Lion form. For starters, it didn't have a mane and it was obviously female. Nodoka said, "This is a cyber lioness. I figured that, if Chris is our alpha male, we should all be lionesses at his side."

Chris laughed at the thought of this, but also thought that Nodoka's idea was a good one. "Don't worry," Nodoka went on to explain, "these are so simple to use that a child can use them." And to prove her right, Pie-way stepped up and climbed into the mech suit. As she did, everyone could hear the sound of the suit's power roaring to life. It was almost like seeing Chris's Cyber Lion form. It was overwhelming. As Pie-way took a step forward, everyone took a step back, a little scared that she might fall. But she moved in the suit as if she and the mech were one.

Nodoka then explained more about the mech's power. Chris enjoyed the demonstration, but then he turned and headed off alone to think. There was going to be a war. Only one side would survive. This was going to take everything he had, and he had to be mentally and physically ready.

He headed for the gym, for it was the only place on the ship where he could be alone.

Soon, Neneko noticed that Chris was gone. Jura noticed too and asked Neneko where she thought he might be. "I think he probably went to the gym," Neneko told Jura. "He's either angry or he's worried about this fight."

"What do you think is wrong?" Jura asked.

Neneko shook her head. "He must be doubting himself again."

"You know," Jura said, "for a man who is honorable to a fault, he sure has issues about fighting!"

"You don't get it, do you?" snapped Neneko. "Chris-chan hates fighting. He always did! He's afraid that, if he starts to like it, he might become that which he hates the most."

Lorelei was watching Neneko and Jura and overheard their conversation. She thought of a great idea to help Chris relax before the big fight. *Oh, I am such a genius!* she thought to herself. *And I'll get the other members of the crew involved as well.*

When Lorelei had everyone gathered together, she began,' "I have been thinking of something important. As you all know, we are going to fight the Titan again. We women will probably end up fighting his beast men, and Chris will fight the Titan directly." She now had their attention. "Also as you know, Chris is the only man on this ship, so we should all help in providing his well-being." Lorelei then suggested something that made most of them blush crimson. Others yelled out in rage, for they were not going to even think of doing what she was suggesting. But Lorelei did her best to explain that this was so their great warrior would remember who and what he' was fighting for. It would also help to ready him for combat.

Chris was in the middle of his tai chi routine when, all of a sudden, something hit the back of his head. He fell to the floor the second it hit him, for he was so preoccupied in what he was doing, he didn't even sense it coming. Neneko then appeared next to him as she told the others to help her get him up.

"What hit me?" Chris said aloud as he awoke with a bad headache. He looked around and found himself in the spa area of the ship. He was in a hot tub! He could have sworn he had been in the gym! But then he noticed something else—he had been striped down to his boxers! Part of him was angry, and the other part was wondering what these girls had in mind. The thing was that they all knew his policy about things like this—they knew that he would never do anything that would anger any of the women on the ship, so why had they done this to him?

He got his answer when Neneko appeared next to him wearing nothing but a towel. She was holding a tray of food. She set the tray on the edge of the hot tub he was sitting in.

"What is going on here, Neneko-chan?" he asked her with only a little rage in his voice. He knew she had been the one who hit him and put him in here. She was the only one in the ship who could turn invisible—and who dared to sneak up him.

"We all thought that you were feeling down after that last fight," Neneko told him, "and we're going to be fighting the Titan again real soon, so we all wanted to show our appreciation to you by throwing this party. We thought it might lessen the tension we've all been feeling, knowing where we're going."

"A party, ah?" Chris said. He thought it was a bit unusual, but then he realized what Neneko meant by "we're all"—the entire crew was there!

When he looked around, he saw that he was right. It looked as if about half the ship's crew were in the spa area relaxing. He could not believe that they would agree to this, knowing that he was in there.

Lorelei came up behind him. "Did you forget that you are allowed in here any time? That was the arrangement we all made with you!"

"I hadn't forgotten," said Chris, 'but it still it was wrong for him to intrude—it lacked decency.

"Chris-chan, stop acting like an honorable warrior for once in your life, and act like a shallow male for once. You always have to act so respectfully to everyone! But what do you do when a women asks you to do something indecent?" Neneko stated, as she got up close to him.

Chris had to think hard on that one, for his honor code stated that he had to be kind and decent toward women. Being asked to be indecent was usually not an issue because they never asked! Chris had never understood women that well. He avoided them like the plague. Heck, the only women he had ever been close to were Minawa and Neneko, and Minawa was the first woman he had ever been with. And he had been close with Neneko—once. Leo was proof of that.

"Well, Chris-chan, what do you say? Will you have some fun with us or what?" Neneko said with a big smile and seductive tone that almost scared him.

"All right then. I know when I'm beat," Chris said with a laugh. A feeling of freedom that he had never felt before came over him as he yelled out, "Let's party!"

Some time later, after they had partied till they'd almost dropped, Lorelei was sitting peacefully at one of the tables in the spa, when she notice Jura watching the Cyber Lion as he slept closely to Neneko and several members of the ship's crew. He had transformed during the party, and fallen asleep like that.

"What are you looking at Jura?" Lorelei said, half asleep herself.

Jura was startled, but didn't show it much as she turned to Lorelei, "I was just thinking how wrong we were to think that all men are evil," Jura said almost to herself.

"I know," Lorelei answered as she offered a seat next to her. As Jura sat down, Lorelei smiled as she said, "You know that big fool is unbelievable. He has not only freed us all from the grip of the Titan, but now he has won the hearts of this crew."

"But Mistress Lorelei …" Jura stated fighting back the feeling that she was right, but Lorelei spoke again before Jura could say anything else.

"It's true you know, and he's even worked his way into your heart, as well. Now that's a feat in itself!" She laughed because, at first, Jura had been the one who had least liked the idea of Chris staying on the ship. Now, it was Jura who had managed to talk so many crew-members to join them for this party.

Once again, they looked at the large lion sleeping soundly on the floor with at least four others sleeping on or around him. With steam rising up from the heat of the 'hot tubs around them, the scene looked almost heavenly.

Jura smiled at them thinking they might have had the right idea. For, even though this might be their last chance to be with the Super Cyborg, the sight of the large lion seemed to put her mind at ease, and seemed to give hope for the future.

They had traveled around the universe looking for the Titan, but they would never have thought that he would have gone to Earth. As their ship flew to the location that Blade had given them, their shock was apparent that the Titan would choose to attack the Earth to get back at the cyborg who had beaten him.

xxx

The Titan's ship loomed in front of them; the sheer size of it was incredible. When the sun turned to show this ship, Chris and the others were almost overwhelmed by sight before them. It made their ship seem so small in comparison.

"Well, there's a guy who still believe that size matters," Lorelei stated as she stared out in shock.

"Well, we're going to bring him down a peg," Chris said. Then he activated the intercom and spoke to the crew. "This is it! Prepare for battle!"

The women warriors climbed into their lioness mech's as Chris ran into the hangar. As he ran, he transformed into his humanoid Cyber Lion. He would lead the others out into space.

xxx

Flying close to the large ship, Chris and the lioness crew-members looked almost like a pride of lions heading for their prey. Unknown to them, the Titan was ready for them. He had monitored the fight between the Super Cyborg and Blade. And now, his last two remaining generals and his fleet of ships were ready. They were cloaked so any fear he had was gone. He knew full well that the Cyber Lion was headed straight into his trap.

Chris turned and pointed, signaling for the lionesses to spread out around him. Just as he was about to order them to attack, hundreds of ships appeared, completely surrounding them. Even more ships surrounded their main ship, which, in a mad moment during their pre-battle party, they had renamed *The Minawa*. Chris and the lionesses were cut off from escape. They had two choices: win or go down fighting.

"What do we do, Chris-chan?" Neneko asked. She was leading the mechs. Chris looked around for a moment then raised his hand in the air. At first they thought that he was going to surrender, but then, facing

518

the lead ship, he clapped both hands together into a fist as he yelled out, "Take them down, ladies!" He fired a power shotgun that traveled easily right through a large number of ships, destroying them all and opening a path to the Titan's main ship. Chris shot off toward the ship. Then a firefight in space began. They were all determined to fight as hard as they could for everything that they had.

Chris shot among the burning ships yelling out, "Titan, I'm coming for you, you monster!"

xxx

Titan was watching the activity from inside the main ship. He was sitting on a throne surrounded by mimetic beasts and cybernetic women, all of whom were seductively stroking his large body.

"Come and get me, you fool," Titan roared out,knowing that the Cyber Lion would hear his every word. "There is no way you can beat me, for I am indestructible!" He then rose as he dismissed everyone around him so he could fight the so-called Super Cyborg alone. He didn't have to wait long for Chris smashed right into his throne room.

"*Titan!*" Chris yelled out in a furious rage ready to fight or die. He had had as much of the Titan as he could stand. He landed on the floor of the throne room and started to walk up the steps to the throne. At the top, he stood right in front of the Titan for what he determined would be the last time.

"Well," said Titan in a fake warm voice. "It's nice to see you again, Cyborg." They stared each other down. "I suppose you're going to go on about honor and its foolish meaning and all that nonsense."

"Honor this," Chris said as he punched Titan right in the face. Titan went flying through his throne and crashed through half his ship.

Shaking his head a bit, Titan looked up in time to see Chris flying right at him, yelling out *"Screaming Fist of the Beast King!"* Chris punched the Titan harder than he had ever been punched in his life. The power of this punch sent the Titan flying through the rest of his ship and out into space where Chris again appeared in front of him.

Chris hit the Titan with a barrage of punches, sending sparks flying with each punch. It was a fireworks display in space.

xxx

Neneko had just destroyed another one of the Titan's ships with a crushing display of her force fields, but that was still only one ship out of the hundreds that still threatened her and those she cared for. She looked at the destruction thinking, *Has there ever been such a battle?*

Then she turned as she saw one of the ships open up. Hundreds of mimetic beasts flew out of the ship— they looked like a demonic army being set free.

"Heaven help us!" Neneko said. She knew she had no choice but to give it all she had. She focused each one of her powers. Even though she could survive in space, she was using a lioness mech because it gave her the added advantage of focusing her powers to a new level.

Neneko mimicked herself over a dozen times, splitting her powers into each version of herself. It shocked her to see that each one seemed to be a different color. Once they shot off in different directions, Neneko was able take down the enemy beasts faster than the mimetic beasts could think.

xxx

Lorelei was still in the main ship, *The Minawa*, watching all this unfold. She had no idea that Neneko could split in that many directions at once. She was amazed as she watched one of the Neneko doubles blast about a dozen of the mimetic beasts, vaporizing them. Another was pounding down on one of the ships, while another was absorbing the power out of most of the beasts that came near her. For some time, Neneko seemed to have become a one-woman army, and it had only taken her a split second.

The Titan landed back on top of his main ship, arrogantly named *The Universe*. He looked around trying to find where that lion cyborg had gone, but he was nowhere to be found. But then, the Titan detected something coming from behind. He turned in time to block another screaming fist, but still the force of the impact forced his feet into the hull of *The Universe.*

Chris and the Titan then vanished in a flash as they fought again at light speeds, making explosions in space as each punch hit.

The Titan was a little impressed, for the cyborg seemed to have improved a little since their last encounter. But, the Titan knew that it was still futile for Chris to fight him. And, to prove it, he punched Chris right in the solar plexus.

The punch caught Chris off guard, for he didn't think that the Titan was that strong. As he flew back, he coughed up blood and just glared at warrior.

Titan didn't give him any time to recover. He just started to beat down on Chris with one punch after another, pushing him right back into *The Universe.*

Chris slammed into the side of the ship with monstrous force, but that didn't stop the Titan as he still pounded down on the Super Cyborg, pushing him into the hull.

Once the Titan was finished, he flew back a bit to admire his work, and then one of the dragon heads on his upper arms moved down and covered his hand, and he faced it at the cyborg and said, "Well, I have to say you put up a good fight, but, in the end, I always win. No matter what you think, no one can beat me." And with that he fired a blast at the cyborg that engulfed him and blasted him right through the ship, causing it to momentarily veer off course.

Inside *The Universe*, the Titan's crew was going nuts yelling out as the whole ship seemed to be falling apart at the seams.

xxx

"Miss Lorelei, something went right through the Titan's ship! What do you think it was?" a crew-member asked.

"I don't know," answered Lorelei.

"Well," said the crew-member, "whatever it was, it blasted right through the ship's hull as if it was nothing."

Lorelei then heard Nodoka on the intercom. "Attention," she said, "The main power grid is about to go out. We will be adrift in space in a few minutes." Lorelei was about to ask how long they had when the lights went out and the ship swerved. She slammed both hands on the consol in front of her. *This is bad*, she thought. *We need Chris more than ever, but where is he?*

xxx

Chris was still traveling on the Titan's beam of energy. Suddenly, he slammed hard into an asteroid. The impact forced him back to his normal form. *Talk about being stuck in a loop*, Chris thought as he remembered the last time he hit an asteroid in a fight with the Titan. Then the Titan appeared in front of him.

"You're finished!" Titan stated as he pointed his hand at Chris. The dragon's head on the Titan's hand glared at Chris, who just laughed as he forced himself up. "If I had a dollar for every time I heard that," Chris said. He laughed again as he slumped over hanging his arms in front of him as if he were dead.

"You would still be dead!" Titan said as he fired point blank right at Chris, blasting him straight back against the asteroid. The pain that Chris was experiencing was like nothing he had felt before. He screamed out into the blackness.

xxx

The Neneko doubles were still fighting it out. Suddenly, one of them stopped. It could hear Chris's cries of pain.

"Hey," she cried out, "did you hear that?"

Another answered, "Yeah, I did." They all gathered together and fused back into one and took off fast.

xxx

Inside *'The Minawa*, Lorelei and the crew were still trying to stabilize the ship. They had switched to backup power, but that wouldn't last long. One of the crew-members yelled out to Lorelei to come look out the window.

"Chris!" Lorelei cried as she saw him get slammed into an asteroid and then blasted by the Titan.

"This doesn't look good," another crew-member said.

Secretly, Lorelei agreed. Chris was the only one who could fight the Titan. If he failed, the Titan would lay waste to them in a matter of moments. "May the gods help us all," she whispered.

xxx

Chris fell back to the surface of the asteroid. He was burnt, battered, and bruised. The Titan walked over and kicked him a couple of times to make sure he was dead, but, after the second kick, Chris grabbed the Titan's leg and looked up at him. His cybernetic eye was flashing off and on as he stuttered out, in an almost growl, "I w-will never give up!"

"Such heroic nonsense," Titan stated as he sent a blast right through Chris's body. The blast went right through the asteroid. It was followed only by deathly silence, for, at last, the Titan had won.

Neneko appeared just as the Titan had finished off Chris. "You son of a bitch!" she screamed. "I'll kill you for that!" And she blasted him with one of Jennifer's killer light rays. But it had little or no effect on Titan's body. He vanished momentarily, and appeared right in front of her saying, "It's too bad that your so-called savior was destroyed. I guess that makes me the top dog again."

With one hand, Titan grabbed both of the girl's arms. He held her out and said, "It will be fun to train you as my personal sex toy." Neneko struggled to get free, but his grip was too strong.

"I would rather die than do anything like that. Besides, I bet you're nothing compared to Chris-chan. He knew how to please a woman!" Neneko suddenly broke out of her mech and shot out into space. She powered up and fired everything she had at the monster.

"You contemptuous little bitch!" Titan yelled as he plowed through her beams and punched her straight back, beating on her as he pursued her.

xxx

Chris seemed to be lying on a sea of black. As he regained consciousness, he slowly stood and looked at himself. He was human again. *This must be another illusion*, he thought. He tried to focus through the illusion, but he couldn't. Just as he realized that he was experiencing reality, he felt an enormous power behind him. He turned to see only a dark silhouette of someone large. Even though he could not see what or who it was, he could tell that it wasn't human at all. In fact, it looked like some kind of shark man.

"Who are you?" asked Chris. "Are you here to take me to the afterlife?" He tried to get a better look at the

creature.

"No, I'm not here for that," the creature said flatly. "I'm here to tell you that the women you have sworn to protect need you to keep fighting."

"But I have lost. And look at me! I can't beat him as I am!" Chris said he fell to his knees in despair.

"Did you think this battle was going to be as easy as the other battles you've fought? This isn't about you at all. This is about what is right, and doing everything in your power to win. Besides, don't you have help fighting? What about Mina and Dita? Or did you forget their sacrifice."

"No, but what good is it against a force like the Titan? I mean, I beat him once, but that was a long time ago, and I let him live because I thought it was right thing to do. But I was wrong." Chris then slammed his fist to the ground, as he cried out, "What good is my honor? What good is it if I can't fight anymore?"

The being in front of Chris walked forward, and, even though he was now standing in front of him Chris still could not make out his face. It was as if the creature didn't want him to know who he was. "Tell me, boy," said the creature, "you always say that you fight for honor, but what does it mean? What is your honor?"

Hearing this, Chris looked at the large being in front of him. He had never thought to define his honor. He had always thought that honor was honor.

"Fool!" the being yelled as he turned his back on Chris. "If you can't find out what honor is to you, then why do you keep talking about it all the time? You need to find the meaning of your honor, and then you will be able to beat the Titan once and for all!" The large shark-man walked out of sight leaving Chris alone in the void.

Chris looked at his hands—his human hands. *Whoever that was,* he thought, *was right! I must find the meaning of my honor.* "But what is it?" he yelled it out to the void. Then memories of his life came rushing through his mind … memories of the twelve girls he started with. He remembered how they always had fun … how they fought together … and how they fell loving him. He remembered Neneko. And he remembered his son and daughter, who were still on Earth.

Thinking back at all these things made him realize that his honor wasn't anything like he had thought of before—it was the people he loved, who were always with him. That's what his honor really was! Not the fact that he protected them, but that he *loved* them—and they loved him.

This realization woke him right up. He found himself still lying on the asteroid where the Titan had left him. Chris roared out as he stood. He was still beaten up, and a few parts flew off him as he moved. But that didn't matter to him anymore. There was only one thought going through his mind—and that was to take down the Titan no matter the cost.

xxx

Neneko's small frame was beaten and bleeding. She was no way a match for the Titan. He was just too strong. Even with her training and the eleven powers that she possessed, her battle with the Titan could only be compared to a mouse trying to fight a tiger.

"This has been interesting," Titan said as he looked at Neneko's torn clothing as she tried to keep herself covered. From out of nowhere, the rest of the cyber lionesses came flying right at them. The lead lioness yelled. "Titan, you will pay for hurting Chris and Neneko!" For Lorelei had just informed them that Chris had been killed by the Titan '

"Women are truly foolish creatures, aren't they?" said the Titan. "Haven't they realized yet that I am indestructible?" Titan shrugged, but then the lioness driven by Jura yelled out, "Indestructible this!" as she punched him hard. Her maddening, furious strength sent the Titan faltering back.

The Titan shook off the impact wondering, *Where did that came from?* Looking back up, he could see the determination and will in every lioness. This was a will he had never seen in them before, for they never before had tried to fight him. For this, he blamed that so-called Super Cyborg. The Titan turned to the area where he had left the body of the Super Cyborg, but then he turned back to the small group of lionesses in front of him. He smirked. *I will enjoy destroying their new determination*, he told himself.

"You will feel the same pain I gave to your so-called great warrior!" Titan yelled out as he transformed to his three-headed dragon form and fired out at them.

The blast that the women saw coming at them was greater than they could ever have thought, but then something shot in front of it and punched it away with one punch. They heard the familiar yell, *"Screaming Bullet!"*

After the blast shot away, the women looked at their savior—it was Chris! But he was still badly hurt, and it looked as if that last punch had almost shattered his arm. He was breathing hard as he faced the Titan, still willing to fight no matter the cost.

The Titan was in shock to think that the cyborg was still alive—if one could call his current state alive. He looked almost like a cybernetic corpse! His flesh was burnt. The flesh side of his face looked almost skeletal. Indeed, his skull was even visible.

His clothing appeared to be almost burnt to his body, and right now the only thing holding him up was his will to fight on.

Jura's group could not believe how Chris looked either. One of them almost got sick in her mech. The thought that he could still be fighting moved them deeply. Jura and Neneko wanted nothing more than to wrap their arms around him and comfort him in this, his hour of need.

Neneko could not help but yell out to her Chris-chan, "Stop fighting!"

But then he turned to her and, with what looked like a smile from his skeletal face, said, "It's okay. I now know what my honor is—it's all of you, my most precious gems. And, for my honor, I will fight on."

xxx

Lorelei was still trying to get the power back on. She was now in the main power room, and it seemed that no matter what she did, nothing worked.

In frustration, she kicked the main console and yelled out, "Work!" The power shot on. Lorelei smiled. "That's all it needed," she said, "a little finesse!"

Suddenly the intercom buzzed. "Lorelei to the bridge. Lorelei to the bridge," came the professional voice, "*It's Chris!*"

"Chris?" Lorelei ran as fast as she could to the bridge. She was shocked to see Chris—alive—on the monitor. She was watching his conversation with Neneko. The shock of seeing Chris in such a state brought tears to her eyes. She fell to the ground thinking, *This can't be happening! This has to be a bad dream!* But it wasn't a dream. This was real, and Chris was standing forward again in a fight–ready stance.

xxx

The Titan laughed. It would not even be a challenge to fight Chris when he was in such a state. With one more blast at full power, the Titan could end this foolish farce!

Chris stood ready for anything. He knew his chances—it didn't take a genius to know that he was going to die in this fight, but he was still determined to sacrifice everything. Just as the Titan fired, Chris heard the voice of the shark-man who had talked to him in his dream.

"Chris Striker, do you remember what Lorelei said? That, if anyone touches your flesh, you will gain a special connection with them?"

"Yeah, I know, but kissing has to be involved, right?"

"No, you just have to have flesh-to-flesh contact. The kissing was just Lorelei's little joke. So, tell me how many of them have touched the flesh of your body?"

Chris remembered the party and said, "They all have."

"Good. Now focus that power … use it to make yourself stronger than you could ever imagine. Their love and their power is yours. Use it to stop the Titan once and for all. And remember, there is a power in you that you are not even aware of … a power so great that even the strongest of warriors will fall because of it.

After hearing the pep talk and thinking about what the shark-man had said, Chris focused his power to the women in *The Minawa* and the others, who were still in space. He could feel their power entering him. It was like nothing he had ever felt before.

xxx

Inside *The Minawa*, Lorelei and the crew-members all felt something strange. It was as if they could sense the battle that Chris was in. They could almost feel what he was doing. He seemed to be calling to them, asking them to give him their power … their strength.

"Miss Lorelei," said one of the crew-members, "what is it? It feels like Chris is calling us."

"He is," Lorelei said. She held her hand up and called out to Chris as if he was standing right next to her. "Take him down!" she shouted.

xxx

Meanwhile the Titan's battleships were surrounding *The Minawa*, preparing to fire. Just as they fired, *The Minawa* was engulfed in a shield of light. The attack beams bounced off the shield as if they were nothing. The warriors in the Titan's ships had no idea what was happening, but the crew in *The Minawa* did—Chris was protecting those he held dear to him. The Super Cyborg was glowing like a beacon in space.

His body started to heal as his flesh regenerated around his metal parts. The Titan, who was watching this miracle, stepped back from firing his cannon, for what he was seeing seemed to be impossible.

Chris stretched out his arms and legs as he roared out and changed into his Alpha Omega Cyber Lion mode. His body then changed again as he focused the power that Mina and Dita had given him, and he changed into his Silver Cyber Lion mode.

Roaring out into space, he then stood in a fighting stance. "This is where it ends, Lord Titan! And this time I'm not going to stop until you're nothing but a greasy smear on my fists!"

Titan could not believe what he was seeing. The cyborg was glowing like a silver star. His body had healed completely. Not only that, but the lionesses behind him seemed to be glowing as well. It was as if they were all connected to him. Still determined to win, Titan roared. His three dragon heads fired blasts at Chris, but the blasts did nothing. Chris's look never changed from the icy stare.

"This can't be happening. I will not be beaten a second time!" Titan roared out as he transformed back to his humanoid form and punched Chris once in the face and then in the stomach. But nothing happened. The Super Cyborg didn't react at all.

"Don't you see? Titan," said Chris. "All the hurt you have caused others has bought you to this moment. You don't have a chance against me. And you have done this to yourself. It's payment for all the years you have treated these wonderful women as your personal property."

"What are you talking about?" yelled the Titan. "I am stronger than all them. The weak must die so the strong can survive!" Titan drifted slightly away from the Super Cyborg Lion.

"If that's truly the way you think, Titan, then we'll play by your rules."

And Chris attacked with cruel rage, pounding on the Titan. The others watched with a feeling of power that they had never felt before. They turned to each other, knowing that they still had a battle of their own to get back to. They flew faster than they thought possible as they started their campaign to finish off the remainder of the Titan's forces.

XXX

As the Titan's last two remaining generals watched from inside *The Universe*, they were freaking out. They did not know what to do. Their leader was being beating back, and all of their forces had almost been taken out. There was nothing standing between them and destruction.

XXX

Jura and Neneko, meanwhile, knew that Chris had the Titan under control, and the other women warriors had the last of the Titan's battleships under control, so they decided to concentrate on *The Universe*. Lorelei had found out that the Titan's last two generals were hiding out there. Jura and Neneko each commandeered a battleship. Neneko made it to *The Universe* and tore into it, yelling out, "This is the end!" Then she yelled out *"Power Explosion!"* and the entire spaceship blew as if it was a super nova. The only thing left was the main power core.

Inside the other battleship, Jura saw the explosion that Neneko had caused. *That girl's got to learn some restraint!* she thought.

Jura then piloted her battleship to the main power core. She was about to blast it, when three mimetic beasts attacked her. But she had no time for them. She just fired a shotgun blast right into the main power core, blowing into oblivion. The entire ship was now gone. Neneko and Jura flew out unharmed signaling each other with a thumbs up. Each headed to another battleship.

XXX

Chris had truly had enough of the Titan and was ready to finish this battle with one more hit. He stood ready in front of the Titan.

"Ha, ha!" the Titan laughed darkly as he floated in front of Chris. "You truly are a hopeless fool if you think this is over."

Chris had no idea what the Titan was talking about. There was nothing left for the Titan to throw at him, but then the Titan raised both his dragon-handed arms in the air and focused the power from each dragon into a ball of energy above him.

"Do you think I didn't plan for this? I was a step ahead of you all the way!" Titan yelled out as he fired each energy blast at Chris. *"Hellfire Ball!"* yelled the Titan, but the Super Cyborg was unfazed as he took the blast head-on.

The Titan's balls of black energy shot at Chris, engulfing him. He roared out in pain, "I will not be beaten by this!" As the energy threatened to vaporize him, he was beyond pain.

Chris roared out as the balls of energy seemed to shrink into him, until they disappeared completely.

The Titan stepped back in shock.

"Why won't you die?" Titan yelled out as he fired at Chris again and again. But each blast just bounced off him. Chris then reared back. The top of his fist opened revealing a circler spinning light. As Chris reared back, the light spun faster.

Titan prepared for the blast.

"Screaming Fist of the Beast King!" Chris yelled out as he shot forward.

"Super Dragon Fist!" the Titan yelled as he also moved forward.

Their punches hit like lighting striking together in space. The force sent out shock waves that seemed to stretch out for miles. The two warriors' powers seemed to be even. No one could tell who was winning. But, suddenly, as they were both roaring like two mad animals, something cracked.

Titan looked at Chris. Then he looked at his own arm where a crack had appeared. The crack moved up his arm. "You will not win, Striker. There is no hope." More cracks appeared on the Titan's body.

As they clashed again, their force waves increased even more. They were both determined, both ready to die for their beliefs and desires. One was a beast who wanted to lay waste to an entire race, and the other was a man who believed in honor and love.

Chris roared. "I will not lose! There are a hundred and fifty sprites, all of whom are telling me to finish you off for good!"

Right then, an enormous super nova erupted between the two warriors. It seemed to shake the very fabric of space. On that day, for one brief shining moment, after all the pain he had gone through, after all the suffering, one man challenged all the odds and achieved the impossible.

Chris roared out as a light surround him and he tore through the Titan's body vaporizing him, but once again leaving the head intact.

The Titan thought that Chris would spare his life again, but he was wrong. Chris's body still embraced in the brilliant, shining light, grabbed the head. Chris Striker crushed the head of the Titan, which gave off one last sickening yell. Chris had ended the reign of the Titan for good. Chris blasted the Titan's remains with a single shotgun blast.

Chris then turned to the remainder of the Titan's armada. The battle still raged on. The warriors on both sides had not seen the final battle between Chris and the Titan. Chris knew it was time to finish this once and for all. He clapped his hands together and fired a power shotgun.

The beams of his attack sought out and destroyed the Titan's remaining battleships and didn't even touch any of the Chris's gems.

After the blasts subsided, there was nothing left of the Titan's armada but space junk. Chris found himself floating in space surrounded by his lionesses.

In the blink of an eye, Chris and the lionesses appeared inside the hangar of *The Minawa*. All of the women were amazed at the power that the cyborg had just displayed, and they all started gathering around him. They were so very happy that he was okay, but they saw that something was wrong—he still had an odd look about him.

Neneko was the first to speak to him. '

"Chris-chan, you just beat the Titan once and for all! You should be happy, what's wrong?"

Chris turned to her and then turned back the bay doors of the hangar. "There is one thing that is still bothering me. Just who was it that rebuilt 'the Titan the last time?"

CHAPTER 64

After the Titan was gone, the few of his men who were left scattered like rats from a sinking ship. They knew that, if the Titan was beaten, there was no way that they could beat any of his destroyers.

So Chris's gems and the Super Cyborg himself had one thing left to do—and that was to fix *The Minawa* and find their place in the Universe. With Chris by their side, there was nothing that they couldn't handle. That's when they decided to stay on Earth until they got *The Minawa* repaired. Chris hoped he could see his family again, and he and Neneko hoped to see Maylu and Leo.

xxx

The city of Tokyo seemed quiet. The people were going about their daily lives, but little did they know that, under their feet, deep underground, a plan was being made.

"So he's back," one of these planners said to another.

"Yes he is. In fact, he's about to run into some of the ones I hired to test his powers. And, if he is as powerful as I think he is, this is going to be fairly interesting."

"Well, I say the stronger he is, the better, if you ask me."

xxx

Meanwhile, Chris was sitting in an expensive-looking car near an exclusive shopping area. He was waiting for Pie-way and Destiny, who had decided to celebrate their victory by indulging in a little shopping extravaganza.

Chris was enjoying the music playing in his car when a young woman tapped at his window. His sunglasses, trench coat, and gloves covered his bionics, so he didn't mind responding to the summons.

"Is there something I can do for you, young lady?" Chris asked politely.

"Well," the girl said pointing to a car parked a few feet away from Chris's, "my car got a flat, and I was wondering if you could help me out."

Chris looked over at her car and said, "Sure thing." But, as he got out of the car, four big guys came out of her car, and the girl held a gun to Chris's head.

Chris didn't move as the guys got into his car. Chris then looked over to the girl holding the gun to his head and asked, "Does your mother know the kind of company you're keeping?"

The girl sneered at him. "Shut up," she said.

The thug who was sitting in the driver's seat of Chris's car tried to start the car. But nothing happened. He kept trying, with no luck. Finally, he turned to Chris and said, "Hey, what's the deal?"

"That car was made especially for me," Chris told him. "It will only start if I am in the driver's seat."

The four guys were furious as they got out of the car and circled around Chris like a bunch of sharks. The largest of the four grabbed Chris from behind and yelled, "I've got him!"

Chris just smiled and said, "Really?" Then he ducked down and sweep-kicked the guy to the ground. Then he dispatched two of the others—each one with a single move as he attacked.

The last of the guys pulled out a knife thinking that it would give him an edge, but Chris kicked the knife out of the guy's hand and into the air. Chris caught the knife as it came back down and held it at the guy's throat. Then, in one move, he closed the knife and hit the guy with his elbow knocking him to the ground.

Chris turned and looked at them all where they lay on the ground unconscious but alive. He shook his head as he started to walk back to his car. But the girl with the gun got in front of him. "Stop!" she yelled. But he kept moving. She fired one shot at him point blank, but, in a move too fast to see, Chris caught the bullet. "Don't do that," he said to the girl as he handed her the bullet. Before he walked off, he said to her, "Go home, and try to do something meaningful with your life."

The girl fell to her knees in shock as Chris walked off. Just then, Pie-way and Destiny arrived. They were laughing, having seen a little of what had gone on. "What took you so long?" asked Destiny.

Chris shook his head. "Just get in the car," he said, and they took off.

xxx

As Chris and the girls drove off, someone came out of the shadows and walked over to the still unconscious gang. He nudged one of them with his foot as he got out a cell phone and punched in a series of numbers. "He's coming your way," he said into the phone, "and he's even stronger than we thought, so be prepared."

Chris was listening to the radio in the car as the two girls in the back were chatting together. Suddenly, out of nowhere, something slammed into the side of the car sending it crashing into a guardrail.

The cyborg turned to the girls in the back. "Are you okay?" he asked.

"We're okay," said Pie-way. "What hit us?"

"I don't know!" Chris said, and he stepped out of the car. "Stay in the car," he said. Chris almost couldn't believe what he saw, for it was the Titan—but he was back to the way he had been when they first fought together.

"It can't be!" Chris said with a shaky voice.

"I am not the Titan," said the lookalike in a metallic tone devoid of emotion. "I am designed from him, though. I am known as Bulldozer, and I am here to take you to the creator."

The two girls in the car heard this. They were about to get out to help, but a look from Chris told them to stay put. Chris readied himself, but he was about to find out that this robot was more than he appeared to be.

As the Titan lookalike robot ran straight at Chris with incredible speed, it started to transform into a large cyber bull. Before Chris could react, it came running at him and slammed him into the wall of a nearby building, burying him in a mountain of rubble.

The Cyber bull, Bulldozer, snorted and raked his left hoof across the ground ready to strike again. But a roar erupted from the rubble as Chris burst out glowing in his hyper mode. He removed his sunglasses, which had broken in the impact, and threw them aside. He glared at the large robotic beast.

Bulldozer snorted again, and charged forward as Chris shot forward yelling out, *"Screaming Bullet!"*

They both struck head-on in a power struggle, but, as they fought for control, Bulldozer changed again. And Chris changed into his Cyber Lion form, Bulldozer stood up on two legs. His front hoofs became three-fingered hands. He grabbed Chris by the leg, picked him up, and swung him around. Then he slammed him into the street.

Bulldozer wasn't finished with Chris yet, though. He grabbed Chris's face and picked him up again, then slammed him back to the ground with even more force than before.

Bulldozer snorted again at Chris as he lay there. Without warning, Chris shot up and punched at the eight- foot beast-man.

Bulldozer felt the blow, but the force of the strike cracked Chris's hand. All it had done to the beast-man was push him back a bit.

Chris knew that he had to transform to his Alpha Omega Cyber Lion mode or he was finished. As he roared out and was halfway through the transformation, Bulldozer's horns started to glow red. Before Chris had a chance, electrical beams shot out of the horns at him. They were so hot they burned the clothes off his back and sent him into a wall, turning the bricks around him into dust.

Pie-way and Destiny had seen enough of this. They jumped out of the car and ran over to Chris as he lay unconscious.

Destiny was about to touch him when Pie-way grabbed her hand back. "No!" she said. "He's still too hot!" Just then, Bulldozer started to move over to them ready to take the cyborg back to his creator.

The two girls stood between Chris and the beast-man determined to protect Chris. But Bulldozer just brushed them off easily. He grabbed the cyborg by the leg and pulled him out of the rubble and brick dust. Then he jumped into the air and landed on the far side of the destroyed building. From there, he jumped off from building to building leaving the two girls alone and crying for him to bring Chris back.

xxx

Later, Chris awoke in a dark room. His arms and legs were strapped to a table. He was unable to move. No matter how hard he tried, he couldn't brake the bonds that held him. And, when he tried to transform, he was instantly given a huge jolt of electricity.

He struggled with his bonds, but he stopped when he heard a female voice say, "It's no use. No matter how strong your cybernetics are, you can never break those bonds. You can also forget about transforming to that Cyber Lion form of your's. It will only end in pain."

As the woman stopped speaking, she moved into the light, and Chris finally got a look at his captor. She was a young women in her early twenties. She was quite beautiful, but there was a dark side to her beauty. Chris could tell that this woman wanted something from him, but the question was, what?

The woman answered his question when she opened a panel in his head. Chris was about to ask her what she was doing, but it was too late. She connected a cable to his head. The Super Cyborg could feel only one thing'—*pain.*

xxx

When Pie-way and Destiny made it back to Cyber Corp, they were in tears. As they told their story to Lorelei and Neneko, Lorelei tried her best to calm them down, but they were both very upset.

Finally, after the girls had explained the gist of what had happened, Neneko said, "We have to find him!"

Lorelei said, "We will do everything in our power to find him."

They searched for two days without any luck. Then, one of the crew-members visited a Web site on the Internet.

There they saw Chris being tortured in ways that made them sick. They were slowly removing his body parts while he was still alive.

Sparks were flying out as machinery tore into his body. When it tore into his flesh, he screamed out in pain as blood poured over the machinery.

Lorelei did not move as she watched. She just stared with a horrified look on her face. But, suddenly she spoke.

"This is an outrage!" she yelled. The women around her stepped back. "Find out who is responsible for this! *Now!*" she cried. '

When Lorelei screamed out the last part of her command, everyone scrambled out of the room. They headed for every corner of the city to hunt down any clues as to where their cyborg was.

For three sleepless days and nights, they found nothing. On the fourth day, Jura was on watch duty outside the Cyber Corp building when a limo nearly ran her over. She jumped back in time as the door opened and a large bag was thrown out onto the street. Then the limo drove off, fast.

As she looked at the bag, she noticed that a metal spike was sticking out of it. And she noticed that it looked like a hand.

As Jura walked closer to the bag, the hand started to move. She jumped back for a second, but then slowly moved toward the bag again. With shaking hands, she tore at the cloth. What she saw made her throw up on the sidewalk. For, in the bag, was what was left of Chris Striker's body.

Chris's head started to shake back and forth. His mouth opened and closed as he tried to speak, but no sound came out. He moved the metal stubs that were once his arms.

Jura could barely hold herself up after she emptied her stomach. She finally screamed out as she fell over in a dead faint.

xxx

It was about a week later. Chris's upper torso was suspended by wires in Lorelei's lab. She, Destiny, and Pie-way had been working on him steadily since he had been found. Most of his body was still in pieces, but the women had faith that they could keep their protector alive.

The whole crew was watching as the three women worked on him. They were worried greatly for him, because he was their life and hope. Seeing him like this was heartbreaking, and they all agreed that they would do whatever it took to get the one who had done this to him.

Neneko entered the lab. "Is he going to be okay?" she asked for the hundredth time. But Lorelei turned to her and said, "I honestly don't know. So much of his body is torn up pretty badly. Whoever did this left him for dead."

Hearing this made them all cringe. What type of monster would to this? And the fear of losing him was too much to bear.

As they were working, a male Cyber Corp board member visited Lorelei's lab. "What is going on?" he asked.

When the crew turned to the man, they noticed that he was one of the men 'who had been trying to take the company away from them ever since Samantha Ivy had left Japan with Chris's son and daughter.

"We are trying to save Chris Striker's life," Jura told him. She was constantly in the lab following Chris's progress.

The well-dressed man walked over to Chris's body. He could see the cyborg twitch as the two women worked on him. He sneered as he asked, "Why work on him so hard? It's not like he still alive!"

Then he continued. "He's nothing but a machine anyway. Quite a few board members feel that it isn't cost effective to fix him—it would be more economical to just trash him."

'The moment the man said this, he felt killer intent all around him. The air in the room became thick, as if he was in a dark sea. He turned to see the faces of every woman in that room. They were staring him down, all of them giving off an aura that would crush any man and reduce him to a quivering mass of jelly.

Seconds later, the board member was thrown out of room bruised and beaten and fired from the company.

xxx

Meanwhile, in another lab, at a rival corporation, a woman was looking at a monitor. As it came to life, she looked at the face of an old enemy. He shot around the screen trying to free himself from the limited space he was in.

The woman spoke into a microphone to get the attention of the one on the screen. "Hello?" she said.

"Who are you, and where am I?" the one on the screen said as he looked around the room.

"Well, is that any way to greet the one who got you out of your prison?" the woman said as she sat back in her chair.

"Well, not that I'm not grateful," said the man. "But this place you've got me in has no cyberspace where I can move about, so this is like a prison too. Though I think I would take this prison over the other one. You don't know what it's like in that other prison, I was being chased by a big black, demonic lion for who knows how long!"

"Well, that's kind of what I want to talk to you about—that prison you were in, and the beast that chased you," the woman said. "I believe that beast was a true demon, one that has been locked inside that cyborg's metal for over a thousand years. I have studied the metal's properties for some time now, and I've learned that it is, in reality, a container for something very powerful. And I want it! So, here's the deal: You work for me, and I'll give you a real body."

"Why should I? And, didn't you just capture him and then let him go?"

"Yes, I did capture him, but I needed to make sure I was right about him, so I took him apart to get a piece of his metal. I made sure he would stay away while I work on this," the woman said as she held up a glowing piece of metal that she had retrieved from the cyborg.

"So you already got a piece of him. What do you need me for?"

"Well, my friend," said the woman. "I need you to keep the cyborg and his friends busy while I finish getting what I need from this fragment of his body. If you haven't noticed, this fragment is not just glowing. It's giving off its own life force as if it were alive."

"Well, lady, how do you expect me to do anything when you've got me trapped inside this box?"

"I was hoping you would ask," the woman said. She went over to a control panel and pressed a button that sent an electrical current into the monitor, shaking it violently until it exploded. What seemed to be living lighting was released from the explosion. It bounced wildly around the room until it finally struck the ground next to the woman. Then it assembled itself into a form.

Viral stood up in his new body. He looked at his hands, and then looked at the woman. He smiled and said, "You gave me a mimetic electrical body like the mimetic beasts that Lord Titan had."

"Yes," she responded. "But, unlike those primitive beasts, your body can change into anything. And I mean anything. The best part is that you can still jump into any electrical device you desire."

Viral looked back at the woman and smiled again. Then he knelt down before her and said, "I am under your complete control. What might I call my new master?"

"Vox," the woman clearly stated.

xxx

Two days later, late at night, Nodoka was watching over Chris's body. He had yet to respond to anything. Just then, though, as Nodoka was reading a book, the cyborg roared out, shaking like mad on the wires that still held up his body.

Nodoka was so scared when this happened that she almost fell out of her chair. She looked over to Chris and saw him shaking and moving about on the lines that were holding him up.

That's when he yelled out as a black aura surrounded him. The wiring that was still sticking out of him lashed out. The black aura started a healing process. The flesh began to heal, and the wiring and the metal started regenerating.

Nodoka was in such awe as she watched this that she forgot to call the others. When she was able to shake off the shock, she ran over to the com system and called everyone to the lab. If her call didn't get everyone there, the roars of the lion would. Chris had awakened everyone.

Lorelei was the first one there. She could not explain what she was seeing. Chris's body was fixing itself. But the thing that took her off guard was the black aura surrounding him. It felt wrong for Chris. It felt evil and dark—almost as if some demon had been awakened. It brought fear down to her very core.

By the time everyone got to the lab, Chris's body had been completely regenerated. But, when he stood up, there were a few red faces in the room, for he was naked. Lorelei approached him. "How do you feel?" she asked him. But he didn't answer. He just stood there not moving.

Then it hit her—his mind was still in status lock. That meant that his body had regenerated on its own. But that made no sense. Finally, she covered him because some of the others were still a little uncomfortable.

Then she turned to face him. She knew that the computer side of his brain was activated, so she asked him, "What happened to you?"

Chris didn't respond. Lorelei thought for a minute, then stated her question differently, as if she was giving an order, "Report status!" she ordered.

This time, he responded in a robotic tone, "This unit was dismantled by an unknown party. A large part of this unit's mind was tampered with."

"Which part of the mind was tampered with?" Lorelei asked fearing the worst.

"Viral containment."

Hearing this Lorelei almost fell backwards, but Neneko braced her up and asked her, "What's wrong? What does viral containment mean?"

Lorelei was white as a sheet as she told her, "It means that they took the living computer virus—Viral." When Lorelei said this, the room went deadly quiet. They all knew the trouble that Viral could cause in a city that depended more on electronics than almost any other one in the world.

xxx

Viral was out on the town, walking around enjoying the freedom given to him by his new body. He looked at the people with a big grin on his face thinking about what bad things he was going to do to them.

He stopped at a corner and put his hand on a building. Then he walked along raking his hand across the surface of the building. As he did, electricity shocked through the walls and blew up every electrical device in the building. An explosion erupted around the building as he walked along just humming an eerie tune. He moved beyond the building destroying everything he touched.

A police officer stopped him realizing that Viral was the one that was causing the chaos.

Viral turned to the officer and smiled innocently. The cop yelled, "Stop where you are and put your hands on the ground!"

Once again, Viral just smiled as he complied. He placed his hands to the ground, but, when he did, the street exploded.

Large electrical wires shot out of the ground whipping around like mad under Viral's control.

One cable wrapped itself around the officer. The officer was electrocuted in a shower of sparks. Other cops arrived on the scene, ready for the mad man, but his control over anything electrical made him a force to be reckoned with. With Chris being out of commission, things didn't look good for the city.

xxx

Lorelei was trying to determine why Chris was still not waking up, when Mary, one of the crew-members, ran into the lab. "Miss Lorelei, there is a powerful electrical mimic man in the middle of the city! He's wrecking everything!" Lorelei turned to a monitor to see for herself. Using a satellite, she focused in on the chaos that was erupting as the mimic beast-man tore apart the city.

She recognized him right away. "Viral," she said in a shaky voice. Then she turned to Mary. "Go get Jura and Neneko please." And she turned to Chris in one last effort to reactivate him.

Lorelei turned on the link to *The Minawa*. Maybe Minawa might have an idea.

xxx

Jura and Neneko had heard about the mimic man who was trying to destroy the whole city. They were on their way to see if they could stop him.

Jura was climbing into one of the lioness mech's. Neneko had just flown off without a mech, using her own powers.

"Show off!" Jura yelled as she settled herself in the mech and took off.

xxx

Meanwhile, Viral had just torn through a bus. It had exploded into flames, the people inside screaming in fear. The cops had been unable to stop him with conventional weapons. Their bullets just went right through him. They had little chance of beating him.

Viral walked out of the flames of the burning bus. Suddenly, out of nowhere, two beams hit him into a far wall. As Neneko landed near the flames, she used her water capabilities to put out the fire. Jura landed in her mech. Viral was getting up to see what had hit him when that something hit him deeper into the wall. The punches continued, each one sending him deeper into the wall until his head blew up in a mass of electrical energy.

Jura took a step back to see if the freak was going to stay down; most of their enemies never seemed to want to die!

Viral's body moved forward without its head. Being headless didn't seem to bother him, because he started to move toward her. As Viral struck at her, his head came back in a flash of light. He punched her again, skidding into a building.

"So it seems 'Striker's bitches are doing his dirty work now!" Viral called out. "Is he still in the catatonic state that Vox left him in?"

When Jura heard the mimic man say this, something clicked. She blasted her way out of the building and came out fist first yelling out her own screaming bullet. Though the bullet wasn't as powerful as Chris's it still could shatter a building in one hit.

Seeing the lioness Jura coming, Viral just raised his hand and caught her fist with one hand. He laughed that she had thought her low-grade punch could damage him in his new form.

Jura was shocked to say the least, for how could he have become so strong? But she had no time to think of this. Viral's 'body changed shape faster than she could follow. In seconds, Viral had wrapped his body around her mech.

Jura did her best to shake the freak off her, but he was too strong. He laughed as he sent electricity throughout the mech's body electrocuting her—he was cooking her inside her own mech.

Jura had to think fast or she was as good as dead. Just when it looked as if Viral was about to finish her, an electrical blast shot Viral off of her. He squirmed around as the electrical charge shot through his mimic body.

"Are you all right?" Neneko asked as she ran over to Jura.

"Yeah, I'm fine … just get him before he gets away!" Jura said as she stood back up.

Neneko vanished in a flash, and reappeared in front of Viral. As he got to his feet, Neneko charged her fists with electricity and she punched him.

Each punch that contacted seemed to strip away at Viral's body.

"I figured that an electrical punch would put a few dents in your mimic body," Neneko stated, as she continued to wail on the freak. Suddenly, however, as fast as a flash of light, Viral vanished, and Neneko's final punch connected with nothing but air.

In the second it took Neneko to realize that Viral had vanished, he reappeared behind her.

Neneko heard the sound of flesh being torn and felt unimaginable pain as four fingers like blades pressed through her body. The cyborg women coughed up blood as she started to fall forward. To Viral's surprise, however, she vanished out of sight and reappeared behind Viral.

The mimic man didn't know what had happened, but Neneko did—she had substituted a hologram for herself just as Viral had struck her.

Neneko blasted Viral with a fireball that sent him flying, and then she vanished again and reappeared on top of him. She focused all her powers as she hit the mimic man into the ground as hard as she could.

Viral impacted the ground with incredible force. Then Neneko fired everything she had at the freak screaming out as she fired down on him.

Rubble and debris flew everywhere. As the dust started to clear, Neneko was breathing hard. She looked around at the destruction in the area where she had fired blast after blast, but she couldn't find any sign of Viral anywhere. "Wow!" she said. "I must have gotten him."

As she started her descent to the ground, Neneko heard the voice of the one she cared for the most in her life. "Good job!" She turned to see her Chris-chan standing in the street arms open wide as if he was welcoming her home. She was so happy to see him that she flew straight to him and wrapped her arms around his neck. He was alive! But, when she looked at him, something seemed off.

"Chris-chan, are you okay?" Neneko asked taking a good look at him as she took a step back.

He smiled at her and as he said, "Why do you ask, Neneko? It's me, Chris. Everything is okay."

As Chris said this, Neneko was sure something was wrong. She could see it in his eyes. They didn't show the normal look of kindness that she had known all her life. And something about his smile didn't seem genuine.

Right as she was thinking this, Chris's smile faded. He pulled back his fist for a punch as Neneko looked at him. She was confused. Suddenly, however, Jura yelled out, "He's not the real Chris!"

Neneko jumped back just as Jura came forward and punched the fake Chris out of the way, sending him flying into the wall of a nearby building.

"Thanks!" Neneko said to Jura. "But how did you know?" Jura just pointed behind her to where Chris and Lorelei were standing.

Neneko took one step toward them, but saw Chris's expression. He still 'didn't seem like himself yet.

Viral managed to get to his feet when he saw Chris. At first he thought that maybe the Super Cyborg had awakened, but, judging by the emotionless expression on his face, he realized he was probably wrong. He smiled. This was going to be easy.

Neneko made it to Lorelei as Viral shot forward at them, electrifying the area as he went. Just as he was about to slam into them, Lorelei yelled into a wrist computer, "Chris, stop him!"

The Super Cyborg reacted immediately. He grabbed the mimic man's hand in mid punch.

Lorelei then ordered Chris, "Kill Viral at any cost."

"Affirmative," Chris stated in a mundane tone that didn't match his normal tone. What they witnessed next was incredible. Chris kicked Viral back and then shot forward in a flash and punched at Viral at impossible speeds, even for him.

"Lorelei, what's going on?" asked Neneko in astonishment. "I have never seen Chris-chan move so fast before!"

"Well," said Lorelei, "it's the fact that he has no restrictions holding him back—no emotions. Chris was always the type to hold back no matter who he fought. Now that he is in this state, there's nothing holding him back."

After Neneko and Jura heard this, they all watched as Chris beat Viral as if the mimetic beast was standing still. They had never seen Chris fight with such cruelty and violence before. It was like watching someone else fight rather than the man they knew.

As they watched, something seemed to be happening to Chris. He seemed to be powering up as he fought Viral. After one last punch to Viral's face, which sent him flying, Chris changed to his Alpha Omega Cyber Lion mode.

Lorelei was in shock. He shouldn't have been able to do that in his current state of mind. And something else was wrong—the mane of the lion had become flames that flashed from red to black and back again.

This made no sense to her or the others, but, when Viral looked up from where he landed and saw this transformation, he seemed to go into a panic as if he knew what was happening.

Viral stood 'quickly. "You stay away from me, you son of a bitch! You're not getting me this time!" Then he slammed his hands into the ground, creating an electrical blast that sent metal and debris flying at the Cyber Lion, who fell crashing to the ground. A pile of debris accumulated over him.

Viral was breathing hard after this attack, but he started to laugh at the thought that he had gotten Striker. But he knew his victory celebration was premature when he heard a metallic lion's roar that seemed to echo around the whole city. Right then, the beast blasted out from under the debris in a black flame that surrounded the Cyber Lion in a dark display of power. Everyone was in shock as they saw his face, for it seemed as if Chris had finally awakened. But those who were close to him knew that something was wrong. The grin on his face seemed to predict the end of everything, and Viral seemed to be going to a panic as he watched the lion's form change. The mane seemed to be made of black fire as it moved with a life of its own.

The fur of the beast was black as night, and his whole body seemed to radiate evil—something they had never seen in Chris before.

"Chris-ch-chan?" Neneko stuttered out as she witnessed this transformation in the man she loved.

The cyber beast-man—the Black Flame Lion—stepped forward, the black flames dancing a dance of death around him as he moved toward the mimic man that once had been a living computer virus.

Viral had no intention of dying. He took off as fast as his feet could take him, but, when he began to run, the Black Flame Lion appeared in front of him. Viral turned to go another way, and the beast was there again. It seemed that, no matter where he turned, the Black Flame Lion was there.

"Get away from me, you freak!" Viral yelled out as he took to the air in an attempt to fly away from the Black Flame Lion. But Chris smirked at this game of cat and mouse, and vanished in a black flash.

Lorelei, Neneko, and Jura could not figure out what was going on. Chris's body seemed genuine enough. But 'the way he was acting was definitely not like the Chris Striker they knew. This one was ruthless and enjoyed the thought of hunting down Viral. At that moment, they watched as the Super Cyborg Black Flame Lion caught up to Viral in the sky.

"This time, Viral, there is no escape," The Black Flame Lion said in a voice that sent chills down everyone's spine.

No one could believe the rumble that seemed to erupt when the cyborg spoke. All the hairs on their necks stood up at the sound of the demonic voice that came from the black lion. And, at that moment, they knew that the Black Flame Lion was not the Chris they knew—but who was he?

"Get away from me!" Viral screamed as he flew off in the opposite direction. The Black Flame Lion just smirked, and the black flame started to burn higher around him until it focused around his fist. "*Fist of the Black Flame!*" he roared out.

The Black Flame Lion punched forward as a fist made of black flames shot out from his extended arm, heading straight to it's target. Viral saw it coming. He yelled out as it flew at him. When the fist hit, it seemed as if it was feeding on him. It consumed him in blackness and then it just exploded in a shockwave.

As the dust in the air cleared, the Black Flame Lion was laughing at his destruction of Viral. As he laughed, what was left of Viral fell to the ground in an electrical charge.

All that was left of him was his upper torso, right arm, and half his head, but, not being human, he was still alive.

The three women ran over to where Viral had landed and looked at his remains. Even now he was trying to get away. When he saw the three of them, he begged them, "Please help me. I don't want to "be destroyed by that Black Lion.

"You know what that thing is?" Lorelei asked Viral.

"Yes," he said. "That is the beast that chased me during the time I was contained inside your so-called Super Cyborg's head." He was still trying to pull himself together so he could get away.

Neneko looked back up at her Chris wondering just what this beast was. Viral continued to tell them about the time he was contained inside Chris's mind. He told them how, right before Chris contained him, he had stated, "We all have our inner demons, and this lion is my inner demon."

Right when Viral said *demon*, Lorelei remembered the legend of the Black Flame Lion. She had always thought it was just a legend, but she didn't have time to think about it right now, for the Black Flame Lion found them, and was charging up another attack that would most definitely finish them all.

Lorelei had to think quickly. She pulled out a devise from her pocket and pointed it at Chris. "I'm so sorry," she said 'as she pushed a button. As soon as she did, the Black Flame Lion stopped in his tracks. He looked as if he had just had a heart attack. Slowly, he reverted back to normal and crashed down to the ground.

"What did you do, Lorelei?" Neneko asked in disbelief.

"It's a kill switch," Lorelei stated as she held up the devise in question. "It's for use in case something like this happens, but it's very dangerous to use because it completely shuts him down for a split second. If I use it too much, it could kill him."

"Is it like what happened to him when that Doctor Connor got a hold of him?" asked Neneko.

"Something like that," answered Lorelei. "But this one is more like a reboot switch as well. With any luck, when he comes around, he should be back to normal."

Hearing this, Neneko took off as fast as her feet could take her, and in seconds she was next to Chris trying to wake him.

xxx

Meanwhile, deep within Chris's mind, a human Chris Striker was unsure of what had happened to him. He found himself walking through what seemed like a dark prison of some kind. There seemed to be nobody there, until he heard a low growl rumbling around him. At first he could not tell where it was coming from. Then he passed one of the larger cells. If it were not for his fast reflexes, he would have been slashed by the claws that shot out between the bars.

He turned back to the cell and realized that was where the growl was coming from. As he slowly got closer to the cell, he saw two glowing red eyes. And, as the light from the ceiling started swinging back and forth in the cell, he saw what could only be called a demon.

But it can't be a demon, he reasoned. *There is no such thing, right?* But the beast started to laugh, and then it spoke.

"You don't believe in me, but you believe in beings from other planets, right?"

"That's different."

"But it is a fact that I am a demon. It is also a fact that I was close to being free. But your little bitch stopped me."

Hearing this made Chris react. "Did you hurt them?" he yelled. "For, so help me, if you did, I'll—"

But Chris was stopped there by the demon as it started to laugh again.

"Know that I didn't hurt them, but I was about to. One of them pulled out a device that shut down your body and reversed us back to the way we were—with me in here, and you out there."

Chris thought about this, and realized that the demon was right. For some time he had been in that cell unconscious. But he remembered what had happened when that woman took him apart. She had taken Viral out of him. He had fallen into that cell and lost his way, and that let this demon lion out.

Chris then wondered something—how had the demon gotten inside him in the first place? As if the demon lion could read his mind, which, in fact, it could, it started to tell him about the metal he was made of and where it had really came from.

"Centuries ago," began the lion demon, "my power reigned across the universe. My power was said to be unstoppable. I was able to burn away anything in my path. I could destroy whole solar systems with just a roar. But, one day, a warrior came. He was said to be the protector of the universe—an immoral being with powers as great as any demon. With the help of the warrior, my power was contained inside an asteroid. Decades later, the asteroid crashed onto the planet you now call Gem. Your Minawa found it and discovered that the metal had unique properties. It even gave off its own life force. She did not realize that the life force was, in fact, *my* power.

"When she brought the metal to Earth, she used it to make a Super Cyborg. She never realized that, one day, my power of the Black Flame Lion would be released. Each time you got enraged, I came through a little stronger. What I did not expect was that your son also contains my power.

"And it is your anger and your son's anger—your will to kill— that frees me. And, let me tell you, you and your son have two of the strongest tempers I have ever seen!"

"You lie!" Chris yelled out. "I do *not* have that kind of temper. I am a pacifist at heart, not a short-tempered demon in any way. That goes for my son too!"

"Ha, ha, ha," the black lion laughed. "You don't get it, do you? Your rage is greater than you'll ever know, and so is your son's."

Hearing the demon say things about his son made Chris stiffen. *What does my son have to do with this?* he thought. And then he remembered how his son had managed to stop Akurei. And how his strength kept increasing. All 'this time, it had been his own anger feeding this demon's power. Every time he fought and got enraged, the demon became stronger. But Chris couldn't figure out how this demon was able to get stronger through his son too.

Then he realized that the metal that he was made of was also growing in his son's body, which meant that the demon was in him too. That was why his son was strong despite the fact that he was so young.

Chris looked back to the demon in the cage. "What about my son?"

The beast laughed again so hard and shook the area around him. "If you ever come in contact with your son again, I will truly be free. Nothing will ever stop me again—not even that warrior from long ago."

Chris yelled out as he transformed himself into his Cyber Lion mode. He roared out in pure rage as he realized that he could never go near his son again without risking freeing this demon.

"Why are you telling me all this?" Chris asked the demon. "Wouldn't it benefit you more to keep this from me?"

"Fool, I'm a demon! I live to make others suffer … to see their hope slowly drain to nothing. I'm hoping to see you try and stop me, only to watch as you fail." The demon laughed as he watched Chris's anger rise. Chris was so enraged, he ripped out of this prison world. He jumped up and began to change into his beast form. As he roared in frustration, the girls appeared and tried their best to calm him, but they could do little to help him, for he was just to strong.

xxx

"My son!" screamed Chris. "I can never see my son, again!" He finally started to revert back to normal, but fell to his knees in exhaustion.

He turned to the women he had grown to love. When they asked what had happened to him, he told them about the demon that was contained inside the metal he was made of. He told them that his son had that same demon in him. He told them how, if he and his son ever came into contact again, the demon would be truly free—free to destroy everything in its path.

Neneko was devastated, for Leo was her son too. And she knew that her Chris-chan wanted to be there for his son and to teach him and his daughter the lessons that he had learned from her grandfather. But now there was no way he could ever see his son again.

Neneko knelt next to Chris and wrapped her arms around him. She knew that they still had no idea who had given Viral his mimic body. Slowly, Chris managed to get himself back together. He stood up and walked over to where they were keeping what was left of the freak Viral.

Viral was lying on a lab table. The blast that he had taken from the Black Flame Lion had nearly destroyed the data that made up his body, so there wasn't much left of him, but, when Chris and Neneko came in, he went into a panic. He was afraid that the cyborg was still under the control of the Black Flame Lion, but then Chris told him, "Don't worry, I'm myself again."

"Ha!" Viral laughed. "You think you're yourself. You'll never be yourself again if that demon has anything to say about it."

"How do you know about this demon?"

"Don't you remember what you told me, when you trapped me inside that thick skull of yours?"

"Refresh my memory," Chris stated with a sneer as he leaned over Viral's torn body.

"You told me that we all have our inner demons, and then you said that you were going to show me yours.

That's when I saw that black lion thing. Do you know that thing chased me throughout cyberspace *for almost a year?*" Viral almost yelled the last part of his sentence.

Chris stood up and looked up to the ceiling in deep thought. Then he turned back to Viral and said, "All right then, buddy, tell me this— who gave you that mimic body?"

"I'll tell you if you if you promise to stay away from me," Viral said. He was shaking a bit because, when Chris looked at him, his cyber eye changed briefly into a feral slit and then changed back again.

"You'll tell me or I'll rip your throat out!" Chris's rage increased every second as he slammed his hand against the lab table, shaking the room.

Lorelei and the others in the room stepped back in shock. They so rarely saw their Chris show so much anger. They had never seen him like this—it was as if he was still possessed or something.

Neneko stepped in and put a hand of Chris's shoulder, trying to calm him down. But, when she touched him, he quickly turned to her, both his eyes glowing a demonic red. He was breathing hard as well. But Neneko slapped him across the face, snapping him out of it. "Calm down!" she yelled.

He shook his head a little as he turned back to her. He was looking a little uneasy, and then he walked out of the room.

Lorelei motioned for Neneko to follow him to make sure he was all right. Lorelei and the others in the room finished getting what they needed from Viral.

Neneko then followed Chris out of the room.

Chris had stopped at the corner in the hall. He stood with his head against the wall trying to clear his head. Ever since he had met that demon lion, he hadn't felt right. He felt as if he was being torn apart from the inside out. And, when he felt Neneko next to him, without her even saying anything, he knew what she was going to ask, but he let her ask anyway.

"Chris-chan, are you all right? Ever since you woke up, you haven't been yourself. I mean, I have never seen you so angry before. It was like you were a different person. Are you sure you're all right Chris-chan?"

"I'm just a little tired, Neneko-chan," he said in a sad tone. "I just need some time to think things through. I'm going to my room to try and sort thing out." And, with that, he walked off only stopping now and again to put his hand against a wall to steady himself.

Neneko watched him go and feared that something terrible was happening to the man she loved. She could feel it, and the original eleven inside her stirred a bit at this feeling.

xxx

Meanwhile, Lorelei had just asked Viral again who had given him his mimic body. Just as he was about to tell her, his body started to electrify. He yelled out in agony as his body began to self-destruct.

"Everyone, get *down!*" Lorelei yelled. Viral's 'body blew up. The explosion not only blew up the lab table that he was on, it blew up half the lab as well.

Neneko ran into the lab as soon as she heard the explosion. "Is everyone all right?" She quickly put out the fire that erupted. Everyone was slowly getting back up from wherever they had been blown. Lorelei was the first to look to see what was left of Viral. As she looked through the wreckage of the lab table, she picked up a small chip that had made up his body. "Does this mean we won't find out who made Viral's mimic body?" Neneko asked her.

Lorelei turned to her and said, "I think there might still be a way." And she quickly walked off into the next room, and shut the door leaving Neneko and the some of the others to clean up the mess.

CHAPTER 65

It had been a couple of hours since Viral had blown up, and Chris was lying on his futon, a look of pain on his face, as he dreamed he was floating in space. He watched as a battle unfolded. He saw the one that had appeared before him when he last fought the Titan. But he still could not tell who or what it was. All he saw was an outline or a shadow of a man or a beast—or was it a shark?

Whatever—or whoever—it was, he was fighting against the Black Flame Lion. Chris could see the battle in his mind, but he didn't know that there, behind the Black Flame Lion, was someone calling out and giving it commands, as if it was the beast's owner or a tamer.

Chris 'watched the fight unfold.

The one fighting the Black Flame Lion was incredible. His style of fighting was unmistakably familiar, then Chris realized it was the very same art he himself had learned from his sensei.

Suddenly, the shark-man did something amazing—as he stretched back both his arms, his hands started to electrify. At that moment, he flung both arms forward yelling his attack, which Chris' couldn't hear from his position. The throw, which looked like a mass of twirling light spinning right at the Black Flame Lion, hit it dead on in a powerful explosion.

The lion roared out in pain. Right then another combatant' appeared. This one was female by the look of her. She made a few hand signs that the cyborg couldn't see clearly, and then forced her hands at the beast pushing it toward a large asteroid. In an instant, the battle was over as the beast was sucked into the asteroid. But Chris could still see and hear the one who was commanding the beast.

Even though this entity's body looked male, the voice sounded female. It yelled to the two that contained her pet, "One day I will free my pet, and, on that day, the universe will be mine. For I will find both of you and destroy you."

Hearing and seeing all this unfold, Chris wondered how could he know about this. He got his answer as he heard the laugh of the Black Flame Lion behind him.

Turning around, he saw the beast as the world around him changed to the prison where he had first seen the black beast.

"So you saw it, didn't you? You saw what happened on the day I was contained inside that asteroid all those years ago," said the Black Flame Lion. "What did you think? Amazing, isn't it?"

"Amazing, yes," Chris told the demon beast behind the bars of his cell. "But hardly enough to scare me if that was what you are trying to do."

"I wasn't trying to scare you. I'm trying to tell you that your time is up ... that soon I will be free to serve my mistress again."

"Not while I live!" Chris yelled into the cage. But the lion smirked at him and then roared out, "You don't have a choice, fool! This body of yours will be mine! One way or another, I will be free!"

"*No!*" Chris yelled out aloud as he woke up. He put a hand to his head as he tried to shake the feeling of dread out of his system.

xxx

Lorelei was still examining the chip that housed the mind of Viral and gave him his mimic body. She put it under a microscope trying to find any clue as to who made it, but the chip was burned out beyond recognition. But then she saw three letters on the corner of the chip: VOX.

She froze in her place as memories came flooding back … memories of a lab assistant she had banished from her world many years ago for conducting monstrous experiments.

Lorelei put her hands against her lab table in disbelief, for, if it really was Vox, things were about to get really bad.

xxx

Chris stood on the roof of the Cyber Corp building staring out into the night sky. The nightmares were still fresh in his mind. Who was it that that contained the Black Flame Lion? And who was the one who was giving the Black Flame Lion commands?

A thought crossed his mind. *If I take* out the one *'who has been giving the orders to the lion, maybe the beast will go quiet again. But how will I find her—or it? I have no clues.*

As he was thinking about this, someone landed near him. Since his mind was elsewhere, he didn't even sense the attack coming until she was right on him.

He turned around right at the very moment the attack struck him sending him flying into a far wall on the other side of the roof. He looked up and saw a women walking toward him.

"What do you want from me?" he asked as he got up fast.

But she smiled at him and said, "I want what's inside you. I want my pet back."

"So you are the mistress of that thing, are you?" Chris said. "Well, you can forget it! For, even though I don't want the beast, it's staying where it is. There is' no way that I'm going to let *you* have it! That would be too dangerous."

"'It is *my* pet! And I know exactly what it can do. That's the reason I want it back!" Right after the woman finished saying this, she vanished, moving at incredible speeds, and appeared again in front of the cyborg. She moved so fast, he couldn't even make a move. She struck him right in the stomach sending him flying skyward out of control.

Right as Chris regained his control, she appeared behind him. She hit him again, sending him hurtling back to the ground with an impact that shook the ground.

Chris managed to pull himself up onto his elbows. She appeared standing before him. He wondered about her—she seemed to have greater strength than his own.

The woman picked him up by his neck, grinning at the pain that he was in. Then she kicked him into a wall with monstrous force. The impact caused the building to crumble and fall on him.

"Do you see the difference in our power, Cyborg?" the women yelled. "If you don't give me what I want, I will kill you to get it out. I was hoping that Viral would manage to make you angry enough to release my pet, but he failed, so now I must do it myself."

Chris pulled himself out of the rubble. His eyes glowed red. His pupils turned to feral slits. He stood up and roared out a metallic roar that echoed around him.

"Well it seems that I'm getting close to my goal," the woman said as she saw his rage. He stared at her ready to attack, but then another woman's voice yelled out, and, suddenly, Chris's attacker was hit by a fireball, which blasted her away.

Neneko landed. "Chris, snap out of it!" she said sharply. "This is exactly what Vox wants you to do! You have to stop!" But, no matter what she said, she wasn't getting through to him. This time, his rage had gotten the best of him. Being in close proximity to the Black Flame Lion's owner had awakened his anger, and the demon wanted out.

Chris roared out, his power shooting out of him as rubble and dust blew around him. Neneko tried to calm him, but he was slowly losing his mind in rage.

"Forget it, girly," Vox said as she walked toward Neneko. "He's mine now, and soon my pet will be free."

As Neneko looked back at Chris and then back at Vox, she could not believe that her Chris-chan could ever become a monster. But then he turned to her, reared his fist back, and punched her. Neneko flew into the air as a black flame aura surround him.

Chris turned back to the woman. He seemed to be smiling as he took his first steps toward her.

"Yes, my pet, come to me," the woman said as she motioned Chris to move toward her. As he walked toward her, the fiery glow started to burn higher, and the flames themselves seemed to have a life force of their own as he moved to her seemingly in a trance.

Chris knelt before her, and she held out her hand, expecting him to take it to show his loyalty. But when he did, he quickly looked up at her. Her eyes were still burning red as he started to crush her hand.

She screamed as the bones in her hand cracked, and she went down on her knees as he stood up. "How did you—" was all she got out as he roared, changing to his Alpha Omega Cyber Lion mode.

"You just don't get it, do you?" the Super Cyborg said. "This is *my* body, and no one will take it from me!"

"But you hit your woman!" She blurted out.

"Did I?" Chris simply stated as he turned to where Neneko lay. Neneko stood and dusted herself off. It was then obvious to Vox that the cyborg and Neneko had played a charade to 'deceive her.

"This can't be!" shrieked Vox. "My pet is stronger than you!"

"You thought wrong, bitch!" Neneko said as she jumped and landed next to the Cyborg Lion.

"Neneko!" Chris said with a grin, " language!" Then he turned to the woman he held by one arm. But she seemed to be giving off the same black flame that he was. As she stood up, she reared back with her free hand, and punched Chris, sending him flying in the opposite direction.

Neneko watched him go flying, and then turned back to Vox. But Vox was ready. She hit Neneko and sent her flying just like the Super Cyborg.

Chris, on his way down, skipped off a building and crashed hard into the ground. He pushed himself up just as he saw Neneko headed right toward him. He quickly moved to catch her. But Vox shot over. Chris moved Neneko behind him so he wouldn't be hurt. In what seemed like slow motion, Vox hit him in the back so hard that he coughed up blood.

He was sent flying again, but this time the impact had also knocked him out cold. He slammed hard into a building, shattering half the building, and sending the people into the street running away screaming.

Vox flew up into the sky and clapped her hands together charging an attack. If she could not have her pet back, she was going to make sure that nobody was going to have him.

The power orb that she made had enough power to take down the city, but, right as she was about to let it go, a lioness mech slammed into her making her throw the orb into the sky. It flew off and fell harmlessly into the ocean miles away. But the explosion that it made erupted and rained down over the city.

Vox turned to her assailant and said, "So, Lorelei, how long has it been? Two? Three hundred years?"

"Not long enough, Vox, and you're still the same even after all these years," Lorelei said. "You still quest for power."

"Can you blame me?" retorted Vox. "I mean, after you built Titan, I had to have that kind of power for myself."

"So how did you do it anyway?" Lorelei asked.

Vox smiled as she said, "It was simple really. I found a race of beings with incredible power, and they gave me the power I wanted. In return I, cyberized most of their armies making them stronger."

"Did they also give you that Black Flame Lion?"

"As a matter a fact, they did," said Vox. "But someone managed to trap him inside an asteroid a few years back. When I found out that the metal in the asteroid was used to make your cyborg friend, I knew I had a chance to get him back."

"Well, Vox, judging from what I saw, it would seem that the cyborg has learned how to control your little pet, from the inside. My guess is that he'll be back up here in a few minutes. And, when he gets here, he's going to rip you apart for what you did to Neneko."

When Lorelei said this, Vox turned to the building where she had last seen Neneko. There was the Cyber Lion, holding Neneko in his arms. He shot a glare at her with enough killer intent to bring the Devil to his knees.

Vox could tell when she was outmatched. She turned back to Lorelei and said, "Next time we'll finish this," and she spun around and disappeared out of sight. Lorelei took a breath and then flew over to land next to Chris. "Are you two okay?" she asked.

Chris looked at her still with those blood-red eyes. He was still not completely in control of his actions.

"Chris, it's all right now," Lorelei said, trying to calm him down.

He looked at her and then back to the sky where Vox had disappeared. "Who—or what—was that?" he asked in a shaky, but firm tone.

"That was Vox," Lorelei told him, "She was once one of us, but she found an incredible power that changed her. I doubt that she is even still human."

"We should go home. It appears that you have a lot to tell me. And Neneko needs you," Chris said as he turned to fly, Neneko cradled in his arms.

Still in the lioness mech, Lorelei watched. She wondered if he was still Chris Striker or if the Black Flame Lion had managed to take his soul from him. Only time would tell.

xxx

The next day, Chris went straight to Lorelei's lab. He flung the doors open as he went in.

Lorelei and Destiny were currently working on Neneko. She had taken a considerable amount of damage. "She's going to need a lot of rest," Destiny stated.

Chris stepped over to Lorelei and said, "We need to talk." He grabbed her arm and pulled her over to the far corner.

"Okay, Lorelei, just who or what was that thing I fought yesterday? And how did she know so much about the metal?"

Lorelei sighed before she spoke, "Her name is Vox. She was once one of us until she betrayed us, a few years before the Titan took control. In fact, there is something else you should know about her that is very important."

"And what would that be?"

"She and Minawa are sisters."

When Chris heard this, he took a step back, and then looked to the ceiling. "Minawa!" he called out. He knew that she was still connected to the computer in the building as well as in *The Minawa*.

When she answered, he asked, "Is what Lorelei saying true? Is Vox really your sister?"

"Yes, Chris, she is, but you have to realize that she cut away all relations when she left our planet in search of power. We believe she found it in a race that was unknown to us—and still is—for she was no longer human when she came back with that Black Flame Lion and powers we had no defense against. But, two strangers who came to our planet managed to save us by containing the Black Flame Lion inside an asteroid. We were very grateful for that."

"And, let me guess," said Chris in a cold tone, "you took metal from that asteroid and used it to make me, right?"

"Yes, but what you don't understand is that the strangers who saved our planet insisted that I make a cyborg out of the metal. They were hoping that the power of the Black Flame Lion would be used for good, and they also said that only the pure of heart could control that power."

"Well that explains everything doesn't," said Chris, "for it seems that I'm not pure of heart enough to completely control the lion's power."

Just as he said this, he heard Neneko say to him, "Chris, you are probably the most pure hearted person in the world." He turned to her, surprised that she was awake after the blast she had taken.

Neneko sat up despite the pain and said, "You can't doubt yourself now, for if you do there will be no hope for anyone." She slipped off the bed and stood unsteadily.

With Destiny's help, she slowly walked to Chris. When she reached him, she fell on him. He held her close. "What do you think you're doing? You're in no shape to be walking around."

But, no matter what he said to her, she had to have her say. She pulled herself away from his arm and stood on her own two feet. "You are the only one who can fight Vox, and she knows it. Didn't you see the way she pulled back when it looked like you were going to attack?"

"Yes, but what good will it do if I defeat her? What if I lose control of that power, and go on a rampage of my own?"

"That won't happen," Destiny said as she joined the conversation, "because we are always here. And, besides, it's not like you're alone when you fight—or did you forget about the two who gave their lives to give you an extra boost?"

Chris looked at the gems on his hands. They represented the two mimetic beings that had given up their lives to give their powers to him: Mina of the wing and Dita of the blade.

"How could I forget them?" Chris said humbly. "They're the ones who really helped me defeat the Titan." Chris then looked back up to the girls around him. He smiled and said, "You're right, I've been doubting myself again. I should be stronger than what I've been."

"Chris-chan," Neneko said. She smiled, but backed off and became serious when she thought she detected an unusual presence in the building.

"What's wro—" Chris began. But, suddenly, the beast-man Bulldozer slammed through the ceiling. He landed on Chris and they both crashed right through the floor.

"What the hell, was that?" Lorelei yelled as she looked down the hole as the two fought it out, crashing through one floor after another.

"That was the cyber beast that took Chris a few weeks ago," Destiny said as they headed out the door to try and find out what was happening below them.

xxx

Chris and Bulldozer had fought their way all the way down to the boiler room in the basement of the building.

Chris looked up as the cyber beast jumped in the air. Chris rolled out of the way just as the beast was about to come down on one knee and crush him. Bulldozer's knee cracked the ground.

Chris jumped to his feet. He was ready this time for this freak. The behemoth then turned as electricity charging from his horns. But

Chris looked right above the bull cyborg. His eyes went wide as he shouted, "*Gas!*"

Then he yelled, "*No!* Don't fire that blast!" But he was too late. As the bull fired at him, the whole building shook violently as if an A-bomb had just gone off. All the lights went out. The emergency lights came on, and the fire alarms went off.

xxx

"What the heck was that?" Jura said as she came out of her room just as Lorelei and the others ran by.

"Chris is fighting at bottom of the building," Lorelei called back to her. "Some behemoth crashed through the roof and slammed him into the basement."

For a second, Jura stood shocked at this, but then she shook it off and ran after them.

xxx

Meanwhile, Chris extricated himself from the dust and rubble in the basement. His clothes were torn—his trench coat was in sheds. At first he didn't see Bulldozer. But, suddenly, something shot out of the rubble. Chris looked at the cyber bull and sighed. "Come on! What's it take to stop you, you freak?"

Bulldozer snorted and charged. But, having learned from his mistakes, Chris jumped over the horned beast, landing behind him. Then he charged up a Power Shotgun blast before the beast could turn around.

He fired it right as Bulldozer began his turn. The blast sent the behemoth slamming into the wall with a monstrous roar as the building shook for a second time.

xxx

The women were still running when they felt the second blast and realized those two were going to bring the building down on them at

565

any minute. Lorelei stopped short and turned to the others. "Forget about Chris! He can take care of himself! Right now we have to evacuate the building!"

xxx

This time when Chris pulled out of the rubble, he cursed to himself for not planning that better. He should have thought about his friends who were still in the building. Just as he thought about this, the area where he had hit Bulldozer started to shake.

"Oh, you have got to be kidding me!" Chris said just as the behemoth shot out of the wall he had been blasted into, and slammed right into Chris.

Bulldozer grabbed him in mid run. He spun around and then threw Chris with all he had, sending the Super Cyborg through the ceiling and up through the floors of the building.

In her lab, Lorelei was on the intercom telling everyone to evacuate the building. Just as she finished the transmission, Chris shot through the floor. He startled them as he flew out of the building and crashed right onto the roof of the building next door.

"Chris-chan!" Neneko yelled out. Then Bulldozer crashed through the floor and jumped across to the building where Chris was.

"This is the craziest thing I have ever seen!" Neneko said as she scanned the building to see what was happening.

But then Lorelei put a hand on her shoulder and said, "We don't have time for this. We have to evacuate the building."

"But what about Chris-chan?" Neneko asked as she turned back to the fight that had broken out on the roof of the other building.

"He'll be fine," Lorelei told her. "When has he not been okay in a fight?" Lorelei turned back to others, "Right now we have to get everyone out of the building as fast as we can."

xxx

Meanwhile, people in the building where Chris and the cyber bull were fighting thought a thunderstorm had broken out. At first the battle was matched fist to fist and stride for stride until Chris broke off and backflipped right off the building. He knew that this fight was getting out of hand, and, if he didn't stop it now, people were going to get hurt.

As he fell, Chris looked up and saw Bulldozer roar out as he jumped after him streamlining his body to catch up.

Chris grabbed the side of the building skidding to a stop, and then pushed himself off, and slammed head first into Bulldozer's chest. Then he punched hard into the gut of the behemoth sending him skyward, spiraling out of control. Chris grinned, vanished, and reappeared above Bulldozer, but, when he punched down at him, he got nothing but air—Bulldozer had disappeared.

Chris was floating for moment wondering where the behemoth had gone, when it slammed into him with so much force that it knocked them both out. They both fell back to the ground.

xxx

Lorelei had just finished evacuating the building when she noticed Neneko staring up into the sky. "What's going on?" she asked. Neneko just pointed to the sky with a terrified look in her eyes. When Lorelei looked to where she was pointing, she saw two objects falling toward Earth. It took a minute for Lorelei to recognize who it was, but, as soon as she did, she yelled out, "Everybody get out of the way!"

Right then, the Super Cyborg and Bulldozer both slammed into the Cyber Corp building again. The whole building shook violently as they slammed down through each floor once again. It was a wonder that the building still stood at all with the damage it had taken already.

Chris awoke in a lot of pain. It was no wonder considering how far he had fallen. Sparks flew violently from his body as he stood and looked around. His left eye started flashing off and on as he started to walk to the edge of the floor he was on. There used to be a window where he was standing. He looked around still wondering if Bulldozer was alive.

He got his answer when he heard a low snort from behind him. He turned to see Bulldozer still standing, but his right arm was gone and his face was torn up. Nevertheless, he still looked as if he was going to attack.

Chris steadied himself as best as he could, considering how damaged he was, as Bulldozer raked his foot against the floor. He was going to charge.

Chris was wobbly, but he stood as firmly as he could, ready to take anything the beast had, when he heard a voice say, "It looks like you have reached the end of the line, Super Cyborg."

Chris looked over to where the voice came from to see Vox come out of the shadows. She stepped over to Bulldozer and touched him, and, when she did, he was immediately covered in a dark red glow. Parts of him that had fallen off flew out of the rubble and started to reattach to him. In seconds, he was back to normal strength.

"Oh crap," Chris stated with a sigh.

xxx

Lorelei and the others stood outside the Cyber Corp building looking on, waiting for something to happen. They had seen Chris hit the building, and it seemed forever until they saw him look out from the broken window. Now he had turned back to something that they could not see.

Neneko had had enough. She jumped into the air and tried to fly up to Chris, but she fell back to the ground for she had not yet fully recovered. She just looked up helplessly. Tears started to swell in her eyes as she prayed that he would be all right.

xxx

At that moment, something hit Chris hard and sent him to his knees. He had been trying to figure out some way he could beat these two when Bulldozer slammed into him so fast that he had no time to react. As he fell, he looked up to see Vox grin at him knowing now she had him right where she wanted him.

He looked down to the ground still trying to find a way out, when, suddenly, he found himself staring at the Black Flame Lion's prison cell. As Chris watched, still hurting all over, the beast walked over to the bars.

"Do you see now how hopeless it is to fight?" said the beast. "You should just let me have your body, and call it a day."

The beast reached his paw out and tried to grab Chris, but Chris stood tall before the monster and then grinned at the beast.

"Do you truly think that I would give up after everything that I've been through already?" Chris asked the beast. "I've beaten tyrants across nameless galaxies, and still come through. I've liberated a world of people. I've watched as the people I love become stronger, and I've seen my own son punch down a warrior twice his size. So it doesn't matter that I can't see him ever again because I know he will find a way to beat you too! But, if you think I'm going to stop fighting just because it looks hopeless, well guess again. I'm *never* going to give up—as long as my gems stand by my side, there is nothing I can't do! In fact, I don't need your help, for I have everything that a man needs to win against the toughest odds."

"And what would that be?" the beast in his prison asked.

Chris shot up at him, growing larger in this world of the mind. He transformed quickly through all his phases until he reached the Silver Cyber Lion form. This time, his mane burned not with black flames, but with gold flames as he roared out', "For the love of the people in my life and for my honor!"

The cyber beast's roar shook the reality of the mind as the Black Flame Lion's world shrank into nothing. Just before he disappeared he yelled out, "Your son's soul is my salvation! I will be back!" Then the beast vanished into the void, for the beast knew that, if Striker ever went near Leo, his son, the beast would be complete again.

Chris roared out, "I will never give up!" As he spun around in mid air, his wounds and body repaired themselves. The women he loved, and people on the ground, watched in amazement.

The cyber beast-man roared out as he shot back to Vox and Bulldozer, who were still in the building. He stopped in the air and stared them down as he let out a low growl.

"Well," Vox exclaimed, "it would seem that you have found a way to purify my pet's power and make it your own. That means he can never be himself again, but it also means that you must die!" There was monstrous venom in her voice as she yelled out to Bulldozer to attack.

The Super Cyborg readied himself as Bulldozer shot forward. The two collided and fought at speeds that had once been impossible for the cyborg. But now, with the new power that he had obtained from the Black Flame Lion, he was fighting at a new level.

As the women who loved him watched from the ground, they worried because Chris was on his own now. None of them had the power to fight with him, for their equipment was now buried under a mountain of rubble. And poor Neneko was still in no condition to fight

As Chris fought Bulldozer, he realized that something felt very different. He was completely calm. And every one of his punches 'seemed to do an incredible amount of damage to Bulldozer, compared with his punches from before, which had barely done any damage at all.

Bulldozer, however, was not enjoying similar thoughts. He was only thinking of crushing the man in front of him, and bringing his head to his mistress. To this end, Bulldozer reared back and punched the Super Cyborg right in the head. Bulldozer smiled wide thinking that he had finished the cyborg. But his smile disappeared when Chris grabbed his hand and pulled' it away from his face. Bulldozer saw that his punch had not left any mark on his enemy.

This realization made Bulldozer furious. He punched madly at the Cyber Lion, who stood there taking each punch as if it was nothing. Suddenly, though, in a flash, Chris moved behind Bulldozer. In one move, he punched right through the behemoth with a screaming bullet. Bulldozer exploded in a fiery display.

Vox was furious when she saw this. She glared at the Super Cyborg for now, not only had the cyborg taken one of her pets, he had taken both. The Super Cyborg was going to die.

Chris looked down at the girls after the explosion and smiled and waved at them. But they were waving back, trying to tell him something. He looked around trying to detect what they were yelling about. He turned back to where Vox had been, but she was gone. And then he felt an enormous power rising. He didn't have the time to turn as something hit him hard in the back sending him crashing hard to the ground.

Neneko, Lorelei, Destiny, and Jura all ran to him. As they did, Vox yelled out, "It is time for all of you to die."

Energy charged in her hands faster than anything they had ever seen. She pointed her hand down as she fired the blast, which came down on them like a bad omen.

As Vox's deadly charge came within inches of the women, Chris shot down to where the women were and punched at the blast with all his might. The two powers clashed like mad, lighting up the area with incredible power. The women had to close their eyes against the blinding light.

"I won't let you hurt them!" Chris yelled out in frustration. The blast seemed to be slowing down, but it was still difficult for Chris to hold it back. It was still aimed right at the women. Neneko put her hand on his. He turned to her as she smiled a kind smile that didn't match the situation they were in. As Vox's blast inched closer to them, Neneko said, "You can do this, Chris-chan, for this should be nothing to you."

Those words seemed to do the trick. Then Lorelei, Destiny, and Jura all touched him as well. Each touch from his precious gems seemed to empower him ... they were the reason for his existence, his being, his strength.

That was all the encouragement he needed. He pushed forward, slowly pushing back the blast that had almost engulfed them. His gems watched, feeling stronger themselves as they let him go and watched the Cyber Lion–man push back the blast as he roared.

He pushed the blast right back up to Vox. He engulfed her in her own blast. The energy went right through Vox, ending in a massive explosion that blackened the skies.

Minutes seemed to pass like hours. As the smoke blew away, everyone was sure that Vox was gone— destroyed by her own blast. But, in the last wisps of smoke, they saw someone. Vox was alive, but she didn't look the same. Her body now looked cybernetic, even though it still had an organic look to it. When she came forward and looked at Chris, he drifted back a bit, shocked at her appearance. For now she looked exactly like the one who was giving the Black Flame Lion orders in his dream. She looked demonic … as if she had just stepped out of a horror movie.

She had not one, but two jaws—one going up and down, and another going from side to side. The only indication that she was female was her voice, for the rest of her was sexless.

She looked at the Super Cyborg, pointed a single finger at him, and fired a single blast right at his face. He flew back with an incredible force that shocked the others. They could now barely see him, but Neneko could see and she told them what was happening. If just one small blast from Vox was able to send Chris flying like that, what would a full-power blast do to him?

Chris managed to straighten himself out before Vox's 'second attack. She punched him across his face with a monstrous crack that sent him flying. He couldn't stop himself.

Vox watched him fly off, and then she shot off after him, leaving everyone in shock'. Chris's gems watched in horror; all they could do was hope that Chris was going to be all right.

Chris was still flying through the air after that last punch. He was out of control … unable to stop. But that didn't matter because 'Vox appeared behind him. Raising her fists in the air, she struck him, knocking him to the ground right in a vacant lot in the middle of New York—her power had been such that she had punched him half way around the globe.

The cyborg lay in the crater that he had made upon impact. He moved one arm as he tried to pull himself up. Vox, however, shot down and slammed into his back with power and strength that he had never felt before. His scream of pain echoed, unheard, in the empty area. The demon women pounded down on him like mad, tearing at his metal, shredding it as she punched on him, faster than human the eye could see.

xxx

Meanwhile, Neneko and Destiny both stopped in their tracks. Their connection with Chris was still stronger than Lorelei and Jura's connection with him. They could all tell that he was in danger, but they could not tell where he was. Suddenly, Neneko and Destiny fell screaming to the ground feeling all his pain. They could almost feel someone tearing off his limbs. Lorelei and Jura also began feeling Chris's pain, and their connection to him felt stronger as well, although Neneko and Destiny's connection remained stronger, as they had had it longer. '

When Jura fell from the pain, she stuttered to Lorelei asking, "W-what are we going to do?"

But Lorelei had already passed out from the pain. The others would soon follow. Things didn't seem good for them, for, if Chris died, the shock would surely kill all of them. This was truly now their darkest hour.

After Vox had finished beating the cyborg, she stood to verify that he was dead. But she saw his cybernetic eye flash on and off weakly. She knew that he was still alive.

"Why do you keep fighting?" Vox asked the broken body that was once known as the Super Cyborg. "You have been fighting a losing battle to begin with! You can't fight me! I made the Black Flame Lion, one of the most powerful beasts in the universe. Even the beings that fought him couldn't beat him—instead they had to seal him inside the metal that you are now made of. But it isn't in you to know when to quit, I guess." She paused for a moment and kicked his broken body. "You should know," she continued, "that, after I finish you, I'm going to find that son of your's. If I can't get my pet out of you, I might have better luck with your son."

Chris heard every word of Vox's little speech. Even in his broken state, he remembered what the Black Flame Lion had told him—that if the beast could not have the Super Cyborg's body he would take the body of his son. But Chris knew his son. He knew that his son would find a way to beat the beast. Also, Leo wasn't by himself. He had an ally in Hinata, the amazing girl that Chris had saved from General Bishop's daughter. *Even if I can never see my son again*, thought Chris, *I know that he will be safe. Dying isn't 'going to be too hard.*

When Vox finished her speech, she turned to the cyborg and raised her hand to the sky, charging up an attack that would blow up the cyborg and send him to his grave. But, as the Super Cyborg lay there knowing he was going to die, he felt something … the same thing that he had felt when he fought the Titan. He felt the presence of the all the women he had protected. He felt their pain. Then he realized—they were feeling everything *he* was feeling. And that meant that, if he died, they would die too, from the shock of his death.

Knowing these consequences of his death—that he would take over a hundred and fifty innocent lives with him—he could not die. He had to fight—and he had to win. But his body was shattered. Well, that hadn't stopped' him before. If he had been able to find the power to regenerate once, he could do it again. "

Right as Vox was about to fire her finishing blow, she felt the cyborg's power rising to the surface. But this was different—for some reason, she was feeling more than the power of one fighter. It was as if 'there were hundreds backing him up. In amazement, she watched his body fix itself. She had to act fast; he was going to be back on his feet in seconds.

"Die, Super Cyborg!" Vox yelled as she blasted down into the crater in which he lay. She created a massive explosion that covered half a mile in each direction. But then, out of the dome of power from the eruption, the Cyber Lion emerged. His mane was a burning flame of power. His face showed a determination to win no matter the cost. His body was completely repaired.

The Cyber Lion punched hard right in the demonic women's face. She was knocked back, but not as far as he would have liked. She recovered fast from the blow, and just stared at him with an icy resolve meant to send chills down his spine. But the Super Cyborg was different. He just stared her down. Slowly, Vox saw something unexpected. It appeared that all of the women to whom the cyborg was so loyal were all standing behind him.

"W-what is this?" stuttered Vox.

The Cyborg Lion–man smiled as he stated, "So, you can see them! Don't you know the women that I protect? They are the most precious things in my life—my gems. We all fight together no matter the odds. They are what give me my strength—the strength to beat any odds."

"This is some kind of joke," Vox said shakily. "My power is one of the greatest in the universe. I cannot be beaten by a fool like you—or your so-called precious gems. They are nothing to me! My power was given to me by the greatest power in the universe—Satan himself!" Vox roared out those last words as if they were her ultimate power … as if she could still find the power to stop this so-called Super Cyborg.

"You are nothing to me!" Vox yelled out again, and she attacked again. The two shot through the landscape. Anyone watching saw them only as two streaks of light fighting each other as their powers vied for superiority.

This was truly it—the battle to end it all. They were both fighting with everything they had, each punch that hit echoed around them like thunder.

They both shot out of the city. Into the valleys and through the mountains they fought on, until they hit the ocean. Their speed was increasing now as they flew across the ocean. Vox sent Chris flying with a blow, only to be punched into the water by his counterattack. Vox then hit Chris, launching him into orbit.

The Super Cyborg shook it off fast as Vox appeared next to him, still punching. He dodged her blow with incredible timing, then threw her over his shoulder, sending her flying farther into space.

Vox stopped herself. She roared out her frustration in a demonic scream that seemed to shake space itself, but then the Cyber Lion–man appeared in front of her, and they continued exchanging blows.

xxx

Back on Earth, Chris's gems started to move. People had gathered around and tried to help them, and to find out what had destroyed the building. But, when the women just started to recover as if nothing had happened to them, the people really started to wonder just what was going on. But Chris's gems knew that, if they were okay, Chris was going to be okay. Suddenly, Neneko detected power levels going crazy above them in space.

xxx

That was an understatement. For Chris and Vox were 'letting off enough power to light up a large city for a hundred years, and space was truly the only place in the world that these powers could be expended without hurting innocent people. That had been Chris's plan in the first place.

Vox was really starting to lose it. Somehow, her opponent seemed evenly matched with her, and this alone was making her fight harder. She believed that the power she had was unstoppable—that nothing in this universe could stop her. But Chris had a different idea. For he was not fighting for power or control, he was fighting to protect. And that alone made him stronger than ever.

Vox punched hard at the cyborg screaming out, "You cannot win!"

Chris smiled as he said, "Lady, you're not the first one to tell me that. All the others finally learned that their quest for power was the thing that destroyed them!"

Vox screamed out again as she swung at him, but he vanished before she hit. Then he appeared right next to her and hit her right back.

The fight then moved on. The warriors were like two shooting stars striking each other.

Vox smiled as she asked the cyborg, "Doesn't this go against that code of honor of yours? I mean striking a woman and all?" She smiled again with that doubled mouth of hers.

"Well, yeah, it kind of does," Chris called back. "But I figured that, since my code of honor states specifically that I 'should not strike a 'lady,' it's okay because you are *no* lady." The Super Cyborg half laughed making the demonic women even more furious.

They both broke away fast. Vox spread both her arms out as power started to gather in her hands. She was ready to finish this—with one last shot … with everything she had.

"This is it, Cyborg," she screamed. "I'm done fighting you, so I'm just going to blow everything up!" As she yelled, her power gathered together in two balls of energy. She held one in each hand.

She's not kidding! Chris thought. The power she was generating could easily destroy him. But, he turned to look behind him at the

Earth—after her balls of energy went through him, they would keep on going and destroy the Earth as well! He knew he had to stop her before she finished everything.

Chris shot toward Vox at top speed, but it wasn't enough, for, right as he went to punch her, she threw her hands together and fired her balls of energy right in his face. Instantly, he was blasted down to Earth.

Vox laughed at the fool. She watched him head straight to the Earth. This blast was going to destroy all her problems in one blow!

xxx

Neneko had detected the blast as it was fired. She was shaking all over as the beam that held her Chris-chan was heading right for them. The pain was becoming overwhelming as Chris was being torn apart again.

Lorelei finally stood. "Neneko, what's happening?" she asked. "Why are we all in such pain?"

Neneko, who was as white as a sheet, said plainly, "We're all going to die."

xxx

The Cyber Lion–man was having a difficult time staying conscious as Vox's beam of energy blasted him back to Earth. He knew this was it. He had thought he had the upper hand, but it seemed that it was futile to fight Vox. She was, indeed, a demon from the darkest regions of hell. He was no match for her.

"So that's it? You're just going to throw in the towel after you came so far?" It was Minawa's voice shooting through every circuit of his body.

"Minawa, I did the best I could. There's nothing left but death."

"Bullcrap!" Minawa yelled. "You've got to fight on! What happened to that honorable man that I fell in love with. He would not have given up this easily."

Chris thought about all the things he had been through. He thought about all the people he had met. He thought about the love of his family and friends. Then he yelled, "*No!* I'm not giving up—not even if my whole body is destroyed!"

He pulled himself away from the beam, but, when he did, the beam shot faster. "Crap!" he yelled as he shot down as fast as he could.

xxx

Lorelei, Destiny, Neneko, and Jura felt the pain go away. Everyone in the streets saw the beam coming at them. People ran screaming, not knowing what to do, just realizing they were probably all about to die. The beam shot toward the city. Just as it was about to hit the skyscrapers, it stopped dead. People uncovered their eyes to see Chris attacking the beam. "*Screaming Fist!*" he cried out. He was just barely able to hold the beam back, as the streets and the buildings shook from the force of the energy.

The Super Cyborg roared out as he yelled, "*I will never give up!*" He hit the beam with one screaming bullet after another, until he finally knocked it away from the planet. At that final moment, he turned to look briefly at everyone in the street, and then he shot back to space like a crazed lighting bolt, his fist pointed out in front of him.

After Vox saw Chris reflect her blast, she screamed out, "This isn't over." As she too shot forward at the Cyber Lion–man.

The two headed for a collision that would be the end for one of them. They both became red hot as they came closer to each other until, when they hit, the heavens were illuminated in a display of fiery lights. All of space seemed to shake from the impact, but, after the lights faded, they both seem unharmed.

Chris slowly looked up at the demonic beast in front of him. His face looked tired and drained of life. He fell back unable to fight anymore. Vox was still floating. She slowly watched him fall back to Earth. "You see?" she cried out. "I told you, you couldn't beat me!" As she spoke, she felt the bullet. She screamed out in pain as the back of her body blew into smithereens. As the rest of her body blew up, she screamed "How could he have beaten me? Lord Satan!" She then vanished from existence.

As Chris fell, he allowed a grin to come across his face, knowing that he had won. But, also as he fell, his body changed back to normal. Now the big question was, would he survive this fall?

XXX

The explosion had lit up the sky. As the light subsided, everyone was still wondering if the world was going to blow up on them. Then Neneko saw something familiar falling from the sky at monstrous speed.

"It's Chris-chan!" Neneko yelled out as she jumped up trying to fly. But she fell back to the ground. She cursed herself as she got back up, and yelled out, "Come on, body, *work!*"

She yelled again as she finally jumped into the sky as fast as she could go, but still, even at the pace she was going, she knew she wouldn't make it before he hit. But then Destiny appeared right next to her. Suddenly, they both disappeared, and then reappeared right next to Chris. Neneko shook off the shock as she quickly grabbed Chris to slow down his descent.

All three of them landed safely. Neneko turned to Destiny as she remembered that Destiny had the power of teleportation. "Thank you for your help Destiny," she said. "Can you get us back to the Cyber Corp building?"

Meanwhile, Chris's gems were still in shock from seeing Chris fall from the sky, and they wondered if he had managed to beat Vox, or were they all still in danger. The rest of the people in the streets just wanted to know what was going on! As TV crews came to get the story of what had happened to the Cyber Corp building, Chris's gems didn't answer the questions for they were waiting for any word on Chris. They didn't care about anything else. Then, 'out of nowhere, Destiny and Neneko appeared. Neneko had one of Chris's arms around her shoulder as she held him up. The others ran to him as Lorelei looked him over.

He was alive, but exhausted. He had used everything he had fighting Vox. Lorelei related his status to the others members of her crew. They all were just happy that he was alive. They also knew they had to get out of there before things got complicated. Lorelei turned to Destiny, who already knew what Lorelei was going to ask her. They all held hands, and together they all disappeared in a flash leaving the public to figure out on their own what had happened.

xxx

They all appeared in the cargo hold of *The Minawa*. "Stations, everyone," Lorelei commanded. "We're getting out of here!"

As Neneko followed Lorelei to the infirmary, she asked, "Is the ship repaired?"

Lorelei turned and smiled as she said, "The ship his been fixed for at least a week."

This meant that they were leaving the earth again. It also meant that they were probably never coming back, knowing all the damage they had caused. They could be paying for it for the rest of their lives.

CHAPTER 66

Chris was back on his feet in no time thanks to Destiny and Nodoka. He was thinking the same thing they had been thinking—it was time for them to move on, but there was one last thing he had to do, and he had enlisted Destiny's help.

He was standing next to Destiny ready to go. They both vanished, and reappeared right in front of Samantha's secret lab. Chris had a favor to ask of Sam, and he knew it was safe because his son and daughter were not in the lab right now.

He knocked on the door. When it opened, Sam almost had a heart attack. She threw herself into his arms and hugged him. He returned the hug saying, "It's good to see you too! But we're not here to say hi."

When he broke off the hug, he told her, "I want you to take care of my son, my daughter, and Hinata until I find a way to see them again."

Sam understood and said, "I will respect your last wish."

"Thank you," he said, "I promise I will return one day, but, until then, it's still too dangerous. I must not get near my son. If we get too close, that Black Flame Lion that resides inside the metal that Leo and I are made from could get loose again. The best idea is to put as much distance between me and my son as possible."

"Good-bye Chris Striker, the Super Cyborg," Sam said as she gave him one last hug. She waved good-bye as they disappeared.

When they made it back to the ship, Chris headed for the bridge. "All right," he said, "let's get going! There's a lot space out there, and we still have to find a new world for all of you."

As *The Minawa* shot off into space, something shook the ship violently. "What's going on?" asked Chris. '

One of his crew-members said, "There's been an explosion on the Earth. What we felt was just the shock- wave."

The main monitors showed them the Earth. An enormous beam of black energy was shooting out of the planet.

"What the heck is that?" Chris asked in shock. None of them had ever seen anything like this before.

As they watched, someone appeared out of nowhere on the bridge. When Chris turned to the visitor, he could not believe his eyes, for there was a large, gargoyle-like cyborg standing right there. His body looked as if it was almost completely made of bronze. The only part of him that still seemed flesh was his head.

The gargoyle-like cyborg turned to Chris, and clearly stated, "Chris Striker, the Super Cyborg, you are needed."

To be continued, in volume 6 of the Omega Chronicles.

In volume two we go to sunny California to introduce the two most powerful vampires in existence. Get ready for the Be-Yonder Vampires—the Demon and the Flame.

www.ingramcontent.com/pod-product-compliance
Lightning Source LLC
Chambersburg PA
CBHW060422310726
48977CB00001B/8